RHYTHM
OF WAR

BY BRANDON SANDERSON

THE STORMLIGHT ARCHIVE

The Way of Kings
Words of Radiance
Edgedancer
Oathbringer
Rhythm of War

THE MISTBORN SAGA

The Final Empire
The Well of Ascension
The Hero of Ages
The Alloy of Law
Shadows of Self
The Bands of Mourning
Misborn: Secret History

LEGION

Legion
Legion: Skin Deep
Legion: Lies of the Beholder

COLLECTIONS

Legion: The Many Lives of Stephen
Leeds
Arcanum Unbounded: The Cosmere
Collection
Legion and the Emperor's Soul

ALCATRAZ VS THE EVIL LIBRARIANS

Alcatraz vs the Evil Librarians
The Scrivener's Bones
The Knights of Crystallia
The Shattered Lens
The Dark Talent

THE RECKONERS

Steelheart
Mitosis
Firefight
Calamity

SKYWARD

Skyward
Starsight

Elantris
Warbreaker
The Rithmatist
Snapshot

GRAPHIC NOVELS

White Sand
Dark One

BRANDON SANDERSON

RHYTHM OF WAR

PART TWO

Book Four of

THE STORMLIGHT ARCHIVE

This edition first published in Great Britain in 2022 by Gollancz

First published in Great Britain in 2020 by Gollancz
an imprint of The Orion Publishing Group Ltd
Carmelite House, 50 Victoria Embankment
London EC4Y 0DZ

An Hachette UK Company

3 5 7 9 10 8 6 4

A CIP catalogue record for this book is
available from the British Library.

ISBN (Mass Market Paperback) 978 0 575 09342 3

Typeset by Input Data Services Ltd, Somerset

Printed in Great Britain by Clays Ltd, Elcograf S.p.A

www.gollancz.co.uk

For Isaac Stewart,
Who paints my imagination.

CONTENTS

Part Three: Songs of Home   13

Interludes   303

Part Four: A Knowledge   321

Interludes   557

Part Five: Knowing a Home of Songs, Called Our Burden   573

Epilogue: Dirty Tricks   737

Endnote   743

Ars Arcanum   744

ILLUSTRATIONS

NOTE: *Many illustrations, titles included, contain spoilers for material that comes before them in the book. Look ahead at your own risk.*

Map of Eastern Makabak   44

Shallan's Sketchbook: Reachers   108

Folio: Envoyform Fashion   186

Shallan's Sketchbook: Highspren   304

Alethi Glyphs Page 2   322

Shallan's Sketchbook: Peakspren   337

Shallan's Sketchbook: Inkspren   374

Navani's Notebook: Dagger   435

Navani's Notebook: Experiments   541

Roshar

Endless Ocean

QUIL

Rall Elorim

RESHI

Kasitor

IRI

R·I·R·A

Kurth

Reshi

Eila

BABATHARNAM

D·A·R·A·B·E·T·H

The Misted Mountains

Panatham

The Purelake

SHINOVAR

YULAY

Fu Nam

DESH

AZIR

Aïmian Sea

ALM

UEZIER

Azimir

Urithiru

AIMIA

The Valle

LIAFOR

Yeddaw

TASHIKK

EMUL

GREAT

HEX

STEEN

Sesemalex Dar

Icewater

TUKAR

MARA

N

LEEWARD

STORMWARD

SOUTHERN DEPTHS

S

STEAMWATER OCEAN

ISLES

Sea

ATAK

SUMI

AKAK

HERDAZ

Northgrip

Mourn's
Vault

Varikev

Ru Parat

Elanar

JAH KEVED

Kholinar

TU
BAYLA

Valath

Shulin

UNCLAIMED HILLS

Homewater Peaks

BAVLAND

ALETHKAR

Rathalas

Dawn's
Shadow

Silnasen

TU
TRIAX

Vedenar

Dumadori

Karanak

Shattered
Plains

TU
FALLA

Tarat Sea

FROSTLANDS

New Natanan

Kharbranth

Longbrow's
Straits

Thaylen City

Klna

The Shallow Crypts

THAYLENAH

OCEAN OF ORIGINS

FOR HIS ROYAL MAJESTY KING GAVILAR
BY HIS ROYAL HIGH CARTOGRAPHER
ISASIK SHULIN KAPHEIN
1167

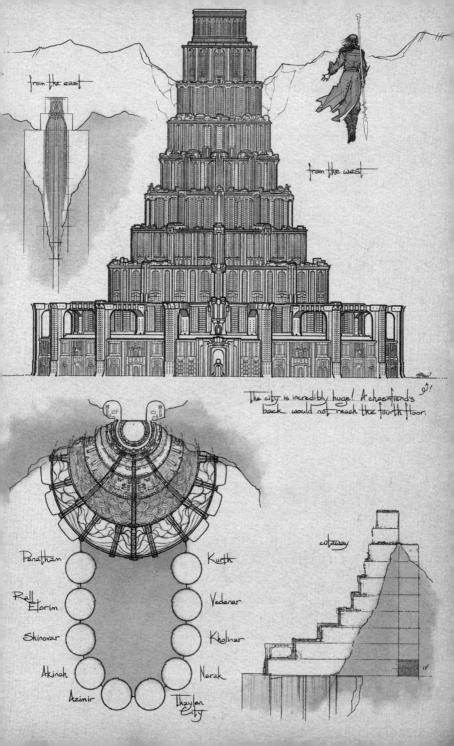

from the east

from the west

The city is incredibly huge! A chasmfiend's
back would not reach the fourth floor.

cutaway

Panatham

Rall
Elorim

Shinovar

Akinah

Azimir

Kurth

Vedenar

Kholinar

Narak

Thaylen
City

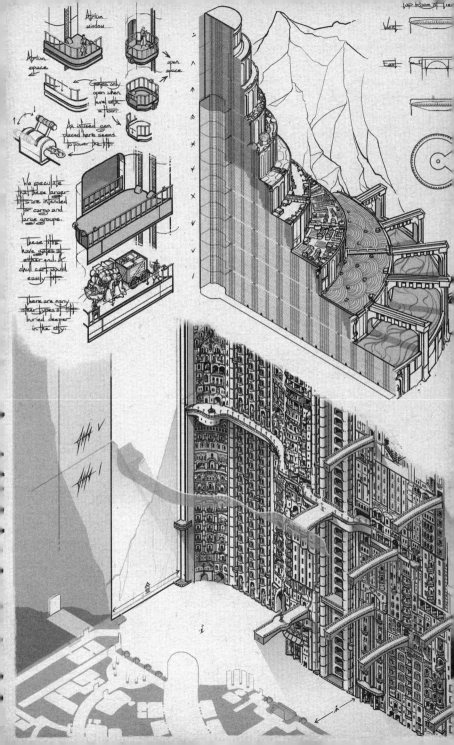

Atrium window

Atrium space

open space

Gates only open when level with floor

An infeed gem placed here seems to power the lift

We speculate that these larger lifts are intended for cargo and large groups.

These lifts have gates at either end. A chull cart would easily fit.

There are many other types of lift buried deeper in the city.

West

East

PART

THREE

Songs of Home

KALADIN • NAVANI • DALINAR •
VENLI • ESHONAI • JASNAH • RENARIN

44

TINDER WAITING
FOR THE SPARK

I find this format most comfortable, as it is how I've collaborated in the past. I have never done it in this way, and with this kind of partner.

—From *Rhythm of War*, page 1

Kaladin jogged through the dark tunnels of Urithiru, Teft across his shoulders, feeling as if he could *hear* his life crumbling underfoot with each step. A phantom cracking, like glass shattering.

Each painful step took him farther from his family, farther from peace. Farther into the darkness. He'd made his decision. He would *not* leave his friend to the whims of enemy captivity. But though he'd finally thought to take off his bloodied shoes—and now carried them with the laces looped around his neck—he still felt as if he were leaving stained tracks behind him.

Storms. What did he think he could accomplish by himself? He was effectively disobeying the queen's order to surrender.

He tried his best to banish such thoughts and keep moving. He would have time later to ruminate on what he'd done. For now, he needed to find a safe place to hide. The tower was no longer home, but an enemy fortress.

Syl zipped out in front of him, checking each intersection before he arrived. Stormlight kept him moving, but he worried what would happen when it ran out. Would his strength fail him? Would he collapse in the center of the corridor?

Why hadn't he collected more spheres from his parents or Laral before leaving? He hadn't even thought to take the stormform's axe. That left him unarmed, save for a *scalpel*. He was too used to having Syl as his Shardspear, but if she couldn't transform—

No, he thought to himself. *No thoughts. Thoughts are dangerous. Just move.*

He pushed forward, relying on Syl, who sped toward a stairwell. The easiest way to lose themselves would be to find a hiding place on the uninhabited floors, perhaps somewhere on eleven or twelve. He took the stairs two at a time, propelled by the pulsing Light in his veins. His glow was enough to see by. Teft began muttering quietly, perhaps responding to the jostling.

They reached the seventh floor, then started straight up toward the eighth. Here, Syl led him farther inward. Try as he might to ignore them, Kaladin continued to hear the echoes of his failure. His father's shouts. His own tears . . .

He'd been so close. So *close*.

He lost track of their location in the endless tunnels. The floor here wasn't painted to give directions, so he trusted in Syl. She zipped ahead to an intersection, spun around in a circle a few times, then shot to the right. He kept pace with her, though he was feeling Teft's weight more and more.

"Just a second," he whispered to her at the next intersection, then rested against the wall—Teft still weighing heavily on his shoulders— and fished a chip from his pouch. The small topaz was barely enough to see by, but he needed it as the Stormlight he was holding finally gave out. And he didn't have many spheres left.

He grunted under the weight of his friend, then pushed himself to stand up straight, clinging tightly to Teft with both hands while gripping the sphere between two fingers. He nodded to Syl, then continued after her, pleased that his strength was holding. He could manage Teft without Light. Despite Kaladin's last few weeks spent as a surgeon, his body was still that of a soldier.

"We should go higher," Syl said, floating alongside his head as a ribbon of light. "Can you manage?"

"Get us to floor ten at least," Kaladin said.

"I'll have to take us up stairwells as I see them. I don't really know this section of the tower. . . ."

He let himself sink into an old familiar mindset as they continued. Teft's weight across his shoulders wasn't that different from carrying a bridge. It brought him back to those days. Running bridges. Eating stew.

Watching his friends die . . . feeling terror anew each day . . .

Those memories offered no comfort. But the rhythm of steps, carrying a burden, working his body on an extended march . . . it was at least familiar.

He followed Syl up one set of steps, then another. Then across another long tunnel, the strata here waving vigorously like ripples in a churning pond. Kaladin kept moving.

Until suddenly he came alert.

He couldn't pinpoint what alarmed him, but he moved on instinct to immediately cover his sphere and duck into a side passage. He stepped into a nook and knelt to slide Teft off his shoulders. He pressed his hand against the unconscious man's mouth to silence his mumbling.

Syl darted over a moment later. He could see her in the darkness, but she didn't illuminate things around her. He shoved his other hand in his pocket, tightly holding the sphere so it couldn't give off any betraying illumination.

"What?" Syl asked.

Kaladin shook his head. He didn't know, but didn't want to speak. He huddled there—hoping Teft wouldn't mutter or shift too loudly—his own heartbeat thumping in his ears.

Then, faint red light crept into the hallway he'd left. Syl immediately zipped to hide her light behind Kaladin's dark form.

The light approached, revealing a single ruby along with a pair of glowing red eyes. Those illuminated a terrible face. Pure black, with hints of marbled red under the eyes. Long dark hair, which appeared woven into his simple wrap of clothing. It was the creature Kaladin had fought in Hearthstone, the one he'd killed in the burning room of the mansion. Though the Fused had been reborn into a new body, Kaladin knew from the skin patterns that it was the same individual. Come for revenge.

The Fused didn't seem to spot Kaladin hiding in the darkness, though he did pause at the intersection for an extended period of time. He moved on, thankfully, going deeper along the path Kaladin had been taking.

Storms . . . Kaladin had defeated the thing last time without any Stormlight, but he had done so by playing on its arrogance. Kaladin doubted it would let him get such an easy kill again.

Those singers in the clinic . . . one of them mentioned that a Fused was looking for me. They called him the Pursuer. This thing . . . it had come to the tower *specifically* to find Kaladin.

"Follow it," he mouthed, turning to Syl, counting on her to understand his meaning. "I'll find someplace more secluded to hide."

She wove her line of light into a brief luminescent representation of a *kejeh* glyph—meaning "affirmative"—then zipped after the Pursuer. She couldn't get too far from Kaladin anymore, but she should be able to follow for a while. Hopefully she could do so circumspectly, as some of the Fused could see spren.

Kaladin hauled Teft back up onto his shoulders, then struck out into the darkness, barely allowing himself any light. There was always something oppressive about being deep in the tower, feeling so far away from the sky and the wind—but it was worse in the darkness. He could all too easily imagine himself trapped in here without spheres, left to wander forever in a tomb of stone.

He wove through a few more turns, hoping to find a stairwell up to another floor. Unfortunately, Teft started muttering again. Gritting his teeth, Kaladin ducked into the first room he found—a place with a narrow doorway. Here he set Teft down, then tried to stifle his noises.

Syl darted into the room a moment later, which made Kaladin jump.

"He's coming," she hissed. "He went only a short distance down the wrong hallway before he stopped, inspected the ground, then doubled back. I don't think he saw me. I followed long enough to see him stop at the place where you hid a bit ago. He found a little smear of blood on the wall there. I hurried ahead of him, but he knows you're nearby."

Storms. Kaladin glanced at his bloody clothing, then at Teft—who was muttering despite Kaladin's attempts to quiet him.

"We need to lead the Pursuer away," Kaladin whispered. "Be ready to distract him."

She made another affirmative signal. Kaladin left his friend as a restless lump in the darkness, then backtracked a little. He pulled up near an intersection, gripping his scalpel. He allowed no light other than Syl's, his few remaining infused spheres tucked away in his black pouch.

He took a few deep breaths, then mouthed his plan to Syl. She sailed farther away through the black corridor, leaving Kaladin in total darkness.

He'd never been able to find the pure emptiness of mind that some soldiers claimed to adopt in battle. He wasn't certain he'd ever want something like that. However, he did compose himself, making his breathing shallow, and came fully alert, listening.

Loose, relaxed, but ready to come alight. Like tinder waiting for the spark. He was ready to breathe in his last spheres of Stormlight, but wouldn't until the last moment.

Footsteps scraped the corridor to Kaladin's right, and the walls slowly bled with red light. Kaladin held his breath, ready, his back to the wall.

The Pursuer froze just before reaching the intersection, and Kaladin knew the creature had spotted Syl, who would have zipped past in the distance. A heartbeat later, scraping noises announced the Pursuer dropping his body as a husk—and a red ribbon of light rushed after Syl. The distraction had worked. Syl would lead him away.

As far as they knew, the Fused couldn't harm spren naturally—the only way to do so was with a Shardblade. Even that was temporary; cut spren with a Shardblade, even rip them to pieces, and they eventually re-formed in the Cognitive Realm. Experiments had proven that the only way to keep them divided was to store separate halves in gemstones.

Kaladin gave it ten heartbeats, then brought out a small sphere for light and dashed into the corridor—sparing a brief glance at the Pursuer's discarded body—before running for the room where he'd put Teft.

It was amazing what a jolt of energy came from being so close to a fight. He heaved Teft on his shoulders without trouble, then was jogging away in moments—almost as if he were infused with Stormlight again. Using the light of the sphere, he soon found a stairwell. He almost rushed up it, but a faint light from above made him stop fast.

Voices speaking to rhythms echoed from above. And from below, he realized. He left that stairwell, but two hallways over he saw distant lights and shadows. He pulled into a side corridor, sweating in streams, fearspren—like globs of goo—writhing up through the stone beneath him.

He knew this feeling. Scurrying through the darkness. People with lights searching in a pattern, hunting him. Breathing heavily, he hauled Teft through a different side passage, but soon spotted lights in that direction as well.

The enemy was forming a noose, slowly tightening around his position. That knowledge sent him into flashbacks of the night when he'd failed Nalma and the others. A night when, like so many other times, he'd survived when everyone else had died. Kaladin wasn't a runaway slave anymore, but the sensation was the same.

"Kaladin!" Syl said, zipping up to him. "I was leading him toward the edge of the level, but we ran into some regular soldiers and he turned back. He seemed to figure out I was trying to distract him."

"There are multiple squads up here," Kaladin said, pulling into the darkness. "Maybe a full company. Storms. The Pursuer must have repurposed the entire force sent to go through homes on the sixth floor."

He was shocked at the speed with which they'd set up the trap. He had to admit that was likely the result of him letting a soldier run and tell the others.

Well, he doubted the enemy had found the time to appropriate one of Navani's maps of this level. They couldn't have managed to place people in every hallway or stairwell. The net closing around him *had* to have gaps.

He began searching. Down a side corridor, he found shadowy figures approaching. And in the next stairwell. They were relentless, and everywhere. Plus, he didn't know this area any better than they did. He twisted around through a group of corridors until he reached a dead end. A quick search of the nearby rooms showed no other exits, and he looked over his shoulder, hearing voices calling to one another. They spoke Azish, he thought—and to the rhythms.

Feeling a sense of growing dread, he set Teft down, counted his few spheres, and took out his scalpel once more. Right. He'd . . . he'd need to take a weapon from the first soldier he killed. A spear, hopefully. Something with reach if he was going to survive a fight in these corridors.

Syl landed on his shoulder and took the shape of a young woman, seated with her hands in her lap.

"We have to try to punch through," Kaladin whispered. "There's a chance they'll send only a couple men this direction. We kill them, then slip out of the noose and run."

She nodded.

It didn't sound like a "couple men" though. And he was reasonably certain he caught a harsher, louder voice among them. The Pursuer was still tracking him, possibly by the faint marks of blood smeared on the walls or floor.

Kaladin pulled Teft into one of the rooms, then positioned himself in the doorway to wait. Not calm, but prepared. He gripped his scalpel in a reverse grip—a hacking grip—for ramming into the space between carapace and neck. Standing there, he felt the weight of it all pressing down on him. The darkness, both inside and out. The fatigue. The dread. Gloomspren like tattered pieces of cloth faded in, as if banners attached to the walls.

"Kaladin," Syl said softly, "could we surrender?"

"That Fused isn't here to take me captive, Syl," he said.

"If you die I'll be alone again."

"We've slipped out of tighter problems than this. . . ." He trailed off as he glanced at her, sitting on his shoulder, seeming far smaller than usual. He couldn't force the rest of the words out. He couldn't lie.

Light began to illuminate the corridor, coming toward him.

Kaladin gripped his knife more tightly. A part of him seemed to have always known it would come to this. Alone in the darkness, standing with his back to the wall, facing overwhelming numbers. A glorious way to die, but Kaladin didn't want glory. He'd given up on that foolish dream as a child.

"Kaladin!" Syl said. "What's that? On the floor?"

A faint violet light had appeared in the crook of the rightmost corner. Almost invisible, even in the darkness. Frowning, Kaladin left his post by the door, inspecting the light. There was a garnet vein in the stone here, and a small portion of it was glowing. As he tried to figure out why, the glow moved—running along the crystal vein. He followed it to the doorway, then watched it cross the hallway to the room on the other side.

He hesitated only briefly before putting away his weapon and hauling Teft onto his shoulders once again. He stumbled across the hallway outside—and one of the approaching people said something in Azish. It sounded hesitant, as if they hadn't caught more than a glimpse of him.

Storms. What was he doing? Chasing phantom lights, like starspren in the sky? In this small chamber, the light moved across the floor and up the wall, revealing what appeared to be a gemstone embedded deeply in the stone.

"A fabrial?" Syl said. "Infuse it!"

Kaladin breathed in some of his Stormlight, then glanced over his shoulder. Voices outside, and shadows. Rather than hold his Stormlight for that fight, however, he did as Syl told him—pressing the Light into the gemstone. He had maybe two or three chips' worth left after that. He was practically defenseless.

The wall split down the center. He gaped as the stones *moved*, but with a silence that defied explanation. They cracked open just wide enough to admit a person. Carrying Teft, he entered a hidden corridor. Behind him, the doorway smoothly slid shut, and the light in the gemstone went out.

Kaladin held his breath as he heard voices in the room behind. Then he pressed his ear against the wall, listening. He couldn't make out much—an argument that seemed to involve the Pursuer. Kaladin worried they had spotted the door closing, but he heard no scraping or pounding. They would spot the spren he'd drawn though, and would know he was close.

Kaladin needed to keep moving. The little violet light on the floor twinkled and moved, so he lugged Teft after it through another series of corridors. Eventually they reached a hidden stairwell that—blessedly—was undefended.

He climbed that, though each footfall was slower than the one before it and exhaustionspren hounded him. He kept moving somehow, as the light led him to the eleventh floor, and then into another dark room. The oppressive silence told him he'd reached a portion of the tower the enemy wasn't searching. He wanted to collapse, but the light pulsed insistently on the wall—and Syl encouraged him to look.

Another embedded gemstone, barely visible. He used the last of his Stormlight to infuse it, and slipped through the door that opened. In absolute darkness, Kaladin set Teft down, feeling the door closing behind.

He didn't have the strength to inspect his surroundings. He instead slid to the cold stone floor, trembling.

There, he finally let himself drift to sleep.

45

A BOLD HEART, A KEEN AND CRAFTY MIND

NINE YEARS AGO

Eshonai had been told that mapping the world removed its mystery. Some of the other listeners insisted the wilderness should be left uncharted—the domain of the spren and the greatshells—and that by trying to confine it to paper, she risked stealing its secrets.

She found this to be flat-out ridiculous. She attuned Awe as she entered the forest, the trees bobbing with lifespren, bright green balls with white spines poking out. Closer to the Shattered Plains, most everything was flat, grown over by only the occasional rockbud. Yet here, not so far away, plants thrived in abundance.

Her people made frequent trips to the forest to get lumber and mushrooms. However, they always took the exact same route. Up the river a day's walk inward, gather there, then return. This time she'd insisted on leaving the party—much to their concern. She'd promised to meet them again at their normal camp, after scouting the outer perimeter of the forest all the way around.

After hiking around the trees for several days, she'd encountered the river on the other side. Now she could cut back through the heart of the forest and reach her family's camp from that direction. She'd bear with her a new map that revealed exactly how large the forest was, at least on one side.

She started along the stream, attuned to Joy, accompanied by swimming riverspren. Everyone had been so worried about her being out in the storms alone. Well, she had been out in storms a dozen times in her life, and had survived with no trouble. Plus, she'd been able to move in among the trees for shelter.

Her family and friends were concerned nonetheless. They spent their lives living in a very small region, dreaming of the day they could conquer one of the ten ancient cities at the perimeter of the Shattered Plains. Such a small-minded goal. Why not strike out, see what else there was to the world?

But no. Only one possible goal existed: win one of the cities. Seek shelter behind crumbling walls, ignoring the barrier the woods provided. Eshonai considered it proof that nature was stronger than the creations of listeners. This forest had likely stood when the ancient cities had been new. Yet this forest still thrived, and those were ruins.

You couldn't steal the secrets from something so strong just by exploring it. You could merely learn.

She settled down near a rock and unrolled her map, made from precious paper. Her mother was one of the few among all the families who knew the Song of Making Paper, and with her help, Eshonai had perfected the process. She used a pen and ink to sketch the path of the river as it entered the forest, then dabbed the ink until it was dry before rerolling the map.

Though she was confident, Resolve attuned, the others' complaints had been particularly bothersome lately.

We know where the forest is and how to reach it. Why map its size? What will that help?

The river flows this direction. Everyone knows where to find it. Why bother putting it on paper?

Too many of her family wanted to pretend the world was smaller than it was. Eshonai was convinced that was why they continued to squabble with the other listener families. If the world consisted only of the land around the ten cities, then fighting over that land made sense.

But their ancestors hadn't fought one another. Their ancestors had turned their faces to the storm and marched away, abandoning their very gods in the name of freedom. Eshonai would use that freedom. Instead of sitting by the fire and complaining, she would experience the beauties

Cultivation offered. And she would ask the best question of them all.

What will I discover next?

Eshonai continued walking, judging the river's course. She used her own methods of counting the distance, then rechecked her work by surveying sights from multiple angles. The river continued flowing for days once a storm passed. How? When all other water had drained away or been lapped up, why did this river keep going? Where did it start?

Rivers and their carapace-covered spren excited her. Rivers were markers, guideposts, roadways. You could never get lost if you knew where the river was. She stopped for lunch near one of the bends, and discovered a type of cremling that was *green,* like the trees. She'd never seen one that shade before. She'd have to tell Venli.

"Stealing nature's secrets," Eshonai said to Annoyance. "What is a secret but a surprise to be discovered?"

Finishing her steamed haspers, she put out her fire and scattered the flamespren before continuing on her way. By her guess, it would take her a day and a half to reach her family. Then, if she left them again and rounded the *other* side of the forest, she'd have a finished picture of how it looked.

There was so much to see, so much to know, so much to *do.* And she was going to discover it all. She was going to . . .

What was that?

She frowned, halting in her tracks. The river wasn't strong now; it would likely slow to a trickle by tomorrow. Over its gurgling, she heard shouts in the distance. Had the others come to find her? She hurried forward, attuning Excitement. Perhaps they were growing more willing to explore.

It wasn't until she was almost to the sounds that she realized something was very wrong with them. They were flat, no hint of a rhythm. As if they were made by the dead.

A moment later she rounded a bend and found herself confronted by something more wondrous—and more terrible—than she'd ever dared imagine.

Humans.

"'. . . dullform dread, with the mind most lost,'" Venli quoted. "'The lowest, and one not bright. To find this form, one need banish the cost. It finds you and brings you to blight.'"

She drew in a deep breath and sat back in their tent, proud. All ninety-one stanzas, recited *perfectly*.

Her mother, Jaxlim, nodded as she worked the loom. "That was one of your better recitations," she said to Praise. "A little more practice, and we can move to the next song."

"But . . . I got it right."

"You mixed up the seventh and fifteenth stanzas," her mother said.

"The order doesn't matter."

"You also forgot the nineteenth."

"No I didn't," Venli said, counting them in her head. Workform? ". . . Did I?"

"You did," her mother said. "But you needn't be embarrassed. You are doing fine."

Fine? Venli had spent *years* memorizing the songs, while Eshonai barely did anything useful. Venli was better than *fine*. She was *excellent*.

Except . . . she'd forgotten an entire stanza? She looked at her mother, who was humming softly as she worked the loom.

"The nineteenth stanza isn't that important," Venli said. "Nobody is going to forget how to become a worker. And dullform. Why do we have a stanza about that? Nobody would *willingly* choose it."

"We need to remember the past," her mother said to the Rhythm of the Lost. "We need to remember what we passed through to get here. We need to take care not to forget ourselves."

Venli attuned Annoyance. And then, Jaxlim began to sing to the rhythms in a beautiful voice. There was something amazing about her mother's voice. It wasn't powerful or bold, but it was like a knife—thin, sharp, almost liquid. It cut Venli to the soul, and Awe replaced her Annoyance.

No, Venli wasn't perfect. Not yet. But her mother was.

Jaxlim sang on, and Venli watched, transfixed, feeling ashamed of her earlier petulance. It was just so hard sometimes. Sitting in here day after day, memorizing while Eshonai played. The two of them were nearly adults, only a year off for Eshonai and a little more than two for Venli. They were supposed to be responsible.

Her mother eventually trailed off, after the tenth stanza.

"Thank you," Venli said.

"For singing something you've heard a thousand times?"

"For reminding me," Venli said to Praise, "of what I am practicing to become."

Her mother attuned Joy and continued working. Venli strolled to the doorway of the tent and peered out, where family members worked at various activities, like chopping wood and felling trees. Her people were the First-Rhythm family, and had a noble heritage. They were thousands strong, but it had been many years since they'd controlled a city.

They kept talking of winning one back soon. Of how they'd strike out of the forest and attack before a storm, claiming their rightful seat. It was an excellent and worthy goal, yet Venli found herself dissatisfied as she watched warriors making arrows and sharpening ancient metal spears. Was this really what life amounted to? Fighting back and forth over the same ten cities?

Surely there was more for them. Surely there was more for *her*. She had come to love the songs, but she wanted to use them. Find the secrets they promised. Would Roshar create someone like Venli, only to have her sit in a hogshide tent and memorize words until she could pass them on, then die?

No. She had to have some kind of destiny. Something grand. "Eshonai thinks we should draw pictures to represent the verses of the songs," Venli said. "Make stacks of papers full of pictures, so we won't forget."

"Your sister has a wisdom to her at times," her mother said.

Venli attuned Betrayal. "She shouldn't be off away from the family so much, being selfish with her time. She should be learning the songs like me. It's her duty too, as your daughter."

"Yes, you are correct," Jaxlim said. "But Eshonai has a bold heart. She merely needs to learn that her family is more important than counting the number of hills outside the camp."

"I have a bold heart!" Venli said.

"You have a keen and crafty mind," her mother said. "Like your mother. Do not dismiss your own talents because you envy those of another."

"Envy? Her?"

Venli's mother continued weaving. She wasn't required to do such

28

work—her position as keeper of songs was lofty, perhaps the most important in the family. Yet her mother always sought to keep busy. She said working her hands kept her body strong, while going over songs worked her mind.

Venli attuned Anxiety, then Confidence, then Anxiety again. She walked to her mother and sat on the stool next to her. Jaxlim projected Confidence, even when doing something as simple as weaving. Her complex skin pattern of wavy red and black lines was among the most beautiful in the camp—like true marbled stone. Eshonai took after their mother's colorings.

Venli, of course, took after her father—primarily white and red, her own pattern more like swirls. In truth, Venli's pattern had all three shades. Many people claimed they couldn't see the small patches of black at her neck, but she could pick them out. Having all three colors was very, very rare.

"Mother," she said to Excitement, "I think I've discovered something."

"And what would that be?"

"I've been experimenting with different spren again. Taking them into the storms."

"You were cautioned about this."

"You didn't forbid me, so I continued. Should we only ever do as we are told?"

"Many say we need no more than workform and mateform," her mother said to Consideration. "They say that courting other forms is to take steps toward forms of power."

"What do *you* say?" Venli asked.

"You are always so concerned for my opinions. Most children, when they reach your age, start to defy and ignore their parents."

"Most children don't have you as a mother."

"Flattery?" Jaxlim said to Amusement.

"Not . . . entirely," Venli said. She attuned Resignation. "Mother, I want to use what I've learned. I have a head full of songs about forms. How can I *help* wanting to try to discover them? For the good of our people."

Jaxlim finally stopped her weaving. She turned on her stool and scooted closer to Venli, taking her hands. She hummed, then sang softly to Praise—just a melody, no words. Venli closed her eyes and let the song wash over her, and thought she could feel her mother's skin vibrating. Feel her soul.

Venli had done this as long as she could remember. Relying on her, and her songs. Ever since her father had left, seeking the eastern sea.

"You make me proud, Venli," Jaxlim said. "You've done well these last few years, memorizing after Eshonai gave up. I encourage you to seek to improve yourself, but remember, you must not become distracted. I need you. *We* need you."

Venli nodded, then hummed the same rhythm, attuning Praise to be in sync with her mother. She felt love, warmth, acceptance from those fingers. And knew whatever else happened, her mother would be there to guide her. Steady her. With a song that pierced even storms.

Her mother returned to her weaving, and Venli began to recite again. She went through the entire thing, and this time did *not* miss a stanza.

When she was done, she waited, taking a drink of water and hoping for her mother's praise. Instead, Jaxlim gave her something better. "Tell me," she said, "of these experiments with spren you've been doing."

"I'm trying to find *warform*!" Venli said to Anticipation. "I've been staying near the edge of the shelter during storms, and trying to attract the right spren. It is difficult, as most spren flee from me once the winds pick up.

"However, this last time I feel I was close. A painspren is the key. They're always around during storms. If I can keep one close to me, I think I can adopt the form."

If she managed it, she'd become the first listener to hold warform in many generations. Ever since the humans and the singers of old destroyed one another in their final battle. This was something she could bring her people, something that would be remembered!

"Let's go speak with the Five," Jaxlim said, standing up from beside the loom.

"Wait," Venli said, taking her arm and attuning Tension. "You are going to tell them what I said? About warform?"

"Naturally. If you are going to continue on this path, we will want their blessing."

"Maybe I should practice more," Venli said. "Before we tell anyone."

Jaxlim hummed to Reprimand. "This is like your refusal to perform the songs in public. You are afraid of exposing yourself to failure again, Venli."

"No," she said. "No, of course not. Mother, I just think this would be better if I knew for certain it worked. Before causing trouble."

Why *wouldn't* someone want to be certain before inviting ridicule by failing? That did *not* make Venli a coward. She'd adopt a new form when nobody else had. That was *bold*. She wanted to control the circumstances, that was all.

"Come with me," Jaxlim said to Peace. "The others have been discussing this—I approached them after you asked me before. I hinted to the elders that I thought adopting new forms might be possible, and I believe they are willing to try."

"Really?" Venli asked.

"Yes. Come. They will celebrate your initiative. That is too rare for us, in this form. It is far better than dullform, but it *does* affect our minds. We need other forms, despite what some may say."

Venli felt herself attuning Excitement as she followed her mother out of the tent. If she *did* obtain warform, would it open her mind? Make her even more bold? Quiet the fears and worries she often felt? She hungered for accomplishments. Hungered to make their world better, less dull, more *vibrant*. Hungered to be the one who carried her people to greatness. Out of the crem and toward the skies.

The Five were gathered around the firepit amid the trees, discussing offensive tactics for the upcoming battle. That mostly equated to which boasts to make, and which warriors to let cast their spears first.

Jaxlim stepped up to the elders and sang a full song to Excitement. A rare delivery from the keeper of songs, and each stanza made Venli stand taller.

Once the song was finished, Jaxlim explained what Venli had told her. Indeed, the elders were interested. They realized that new forms were worth the risk. Confident that she would not be rejected, Venli stepped forward and attuned Victory.

As she began, however, something sounded outside of town. The warning drums? The Five hastened to grab their weapons—ancient axes, spears, and swords, each one precious and passed down for generations, for the listeners had no means of creating new metal weapons.

But what could this be? No other family would attack them out here in the wilderness. It hadn't happened in generations, since the Pure-Song family had raided the Fourth-Movement family in an attempt to steal their weapons. The Pure-Songers had been thoroughly shunned for that action.

Venli stayed back as the elders left. She didn't wish to be involved in a skirmish—if indeed that was happening. She was an apprentice keeper of songs, and was far too valuable to risk in battle. Hopefully whatever this was, it would be over soon and she could return to basking in the respect of the elders.

So it was that she was one of the last to hear about Eshonai's incredible discovery. Among the last to learn that their world had forever been changed. And among the last to learn that her grand announcement had been utterly overshadowed by the actions of her reckless sister.

I approach this project with an equal mixture of trepidation and hope. And I know not which should rule.

—From *Rhythm of War*, page 1

Raboniel denied Navani servants. The Fused apparently thought it would be a hardship for Navani to live without them. So Navani allowed herself a small moment of pride when she stepped out of her rooms on the first full day of Urithiru's occupation. Her hair was clean and braided, her simple havah pressed and neat, her makeup done. Washing in cold water hadn't been pleasant, but the fabrials weren't working, so it wasn't as if she could expect warm water even if she had servants.

Navani was led down to the library rooms in the basement of Urithiru. Raboniel sat at Navani's own desk, going through her notes. Upon arriving, Navani bowed precisely, just low enough to indicate obedience—but not low enough to imply subservience.

The Fused pushed back the chair and leaned an elbow on the desktop, then made a shooing motion with a hummed sound to dismiss the guards.

"What is your decision?" the Fused asked.

"I will organize my scholars, Ancient One," Navani said, "and continue their research under your observation."

"The wiser choice, and the more dangerous one, Navani Kholin." Raboniel hummed a different tone. "I do not find the schematics for your flying machine in these notes."

Navani made a show of debating it, but she'd already considered this issue. The secrets of the flying platform would be impossible to keep; too many of Navani's scholars knew them. Beyond that, many of the new style of conjoined fabrials—which allowed lateral motion while maintaining elevation—were already in use around the tower. Though fabrials didn't work, Raboniel's people could surely discern their operation.

After a long debate with herself, she'd come to the conclusion that she needed to give up this secret. Her best hope in escaping the current predicament was to appear to be willing to work with Raboniel, while also stalling.

"I intentionally don't keep priority schematics anywhere but in my own head," Navani lied. "Instead I explain each piece I need built to my scholars as I need them. Given time, I can draw for you the mechanism that makes the machine work."

Raboniel hummed to a rhythm, but Navani couldn't tell what it represented. However, Raboniel seemed skeptical as she stood and waved for Navani to sit down. She placed a reed in Navani's hands and folded her arms to wait.

Well, fine. Navani began drawing with quick, efficient lines. She made a diagram of a conjoined fabrial, with a quick explanation of how it worked, then she drew the expanded vision of hundreds of them embedded into the flying machine.

"Yes," Raboniel said as Navani sketched the last portions, "but how do you make it move laterally? Surely with this construction, you could raise a machine high in the air—but it would have to remain there, in one place. You don't expect me to believe that you have a ground machine moving in exact coordination to the one in the sky."

"You understand more about fabrials than I assumed, Lady of Wishes."

Raboniel hummed a rhythm. "I am a quick learner." She gestured to the notes on Navani's desk. "In the past, my kind found it difficult to persuade spren to manifest themselves in the Physical Realm as devices.

It seems Voidspren are not as naturally . . . self-sacrificing as those of Honor or Cultivation."

Navani blinked as the implications of that sank in. Suddenly a dozen loose threads in her mind tied together, forming a tapestry. An *explanation*. That was why the fabrials of the tower—the pumps, the climbing mechanisms—didn't have gemstones with captive spren. Storms . . . that was the answer to Soulcasting devices.

Awespren burst around her in a ring of blue smoke. Soulcasters didn't *hold* spren because they *were* spren. Manifesting in the Physical Realm like Shardblades. Spren became metal on this side. Somehow the ancient spren had been coaxed into manifesting as Soulcasters instead of Blades?

"You didn't know, I see," Raboniel said, pulling a chair over for herself. Even sitting, she was a foot taller than Navani. She made such an odd image: a carapace-armored figure, as if prepared for war, picking through notes. "Odd that you should have made so many advances that we never dreamed of in epochs past, yet you've forgotten the far simpler method your ancestors used."

"We . . . we didn't have access to spren who would talk to us," Navani explained. "Vev's golden keys . . . this . . . I can't believe we didn't see it. The implications . . ."

"Lateral movement?" Raboniel asked.

Feeling almost in a daze, Navani sketched out the answer. "We learned to isolate planes for conjoined fabrials," she explained. "You have to use this construction of aluminum wires, rigged to touch the gemstone. That maintains vertical position, but allows the gemstone to be moved horizontally."

"Fascinating," Raboniel said. "Ralkalest—you call it aluminum in your language—interfering with the Connection. That's quite ingenious. It must have taken a great deal of testing to get the correct configuration."

"Over a year's worth," Navani admitted. "After the initial possibility was theorized. We have a problem that we can't move vertically and laterally at the same time—the fabrials that move us upward and downward are finicky, and we have been touching aluminum to them only after locking them into place."

"That's inconvenient."

"Yes," Navani said, "but we've found a system where we stop, then do our vertical motions. It can be a pain, since spanreeds are very difficult to make work in moving vehicles."

"It seems there should be a way to use this knowledge to make spanreeds that can be used while moving," Raboniel said, inspecting Navani's sketch.

"That was my thought as well," Navani said. "I put a small team on it, but we've been mostly occupied by other matters. Your weapons against our Radiants still confuse me."

Raboniel hummed to a quick and dismissive rhythm. "Ancient technology, barely functional," she said. "We can suck the Stormlight from a Radiant, yes—so long as they remain hanging there impaled by one of our weapons. This method does nothing to prevent the spren from bonding a new Radiant. I should like it if your spren were easier to capture in gemstones."

"I'll pass the request along," Navani said.

Raboniel hummed to a different rhythm, then smiled. It was difficult not to see the expression as predatory on her marbled face, with its lean danger. Yet there was also something tempting about the efficiency of this interaction. A few minutes of exchange, and Navani knew secrets she'd been trying to crack for decades.

"This is how we end the war, Navani," Raboniel said, standing. "With information. Shared."

"And this ends the war how?"

"By showing everyone that our lives will all be improved by working together."

"With the singers ruling."

"Of course," Raboniel said. "You are obviously a keen scholar, Navani Kholin. If you could improve the lives of your people manyfold, is that not worth abandoning self-governance? Look what we've done in mere minutes by sharing our knowledge."

Shared only because of your threats, Navani thought, careful not to show that on her face. This wasn't some free exchange. *It doesn't matter what you tell me, Raboniel. You can reveal any secret you desire—because I'm in your power. You can just kill me once you have everything you want.*

She smiled at Raboniel, however. "I would like to check on my scholars, Lady of Wishes, to see how they're being treated, and find out the extent of our . . . losses." That made one point clear, Navani hoped.

Some of her friends had been murdered. She was not simply going to forget about that.

Raboniel hummed, gesturing for Navani to join her. This was going to require a delicate balance, with both of them trying to play one another. Navani had to be explicitly careful not to let herself be taken in by Raboniel. That was one advantage Navani had over her scholars. She might never be worthy to join them, but she did have more experience with the real world of politics.

Raboniel and Navani entered the second of the two library rooms—the one with more desks and chairs. Navani's best—ardents and scholars alike—sat on the floor, heads bowed. They'd plainly been made to sleep here, judging by the spread-out blankets.

A few looked up to see her, and she noted with relief that Rushu and Falilar were both unharmed. She did a quick count, immediately picking out the notable exceptions. She stepped over to Falilar, squatting down and asking, "Neshan? Inabar?"

"Killed, Brightness," he said softly. "They were in the crystal pillar room, along with both of Neshan's wards, Ardent Vevanara, and a handful of unfortunate soldiers."

Navani winced. "Pass the word," she whispered. "For the time being, we are going to cooperate with the occupation." She stopped by Rushu next. "I am glad you are well."

The ardent—who had obviously been crying—nodded. "I was on my way down here to gather some scribes to help catalogue the destruction up in that room, when . . . this happened. Brightness, do you think it's related?"

In the chaos, Navani had nearly forgotten the strange explosion. "Did you by chance find any infused spheres in the wreckage?" *Specifically, a strange Voidlight one?*

"No, Brightness," Rushu said. "You saw the place. It was in shambles. But I did darken it to see if anything glowed, and saw nothing. Not a hint of Stormlight, or even Voidlight."

As Navani had feared. Whatever that explosion had been, it had to be tied to the strange sphere—and that sphere was likely now gone.

Navani stood and walked back to Raboniel. "You didn't need to kill my scholars during your attack. They were no threat to you."

Raboniel hummed to a quick-paced rhythm. "You will not be warned again, Navani. You will use my title when addressing me. I do not want to see you harmed, but there are proprieties thousands of years old that you *will* follow."

"I . . . understand, Lady of Wishes. I think putting my remaining people to work immediately would be good for morale. What would you like us to do?"

"To ease the transition," Raboniel said, "have them continue whatever they were doing before my arrival."

"Many were working on fabrials, which will no longer function."

"Have them do design sketches then," Raboniel said. "And write about the experiments they'd done before the occupation. I can see that their new theories get tested."

Did that mean there was a way to get fabrials working in the tower? "As you wish."

Then she got to work on the real problem: planning how she was going to get them out of this mess.

⁂

Kaladin was awakened by rain. He blinked, feeling mist on his face and seeing a jagged sky lit by spears of lightning frozen in place—not fading, just hanging there, framed by black clouds in a constant boil.

He stared at the strange sight, then rolled to his side, half submerged in a puddle of frigid water. Was this Hearthstone? The warcamps? No . . . neither?

He groaned, forcing himself to his feet. He didn't appear to be wounded, but his head was pounding. No weapons. He felt naked without a spear. Gusts of rain blew around him, the falling water moving in sheets—and he swore he could see the outlines of figures in the rainfall. As if it were making momentary shapes as it fell.

The landscape was dark, evoking distant crags. He started through the water, surprised to see no spren around—not even rainspren. He thought he saw light atop a hill, so he started up the incline, careful not to lose his footing on the slick rock. A part of him wondered why he could see. The frozen jagged lightning bolts didn't give off much illumination. Hadn't he been in a place like this once? With omnipresent light, but a black sky?

He stopped and stared upward, rain scouring his face. This was all . . . all wrong. This wasn't real . . . was it?

Motion.

Kaladin spun. A short figure moved down the hill toward him, emerging from the darkness. It seemed composed entirely of swirling grey mist with no features, though it wielded a spear. Kaladin caught the weapon with a quick turn of his hand, then twisted and pushed back in a classic disarming move.

This phantom attacker wasn't terribly skilled, and Kaladin easily stole the weapon. Instinct took command, and he spun the spear and rammed it through the figure's neck. As the short figure dropped, two more appeared as if from nothing, both wielding spears of their own.

Kaladin blocked one strike and threw the attacker off with a calculated shove, then spun and dropped the other one with a sweep to the legs. He stabbed that figure with a quick thrust to the neck, then easily rammed his spear into the stomach of the other one as it stood up. Blood ran down the spear's shaft onto Kaladin's fingers.

He yanked the spear free as the smoky figure dropped. It felt good to hold a spear. To be able to fight without worries. Without anything weighing him down other than the rainwater on his uniform. Fighting used to be simple. Before . . .

Before . . .

The swirling mist evaporated off the fallen figures and he found three young messenger boys in Amaram's colors, killed by Kaladin's spear. Three corpses, including his brother.

"No!" Kaladin screamed, ragged and hateful. "How dare you show me this? It didn't happen that way! I was there!"

He turned away from the corpses, looking toward the sky. "I didn't kill him! I just failed him. I . . . I just . . ."

He stumbled away from the dead boys and dropped his spear, hands to his head. He felt the scars on his forehead. They seemed deeper, like chasms cutting through his skull.

Shash. Dangerous.

Thunder rumbled overhead and he stumbled downhill, unable to banish the sight of Tien dead and bleeding on the hillside. What kind of terrible vision was this?

"You saved us so we could die," a voice said from the darkness.

He knew that voice. Kaladin spun, splashing in the rainwater, searching for the source. He was on the Shattered Plains now. In the rain he saw the *suggestions* of people. Figures made by the falling drops, but somehow empty.

The figures began attacking each other, and he heard the thunder of war. Men shouting, weapons clashing, boots on stone. It surrounded him, overwhelmed him, until—in a flash—he emerged into an enormous battle, the suggested shapes becoming real. Men in blue fighting against other men in blue.

"Stop fighting!" Kaladin shouted at them. "You're killing your own! They're all our soldiers!"

They didn't seem to hear him. Blood flowed beneath his feet instead of rainwater, sprays and gushes melding as spearmen climbed eagerly over the bodies of the fallen to continue killing one another. Kaladin grabbed one spearman and pushed him away from another, then seized a third and pulled him back—only to find that it was Lopen.

"Lopen!" Kaladin said. "Listen to me! Stop fighting!"

Lopen bared his teeth in a terrible grin, then knocked Kaladin aside before launching himself at yet another figure—Rock, who had stumbled on a corpse. Lopen killed him with a spear through the gut, but then Teft killed Lopen from behind. Bisig stabbed Teft, and Kaladin didn't see who brought him down. He was too horrified.

Sigzil dropped nearby with a hole in his side, and Kaladin caught him.

"Why?" Sigzil asked, blood dribbling from his lips. "Why didn't you let us sleep?"

"This isn't real. This can't be real."

"You should have let us die on the Shattered Plains."

"I wanted to protect you!" Kaladin shouted. "I *had* to protect you!"

"You cursed us . . ."

Kaladin dropped the dying body and stumbled away. He ducked his head, his mind cloudy, and started running. A part of him knew this horror wasn't real, but he could still hear the screaming. Accusing him. *Why did you do this, Kaladin? Why have you killed us?*

He pressed his hands to his ears, so intent on escaping the carnage that he nearly ran straight into a chasm. He pulled up, teetering on the edge. He stumbled, then looked to his left. The warcamps were there, up a short slope.

He'd been here. He remembered this place, this storm, lightly raining. This chasm. Where he'd nearly died.

"You saved us," a voice said, "so we could suffer."

Moash. He stood on the edge of the chasm near Kaladin. The man turned, and Kaladin saw his eyes—black pits. "People think you were merciful to us. But we both know the truth, don't we? You did it for you. Not us. If you were truly merciful, you'd have given us easy deaths."

"No," Kaladin said. "No!"

"The void awaits, Kal," Moash said. "The emptiness. It lets you do anything—even kill a king—without regret. One step. You'll never have to feel pain again."

Moash took a step and dropped into the chasm. Kaladin fell to his knees on the edge, rain streaming around him. He stared down in horror.

Then started awake someplace cold. Immediately, a hundred pains coursed through his joints and muscles, each demanding his attention like a screaming child. He groaned and opened his eyes, but there was only darkness.

I'm in the tower, he thought, remembering the events of the previous day. *Storms. The place is controlled by the Fused. I barely got away.*

The nightmares seemed to be getting worse. Or they'd always been this bad, but he didn't remember. He lay there, breathing deeply, sweating as if from exertion—and remembered the sight of his friends dying. Remembered Moash stepping into that darkness and vanishing.

Sleeping was supposed to refresh you, but Kaladin felt more tired than when he'd collapsed. He groaned and put his back to the wall, forcing himself to sit up. Then he felt around in a sudden panic. In his addled state, a part of him thought for sure he'd find Teft dead on the floor.

He let out a sigh of relief as he located his friend lying nearby, still breathing. The man had wet himself, unfortunately—he'd grow dehydrated quickly if Kaladin didn't do something, and the potential for rotspren was high if Kaladin didn't get him cleaned up and properly situated with a bedpan.

Storms. The weight of what Kaladin had done hung above him, nearly as oppressive as the weight of the tower. He was alone, lost in the darkness, without Stormlight or anything to drink—let alone proper weapons. He needed to take care of not only himself, but a man in a coma.

What had he been thinking? He didn't believe the nightmare—but he couldn't completely banish its echoes either. Why? Why couldn't he have let go? Why did he keep fighting? Was it really for them?

Or was it because he was selfish? Because *he* couldn't let go and admit defeat?

"Syl?" he asked in the darkness. When she didn't answer him, he called again, his voice trembling. "Syl, where are you?"

No reply. He felt around his enclosure, and realized he had no idea how to get out. He'd entombed himself and Teft here in this too-thick darkness. To die slow deaths alone . . .

Then a pinprick of light appeared. Syl, blessedly, entered the enclosure. She couldn't pass through walls—Radiant spren had enough substance in the Physical Realm that they were impeded by most materials. Instead she appeared to have come in through some sort of vent high in the wall.

Her appearance brought with it a measure of his sanity. He released a shuddering breath as she flitted down and landed on his outstretched palm.

"I found a way out," she said, taking the shape of a soldier wearing a scout's uniform. "I don't think you'd be able to get through it though. Even a child would be cramped.

"I looked around, though I couldn't go too far. Guards are posted at many stairwells, but they don't seem to be searching for you. These floors are big enough that I think they've realized finding one man in here is virtually impossible."

"That's some good news, I guess," Kaladin said. "Do you have any idea what that light was that led me in here?"

"I . . . have a theory," Syl said. "A long time ago, before things went poorly between spren and humans, there were three Bondsmiths. One for the Stormfather. One for the Nightwatcher. And one other. For a spren called the Sibling. A spren who remained in this tower, hidden, and did not appear to humans. They were supposed to have died long ago."

"Huh," Kaladin said, feeling at the door that had opened to let him in. "What were they like?"

"I don't know," Syl said, moving to his shoulder. "We've talked to Brightness Navani about this, answering her questions, and the other Radiant spren didn't know more than I just said. Remember, many of the spren who knew about the old days died—and the Sibling was always secretive. I don't know what kind of spren they were, or why they could create a Bondsmith. If they are alive though, I don't know why so much in the tower doesn't work."

"Well, this wall worked," Kaladin said, finding the gemstone in the wall. The gem was dark now, but it was also much more prominent on this side. He could easily have missed it from the other direction. How many other rooms had such gemstones embedded in the wall, hiding secret doors?

He touched the gemstone. Despite the fact that he didn't have any more Stormlight, light appeared deep inside it. A white light that twinkled like a star. It expanded into a small burst of Stormlight, and the door silently split open again.

Kaladin let out a long breath and felt a little of his panic wash away. He wouldn't die in the darkness. Once the gemstone was charged, it worked like any other fabrial, continuing to function so long as it had remaining Stormlight.

He looked to Syl. "Think you can find your way back here to Teft if we leave and do some scouting?"

"I should be able to memorize our path."

"Great," Kaladin said. "Because we need supplies." He couldn't afford to think about the long term yet. Those daunting questions—what he was going to do about the tower, the dozens of Radiants in enemy captivity, his family—would need to wait. First he needed water, food, Stormlight, and—most importantly—a better weapon.

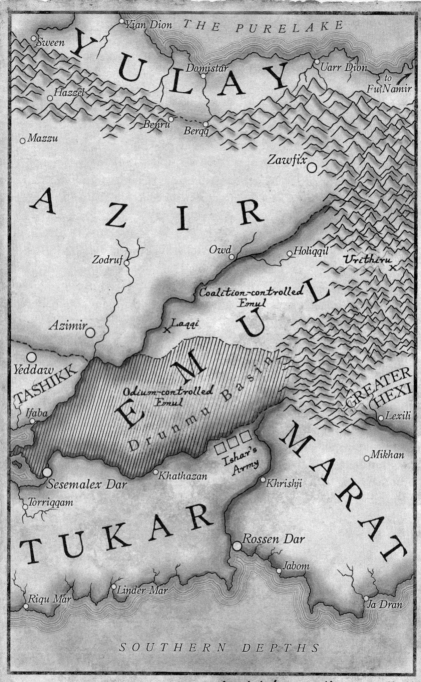

Annotated map of the war in Emul.

I approach this project with inspiration renewed; the answers are all that should matter.

—From *Rhythm of War,* page 1 undertext

The wood lurched under Dalinar's feet, and he grabbed a railing to steady himself. "Skybreakers!" he shouted. "Trying to get at the fabrial housings!"

Two figures in blue leaped off the deck nearby, bursting with Light as the platform continued to shake. Two wouldn't be able to handle this. Storm it, where was—

Sigzil and his force of ten Windrunners came swooping back, striking at the underside of the flying platform. It wasn't truly a flying machine like the *Fourth Bridge,* but these platforms were nevertheless an excellent vantage for viewing a battlefield. Assuming they didn't get attacked.

Dalinar held firm to the railing, glancing at the Mink—who was tethered to Dalinar with a rope. The shorter man was grinning wildly as he clung to the railing. Fortunately, the platform soon stopped lurching and the Skybreakers scattered, trailed by figures in blue with spears.

Fewer Heavenly Ones than I'd have expected, Dalinar noted as the wind ruffled his hair. He picked out only four of the flying Fused watching the battlefield from above and occasionally delivering instructions to the ground troops. They didn't engage. *They're leaning on the Skybreakers for this battle.* Perhaps the bulk of the Heavenly Ones were with the main enemy forces, stationed several days' march away.

The Mink leaned out over the side of the platform, trying to get a view directly beneath—where Radiants were clashing. He didn't seem at all bothered by the three-hundred-yard drop to the ground. For a man who always seemed so paranoid, he could certainly be cavalier regarding danger.

Beneath them, the battle lines held formation. Dalinar's troops, augmented by ranks of Azish, fought Taravangian's treasonous forces—who had tried to strike inward to rescue their king. The Vedens were accompanied by a small number of Fused and some singer troops, a small enough force to have moved in close without detection before the betrayal.

On Dalinar's platform, some fifty archers re-formed their ranks following the chaos of the sudden Skybreaker attack. In moments, they were sending a hail of arrows on the Vedens.

"They'll break soon," the Mink said softly, surveying the battlefield. "Their line is bowing. Those Azish fight well. Better than I thought they would."

"They have excellent discipline," Dalinar agreed. "They simply needed proper direction." Any given Azish soldier was no match for an Alethi, but after witnessing their discipline this last year, Dalinar was grateful he'd never had to face their infantry in battle. The vast blocks of Azish pikes were less mobile than the Alethi equivalent, but were impeccably coordinated.

They were a tremendous addition to an Alethi system, which had far more flexibility and a variety of specialized troops. Using Azish blocks like wedges, and Alethi tactics, they'd been able to stand against the enemy despite their natural advantages, like carapace armor and stronger builds.

And the Veden traitors? Well, the Mink was right. The enemy line was beginning to bow and crack. They had no cavalry, and the Mink made a quiet order to one of the waiting scribes, who transferred it. Dalinar guessed—correctly—he'd ordered a harrying strike of light riders along the left flank. Those filled the Veden back rows with arrows, distracting them to further stress the wavering lines.

"I do have to admit," the Mink said to Dalinar as they watched, bow-strings snapping behind them, "this is an excellent way to oversee a battlefield."

"And you were worried about there being no escape."

"Rather," the Mink said, looking toward the ground below, "I was worried about all avenues of escape being interrupted by an unfortunate collision with the ground. Still don't know the wisdom of putting us both up here; seems like we should be on separate platforms, so that if one falls, the other can continue to lead our forces."

"You mistake my purpose, Dieno," Dalinar said, tugging on the rope that bound them. "My job in this battle isn't to command if you are killed. It's to get you out *before* you are killed."

One of Jasnah's escape boats waited on the other side, in Shadesmar. In an emergency, Dalinar could get himself and the Mink through the perpendicularity. They'd drop a short distance—but not nearly as far as they would on this side—into a padded ship with mandras hooked in place.

The Mink, unsurprisingly, didn't like that escape route. He couldn't control it. In truth, Dalinar wasn't a hundred percent comfortable with it himself—he didn't fully trust his powers yet. His mastery over them was tenuous.

He opened the perpendicularity as the Windrunners approached for more Stormlight. He managed to open it only a sliver, renewing those nearby, but preventing the Skybreakers from partaking. They retreated; Skybreakers couldn't match Windrunners who were being constantly renewed, and were usually deployed on battlefields where Dalinar was not present.

As the Mink took casualty reports—which included two Windrunner squires, unfortunately—a young scribe stepped up to Dalinar with a sheaf of papers and a blinking spanreed. "Word from Urithiru, Brightlord," she said. "You wanted to know as soon as we heard something, and we have."

Dalinar felt a huge weight slide off his shoulders. "Finally! What is happening?"

"Trouble with the tower fabrials," the scribe reported. "Brightness Navani says that some kind of strange defensive aura has been deployed, preventing Radiants from using their powers. It also interferes with fabrials. She had to send a scouting team out along the ridge into the mountains before they were able to deliver her message.

"Everyone is safe, and she's working on the problem. That is why the Oathgates have stopped working, however. She begs for your patience, and asks if anything strange has happened here."

"Tell her about Taravangian's betrayal," Dalinar said, "but report that I'm safe, as is our family. We are fighting the traitors, and should soon win the day."

She nodded and went to send the message. The Mink stepped closer; he'd either overheard, or had received a similar report.

"They're trying to confuse and distract us during the betrayal," he said. "Heaping attacks on multiple fronts."

"Another ploy to negate the Oathgates," Dalinar agreed. "That device they used on Highmarshal Kaladin must have been some sort of test. They've knocked out Urithiru for a while to isolate us."

The Mink leaned out, squinting at the armies below. "Something about this smells wrong, Blackthorn. If this was merely a ploy to isolate the fighting in Azir and Emul, they've made a tactical mistake. Their forces in this part of the land are exposed, and we have the upper hand. They wouldn't go through so much effort to block us from the Oathgates unless it were *truly* cutting off our escape route. Which it won't because we're not going to need one."

"You think this is a distraction from something else?"

The Mink nodded slowly. Far below, the cavalry did another sweep. The line of the traitors buckled further.

"I'll tell the others to watch out," Dalinar said, "and send scouts to investigate Urithiru. I agree, something about this is off."

"Make certain the armies we're going to fight in Emul haven't been secretly reinforced. That could be terrible for us—the only true disaster I can envision here is Azimir being besieged, and unable to be resupplied via the Oathgates. Having seen that city, I'd hate to be trapped there."

"Agreed," Dalinar said.

The Mink leaned out further, precariously, as he watched the battle-field below. It was hard to hear—muffled clangs, shouts from far away. Men moved like lifespren.

But Dalinar could smell the sweat. Could hear the roar. Could *feel* himself standing among the struggling, screaming, dying bodies and *dominating* with Blade in hand. Once you'd tasted the near invincibility of wearing Plate and wading in among mortals, it was a . . . difficult flavor to forget.

"You miss it," the Mink said, eyeing him.

"Yes," Dalinar admitted.

"They could use you on the ground."

"Down there, I'd be merely another sword. I can do more in other positions."

"Pardon, Blackthorn, but you were *never* merely another sword." The Mink crossed his arms, leaning against the wooden railing. "You keep saying you're more use elsewhere, and I suppose you make a pretty good storm for renewing spheres. But I can sense you stepping away. What are you planning?"

That was the question. He sensed there was so much more for him to do. Greater things. Important things. The tasks of a Bondsmith. But getting to them, figuring them out . . .

"They're breaking," the Mink said, standing up straight. "You want to let them go, or pin them and crush them?"

"What do you think?" Dalinar asked.

"I hate fighting men who feel they have no way out," the Mink said.

"We can't afford to let them reinforce the enemy to the south," Dalinar said. That would be their true battlefield, once this skirmish was over. The war for Emul. "Keep pressing them until they surrender."

The Mink began giving the orders. From below, drums washed over the battlefield: the frantic attempts by enemy commanders to maintain discipline as the lines disintegrated. He could almost hear their shouted, panic-tinged cries. Desperation in the air.

The Mink is right, Dalinar thought. *They made a real effort here to strike at us—but something is wrong. We're missing a piece of the enemy's plan.*

As he was watching, a nondescript soldier stepped up beside him. Dalinar had brought only a handful of bodyguards today: three men from the Cobalt Guard, and a single Shardbearer. Cord, the Horneater woman, who had taken it upon herself to join his guards for reasons he didn't quite understand.

He also held a hidden weapon—the man who stood beside him, so ordinary in his Alethi uniform, holding a sheathed sword that was admittedly longer than regulation. Szeth, the Assassin in White, wearing a false face. He didn't speak, though the complex Lightweaving he wore would disguise his voice. He simply watched, his eyes narrowed. What did he see in this battlefield? What had caught his attention?

Szeth suddenly grabbed Dalinar by the front of his uniform and towed him to the side. Dalinar barely had time to shout in surprise as a glowing figure rose up beside the archer platform, radiant with Stormlight and bearing a silvery Blade. Szeth stepped between Dalinar and the Skybreaker, hand going to his sword. But Dalinar caught him by the arm, preventing him from drawing it. Once that weapon came out, dangerous things happened. They would want to be absolutely certain it was needed before unleashing it.

The figure was familiar to Dalinar. Dark brown skin, with a birthmark on his cheek. Nalan—called Nale. Herald and leader of the Skybreakers. He had shaved his head recently, and held out his Blade in a defiant—perhaps challenging—posture as he addressed Dalinar.

"Bondsmith," Nale said, "your war is unjust. You must submit to the laws of the—"

An arrow slammed into his face, dead center, interrupting him. Dalinar glanced back, then stopped Cord, who was drawing her Shardbow again. "Wait. I'd hear him."

Nale, with a suffering expression, pulled the arrow free and dropped it, letting his Stormlight heal him. Could this man be killed? Ash said the enemy had somehow killed Jezrien—but before, when Heralds died, their souls had returned to Damnation to await torture.

Nale didn't continue his diatribe. He lightly stepped up onto the railing of the platform, then dropped to the deck. He tossed his Blade away, letting it vanish to mist in midair.

"How are you a Bondsmith?" Nale asked Dalinar. "You should not exist, Blackthorn. Your cause is not righteous. You should be denied the true Surges of Honor."

"Perhaps it is a sign that *you* are wrong, Nalan," Dalinar said. "Perhaps our cause *is* righteous."

"No," Nale said. "Other Radiants can lie to themselves and their spren. So-called honorspren prove that morality is shaped by their perceptions. You should be different. Honor should not allow this bonding."

"Honor is dead," Dalinar said.

"And yet," Nale said, "Honor still should prevent this. Prevent *you*." He looked Dalinar up and down. "No Shardblade. Fair enough."

He launched forward, reaching for Dalinar. Szeth was upon him in a moment, but hesitated to draw his strange Blade. Nale moved with a skyeel's grace, twisting Szeth about and slamming him to the deck of the wooden platform. The Herald slapped aside Szeth's sheathed sword, punching him in the crook of the elbow and making him drop his weapon. Nale casually reached up and caught the arrow launched from Cord's Shardbow mere feet away—an inhuman feat.

Dalinar pressed his hands together, reaching beyond reality for the perpendicularity. Nale leaped over Szeth toward Dalinar as the others on the platform shouted, trying to react to the attack.

No, the Stormfather said to Dalinar. *Touch him.*

Dalinar hesitated—the power of the perpendicularity at his fingertips—then reached out and pressed his hand to Nale's chest as the Herald reached for him.

Flash.

Dalinar saw Nale stepping away from a discarded Blade rammed into the stone.

Flash.

Nale cradling a child in one arm, his Blade out as dark forces crawled across a ridge nearby.

Flash.

Nale standing with a group of scholars and unrolling a large writ, filled with writing. "The law cannot be moral," Nale said to them. "But *you* can be moral as you create laws. Ever must you protect the weakest, those most likely to be taken advantage of. Institute a right of movement, so that a family who feels their lord is unrighteous can leave his area. Then tie a lord's authority to the people who follow him."

Flash.

Nale kneeling before a highspren.

Flash.

Nale fighting on a battlefield.

Flash.

Another fight.

Flash.

Another fight.

The visions came faster and faster; Dalinar could no longer distinguish one from another. Until

Flash.

Nale clasping hands with a bearded Alethi man, regal and wise. Dalinar knew this was Jezerezeh, though he couldn't say how.

"I will take this charge," Nale said softly. "With honor."

"Do not consider it an honor," Jezerezeh said. "A duty, yes, but not an honor."

"I understand. Though I had not expected you would come to an enemy with this offer."

"An enemy, yes," Jezerezeh said. "But an enemy who was correct all along, making me the villain, not you. We will fix what we've broken. Ishar and I agreed. There is no person we would welcome more eagerly into this pact than you. You are the single most honorable man I have ever had the privilege of opposing."

"I wish that were true," Nale said. "But I will serve as best I can."

The vision faded and Nale lurched away from Dalinar, gasping, his eyes wide. He left a line of light stretching between him and Dalinar.

Bondsmith, the Stormfather said in Dalinar's mind. *You forged a brief Connection with him. What did you see?*

"His past, I think," Dalinar whispered. "And now . . ."

Nale scratched at his head, and Dalinar saw a skeletal figure overlapping him. Like the echo of light that followed Szeth, only worn, dim. Dalinar stepped forward, walking among his stunned bodyguards, noting eight lines of light extending from Nale into the distance.

"I see the Oathpact, I think," Dalinar said. "The thing that bound them together and made them capable of holding the enemy in Damnation."

A cage, forged of their spirits, the Stormfather said in his mind. *It was broken. Even before Jezrien's death, they shattered it by what they did long ago.*

"No, only one line of it is completely broken. The rest are there, but weak, impotent." Dalinar pointed to one line, bright and powerful. "Except one. Still vibrant."

Nale looked up at him, then ripped free of the line of light Connecting him to Dalinar and threw himself off the platform. The Herald burst alight and shot away as—belatedly—a few Windrunners came to Dalinar's aid.

You wield the power of gods, Dalinar, the Stormfather said. *I once thought I knew the extent of your abilities. I have abandoned that ignorant supposition.*

"Could I reforge it?" Dalinar asked. "Could I remake the Oathpact, and bind the Fused away again?"

I do not know. It may be possible, but I have no idea how. Or if it would be wise. The Heralds suffer for what they did.

"I saw that in him," Dalinar said, watching as Nale vanished in the distance. "He is burdened with a terrible pain that warps how he sees reality. An insanity unlike the ones that afflict ordinary men—an insanity that has to do with his worn soul . . ."

Szeth recovered his sword, seeming ashamed he'd been so easily bested. Dalinar did not fault him, nor the others, who insisted that he and the Mink retreat from the battlefield, now that the rout of Taravangian's troops was fully in progress.

Dalinar let the Windrunners spirit him away. All the while, he was lost in thought.

He needed to understand his powers. His duty was no longer to stand with a sword held high, shouting orders on the battlefield. He instead needed to find a way to use his abilities to solve this war. Reforge the Oathpact, or barring that, find another solution—one that included binding Odium once and for all.

SCENT OF DEATH, SCENT OF LIFE

NINE YEARS AGO

There was more than one way to explore. It turned out you could do it from the center of your own tent, if a group of living relics walked out of the forest and came to visit.

The humans thrilled Eshonai. They *hadn't* been destroyed after all. And their ways were so strange. They spoke without rhythm, and couldn't hear the songs of Roshar. They made carapace out of metal and tied it to themselves. Though she first assumed they had lost their forms, she soon realized that they had only a *single* form, and could never change. They had to deal with the passions of mateform *all the time*.

More intriguing, they brought with them a tribe of dullform creatures who also had no songs. They had skin patterns like the listeners, but didn't talk, let alone sing. Eshonai found them fascinating and disturbing. Where had the humans found such strange individuals?

The humans made camp across the river in the forest, and at first the Five let only a few listeners come to meet them. They worried about frightening away the strange humans if the entire family came to bother them.

Eshonai thought this foolish. The humans wouldn't grow frightened. They knew ancient things. Methods of forging metal and of writing sounds on paper. Things that the listeners had forgotten during the long sleep, the time they'd spent wearing dullform, memorizing songs by sheer force of will.

Eshonai, Klade, and a few others joined a few human scholars, trying to decipher one another's tongues. Preserved in the songs, fortunately, were human phrases. Perhaps her past with the songs was what helped Eshonai learn faster than the others. Or maybe it was her stubbornness. She spent evenings sitting with the humans, making them repeat sounds over and over late into the night by the light of their brilliant glowing gemstones.

That was another thing. Human gemstones glowed far more brightly than listener ones. It had to do with the way the gemstones were cut and shaped. Each day with the humans taught her something new.

Once the language barrier began to fall, the humans asked if they could be taken out onto the Shattered Plains. So it was that Eshonai led the way, though she kept them far from the ten ancient cities and the other listener families, for now.

Using one of Eshonai's maps, they approached from the north and walked along the chasms until they reached an ancient listener bridge. The rift in the stone smelled of wet rotting plants. Pungent, but not unpleasant. Where plants rotted, others often soon grew, and the scent of death was the same as the scent of life.

The humans followed gingerly across the bridge of wood and rope, the guards going first—wearing their buffed metal carapace breastplates and caps. They seemed to expect the bridge to collapse at any moment.

Once across, Eshonai stepped up onto a boulder and took a deep breath, feeling the winds. Overhead, a few windspren swirled in the sky. Once the guards had crossed, some of the others started over as well. Everyone had wanted to come see the Plains where the monsters of the chasms lived.

One of the attendants was a curious woman who was the surgeon's assistant. She climbed up onto the rock beside Eshonai, though her clothing—which enveloped her from neck to ankles and covered up her left hand for some reason—wasn't particularly good for exploring. It was nice to see that there were some things that the listeners had figured out that the humans hadn't.

"What do you see?" she asked Eshonai in the human tongue. "When you look at the spren?"

Eshonai hummed to Consideration. What did she mean? "I see spren," Eshonai said, speaking slowly and deliberately, as her accent was sometimes bad.

"Yes, what do they look like?"

"Long white lines," Eshonai said, pointing at the windspren. "Holes. Small holes? Is there a word?"

"Pinpricks, perhaps."

"Pinpricks in sky," Eshonai said. "And tails, long, very long."

"Curious," the woman said. She wore a lot of rings on her right hand, though Eshonai couldn't tell why. It seemed like they would get caught on things. "It *is* different."

"Different?" Eshonai said. "We see different?"

"Yes," the woman said. "You seem to see the reality of the spren, or closer to it. Tell me. We have stories, among the humans, of windspren that act like people. Taking different shapes, playing tricks. Have you ever seen one like that?"

Eshonai went over the words in her mind. She *thought* she understood some of it. "Spren like people? Act like people?"

"Yes."

"I have seen this," she said.

"Excellent. And windspren that talk? That call you by name? Have you met any like this?"

"What?" Eshonai said, attuning Amusement. "Spren talking? No. It seems . . . not real? Fake, but a story?"

"'Fanciful' is perhaps the word you want."

"Fanciful," Eshonai said, examining the sounds in her mind. Yes, there was more than one way to explore.

The king and his brother finally crossed onto the plateau. "King" was not a new word to her, as it was mentioned in the songs. There had been debate among the listeners whether they should have a monarch. It seemed to Eshonai that until they managed to stop squabbling and became a single unified people, the discussion was silly.

The king's brother was a brutish man who seemed like a slightly different breed from everyone else. He was the first she'd met, along with a group of human scouts, back in the forest. This human wasn't simply larger than most of the others, he walked with a different step. His face was harder. If a human could ever be said to have a form, this man was warform.

The king himself though . . . he was proof that humans didn't have forms. He was so erratic. Sometimes loud and angry, other times quiet and dismissive. Listeners had different emotions too, of course. It was just that this man seemed to defy explanation. Perhaps the fact that the humans spoke with no rhythms made her more surprised when they acted with such passion. He was also the only male in the group who wore a beard. Why was that?

"Guide," the king said, walking up to her. "Is this where the hunts happen?"

"Sometimes," she said. "Depends. It is season, so maybe they come. Maybe not."

The king nodded absently. He had taken little interest in her or any of the listeners. His scouts and scholars, however, seemed as fascinated by Eshonai as she was with them. So she tended to spend time with them.

"What kinds of greatshells can live here?" the brother asked. "There doesn't seem to be space for them, with all these cracks in the ground. Are they like whitespines? Jumping from place to place?"

"Whitespine?" she said, not knowing the word.

The woman with the rings brought out a book with a drawing in it for her.

Eshonai shook her head. "No, not that. They are . . ." How to explain the monsters of the chasms? "They are great. And large. And powerful. They . . . these lands are theirs."

"And do your people worship them?" one of the scholars asked.

"Worship?"

"Reverence. Respect."

"Yes." Who wouldn't respect a beast so mighty?

"Their gods, Brightlord," said the scribe to the king. "As I suspected, they worship these beasts. We must take care with future hunts."

Eshonai hummed to Anxiety, to indicate she was confused—but they didn't recognize this. They had to say everything with words.

"Here," the king said, pointing. "This plateau seems a good enough place for a break."

The human attendants began unpacking their things—tents made of a marvelous tough cloth, and a variety of foods. They enjoyed their lunches, these humans. Their traveling luxury was so opulent, it made Eshonai wonder what their *homes* were like.

Once they left, she intended to see. If they'd made it here without a properly durable form such as workform, then they must not have come that far. She attuned Amusement. After all these years with no contact, she likely would have found her way to their home on her own, given a few more months.

Eshonai kept busy by helping erect the tents. She wanted to figure out the pieces. She was fairly certain she could carve poles like the ones used for holding up the roof. But the cloth was lighter, smoother, than what the listeners could create. One of the workers was having trouble with a knot, so Eshonai took out her knife to cut it free.

"What is that?" a voice said from behind her. "Do you mind showing me that knife?"

It was the woman with the rings. Eshonai had thought she might be once-mates with the king, considering how often she spoke with him. But apparently there was no relation.

Eshonai glanced down, realizing that she'd brought out her good hunting knife. It was one of the weapons her ancestors had salvaged from the ruins at the center of the Plains, with beautiful metal that had lines in it, and a carved hilt of majestic detail.

She shrugged and showed it to the woman. The strange woman, in turn, waved urgently to the king. He left the shade and stepped over, taking the knife and narrowing his eyes as he studied it.

"Where did you get this?" he asked Eshonai.

"It is old," she said, not wanting to say too much. "Handed down. Generations."

"Lasting back to the False Desolation, perhaps?" the woman asked the king. "Could they really have weapons two thousand years old?"

The listener Shardblades were far more marvelous, but Eshonai didn't speak of those. Her family didn't own any anyway.

"I would like to know," the king said, "how you—"

He was interrupted by a trumping in the near distance. Eshonai spun, attuning Tension. "Monster of Chasms," she said. "Get soldiers! I did not think one would come close."

"We can handle a . . ." the king began, but trailed off, and his eyes became wide. An awespren approached—a floating blue ball of a creature that expanded with great enthusiasm.

Eshonai turned and saw a distant shadow emerging from a chasm.

Sleek yet strong, powerful yet graceful. The beast walked on numerous legs, and didn't bestow the humans with a glance. They were to it as it was to the sun—indeed, it turned upward at the light to bask. Gorgeous and mighty, as if the Rhythm of Awe had been given life.

"Blood of my fathers . . ." the king's brother said, stepping up. "How big *is* that thing?"

"Bigger than any we have in Alethkar," the king said. "You'd have to make your way to the Herdazian coast to come across a greatshell so large. But those live in the waters."

"These live in chasms," Eshonai whispered. "It doesn't seem angry, which is our fortune."

"It might be far enough away that it hasn't noticed us," the king's brother said.

"It noticed us," Eshonai said. "It simply doesn't care."

Others gathered around, and the king hushed them. Finally, the chasmfiend turned and looked them over. Then it slunk down into the chasm, trailed by a few shimmering chasmspren, like arrows in flight.

"Storms," the king's brother said. "You mean at any time, standing on these plateaus, one of *those* might be right below? Prowling about?"

"How can they live in those chasms?" one of the women asked. "What do they eat?"

It was a more solemn and quick group that returned to their lunch. They were eager to finish and leave, but none of them said it, and none hummed to Anxiety.

Of them all, only the king seemed unperturbed. While the others busied themselves, he continued studying Eshonai's knife, which he hadn't returned to her.

"You truly kept these for thousands of years?" he asked.

"No," she admitted. "We found them. Not my parents. Their parents' parents. In the ruins."

"Ruins, you say?" he looked up sharply. "What ruins? Those cities the other guide mentioned?"

Eshonai cursed Klade softly for having mentioned the ten cities. Deciding not to clarify that she meant the ruins at the center of the Plains, she attuned Anxiety. The way he inspected her made her feel like she was a map that had been drawn wrong. "My people built cities," she said. "Old parents of my people."

"You don't say . . ." he said. "Very curious. You remember those days then? You have records of them?"

"We have songs," she said. "Many songs. Important songs. They talk of the forms we bore. The wars we fought. How we left the . . . I don't know the word . . . the ones of old. Who ruled us. When the Neshua Kadal were fighting, with spren as companions, and had . . . had things . . . they could do . . ."

"Radiants?" he said, his voice growing softer. "Your people have stories about the *Knights Radiant*?"

"Yes, maybe?" she said. "I can't words, yet. Of this."

"Curious, curious."

As she'd expected, the humans decided to return to the forest soon after their meal. They were frightened—all but the king. He spent the entire trip asking about the songs. She had plainly been mistaken when she'd assumed he didn't care much about the listeners.

For from that moment on, he seemed very, *very* interested. He had his scholars interrogate them about songs, lore, and whether they knew of any other ruins. When the humans finally left for their lands several days later, King Gavilar gave Eshonai's people a gift: several crates of modern weapons, made of fine steel. They were no replacement for the ancient weapons, but not all of her people had those. No family had enough to outfit all their warriors.

All Gavilar wanted in exchange was a promise: that when he returned in the near future, he wanted to find Eshonai's people housed in one of the cities at the edge of the Plains. At that time, he said, he hoped to be able to hear from the keepers of songs in person.

SOUL OF DISCOVERY

In my fevered state, I worry I'm unable to focus on what is important.

—From *Rhythm of War*, page 3

Navani set to work organizing her scholars under the careful supervision of a large number of singer guards.

The situation left Navani with a delicate problem. She didn't want to give away more than was absolutely necessary. But if she failed to make progress, Raboniel would eventually notice and take action.

For now, Navani set the scholars to doing some busywork. The singers kept her people enclosed in a single one of the two library rooms, so Navani had the wards and younger ardents begin cleaning the room. They gathered up old projects and boxes of notes, then carried them out to stack in the hallway. They needed to make space.

She assigned the more experienced scholars to do revision work: going back over projects and either checking calculations or drawing new sketches. Ardents brought out fresh ledgers to go over figures, while Rushu unrolled large schematics and set several younger women to measuring each and every line. This would take up several days, perhaps longer—and it was also quite a natural thing to do. Navani frequently ordered recalculations after an interruption. It restored the scholars to a proper mindset, and they sometimes found legitimate errors.

Soon enough, she had an orderly room full of calming sounds. Papers shuffling, pens writing, people quietly discussing. No creationspren or logicspren, as often attended exciting work. Hopefully the singers in the room wouldn't realize that was odd.

Those singers were always underfoot, lingering close enough to overhear what Navani told her people. She'd grown accustomed to a clean workspace—giving her people enough freedom to innovate, but also enough careful corralling to keep them innovating in the proper direction. All of these guards undermined that effort, and Navani often caught her scholars glancing up and staring at some armed brute standing nearby.

At least most were merely common soldiers. Only one Fused—other than Raboniel—stayed near the scholars, and she wasn't one of those unnerving ones who could meld with the rock. No, this was a Fused of Raboniel's same type, a tall Fused with a topknot and a long face marbled white and red. The femalen sat on the floor, watching them, her eyes glazed over.

Navani kept covert watch over this Fused during the morning work. She had been told that many Fused were unhinged, and this one seemed to fit that description. She often stared off into nothingness, then giggled to herself. She would let her head flop from one side to the other. Why would Raboniel put this one here to watch them? Were there possibly so few sane Fused left that there was no other choice?

Navani leaned against the wall, touching her palms to the stone—where a vein of garnet ran almost imperceptibly along one line of strata—and pretended to watch as several young women carried boxes of papers out into the hallway.

You didn't talk to me last night, the Sibling said.

"I was being watched," Navani said under her breath. "They didn't let me stay in my own rooms, but took me to a smaller one. We'll need to talk here. You can hear me if I speak very softly like this?"

Yes.

"Can you see what Raboniel is doing?"

She had some workers set up a desk near the shield, where she is doing tests upon it to see if she can get through.

"Can she?"

I don't know. This is the first time it has been deployed. But she doesn't seem to realize you were the one who activated it. She explained to several others that she must have triggered some unknown fail-safe left by the ancient Radiants. She thinks that I must be dead after all this time, since the tower doesn't work.

"Curious," Navani said. "Why would she think that?"

The Midnight Mother told her. That Unmade who infected me for so many years, the one your Radiants frightened away? I remained hidden from her all that time, never fighting back, and so she thinks I died.

"All that time?" Navani asked. "How long?"

Centuries.

"Wasn't that hard?"

No. Why? Centuries mean nothing to me. I do not age.

"Other spren act like time has meaning."

Radiant spren, yes. Radiant spren put on a show, pretending as if they are male or female, malen or femalen, when they are neither. They think like humans because they want to be like humans.

I do not pretend. I am not human. I do not need to care about time. I do not need to look like you. I do not need to beg for your attention.

Navani cocked an eyebrow at that, considering that the Sibling *had* needed to beg for her help. She held her tongue. How to best use this advantage? What was the path to freedom? Navani liked to think that she could see patterns, that she could make order from chaos. There *was* a way out of this mess. She had to believe that.

Treat it like any other problem, Navani thought to herself. *Approach it systematically, breaking it down into manageable pieces.*

Last night, she'd decided on a few general courses of action. First, she had to maintain the ground she'd already obtained. That meant making certain the Sibling's shield remained in place.

Second, she had to get word to Dalinar and those on the outside, apprising them of what had happened.

Third, Navani needed to figure out what the enemy had done to negate Radiant powers. According to the Sibling, it involved a corruption of ancient tower protections. Navani needed to deactivate it.

Finally, she needed to turn that power upon the invaders. Barring that, she needed to use the awakened Radiants to mount a counterattack.

Standing here, trapped in the basement and constantly watched, those seemed impossible tasks. But her scholars had made a ship fly. She could do this, with their help.

Navani counted off the singer guards as they strolled through the room, looking over the shoulders of working scholars. One stopped the girls carrying out notes and checked through the boxes. That one Fused—the one who kept moving her head from one side to the other, humming a loud rhythm—was watching Navani at the moment. Navani tried not to let that unnerve her, and turned her head so her lips wouldn't be visible, then continued talking under her breath.

"Let's assume," she said, "that Raboniel is smart enough to figure out what those ancient Radiants did in creating this shield for you. What would be the best way for her to go about circumventing it?"

The Sibling didn't respond, and Navani began to worry. "Has something happened? Are you well?"

I am fine, the Sibling said. *But we are not friends, human. You are a slaver. I do not trust you.*

"You've trusted me so far."

Out of necessity. I am safe now.

"And for how long will you be safe? You're saying there is *no* way for Raboniel to get through?"

The Sibling didn't respond.

"Fine," Navani said. "But I can't plan a way to help you if I don't know your weaknesses. You'll be alone, subject to whatever Raboniel decides to do."

. . . I hate humans, the Sibling eventually said. *Humans twist what is said and always make themselves out to be right.*

How long until you demand that I bond a human, give up my freedom, and risk my life? I'm sure you'll have wonderful explanations as to why I should absolutely do that.

This time Navani was the one who remained silent. The Sibling could create another Bondsmith, and considering how useful Dalinar's powers were to the war effort, Navani would be foolish not to seize the opportunity. So she *would* need to find a way to make the Sibling bond a human again. She'd have to find someone completely unthreatening. Someone who didn't work with fabrials, someone who wasn't a politician. Someone the Sibling would like.

For now, Navani didn't prod. The Sibling clearly had some strange ways, but their interactions so far had been quite human, despite what they claimed. And Navani would expect a human to . . .

The shield we created is something Raboniel might have heard about, the Sibling said at last. *Therefore, she might understand how to circumvent it.*

"Tell me more," Navani said.

The shield is an extrapolation of the Surge of Soulcasting. It solidifies the air in a region by persuading it that it is glass. For the shield to be maintained, the system needs to be fed by external sources of Stormlight. Raboniel might realize this—especially if she researches the remnants of the node you used to activate the shield.

There are other nodes like that one, with crystals connected directly to my heart. There were four. You destroyed one. If she finds one of the other three, she could use it to corrupt me from the outside.

"So we need to find them first," Navani said, "and destroy them."

No. NO! That will weaken the shield, then destroy it. We need to defend them. Breaking one was bad enough. Do not think because I gave you permission once, you can continue to do this. Humans always break things.

Navani took a deep breath. She had to speak very carefully. "I won't break any of them unless it's absolutely necessary. Let's talk about something else. How did you contact me earlier? Can you work a spanreed?"

I hate the things. But using one was necessary.

"Yes, but how? Do you have hands somewhere?"

Just helpers. There is an insane woman, locked in a monastery, who I contacted. Those isolated, those with permeable souls, respond better to spren sometimes. This one, however, only wrote down everything I said—never responding. I had Dabbid bring her a spanreed, and I communicated through her.

Drat. That didn't seem particularly useful, at least now that spanreeds weren't working. "How is it that the enemy knocked the Radiants unconscious?" Navani asked.

It is an aspect of Ur, the Tower, the Sibling said. *A defense set up to prevent the Fused—and the Unmade, depending on circumstances—from entering it.*

"I encountered a fabrial designed to do the same—one I think must have been modeled after part of the crystal pillar. I don't mean to be rude, but did you not consider activating this defense when they attacked?"

The Sibling fell silent for a time, and Navani wondered if she had pushed the spren too far. Fortunately they spoke again, softly. *I have . . . been wounded. Thousands of years ago, something happened that changed the singers. It hurt me too.*

Navani covered her shock. "You're speaking of the binding of that Unmade, which made the singers lose their forms?"

Yes. That terrible act touched the souls of all who belong to Roshar. Spren too.

"How have no spren mentioned this?"

I don't know. But I lost the rhythm of my Light that day. The tower stopped working. My father, Honor, should have been able to help me, but he was losing his mind. And he soon died . . .

There was enough sorrow in the Sibling's voice that Navani didn't push them for answers. This changed everything.

When that Fused touched me, the Sibling continued, *she corrupted part of me to the tone of Odium. This wouldn't have been possible, once—but it is now. She fills my system with his Light, ruining me. Corrupting me.*

"So . . ." Navani said. "If we could find a way to destroy the Voidlight inside you, or somehow recover the rhythm you lost, you could reactivate the tower to our defense?"

I suppose. It doesn't seem possible. I feel . . . like we're doomed.

The mood shift seemed familiarly human. Indeed, Navani felt a little of the same. She rested her head against the wall, closing her eyes.

Break it down into little pieces, she reminded herself. *Protect the Sibling long enough to figure out the other problems. That's your first task.*

You didn't fill out a map all at once. You did it one line at a time. That was the soul of discovery.

But . . . the Sibling said.

"But?" Navani said, opening her eyes. "But what?"

But we might not need to wake up any Radiants. There are two in the tower who are still awake.

Again Navani nearly broke her calm facade. Why hadn't the Sibling mentioned this immediately? "How?"

One makes sense to me, the Sibling said. *She is awake because she was created oddly, to use Light differently from others. She was made by my mother for this purpose. But I have lost track of her, and I do not know where she is. A young woman. Edgedancer.*

"Lift," Navani said. That one always *had* been strange. "You can't see her anymore?"

No. I think one reason I can see parts of the tower has to do with Radiants, who are Connected to me. I caught glimmers of this Edgedancer girl for a while, but she vanished yesterday. She was in a cage, and I suspect they surrounded her with ralkalest.

But there is one other. A man. He must be of the Fourth Ideal, but he has no armor. So . . . maybe of the Third, but close to the Fourth? Perhaps it is something about his closeness to my father—and his closeness to the Surge of Adhesion—that keeps him conscious. His power is that of bonds. This man is a Windrunner, but no longer wears a uniform.

Kaladin. "Can you contact him?"

⁂

Kaladin's first goal was Stormlight. Fortunately, he knew exactly where to find some infused spheres. Workers frequently erected gemstone lanterns in busier corridors, pushing away the darkness and making the interior more welcoming and comfortable. One such project had been happening on the sixth floor, far enough from his family's clinic that he felt it wasn't too dangerous to try approaching.

He started by feeling his way through the darkened hallways near his hiding place on the eleventh floor. Together with Syl, he made a mental map of the area, then inched to the perimeter. Kaladin felt like he was leaving a slaver's cage when he saw that first glimmer of sunlight in the distance, and had to keep himself from running all-out to reach it.

Slow, steady, careful. He let Syl explore on ahead. She snuck up to the balcony, then peeked out. Kaladin crouched in the darkness waiting, watching, listening. Finally she darted back and made a swirl in the air, the signal that she hadn't seen anything suspicious.

He emerged into the light. He tried to memorize the strata here in this outermost hallway, then glanced over his shoulder back into the bowels of the eleventh floor. That corridor was basically a straight shot to his hiding place. His stupid brain imagined forgetting the way and leaving Teft to die, wasting away, perhaps waking at the end. Alone, trapped, terrified . . .

Kaladin shook his head, then inched out into a balcony room where he could survey the exterior of the tower. They hadn't seen a single guard while walking here. Glancing out, he didn't see a single Heavenly One flying. What was happening? Had they *retreated* for some reason?

No. He still felt the oppressive dullness, the sign of whatever they'd done to suppress the Radiants. Kaladin leaned out farther. On the plateaus, he saw figures in blue uniforms guarding the Oathgates in their usual locations. He felt a spike of relief, and even disbelief. Had it *all* been some terrible nightmare?

"Kaladin!" Syl hissed. "Someone's coming."

The two of them pressed their backs to the nearby wall as a group of figures passed through the hallway outside. They were speaking to the rhythms, in Azish. Singer guards—Kaladin caught a glimpse of them carrying spears. He almost jumped them, but restrained himself. There would be an easier and less blatant way of getting a proper weapon.

The enemy was clearly still in control. And as he considered it, the truth occurred to him.

"They're making the outside of the tower look like nothing has happened," he whispered to Syl after the patrol had passed. "They know Dalinar will send Windrunners to scout the tower once communication fails, so the enemy is trying to pretend the place hasn't been conquered. Those are either Fused illusions, or human sympathizers—perhaps the remnants of Amaram's army—wearing stolen uniforms."

"And Windrunners won't be able to get close enough to discover the truth, lest their powers fail," Syl said.

"That part will be suspicious," Kaladin said. "The enemy can't keep this going for long."

The two moved to a nearby stairwell. It didn't seem to be guarded, but he sent Syl ahead to check anyway. Then they started down, finding the tenth, ninth, and eighth floors relatively unguarded. There was simply too much space up here to watch it all. Though they did spot one other patrol at the tower's perimeter, it was easy going until they reached the seventh floor. Here, leading down to the more populated sixth floor, they found guards at the bottom of the first five stairwells they tried.

They had to move inward and find a small out-of-the-way stairwell that Syl remembered. Reaching it meant entering the darkness again. To Kaladin, sunlight was as vital as food or water. Leaving it was agony, but he did it.

And as hoped, the smaller stairwell was unguarded. They emerged onto the sixth floor in quiet darkness. It seemed most of the tower's human population was still confined to quarters. The enemy was working on how to rule this place, which should leave Kaladin with an opening. With that in mind, he sent Syl on a task.

She zipped out toward the balcony rooms, leaving him crouched in the stairwell, armed with his scalpel. Kaladin shivered, wishing he had a coat or jacket. It felt colder now than it ever had in the tower. Whatever the enemy had done to stop the Radiants had also interfered with the tower's other functions. That made him worry about the people.

Syl eventually returned. "Your family is confined to quarters like everyone else," she said softly. "But there are actual guards at their door. I didn't dare try to talk to your father or mother, but I saw them together through the window. They look healthy, if frightened."

Kaladin nodded. That was the best he could have hoped for, he supposed. Hopefully his father had talked his way out of trouble, as he'd said. Together, Kaladin and Syl snuck inward to the hallway where the lanterns were being installed. The workers had left a pile of lanterns here, along with tools for drilling their mountings into the rock.

They hadn't left gemstones in the equipment piles, and the lanterns in this particular corridor were empty. But in the next corridor over, the lanterns had been fitted with amethysts—midsized gemstones for light, a little larger than a broam. That meant a lot of Stormlight, if he could get it out.

"What do you think?" Kaladin asked Syl. "Grab a crowbar and snap them quickly, then run for it?"

"Seems like that would make a lot of noise," she said, landing on one of the lanterns.

"I could just steal the Stormlight and infuse the spheres I've been carrying. I wish I could get some of these gemstones though. I need a better reserve."

"We could try to find the lampkeeper and get her keys," Syl said.

"The one assigned to this floor is a lighteyed woman who lives somewhere on the third floor, I think. Lopen tried to get her to go to dinner with him."

"Of course he did," Syl said. "But . . . as I think about it, trying to find her seems like it would be difficult and dangerous."

"Agreed."

She stood on the top of the glowing lantern, then flitted around to the side, becoming a ribbon of light, and zipped in through the lantern's small keyhole. Although she couldn't pass through solid objects, squeezing through a crack or hole usually served well enough.

Her ribbon wound around inside the lantern. These were sturdy iron devices built to resist break-ins. They had glass sides, but those were reinforced with a lattice of metal. A key would unlock one of the faces, letting you swing it open and access the inside. The other faces of the lantern could be unlatched from the inside, and could open as well.

Syl flew over to one of these latches and formed into a person again. Theoretically, if you didn't have a key, you could break the glass and use a wire to manually turn the inside latches to open one of the faces. But the device had been designed to make this difficult, with thick glass and that iron webbing behind.

Syl tried pushing on the latch, but it was too heavy for her. She put her hands on her hips, glaring at it. "Try a Lashing," Syl called, her voice echoing against the glass, louder than her tiny form would have suggested.

"Lashings don't work," Kaladin said softly, keeping an eye down the corridor for guard patrols.

"Gravitational Lashings don't work," Syl said. "The other ones do though, right?"

Windrunners had three varieties of Lashings. Most commonly he used the gravitational Lashing, where you infused an object or person and changed the direction gravity pulled them. But there were two others. He'd tested a Full Lashing while carrying Teft to the clinic during the invasion. That Lashing allowed you to infuse an object with Light and command it to stick to anything that touched it. He'd used it during his early days as a bridgeman to stick rocks to a chasm wall.

The last Lashing was the most strange and arcane of the three. The Reverse Lashing made something *attract* other objects. It was like a hybrid of the other two. You infused a surface, then commanded it to pull on specific items. They were drawn to it. As if . . . as if the object you infused had become the *source* of gravity. As a bridgeman, Kaladin had unknowingly used this Lashing to pull arrows through the air to his bridge, making them swerve to miss his friends.

"What you call 'Lashings,'" Syl said to him, "are really two Surges working together. Gravitation and Adhesion, combined in different ways. You say Gravitation Lashings don't work, and Adhesion ones do. What about a Reverse Lashing?"

"Haven't tried," Kaladin admitted. He stepped to the side and drew the Stormlight out of a different lantern. He felt the energy, the power, in his veins—something he'd been yearning for. He smiled and stepped back, alight with power.

"Try making the glass attract the latch," Syl said, gesturing. "If you can get the latch to move toward you, it will pop out and unlock."

He touched the side of the lantern housing. During the last year, he'd practiced his Lashings. Sigzil had monitored, making him do experiments, as usual. They'd found that a Reverse Lashing required a command—or at least a visualization of what you wanted. As he infused the glass, he tried to imagine the Stormlight attracting things.

No, not things. The latch specifically.

The Stormlight resisted. As with the basic gravitational Lashing, he could feel the power, but something blocked it. However, the blockage was weaker here. He concentrated, pushing harder, and—like a floodgate opening—the Light suddenly burst from him. A Reverse Lashing didn't glow as brightly as it should, considering the Stormlight. It was kind of inverted, in a way. But Kaladin's actions were followed by a faint *click*.

The power had attracted the latch, which—pulled by that unseen force—had popped free of its housing. Eager, Kaladin slipped the front of the lantern open, then plucked the gemstone out and slipped it into his pocket.

Syl zipped out. "We need more practice on these, Kaladin. You don't use them as instinctively as the other two."

He nodded, thoughtful, and reclaimed the Stormlight he'd pressed into the lantern housing. Then the two of them moved furtively along the corridor, dropping it into darkness with each gemstone stolen.

"Reverse Lashings take effort," Kaladin told Syl softly. "It makes me wonder though, if I could somehow make basic gravitational Lashings function." He'd come to rely on those in a fight—the ability to leap into the air, to send his opponent flying off. Even the simple ability to make himself lighter so he flowed more easily through the battle.

He finished off the last of the lanterns, satisfied with the healthy pocketful of Stormlight. A fortune by Hearthstone terms, though he'd started to grow accustomed to having that much on hand. With these gemstones secured in a dark pouch so his pocket wouldn't glow, the two of them set off on their next task. Supplies.

They kept to the inner part of the floor this time, where they'd be able to see a patrol coming by the light it carried. Kaladin led Syl down some steps, as he had a good idea of where to get food and water.

As he'd hoped, the monastery in the middle of the fourth floor wasn't a high priority to guard. He found a pair of singers in uniform occupying one watchpost along the way, but was able to sneak down a side corridor and find a completely unguarded door.

Kaladin and Syl entered, then crept through a corridor lined with cells. He still thought of them that way, even though the ardents here insisted they weren't a prison. Of course, the rooms the ardents *themselves* stayed in were properly lit, furnished, and downright homey. Kaladin found one of these by the light under the door, checked the glyph painted on the wood, then slipped in.

He startled the ardent inside, the same man he'd met during his earlier visit to this place. Kuno, Kaladin had learned his name was. The ardent had been reading, but scrambled—and failed—to pull his spectacles down onto his eyes as Kaladin crossed the room in a rush and made a shushing gesture.

"Are there other guards?" Kaladin whispered. "I saw two at the front gate."

"N-no, Brightlord," Kuno said, spectacles dangling loosely from his fingers. "I . . . How? How are you here?"

"By the grace of god or luck. I haven't decided which. I need supplies. Rations, jugs of water. Medical supplies if you have any."

The man stuttered, then leaned close, ignoring the spectacles in his hand as he squinted at Kaladin. "By the Almighty. It really *is* you. Stormblessed . . ."

"Do you have the things I need?"

"Yes, yes," Kuno said, rising and running his hand across his shaved head, then led the way out of the room.

"You were right," Syl said from Kaladin's shoulder as he followed. "They probably secured all the guard posts, clinics, and barracks.

But an out-of-the way sanitarium . . ."

Kuno took them to a little storeroom. Inside, Kaladin was able to find almost everything he needed. A hospital robe and bedpan for Teft. Various other articles of clothing. A sponge and washbasin, even a large syringe for feeding someone unconscious.

Kaladin packed these into a sack along with bandages, fathom bark for pain, and some antiseptic. Some dried rations followed, mostly Soulcast, but they'd do. He tied four wooden jugs of water to a rope he could sling around his neck, then noticed a bucket with some cleaning supplies in it. He picked out four brushes with thick bristles and sturdy wooden handles, used for scrubbing floors.

"Need to . . . wash some floors, Radiant?" the ardent said.

"No, but I can't fly anymore, so I need these," Kaladin said, stuffing them in his bag. "You don't have any broth, do you?"

"Not handy," Kuno said.

"Pity. What about a weapon?"

"A weapon? Why would you need one? You have your Blade."

"Doesn't work right now," Kaladin said.

"Well, we don't keep weapons here, Brightlord," Kuno said, wiping his face, which was dripping with sweat. "Storms. You mean . . . you're going to fight them?"

"Resist them, at least." Kaladin put the rope with the jugs around his neck, then stood with some effort and settled the weight so the cord didn't bite *too* harshly. "Don't tell anyone about me. I don't want you getting taken in for questioning. I will need more supplies."

"You . . . you're going to return? Do this . . . regularly?" The man pulled his spectacles off and wiped his face again.

Kaladin reached out and put his hand on the man's shoulder. "If we lose the tower, we lose the war. I'm not in any shape to fight. I'm going to do it anyway. I don't need you to lift a spear, but if you could get me some broth and refill my water jugs every couple of days . . ."

The man nodded. "All right. I can . . . I can do that."

"Good man," Kaladin said. "As I said, keep this quiet. I don't want the general public getting it into their heads that they should pick up a spear and start fighting against Fused. If there's a way out of this mess, it will involve me either getting word to Dalinar or somehow waking the other Radiants."

He drew in a little Stormlight. He would need it to help him carry all this, and seeing the glow gave the ardent an obvious boost of confidence.

"Life before death," Kaladin said to him.

"Life before death, Radiant," Kuno said.

Kaladin picked up his sacks and started out into the darkness. It was slow going, but he eventually arrived on the eleventh floor. Here he oriented himself while Syl poked around to see if she could remember the way. They needn't have worried—a small spark of light appeared in a vein of garnet on the floor.

They followed the light to the room where they had left Teft. The door opened easily, without needing more Stormlight. Inside, Kaladin set down his supplies, checked on his friend, then started a better inventory of what he'd grabbed. The garnet light sparkled on the floor beside him, and he brushed the crystal vein with his fingers.

A voice immediately popped into his head.

Highmarshal? Is it true? Are you awake and functioning?

Kaladin started. It was the queen's voice.

∴

Brightness Navani? Kaladin's voice said in Navani's head. *I am awake. Basically functioning. My powers are . . . acting strange. I don't know why I'm not comatose like the others.*

Navani drew in a long, deep breath. The Sibling had watched him sneak to the fourth floor, then raid a monastery for supplies. While he'd been returning, Navani had done several circuits of her room—talking to her scholars and giving them encouragement—to not draw suspicion. Now she was back in position, resting against the wall, trying to look bored.

She was anything but. She had access to a Knight Radiant, perhaps two if the Sibling could locate Lift. "That is well," she whispered, the Sibling transferring her words to Kaladin. "For now, I am reluctantly working with our captors. They have me and my scholars locked away in the eastern basement study room, near the gemstone pillar."

Do you know what's wrong with the Radiants? he asked.

"To an extent, yes," she whispered. "The details are somewhat technical, but the tower had ancient protections to defend it from enemies who were using Voidlight. A Fused scholar inverted this; it now suppresses those who would use Stormlight. She did not complete the tower's corruption, however. I narrowly prevented her from doing so by erecting a barrier around the pillar. Unfortunately, that same barrier prevents me from undoing the work she did there."

So . . . what do we do?

"I don't know," Navani admitted. Dalinar would have probably told her to act strong, to pretend she had a plan when she didn't—but she wasn't a general. Pretending never worked with her scholars; they appreciated honesty. "I've barely had time to plan, and I'm still dragging from yesterday."

I know that feeling, Kaladin said.

"The enemy has made the Oathgates work somehow," Navani said, a plan forming in her mind. "My first goal is to continue protecting the Sibling, the spren of the tower. My second goal is to get word to my husband and the other monarchs. If we could figure out how the enemy is making the Oathgates work, I might be able to get my spanreeds functioning and send warning."

That sounds like a pretty good start, Brightness, Kaladin said. *I'm glad to have a direction to work toward. So you want me to find out how they're operating the Oathgates?*

"Exactly. My only guess is that they are powering them with Voidlight somehow—but I tried to make fabrials use Voidlight in the past, and failed. I know for a fact, however, that the enemy has functional spanreeds. I haven't been able to get a good look at one of those—but if you could find out how they're using the Oathgates, or other fabrials, that would give me something to work with."

I'd need to get close to the Oathgates to do that, Kaladin said. *And not be seen doing so.*

"Yes. Can you manage that? I know you said your powers aren't functioning completely."

I . . . I'll find a way, Brightness. I suspect the enemy won't be using the Oathgates until nighttime. I think they're trying to keep up a front of nothing being wrong with the tower, in case Dalinar sends scouts. They have some humans wearing Alethi uniforms patrolling outside. At night, even distant Windrunners trying to watch would be visible in the darkness. I suspect they'd find this a safer time to use the Oathgates.

Curious indeed. How long did Raboniel realistically think she could keep up such a subterfuge? Surely Dalinar would withdraw from the battlefield in Azir and focus everything on discovering what was wrong with Urithiru. Unless there were aspects to this that Navani wasn't considering.

The implications of that frightened her. She was blind, locked away in this basement.

"Highmarshal," she said to Kaladin, "I'll try to contact you again tomorrow around the same time. Until then, be warned. The enemy will be seeking a way to disrupt the shield I erected. There were four nodes hidden in the tower, large gemstones infused with Stormlight to maintain the barrier, but the first has been destroyed. The Sibling won't say where the other three are.

"These nodes are direct channels to the heart of the tower, and as such are great points of vulnerability. If you find one, tell me. And be aware, if the enemy gains access to it, they can complete the tower's corruption."

Yes, sir. Er. Brightness.

"I need to go. Lift is awake somewhere too, so it would be worth keeping an eye out for her. At any rate, take care, Highmarshal. If the task proves too dangerous, retreat. We are too few right now to take unwise risks."

Understood. After a moment's pause, the Sibling's voice continued, *He has gone back to unpacking his supplies. You should be careful though, how you ask after fabrials. Do not forget that I consider what you have done to be a high crime.*

"I've not forgotten," Navani said. "But surely you don't oppose the Oathgates."

I do not, the Sibling said, sounding reluctant. *Those spren have gone willingly to their transformations.*

"Do you know why it works? Powering the Oathgates with Voidlight?"

No. The Oathgates are not part of me. I will leave you now. Our talking is suspicious.

Navani didn't press the matter, instead making another circuit around her scholars. She wasn't certain whether she trusted what the Sibling said. Could spren lie? She didn't think she'd ever asked the Radiants' spren. A foolish oversight.

At any rate, in Kaladin she at least had a connection to the rest of the tower. A lifeline. That was one step forward in finding a way out of this mess.

When in such a state, detachment is enviable. I have learned that my greatest discoveries come when I abandon lesser connections.

—From *Rhythm of War*, page 3 undertext

Two days after defeating Taravangian's traitors, Dalinar stood in the war tent, helping prepare for the larger offensive against the singers in Emul. Just behind him stood Szeth in disguise. Nobody gave the man a second glance; Dalinar often had members of the Cobalt Guard with him.

Dalinar surveyed the war table with its maps and lists of troop numbers. So many different pieces, representing the state of their fighting across many different battlefronts. When he'd been younger, these types of abstractions had frustrated him. He'd wanted to be *on* the battlefield, Blade in hand, smashing his way through enemy lines and making such maps obsolete.

Then he'd begun to see the armies behind the little squares on the sheets of paper. Begun to truly grasp how the movement of troops—supplies, logistics, large-scale tactics—was more important than winning a given battle in person. And it had excited him.

Somehow he'd moved beyond that now. War—and all its facets—no longer excited him. It was important, and it was a thing he would do. But he had discovered a greater duty.

How do we win? Truly win, *not merely gain an advantage for a time?*

He mused on these thoughts as his generals and head scribes presented their final conclusions on the Veden betrayal.

"Our troops in southern Alethkar were successfully supported by the Thaylen ships, as you advised," Teshav said. "Our generals along the coast were able to retreat through a series of fortresses as you directed. They have regrouped at Karanak—which we control. Because none of our battalions were completely surrounded by Vedens, we suffered virtually no losses."

"Our navy locked the Veden ships into their ports," said Kmakl, the aging Thaylen prince consort. "They won't break our blockade anytime soon, unless the Fused and Skybreakers give them heavy air support."

"We destroyed almost all the Vedens who betrayed us here," said Omal, a short Azish general who wore a brightly colored patterned sash across his uniform coat. "Your leadership on the battlefield was excellent, Blackthorn—not to mention the timeliness of your warnings before the battle. Instead of burning our supply dumps and rescuing their king, they were nearly eliminated."

Dalinar looked across the table at the Mink, who was smiling with a gap-toothed sense of satisfaction.

"This was very well handled, Uncle," Jasnah said to him, surveying the war table map. "You averted a catastrophe."

Noura conferred with the Azish emperor, who sat on a throne near the side of the battle tent, then walked over. "We regret the loss of such an important ally in Taravangian," she said. "This betrayal will be felt— and prosecuted—by the Azish for generations. That said, we too approve of your handling of the situation. You did well to remain suspicious of him all these months, and we were unwise to think his treachery was all in the past."

Dalinar leaned over the table, which was lit with spheres. Though he missed the large illusory map he could create with Shallan, there was something about the tangible feeling of *this* map, the paper marked up with the thoughts of his best generals, that spoke to him. As he stared, everything but the map seemed to fade from his view.

Something was still wrong. Taravangian had been so *subtle* for so many months. Yet now he let himself be captured?

His armies in Jah Keved seem not to care much about him, Dalinar thought, reading the displayed battle reports and figures as if they were whispered explanations in his ears. *The Veden highprinces will be happy to put their own men in charge. And they seem quick to side with the singers, as the Iriali were.*

Kharbranth, led by Taravangian's daughter Savrahalidem, had disavowed their former ruler and proclaimed themselves neutral in the conflict—with their surgeons willing to continue serving whichever side petitioned their aid. Dalinar would have his ships blockade them just in case—but he wasn't about to land troops there and fight a costly battle for such a relatively unimportant target. They likely knew that.

The real prize was Taravangian himself. Someone Dalinar already held captive. After the elderly king's careful posturing over the years, how had he let his empire collapse practically overnight?

Why? Why risk it now?

"What news of Urithiru?" Dalinar asked.

"Windrunners should return soon with their latest visual on the tower," Teshav said from the dim perimeter of the table. "But Brightness Navani's most recent spanreed letter indicates that our people there are managing well."

Navani continued to send soldiers hiking along the outside of the mountain faces to deliver messages. Each new bit told them a little more. Some of Taravangian's scholars had activated a device like the one Highmarshal Kaladin had found. A separate collapse of the tunnels below—likely the work of saboteurs—made getting in and out that way impossible.

The device was hidden, and Navani hadn't been able to find and deactivate it. She worried the search would take weeks. Unfortunately, Dalinar's scouts had proven the device's effectiveness. If they drew too close, they not only lost their powers, but dropped unconscious.

For now though, it seemed that everyone was safe—though inconvenienced. If Dalinar hadn't been anticipating the betrayal, things could have gone very differently. He could imagine a version of events where Taravangian's betrayal threw the coalition into chaos, allowing the singer military to surge forward and push Dalinar's troops all the way back to Azimir. There, without proper resupply and support, they could have been crushed.

Perhaps that's it, he thought. *Perhaps that was what Taravangian was intending—why he risked so much.* The king, so far, had remained silent during interrogations. Perhaps Dalinar could speak to him directly and get more information. But he worried that somehow all of this was according to Taravangian's plans, and Dalinar was second-guessing himself at every point.

"Monarchs," Dalinar said to the group, "I suggest we continue our battle for Emul until we have more information about Urithiru."

"Agreed," the Azish emperor said immediately.

"I will seek approval from the guilds of Thaylenah and the queen," Prince Kmakl said, scanning through naval reports. "But for now, I have no problem with continuing to let the Alethi generals lead. However, Brightlord Dalinar, you realize this betrayal is going to make recovering your homeland even more difficult."

"I do," Dalinar said. "I still believe that the best thing we can do for Alethkar's eventual recovery is to first secure the West."

Each of those words was a knife stabbing at his heart. It meant giving Alethkar up for years. Perhaps longer. With Jah Keved as a staging area, he'd been able to entertain dreams of striking right for Kholinar. No longer.

Storming Taravangian. Damnation take you.

With Kmakl and the Azish weighing in, the sole monarch who hadn't spoken up was Jasnah. She inspected the maps, Wit—as ever—standing at her shoulder.

"I assume, Uncle," she said, "that you will be letting the Mink prosecute this campaign?"

"This is a larger conflict than one man can direct on his own," Dalinar said. "But after his handling of the battle two days ago, I think he's proven his worth. One of the reasons I worked so hard to recruit him was to have his particular genius directing our strategy."

"At the will of the monarchs," the Mink said, "I'll do this—but remember your promises. I won't have you escape them. Once we inevitably liberate Alethkar, my kingdom is next."

Jasnah nodded. "I would like to see your battle plans, General Dieno. I give my initial approval to our continued offensive into Emul, but I will want details. Losing access to the Oathgates is going to prove disruptive."

With that, Dalinar called an end to the meeting. People began to uncover spheres around the perimeter of the war pavilion—revealing how enormous it truly was. It had to be large enough to accommodate everyone's entourages, and so the map table looked small once everyone started retreating to their sections of the tent.

Kmakl made his way over to the Thaylen scribes, where they used spanreeds to send minutes of the meeting home to Fen and the Thaylen guildmasters. Dalinar shook his head. He agreed with Fen's decision to stay behind, and wished that Jasnah had made the same choice. Too many monarchs in one location made him nervous.

It also bothered him that so much of what Queen Fen did was subject to the whims of a bunch of merchants and guildmasters. If they did win this war, he'd see if he could find a way to help her wrest control of her kingdom from those eels.

The Azish and Emuli contingents began to vacate the war tent, letting in some fresh air. Dalinar used a handkerchief to mop at the sweat on the back of his neck—this region of Roshar wasn't as muggy as the parts around the Reshi Isles, but the summer weather here was still too hot for his taste. He almost wanted to have one of the Windrunners fly him up to a higher altitude where he could get some proper cold air and think clearly.

He settled for stepping outside the tent and surveying the camp. They'd commandeered a small town named Laqqi, just inside the Emuli border, not too far from Azimir. That placed it about a three-day march from the battlefront, where their lines—soon to be reinforced—held against the enemy forces to the south.

Little more than a village, Laqqi had been overrun by troops setting up supply stations and command tents. Workers reinforced the eastern approach to block storms, and Windrunners soared through the air. This position made for an excellent command center, close enough to the battlefront to be reached by short flight, but far enough away to be protected from ground assault.

Dalinar took some time out here, after checking that little Gav was playing happily with his governess, to think about Evi. Storms, he'd been so proud at Adolin's birth. How had he let himself miss so much of his son's childhood?

He turned those memories over in his head. At first, he'd found being able to remember Evi to be novel—but the more the memories settled with him, the more they felt comfortable, like a familiar seat by the fire. He was ashamed of so much of what he'd remembered about himself, but he would not trade these memories again. He needed them. Needed her.

He enjoyed the fresh air for a time, breathing deeply, before he returned to the tent to get something to drink. Szeth followed with his hand on his oversized sword—the silver sheath and black hilt were masked by a disguise. Szeth didn't say anything, but Dalinar knew that he considered his defeat by Nale to be shameful. In Dalinar's estimation, it spoke more of the Herald's skill than anything else. Why was it Nale so often stayed out of battles, overseeing his Skybreakers from afar?

Jasnah joined Dalinar as he poured himself some wine in the tent, by the bar. She knew what Szeth really was, but she was too politic to give him so much as a glance.

"You're stepping away from the fight, Uncle," she noted quietly. "I expected you to lead the war effort here personally."

"I have found someone more capable to do the job."

"Pardon, Uncle, but you should find a better lie. You *never* let go of something you're interested in doing yourself. It's one of your more consistent behaviors."

He stilled himself, then glanced about the room. She shouldn't have confronted him here, where representatives of the other monarchs might hear. Knowing Jasnah, that was part of the reason she had done so. With her, every conversation was a little contest, and she always considered the terrain.

"I'm beginning to realize something," he said softly, stepping her over to the side, away from the bar. Szeth stayed close, as did Wit. Others gave them space. "My powers as a Bondsmith are more valuable than we have known. I told you about how, in the battle, I touched Nalan and saw his past."

"A feat you've been unable to replicate with Shalash or Talenelat."

"Yes, because I don't know what I'm doing!" Dalinar said. "I am a weapon we haven't fully investigated. I need to learn how to use these powers—use them for more than merely renewing spheres and opening the perpendicularity."

"I appreciate someone wanting to learn, Uncle," Jasnah said. "But you are *already* a powerful weapon. You are one of our greatest military minds."

"I need to become something more," Dalinar said. "I'm worried that this war is going to be an endless give-and-take. We seize Emul, but lose Jah Keved. Back and forth, back and forth. How do we *win*, Jasnah? What is our end goal?"

She nodded slowly. "We need to push Odium to an accord. You think learning about your powers can help you achieve this?"

Over a year had passed since Odium had agreed to a contest by champions—but since then, Dalinar hadn't seen the being. No visits. No visions. Not even a messenger.

"Rayse—Odium—is not one to be pushed into anything," Wit said from over Jasnah's shoulder. "He might have agreed to a contest in theory, Blackthorn, but he never set terms. And he won't, as long as he thinks he's winning this war. You need to frighten him, convince him that he might lose. Only then will he proceed with a contest of champions—as long as the terms limit his losses."

"I would rather a complete victory than something that allows Odium to hedge his bets," Dalinar said.

"Ah, delightful," Wit replied, holding up his palm and mimicking writing something down. "I'll just make a note that you'd like to win. Yes, how *foolish* of me not to realize that, Blackthorn. Total victory. Over a god. Who is currently holding your homeland, and recently gained the allegiance of one of the strongest militaries on the planet. Shall I also have him bake you something sweet as an apology for this whole 'end of the world' mess?"

"That will do, Wit," Dalinar said with a sigh.

"The baking thing is an actual tradition," Wit added. "I once visited a place where—if you lose a battle—your mother has to bake the other fellow something tasty. I rather liked those people."

"Pity you didn't remain with them longer," Dalinar said.

"Ha! Well, I didn't think it wise to stay around. After all, they were cannibals."

Dalinar shook his head, focusing back on the task at hand. "Wit says we have to somehow persuade Odium we're a threat. But *I* think the enemy is manipulating us. This entire trick with Taravangian has me unsettled. We're dealing with a god, but we aren't using all the tools at our disposal."

He held up his palm. "With this, I can touch his world, the Spiritual Realm. And when I was fighting Nalan, I felt something, saw something. What if I could reforge the Oathpact? If the Fused stopped being reborn, would that not give us—at last—an edge over Odium? Something to *force* him to negotiate on our terms?"

Jasnah folded her arms, pensive. Wit, however, leaned in. "You know," Wit whispered, "I think he might be right. I feel ashamed to admit it, but the Blackthorn has seen further than we have, Jasnah. He is more valuable as a Bondsmith than as a general—or even a king."

"You make a good argument, Uncle," Jasnah admitted. "I'm simply worried. If your powers are so incredible, it feels dangerous to experiment with them. My own first forays into Soulcasting were deadly at times. What will your greater abilities do, by accident, in similar situations?"

It was a valid point, one that left them solemn as they picked up cups of wine and drank in silence, thinking. As they stood there, Prince Kmakl passed by on his way out of the tent, listening as a scribe read him a draft of a letter to the merchant lords of Thaylen City.

"Another topic, Uncle," Jasnah noted. "Lately, I see your eyes narrow when you look at Prince Kmakl. I thought you liked Fen and her husband."

"I do like them," he said. "I just don't like how much bureaucracy Fen has to go through before anything gets done. The Azish are even worse. Why name your ruler an 'emperor' if he has to get approval from a dozen different functionaries to do his job?"

"One is a constitutional monarchy, the other a scholarly republic," Jasnah said, sounding amused. "What did you expect?"

"A king to be a king," he muttered, drinking the rest of his wine in one gulp.

"Both of their governments go back centuries," Jasnah said. "They've had generations to refine their processes. We'd do well to learn from them." She eyed him, thoughtful. "The days of absolute power in one person's hands will likely soon pass us by. I wouldn't be surprised if I'm the last true Alethi monarch."

"What would your father say, hearing you talk like that?"

"I suspect I could make him understand," she said. "He was interested in his legacy. Building something that would span generations. His goals were laudable, but his methods . . . well, our kingdom has been difficult to maintain. A king ruling by the gauntlet and sword can easily see it slip away when he weakens. Compare this to the Azish system, where a bad Prime is unable to single-handedly ruin their government."

"And a good one is unable to accomplish much," Dalinar said, then held his hand up to forestall further argument. "I see what you're saying. But I find nobility in the traditional way of rule."

"Having read the histories, I believe the nobility you imagine is created from stories *about* the inhabitants of ancient days, but rarely possessed by said inhabitants. Those kings tended to live short, brutal lives. No matter. Once we win this war, I expect to have decades to persuade you."

Kelek help him. Dalinar poured himself more orange wine.

"I will think on what you said about your powers," Jasnah said, "and I will see if I can offer any advice on how to proceed. For now, Uncle, know that I trust your judgment in this, and will help support the Mink if you take a smaller role in war planning. You are right, and I was wrong to question."

"One is never wrong to question," Dalinar said. "You taught me that."

She patted his arm fondly, then walked off to turn her attention to the maps the Mink was marking up on the war table.

Wit lingered, smiling at Dalinar. "I agree with her," he whispered. "And on the topic of monarchs, I will have you know that *I* find you to be an endearing despot. You're so pleasant, I *almost* don't find it horrifying that I'm living among a people willing to trust a single man with near-absolute power over the lives of hundreds of thousands—while completely ignoring proper checks and balances upon his potential greed, jealousy, or ambition."

"Did you really have to come with us, Wit?" Dalinar asked. "I . . ." He trailed off. Then shook his head.

"What?" Wit asked.

"Never mind. Saying anything would provide you with more rocks to throw at me."

"And you're supposed to be the dumb one," Wit said, grinning. "When have I ever mocked you, though?"

"All the time, Wit. You mock everyone."

"Do I? Do I really? Hmmm . . ." He tapped his chin. "I'm gainfully employed as Queen's Wit, and she expects me to provide only the best of mockery on her behalf. I need to be careful about simply giving it away. Who is going to buy the cow, and all that."

Dalinar frowned. "What is a cow?"

"Big, juicy, delicious. Wish I could still eat them. You don't seem to have them around here, which I find amazing, as I'm sure there was one somewhere in Sadeas's lineage. Paternal grandfather perhaps. Watch the highprinces. There's almost certainly going to be a show." He sauntered off to take his customary position near Jasnah.

Watch the highprinces? What did that mean? For the most part, they were becoming a useful lot. Aladar kept reinforcing Dalinar's trust in him, and Dalinar had sent him to oversee the withdrawal in Alethkar. Hatham had fallen into line, and Dalinar had him watching the supply chain from Azimir. Bethab was proving quite useful as an ambassador stationed in Thaylen City—or, well, his wife was the useful one, but they were both proving helpful. Roion was dead with honors, his son carefully chosen to not make things difficult. Even *Sebarial* was relevant these days.

One highprince was currently with Dalinar in Emul. Ruthar. Dalinar focused on the brawny, bearded man. He was the worst of those left; he fancied himself a soldier, but had never worn a proper uniform in his life. Today he hovered near the far end of the bar, by the strong wines. At least he'd learned to stop contradicting Dalinar in front of the other monarchs.

Dalinar narrowed his eyes toward Jasnah, who was making a display of going over the battle plans with the Mink. *She's putting on a show,* he thought, noting how she specifically called out details on the maps, suggesting troop arrangements. She did a fair job, though she was no general.

The Mink listened to her suggestions, but likely wouldn't take many of them. He seemed to find her fascinating. Well, Jasnah was a rare gemstone for certain. Was her show for the Mink? No . . . this had to do with Ruthar, didn't it?

Further musings were interrupted as a figure in blue entered the tent. Lyn the Windrunner wore her hair in a braid, though wisps had pulled free during her flight. She'd led the most recent scouting of Urithiru.

Dalinar waved her over, and noted Jasnah at the map table quieting and turning to listen as Lyn gave her report.

"We met with the soldier the queen sent," the Windrunner explained, saluting. "I myself tried to step through the invisible barrier and approach. I dropped to the snow like I'd taken a hit straight to the jaw. The soldier had to drag me out to the others."

"Did you see my wife?"

"No, sir," Lyn said. "But that hike . . . it looks brutal. Radiants can't get within hundreds of yards of the tower, so this soldier has to march all the way back and forth along the ridges for hours to get to where he can send messages."

Dalinar rubbed his chin in thought. Navani's messages seemed trustworthy, and she cautioned patience. But passcodes were not foolproof, and something about this just felt wrong. "What can you see from a distance? Anything?"

"We had to use spyglasses," Lyn said. "There weren't as many people out as usual, but there were some Windrunners on the roof, and I think I made out Teft up there, and Isom the Lightweaver. They held up a big sign, with glyphs that we *think* read 'patience' and 'progress.'"

Dalinar nodded. "Thank you, Radiant. Go give a full report, with details, to Brightness Teshav, then get something to eat."

"Thank you, sir," she said. She started toward the exit.

Something nagged at Dalinar, however. That weight hadn't *completely* eased. "Lyn?" he called.

"Sir?"

"The enemy has Lightweavers. Or at least something similar."

"Yes, sir," she said. "Though the only confirmed report we have of them is that incursion at the Thaylen vault a year ago."

He resisted shooting a glance at Szeth—so quiet, so easy to forget—standing nearby, wearing the face of an Alethi man.

"Ask Companylord Sigzil to send another team of scouts later tonight," Dalinar said. "I'll infuse the traveling gemstones for another run. Have this new team watch the tower from a distance, hidden, then report anything suspicious they might see."

"Wise suggestion, sir," Lyn said, then bowed and retreated.

Jasnah nodded to him, then returned to her exaggerated discussion of the maps. Yes, she *was* acting a role here.

Dalinar glanced at Ruthar, whose face was steadily growing redder. Perhaps he'd had a few drinks too many while waiting for the monarchs to finish their planning, but plainly he did *not* like how Jasnah was blatantly interjecting herself into the war plans. It was a masculine art, and Ruthar had been forbidden from participating in the planning today.

Looking at him, it was hard not to agree with what Jasnah had said about Alethkar. Gavilar's grand unification of the kingdom hadn't lasted ten years past his death before essentially breaking into civil war. Alethi squabbling had ended up favoring men like Ruthar. Oily, belligerent, aggressive. The last representation of old Alethkar.

Jasnah was making herself into bait. And Ruthar bit. Hard.

"Am I the only one seeing this?" Ruthar asked a little too loudly to his attendants. "I didn't say anything when she was made queen. Other nations have queens. But are any of *them* in this room interrogating a general?"

One of his companions tried to calm him, but he brushed her off, shouting, "It's a disgrace! Dalinar writing? He might as well put on a havah and start painting. We *deserve* the judgments of the Almighty, after giving the throne to a godless wh—" He stopped himself just in time, perhaps realizing how still the tent had grown.

Dalinar stepped forward to berate the man. There was nothing for it now but to—

"Wit," Jasnah said, her voice cold.

Wit strode forward, his hands spread to the sides, as if stepping out from behind curtains to face an adoring crowd. "I see you're envious of those more skilled in the masculine arts than you, Ruthar," Wit said. "I agree, you could use lessons on how to be a man—but those in this room would teach lessons far too advanced. Let me call in a eunuch to instruct you, and once you've reached his level, we'll talk further."

"Harsher," Jasnah said.

"You speak of honor, Ruthar, though you've never known it," Wit said, his voice rising. "You'll never find it though. You see, I hid your honor in a place you could never find it: in the arms of someone who truly loves you."

"Wit," Jasnah said. "*Harsher.*"

"I've been speaking to your children, Ruthar," Wit said. "No, this part isn't a joke. Relis, Ivanar. Yes, I know them. I know a lot of things. Would you like to explain to the queen where Ivanar's broken arm last month *truly* came from? Tell me, do you beat your children because you're a sadist, or because you're a coward and they are the only ones who won't dare fight back? Or . . . oh, silly Wit. It's both, isn't it?"

"How *dare* you!" Ruthar roared, shoving away the attendant who tried to control him. Angerspren rose around his feet, like pools of bubbling blood. "I demand trial by swords! Me versus you, stupid fool. Or me against your champion, if you're too much of a coward to face me!"

"Trial by combat accepted," Wit said lightly, undoing his belt and sliding free his sheathed sword. "Shall we?"

"Fine!" Ruthar said, drawing his sword, causing many of the women and attendants to scatter to the sides of the large tent.

"This is idiocy," Dalinar said, stepping between them. "Ruthar, you've been baited. Killing a Queen's Wit is punishable by exile and forfeit of title. You *know* this."

Ruthar grunted, the words sinking in.

"Besides," Dalinar said, glancing over his shoulder, "that man is no simple Wit. I'm not sure if you *can* kill him."

"You tell me I'd forfeit my title," Ruthar growled. "What title? What *lands* do I hold? And exile? We are *in* exile, Blackthorn. Maybe I should challenge you. You've lost our kingdom, and now you expect me to waste my time in foreign lands? Protecting those we should have conquered? We *would* have, if your nephew had been half the man his father was."

"Ruthar," Wit said, "you don't need to fight him. Or me. I accept your challenge, but I exercise my right to choose a champion. You won't risk losing your lands by killing a Wit."

"Excellent," Ruthar said. "I accept. Stop trying to interfere, Blackthorn."

Dalinar reluctantly stepped to the side. He felt a mounting dread, but there was nothing illegal here. And he doubted any action he could take would prevent this trap from springing.

"So," Ruthar said, brandishing his sword. "Wit. You call *me* coward, then wiggle out of a challenge? So be it! Who do you want me to kill, then?"

"Your Majesty?" Wit said. "If you don't mind?" He cocked his sheathed sword to the side, hilt out, as Jasnah brushed past and drew the weapon—a thin, silvery blade that Dalinar didn't think he'd ever seen unsheathed.

Dalinar's dread deepened as Jasnah stepped into striking range, batting aside Ruthar's sword. He recovered from his shock and blocked her next strike. She was better than Dalinar might have expected, but her stance was uncertain, and she overreached. At best, she was equal to a promising student.

She had two distinct advantages though. She was Radiant. And Ruthar was an idiot.

"I refuse this," he said, tossing his sword aside. "I will not face a woman in combat. It is demeaning."

And so, Jasnah stabbed him straight through the throat.

This lunge was better than the previous one, but it was not her skill that won the fight—it was the fact that Ruthar underestimated how far she would go. Indeed, Ruthar's eyes bulged as shockspren shattered around him as yellow glass. He stumbled back, gushing lifeblood across his beautiful doublet.

"Renarin!" Jasnah called.

Dalinar's younger son scrambled into the tent from outside, and the full level of her preparation became manifest. The twisting feeling in Dalinar's stomach began to release. He'd been preparing to lock down the tent, send guards for Ruthar's next of kin, and institute martial law.

Renarin scurried forward and used his powers as a Truthwatcher to heal Ruthar, sealing up the wound in the man's neck before he bled out. Still, Dalinar caught the eye of Fisk, the current captain of the Cobalt Guard. He was a solid fellow, bearer of the Blade Loremaker. Fisk nodded in understanding, and covertly signaled his soldiers to create a perimeter around the tent—nobody in or out—until Dalinar was ready to let news of this incident spread.

Jasnah held Wit's sword out to her side, and he took it, clicking his tongue. "Not willing to wipe the blood off first, Brightness? I suppose this is the sword's first kill. Adonalsium knows, I could never give her that myself. Still." He wiped the weapon clean with a white handkerchief, glancing at Ruthar. "I'll be billing you for a new handkerchief."

Both Wit and Jasnah pointedly ignored the horrified expressions of the room's attendants. The standout exception was the Mink, who was grinning at the show. Dalinar almost expected him to begin applauding.

Dalinar felt no such mirth. Although she hadn't gone all the way, he didn't like Jasnah's statement. Duels of passion were—if not common—an accepted part of Alethi culture. He himself had killed more than one man at a feast or other gathering. It was reminiscent, however, of their barbaric days as broken princedoms. Times that the Alethi tried to pretend had never happened. These days, this sort of thing was supposed to be handled in a more civilized way, with formal challenges and duels in arenas days later.

"Ruthar," Jasnah said, standing above him. "You have insulted me thrice tonight. First, by implying a queen should not take concern for the welfare of her own armies. Second, by threatening to assault my Wit, a man who is an extension of the royal will. Third and worst of all, by judging me unfit to defend myself, despite my calling as a Knight Radiant.

"As you have died tonight, and I have bested you legally in combat, I name you forfeit of your title. It will pass to your eldest son, who has been speaking quite frankly with Wit recently. It seems he will make a far more fitting highprince."

"That bastard!" Ruthar croaked. "That traitorous bastard!"

"Not yours then, is he?" Wit said. "That explains why I like him."

"What you do from here is your choice," Jasnah said. "Unfortunately, by the time you leave this tent, you will find that your princedom has quite thoroughly moved on. You'll be barred entrance to your own camp, should you try to return. I suggest you join the military as a new recruit. Alternatively, you may take up the queen's charity at the Beggars' Feasts and poorhouses."

She left him gaping on the floor and touching his healed neck—still wet with blood. Renarin awkwardly hurried after Jasnah as she moved over to the map table.

Wit dropped his bloody handkerchief before Ruthar. "How remarkable," he said. "If you spend your life knocking people down, you eventually find they won't stand up for you. There's poetry in that, don't you think, you storming personification of a cancerous anal discharge?"

Dalinar marched up beside Jasnah at the table. Szeth stayed close behind him, carefully watching Ruthar, silent but making certain Dalinar's back was guarded. Renarin stood with his hands in his pockets and refused to meet Dalinar's gaze. The boy likely felt guilty for keeping this little plan quiet, though Dalinar wasn't angry at him. Denying Jasnah was next to impossible in situations like this.

"Don't glare at me, Uncle," Jasnah said softly. "It was a lesson I had to give. Ruthar was a mouthpiece for many other discontented grumblings."

"I had assumed," he said, "that you of all people would wish to teach your lessons *without* a sword."

"I would much prefer it," she said. "But you cannot tame a feral axehound with kind words. You use raw meat."

She eyed the still-stunned people in the tent. They were all quite deliberately staying away from Ruthar. Dalinar met Fisk's eyes, then nodded again. The lockdown could be eased. Ruthar's closest allies were fickle, and would see his fallen state as a disease to be avoided. Jasnah had already secured the loyalty of those who could have been dangerous—his family and military advisors.

"You should know," Dalinar said, "that I found this entire experience distasteful. And not only because you didn't warn me it was going to happen."

"That is *why* I didn't warn you," Jasnah said. "Here. This may calm you." She tapped a paper she'd set onto the map table, which the Mink picked up and began reading with great interest. He looked like he hadn't been so entertained in years.

"A draft of a new law," the short man said. "Forbidding trial by sword. How unexciting."

Jasnah plucked the paper from his fingers. "I will use my own *unfortunate* experience today as an example of why this is a terrible tradition. Ruthar's blood will be the last such spilled. And as we leave this era of barbarism, each and every attendant at court will know that Alethkar's first queen is a woman unafraid of doing what needs to be done. Herself."

She was firm, so Dalinar tucked away his anger, then turned to leave. A part of him understood her move, and it *was* likely to be effective. Yet at the same time, it displayed that Jasnah Kholin—brilliant, determined—was not perfect. There were things about her that unnerved even the callous soldier that lived deep inside him.

As he walked away, Renarin hurried over. "Sorry," the boy whispered. "I didn't know she hadn't told you."

"It's all right, son," Dalinar said. "I suspect that without you, she'd have gone through with the plan anyway—then left him to bleed out on the floor."

Renarin ducked his head. "Father. I've . . . had an episode."

Dalinar stopped. "Anything urgent?"

"No."

"Can I find you later today, maybe tomorrow?" Dalinar asked. "I want to help contain the fallout from this stunt."

Renarin nodded quickly, then slipped out of the tent. Ruthar had stumbled to his feet, holding his neck, his gaudy yellow outfit now ruined. He searched around the room as if for succor, but his former friends and attendants were quietly slipping away—leaving only soldiers and the queen, who stood with her back to him. As if Ruthar were no longer worth attention.

Wit stood in his jet-black suit, one hand on the map table, leaning at a nearly impossible angle. Dalinar often found Wit with a grin on his face, but not today. Today the man looked cold, emotionless. His eyes were deep voids, their color invisible in the dim light.

They maneuvered Ruthar expertly, Dalinar thought. *Forced him to make all the wrong moves. Could . . . I do something similar in facing Odium?* Anger the god somehow, forcing him to accept a reckless agreement?

How did one intimidate a creature as powerful as Odium? What, on all of Roshar, could a god possibly fear or hate so much? He'd have to bring up the matter with Jasnah and Wit. Though . . . not today.

Today he'd had enough of their machinations.

This song—this tone, this rhythm—sounds so familiar, in ways I cannot explain or express.

—From *Rhythm of War*, page 5

Only the femalens among your staff read?" Raboniel asked to Craving as they stood in the hallway outside the room with the crystal pillar. "I would have thought better of your instruction, Venli, considering how capable you are in other areas. Your staff shouldn't follow foolish human customs."

Venli's staff of singers—the ones carefully recruited in Kholinar over the last year—had arrived in Urithiru via the Oathgate transfers early this morning. Raboniel had immediately put them to work. Nearby, the femalens were sorting through the boxes of notes and equipment the human queen had moved out into the hallway. Young human scribes were adding to that, repositioning boxes, making a general scene of chaos.

Venli's staff, at Raboniel's order, were doing their best to make sense of it—and to read through the pages and pages of notes to try to find important points to bring to Raboniel's attention. They would soon take scholarform to help, but the task was still difficult. Venli had instructed them to do their best.

Today, Raboniel stood with her back to the blue shield, watching the confusion in the hallway and humming to herself.

Venli hummed to Indifference. "Ancient One," she said, "my staff are good—but they are culturally Alethi. My own people, the listeners, would have happily taught them a better way—but the listeners were taken by Odium, in his wisdom."

"Do you question Odium, Venli?" Raboniel said to Craving.

"I have been taught that Passion does a person credit, Ancient One," Venli said. "And to wonder, to question, is a Passion."

"Indeed. Yet there are many among the Fused who think such Passions should be denied to everyone but themselves. You might find Odium shockingly like one of us in this regard. Or perhaps instead we are like him." She nodded toward the mess of human scribes and Venli's staff, working in near-perpetual motion like a pile of cremlings feasting after the rain. "What do you think of this?"

"If I had to guess, the human queen seems to be *trying* to make a mess."

"She's creating ways to stall that won't appear like purposeful interference," Raboniel said to Ridicule, though she seemed more amused than angry. "She complains that she doesn't have enough space, and constantly reshuffles these boxes to buy time. Also, I suspect she's trying to establish a presence outside the room—even if just in this hallway—so that she has a better chance of putting her people where they can overhear what we're saying. She seems to be getting more information than I expected; some of her people might be able to speak my language."

"I find that difficult to believe, Lady of Wishes. From what I've been led to understand, it wasn't but a year ago that they finally figured out how to read the Dawnchant."

"Yes, curious," Raboniel said, smiling and speaking to Craving. "Tell me, Venli. Why is it you serve so eagerly after knowing what Odium did to your people?"

Timbre pulsed in worry, but Venli had already prepared an answer. "I knew that only the very best among us would earn his favor and reward. Most were simply not worthy."

Raboniel hummed softly, then nodded. She returned to her own work, studying the shield around the pillar. "I'm waiting on reports of the Pursuer's sweep of the upper floors of the first tier. As well as news of his search for Radiants."

"I will go immediately and ask, Ancient One," Venli said, stepping away.

"Venli," Raboniel said. "Many mortals in the past sought elevation to stand among the Fused. You should know that, after our initial elevation, he never again granted such a lofty gift to a mortal."

"I . . . Thank you, Ancient One." She hummed to Tribute and withdrew, picking her way through the increasingly cluttered hallway. Within her, Timbre pulsed to Amusement. She knew that Venli had no aspirations of becoming a Fused.

"Do not be so quick to laud me," Venli whispered to the spren. "The person I was not so long ago would have been *thrilled* by the possibility of becoming immortal."

Timbre's pulses seemed skeptical. But she hadn't known Venli during that time—and as well she hadn't.

As Venli reached the end of the hallway, she was joined by Dul, the tall stormsetter who was in Venli's inner group of singers. The ones she'd been promising, over the last year, that she would help escape the Fused.

Today Dul wore mediationform, with an open face and smooth, beautiful carapace. He had a mostly red skin pattern with tiny hints of black, like submerged rocks in a deep red sea. He fell into stride with Venli as they walked out into the chamber with the stairs. As far as she knew, this large open room—in the shape of a cylinder—was the sole way up from the basement. They marched up the stairs that wound around the outside, passing over a section of hastily rebuilt steps, until they were far enough from others that no one would be able to overhear them.

She quickly checked Shadesmar. That place was strange, with glowing light suffusing everything, but best she could tell, no Voidspren were watching them. Here, isolated on the steps, she felt reasonably safe chatting.

"Report," she whispered.

"As you hoped," he replied as they walked, "we have been able to arrange the supply dumps from Kholinar to our benefit. Alavah and Ron are covertly making packs of supplies that will be easy to grab and take if we need them."

"Excellent," Venli said.

"I don't know how we'll escape without being spotted," Dul said. "Everyone is on edge in this place, and they have guards watching carefully outside for Alethi scouts."

"Something is going to happen, Dul," Venli said to Determination. "The humans will try to revolt, or an attack will come, or perhaps that captive queen will find a way to turn fabrials against the Fused.

"When that happens, whatever it is, we're going to be ready to run. I was led here through the mountains, and I memorized the route. We can sneak through those valleys, hiding from the Heavenly Ones in the tree cover. There *has* to be some out-of-the-way location up here in these wilds where a few dozen people can lose themselves to the world."

Dul paused on the steps, and hummed to Hope. He nearly seemed to have tears in his eyes.

"Are you all right?" Venli asked, stopping beside him.

He hummed a little louder. "After all this time, I can taste it, Venli. An escape. A way out."

"Be careful," she said. "We will need some kind of ploy to convince everyone we died, so they don't search for us. And we have to be very careful not to draw suspicion before that."

"Understood," he said, then hummed to Tension. "We've had a problem with Shumin, the new recruit."

She hummed to Reprimand.

"She tried recruiting others," Dul explained. "She's been implying she knows someone planning to start a rebellion against the Fused."

Venli hummed to Derision. She didn't normally use Odium's rhythms with her friends, but it fit the situation too well.

Dul sighed like a human. "It's the same old problem, Venli. The people willing to listen to us *are* going to be a little unreliable—if they were fully capable or smart, they wouldn't dare keep secrets from the Fused."

"So what does that say about you and me?" Venli asked.

"Pretty sure that was clearly implied," Dul said with a grin, speaking to Amusement.

"Isolate Shumin," Venli said. "We don't dare return her to Kholinar without supervision, but see if you can get her assigned to some kind of menial task without much time to interact with others. And emphasize to her *again* that she's not to recruit."

"Understood," he said softly to Consolation. He glanced upward, along the wide set of winding steps. "I hear the humans almost won here on these steps. No Radiants, and they stood against Fused and Regals."

"Briefly," Venli said. "But . . . yes, it was a sight. I almost wanted them to win."

"Is there a path for us there, Venli?" he asked to Pleading. "Go to them, help them, and get help in return?"

"You know far more about humans than I do," Venli said. "What do your instincts say?"

He glanced away. "They don't see us as people. Before, they wouldn't let me and Mazish marry. One of the only times I spoke to my master was to make that request—a single word, with as much passion as I could muster. He was angry that I *dared* talk to him. One storming word . . ."

He attracted an angerspren that prowled up the steps below him, like sparking lightning. Timbre pulsed morosely. Her kind had been treated similarly. Yet Venli found herself thinking about the fight on these steps. They were valiant, these humans. Though you obviously had to be careful not to let them get too much power over you.

"When you get back to the others," Venli said, continuing to climb, "put a few of our people on the crews that are gathering and caring for the unconscious Knights Radiant. We should watch them for an opportunity, just in case."

She had originally hoped they would be able to train her in her powers—but that seemed impossible now. She still didn't know if she'd be able to use them here without being detected, and was trying to think of a way to find the answer to that.

"Understood, Brightness." He nodded to her as they reached the top of the steps, then parted ways.

Venli hummed to Longing. She hoped she wasn't causing Dul to sing hopeless songs; though she spoke to Confidence, she didn't know whether there would be a chance for them to escape in the coming weeks. And the more time she spent with Raboniel, the more she worried. That Fused saw things she shouldn't be able to, piercing plots with keen eyes.

Each day Venli's people lived in secret was another chance for them to be exposed, taken quietly in the night, and either executed or forced to become hosts for the Fused. They needed what she'd promised: to live on their own, as their own nation. Could she really provide that though? Venli, who had never touched anything in her life without making a storm of it. She had gotten one people destroyed already.

Timbre pulsed consoling ideas as Venli made her way through the corridors.

"I wish I could believe, Timbre," she said softly. "I really wish I could. But you don't know what you're working with in me. You don't understand."

Timbre pulsed, inquisitive. She wanted to know. Venli had long remained silent about the more difficult parts of her past.

The time to share them, however, was long overdue. "The worst of it began," Venli whispered, "when the humans visited us the second time. . . ."

52

A PATH
TOWARD SAVING

EIGHT AND A HALF YEARS AGO

A delicate touch . . .'" Jaxlim said. "'To . . . To . . .'"

Venli froze. She looked up from her place by the wall, where she was using some paper—a gift from the humans—to play with letters and beats. Representations of sounds in a possible written language, like the humans used.

Her mother stood by the window, doing her daily recitations. The same calming songs, performed by the same beautiful voice that had been Venli's guide all her days. The foundation upon which she'd built her life.

"'A delicate touch . . .'" Jaxlim began again. But again she faltered.

"'Nimbleform has a delicate touch,'" Venli prompted. "'Gave the gods this form to many . . .'"

But her mother didn't continue singing. She stared out the window, silent, not even humming. It was the second time this week she'd completely forgotten a stanza.

Venli rose, setting aside her work and taking her mother's hand. She attuned Praise, but didn't know what to say.

"I'm merely tired," Jaxlim said. "From the stress of these strange days and their stranger visitors." The humans had promised to return, and since their departure months ago, the family had been abuzz with different ideas of what to do about the strange creatures.

"Go," Jaxlim said. "Find your sister. She said she'd come listen to a recitation, and at least learn the Song of Listing. I will get some sleep. That's what I need."

Venli helped her mother to the bed. Jaxlim had always seemed so strong, and indeed her body was fit and powerful. Yet she wobbled as she lay down, shaken. Not on the outside, but deep within.

Until recently, Jaxlim had *never* forgotten songs. To even suggest it would have been unthinkable.

Once her mother was situated, Venli attuned Determination and stepped out of their home—not into a forest clearing, but into a city. One of the ten ancient ones, surrounded by a broken wall and populated by the remnants of buildings.

Finding the humans had emboldened Venli's family. Bearing newly bestowed weapons, they'd marched to the Shattered Plains and claimed a place among the ten, defeating the family who had held it before them. Once, Venli would have walked tall and proud at that victory.

Today, she was too unsettled. She went searching, ignoring cries to Joy in greeting. Where was Eshonai? Surely she hadn't gone off again, not without telling her sibling and mother. . . .

Fortunately, Venli found her at a scouting tower, built up along the broken wall near the front gates of the city. Eshonai stood on the very top, watching out to the northwest, the direction the humans had come from.

"Venli!" she said, grabbing her arm and pulling her to the front of the flimsy wooden scout tower. "Look! That seems like smoke in the distance. From their campfires perhaps?"

Venli looked down at the wobbly tower. Was this safe?

"I've been thinking about what we can learn from them," Eshonai said to Excitement. "Oh, it will feel so good to show them to the rest of the families! That will stop everyone from doubting our word, won't it? Seeing the humans themselves!"

"That will feel good," Venli admitted. She knelt, holding to the wooden floor while Eshonai stood up on her toes. Storms! It looked like she was about to climb onto the railing.

"What must their cities be like?" Eshonai said. "I think I will leave with them this time. Travel the world. See it all!"

"Eshonai, no!" Venli said. And the true panic in her rhythm made Eshonai finally pause.

"Sister?" she asked.

Venli searched for the right words. To talk to Eshonai about their mother. About what . . . seemed to be happening. But she couldn't confront it. It was as if by voicing her fears, she'd make them real. She wanted to pretend it was nothing. As long as she could.

"You were supposed to come today," Venli said, "and listen to one of the songs. Maybe learn one again."

"We have you and Mother for that," Eshonai said, looking toward the horizon. "I haven't the mind for it."

But I need you with me, Venli thought. *With us. Together.*

I need my sister.

"I'm going to lead a scout group to go investigate that smoke," Eshonai said, moving toward the ladder. "Tell Mother for me, will you?"

She was gone before Venli could say anything. A day later, Eshonai came back triumphant. The humans had indeed returned.

·⋆·

It didn't take long for Venli to find the humans tedious.

Though they'd barely noticed her on the first visit, this time they wouldn't leave her alone. They wanted to hear the songs over and over. It was so frustrating! They couldn't replicate the songs if they *did* memorize them—they couldn't hear the rhythms.

Worse, when she performed, the humans kept interrupting and asking for more information, more explanations, more accurate translations. *Infuriating,* she thought, attuned to Irritation. She'd started to learn their language because Jaxlim insisted, but it didn't seem a good use of her time or her talents. The humans should learn *her* language.

When they finally let her go for the day, she stepped out of the building and welcomed the sunlight. Sitting outside were three of those dull-minded, stupid "parshmen" who didn't have songs. Seeing them made Venli uncomfortable.

Was that what the humans thought *she* was like? Some simpleton? Some of her family tried to talk to the parshmen, but Venli stayed away.

She didn't like how they made her feel. They weren't her people, any more than the humans were.

She scanned the bustling city, noting the crowds of listeners nearby. The humans drew so many gawkers. Listeners from many families—even lowly ones who didn't have a city—came to catch a glimpse. Lines of people of all varieties of skin patterns stuffed the streets, meaning that Venli was crowded as she pushed through them.

"They probably won't come out for a while yet," she said to Reprimand to a group of listeners she didn't recognize.

"You are the apprentice keeper of songs," one of them said, "of the family who discovered the humans." He said it to Awe, which made Venli pause. So he knew of her, did he?

"I am no apprentice," she said. "I am simply waiting, as is respectful, upon my mother's word before I take my place."

She glanced back toward the building she'd left. Like many in the city, it was made of ancient walls covered in crem, with a roof of carapace. The humans had been allowed to make camp here, *inside* the walls, with their tents and their strange wooden vehicles that could withstand a storm. It seemed unfair that their *moving* structures should last better than the buildings the listeners built.

"I've spent many hours with them so far," Venli said to Consideration. "What would you know of them? I can tell you."

"Do they really lack souls?" asked a female in mateform. Silly things. Venli intended to never adopt that form.

"That's one theory," Venli said. "They can't hear the rhythms, and they seem dull of speech and mind. Makes me wonder why they were so difficult for our ancestors to fight."

"They work metal as if it were wax," another said. "Look at that armor."

"Far less practical than carapace would be," Venli said.

"We don't have carapace armor anymore," another said.

That was true, of course; their current forms *didn't* have much carapace. Most of what they knew about grander forms such as warform came from the songs. And Venli, infuriatingly, hadn't made progress in discovering that one.

Still, wouldn't growing your own armor be much better than what the humans did? Well, she answered a few more questions, though she wished for the listeners to notice how tired she was from reciting songs all day. Couldn't they at least have fetched her something to drink?

Eventually she moved on, and tried to push through her bad mood. She should probably enjoy reciting songs for the humans—she did enjoy the music. But she didn't miss that Jaxlim always had them come to Venli. Her mother didn't want to be seen making a mistake by anyone, particularly not these humans.

Deep down, that was probably the real source of Venli's irritation. The knot of worry that festered in her gut, making her feel helpless. And alone.

Nearby, on the street, listeners changed their rhythms. Venli suspected what it was before she turned and saw Eshonai striding down the street. Everyone knew her, of course. The one who had discovered the humans.

Venli almost went to her. But why? There was never any comfort to be found in her presence. Only more talk of the human world, their cities and their mystery. And no talk of the real problems at home Eshonai continued to ignore.

So instead, Venli slipped between two small buildings and emerged onto a street on the other side. Maybe she could go to the fields and see Demid. She started that way . . . then stopped. No, they had decided not to show the humans how they used Stormlight to grow plants. The songs cautioned that this secret should not be shared. So they weren't working the fields, and Demid wouldn't be there.

Instead Venli made her way down to the plateaus, where she could be alone. Just her and the lifespren. She attuned Peace to check the time, then settled down and stared over the broken plateaus, trying to soothe her worry about her mother. Worry that she would have to take over being keeper of songs, as she'd claimed she was to those listeners—a boast that now seemed far too puffed up.

Venli didn't want to replace Jaxlim. She wanted to go back to the way things had been before the humans arrived.

The moment she thought that, she saw a human female leave the city above and come walking in her direction. Venli sighed. Couldn't they leave her for one movement? Well, they all assumed she couldn't speak their language, and so she could play dumb. And . . . it wouldn't require much pretending. Their rhythmless dead language was hard to understand.

The female gestured for permission, then sat next to Venli. She was the one with the rings on her exposed hand. Some kind of surgeon, Venli had been told. She didn't seem important. Most everyone ignored her—she was basically one of the servants.

"It's quite impressive, isn't it?" the human said *in the listener tongue*, looking over the Shattered Plains. "Something terrible must have happened here. Doesn't seem like those plateaus could have formed naturally."

Venli attuned Anxiety. The woman spoke the words without a rhythm, yes, but they were perfectly understandable.

"How . . ." Venli said, then hummed to Betrayal.

"Oh, I've always been good with languages," the female said. "My name is Axindweth. Though few here know me by that name, I give it to you."

"Why?"

"Because I think we're going to be friends, Venli," she said. "I've been sent to search out someone like you. Someone who remembers what your people used to be. Someone who wants to restore the glory that you've lost."

"We *are* glorious," Venli said, attuning Irritation and standing.

"Glorious?" Axindweth said. "Living in crem huts? Making stone tools because you've forgotten how to forge metal? Living all your lives in two forms, when you used to have dozens?"

"What do *you* know about any of this?" Venli said, turning to leave. Her mother would be very interested to hear one of the humans had been hiding the ability to speak their language.

"I know much about too many things," the woman said. "Would you like to learn how to obtain a form of power, Venli?"

Venli looked back. "We abandoned those. They are dangerous. They let the old gods control our ancestors."

"Isn't it odd," Axindweth said, "how much stock you put in what your ancestors said? A dusty old group of people that you've never met? If you gathered a collection of listeners from the other families, would you let *them* decide your future? That's all they were, your ancient ancestors. A random group of people."

"Not random," Venli said to Praise. "They had strength. They left their gods to find freedom."

"Yes," Axindweth said. "I suppose they did."

Venli continued on her way. Stupid human.

"There were forms of power that could heal someone, you know," the human said idly.

Venli froze in place. Then she spun, attuning Betrayal again. How did she know about Venli's mother?

"Yes," Axindweth said, toying with one of her rings, staring out away from Venli. "Great things were once possible for your people. Your ancestors, the ones you revere, might have been brave. But have you ever asked yourself about the things they didn't leave you in songs? Have you seen the holes in their stories? You bear the pain of their actions, living without forms for generations. Exiled. Shouldn't *you* have the choices they did, weighing forms of power against your current life?"

"How do you know all these things?" Venli demanded, walking back. "How do you know about forms of power? Who *are* you?"

The woman removed something from within her covered sleeve. A single glowing gemstone. Blood red.

"Take that into a storm," the woman said. "And break it. Inside, you will find a path toward saving those you love."

The woman stood and left the gem sitting on the rock.

Reacher skin appears to be made of polished bronze metal, but moves as smoothly as flesh. The faint grooves that trace their surface are unique to each individual.

Their pupils dilate, despite appearing to be holes poked in bronze orbs.

They have no eyelashes. When they have eyebrows, they are shaped of the same bronze substance as their skin.

Most Reachers maintain a form that closely matches human physiognomy, but on occasion there are unique variations.

The muscularity of their form does not appear to correlate directly with their relative strength. They do not require exercise or nutrition.

Their clothing choices are quite eclectic. From Azish wraps and patterns to Thaylen sailor garb, there seems to be no cohesive style to what they wear.

They appear in the Physical Realm as a small ball of white fire that pulses, emitting little rings of light in bursts. When they move they leave behind a glowing trail like that of a comet.

I am led to wonder, from experiences such as this, if we have been wrong. We call humans alien to Roshar, yet they have lived here for thousands of years now. Perhaps it is time to acknowledge there are no aliens or interlopers. Only cousins.

—From *Rhythm of War*, page 5 undertext

Timbre was uncharacteristically silent as Venli finished her account. Venli had taken the long way up to the sixth floor to gather reports for Raboniel, and had spent the time explaining about that day—the day she'd made her first choice down this path. The day she'd taken that gemstone, and hidden it from her mother and her sister.

Venli could tell herself all she wanted that her motives had been noble. She knew the truth. She'd kept that secret because she'd been afraid of losing the glory of discovering a new form to her sister.

Instead, the reverse had happened; Venli lived her sister's destiny. *Venli* had ended up with Timbre. *Venli* had become Radiant. Venli had *lived*. These were proof that the cosmere made mistakes.

Venli entered the refreshingly cool sixth-floor balcony room where scouting operations had been set up. Raboniel thought the humans had deliberately destroyed maps of the tower, so this group was making their own. Ruling this place was going to be a huge chore, one Venli was glad she didn't have to organize.

The singers here hummed to Praise as Venli entered, showing her respect. Even the two relayform Regals gave deference to a Voice such as Venli. She asked for, and was given, a wide range of reports on the activities up here.

Everything from the seventh floor up was unoccupied. Consequently, they were setting up checkpoints at each stairwell on the sixth floor, worried that panicked humans might try to hide on the many upper floors once confinement to quarters was relaxed. And confinement to quarters *would* need to be relaxed soon. The humans were running out of food and water. Venli suspected Raboniel would give the word for normal operations to recommence by the end of the day.

They'd found a large number of unconscious Radiants, many of whom had been in the homes of people trying to protect or hide them. Venli hummed to Derision as she scanned the list. The foolish people were lucky; Raboniel was more lenient than some Fused. She had ordered that anyone found keeping Radiants would be punished, and the Radiants executed—but that any Radiants revealed willingly would be spared.

It had been a wise move: many Radiants had been offered up after her announcement. The few found *later* had been executed, along with one member of each family hiding them. A stern but just application of the law. Timbre found it horrifying. Venli found it amazing Raboniel hadn't executed them all.

She wants these Radiants for something, she thought. *Something to do with her plans, her experiments.* Venli had not forgotten what had earned the Lady of Wishes her terrible reputation: an attempt long ago to create a disease that would end the war by exterminating all of humankind.

Well, Venli might have her own use for these Radiants. She listened with half an ear to the reports, until the relayform said something that drew her full attention.

"Wait," Venli said. "Repeat that?"

"A human surgeon killed one of our number during the investigations the other night," the malen said.

"I haven't heard of this," Venli said.

"We reported it at the time, and a Fused took charge immediately, so we assumed it had gotten back to Raboniel. This human took an unconscious Windrunner with him when he fled."

"Which Fused did you report this to?"

"The Pursuer."

Timbre pulsed worryingly.

"Do we have a description of this human surgeon?" Venli asked.

"Tall male," the Regal said. "Shoulder-length wavy hair. Slave brands. The soldier who witnessed the event claimed the human was glowing with Stormlight, but we suspect our soldier was merely rattled. He proved to be a coward, and has been assigned to waste detail."

Venli hummed to Thoughtfulness, though she felt a mounting dread. Kaladin Stormblessed was in the tower; he hadn't gone with the main bulk of his kind to the war in Emul. And he was . . . somehow still conscious? Leshwi would want to know that. She had asked Venli to watch over Raboniel specifically, but surely this was a matter deserving of her true master's attention.

"I see," Venli said to Thoughtfulness. "Has this human been found?"

"He fled to the upper floors," the Regal explained to Spite. "We searched and found nothing—even the Pursuer, who was certain the human was close, was unable to locate him."

"The Lady of Wishes will find this interesting," Venli said. "Send me word if anything more is discovered."

The Regal hummed to Command in acknowledgment, then gave Venli a list with descriptions of all the other Radiants surrendered to this group. Raboniel wanted them kept all in one room, being watched. Venli would have to put her people to work looking for a suitable location.

One conscious Windrunner, when all the others remained unconscious. Yes, she'd find a way to send a note about this to Leshwi. "The singer who saw the human kill our soldier," Venli said, moving to leave. "Give me his name and station. The Lady of Wishes may want me to interrogate him."

The Regal hummed to Derision. "The coward won't be able to tell you much. If the Lady of Wishes is truly interested in this murderous human, she should wait until this evening for another report."

"Why?"

"By then the Pursuer will have interrogated the human's family," the

Regal said. "And will have exacted revenge for the death of our soldier."

The rhythms went silent. Timbre, hidden deep within Venli's gemheart, seemed to be holding her breath.

"We captured them, then?" Venli said.

"They're locked in the clinic a short way from here," the Regal said to Craving. "A surgeon, his wife, one child. We only now discovered they are the murderous human's family. It's a pity the Lady of Wishes has ordered us to be so tame during this occupation, but at least we'll get a little blood tonight."

Venli tried to hum to Conceit as she left, but found nothing. No rhythms at all—it was unnerving. She shoved the list of descriptions in her pocket, and as soon as she was a short way from the scout post she hissed, "What are you doing?"

Timbre pulsed, and the rhythms slowly returned. Venli relaxed. For a moment she'd worried something was wrong.

Timbre pulsed morosely. To her, something *was* wrong.

"I agree that it's unfortunate about the Windrunner's family," Venli said. "But at the same time, their son *was* involved in killing one of our troops."

Timbre pulsed again.

"I suppose they *aren't* our troops," Venli agreed. "But why do you care so much? Don't you hate humans?"

That drew a sharp rebuke. Just because Timbre and the other Reachers had decided not to bond humans any longer, it didn't mean she *hated* them. And killing someone's family because they resisted? That *was* terrible. Many Fused wouldn't take that step, but the Pursuer—and his troops . . . well, she'd heard the bloodthirst in that relayform's rhythms.

Venli walked in silence, troubled. She had her own business to see to, her own problems. Yet Timbre continued to pulse softly, urging her. Venli had seen the Blackthorn once in a vision. The Bondsmith. He'd shown her kindness. And so many of the humans of this tower, they were just people trying to live their lives.

Eshonai would have done something.

"I'm a fraud, Timbre," Venli whispered. "A fake Radiant. I don't know what I'm doing."

Timbre pulsed. The meaning was clear.

I do.

It was enough. Venli turned and started down the steps, picking up speed as she went. There wasn't much Venli could do directly to help the family. Her authority as Voice certainly wouldn't extend to countering the will of the Pursuer.

Instead she made her way to the majestic atrium of the tower. This enormous opening far within the tower reminded her of the shaft that led to the basement—a circular breach in the stone. Only this was on a far grander scale, over a hundred feet wide. It stretched tall, high into the darkness above, and seemed to reach all the way to the very top.

Lifts ran up and down the inside of the atrium, though they needed Voidlight to work now. The far wall—pointed directly east—was not stone, but instead a flat glass window. Amazingly large, it showed snow-covered peaks and provided natural light to the entire atrium.

The lifts were barely in use, as the singers were focused on establishing control of the lower floors. To avoid alerting human Windrunner scouts, the *shanay-im* were forbidden from soaring around outside. They'd taken up residence here instead, within this grand hall, hovering in the open air. Venli used her authority to commandeer a lift, then made her way up to the fifteenth floor. Here she found Leshwi meditating with her long clothing drifting beneath her, with only two servants to see to her needs. She'd donated the others to Raboniel.

Leshwi noticed Venli immediately, cracking an eye. Venli sent the two servants away and hummed to Craving, standing patiently and waiting for her mistress to formally acknowledge her. Leshwi drifted over to the balcony and rested one hand on the railing.

Venli approached quickly, humming to Tribute.

"Why have you not approached in secret, as I explained?" Leshwi demanded.

Leshwi had set up a method for Venli to clandestinely deliver notes about Raboniel. Venli found the whole thing a baffling part of Fused politics. Raboniel knew that Venli was spying, and Leshwi knew that Raboniel knew, yet they both pretended the subterfuge was unknown.

"The Windrunner you wish to defeat is here in the tower," Venli said, "and I have reason to believe he did not fall unconscious. In fact, he still has access to his powers."

Leshwi hummed abruptly to Exultation. A telling choice.

"Where?" Leshwi said.

"He killed a soldier who was trying to collect the unconscious Radiants," Venli said, "then escaped into the tower. He rescued one other Windrunner."

"Honor propels him," Leshwi said, "even now. Even after his god's death. This is excellent news, Venli. You did well to break protocol to bring me this. Does the Pursuer know?"

"Yes, unfortunately."

"Raboniel will let him ignore my prior claim," Leshwi said. "He won't even be reprimanded for it, so long as it is in service of hunting a fugitive. Poor Stormblessed. He has given them the spear by which to impale him. If I wish to fight him myself, I will need to locate him first."

"And *do* you wish to fight him, Ancient One?" Venli asked. "Is that truly why you want to find him? To kill him?"

"Why would you ask this?" Leshwi asked to Craving.

Venli would have let it die at that, feeling foolish. But Timbre pulsed, nudging her.

"You seem to respect him," Venli said.

Leshwi hummed softly, but Venli did not catch the rhythm. Odd. Her powers normally let her understand anything her mistress said or implied. There *was* something familiar about that rhythm though.

"It is rare to find a human who can fight in the skies well enough to be a challenge for me," Leshwi said. "And his spren . . . I hear she is ancient. . . . But never mind that. You will not raise this matter with me again."

Timbre pulsed, indicating Venli should *tell* her mistress. About them. About being *Radiant*.

Stupidity. Venli immediately shied back at the idea. Leshwi would kill her.

"Is there something else?" Leshwi said to Command.

"Stormblessed's family is being held by the Pursuer's guards," Venli said. "They are on the sixth floor, in a clinic at the perimeter, near the main corridor. The Pursuer plans to interrogate them, and I fear it will turn ugly. Many of his troops are angry they were forbidden to kill during the incursion. They are . . . excitable."

"Violent and bloodthirsty, you mean."

"Yes, Ancient One. The . . . the family of the Windrunner would be an excellent resource for us, mistress. If you wish to find him before the

Pursuer, then perhaps holding them would give us an advantage."

Leshwi hummed to Thoughtfulness. "You are merciful, Venli. Do not reveal this Passion to others. Wait here."

Leshwi pushed off and soared downward, doing a loop and turning gracefully into the lit central corridor on the sixth floor. Venli waited, Timbre pulsing in concern.

It took a good hour for Leshwi to finally return, soaring upward from the direction of the large market on the ground floor.

"What did you do?" Venli asked.

"I took the Windrunner's family into my custody," Leshwi said. "My position gives me authority over the Pursuer."

"You didn't hurt them, did you?" Venli asked to Pleading.

Leshwi stared at her, and only after a moment did Venli realize she'd slipped and used one of the old rhythms. Pleading was one of Roshar's rhythms, not Odium's.

"I did not," Leshwi said. "And now that I've moved—and extended myself in this way—the Pursuer won't dare harm them. At least not unless the power dynamic shifts in the tower. I placed the family in a safe location and told them to remain hidden. We might need them, as you indicated."

Venli hummed to Subservience.

"Find a place where we can watch them, then send me a note. I will consider if there is a way to use them to find Stormblessed, and for now will spread a rumor that I have disposed of them. Even if the Pursuer finds the truth, though, they should be safe for the time being. That said, I give warning again: You must *not* let others see your compassion for humans. It will be misconstrued, particularly with you being the child of traitors."

"Yes, Ancient One."

"Go," she said. "I consider what I have done here today a favor to you. Do not forget it."

Venli hummed to Subservience and left quickly. Timbre pulsed encouragingly.

"I *am* a false Radiant," Venli said. "You know this."

Timbre pulsed again. Perhaps. But today had been a step in the right direction.

THE FUTURE
BECOME DUST

*It would have been so easy if Voidlight and Stormlight destroyed
one another. Such a simple answer.*

—From *Rhythm of War*, page 6

G rampa," little Gavinor asked. "Was my daddy brave when he
died?"

Dalinar settled down on the floor of the small room, setting aside the wooden sword he'd been using to play at a greatshell hunt.
Had Adolin ever been this small?

He was determined not to miss so much of Gav's life as he had his
sons'. He wanted to love and cherish this solemn child with dark hair
and pure yellow eyes.

"He was very brave," Dalinar said, waving for the child to come sit in his
lap. "So very brave. He went almost alone to our home, to try to save it."

"To save me," Gav said softly. "He died because of me."

"No!" Dalinar said. "He died because of evil people."

"Evil people . . . like Mommy?"

Storms. This poor child.

"Your mother," Dalinar said, "was also brave. She didn't do those
terrible things; it was the enemy, who had taken over her mind. Do you
understand? Your mother loved you."

Gav nodded, serious beyond his years. He did like playing at great-shell hunts, though he didn't laugh during them like other children would. He treated even play as a somber occasion.

Dalinar tried to restart the pretend hunt, but the boy's mind seemed overshadowed by these dark thoughts. After just another few minutes, Gav complained that he was tired. So Dalinar let his nursemaid take him to rest. Then Dalinar lingered at the doorway, watching her tuck him into bed.

What five-year-old *wanted* to go to bed? Though Dalinar had not been the most dutiful parent, he did remember lengthy complaints from both Adolin and Renarin on evenings like this, when they insisted they *were* old enough to stay up and they did *not* feel tired. Gav instead clutched his little wooden sword, which he kept with him at all times, and drifted off.

Dalinar left the small home, nodding to the guards outside. The Azish thought it strange that the Alethi officers brought families to war, but how else were children to learn proper military protocol?

It was the evening following Jasnah's stunt with Ruthar, and Dalinar had spent most of the day—before visiting Gav—speaking via spanreed to highlords and highladies, smoothing over their concerns about the near execution. He'd made certain the legality of Jasnah's actions would not be questioned. And he'd personally talked to Relis, Ruthar's son.

The young man had lost a bout to Adolin back in the warcamps, and Dalinar had worried about his motivations now. However, it seemed that Relis was eager to prove he could be a loyalist. Dalinar had made certain that his father was taken to Azimir and given a small house there, where he could be watched. Regardless of what Jasnah said, Dalinar wouldn't have a former highprince begging for scraps.

Finally—after smoothing things over with the Azish, who did *not* appreciate Alethi trials by sword—he was feeling he had the situation under control. He stopped in the middle of the camp, thoughtful. He'd almost forgotten Renarin's talk of his episode the day before.

Dalinar turned and strode through the warcamp—a bustling illustration of organized chaos. Messengers ran this way and that, mostly wearing the patterned livery of the various Azish scribe orders. Alethi captains had their soldiers hauling supplies or marking the stone ground with painted lines to indicate directions.

A trail of wagons snaked in from the northwest, a lifeline to populated lands and fertile hills untouched by war. Fearing that this camp was already a big target, Dalinar had posted many of his Soulcasters in Azimir.

The landscape was different from what he knew. More trees, less grass, and strange fields of shrubs with interlocking branches that created vast snarls. Despite that, the signs he saw in this village were all too familiar. A bit of cloth trapped in the hardened crem beside the roadway. Burnt-out buildings, torched either out of a sadistic amusement, or to deny beds and stormshutters to the army that had moved in next. Those fires had been fed by homes with too many possessions left behind.

Engineers had continued to shore up the eastern stormwall, where a natural windbreak created a cleft. Normally this shoring process would have taken weeks. Today Shardbearers cut out stone blocks, which Windrunners made light enough to push into position with ease. The ever-present Azish functionaries were supervising.

Dalinar turned toward the Windrunner camp, troubled. Jasnah's stunt had overshadowed their conversation about monarchs and monarchies—but now that he dwelled on it, he found it as disturbing as the duel. The way Jasnah had talked . . . She had seemed *proud* of the idea that she might be Alethkar's last queen. She intended to see Alethkar left with some version of a neutered monarchy, like in Thaylenah or Azir.

How would the country function without a proper monarch? The Alethi weren't like these persnickety Azish. The Alethi liked real leaders, soldiers who were accustomed to making decisions. A country was like an army. Someone strong needed to be in charge. And barring that, someone *decisive* needed to be in charge.

The thoughts persisted as he neared the Windrunner camp and smelled something delicious on the air. The Windrunners continued a tradition begun in the bridge crews: a large communal stew available to anyone. Dalinar had originally tried to regulate the thing. However, while he usually found the Windrunners agreeable to proper military decorum, they had absolutely refused to follow proper quartermaster requisition and mess requirements for their evening stews.

Eventually Dalinar had done what any good commander did when faced by such persistent mass insubordination: He backed down. When good men disobeyed, it was time to look at your orders.

Today he found the Windrunners visited by an unusual number of Thaylens. The stews tended to attract whichever soldiers felt most out of place, and Dalinar suspected the Thaylens were feeling that way, being so far from the oceans. Companylord Sigzil was taking a turn at storytelling. Renarin was there too in his Bridge Four uniform, watching Sigzil with rapt attention. Regardless of war or storm, the boy tried to find his way to this fire every evening.

Dalinar approached, and only then did he realize the stir he was causing. Soldiers nudged one another, and someone ran to get him a stool. Sigzil paused in his story, saluting smartly.

They think I've come to approve of the tradition, Dalinar realized. They seemed to have been waiting for it, judging by how eagerly one of the Windrunner squires brought him a bowl. Dalinar accepted the food and took a bite, then nodded approvingly. That inspired applause. After that, there was nothing to do but settle down and keep eating, indicating that the rest of them could go on with their ritual.

When he glanced over at his son, Renarin was smiling. A reserved grin; you rarely saw teeth from Renarin. However, the lad didn't have his box out, the one he often used to occupy his hands. He was relaxed here among these people.

"That was good of you, Father," Renarin whispered, moving closer. "They've been waiting for you to stop by."

"It's good stew," Dalinar noted.

"Secret Horneater recipe," Renarin said. "Apparently it has only two lines of instructions. 'Take everything you have, and put him in pot. Don't let anyone airsick touch seasonings.'" Renarin said it fondly, but he hadn't finished his bowl. He seemed distracted. Though . . . he always seemed distracted. "I assume you're here to talk about . . . what I told you? The episode?"

Dalinar nodded.

Renarin tapped his spoon against the side of his bowl, a rhythmic click. He stared at the cookfire flamespren. "Does it strike you as cruel of fate, Father? My blood sickness gets healed, so I can finally be a soldier like I always wanted. But that same healing has given me another kind of fit. More dangerous than the other by far."

"What did you see this time?"

"I'm not sure I should say. I know I told you to come talk to me, but . . . I vacillate. The things I see, they're of him, right? I think *he* shows me what he wants. That's why I saw you becoming his champion." He glanced down at his bowl. "Glys isn't convinced the visions are bad. He says we're something new, and he doesn't think the visions are specifically from Odium—though perhaps his desires taint what we see."

"Any information—even if you suspect your enemy is feeding it to you—is useful, son. More wars are lost to lack of information than are lost to lack of courage."

Renarin set his bowl beside his seat. It was easy to fall into the habit of underestimating Renarin. He always moved in this deliberate, careful way. It made him seem fragile.

Don't forget, part of Dalinar thought. *When you were broken on the floor, consumed by your past, this boy held you. Don't forget who was strong, when you—the Blackthorn—were weak.*

The youth stood up, then gestured for Dalinar to follow. They left the circle of firelight, waving farewell to the others. Lopen called out, asking Renarin to "look into the future and find out if I beat Huio at cards tomorrow." It seemed a little crass to Dalinar, bringing up his son's strange disorder, but Renarin took it with a chuckle.

The sky had grown dim, though the sun wasn't fully set yet. These western lands were warmer than Dalinar liked—particularly at night. They didn't cool off as was proper.

The Windrunner camp was near the edge of the village, so they strolled out into the wilderness near some snarls of bushes and a few tall trees—with broad canopies—that had grown out of the center, perhaps somehow using the bushes for extra strength. This area was relatively quiet, and soon the two of them were alone.

"Renarin?" Dalinar asked. "Are you going to tell me what you saw?"

His son slowed. His eyes caught the light of the now-distant campfire. "Yes," he said. "But I want to get it right, Father. So I need to summon it again."

"You can *summon* it?" Dalinar said. "I thought it came upon you unexpectedly."

"It did," Renarin said. "And it will again. But right now, it simply is." He turned forward and stepped into the darkness.

⸙

As Renarin stepped forward, the ground beneath his feet became dark glass, spreading from the heel of his boot. It cracked in a web of lines, a purposeful pattern, black on black.

Glys, who preferred to hide within Renarin, grew excited. He'd captured this vision as it came, so they could study it. Renarin wasn't quite so enthusiastic. It would be so much easier if he were like other Radiants.

Stained glass spread out around him, engulfing the landscape, a phantom light shimmering and glowing from behind in the darkness. As he walked, each of his footsteps made the ground pulse red, light shining up through the cracks. His father wouldn't be able to see what he did. But hopefully Renarin could describe it properly.

"I see you in this vision," Renarin said to his father. "You're in a lot of them. In this one you stand tall, formed as if from stained glass, and you wear Shardplate. Stark white Shardplate, though you are pierced with a black arrow."

"Do you know what it means?" Dalinar said, a shadow barely visible from behind the glass window depicting him.

"I think it might be a symbol of you, who you were, who you become. The more important part is the enemy. He makes up the bulk of this image. A window of yellow-white light breaking into smaller and smaller pieces, into infinity.

"He is like the sun, Father. He controls and dominates everything—and although your figure raises a sword high, it's facing the wrong direction. You're fighting and you're fighting, but not him. I think I understand the meaning: you want a deal, you want a contest of champions, but you're going to keep fighting, and fighting, and fighting distractions. Because why would the enemy agree to a contest that he can theoretically lose?"

"He already agreed," Dalinar said.

"Were terms set?" Renarin asked. "A date picked? I don't know if this vision is what he wants us to see. But either way . . . I don't think he's worried enough to agree to terms. He can wait, keep you fighting, keep *us* fighting. Forever. He can make this war so it never ends."

Dalinar stepped forward, passing through the stained glass that represented him—though he wouldn't know he had done so.

It seemed to Renarin as if his father never aged. Even in his earliest memories, Renarin remembered him looking like this—so powerful, so unchanging, so strong. Some of that was from the things his mother had told Renarin, building an image in his head of the perfect Alethi officer.

It was a tragedy that she hadn't lived to see Dalinar become the man she'd imagined him to be. A shame that Odium had seen her killed. That was the way Renarin *had* to present it to himself. Better to turn his pain against the enemy than to lose his father along with his mother.

"I have stared Odium in the eyes," Dalinar said. "I have faced him. He expected me to break. By refusing, I've upended his plans. It means he can be defeated—and equally important, it means he doesn't know everything or see everything."

"Yes," Renarin said, walking across broken glass to look up at the enormous depiction of Odium. "I don't think he's omnipresent, Father. Well, part of him is everywhere, but he can't access that information— any more than the Stormfather knows everything the wind touches. I think . . . Odium might see like I do. Not events, or the world itself, but *possibilities.*

"This war is dangerous for us, Father. In the past, the Heralds would organize our forces, fight with us for a time—but would then return to lock away the souls of the Fused in Damnation, preventing their re-births. That way, each Fused we killed was an actual casualty. But the Oathpact is broken now, and the Fused cannot be locked away."

"Yes . . ." Dalinar said, moving to stand beside Renarin. "I've been thinking about this myself. Trying to determine if there was a way to re-store the Oathpact, or to somehow otherwise make the enemy fear. This is new ground, for both us and Odium. There must be something about this new reality that unnerves him. Is there anything else you see?"

See the blackness that will be, Renarin? Glys said.

"Friction between the two of you," Renarin said, pointing up at the stained glass. "And a blackness interfering, marring the beauty of the window. Like a sickness infecting both of you, at the edges."

"Curious," Dalinar said, looking where Renarin had pointed, though he'd see only empty air. "I wonder if we'll ever know what that represents."

"Oh, that one's easy, Father," Renarin said. "That's me."

"Renarin, I don't think you should see yourself as—"

"You needn't try to protect my ego, Father. When Glys and I bonded, we became . . . something new. We see the future. At first I was confused at my place—but I've come to understand. What I see interferes with Odium's ability. Because I can see possibilities of the future, my knowledge changes what I will do. Therefore, his ability to see my future is obscured. Anyone close to me is difficult for him to read."

"I find that comforting," Dalinar said, putting his arm around Renarin's shoulders. "Whatever you are, son, it's a blessing. You might be a different kind of Radiant, but you're Radiant all the same. You shouldn't feel you need to hide this or your spren."

Renarin ducked his head, embarrassed. His father knew not to touch him too quickly, too unexpectedly, so it wasn't the arm around his shoulders. It was just that . . . well, Dalinar was so accustomed to being able to do whatever he wanted. He had written a storming *book*.

Renarin held no illusions that he would be similarly accepted. He and his father might be of similar rank, from the same family, but Renarin had never been able to navigate society like Dalinar did. True, his father at times "navigated" society like a chull marching through a crowd, but people got out of the way all the same.

Not for Renarin. The people of both Alethkar and Azir had *thousands* of years training them to fear and condemn anyone who claimed to be able to see the future. They weren't going to put that aside easily, and particularly not for Renarin.

We will be careful, Glys thought. *We will be safe.*

We will try, Renarin thought to him.

Out loud, he merely said, "Thank you. It means a lot to me that you believe that, Father."

You will ask him? Glys said. *So my siblings can be?*

"Glys wants me to note," Renarin said, "that there are others like him. Other spren that Sja-anat has touched, changed, made into . . . whatever it is we are."

"What she does is not right. Corrupting spren?"

"If I'm a blessing, Father, how can we reject the others? How can we condemn the one who made them? Sja-anat isn't human, and doesn't think like one, but I believe she *is* trying to find a path toward peace between singers and humans. In her own way."

"Still . . . I've felt the touch of one of the Unmade, Renarin."

And by one, you judge the others? Renarin didn't say it though. People too often said things as soon as they popped into their heads. Instead he waited.

"How many corrupted spren are we talking about?" Dalinar finally asked.

"Only a handful," Renarin said. "She won't change intelligent spren without their consent."

"Well, that's valuable to know. I'll consider it. Are you . . . in contact with her?"

"Not in months. Glys is worried at how silent she's become, though he thinks she is somewhere near right now."

She creates in us a faction loved by neither men nor Odium, Glys agreed. *No home. No allies. She might be destroyed by either. We will need more. Like you and like me. Together.*

Around Renarin, the stained glass windows began to crumble. It took Stormlight and effort by Glys to re-create them—and he was plainly getting tired. Gradually, Renarin's world became normal.

"Let me know if she contacts you," Dalinar said. "And if any of these episodes come upon you, bring them to me. I know a little of what it is like, son. You aren't as alone as you probably think."

He knows you, Glys said, thrilled by the idea. *He does and will.*

Renarin supposed that maybe he did. How unusual, and how comforting. Renarin—tense at first—leaned against his father, then accepted the offered strength as he watched the future become dust around him.

We need more, Glys said. *We need more like us, who will be. Who?*

I can think of one, Renarin said, *who would be a perfect choice. . . .*

We must not let our desires for a specific result cloud our perceptions.

—From *Rhythm of War*, page 6 undertext

With Stormlight, Kaladin had been able to investigate his little hideout, finding it slightly larger than he'd pictured. A stone shelf along one wall gave him a place to put Teft. He'd washed the man, then dressed him in the loose robe, with bedpan in place. One of the sacks Kaladin had taken from the monastery— stuffed with clothing—made a makeshift pillow. He'd need to find blankets, but for now his friend seemed as comfortable as Kaladin could make him.

Teft was still willing to take water, sucking it from the large metal syringe Kaladin brought back. Indeed, Teft lapped up the contents eagerly. He seemed so close to coming awake, Kaladin expected him to start cursing at any moment, demanding to know where his uniform had gone.

Syl watched, uncharacteristically solemn. "What will we do if he dies?" she asked softly.

"Don't think about that," Kaladin said.

"What if I can't help thinking about it?"

"Find something to distract you."

She sat on the stone shelf, hands in her lap. "Is that how you stand it? Knowing everyone is going to die? You just . . . don't think about it?"

"Basically," Kaladin said, refilling his syringe from the wooden water jug, then putting the tip into Teft's mouth and slowly emptying it. "Everyone dies eventually."

"I won't," she said. "Spren are immortal, even if you kill them. Someday I'll have to watch you die."

"What brought this on?" Kaladin asked. "This isn't like you."

"Yup. Right. Of course. Not like me." She plastered a smile on her face. "Sorry."

"I didn't mean it that way, Syl," Kaladin said. "You don't have to pretend."

"I'm not."

"I've used enough fake smiles to not be fooled by one. You were doing this earlier too, before the problems in the tower started. What happened?"

She looked down. "I've . . . been remembering what it was like when Relador, my old knight, died. How it made me sleep for so many years, straight through the Recreance. I keep wondering, will that happen to me again?"

"Do you feel a darkness?" Kaladin asked. "A whisper that everything will always turn out for the worst? And at the same time a crippling— and baffling—impulse pushing you to give up and do nothing to change it?"

"No," she said, shaking her head. "Nothing like that. Just a worry in the back of my mind that I keep circling around to. Like . . . I have a present I want to open, and I get excited for a little while—only to remember I already opened it and there was nothing inside."

"Sounds like how I used to feel when I remembered Tien was dead," Kaladin said. "I'd get used to living life as normal, feeling good—only to be reminded by seeing a rock in the rain, or by seeing a wooden carving like the ones he used to do. Then my whole day would come crashing down."

"Like that! But it doesn't crash my day down. Just makes me settle back and think and wish I could see him again. It still hurts. Is something wrong with me?"

"That sounds normal to me. Healthy. You're dealing with the loss when you never really did so before. Now that you're coming fully back to yourself, you're finally confronting things you've been ignoring."

"You just told me not to think about it though," Syl said. "Will that actually help?"

Kaladin winced. No, it wouldn't. He'd tried. "Distractions *can* be helpful. Doing something, reminding yourself there's a lot out there that's wonderful. But . . . you do have to think about these things eventually, I guess." He filled the syringe again. "You shouldn't ask me about this sort of problem. I'm . . . not the best at dealing with them myself."

"I feel like I shouldn't *have* to deal with them," Syl said. "I'm a spren, not a human. If I'm thinking like this, doesn't it mean I'm broken?"

"It means you're alive," Kaladin said. "I'd be more worried if you *didn't* feel loss."

"Maybe it's because you humans created us."

"Or it's because you're a little piece of divinity, like you always say." Kaladin shrugged. "If there *is* a god, then I think we could find him in the way we care about one another. Humans thinking about the wind, and honor, might have given you shape from formless power—but you're your own person now. As I'm my own person, though my parents gave me shape."

She smiled at that, and walked across the shelf wearing the form of a woman in a havah. "A person," she said. "I like thinking like that. Being like that. A lot of the other honorspren, they talk about what we were *made* to be, what we *must* do. I talked like that once. I was wrong."

"A lot of humans are the same," he said, leaning down so he was eye level with her. "I guess we both need to remember that whatever's happening in our heads, whatever it was that created us, we get to choose. That's what makes us people, Syl."

She smiled, then her havah bled from a light white-blue to a deeper blue color, striking and distinct, like it was made of real cloth.

"You're getting better at that," he said. "The colors are more vibrant this time."

She held up her arms. "I think the closer I get to your world, the more I can become, the more I can change."

She seemed to like that idea and sat, making her dress fade from one shade of blue to another, and then to a green. Kaladin finished giving Teft the syringe of water, then held it up. The sides of the metal had fingerprints in them, sunken into the surface. This device had been Soulcast into metal after first being formed from wax—the fingerprints were a telltale sign.

"You can become more things," he said. "Like a syringe maybe? We talked about you becoming other tools."

"I think I could do it," she said. "If I could manifest as a Blade right now, I could change shape to be like that. I think . . . you imagining it, me believing it, we could do even more. It—"

She cut off as a faint scraping sounded outside, from near the doorway. Immediately Kaladin reached for his scalpel. Syl came alert, zipping up into the air around him as a ribbon of light. Kaladin crept toward the door. He'd covered up the gemstone in the wall on this side with a piece of cloth. He didn't know if his light would shine out or not, but wasn't taking any chances.

But he could hear. Someone *was* out there, their boots scraping stone. Were they inspecting the door?

He made a snap decision, slipping his hand under the cloth and pressing it against the stone, commanding it to open. The rocks began to split. Kaladin prepared to leap out and attack the singer on the other side.

But it wasn't a singer.

It was Dabbid.

The unassuming bridgeman wore street clothing, and he stepped away from the door as it opened. He saw Kaladin and nodded to him, as if this were all completely expected.

"Dabbid?" Kaladin said. Other than Rlain, Dabbid was the only original bridgeman who hadn't manifested Windrunner powers. So it made sense he was awake. But how had he found his way here?

Dabbid held up a pot with something liquid inside. Kaladin gave it a sniff. "Broth?" he asked. "How did you know?"

Dabbid pointed at the line of crystal on the wall, where the tower spren's light began to twinkle. Surprising; along with being mute, the man didn't often volunteer information.

Holding the pot awkwardly, Dabbid tapped his wrists together. *Bridge Four.*

"I am *so* glad to see you," Kaladin said, leading him into the room. "How did you get broth? Never mind. Here, come sit by Teft." Dabbid was one of the first men Kaladin had saved when he'd started administering medical aid to the bridgemen. While Dabbid's physical wounds had healed, his battle shock was the strongest Kaladin had ever seen.

Regardless, he was a *wonderful* sight. Kaladin had been worrying about leaving Teft. If Kaladin died on a mission, that would be a death sentence for Teft too. Unless someone else knew about him.

He got Dabbid situated, then showed him the use of the syringe and had him start feeding Teft. Kaladin felt bad, putting the mute bridgeman to work as soon as he arrived, but—by Syl's internal clock—night would soon arrive. Kaladin needed to get moving.

"I'll explain more when I return," Kaladin promised. "Dabbid, can you get this door open? In case you need to fetch more food and water."

Dabbid walked over and put his hand on the door's gemstone; it opened for him as easily as it did for Kaladin. That was somewhat worrisome. Kaladin touched the wall garnet. "Tower spren?" he asked.

Yes.

"Is there a way I can lock these doors, so they can't be opened by just anyone?"

It was once possible to attune them to individuals. These days, I must simply leave a given door so it can be opened by anyone, or lock it so none can open it.

Well, it was good to know that—in a pinch—he should be able to ask the Sibling to lock the door. For now, it was enough that Dabbid could get in and out.

Kaladin nodded to Syl, left one gemstone to give Dabbid light, then slipped out.

．＊．

Navani had asked Kaladin to observe the Oathgates up close as they were activated. To see if he could figure out why they functioned when other fabrials did not.

Unfortunately, Kaladin doubted he'd be able to get all the way down to the Oathgate plateau by sneaking through the hallways of the tower. He had made it to an out-of-the-way monastery on the fourth floor, yes, but that was a long way from the highly populated first two floors. Even if humans weren't confined to quarters, Kaladin couldn't saunter along without getting stopped. Kaladin Stormblessed drew attention.

Instead, he wanted to try climbing along the outside of the tower. Before he'd learned to fly, he'd stuck rocks to the chasm wall and climbed them. He figured he could do something similar now. The enemy had plainly ordered the Heavenly Ones to stay inside, and few people went out on the balconies.

So he made his way onto a balcony on the tenth floor right as dusk was arriving. He'd tied a sack to his belt, and in it he'd stuffed the four scrub brushes he'd gotten from the monastery. Earlier, he'd cut the bristles free with his scalpel, leaving them flat on the front but with a curved handle for holding.

Kaladin couldn't paint his hands with a Full Lashing to stick them to things. Lopen kept sticking his clothing or hair to the floor, but a Radiant's skin seemed immune to the power. Perhaps Kaladin could have rigged some gloves that worked, but the brush handholds seemed sturdier.

He leaned out of the balcony and checked to see if anyone was watching. It was growing dark already. He doubted anyone would be able to see him in the gloom, so long as he didn't draw in too much Stormlight. By keeping it mostly in the brushes attached to the wall, he wouldn't glow so much that he risked being spotted. At least, the risk of that felt far less than the risk of sneaking through the occupied floors.

Best to try it first in a way that wasn't dangerous. Kaladin took out one of the brushes and infused it with Stormlight, then pressed the flat side against a pillar on the balcony. With it affixed in place, he was able to hang his entire weight on it—dangling free—without it pulling off or the handle breaking.

"Good enough," he said, recovering the Stormlight from the Lashing. He took off his socks, but replaced his boots. He scanned the air for Heavenly Ones one last time, then stepped over the side of the balcony and balanced on the little ledge outside. He looked down toward the stones far below, but they were lost in the evening darkness. He felt as if he were standing on the edge of eternity.

He'd always liked being up high. Even before becoming Radiant, he'd felt a certain kinship with the open sky. Standing here, part of him wanted to jump, to feel the rushing wind. It wasn't some suicidal tendency, not this time. It was the call of something beautiful.

"Are you scared?" Syl said.

"No," Kaladin said. "The opposite. I've gotten so accustomed to leaping from high places that I'm not nearly as worried about this as I probably should be."

He infused two of the brushes, then moved to the far left side of the balcony. Here the stone wall made a straight "path" toward the ground between balconies. Kaladin took a deep breath and swung out and slammed one brush against the stone, then the other.

He found footholds on the stone, but they were slippery. Once, there had been a great deal of ornamentation on the rock out here—but years of highstorms had smoothed some of that out. Perhaps Lift could have climbed it without help, but Kaladin was glad he had Stormlight. He infused the toes of his boots through his feet, then stuck them to the wall too.

He started toward the ground, unsticking one limb, moving it, then sticking it back. Syl walked through the air beside him, as if striding down invisible steps. Kaladin found the descent more difficult than he'd anticipated. He had to rely a great deal on his upper-body strength, as it was difficult to get the boots to stick right, with just the toes.

He'd release one brush from the wall, then slide it into place while holding on with only one hand, then move his feet before moving the other. Though Radiant, he was sweating from exertion by the time he reached the fifth floor. He decided to take a break, and—after having Syl check to make sure it was empty—he moved over and swung onto a balcony. He settled down, breathing deeply, a few spiky coldspren moving across the balcony rail toward him, like friendly cremlings.

Syl darted into the hallway to make sure nobody was near. Fortunately, the increasingly cold tower—and the desire for subterfuge— seemed to have convinced most of the invading singers to take quarters far inward. So long as he stayed away from patrols, he should be safe.

He sat with his back to the balcony railing, feeling his muscles burn. As a soldier, then a bridgeman, he'd grown accustomed to the sensation of overexerted muscles. He almost felt cheated these days, because Stormlight's healing made the feeling rare. Indeed, after he sat for a minute, the sensation was completely gone.

Once Syl returned, he resumed his climb. As he did, a couple of windspren drew near: little lines of light that looped about him. As he descended toward the fourth floor, they would occasionally show faces at him—or the outlines of figures—before giggling and flitting off.

Syl watched them with fondness. He wanted to ask her what she was thinking, but didn't dare speak, lest someone inside hear voices coming in through a window. He took care to press his handholds into place quietly.

Kaladin hit a snag as he reached the fourth floor. Syl noticed first, becoming a ribbon and making the glyph for "stop" in the air beside him. He froze, then heard it. Voices.

He nodded to Syl, who went to investigate. He felt her concern through the bond; when Syl was a Blade, they had a direct mental connection—but when she was not in that shape, the connection was softer. They'd been practicing on sending words to one another, but they tended to be vague impressions.

This time, he got a sense of some distinct words. . . . *singers . . . with spyglasses . . . third-floor balcony . . . looking up . . .*

Kaladin hung in place, silent as he could be. He could hear them below and to the left, on a balcony. They had spyglasses? Why?

To watch the sky, he thought, trying to project the idea to Syl. *For Windrunner scouts. They won't want to use the Oathgate until they're certain nobody is watching.*

Syl returned, and Kaladin started to feel his muscles burning again. He wiped his sweaty brow on his sleeve, then carefully—his teeth gritted—drew in Stormlight to release one of his brush handholds. His skin started to release luminescent smoke, but before the light became too obvious, he re-Lashed the brush and stretched out, attaching it to the rock as far to his right as he could reach.

He moved to the side, away from the occupied balcony. He could climb across the next balcony over. As he moved, he heard the singers chatting in Alethi—femalen voices he thought, though some singer forms made gender difficult to distinguish from the voice. Judging by the conversation, they were indeed watching for Windrunners. They did Oathgate transfers at night deliberately—when flying Radiants would be starkly visible, glowing in the night sky.

Kaladin crossed over two balconies to his right, then continued down another open flat corridor of stone. He was on the northern part of the tower, and had moved west to get away from the scouts. Syl kept checking the nearby balconies as Kaladin continued his methodical pace.

Unfortunately, soon after he'd passed the third floor, a dark light flashed from the Oathgates. It was tinged violet like Voidlight, but was brighter than a Voidlight sphere.

Kaladin took a moment to rest, hanging on but not moving. "Syl," he whispered. "Go check on those scouts on the balcony. Tell me if they're still watching the sky."

She zipped off, then returned a moment later.

"They're packing up their things," she whispered. "Looks like they're leaving."

That was what he'd feared. The enemy would use the Oathgates as infrequently as possible, as moving singer troops in and out of the tower would expose them to spying eyes. If the scouts were packing up, it was a fairly solid indication that the Oathgates wouldn't be used again tonight. Kaladin had been too slow.

But the gate had flashed with Voidlight. So he knew they'd done *something* to the fabrial. He'd have to try again tomorrow; he'd moved slower than he'd intended today, but he felt good about the process. A little more practice, and he could probably get down fast enough. But would getting close to the Oathgates tell him anything about what had been done to them? He didn't feel he knew enough about fabrials.

For now, he started climbing back up to see how much more difficult it was. This was slower, but the footholds with his boots were more helpful. As he ascended, he found a fierce pride in the effort. The changes to the tower had tried to keep him confined to the ground, but the sky was *his*. He'd found a way to scale her again, if in a less impressive way. If he . . .

Kaladin paused, hanging from his handholds, as something struck him. Something that he felt profoundly stupid for having not seen immediately.

"The scouts on the balcony," he whispered to Syl as she darted in to see why he'd stopped. "What would they have done if they'd spotted Windrunners in the sky?"

"They'd have told the others to stop the transfer," Syl said, "so the fact that the Oathgate glowed the wrong color wouldn't give away the truth."

"How?" Kaladin asked. "*How* did they contact the Oathgate operators? Did you see flags or anything?"

"No," Syl said. "They were just sitting there writing in the dark. They must have been using . . . a *spanreed*."

One that worked in the tower. Navani was trying to figure out how the enemy was operating fabrials. What if he could hand her one? Surely that would lead to more valuable information than he would get by observing the Oathgates.

Syl zipped over to the balcony the scouts had been using. "I can see them!" she said. "They've packed up, and they're leaving, but they're just ahead."

Follow, Kaladin sent her mentally, then moved as quickly as he could in that direction. He might have missed the night's transfer, but there was still a way he could help.

And it involved stealing that spanreed.

But how can we not, in searching, wish for a specific result? What scientist goes into a project without a hope for what they will find?

—From *Rhythm of War*, page 6 undertext

Venli inspected the large model of the tower. Such an intricate construction, a masterwork of sculpting, bathed in violet moonlight through the window. What had it been used for by the Radiants of old, all those years ago? Was this a forgotten art piece, or something more? She'd heard several Voidspren saying that perhaps it was a scale model for the spren to live in, but—for all its intricacy—it didn't have things like furniture or doors.

She walked around it, passing through the middle, where it was split to show a cross section. For some reason, seeing it in miniature highlighted how impossibly vast the tower was. Even reconstructed like this, it was twice Venli's height.

She shook her head and left the model behind, moving among the fallen Radiants, each of whom lay silent on the floor of this large chamber. According to Raboniel's request, Venli had found a place to keep them all together. She'd wanted them on the ground floor, close enough to the basement rooms to be sent for, but that region of the tower was quite well occupied. So rather than go to the trouble of kicking people out of a chamber to use, Venli had appropriated this newly discovered—and empty—one. It had only one entrance, so it was easy to guard, and the window provided natural light.

There were around fifty of them in total. Perhaps with such low numbers, Raboniel's forces could have taken this place even if the Radiants had fought. Perhaps not. There was something about these modern Radiants. The Fused seemed to be constantly surprised by them. Everyone had expected impotence, inexperience. Roshar had gone centuries without the Radiant bond. These had no masters to train them; they had to discover everything on their own. How did they do so well?

Timbre pulsed her thoughts on the matter. Sometimes ignorance was an advantage, as you weren't limited by the expectations of the past. Perhaps that was it. Or perhaps it was something else. New, younger spren, enthusiastic—pitted against weary old Fused souls.

Venli lingered near the body of a young woman. The Radiants were each lying on a blanket and draped with a sheet, corpselike, leaving only their faces exposed. This Radiant, however, was stirring. Her eyes were closed, but her face twitched, as if she were in the grip of a terrible nightmare. She might be. Odium had invaded Venli's mind in the past; who knew how far his corrupting touch could reach?

Windrunner, Venli thought, reading the markings on the floor next to the woman. They listed whatever Venli's team had been able to learn about the individual Radiants from interrogating the tower's humans. She glanced down the row toward another Radiant whose face was making similar expressions. Also a Windrunner.

She finished her inspection and met up with Dul. It had turned out to be simple for Venli to put her most trusted people in charge of the fallen Radiants, as Raboniel thought it a good use for them.

"The other Windrunners," Venli said softly. "Do they all seem . . ."

"Closer to waking?" Dul asked to Awe. "Yeah. They do. Any time one of the Radiants stirs, it's always a Windrunner. We've caught some of them muttering in their sleep."

"Raboniel asked me specifically to check on this," Venli said to Anxiety. "She seemed to have anticipated it."

"Not hard to guess," Dul said. "The Radiant who is awake—supposedly roaming the tower—is a Windrunner, right?"

Venli nodded, looking along the rows of bodies. Venli's loyalists moved among them, administering broth and changing soiled blankets.

"This was a good maneuver, putting us here," Dul whispered. "Caring for the humans gives us an excuse to collect blankets and clothing for when we leave. I've begun putting away broth paste that should keep."

"Good," Venli said to Anxiety. "When only our people are around, test those Windrunners and see if you can wake one up."

"And if we succeed?" Dul asked to Skepticism. "I think that's a terrible idea."

Venli's first instinct—even still—was to slap him. How dare he question her? She pushed away that instinct, though it warned her that she was the same selfish person, despite it all. A few Words didn't suddenly make her something better.

"Their powers would be suppressed," Venli explained to him. "So they shouldn't be a danger to you. And if they are violent, get away and let it be assumed they woke up spontaneously. That will keep us from being implicated."

"Fine, but why risk it?"

"Escaping and hiding will be far easier with the help of one like these," Venli said. "At the very least, we'll need a distraction to get out. The Windrunners waking and suddenly fighting would provide that."

She glanced at Dul, who still hummed to Skepticism.

"Look," Venli said as they completed a walk around the room, "I don't like humans any more than you do. But if we truly want to escape, we'll need to make use of every advantage we can find." She swept her hand across the room of unconscious Radiants. "This could be a very large one."

Finally, Dul hummed to Reconciliation. "I suppose you're right. It's worth trying, though I'm not sure how to wake these up. What we need is a surgeon. Could probably use one anyway; some of these seem to be getting sores and drawing rotspren. Others won't take any broth, though they have hungerspren buzzing around them."

Venli attuned Peace as an idea occurred to her. "I'm sure I could get you surgeons. In fact, I know of one who might be willing to help our cause. A human. He's in hiding, because of certain matters we shouldn't spread. But I think we could place him here, to help."

Dul nodded, humming to Appreciation. Venli left, stepping out onto the floor of the atrium—with the long vertical shaft running up toward the top of the tower. She passed several Regals standing guard at the door to the room with the model. Leshwi had told her to put the surgeon and his family someplace safe; well, this made sense.

Curfew was nearing, so here on the floor of the atrium, people were hurrying about their last-minute activities. The humans—no longer confined to quarters—had crept from their shells like vines after a storm. Many of them lived around the atrium, and they had pulled out carts, making temporary shops here near the large window. Like spren to the Passions, the humans sought out the sunlight.

Tonight, they walked timidly and kept their distance from Venli, as if they couldn't believe that they were supposed to continue on as if nothing had happened. Venli found a stairwell and hurried up, causing a few human women to pull to one side and gasp softly, drawing wormlike fearspren. Sometimes Venli forgot how fearsome her Regal form looked. She'd grown comfortable with it, and more and more it felt like her natural state—even if there was a Voidspren trapped in her gemheart.

On the second floor, Venli made her way toward a meeting point near the atrium balcony. She was supposed to give service to a team of Fused tonight, in case they needed an interpreter. Many Fused had trouble speaking to modern singers. That made sense, considering how short a time they'd been back. Venli found it odder that some—like Raboniel— had already learned to speak modern Alethi.

Venli arrived at the meeting place, surprised to find several Deepest Ones: the strange Fused with limber bodies and milky-white eyes glowing red from behind. They enjoyed spending their time sunken in rock as much as the Heavenly Ones liked to soar. She had occasionally walked into a room to find one or two of them lingering there, sunken into the floor, revealing only their faces, eyes closed.

Tonight four stood in a clump, attended by a few ordinary singers carrying equipment. The Fused were arguing among themselves in their language.

"I did not think the sand would work," one of the Deepest Ones said to Spite. Their rhythms sounded off. Muted. "I was right in this. You should acknowledge it."

"There are too many different fabrials in the tower," said another. "And too many spren. The device we hunt doesn't leave a strong enough impression to be noticeable, hidden as it is."

"You're searching for the fabrial that is creating the shield around the crystal pillar," Venli guessed. Raboniel had mentioned the field was created by a fabrial—which she theorized would have several gemstones, called nodes, maintaining it, hidden somewhere in the tower.

The Deepest Ones did not directly reprimand her for speaking without first being addressed. As Raboniel's Voice, Venli had a certain amount of authority, even with these. Not to command, but certainly to speak.

"Why not use secretspren?" she asked. "They can find fabrials as easily as they find Radiants, can't they?"

"The entire tower is a fabrial," one of the Deepest Ones said. "The secretspren are useless here; they spin in circles, confused. Asking them to find a specific use of Light in here is like asking them to find a specific patch of water in an ocean."

"Useless spren," another said. "Have you seen the chaosspren?"

Venli had. Those types of Voidspren—normally invisible to anyone but the ones they appeared to—left sparks in the air now, as if somehow responding to the dampening field. In this place, even someone who couldn't look into Shadesmar could know whether they were being watched or not.

As Venli thought on that, she attuned Excitement. No invisible spren . . . and the secretspren were useless. That meant a Radiant in the tower would be free to use their powers without being noticed.

She could use her powers without being noticed.

The implications of it made Timbre begin to thrum to Excitement as well, in time with Venli's attunement. Finally. They could practice.

Dared she, though?

"Voice," one of the Deepest Ones said, waving her over. It was a femalen with pale white skin, swirled with the faintest lines of red. "We need to find these nodes. But without secretspren, we might have to search the entire tower. You will begin interrogating humans, asking if they've seen a large gemstone that seems unattached from any visible fabrial."

"As you wish, Ancient One," Venli said to Abashment. "But if I may say, this seems an inelegant solution. Are the nodes not likely to be hidden?"

"Yes," another said, "but they will also need to be accessible. Their purpose is to let Radiants charge the shield with Stormlight."

"Be that as it may, Ancient One, I am skeptical," Venli said. "Assuming humans answered me truthfully, I suspect they would not know anything. They have not finished mapping all the floors of the tower, let alone its secret places. Do you truly wish us to spend months talking to each human, asking them if they've seen something as vague as a random gemstone?"

The Deepest Ones hummed to Destruction, but otherwise did not contradict her. As with many of the Fused, they did not object out of hand to being challenged, not if the argument was a good one. Venli could learn from them in that regard.

"This is as I said," one said to the others. "We could search this place for *years* and discover nothing."

"Won't the nodes be connected to the crystal pillar?" Venli asked.

"Yes," said one of the Deepest Ones. "By veins of crystal, for transporting Stormlight."

"Then we could follow those," Venli said. "You could sink into the rock and find them, then trace them outward."

"No," said another to Derision. "We cannot see while embedded. We can hear, and we can sing, and the tones of Roshar guide us. But this fabrial is made to be silent to us. To trace the lines, we would need to break apart the stone—and sever all the connections to the pillar. That might destroy the tower's protections entirely, letting the Radiants awaken and defeating our purpose."

"So if you did find a gemstone in the tower," Venli said, "you couldn't know whether it was tied to the protective field. You might break the gemstone and find it was tied to something else entirely."

The Fused hummed at her in Derision. Venli was pushing the boundaries of the interference they would accept. "No, foolish one," the femalen said. "This fabrial of protection is *new*. Added to the tower *after* its creation. There will be few other gemstones like it. The rest of the tower works as a single entity, which is why Raboniel was able to engage its protections by infusing it with Voidlight."

That . . . didn't really explain as much as they seemed to think, but Venli hummed to Subservience to indicate she appreciated the information and the correction. Her mind, however, was still daunted by the implications of what she'd learned earlier. She'd spent all these months being timid about her powers, telling herself she didn't dare use them. Why was she so worried now, though?

Timbre pulsed. Indicating it was all right to be afraid of trying something new. It was natural.

But that wasn't it, not entirely. It seemed that most of Venli's life, she'd been afraid of the wrong things. Her curiosity had led to her people's downfall. And now she played with powers she didn't understand, gathering an entire group of hopefuls who depended on her.

If she made a wrong move, Dul and the others were doomed.

The Deepest Ones conferred. The femalen continued to watch Venli, however. The other three seemed to regard her as their foremost, for they quieted when she spoke.

"You are mortal," she said to Venli. "You are the Last Listener. Few Regals earn a true title, and I find it odd to see the child of traitors developing one. Tell me, where would *you* place these nodes, if you were to do so?"

"I . . ." Venli attuned Agony. "I have no knowledge of the tower. I couldn't say."

"Guess," the Fused prompted. "Try."

"I suppose," Venli said, "I would put it someplace easy to give it Stormlight, but a place no one would search. Or . . ." A thought occurred to her, but she quieted it. She didn't want to help them. The longer it took to fully corrupt the tower, the better it seemed for her people. "No, never mind. I am foolish, Ancient One, and ignorant."

"Perhaps, but you are also mortal—and think like one," the Fused considered. "Mortals are busy. They live short lives, always stuffed with so many things to do. Yet they are also lazy. They want to do none of what they should. Would you not say this is true?"

"I . . . Yes, of course," Venli said. This was not a Fused wanting someone to object.

"Yes," said another Deepest One. "Would they not put the gemstone nodes, at least one of them, where Stormlight could renew it *naturally*?"

"Storms reach this high only occasionally," another said, "but they *do* come up here. So it would make sense to put one in reach of the occasional free infusion of power."

Timbre pulsed to Sorrow inside Venli. This was exactly the idea she'd chosen not to share. Where was the best place for a node? Outside somewhere—but not on the balconies, where it could be spotted.

She looked across the atrium toward the large window. The Deepest Ones had come to the same conclusion apparently, for they flowed away toward the far wall, to look for signs of a gemstone embedded outside.

Timbre pulsed to Disappointment.

"I didn't *try* to help," Venli whispered. "Besides, they mostly figured it out on their own."

Timbre pulsed again. Hopefully it would turn out to be nothing. It was just a guess, after all.

The Fused had left her with no instructions, so she remained with the servants—until she spotted a familiar figure hurrying through the corridor. Mazish, Dul's wife, one of Venli's inner circle.

She stepped forward quickly, intercepting the squat workform—who was humming to Anxiety.

"What?" Venli asked.

"Venli," she said. "Venli, they . . . they've found *another*."

"Another Radiant?" Venli asked to Confusion.

"No. No, not that. I mean." She seized Venli by the arm. "Another one of you. Another *listener*."

CHILD OF ODIUM

EIGHT AND A HALF YEARS AGO

Eshonai found the humans endlessly fascinating.

Between their first and second visits, Eshonai had organized several trips to try to find their homeland. Suddenly, everyone had wanted to join her, and she'd led large expeditions. Those had been all song, and no crescendo, unfortunately—the only thing she'd been able to locate was a solitary human outpost to the west.

They'd told her to expect a second visit soon, but now that visit seemed to be drawing to a close. So Eshonai took every remaining opportunity to watch the humans. She loved the way they walked, the way they talked, even the way they *looked* at her. Or sometimes didn't.

Like today, as she strolled through Gavilar Kholin's camp. His servants barely glanced at her as they packed. She stepped up beside one worker, who was unstringing a large metal bow. The man *must* have seen her standing there—but when he stood up a few minutes later, he jumped to find her beside him.

Such strange behavior. Sometimes she thought she could read the rhythms in the human motions—like that man with the bow would be attuned to Anxiety. Yet they still didn't seem to grasp that listeners could hear something they could not. What would it be like to go about all the time without a rhythm in your head? It must be painful. Or lonely. So empty.

The various humans continued their packing, storing everything in wagons for the day's storm. The humans were good at judging the arrival of those—though they were often wrong on the hour, they were usually right on the day. This, however, was no routine pre-storm packing job. They would soon leave; she could read this in the way they talked to each other, the way they double-checked bindings and folded tents with more precision than usual. They weren't planning to unpack any of it for a while.

She wished they would stay longer—their first interaction had been so short, and now this second visit was over almost before it began. Perhaps she could go with them, as she'd told Venli. She'd asked how far beyond the hills their home was, but they didn't answer, and refused to share their maps.

Eshonai moved to slip out of camp, but stopped as she noticed one man standing off from the rest. Dalinar Kholin looked out, eastward, toward the Origin of Storms.

Curious, Eshonai walked up to him, noting that he had his Shardblade out. He held it lightly before him, the tip sunken into the stone. He seemed to be searching for something, but before him stretched only the Plains—an empty expanse.

Unlike the others, he noticed her approach immediately, turning as she made the slightest scrape on the stones while walking. She froze beneath his gaze, which always seemed to be the stare of a greatshell.

"You're one of the interpreters," he said.

"Yes."

"What was your name?"

"Eshonai," she said, though she had little doubt he'd forget again. The humans didn't seem to be able to distinguish very well between different listeners.

"Have you been out there?" he asked, nodding toward the Plains. "To the center?"

"No," she said. "I'd like to go, but the old bridges . . . they do not stand. It would take work, much work, to put them back. Most of my people don't like . . . what is the word? Going where it is difficult to go?"

"Exploring, perhaps," he said.

"Yes. Exploring. We once exploring. But now, very little exploring."
Until recently.

He grunted. "You're good with our language."

"I like it," she said. "Speaking new ways. Thinking new ways. They are same, yes?"

"Yes, perhaps they are." He turned and looked over his shoulder toward the west. Toward his homeland. "Perhaps your people are afraid to return to where they once lived."

"Why fear that?" Eshonai asked, attuning Confusion.

"Places have power over us, parshwoman," he said. "Places have memories. Sometimes when you go to a place you've never been, it can be wonderful . . . because it lets you be someone else. No expectations. No storming memories."

"I like new places," she said. "Because . . . they are new." She attuned Irritation. That hadn't come out as she'd wanted it to; she felt stupid, speaking their language. It was difficult to express anything deep while speaking it, because the rhythms didn't match the sounds.

"Wise words," Dalinar said.

Wise words? Was he being patronizing? Humans seemed to not expect much from her people, and were surprised whenever a complex conversation happened. As if they were amused that the listeners were not as dull-minded as parshmen.

"I would like to go to see places where you live," Eshonai said. "I would visit you, and have you visit us, more."

Dalinar dismissed his Blade, sending it away with a puff of white fog. She attuned Confusion.

"My brother has taken an interest in you," Dalinar said softly. "This . . . Well, be more cautious with your invitations, parshwoman. Our attention can be dangerous."

"I do not understand," she said. It sounded as if he were warning her against his own.

"I have grown tired of pushing people around," Dalinar said. "In my wake, I've left too many smoldering holes where cities used to be. You are something special, something we've never seen before. And I know my brother—I know that look in his eyes, that excitement.

"His interest could benefit you, but it could have an equal cost. Do not be so quick to share your stormshelter with men you just barely met.

Don't offend, but also don't be too quick to bend. Any new recruit needs to learn both lessons. In this case, I'd suggest politeness—but care. Do not let him back you into a corner. He will respect you if you stand up for yourselves. And whatever you do, *don't* give him any reason to decide he wants what you have."

Be forceful, stand up for themselves, but don't offend their king? How did that make any sense? Yet looking at him—listening to his calm but firm voice—she thought she did understand. His intent, as if given to her by a rhythm.

Be careful with us was what he was saying. *We are far more dangerous than you think.*

He had mentioned . . . burning cities.

"How many cities do your people live in?" she asked.

"Hundreds," he said. "The number of humans in our realm would stagger you. It is many times the number of parshmen I've seen here living with you."

Impossible. That . . . was impossible, wasn't it?

We know so little.

"Thank you," she said to Appreciation. She got it to click, the way of speaking his language but putting a rhythm to it. It *could* work.

He nodded to her. "We are leaving. I realize this visit was short, but my brother needs to return to his lands. You will . . . certainly meet us again. We will send a more permanent envoy. I promise you this."

He turned, moving with the momentum of a shifting boulder, and walked toward his stormwagon.

❖

Venli felt as if the bright red gemstone would burn its way through her clothing. She huddled in one of the stormshelters: a group of wide slits in the ground near the city, which they'd covered over with animal carapace and crem. Each was in the top of a hill, so the sides could drain.

Venli's immediate family gathered together in this one to chat and feast, as was their habit during storm days. The others seemed so cheerful, speaking to Joy or Appreciation while they ate beside the fire, listening as Venli's mother sang songs by the light of uncut gemhearts.

Those could be organic, lumpish things. While they took in Storm-light, none were nearly as bright as the strange gemstone in her pocket. The one the human had given her. Venli felt as if it should be on fire, though it was as cold as a normal gemstone. She attuned Anxiety and glanced at the others, worrying they'd see that too-red glow.

I'm supposed to go out into the storm, she thought, listening to the rain pound distant stone. *Does this count? I can see the storm out there, flashing and making its own rhythm, too frantic. Too wild.*

No, she wasn't close enough. Hiding in one of these shelters wouldn't allow her to adopt mateform, which was the sole transformation they did regularly. No one wanted to go back to dullform, after all.

There *were* other forms to be found. She'd been close to warform. And now . . . this gemstone . . .

She'd carried it for weeks, terrified of what might happen. She glanced at her mother, and the close family members who sat and listened. Enraptured by the beautiful songs. Even Venli, who had heard them hundreds of times, found herself wanting to drift back and sit at her mother's feet.

None of them knew what was happening. To Jaxlim. Mother hid it well. Was it true, that other forms could help her? The humans were leaving now, so this was the last chance Venli would have to try the gemstone, then—if it didn't work—get answers from the human who had given it to her.

Venli attuned Determination and rose from her place, walking toward the end of the shelter, where they'd tied their gemstones to be renewed—close enough to the storm to be given light by the Rider's touch. Several of the others whispered behind her, their voices attuned to Amusement. They thought she had decided to adopt mateform, which she'd always been adamant she would never do.

Her mother had smiled when she'd asked, explaining that few ever *intended* to adopt mateform. She acted as if it was simply something that happened, that an urge overtook you, or you sat too close to the exit during a storm—then poof, the next thing you knew, you'd become a silly idiot looking to breed. It was embarrassing to think others assumed Venli was doing that now.

She reached the wet stone at the edge of the shelter, where rainspren clustered with eyes pointed upward and grasping claws below. The wind and thunder were louder here, like the war calls of a rival family, trying to frighten her away.

Perhaps it would be best just to give the gemstone to her mother, and let *her* go try to find the new form. Wasn't that what this was about?

No, Venli thought, trembling. *No. It's not.*

Months spent trying to find new forms had gotten her nowhere—while Eshonai gained more and more acclaim. Even their mother, who had called her explorations foolish, now spoke of Eshonai with respect. The person who had found the humans. The person who had changed the world.

Venli had done what she was supposed to. She'd remained with her mother, she'd spent endless days memorizing songs, dutiful. But Eshonai got the praise.

Before her nerves betrayed her, Venli stepped out onto the hillside, entering the storm. The force of the wind made her stumble and slide down the slick rock. In an eyeblink she went from sheltered, song-filled warmth to icy chaos. A tempest with sounds like instruments breaking and songs failing. She tried to hold to the Rhythm of Resolve, but it was the Rhythm of Winds by the time she scrambled behind a large boulder and pressed her back against the stone.

From there, her mind devolved to the Rhythm of Pleading, bordering on panic. What was she doing? This was *insanity*. She'd often *mocked* those who went out in the storms without shields or other protections.

She wanted to return to the shelter, but she was too frightened to move. Something large crushed the ground nearby, causing her to jump, but a moment of darkness in the howling tempest prevented her from seeing how close the impact had been. As if the lightning, the wind, and the rain all conspired against her.

She reached into her pocket and took out the gemstone. What had seemed so bright before now seemed frail. The red light barely illuminated her hand.

Break it. She was supposed to break it. With fingers already numb from the cold, she searched around, eventually finding a large stone. The ground was shattered here in a circle the size of a listener. She retreated to the relative shelter of the boulder, shivering as she held the gemstone in one hand, the rock in the other.

Then silence.

It was so sudden, so unexpected, that she gasped. The rhythms in her mind became as one, a single steady beat. She looked upward into pure blackness. The ground around her seemed dry all of a sudden. She slowly turned around, then huddled down again. There was something in the sky, something like a face made from clouds and natural light. The impression of something vast and unknowable.

You wish to take this step? a not-voice said, vibrating through her like a rhythm.

"I . . ." This was him, the spren of highstorms—the Rider of Storms. The songs called him a traitor.

You have spent so long as children of no god, the rhythm said to her. You would make this choice for all of your people?

Venli felt both a thrill and a terror at those words. So there *was* something in the gemstone?

"My . . . my people need forms!" she shouted up toward the vast entity.

This is more than forms. This power changes mortals.

Power?

"You served our enemies!" she called to the sky. "How can I trust what you say?"

Yet you trust the gift of one of those enemies? Regardless, I serve no one. Not man or singer. I simply am. Farewell, child of the Plains.

Child of Odium.

The vision ended as abruptly as it had begun, and Venli was again in the storm. She nearly dropped her burdens in shock, but then—huddling against the gleeful wind—she set the glowing gemstone on the ground. She gripped the rock in her hand, slick with rain. She wavered.

Should she take more care?

What greatness was achieved by being careful, though?

Eshonai hadn't been careful, and she'd discovered a new world. Venli slammed the stone downward and crushed the gem. Light escaped in a puff, and she winced in the pelting rain, bracing herself for a wondrous transformation.

"Finally!" a voice said to the Rhythm of Irritation. "*That* was unpleasant." The red light turned into a tiny human male, standing with hands on hips, glowing faintly in the storm.

Venli pulled her arms in tight, shivering, blinking rainwater out of her eyes. "Spren," she hissed. "I have summoned you to grant me one of the ancient forms."

"You?" he asked. "How old are you? Are there any others I could talk to?"

"Show me this secret first," she said. "Then we will give your form to others. It can heal them, right? That is what I was told."

He didn't reply.

"You will not deny me this!" Venli said, though her words were lost in a sudden peal of thunder. "I've suffered long to accomplish this goal."

"Well, you're certainly *dramatic*," the little spren said, tapping his foot. "Guess we use the tools we find in the shed, even if they've got a little rust on them. Here's the deal. I'm going to take up residence inside of you, and together we're going to do some incredible things."

"We will bring useful forms to my people?" Venli asked, her teeth chattering.

"Well, yes. And also no. For a while, we'll need you to appear as if you are still in workform. I need to scout out how things are on old Roshar these days. It's been a while. You think you can get into Shadesmar, if we need to?"

"Sh-Shadesmar?" she asked.

"Yes, we need to get to the storm there. The newer one in the south? Where I entered that gemstone . . . You have no idea what I'm talking about. Delightful. Right, then. Get ready, we've got *a lot* of work to do. . . ."

⁘

Eshonai attuned Anxiety as she stood by the mouth of the shelter, searching for her sister. She couldn't make out much in the tempest. The flashes of lightning, though brilliant, were too brief to give her a real picture of the landscape.

"She really did it, did she?" Thude asked to Amusement as he stepped up beside her, chewing on some fruit. "After all that complaining, she sauntered out to become a mate."

"I doubt it," Eshonai said. "She's been trying to find warform for months now. She's not looking to become a mate. She's too young, anyway." The humans had been surprised at how young Eshonai and Venli were—apparently, humans aged more slowly? But Venli was still months away from official adulthood.

"Younger ones have made the decision," Thude said, rubbing at his beard. "I've thought about it, you know? There's a certain bond to once-mates."

"You just think it sounds fun," Eshonai said to Reprimand.

He laughed. "I do at that." Thunder shook the enclosure, silencing both of them for a time as they listened to it, both attuning the Rhythm of Winds out of deference. There was something wondrous—if dangerous—about feeling the very vibrations of the storm.

"This isn't the time to be distracted by something silly like mateform," Eshonai said. "The humans are leaving again once this storm ends. We should be talking about sending someone with them."

"You're too responsible for your own good sometimes, Eshonai," Thude replied, his arm up against the top of the enclosure as he leaned forward, letting the rain hit his face.

"Me? Responsible?" she said. "Mother might have words for you on *that* topic."

"And each one would remind me how alike the two of you are," Thude said, attuned to Joy and grinning at the storm like a fool. "I'm going to do it one of these days, Eshonai. I'm going to see if Bila will go with me. Life is meant to be more than working the fields or chopping wood."

With that, Eshonai could agree. And she supposed she could understand someone wanting to do something different with their life. None of them would exist if their parents hadn't decided to become mates.

The idea still made her want to attune Anxiety. She disliked how much that form changed the way people thought. She wanted to be herself, with her own desires and passions, not let some form override her. Of course, there was an argument that she was even now influenced by workform. . . .

She attuned Determination and put that out of her mind. Venli. Where was she? Eshonai knew she shouldn't fear for her sister. Listeners went into the storms all the time, and while it was never strictly safe, she didn't need to hum to Anxiety like the humans did when they talked of storms. Storms were a natural part of life, a gift from Roshar to the listeners.

Though a little piece of Eshonai . . . a part she hated to acknowledge . . . noted how much easier life would be without Venli around, complaining all the time. Without her jealousy. Everything Eshonai did—every conversation, or plan, or outing—was made harder when Venli decided to be involved. Complications would materialize out of calm air.

It was weakness in Eshonai that she should feel this way. She was supposed to love her sister. And she didn't really *want* harm to come to Venli, but it was difficult not to remember how peaceful it had been to explore on her own, without any of Venli's drama. . . .

A figure appeared out of the storm, slick with rain, backlit by lightning. Eshonai felt guilty again, and attuned Joy by force upon seeing it was Venli. She stepped out into the storm and helped her sister the rest of the way.

Venli remained in workform. A wet, shivering femalen in workform.

"Didn't work, eh?" Thude asked her.

Venli looked at him, as mute as a human, her mouth opening a little. Then, unnervingly, she grinned. A frantic, uncharacteristic grin.

"No, Thude," Venli said. "It didn't work. I will have to try many, many more times to find warform."

He hummed to Reconciliation, eyeing Eshonai. She'd been right—it hadn't been about mateform after all.

"I should like to sit by the fire," Venli said, "and warm myself."

"Venli?" Eshonai said. "Your words . . . where are their rhythms?"

Venli paused. Then she—as if it were a struggle—began humming to Amusement. It took her a few tries.

"Don't be silly," Venli said. "You just weren't listening." She strode toward the fire, walking with a swagger that seemed even more confident than normal. The high-headed stroll of a femalen who thought that the storms began and ended upon her whims.

I find this experience so odd. I work with a scholar from the ancient days, before modern scientific theory was developed. I keep forgetting all the thousands of years of tradition you completely missed.

—From *Rhythm of War*, page 6 undertext

Kaladin landed on the balcony with a muted thump. Syl was a glowing ribbon of light farther into the building. He couldn't see the scouts who had packed up and left with the spanreeds, but he trusted Syl was watching them.

He followed into the darkness, putting his Störmlight into a sphere so he didn't glow. He had failed to spy on the Oathgates, but if he could somehow steal one of those Voidlight spanreeds, he could still help Navani.

He crept as quickly as he dared in the darkness, one hand on the wall. He soon neared a hallway with lanterns along the wall; as this was the third floor of the tower, much of it was occupied and lit. The lanterns revealed two femalen singers ahead, wearing havahs and chatting quietly. Syl carefully darted into side tunnels and nooks behind them.

Kaladin trailed far behind, relying on Syl to point out turns, as the two singers were often out of his direct line of sight. This section of the tower was a large laundry facility, where darkeyes could come to use public water and soap. He passed several large rooms without doors where the floor was shaped into a sequence of basins.

It was nearly empty now. The tower's pumps hadn't been changed to work on Voidlight, it seemed. He did have to avoid several water-carrying teams—humans pulling carts, with singer guards—moving through the tunnels. Syl soon came zipping back, so he ducked into a darkened alcove near an empty room full of baskets for laundry. The place smelled of soap.

"Guard post ahead," she whispered. "They went through it. What do you want to do?"

"Any Fused nearby?" Kaladin asked.

"Not that I saw. Only ordinary singers."

"Theoretically, regular guards shouldn't be able to see you unless you let them. Follow those singers with the spanreeds. Hopefully their rooms are nearby. If they split up, pick the one with the blue havah—the embroidery indicates she's the more important. Once you know where her room is, come back, then we can sneak in another way and steal the spanreed."

"Right. If they get too far away from you though, I'll lose myself. . . ."

"Return if you start to feel that," he said. "We can try another night."

Syl soared off without another word, leaving Kaladin hiding inside the room with the baskets. Unfortunately, he soon heard voices—and peeked to see a pair of singers with baskets walking down the hallway. Even an occupying force of ancient evil soldiers needed to do laundry, it seemed. Kaladin closed the door, shutting himself in darkness, then—realizing there was a chance they were coming to dump their baskets in this very room—he grabbed a broom and lashed it across the door.

Since he'd infused the broom on either end, no Stormlight should show through the door. A moment later it rattled as they tried to push it inward. Annoyed voices outside complained in Azish as they tried the door again. He gripped his knife, darkness weighing upon him. The horror of the nightmares, and a fatigue that went far deeper than the earlier strain to his muscles. A tiredness that had been with him so long, he'd accepted it as normal.

When the door rattled again, he was *certain* it was a dark force come to claim him. He heard the sounds of bowstrings, and of Gaz yelling for the bridgemen to run. Screams of men dying, and . . . And . . .

He blinked. The door had fallen still. When . . . when had that happened? He gave it a few minutes, wiping the sweat from his forehead, then un-Lashed the broom and cracked the door. Two abandoned baskets sat nearby, no singers in sight. He let out a long breath, then pried his fingers off his scalpel and tucked it away.

Eventually Syl returned. "They weren't going to their rooms," she said, animatedly dancing around in patterns as a ribbon of light. "They dropped off their spanreed in a room ahead where there are *dozens* of spanreeds, watched over by a couple of senior femalens."

Kaladin nodded, breathing deeply, fighting back the tiredness.

"You . . . all right?" Syl asked.

"I'm fine," Kaladin said. "That's a spanreed hub you found. Makes sense they'd set one up in the tower." Maintaining hundreds of spanreeds could grow unwieldy, so many highlords and highladies would set up hubs. Disparate locations—like guard posts around the tower—could send reports to a central room, where the hub attendants sifted for important information and sent it to those in power.

The singers were keeping their reeds in central locations to be checked out, used, and returned. The reeds wouldn't go home with individual scribes. This wasn't going to be as easy as sneaking into a bedroom to grab one, but the hub might offer other opportunities.

"We need to get past that guard post," Kaladin whispered, burying his fatigue.

"There's something else, Kaladin," Syl said. "Look out the door, down the tunnel."

Frowning, he did as she requested, peeking out and watching down the tunnel. He was confused, until he saw something pass in the air— like rippling red lightning.

"That's a new kind of Voidspren," he said. The ones he'd seen in the past that looked like lightning moved along the ground.

"It's not, though," Syl said. "That spren should be invisible to people, but something is off about its aura. It is leaving a trail that I noted the guards watching."

Curious. So the tower was interfering with spren invisibility? "Did the guards look at you when you passed?"

"No, but they might just not have noticed me."

Kaladin nodded, watching a little longer. That spren in the distance didn't pass again. "It's worth the risk," he decided, "in proceeding. At least we'll know if we're being spied upon."

"But what about that guard post?" she asked.

"I doubt we'll be able to sneak around it," he said. "They'll have all directions guarded for something valuable like a spanreed hub. But a lot of these rooms have small tunnels at the tops for ventilation. Perhaps we can sneak through one of those?"

Syl led him carefully to an intersection. He peered right, to where four guards blocked the way, two at either side of the hallway. Spears at the crooks of their arms, they wore Alethi-style uniforms with knots on the shoulders. Kaladin was able to spot one of the ventilation holes nearby, but this one was far too small for him to squeeze into.

He'd stood on guard duty himself like that on a number of occasions. If these four were well trained, there would be no luring them away with simple distractions. If you wanted a path well protected, you often posted four. Two to investigate any disturbances, two to remain vigilant.

With the hallway this narrow, and with those guards looking as alert as they were . . . Well, he'd been there. The only times when he'd been drawn away, it had involved someone with proper authority commandeering him for another task.

"Syl," he whispered, "you're getting better at changing colors. Do you think you could change your coloring to appear like a Voidspren?"

She cocked her head, standing beside him in the air, then scrunched up her face in a look of concentration. Her dress changed to red, but not her "skin," even though it was simply another part of her. Strange.

"I think this is all I can manage," she said.

"Then make the dress cover your hands with gloves and put on a mask."

She cocked her head, then changed her clothing so she was wrapped in phantom cloth. That bled to a deep red, making her entire form glow with that color.

She inspected her arms. "Do you think it will fool them?"

"It might," Kaladin said. He pulled a length of rope from his sack, then Lashed it to the wall. "Go order all four of them to come with you, then pull them over here to look at this."

"But . . . doesn't that rope risk causing a bigger disturbance? Like, what if they go for backup?"

"We need something reasonable enough to have caused a Voidspren to get riled up. I know guard duty though, and those are common warforms. Regular soldiers. I'm guessing that so long as there's no danger, they'll just make a report on it."

He hid down a side hallway, waiting as Syl flew off toward the guard post. She didn't look exactly like a Voidspren, but it was a reasonable approximation.

She drew near to the post, then spoke loudly enough that he heard her easily. "You there! I am super annoyed! Super, super annoyed! How can you stand there? Didn't you see?"

"Brightness?" one of them said, in Alethi. "Er, Ancient One? We are to—"

"Come on, come on! No, all of you. Come see this! Right now. I'm really annoyed! Can't you tell?"

Kaladin waited, tense. Would it work? Even when acting angry, there was a certain perkiness to Syl's voice. She sounded too . . . lively to be a Voidspren.

The guards followed though—and as he'd hoped, the glowing length of rope on the wall caught their attention entirely. Kaladin was able to sneak out behind them, passing the post.

At the end of this hallway was the door Syl said led into the spanreed room. Kaladin didn't dare slip through it; he'd step directly into the middle of a hub of activity. Instead he prowled into a smaller hallway to the right—and here he finally caught a break. High up on the wall, near the ceiling, a dark cleft indicated a large ventilation shaft in the stone. Maybe big enough for him to squeeze through.

Syl returned—once again white-blue, and likely invisible. "They're sending one of their number to make a report," she said. "Like you said." She peeked into the shaft in the rock Kaladin had found. "What is this?"

Ventilation? he thought, trying to send the idea to her so he wouldn't have to make noise.

It worked. "Seems too big for that," she said. "This place is so strange."

With two of his brushes, Kaladin was able to haul himself up and inspect the cleft in the stone. Syl flew into the darkened shaft toward some light at the other end. He heard the guards talking as they came back, but he was around the corner from them now, out of sight.

This ventilation shaft looked like it turned toward the spanreed room just to the left. It *was* big enough. Maybe.

Syl waved, excited. So he squeezed in. It was more than wide enough to the right and left, but it was barely high enough. He had to move using his brush handholds to pull himself along. He worried the scraping sounds he made would give him away—but he was rewarded when the shaft opened up to the left, revealing a small, well-lit room. The shaft he'd entered ran through the middle of the large thick wall between this room and whatever was on the other side.

That meant Kaladin was able to peek in—hidden mostly behind the stone—at the room from the top of the wall. Spanreeds stood poised on many pieces of paper, waiting for reports. There was no sign of the two singer women from earlier—they'd delivered their spanreed and gone off duty. However, two other femalens in rich dresses maintained the reeds, checking for blinking lights and moving reeds between actively writing on boards and inactive piles on the tables.

Syl entered, and none of them glanced at her, so she seemed to actually be invisible. So, she began reading the reports that were coming in. The door opened and one of the guards entered, requesting a report be sent to his superior. They'd found what appeared to be the sign of a Radiant—something the Pursuer had told everyone to watch for.

Kaladin might not have much time before the creature himself arrived. Best to move quickly. As the guard left, Kaladin quietly maneuvered in the tight quarters, reaching to his waist and pulling out some of his rope. Directly beneath him was a table with a number of spanreeds, including a leather case that had a few nibs sticking out of it.

He needed to wait for the perfect moment. Fortunately, several spanreeds started blinking at once—and they must have been important ones, for the two femalens quickly turned to these and stopped working on the soldier's report. Kaladin Lashed his rope to one of his brushes, then infused the flat of the brush with a Reverse Lashing—commanding it to attract certain objects only. In this instance, that leather case.

The femalens were so preoccupied that Kaladin felt his chance had come. He lowered the brush on the rope toward the table. As the brush drew near, the leather case moved of its own volition, pulled over so it stuck to the brush.

Heart thumping, certain he was about to be caught, Kaladin drew it up, the case sticking to the end, the spanreeds inside clinking softly. Nobody noticed, and he pulled it into the shaft.

Inside the case, he found an entire group of spanreeds—at least twenty. Perhaps they'd just been delivered, as they were still wrapped in pairs, with twine around them. Judging by the way the rubies glowed with Voidlight, he was hopeful that they would work in the tower.

He tucked the large pouch away in his sack. He then spared a thought for all the important information that was likely being relayed through this room. Could he steal some of it?

No. He'd already risked enough today. He sent a quick thought to Syl, who came zipping up to him as he wiggled backward through the ventilation shaft. She flitted on ahead of him, then called from behind, "Hallway is empty."

He eased out of the hole, catching the edge with his fingers and hanging a moment before quietly dropping the last few feet to the floor of the corridor. He peeked back out toward the guard post.

"Now what?" Syl said. "Want me to imitate a Voidspren again?"

He nodded. Part of him wanted to try another path, as he worried that these soldiers might grow suspicious at the same ruse. But he also knew they'd fallen for it once, and he knew a direct way to the perimeter using this path. Safer this way.

As Syl was getting ready, however, Kaladin spotted something farther down this hallway, away from the guards. A flashing light. He held up his hand to stop Syl, then pointed.

"What is that?" she said, zipping off toward the light. He followed more cautiously, stepping up to a blinking garnet light. Frowning, Kaladin pressed his hand against it.

"Brightness Navani?" he asked.

No, a voice said. It had a middling pitch, not necessarily male or female. *I need you, Radiant. Please. They've found me.*

"You?"

One of the nodes! That protect me. Please. Please, you have to defend it. Please.

"How do you know? Have you told Brightness Navani?"

Please.

"Where?" he said.

Second level, near the central atrium. I will lead you. They realized that one of the nodes would be open to the air, to be renewed by Stormlight. They've sent for her. The Lady of Pains. She'll take my mind. Please, Radiant. Protect me.

Syl hovered beside him. "What?" she asked.

He lowered his hand. He was so tired.

But today, he couldn't afford to be tired. He had to be Kaladin Stormblessed. Kaladin Stormblessed fought anyway.

"We're going to need to find me a better weapon," he said. "Quickly."

*This point regarding the Rhythm of War's emotional influence will
be of particular interest to El.*

—From *Rhythm of War,* page 10

Kaladin knew there was a chance he was making a huge mistake. He didn't understand the nature of the tower or what was going on with it and Navani. He was risking a great deal by revealing himself.

However, that garnet light had rescued him from the Pursuer's clutches. And right now, he'd heard something in the spren's voice. A genuine fright. Terror, combined with a plea for protection, was not something Kaladin could ignore.

He was fatigued mentally and physically. As he ran, he drew a field of exhaustionspren, like jets of dust. Worse, a part of him panicked these days every time he went to pick up a weapon. He'd trained himself these last months to function despite those things. He leaned on the spike of energy that coursed through him, even before he drew in Stormlight. He let that control him, instead of the fatigue.

It would catch up to him eventually. But for now, he could pretend to be strong. Pretend to be a soldier again.

The four guards were facing in the other direction, so Kaladin—running at full speed—nearly reached them before the first guard spun around. Kaladin took the chance to burst alight with power, earning him another fraction of a second as the guard panicked, his eyes going wide with fright.

He shouted as Kaladin drew close, hands out before him, waiting for the thrust of the spear. A lot of men were afraid of something sharp coming at them, but as long as his Stormlight held, Kaladin's only real danger was getting outnumbered and overwhelmed.

Kaladin caught the spear as the singer thrust it. He then yanked, throwing the enemy off balance. He'd been taught that maneuver by Hav, who said it was necessary to learn, but almost impossible to execute. Kaladin added his own twist by infusing the shaft with a Full Lashing, making it stick to the guard's hands. Then he shoved the weapon to the side, sticking it to a second guard's spear as he spun.

Kaladin grabbed that spear, infusing it as well, then left both guards stuck to their weapons. As they shouted in surprise, Kaladin held the shafts of the crossed spears—one in each hand—and shoved them upward so the tips struck the ceiling. Then he smoothly ducked through the peaked opening, leaving the two men crying out and struggling as they tried unsuccessfully to free their weapons and hands.

Kaladin slammed his shoulder into the third guard, infusing the singer's coat with a slap to the back. He shoved this guard into the fourth. They fell in a lump, entangled and stuck together. Kaladin danced on his toes, awaiting the next attack. It didn't come. The singers stayed where he'd put them, shouting and railing as they struggled to move.

He kicked a spear up and seized it out of the air. *Hello, old friend. I keep finding my way back to you, don't I?* Perhaps it wasn't *Teft's* addiction he needed to worry about. There was always an excuse for why Kaladin needed the spear again, wasn't there?

This was what he'd been afraid of. This was what made him tremble. The worry that he would never be able to put it down.

He tucked the spear under his arm and took off through the tunnel. A twinkling garnet light appeared on the floor in front of him, moving along one of the strata, leading the way toward a stairwell ahead.

"No," Kaladin said, hoping the tower's spren could hear him. "There will be a guard post at the bottom. I can already hear them responding to those shouts. To reach the second floor, we go out on a perimeter balcony, down the outside, and then head inward. That will lose any tails we pick up."

The spren seemed to have heard, for they sent a light moving along the wall next to him—opposite Syl's blue-white ribbon on his other side. They reached the balcony in a few short minutes, a fraction of the time it had taken to sneak inward. They were at the rim of the tower, but the central atrium was far away at the eastern side. All the way inward. He'd have to cross the entire second floor to reach it.

He heard shouts behind him, so he'd been right about picking up tails. He stuck his spear to his back by infusing part of it and slapping it against his shirt, then he unwound the rope around his waist. A quick infusion on the end let him stick it to the railing as he stepped up in a fluid motion and leaped off, sticking the other end to his shirt in case he slipped, then holding tight.

He swung out and around, then onto the balcony below. This one, unfortunately, was occupied. So after he recovered his rope, he charged through a family's room—leaping and sliding across their dinner table. He was out the door a moment later, spear in hand. He heard a distant shout of anger from outside the balcony, as the singers above realized he'd gone a way they couldn't follow.

The tower's spren found him here and began guiding him. The strata and lines of crystal didn't always run directly down the corridors, so sometimes the light would spiral around him, following the grain of the stone. Other times the light would vanish when there was no direct path for it, but it would always appear ahead of him again, glowing on the floor or wall, urging him onward.

He drew attention, naturally. The late hour meant that he didn't encounter crowds to slow him, but it also meant there wasn't much else to distract the guard patrols. He infused and tossed his spear at a pair of guards who stumbled into the hallway ahead of him—then stole one of their dropped weapons as they struggled and cursed, trying to get his old weapon to stop sticking to their fingers.

The next set weren't so easily defeated. He found them organizing hastily at an intersection—one he had to pass through, or endure a long detour. Kaladin slowed in the corridor, watching them form up with nets in hand. His first instinct was to take to the walls and disorient them. But of course he didn't have access to that ability—he suspected it would be a long time before he internalized that gravitational Lashings didn't work.

He took his spear in a one-handed grip, the butt tucked under his arm, then nodded to Syl. Together, they rushed the blockade. A few soldiers had crossbows, so he infused the wall with his free hand. When those loosed, the bolts swerved toward the stone.

The group with the nets hung back behind singers with axes. The weapons reminded him of the Parshendi, but the singers were dressed like the Azish, with colorful coats, no gemstones woven into the malens' beards.

They knew how to fight Radiants. The axe wielders came in quickly, forcing him to engage, and then the nets started flying. Kaladin swiped one away with his spear, but that exposed him, and an axe bit him in the side—the kind of wound that would spell death for an ordinary soldier.

Kaladin pulled himself free of the axe, the biting pain fading as his Stormlight healed him, but another net came soaring overhead. They wouldn't mind if they caught some of their number in it, so long as they tangled Kaladin long enough for them to start hacking at him.

Feeling his solitude more than ever, Kaladin dodged the net by retreating. He wanted to infuse one of the nets and stick it to the floor so it couldn't be recovered, but he couldn't bend over to touch it.

Maybe I should remove my boots, he thought. That idea flew counter to all of his training, but he didn't fight like he once had. These days, a stubbed toe would be healed instantly—while being able to infuse the ground he walked on would be a huge advantage.

He kept the singers at bay with some careful lunges, then backed up before a net could catch him. Unfortunately, this group was probably meant to stall him while Regals and Fused could be mustered. It was working perfectly. Without a Shardblade, Kaladin was far from unstoppable. He was forced away until he reached another intersection.

"Kaladin," Syl said, hovering beside his head as a ribbon of light. "To your left."

He spared a glance to see a flashing garnet light on the wall farther down the left-hand corridor. Well, he certainly wasn't going to push through these soldiers anytime soon. He took off in a dash toward the light, and the soldiers—rightly timid when facing a Radiant—followed more cautiously. That gave Kaladin time to kick open a door, following the light, and enter an upscale glassmaker's shop.

It seemed like a dead end until he spotted the hint of a gemstone set into the wall behind the counter. He leaped over it and infused the stone, and was rewarded as the wall parted. He slipped through the opening, then set the thing closing behind him.

This put him in a second, larger shop, filled with half-finished dressing dummies. He startled a late-night worker, a human with a Thaylen naval mustache and curled eyebrows. He dropped his adze and leaped to his feet, then clapped his hands.

"Brightlord Stormblessed!" he exclaimed.

"Quietly," Kaladin said, crossing the room and cracking the door to peek out. "You need to hide. When they come asking, you didn't see me."

The hallway outside was clear, and Kaladin was pretty sure he knew where he was. This shortcut had completely circumvented the blockade. Hopefully that would confuse the soldiers as they tried to track him. Kaladin moved to sneak out the door, but the woodworker caught him by the arm.

"Radiant," he said. "How? How do you still fight?"

"The same way you do," Kaladin said. "One day at a time, always taking the next step." He took the man's wrist with his hand. "Don't get yourself killed. But also don't give up hope."

The man nodded.

"Hide," Kaladin said. "They'll come searching for me."

He pulled free and joined Syl. After about ten minutes of jogging, he heard shouting to his right, but nobody came running—and he realized where they thought he was heading: to a set of stairs that led directly toward the larger stairwell, which in turn led to the basement. They thought he was trying to rescue the queen, or maybe reach the crystal pillar.

Their error let him follow some back pathways without meeting any patrols, until he finally drew near the atrium. He'd managed to cross the entire floor, but he was now so deeply embedded within the tower that he was essentially surrounded.

The light led him around to the northern side of the tower, through some residential hallways, with lights under the doors. Rooms near the atrium and its grand window were popular—here, people could still see sunlight, but the atrium was generally warmer than the perimeter, with easy access to lifts.

The area was unnaturally silent, perhaps under curfew. He was used to the atrium region being alive with the sound of people talking all hours of the day, the lifts clanking faintly as they moved. Tonight it was hushed. He crept along the tower spren's path, wondering when he'd find resistance. Surely someone would have put together what he was doing. Surely they would . . .

He stopped in the hallway as he saw bright light ahead. He could have sworn he'd reached the furthermost edge of the tower, the place near the enormous glass window that looked out to the east. There shouldn't be any more rooms here, but ahead and to his right, moonlight spilled through an opening.

He inched up to find the area strewn with rubble. A secret door in the wall had been broken open; when he peeked through, he saw a short tunnel that ended at open air. This *was* the eastern wall of the tower, the flat side of Urithiru. The secret tunnel here was old, not newly cut, and had been created open to the air of the mountains.

The Pursuer was here, standing with another Fused and inspecting a strange device at the end of the short tunnel, right where it ended and opened to the air. A glowing sapphire, easily as large as a chasmfiend's gemheart, had been set into a built-in stand rising from the floor. The entire mechanism was covered over in crem, so it had been here a while, and the Fused had needed to break off a crem crust to reach the gemstone.

The implication struck Kaladin immediately. As the Sibling had hinted, a node to defend the tower had been placed where it could draw in Stormlight naturally from the storms, when they reached this high. The unfamiliar Fused was a tall femalen with a topknot of red-orange hair. She wore practical battle gear, leather and cloth, and stood with her hands clasped behind her back as she inspected the sapphire.

The other was, as he'd noted earlier, the Pursuer. A hulking mountain of chitin and dark brown cloth, with eyes glowing a deep red. All of the spheres had been removed from the lanterns in the hallway behind Kaladin, so the only light came from the sapphire.

"See?" the femalen said in Alethi as they spotted Kaladin. "I told you he'd come. I keep my promises, Pursuer. He's yours."

The red eyes focused on Kaladin, then went dark as a ribbon of crimson light burst from the center of the Pursuer's mass. The body—a discarded husk—collapsed to the floor. Kaladin raised his spear, gauging where the Pursuer would land. He thrust on instinct, hoping to catch the Fused as he materialized.

This time, however, the Pursuer's ribbon jogged and looped a few times, disorienting Kaladin. He thrust again, missing the mark as the Pursuer coalesced to the side of Kaladin's spear. The creature lunged for Kaladin, who danced backward into the darkened hallway outside the tunnel.

The creature stepped into the broken doorway. So, Kaladin infused his spear and tossed it at the Pursuer—who reflexively caught it. That stuck his hands to the spear, and Kaladin leaped forward and shoved himself against the Fused, getting him to step backward. The two ends of the spear stuck to the walls on either side of the opening.

Kaladin leaped away, leaving the creature partially immobilized, awkwardly trying to move with both hands locked into place. Then, of course, the Pursuer just dropped that body as a husk and launched out as a ribbon of light. Kaladin cursed. He was too unpracticed with this kind of fighting—and this kind of opponent. What had worked on the soldiers was a foolish move here. He lunged to grab his spear, but it fell beneath the collapsing husk.

The Pursuer materialized directly behind Kaladin, grabbing him with powerful hands, preventing him from reaching the spear. It was a poor weapon for this fight anyway. The Pursuer obviously excelled at getting in close.

Kaladin twisted, trying to wrench free, but the Pursuer gripped him in a precise hold, executed perfectly, immobilizing both of Kaladin's arms. The creature then pushed, using his superior weight to knock Kaladin to his knees.

The Pursuer didn't try to choke Kaladin. The creature didn't even release him with one hand to grab a knife, as he had during their previous fight. All the Pursuer had to do was hold Kaladin still until his Stormlight ran out. They were deep within the tower, surrounded by other singers and Fused. The longer this fight lasted, the worse it would go for Kaladin.

He struggled, trying to pull free. In response, the Pursuer leaned in and spoke with a thick accent. "I will kill you. It is my right. I have killed every person—human or singer—who has ever killed me."

Kaladin tried to roll them both to the side, but the Pursuer held them stable.

"No one has ever defeated me twice," the creature whispered. "But if you somehow managed such a feat, I would keep coming. We are no longer confined to Braize at the end of the war, and I am immortal. I can follow you forever. *I* am the spren of *vengeance.*"

Kaladin tried to infuse his opponent, as he might have with a gravitational Lashing. The Light resisted, but that wasn't surprising. Fused had powers of their own, and for some reason that made them difficult to infuse.

So he instead stretched and brushed the floor with one hand, infusing the stone. It trapped the Pursuer's feet, but it also stuck to Kaladin's boots, locking them together.

"Let go now," the Pursuer said. "Die, as is *your* right. You will never be able to sleep soundly again, little Radiant. I will always come, always hunt you. As sure as the storms. I will—"

"Put him down!" a stern voice said as a red spren strode across the floor. "Right now! We need him. You can kill him after!"

The Pursuer relaxed his grip, perhaps stunned to be given an order by a Voidspren. Kaladin elbowed the Pursuer in the chin—which hurt like a hammer to the elbow—forcing the creature to let go. That let Kaladin lunge forward and recover some Stormlight by brushing the floor, which in turn set his feet free. He scrambled away, leaving enough Stormlight infused in the floor to keep the Pursuer planted in place.

The creature focused on Syl. "You lie well, for an honorspren," he said. His body crumbled, his ribbon vanishing around a corner. As before, he seemed to need a break after abandoning a third body.

Kaladin suspected that if the Pursuer made a fourth body, he wouldn't have enough Voidlight left to escape it. That might be how you killed him: trap him in the fourth body. Either that, or catch him by surprise and kill him before he could eject, which was what Kaladin had done before.

"Thanks," Kaladin said as Syl turned blue again. He grabbed his spear, then glanced over his shoulder and saw some humans peeking out of their rooms, watching the fight. He waved for them to close their doors, then hopped through the rubble and dashed toward the Fused at the end of the secret tunnel.

As he approached, he spotted a glass globe, perhaps six inches in diameter, set into a small alcove in the wall near the gemstone. At first he thought it was some kind of lighting fixture, but it was wrapped in metal wires like a fabrial. What on Roshar?

He didn't have time to inspect it further, for the Fused was pressing her hand against the sapphire. The gemstone's light had started to fade.

She's corrupting the pillar, Kaladin thought, *using this as a conduit to touch it.* He leveled his spear at her.

She stopped and turned to regard him. "The Pursuer isn't lying," she said in accented Alethi. "He *will* hunt you forever. To the abandonment of all reason and duty."

"Step away from the gemstone," Kaladin said.

"He'll return shortly," she noted. "You should flee. He has placed Voidlight gemstones in stashes nearby, so he can reinfuse himself and make new bodies."

"I said *step away.*"

"You're a Windrunner," she said. "You won't hurt me if I'm not a threat."

"Touching that gemstone makes you a threat. Step away."

She did, which meant walking toward him, clasping her hands behind her. "What is it, do you suppose, that makes you able to continue using your powers? I'll admit, I *had* worried about the Windrunners. They say your Surges are closest to Honor."

Kaladin gripped his spear, uncertain what to do. Stab her? He had to protect the gemstone.

Or destroy it, he thought. Storms, that would weaken the shield Navani had set up—and if the enemy had found *this* one so quickly, how long would it be until they discovered the others? He glanced to Syl on his shoulder, and she shook her head. She didn't know what to do either.

"Ah," the Fused said. "He's back. On with you, then."

Kaladin risked looking over his shoulder, cursing as he saw a distinctly bloodred ribbon of light approaching. Making a snap decision, Kaladin dropped his spear and pulled out his scalpel. Then he quickly sliced the laces on his boots.

The Pursuer appeared inside the tunnel and grabbed for him, but

Kaladin bent—dodging the grip—and infused the floor with a Full Lashing. Then he leaped forward around the Pursuer, leaving his shoes stuck to the stone. The Pursuer couldn't help but land on that floor, trapping him in place.

Kaladin held out his scalpel, barefoot as he backed up into the rubble of the broken wall that had been opened. The Pursuer eyed him, remaining rooted on the ground. Then he grinned and left his body, shooting toward Kaladin.

Kaladin retreated through the opening into the outer corridor, infusing the floor again, using up a large amount of his Stormlight. He was able to roll away from the Pursuer's next attack, which again left the creature rooted. But Kaladin couldn't step forward and reclaim the Light he'd used, not without getting within the Pursuer's reach.

His Stormlight was almost gone, something the Pursuer had clearly figured out. The creature left his second body, the first already starting to crumble. When Kaladin leaped forward to try to retrieve his Stormlight, the Pursuer darted at him as a ribbon of light—like a snapping eel—and Kaladin retreated.

The two watched one another in the dark corridor. The Pursuer could only form one more body before he'd need to renew his Voidlight, or risk fighting in his fourth body and perhaps being killed. But Kaladin's Light was low—and he didn't have a quick way to get more.

Storms. The other Fused—the femalen—had returned to the gemstone and was working on it again.

"We have to destroy it, Kaladin," Syl whispered.

She was right. He couldn't defend this place on his own. He'd simply have to hope that the other nodes were better hidden. Though . . . how could something be better hidden than in the *middle* of a *wall*?

Kaladin took a deep breath, then dashed forward to force the Pursuer to materialize. He did so—but only after zipping back into the center of the second pool of Light Kaladin had made. That let the creature materialize standing on the remnants of his second husk, which was stuck to the Light.

The Fused crouched low, hands out and ready to grab Kaladin if he tried to run past. Kaladin was forced to shy back.

I can't afford to fight him the way he wants, Kaladin thought. *If he gets me into his grip, I'll end up pinned.*

When he'd killed the creature before, Kaladin had used the Pursuer's assumptions against him. This time he wasn't making the same mistake, but he was still so very confident.

Use that. *Let him defeat himself.*

Kaladin turned and started running in the opposite direction.

Behind, the Pursuer began laughing. "That's right, human! Flee! You see it now! Run and be pursued."

Syl zipped up alongside Kaladin. "What's the plan?"

"He's called the Pursuer," Kaladin said. "He loves the chase. When we were doing what humans shouldn't do—trying to fight him—he was deliberate and careful. Now we're fleeing prey. He might get sloppy. But he won't leave that third body until we're far enough away that he's sure we won't just double back and attack that other Fused. Go warn me when he does."

"Right." She darted off to watch.

Kaladin took a few turns in the corridor, then said, "Tower spren, I need you!" A garnet light ahead started flashing quickly as if anxious.

Kaladin jogged to it, and Syl came darting back. "The Pursuer is recharging—but he's not leaving the fabrial unwatched! He's getting Voidlight from the other Fused."

Kaladin nodded as he pressed his hand to the wall. The tower spren spoke in his mind.

SheiskillingmeSheiskillingmeSheiskillingme. Stopitstopit.

"I'm trying," Kaladin said. He dug out some of his gemstones, then infused his Stormlight into them to preserve what he had left. "I'm not convinced I can beat that monster again. Not without a team on a battlefield. He fights too well one-on-one. So, I need another hidden room. One with only a single exit—and with a door that will open and close fast."

You're going to hide? the Sibling said, hysterical. *You can't—*

"I won't abandon you, but you need to do this for me. We don't have much time. Please."

"Kaladin!" Syl said. "He's coming!"

Kaladin cursed, leaving the Sibling and dashing for an intersection in the dark corridors ahead.

"Duck!" Syl said.

Kaladin ducked, narrowly avoiding the Pursuer's grip as he

materialized. As Kaladin darted a different direction, the creature tried again, dropping a husk and shooting ahead of Kaladin.

Trying to play the part of panicked prey, Kaladin turned and ran the other way—though he hated putting his back to the creature like that. He could almost feel him, forming with arms grabbing at Kaladin's neck. . . .

As he dashed through the corridor, people who had been watching snapped their doors shut. Behind him, the Pursuer laughed. Yes, he understood *this* kind of fight. He enjoyed it. "Run!" he shouted. "Run, little human!"

Ahead, garnet light flashed, then began moving down a side hallway. Kaladin scrambled that direction as Syl warned him the Pursuer was coming. The garnet light, fortunately, moved up a wall straight ahead, then flashed, revealing a gemstone hidden in the rock. Kaladin drew in the Light of one of his spheres and infused the gemstone, making the door begin to open. It was faster than previous ones, as he'd asked.

Syl cried, "He's almost here!"

"As soon as I walk in," Kaladin whispered to the tower's spren, "start closing the door. Then lock it."

He glanced back, and saw the red light rapidly approaching. So, taking a deep breath, Kaladin ducked through the once-hidden doorway. As he'd asked, it immediately began to grind closed. Kaladin turned to face outward, anxious as he pulled free his scalpel. He made it look like he intended to stand and fight.

Go for my back again, like you've done before. Please.

The ribbon danced in over his head. Kaladin leaped forward, squeezing through the tight doorway as it closed, right as the Pursuer appeared in the room behind him.

Kaladin fell forward and scrambled across the ground. Behind him, the door thumped closed. He waited, his heart thundering in his chest, as he turned and watched the doorway. Would the Pursuer's ribbon be small enough to squeeze through? These hidden doors sealed so tightly they were almost impossible to see from the outside, and Syl had physical form as a ribbon. He assumed the same rules applied to the Pursuer.

Syl flitted down beside him, taking the shape of a young woman in a Bridge Four uniform. She colored it a dark blue.

Quiet. Followed by a yell of rage, muffled to near silence by the intervening stone. Kaladin grinned, picking himself up. He thought he heard the Pursuer yell, "Coward!"

He gave the closed door a salute, then turned to jog back the way he had come. Again he had to hiss at people to close their doors and stay out of sight. Where was their sense of self-preservation?

Their eyes were hopeful when they saw him. And in those expressions, he understood why they had to look, regardless of the danger. They thought everyone had been conquered and controlled, but here was a Radiant. Their hopes pressed on him as he finally reached the hidden tunnel. The femalen Fused with the topknot stood in a posture of concentration, her hand pressed against the sapphire.

She didn't *seem* to be corrupting it. Indeed, she had brought out a large diamond and was holding it up to the sapphire—drawing light from it. Stormlight, it seemed, although it was tinged faintly the wrong color.

Kaladin scooped a piece of broken rubble from the floor. The sides of the rubble were smoothly cut. The work of a Shardblade.

Kaladin leaped forward and shoved the Fused back, trying to knock her off the cliff. That caused her to exclaim and fall out of her trance, though she grabbed a protruding rock and prevented herself from falling.

Before she could stop him, Kaladin slammed his rubble into the gemstone, cracking it. That was enough—cracked gemstones couldn't hold Stormlight—but he slammed it a few more times to be certain, breaking the sapphire free of its housing and sending it tumbling into the void outside.

It vanished into darkness, plummeting hundreds upon hundreds of feet down the sheer cliff toward the rocks far below. Kaladin felt something when it broke free. A faint sense that the darkness in the tower had grown stronger—or perhaps Kaladin was only now recognizing the results of the Fused's recent attempt at corrupting the tower.

He puffed out, the deed done, and backed away. In that moment though—his Stormlight running low, his energy deflating, the darkness growing stronger—he flagged. He reached out for the wall as his vision wavered, and the fatigue seemed to be almost too much.

A shadow moved in front of him, and he forced himself alert—but not before the Fused in the topknot managed to ram a knife into his chest. He felt an immediate spike of pain and pulled out his scalpel, but the Fused jumped back before he could strike.

Painspren wriggled up from the stone as Kaladin stumbled, bleeding. He drew in the last of his Stormlight and pressed his hand to the wound. Storms. His mind . . . was fuzzy. And the darkness seemed so strong.

The Fused, however, didn't seem interested in striking again. She tucked away her knife and laced her fingers before herself, watching him. Oddly, he noticed that the glass sphere that had been in the little stone alcove was gone. Where had the Fused put it?

"You continue to heal," she noted. "And I saw the use of Adhesion earlier. I assume from the way you move, confined to the ground, that Gravitation has abandoned you. Does your hybrid power work? The one your kind often uses to direct arrows in flight?"

Kaladin didn't respond. He gripped his scalpel, waiting to heal. The pain lingered. Was healing slower than usual? "What did you to do me?" he demanded, hoarse. "Was that blade poisoned?"

"No," she said. "I merely wanted to inspect your healing. It seems to be lethargic, does it not? Hmmm . . ."

He didn't like how she looked at him, so discerning and interested—like a surgeon inspecting a corpse before a dissection. She didn't seem to care that he had destroyed her chance at corrupting the tower—perhaps because Kaladin's attack had furthered her eventual goal of reaching the crystal pillar.

He raised his scalpel, waiting for his storming wound to heal. It continued to do so. Languidly.

"If you kill me," the Fused noted, "I will simply be reborn. I will choose the most innocent among the singers of the tower. A mother perhaps, with a child precisely old enough to understand the pain of loss—but not old enough to understand why her mother now rejects her."

Kaladin growled despite himself, stepping forward.

"Yes," the femalen said. "A true Windrunner, all the way to your gemheart. Fascinating. You had no continuity of spren or traditions from the old ones, I'm led to believe. Yet the same attitudes, the same structures, arise naturally—like the lattice of a growing crystal."

Kaladin growled again, sliding to the side toward his discarded spear and shoes.

"You should go," the Fused said. "If you've killed the Pursuer again, it will make for quite the stir among my kind. I don't believe that's ever been accomplished. Regardless, I have Fused and Regals on their way to join us and finish his work. You might escape them, if you leave now."

Kaladin hesitated, uncertain. His instincts said he should do the opposite of whatever this femalen said, out of principle. But he thought better of it and fled into the corridors—his side aching—trusting in the tower spren and Syl to guide him out of danger and to a safe hiding place.

Who is this person? You used no title, so I assume they are not a Fused. Who, then, is El?

—From *Rhythm of War*, page 10 undertext

Venli felt all rhythms freeze when she saw Rlain in the cell. Like the silence following a crescendo.

In that silence, Venli finally believed what Mazish had told her. In that silence, all of Roshar changed. Venli was no longer the last. And in that silence, Venli thought she could hear something distant beyond the rhythms. A pure tone.

Rlain looked up through the bars, then sneered at her.

The moment of peace vanished. He'd picked up some human expressions, it seemed. Did he recognize her in this form? Her skin patterns were the same, but she and Rlain had never been close. He likely saw only an unfamiliar Regal.

Venli retreated down the hallway, passing several empty cells with bars on the doors. It was the day after the incident with Stormblessed and the destruction of the node. Venli had been on her way to visit Rlain when the event had occurred, drawing her away to attend her master.

Curiously, though Venli had assumed that Raboniel would be furious, instead she'd taken it in stride. She'd almost seemed *amused* at what had occurred. She was hiding something about her motivations. She seemed to not *want* the corruption to happen too quickly.

At any rate, dealing with the aftermath of the incident had involved Venli interpreting late into the night for various Fused. It hadn't been until this morning that she'd been able to break away and come check on what Mazish had told her.

Rlain. Alive.

Near the door, Venli met with the head jailer: a direform Regal with a crest of spikes beginning on his head and running down his neck.

"I didn't realize we *had* a prison," she said to him—softly, and to Indifference.

"The humans built it," he replied, also to Indifference. "I interviewed several of the workers here. They claim they were keeping the assassin in here."

"*The* assassin?"

"Indeed. He vanished right before we arrived."

"He should have fallen unconscious."

"Well, he didn't, and nobody has seen anything of him."

"You should have told me of this earlier," Venli said. "The Lady thinks that certain Radiants might still be able to function in the tower. It's possible this one is out there somewhere, preparing to kill."

The direform hummed to Abashment. "Well, we've been prepping this place in case we need to lock up a Regal with proper comforts. We've got a larger brig for human prisoners. Figured this would be a good place for your friend there, until official word arrived."

Venli glanced along the hall of empty cells, lit by topaz lanterns hanging from the ceiling. They gave the chamber a soft brown warmth, the color of cremstone.

"Why did you lock him away?" she asked.

"He's an essai," the direform said to Derision, using an ancient word they'd picked up from the Fused. It meant something along the lines of "human lover," though her form told her it technically meant "hairy."

"He was a spy my people sent to watch them."

"Then he betrayed you," the direform said. "He claims he'd been held by the humans against his will, but it didn't take much asking around to find the truth. He was friendly with the Radiants—was their servant or something. Could have left at any time, but stayed. Wanted to keep being a slave, I guess." He changed to the Rhythm of Executions—a rarely used rhythm.

"I will speak with him," Venli said. "Alone."

The direform studied her, humming to Destruction in challenge. She hummed it back—she outranked this one, so long as she was Raboniel's Voice.

"I will send again to the Lady of Wishes," he finally said, "to inform her that you have done this."

"As you will," Venli said, then waited pointedly until he stepped out and shut the door. Venli glanced into Shadesmar, as she'd grown into the habit of doing, though she'd learned Voidspren couldn't hide in the tower. It was instinct by now. And she—

Wait. There *was* a Voidspren here.

It was hiding in the body of a cremling. Most spren could enter bodies, if they couldn't pass through other solid objects. She wasn't terribly familiar with all the varieties of Voidspren, but this one must have realized that it couldn't hide in the tower as it once had, so used this method to remain unseen.

She attuned Anxiety, and Timbre agreed. Was it watching her, or Rlain? Or was it simply here to patrol? Had she done anything recently that would give her away?

She maintained her composure, pretending to think as she strolled in the prison chamber. Then she pretended to notice the cremling for the first time, then shooed it away. The thing scuttled down the wall and out under the door. She glanced into Shadesmar, and saw the Voidspren—through the hundreds of shimmering colors that made up the tower—retreating into the distance alongside the tiny speck of light that represented the cremling.

That left her nervous enough that she paced a few times—and checked again—before finally she forced herself to return to the cell. "*Rlain.*"

He looked up at her. Then he frowned and stood.

"It's me," she said to Peace, speaking in the listener language for an extra measure of privacy. "Venli."

He stepped closer to the bars, and his eyes flickered to her face. He hummed to Remembrance. "I was under the impression they had killed all of the listeners."

"Only most of us. What are you *doing* here, Rlain? Last we knew, the humans had discovered you in the warcamps and executed you!"

"I . . . wasn't discovered," he said. He spoke to Curiosity, but his body language—he had indeed picked up some human attitudes—betrayed his true emotions. He obviously didn't trust her. "I was made an example, used as an experiment. They put me in the bridge crews. I don't think anyone ever suspected I was a spy. They just thought I was too smart for a parshman."

"You've been living among them all this time? That guard says you're an ess—a human sympathizer. I can't believe you're alive, and I'm not the . . . I mean . . ." Language failed her, and she ended up standing there, humming the Rhythm of the Lost and feeling like an idiot. Timbre chimed in, giving the same rhythm—and that helped somehow.

Rlain studied her. He'd probably heard that forms of power changed a person's personality—storms . . . they'd always known that. Known they were dangerous.

"Rlain," she said, her voice soft, "I'm me. *Truly* me. This form doesn't . . . change me like stormform did for the others."

Timbre pulsed. Tell him the truth. Show him what you are.

She locked up. *No.* She couldn't.

"The others?" he asked, hopeful. "Remala? Eshonai? She fought Adolin, we think, in battle. Do you know . . . if she is . . ."

"I saw my sister's corpse myself at the bottom of the chasms," she said to Pain. "There aren't any others left but me. He . . . Odium took them, made them into Fused. He saved me because he wanted me to tell stories about our people, use them to inspire the newly freed singers. But I think he was afraid of us, as a group. So he destroyed us."

She hummed to the Rhythm of the Lost again. Rlain eventually joined her and stepped forward until he was right beside the bars.

"I'm sorry, Venli," he eventually said. "That must have been awful."

He doesn't know, she realized, *that I caused all this. How could he? He was among the humans. To him, I'm simply . . . another survivor.*

She found that idea daunting.

"You need to free me," Rlain said. "I hoped they'd accept my story, but I'm too well known in the tower. You stand out when you're the only 'parshman' anyone knows."

"I'll see what I can do," Venli said to Reconciliation. "The guard doesn't trust me—a lot of them don't—and talking to you will make that worse. If I do get you out, what are you going to do? You won't get me into trouble, will you?"

He frowned at her, then hummed to Irritation.

"You *are* a human sympathizer," Venli said.

"They're my friends," he said. "My family, now. They aren't perfect, Venli, but if we want to defeat Odium we're going to need them. We're going to need this tower."

"Do we want to defeat Odium?" Venli asked. "A lot of people like the way things are going, Rlain. We have a nation of our own—not a few shacks in a backwater countryside, but a *real* nation with cities, roads, infrastructure. Things—I might add—that were largely built by the efforts of enslaved singers. The humans don't deserve our loyalty or even an alliance. Not after what they did."

Rlain didn't object immediately. Instead he hummed to Tension. "We find ourselves caught, literally, between two storms," he finally said. "But if I'm going to pick one to walk through, Venli, I'll pick the highstorm. That was once our storm. The spren were our allies. And yes, the humans tried to exploit the listeners, then tried to destroy us—but the Fused are the ones who *succeeded*. Odium chose to destroy our people. I'm not going to serve him. I . . ."

He trailed off, perhaps realizing what he was saying. He'd tried to start the conversation noncommittal, plainly worried she was an agent for Odium. Now he'd confirmed where he stood. He looked to her, and his humming fell silent. Waiting.

"I don't know if any good can be done by fighting him, Rlain," she whispered. "But I . . . keep secrets from Odium myself. I've been trying to build something separate from his rule, a people I could . . . I don't know, use to start a new group of listeners."

Trying, in her own pitiful way, to undo what she'd done.

"How many?" Rlain asked, to Excitement.

"A dozen so far," Venli said. "I have them watching over the fallen Radiants. I have some authority in the tower, but I don't know how far it will extend. It's complicated. The various Fused have different motivations, and I'm wrapped up in the threads of it all. I helped save some humans who were going to be executed—but I'm not interested in allying with them in general."

"Who did you save? The queen?"

"No, someone far less important," Venli said. "A surgeon and his wife, who were—"

"Lirin and Hesina?" he asked to Excitement. "The child too, I hope."

"Yes. How did you—"

"You *need* to get me *out*, Venli," Rlain said. "And get me to Hesina. I have something useful I could show her—and you, if you want to help."

"I've been trying to tell you," Venli whispered, glancing over her shoulder at the door. "I have *some* authority, but there are many who distrust me. I don't know if I can get you free. It might draw too much attention to me."

"Venli," he said to Confidence, "look at me."

She met his gaze. Had he always been this intense? Eshonai had known him better than she had.

"You need to do this," Rlain said to her. "You need to use whatever influence you have and *get me out.*"

"I don't know if—"

"Stop being so insufferably selfish! Do something *against* your own self-interest, for the greater good, for once in your *storming* life, Venli."

She hummed to Betrayal. She didn't deserve that. She'd just told him how she was trying to rebuild the listeners. But he hummed louder to Confidence, so she aligned her rhythm to his.

"I'll try," she said.

◆

Though Raboniel often spent her time down near the crystal pillar—or with the human scholars in the chambers nearby—the Lady of Wishes had indicated she would be about other duties today. By asking around, Venli found that she was for some reason at the Blackthorn's former rooms.

Venli stepped inside, where an unusual number of Fused had gathered and were systematically going through the warlord's belongings—cataloguing them, making notations about them, and packing them away. Venli passed through and saw one crate contained socks: each pair recorded and carefully stored.

They were putting all of his things into storage, but why had they dedicated Fused to such a mundane job? What was more, these were important Fused, none of the more erratic or crazy represented. Leshwi herself had been pressed into the work, and that all together whispered something meaningful: Someone very high up in the singer hierarchy was interested in this man. To the point of wanting to dissect and understand his each and every possession, no matter how ordinary.

Venli moved around the perimeter of the room, careful to stay away from the broad doors or windows leading to the balcony. Those had been draped off, but the rules were strict during daylight hours. No singers were to show themselves outside, lest they accidentally reveal the truth to Windrunner scouts.

She found two humans she didn't recognize at the doorway into the bedroom, watching what occurred inside. There, Raboniel was speaking to a third human. The tall male was dressed in a coat and trousers that seemed elegant to Venli's eyes—though she knew little of their fashion. More striking was the strange creature on his shoulder, an odd thing unlike any Venli had ever seen. It stood on two legs like a person, though its face ended in a beak and it had brightly colored scales that looked *soft*, of all things. When she entered, it turned and stared at her, and she was unnerved by how bright and intelligent its eyes seemed.

The Lady of Wishes sat in a chair by the bed, her face passive, with stacks of papers and books beside her.

Who was this man, and why would Raboniel pause her research to give him an audience? The Lady normally ignored requests from humans, going so far as to have several "important" ones flogged when they demanded audiences. More curious, as Venli edged around the side of the room, she saw that the man's face was scarred in several places, bespeaking a roughness in contrast to his fine clothing.

"The only thing I find remarkable," Raboniel said to Derision, "is how audacious you are, human. Do you not understand how easily I could have you beaten or killed?"

"That would be to throw away a useful opportunity," the man said, loud and bold—a human version of the Rhythm of Determination. "And you are not one who throws away something useful, are you, Ancient One?"

"Use is relative," Raboniel replied. "I will throw away an opportunity I'll never have time to exploit if it is preventing me from something better."

"What is better than free riches?" he said.

"I have Urithiru," she said. "What need have I of spheres?"

"Not that kind of riches," the man said, with a smile. He stepped forward and respectfully handed her a large pouch. Raboniel took it, and it made a soft clink. Raboniel undid the top, and stared inside. She sat there for a long moment, and when she next spoke, her voice was *devoid* of rhythms. "How? Where did you get this?"

"I bring a gift," was all the man said. "To encourage you to meet with my *babsk* to negotiate terms. I had thought to wait until the current . . . turmoil subsided, but my *babsk* is determined. We will have a deal for use of the Oathgates. And we will pay."

"It is . . . a fine gift," Raboniel finally said.

"That is not the gift," he said. "That is a mere advance on our future payments. This is the gift."

He gestured to the side, and the strange creature on his shoulder whistled. The two men that Venli had seen outside entered, carrying something between them—a large cloth-covered box. It barely fit through the door, and was heavy, judging by the *thump* it made when they set it down.

The lead human whipped the cloth off, revealing a small teenage human girl in a box with bars on the sides. The dirty creature growled as she huddled in the center, shadowed. The man gestured dramatically, then bowed and began to walk away.

"Human?" Raboniel said. "I did not dismiss you. What is this? I need no slaves."

"This is no slave," the man said. "But if your master does happen to ever locate Cultivation, suggest that he ask her precisely *why* she made an Edgedancer who is fueled by Lifelight and not Stormlight." He bowed again—a formal military bow—then withdrew.

Venli waited, expecting Raboniel to demand he be executed, or at least flogged. Instead she started humming to Conceit. She even smiled.

"I am confused, Ancient One," Venli said, looking after the man.

"You needn't be," Raboniel said, "for this has nothing to do with you. He *is* dramatic, as I was warned. Hopefully he thinks I was put onto the back foot by his little stunt. Did he *really* deliver me a Radiant who is awake despite the tower's protections?" She peered in at the caged child, who stared back defiantly and growled. "Barely seems tame."

She clapped, and several servants entered. "Take this one to a secure place and do not let her go. Be careful. She might be dangerous." As they took the cage, she turned to Venli and spoke to Craving. "So, was it really another of your people, as the reports say?"

"Yes," Venli said. "I know him. His name is Rlain. A listener."

"A child of traitors," Raboniel said.

"As am I," Venli said, then paused. She took a deep breath and changed her rhythm to Conceit. "I would have him released to my care. I haven't any other kin to speak of. He is precious to me."

"Odium specifically made your kin extinct," Raboniel said. "You are the last. A distinction that you should appreciate, for the way it makes you unique."

"I do not wish uniqueness," Venli said. "I wish to keep this malen alive and enjoy his company. I have served well in several capacities, to multiple Fused. I demand this compensation."

Raboniel hummed to Derision. Venli panicked, and nearly lost her will—but Timbre, always watching, pulsed to *Conceit*. A rhythm of Odium, but the best counterpart to Resolve. The rhythm Venli needed to continue to express now. She did so, humming it, as she didn't trust herself to speak.

"Very well," Raboniel said, picking up her papers to begin reading again. "Your Passion does you credit. He is yours. Be certain he doesn't cause problems, for I will lay them at your charge."

Venli hummed to Tribute, then quickly retreated. Inside, Timbre pulsed to one of the normal rhythms. She seemed in pain, as if using one of the wrong rhythms had been hard for her. But they'd done it. Like she'd freed the Windrunner's family.

Timbre pulsed. Freedom. That was to be her next oath, Venli realized. To free those who had been taken unjustly. She almost said a new oath out loud, right there, but Timbre pulsed in warning.

So she returned to her rooms before going to Rlain. She shut the door to her quarters, then whispered the words.

"I will seek freedom for those in bondage," she said, then waited. Nothing happened. Had it worked?

A distant sensation struck her, a femalen voice, so very far away—but thrumming with the pure rhythm of Roshar.

These words, it said, *are not accepted.*

Not accepted? Venli sank down into a chair. Timbre pulsed to the Rhythm of Confusion. But in her gemheart, Venli realized she knew the reason. She'd just watched a child trapped in a cage be hauled off by Raboniel's servants. It seemed obvious, now that she considered.

She couldn't honestly speak those words. Not when she was concerned with freeing Rlain primarily because she wanted another listener to confide in. Not when she was willing to ignore the need of a child locked in a cage.

If she wanted to honestly progress as a Radiant, she'd need to do as Rlain had said and start thinking about someone other than herself. And it was beyond time for her to begin treating her powers with the respect they deserved.

Singer folios focus on how fashion augments singer forms and skin patterns.
Specifically, this plate illustrates how a Fused might dress their envoyform
Voice in a way that demands attention in a crowded gathering.

In other circumstances, I would be fascinated by this sand to the point of abandoning all other rational pursuits. What is it? Where did it come from?

—From *Rhythm of War*, page 13

Finally, at long last, Navani heard Kaladin's voice.

I'm sorry, Brightness, he said, his voice transmitted via the Sibling to Navani. *I collapsed when I got back last night, and fell asleep. I didn't intentionally keep you waiting.*

Upon arriving at the chamber of scholars in the morning, Navani had discovered—via the Sibling—that she had slept through what had nearly been the end of their resistance. She had then waited several interminable hours to hear from the Windrunner.

"Don't apologize," Navani whispered, standing in her now customary place, her hands behind her, touching the line of crystal on the wall as she surveyed her working scholars. Guards stood at the door, and the strange insane Fused sat in her place by the far wall, but no one interfered directly with Navani. "You did what you had to—and you did well."

I failed, Kaladin said.

"No," Navani said softly, but firmly. "Highmarshal, your job is not to save the tower. Your job is to buy me time enough to reverse what has been done. You didn't fail. You accomplished something incredible, and because of it we can still fight."

His reply was long in coming. *Thank you*, he said, his voice bolstered. *I needed to hear those words.*

"They are true," Navani said. "Given enough time, I'm confident I can flush the tower of the enemy's Light, then instead prime it with the proper kind."

It came down to the nature of Stormlight, Voidlight, and the way the Sibling worked. Navani needed to take a crash course in Light, and figure out exactly what had gone wrong.

Breaking the node seems to have made things worse, Kaladin said. *Healing takes longer now. A Fused hit me with a knife, and it took a good ten minutes before my Stormlight fully healed the wound.*

"I doubt that was due to the breaking of the node," Navani said. "Raboniel was able to corrupt the Sibling further before you stopped her."

Understood. I do feel bad I couldn't protect the node, but Brightness, I think doing so would be impossible. If the others get discovered, we'll have to destroy them too.

"I agree," she said. "Do what you have to in order to give me more time. Anything else to report?"

Oh, right! Kaladin said. *I couldn't get to the Oathgates in time. I thought I'd be able to easily climb down to the ground floor, but it was a longer process than I imagined.*

"You didn't fly?"

Those Lashings don't work, Brightness. I need to use Adhesion to make handholds. I'll need to practice more—or find another way up and down—if you want me to try to reach the Oathgates. Regardless, I did snatch some spanreeds for you. Full sets, it turns out, twelve of them.

Syl has been inspecting them, and she thinks she knows the reason they work. Brightness, the spren inside have been corrupted, like Renarin's spren. The rubies work on Voidlight now, as you suspected, and these spren must be the reason.

Navani let out a long breath. This had been one of her guesses; she hadn't wanted it proven. If she needed to acquire corrupted spren, she was unlikely to be able to get any fabrials working without Raboniel knowing.

"Rest," she told Kaladin, "and keep your strength up. I will figure out a path to reverse what is happening here."

We need to warn Dalinar, Kaladin said. *Maybe we could get half of one of these spanreeds to him.*

"I don't know how we'd accomplish that," Navani said.

Well, I guess it depends on how far down the tower's defenses go. It's possible I could leap off a ledge, fall far enough to get outside the suppression, then activate my Lashings. But that would leave you without access to a Radiant. Honestly, I'm loath to suggest it. I don't know if I could leave, considering how things are.

"Agreed," Navani said. "For now, it's more important that I have you here with me. Keep watch for Lift; the Sibling has lost track of her, but she was awake like you are."

Understood, he said.

"Are you otherwise well? Do you have food?"

Yeah. I have another of my men helping me. He's not a Radiant, but he's a good man.

"The mute?" Navani guessed.

You know Dabbid?

"We've met. Give him my best."

Will do, Brightness. Really though, I don't think I can rest. I need to practice climbing the outside of the tower—but even with practice, I'm worried I won't be fast enough. What if a node is discovered on the fortieth floor? It would take me hours to climb that high.

"A valid worry," she said. "I'll see if I can find a solution. Let's talk tomorrow around this time."

Understood.

She pushed off the wall and strolled through the room. She didn't want to be seen talking to herself; surely the singers knew to watch for signs that someone was Radiant. She conversed softly with Rushu, explaining her plans for the next phase of time-wasting.

Rushu approved, but Navani felt annoyed as she moved on. *I need to do more than waste time,* Navani thought. *I need to work toward our freedom.*

She'd been formulating her plan. Step one was to continue making certain they didn't lose ground, and Kaladin would have to handle that. Step two was getting word to Dalinar. Now that she had spanreeds, perhaps she could find a way.

It was the third step that currently concerned her. In talking to the Sibling, Navani had confirmed a number of things she'd previously suspected. The tower regulated pressure and heat for those living inside— and it had once done a far better job of this, along with performing a host of other vital functions.

Most of that, including the tower's protections against Fused, had ended around the Recreance. The time when the Radiants had abandoned their oaths—and the time when the ancient singers had been transformed into parshmen, their songs and forms stolen. The actions of those ancient Radiants had somehow broken the tower—and Raboniel, by filling the tower with Voidlight, was starting to repair it in a twisted way.

Navani felt smothered by it all. She needed to fix a problem using mechanisms she didn't understand—and indeed had learned about only days ago. She paced, massaging her temples. She needed a smaller problem she could work on first, to give her brain some time away from the bigger problem.

What was a smaller problem she could fix? Helping Kaladin move faster up and down through the tower? Was there a hidden lift that she could . . .

Wait.

A way for one person to quickly get up and down, she thought. *Storms.* She turned on her heel and walked to the other side of the room, suppressing—as best she could—visible signs of her excitement.

The junior engineer Tomor had survived the initial assault. Navani had him recalculating the math on certain schematics. She leaned down beside the young ardent and pointed at his current project, but whispered something else.

"That glove you made," she said. "The one that you wanted to use as a single-person lift. Where is it?"

"Brightness?" he asked, surprised. "In the boxes out in the hallway."

"I need you to sneak it out," she whispered, "when you leave today."

The singers let her lesser scholars move more freely than Navani. What else could they do? Force three dozen people to sleep in this room, without facilities? A few of the key scholars—Navani, Rushu, Falilar— were always escorted, but the subordinates weren't paid as much attention.

"Brightness?" Tomor said. "What if I get caught?"

"You might be killed," she whispered. "But it is a risk we must take. A Radiant still fights, Tomor, and he needs your device to climb between floors."

Tomor's eyes lit up. "My device . . . Stormblessed needs it?"

"You know he's the one?"

"Everyone's talking about him," Tomor said. "I thought it was a fanciful rumor."

"Bring such rumors to me, fanciful or not," Navani said. "For now, I need you to sneak that glove out and leave it hidden somewhere it won't be discovered, but where Kaladin can reasonably retrieve it."

"I'll try, Brightness," Tomor said, nervous. "But fabrials don't work anymore."

"Leave that to me," she said. "Include a quick sketch of a map to the location of the weights on the twentieth floor, as he'll need to visit those too."

With the conjoined rubies Kaladin had stolen in those spanreeds, they could hopefully make the device function. She'd have to coach Kaladin through installing it all. And the rubies would be smaller than the ones Tomor had built into the device; would they be able to handle the weight? She'd need to do some calculations, but assuming Tomor had used the newer cages that didn't stress the rubies as much, it should work.

She rose to go speak to some of the others in the same manner and posture, to hide the importance of her conversation with Tomor. During the second such conference, however, she noticed someone at the doorway.

Raboniel. Navani took a deep breath, composing herself and smothering her spike of anxiety. Raboniel would likely be unhappy about what had happened last night. Hopefully she didn't suspect Navani's part in it.

Unfortunately, a guard soon walked into the room, then made straight for Navani. Raboniel didn't fetch an inferior personally. Navani couldn't banish the anxietyspren that trailed her as she joined the Fused at the doorway.

Raboniel wore a gown today, though of no cut Navani recognized. Loose and formless, it felt like what an Alethi woman would wear to bed. Though the Fused wore it well with her tall figure, it was strangely off-putting to see her in something that seemed more regal than martial.

The Fused didn't speak as Navani arrived. Instead she turned and walked out of the chamber with a relaxed gait. Navani followed, and they entered the hallway with the murals. Down to the left, the shield surrounding the crystal pillar glowed a soft blue.

"Your scholars," Raboniel finally noted, "do not seem to be making much progress. They were to deliver up to my people fabrials to test."

"My scholars are frightened and unnerved, Ancient One," Navani said. "It might take weeks before they feel up to true studies again."

"Yes, and longer, if you continue having them repeat work in an effort to not make progress."

She figured that out faster than I anticipated, Navani thought as the two strolled along the hallway toward the shield. Here a common singer soldier in warform was working under the direction of several Fused. With a Shardblade.

They'd known the singers had claimed some Blades from the humans they'd fought—but Navani recognized this one. It had belonged to her son. Elhokar's Blade, Sunraiser.

Navani kept her face impassive only with great effort, though the anxietyspren faded and an agonyspren arrived instead: an upside-down face carved from stone pressing out from the wall nearby. It betrayed her true emotions. That loss ran deep.

Raboniel glanced at it, but said nothing. Navani kept her eyes forward. Watching that horrible Blade in that awful creature's hand. The warform held the weapon at the ready. It held no gemstone at its pommel; it seemed that the warform didn't have it bonded. Or perhaps the summoning mechanism didn't work in the tower, with the protections in place.

The warform attacked the shield—and contrary to Navani's expectation, the Blade bit into the blue light. The warform carved off a chunk, which evaporated to nothing before it hit the floor—and the shield restored itself just as quickly. The warform tried again, attempting to dig faster. After a few minutes of watching, Navani could tell the effort was futile. The bubble regrew too quickly.

"Fascinating behavior, wouldn't you say?" Raboniel asked Navani.

Navani turned toward Raboniel, steeling herself against the memories brought forth by the sight of the sword. She could cry for her child again tonight, as she had done many nights in the past. For now, she would *not* show these creatures her pain.

"I've never seen anything like that shield, Lady of Wishes," she said. "I couldn't *begin* to understand how it was created."

"We could unravel its secrets, if we tried together," Raboniel said, "instead of wasting our time watching one another for hidden motives."

"This is true, Ancient One," Navani said. "But if you want my cooperation and goodwill, perhaps you shouldn't flaunt in front of me the Blade taken from the corpse of my son."

Raboniel stiffened. She glanced at the warform with the weapon. "I did not know."

Didn't she? Or was this another game?

Raboniel turned, nodding for Navani to follow as they walked away from the shield.

"If I might ask, Ancient One," Navani said, "why do you give the Blades you capture to common soldiers, and not keep them yourselves?"

Raboniel hummed to one of her rhythms, but Navani could never tell them apart. Singers seemed to be able to distinguish one rhythm from another after hearing a short word or a couple of seconds of humming.

"Some Fused do keep the Blades we capture," Raboniel said. "The ones who enjoy the pain. Now, I fear I must make some changes in how you and your scholars operate. You are distracted, naturally, by preventing them from giving me too much information. I have unconsciously put you in a position where your obvious talents are wasted by foolish politicking.

"These are the new arrangements: You will work by yourself at my desk in a separate room from the other scholars. Twice a day, you may give them written directions, which I will personally vet. That should give you more time for worthwhile pursuits, and less for deceit."

Navani drew her lips to a line. "I think that is unwise, Ancient One," she said. "I am accustomed to working directly with my scholars. They are far more efficient when I am personally directing their efforts."

"I find it difficult to imagine them being *less* efficient than they are currently, Navani," Raboniel said. "We will work this way from now on. It is not a matter I care to debate."

Raboniel had a long stride, and used it purposely to force Navani to hurry to match her. Upon reaching the scholars' chambers, Raboniel turned left instead of right—entering the room Navani's scholars had been using as a library.

Raboniel's desk in this chamber had once belonged to Navani. The Fused gestured, and Navani sat as instructed. This was going to be inconvenient—but that was Raboniel's intent.

The Fused went down on one knee, then picked through a box on the floor here. She set something on the desk. A glass globe? Yes, like the one that had been near the first node Navani had activated.

"When we discovered the node operating the field, this was connected to it," Raboniel said. "Look closely. What do you see?"

Navani hesitantly picked up the globe, which was heavier than it appeared. Though it was made of solid glass, she spotted an unusual construction inside. Something she hadn't noticed, or understood, the first time she'd seen one of these. The globe had a pillar rising through the center. . . .

"It's a reproduction of the crystal pillar room," Navani said, her eyes widening. "You don't suppose . . ."

"That's how the field is created," Raboniel said, tapping the globe with an orange carapace fingernail. "It's a type of Soulcasting. The fabrial is persuading the air in a sphere around the pillar to think it is solid glass. That's why cutting off a piece accomplishes nothing."

"That's incredible," Navani said. "An application of the Surge I never *anticipated*. It's not a full transformation, but a half state somehow. Kept in perpetual stasis, using this globe as a model to mimic . . ."

"There must be similar globes at the other nodes."

"Clearly," Navani said. "After this one was detached, did it make the shield seem weaker than before?"

"Not that we can tell," Raboniel said. "One node must be enough to perpetuate the transformation."

"Fascinating . . ."

Don't get taken in, Navani. She wants you to think like a scholar, not like a queen. She wants you working for her, not against her.

That focus was even more difficult to maintain as Raboniel set something else on the table. A small diamond the size of Navani's thumb, full of Stormlight. But . . . was the hue faintly off? Navani held it up, frowning, turning it over in her fingers. She couldn't tell without a Stormlight sphere to compare it to, but it did seem this color was faintly teal.

"It's not Stormlight, is it?" she asked. "Nor Voidlight?"

Raboniel hummed a rhythm. Then, realizing Navani wouldn't understand, said, "No."

"The third Light. I *knew* it. The moment I learned about Voidlight, I wondered. Three gods. Three types of Light."

"Ah," Raboniel said, "but this isn't the third Light. We call that Lifelight. Cultivation's power, distilled. This is something different. Something unique. It is the reason I came to this tower. It is a *mixing* of two. Stormlight and Lifelight. Like . . ."

"Like the Sibling is a child of both Honor and Cultivation," Navani said.

Storms. That was what the Sibling had meant by *their* Light no longer working. They hadn't been able to make the tower function any longer because something had happened to the tower's Light.

"It came out in barely a trickle," Raboniel said. "Something is wrong with the tower, preventing it from flowing." Her rhythm grew more energetic. "But this is proof. I have long suspected that there must be a way to mix and change the various forms of Light. These three energies are the means by which all Surges work, and yet we know so little about them.

"What could we do with this power if we *truly* understood it? This Towerlight is proof that Stormlight and Lifelight can mix and create something new. Can the same be done with Stormlight and Voidlight? Or will that prove impossible, since the two are opposites?"

"Are they, though?" Navani asked.

"Yes. Like night and day or oil and water. But perhaps we can find a way to put them together. If so, it could be a . . . model, perhaps, of our peoples. A way toward unity instead of strife. Proof that we, although opposites, can coexist."

Navani stared at the Towerlight sphere, and she felt compelled to correct one thing. "Oil and water aren't opposites."

"Of course they are," Raboniel said. "This is a central tenet of philosophy. They cannot mix, but must remain ever separated."

"Just because something doesn't mix doesn't make them opposites," Navani said. "Sand and water don't mix either, and you wouldn't call *them* opposites. That's beside the point. Oil and water can mix, if you have an emulsifier."

"I do not know this word."

"It's a kind of binding agent, Ancient One," Navani said, standing. If her things were still in here . . . yes, over at the side of the room, she found a crate holding simple materials for experiments.

She made up a vial with some oil and water, adding some stump-weight sap extract as a simple emulsifier. She shook the resulting solution and handed it to Raboniel. The Fused took it and held it up, waiting for the oil and water to separate. But of course they didn't.

"Oil and water mix in nature all the time," Navani said. "Sow's milk has fat suspended in it, for example."

"I . . . have accepted ancient philosophy as fact for too long, I see," Raboniel said. "I call myself a scholar, but today I feel a fool."

"Everyone has holes in their knowledge. There is no shame in ignorance. In any case, oil and water aren't opposites. I'm not certain what the opposite of water would be, if the word even has meaning when applied to an element."

"The various forms of Light *do* have opposites," Raboniel said. "I am certain of it. Yet I must think on what you've shown me." She reached over and tapped the sphere full of Towerlight. "For now, experiment with this Light. To keep you focused, I must insist you remain in this room until finished each day, except when accompanied to use the chamber."

"Very well," Navani said. "Though if you want my scholars to actually develop something for you, this idea of them drawing plans and you testing them is foolish. It won't work, at least not well. Instead, Ancient One, I suggest you deliver to us gemstones that can power fabrials that work in the tower."

Raboniel hummed for a moment, regarding the emulsion. "I will send such gems to your people as proof of my willingness to work together." She turned to go. "If you intend to use ciphers to give hidden instructions to your scholars, kindly make them difficult ones. The spren I will use to unravel your true messages do like a challenge. It gives them more variety in existence."

Raboniel set a guard at the door, but didn't restrict Navani's access within the room. It was otherwise unoccupied: it held only bookshelves, crates, and the occasional sphere lantern. There were no other exits, but near the rear of the room Navani found a vein of crystal hidden among the strata.

"Are you there?" she asked, touching it.

Yes, the Sibling replied. *I am closer to death than ever. Surrounded by evils on all sides. Men and singers alike seeking to abuse me.*

"Don't create a false equivalency," Navani said. "My kind might not understand the harm we've done to spren, but the enemy *certainly* knows the harm they cause in corrupting them."

Regardless. I will soon die. Only two nodes remain, and the previous one was discovered so rapidly.

"More proof that you should be helping us, not them," Navani whispered, peeking through the stacks to see that she hadn't aroused the guard's attention. "I need to understand more about how these various forms of Light work."

I don't think I can explain much, the Sibling said. *For me, it all simply worked. Like a human child can breathe, so I used to make and use Light. And then . . . the tones went away . . . and the Light left me.*

"All right," Navani said. "We can talk on that more later. For now, you need to tell me where the other nodes are."

No. Defend them once they are found.

"Sibling," Navani said, "if Kaladin Stormblessed can't protect a node, no one can. Our goal should be to *distract* and *mislead,* to prevent the Fused from ever finding them. To do this, I'll need to know where the nodes are."

You talk so well, the Sibling said. *So frustratingly well. You humans always sound so reasonable. It's only later, after the pain, that the truth comes out.*

"Hide it if you wish," Navani said. "But you have to know, after watching Kaladin fight for you, that we are severely outmatched. Our sole hope is to prevent the nodes from being located. If I knew where at least *one* of them was, I could come up with plots to deflect the enemy's attention."

Come up with those plots first, the Sibling said. *Then talk to me again.*

"Fine," Navani said. She slipped a few books off the shelf to hide what she'd been doing, then walked to her seat. There, she began writing down everything she knew about light.

EIGHT YEARS AGO

Eshonai turned the topaz over in her fingers and attuned Tension. A topaz *should* glow with a calm, deep brown—but this one gave off a wicked orange light, like the bright color along the back of a sigs cremling warning that it was poisonous.

Looking closely, Eshonai thought she could make out the spren trapped in it. A painspren, frantically moving around. Though . . . perhaps she imagined the frantic part. The spren was mostly formless when inside the gemstone, having reverted to the misty Stormlight that created all of their kind. Still, it couldn't be *happy* in there. How would she feel if she were locked into a room, unable to explore?

"You learned this from the humans?" Eshonai said.

"Yes," Venli said. She sat comfortably between two of the elders in the small council room, which was furnished with woven mats and painted banners.

Venli wasn't one of the Five—the head elders—but she seemed to think she belonged among them. Something had happened to her these last few months. Where she'd once been self-indulgent, she now radiated egotism and confidence. She hummed to Victory as Eshonai passed the gemstone to one of the elders.

"Why did you not bring this to us earlier, Venli?" Klade asked. The reserved elder took the gemstone next. "The humans have been gone for months now."

"I thought I might be wrong," Venli said to Confidence. "I decided to see if I could trap a spren on my own. Surely you wouldn't have wanted to be bothered by my fancies, should I have been wrong."

"I hadn't heard of this thing they can do," Klade said to Reconciliation. "Do you think you could trap a lifespren? If so, we could better choose when we adopt mateform. That would be convenient."

"Try this stone," Venli said, taking it, then handing it to Varnali next. "I think it might be the secret to warform."

"A dangerous form," Varnali said. "But useful."

"It is not a form of power," Klade said. "It is within our rights to claim it."

"The humans make overtures," Gangnah—foremost among them— said to Annoyance, a rhythm used to elicit sympathy for a frustrating situation. "They act as if we are a nation united, not a group of squabbling families. I wish we could present to them a stronger face. They have accomplished so much during our centuries apart, while we remember so little."

"Pardon, elders," Eshonai said to Reconciliation. "But they have advantages we do not. A much larger population, ancient devices to create metals, a land more sheltered from the storms."

She'd recently returned from her latest exploration efforts—which the elders now fully supported. She'd sought to circumvent the human trading post, then find their home. She'd attuned Disappointment more than once; every place she *thought* she'd find the humans had been empty. They'd found packs of wild chulls, and even spotted a distant and rare group of Ryshadium.

No humans. Not until she'd returned to their trading post, which had been transformed into a small fort—built from stone and staffed by soldiers and two scribes. The humans had a message for her there. The human king wished to "formalize relations" with her people, whom they referred to as "Parshendi."

She'd returned with the message to find this: Venli sitting among the elders. Venli, so *sure* of herself. Venli replicating human techniques that Eshonai—despite spending the most time with them—hadn't heard them discuss.

"Thank you, Eshonai," Gangnah said to Appreciation. "You have done well on your expedition." Workform had carapace only along the backs of the hands in small ridges, and Gangnah's was beginning to whiten at the edges. A sign of her age. She turned to the others and continued. "We will need to respond to this offer. The humans expect us to be a nation. Should we form a government like they have?"

"The other families would never follow us," Klade said. "They already resent how the humans paid more attention to us."

"I find the idea of a king distasteful," added Husal, to Anxiety. "We should not follow them in this."

Eshonai hummed to Pleading, indicating she wished to speak again. "Elders," she said, "I think I should visit the other families and show them my maps."

"What would that accomplish?" Venli asked to Skepticism.

"If I show them how much there is to the world, they will understand that we are smaller as a people than we thought. They will want to unite."

Venli hummed to Amusement. "You think they'd simply join with us? Because they saw maps? Eshonai, you are a *delight*."

"We will consider your proposal," Gangnah said, then hummed to Appreciation—as a dismissal.

Eshonai retreated out into the sunlight as the elders asked Venli additional questions about creating gemstones with trapped spren. Eshonai attuned Annoyance. Then, by force, she changed her rhythm to Peace instead. She *always* felt anxious after an extended trip. She wasn't annoyed with her sister, just the general situation.

She let herself rove outward to the cracked wall that surrounded the city. She liked this place; it was old, and old things seemed . . . thoughtful to her. She walked along the base of the once-wall, passing listeners tending chulls, carrying in grain from the fields, hauling water. Many raised a hand or called to a rhythm when they saw her. She was famous now, unfortunately. She had to stop and chat with several listeners who wanted to ask about her expedition.

She suffered the attention with patience. Eshonai had spent years trying to inspire this kind of interest about the outside world. She wouldn't throw away this goodwill now.

She managed to extract herself, and climbed up a watchpost along the wall. From it, she could see listeners from other families moving about on the Plains, or driving their hogs past the perimeter of the city.

There are more of them about than usual, she thought. One of the other families might be preparing an assault on the city. Would they be so bold? So soon after the humans had come and changed the world?

Yes, they would be. Eshonai's own family had been that bold, after all. The others might assume Eshonai's people were getting secrets, or special trade goods, from the humans. They would want to put themselves into a position to receive the humans' blessings instead.

Eshonai needed to go to them and explain. Why fight, when there was so much more out there to experience? Why squabble over these old, broken-down cities? They could be building new ones as the humans did. She attuned Determination.

Then she attuned right back to Anxiety as she saw a figure walking distractedly along the base of the wall. Eshonai's mother wore a loose brown robe, dull against the femalen's gorgeous red and black skin patterns.

Eshonai climbed down and ran over. "Mother?"

"Ah," her mother said to Anxiety. "I know you. Can you perhaps help me? I seem to find myself in an odd situation."

Eshonai took her mother by the arm. "Mother."

"Yes. Yes, I'm your mother. You are Eshonai." The femalen looked around, then she leaned in. "Can you tell me how I arrived here, Eshonai? I don't seem to remember."

"You were going to wait for me to get home," Eshonai said. "With food."

"I was? Why didn't I do that, then?"

"You must have lost track of time," Eshonai said, to Consolation. "Let's get you home."

Jaxlim hummed to Determination and refused to be budged, seeming to become more conscious, more herself by the second. "Eshonai," she said, "we have to confront this. This is not simply me feeling tired. This is something worse."

"Maybe not, Mother," Eshonai said. "Maybe it . . ."

Her mother hummed to the Rhythm of the Lost. Eshonai trailed off.

"I must make certain your sister knows the songs," Jaxlim said. "We may have reached the riddens of my life, Eshonai."

"Please, come and rest," Eshonai said to Peace.

"Rest is for those with time to spare, dear," her mother said, but let herself be led in the direction of their home. She pulled her robe tight. "I can face this. Our ancestors took weakness upon themselves to bring our people into existence. They faced frailty of body and mind. I can face this with grace. I must."

Eshonai settled her at home with something to eat. Then, Eshonai considered getting out her new maps to show her mother, but hesitated. Jaxlim never did like hearing about Eshonai's travels. It was best not to upset her.

Why did it have to happen like this? Eshonai finally got what she wanted out of life. But progress, change, couldn't happen without the passing of storms and the movement of years. Each day forward meant another day of regression for her mother.

Time. It was a sadistic master. It made adults of children—then gleefully, relentlessly, stole away everything it had given.

They were still eating when Venli returned. She always had a hidden smile these days, as if attuning Amusement in secret. She set her gemstone—the one with the spren—on the table.

"They're going to try it," Venli said. "They are taking volunteers now. I'm to provide a handful of these gemstones."

"How did you learn to cut them as humans do?" Eshonai asked.

"It wasn't hard," Venli said. "It merely took a little practice."

Their mother stared at the gemstone. She wiped her hands with a cloth, then picked it up. "Venli. I need you to return to practice. I don't know how much longer I will be suited to being our keeper of songs."

"Because your mind is giving out," Venli said. "Mother, why do you think I've been working so hard to find these new forms? This can help."

Eshonai attuned Surprise, glancing at their mother.

"Help?" Jaxlim said.

"Each form has a different way of thinking," Venli said. "That is preserved in the songs. And some were stronger, more resilient to diseases, both physical and mental. So if you were to change to this new form . . ."

Her mother attuned Consideration.

"I . . . hadn't realized this," Eshonai said. "Mother, you must volunteer! This could be our answer!"

"I've been trying to get the elders to see," Venli said. "They want young listeners to try the change first."

"They will listen to me," Jaxlim said to Determination. "It is, after all, my job to speak for them to hear. I will try this form, Venli. And if you have truly accomplished this goal of yours . . . well, I once thought that being our new keeper of songs would be your highest calling. I hadn't considered that you might *invent* a calling with even more honor. Keeper of forms."

Eshonai settled back, listening to her sister humming to Joy. Only . . . the beat was off somehow. Faster. More violent?

You're imagining things, she told herself. *Don't let jealousy consume you, Eshonai. It could easily destroy your family.*

I am told that it is not the sand itself, but something that grows upon it, that exhibits the strange properties. One can make more, with proper materials and a seed of the original.

—From *Rhythm of War*, page 13 undertext

Kaladin thrashed, sweating and trembling, his mind filled with visions of his friends dying. Of Rock frozen in the Peaks, of Lopen slain on a distant battlefield, of Teft dying alone, shriveled to bones, his eyes glazed over from repeated use of firemoss.

"No," Kaladin screamed. "No!"

"Kaladin!" Syl said. She zipped around his head, filling his eyes with streaks of blue-white light. "You're awake. You're all right. Kaladin?"

He breathed in and out, taking deep lungfuls. The nightmares felt so *real,* and they *lingered.* Like the scent of blood on your clothing after a battle.

He forced himself to his feet, and was surprised to find a small bag of glowing gemstones on the room's stone ledge.

"From Dabbid," Syl said. "He left them a little earlier, along with some broth, then grabbed the jug to go get water."

"How did he . . ." Maybe he'd gotten them from the ardent at the monastery? Or maybe he'd quietly taken them from somewhere else.

Dabbid could move around the tower in ways that Kaladin couldn't—people always looked at Kaladin, remembered him. It was the height, he guessed. Or maybe it was the way he held himself. He'd never learned to keep his head down properly, even when he'd been a slave.

Kaladin shook his head, then did his morning routine: stretches, exercises, then washing as best he could with a cloth and some water. After that he saw to Teft, washing him, then shifting the way the man was lying to help prevent bedsores. That all done, Kaladin knelt beside Teft's bench with the syringe and broth, trying to find solace from his own mind through the calming act of feeding his friend.

Syl settled onto the stone bench beside Teft as Kaladin worked, wearing her girlish dress, sitting with her knees pulled up against her chest and her arms wrapped around them. Neither of them spoke for a long while as Kaladin worked.

"I wish he were awake," Syl finally whispered. "There's something happy about the way Teft is angry."

Kaladin nodded.

"I went to Dalinar," she said, "before he left. I asked him if he could make me feel like humans do. Sad sometimes."

"What?" Kaladin asked. "Why in the Almighty's tenth name would you do something like that?"

"I wanted to feel what you feel," she said.

"*Nobody* should have to feel like I do."

"I'm my own person, Kaladin. I can make decisions for myself." She stared sightlessly past Teft and Kaladin. "It was in talking to him that I started remembering my old knight, like I told you. I think Dalinar did something. I wanted him to Connect me to you. He refused. But I think he somehow Connected me to who I was. Made me able to remember, and hurt again . . ."

Kaladin felt helpless. He had never been able to struggle through his *own* feelings of darkness. How did he help someone else?

Tien could do it, he thought. *Tien would know what to say.*

Storms, he missed his brother. Even after all these years.

"I think," Syl said, "that we spren have a problem. We think we don't change. You'll hear us say it sometimes. 'Men change. Singers change. Spren don't.' We think that because pieces of us are eternal, we are as well. But pieces of humans are eternal too.

"If we can choose, we can change. If we can't change, then choice means nothing. I'm *glad* I feel this way, to remind me that I haven't always felt the same. Been the same. It means that in coming here to find another Knight Radiant, I was *deciding*. Not simply doing what I was made to, but doing what I *wanted* to."

Kaladin cocked his head, the syringe full of broth halfway to Teft's lips. "When I'm at my worst, I feel like I *can't* change. Like I've *never* changed. That I've always felt this way, and always will."

"When you get like that," Syl said, "let me know, all right? Maybe it will help to talk to me about it."

"Yeah. All right."

"And Kal?" she said. "Do the same for me."

He nodded, and the two of them fell silent. Kaladin wanted to say more. He *should* have said more. But he felt so tired. Exhaustionspren swirled in the room, though he'd slept half the day.

He could see the signs. Or rather, he couldn't ignore them anymore. He was deeply within the grip of battle shock, and the tower being under occupation didn't magically fix that. It made things worse. More fighting. More time alone. More people depending on him.

Killing, loneliness, and stress. An unholy triumvirate, working together with spears and knives to corner him. Then they just. Kept. Stabbing.

"Kaladin?" Syl said.

He realized he'd been sitting there, not moving, for . . . how long? Storms. He quickly refilled the syringe and lifted it to Teft's lips. The man was stirring again, muttering, and Kaladin could almost make out what he was saying. Something about his parents?

Soon the door opened and Dabbid entered. He gave Kaladin a quick salute, then hurried over to the bench near Teft and put something down on the stone. He gestured urgently.

"What's this?" Kaladin asked, then unwrapped the cloth to reveal some kind of fabrial. It looked like a leather bracer, the type Dalinar and Navani wore to tell the time. Only the construction was different. It had long leather straps on it, and a metal portion—like a handle—that came up and went across the palm. Turning it over, Kaladin found ten rubies in the bracer portion, though they were dun.

"What on Roshar?" Kaladin asked.

Dabbid shrugged.

"The Sibling led you to this, I assume?"

Dabbid nodded.

"Navani must have sent it," Kaladin said. "Syl, what time is it?"

"About a half hour before your meeting with the queen," she said, looking upward toward the sky, occluded behind many feet of stone.

"Next highstorm?" Kaladin asked.

"Not sure, a few days at least. Why?"

"We'll want to restore the dun gemstones I used in that fight with the Pursuer. Thanks for the new ones, by the way, Dabbid. We'll need to find a way to hide the others outside to recharge though."

Dabbid patted his chest. He'd do it.

"You seem to be doing better these days," Kaladin said, settling down to finish feeding Teft.

Dabbid shrugged.

"Want to share your secret?" Kaladin asked.

Dabbid sat on the floor and put his hands in his lap. So Kaladin went back to his work. It proved surprisingly tiring—as he had to forcibly keep his attention from wandering to his nightmares. He was glad when, upon finishing, Syl told him the time had arrived for his check-in with Navani.

He walked to the side of the room, pressed his hand against the crystal vein, and waited for her to speak in his mind.

Highmarshal? she said a few minutes later.

"Here," he replied. "But, since I was on my way to becoming a full-time surgeon, I'm not sure I still have that rank."

I'm reinstating you. I managed to have one of my engineers sneak out a fabrial you might find useful. The Sibling should be able to guide you to it.

"I've got it already," Kaladin said. "Though I have no idea what it's supposed to do."

It's a personal lift, meant to levitate you up and down long distances. To help you travel the height of the tower.

"Interesting," he said, glancing at the device laid out on the stone bench. "Though, I'm not one for technology, Brightness. Pardon, but I barely know how to turn on a heating fabrial."

You'll need to learn quickly then, Navani said. *As you'll need to replace the rubies in the fabrial with the Voidspren ones from the spanreeds you stole. We'll need all twelve pairs. Do you see a map in with the device?*

"Just a moment," he said, digging in the sack and pulling out a small folded map. It led to a place on the twentieth floor, judging by the glyphs. "I've got it. I should be able to reach this place. The enemy isn't guarding the upper floors."

Excellent. There are weights in a shaft up there where you'll need to install the other halves of those rubies. A mechanism on the fabrial bracer will drop one of those weights, and that force will transfer through the bracer. You'll be pulled in whatever direction you've pointed the device.

"By my arm?" Kaladin asked. "That doesn't sound comfortable."

It isn't. My engineer has been trying to fix that. There is a strap that winds around your arm and braces against your shoulder, which he thinks might help.

"All right . . ." he said. It was something to do, at least.

But fabrials? He'd always considered them toys for rich people. Though he supposed that was becoming less and less the case. Breeding projects were creating livestock with larger and larger ruby gemhearts, and fabrial creation methods were spreading. It seemed every third room had a heating fabrial these days, and spanreeds were cheap enough that even the enlisted men could afford to pay to send messages via one.

Navani coached him through replacing the rubies. Fortunately, the case of spanreeds he'd stolen included a few small tools for undoing casings. It wasn't any more difficult than replacing the buckles on a leather jerkin.

Once it was done, he and Syl ventured out, sneaking up nine floors. He didn't use any Stormlight; he didn't have enough to waste. Besides, it felt good to work his body.

On the twentieth floor, the garnet light led him to the location the map had described. Inside he found the weights and the shaft, and Navani walked him through installing the matching rubies. He began to grasp how the device worked. The big weights were more than heavy enough to lift a man. Five of the rubies in his fabrial were connected to these weights, binding them together.

The other seven rubies were used to activate and control the weights. The intricate system of pulleys and mechanisms was far more complex than he could understand, but essentially it allowed him to switch to a different weight when one had dropped all the way. He could also slow the weight's fall or stop it completely, modulating how quickly he was being pulled.

Each weight should be able to pull you hundreds of feet before running out, Navani said via a garnet vein on the wall. *These shafts plunge all the way down to the aquifers at the base of the mountain. That means you should be able to soar all the way up from the ground floor to the top of the tower using one weight.*

The bad news is that once all five weights have fallen, the device will be useless until you rewind them. There is a winch in the corner; it's an arduous process, I'm afraid.

"That's annoying," Kaladin said.

Yes, it is mildly inconvenient that we have to wind a crank to experience the wonder of making a human being safely levitate hundreds of feet in the air.

"Pardon, Brightness, but I can usually do it with far less trouble."

Which is meaningless right now, isn't it?

"I suppose it is," he said. He looked at the fabrial, now attached to his left arm, with the straps winding around all the way to his shoulder. It was a little constrictive, but otherwise fit quite well. "So, I point it where I want to go, activate it, and I'll get pulled that way?"

Yes. But we made the device so that it won't move if you let go—it was too dangerous otherwise. See the pressure spring across your palm? Ease off that, and the brake on the line will activate. Do you see?

"Yes," Kaladin said, making a fist around the bar. It had a separate metal portion wrapped around it on one side, with a spring underneath. So the harder he squeezed, the faster the device would pull him. If he let go completely, he'd stop in place.

There are two steps to the fabrial's use. First, you have to turn the device on—conjoining the rubies. The switch you can move with your thumb? That's for this purpose. Once you flip it, your arm will be locked into its current orientation, and won't be able to move the bracer in any direction except forward.

The second step is to start dropping a weight. If a weight falls all the way, swap to the next one using the dial on the back of your wrist. You see it?

"I do," he said.

Once you stop, you'll remain hanging until you disengage the device. But so long as you have another weight that hasn't run out, you can turn the dial to that one, then continue moving upward. Or if you're bold enough, you can disengage the device and fall for a second while you point it another direction, then engage it again and set it to pull you that way instead.

"That sounds dangerous," Kaladin said. "If I'm up high in the air, and need to get over to a balcony or something, I have to drop into free fall for a bit to reset the direction of the device so it can pull me laterally instead of up and down?"

Yes, unfortunately. The engineer who created this has grand and lofty ideas—but not much practical sense. But it's better than nothing, Highmarshal. And it's the best I can do for you right now.

Kaladin took a deep breath. "Understood. I'm sorry if I sounded ungrateful, Brightness. It's been a rough few days. I'm glad for the help. I'll familiarize myself with it."

Excellent. You shouldn't have to worry about the Voidlight in the gemstones running out through practice—conjoined rubies don't use much energy to maintain their connection. But they will run out naturally, over time. We'll have to figure out what to do about that when it happens.

For now, I'm hoping the Sibling will soon trust me enough to tell me where to find the remaining nodes. Once I have that information, I can devise a plan to protect them, perhaps by distracting the enemy's search toward a different region of the tower. It's vital that you keep that shield in place as long as possible, to give me time to figure out what is wrong with the Light in the tower and its defenses.

"Any movement there?" Kaladin asked.

No, but I'm currently focused on filling holes in my understanding. Once I have the proper fundamentals on Stormlight and Voidlight, I hope I'll make more rapid progress.

"Understood," Kaladin said. "I'll contact you again in a few hours, if you can make time, to discuss my experience with this device."

Thank you.

He stepped away from the wall. Syl stood in the air beside him, inspecting the fabrial.

"So?" Kaladin asked her. "What do you think?"

"I think you're going to look *extremely* silly using it. I can't wait."

He walked out to a nearby hallway. Up here on the twentieth floor, he should be safe practicing in the open—assuming he stayed away from the atrium. He walked the length of the hallway, setting out amethysts to light the way. Then he stood at one end, looking down the line of lights. The fabrial left his fingers free, but that bar in the center of his hand would interfere with fighting. He'd have to one-hand his spear, as if he were fighting with a shield.

"We're going to try it here?" Syl asked, darting over to him. "Isn't it for getting up and down?"

"Brightness Navani told me it pulls you in whatever direction you point it," he said. "New Windrunners always want to go up with their Lashings—but the more experience you have, the more you realize you can accomplish far more if you think in three dimensions."

He pointed his left hand down the hallway and opened his palm. Then, thinking it wise, he took in a little Stormlight. Finally, he used his thumb to flip the little lever and engage the mechanism. Nothing happened.

So far so good, he thought, trying to move his hand right or left. It resisted, held in place. Good.

He eased his hand into a fist, squeezing the bar across his palm, and was immediately pulled through the corridor. He skidded on his heels, and wasn't able to slow himself at all. Those weights really *were* heavy.

Kaladin opened his hand, stopping in place. Because the device was still active, when he lifted his feet off the ground, he stayed in the air. However, this also put an incredible amount of stress on his arm, especially the elbow.

Yes, the device in its current state might be too dangerous for anyone without Stormlight to use. He put his feet back down and tapped the toggle with his thumb to disengage the device, and his arm immediately dropped free. The weight—when he went to check on it—was hanging a little further down into the shaft. As soon as he'd disengaged the device, the brakes had locked, holding the weight in place.

He went out into the hallway, engaged the device, and gripped the bar firmly. That sent him soaring forward. He tucked up his feet, straining—with effort—to keep himself otherwise upright. In that moment, difficult though the exercise was, he felt something come alive in him again. The wind in his hair. His body soaring, claiming the sky, albeit in an imperfect way. He found the experience familiar. Even intuitive.

That lasted right up until the moment when he noticed the quickly approaching far wall. He reacted a little too slowly, first trying to Lash himself backward by instinct. He slammed into the wall hand-first and felt his knuckles *crunch*. The device continued trying to go forward, crushing his mangled hand further, forcing it to keep the bar compressed. The device held him affixed to the wall until he managed to reach over with his other hand and flip the thumb switch, releasing the mechanism and setting him free.

He gasped in pain, sucking the Stormlight from a nearby amethyst on the floor. The healing happened slowly, as it had the other day. The pain was acute; he gritted his teeth while he waited—and split skin, broken by bones, made him bleed on the device, staining its leather.

Syl scowled at the painspren crawling around the floor. "Um, I was wrong. That wasn't particularly funny."

"Sorry," Kaladin said, eyes watering from the pain.

"What happened?"

"Bad instincts," he said. "Not the device's fault. I just forgot what I was doing."

He sat to wait, and he *heard* the joints popping and the bones grinding as the Stormlight reknit him. He'd come to rely on his near-instantaneous healing; this was agony.

It was a good five minutes before he shook out his healed hand and stretched it, good as new, other than some lingering phantom pain. "Right," he said. "I'll want to be more careful. I'm playing with some incredible forces in those weights."

"At least you didn't break the fabrial," Syl said. "Strange as it is to say, it's a lot easier to get you a new hand than a new device."

"True," he said, standing. He launched himself down the hallway back the way he had come, this time maintaining a careful speed, and slowed himself as he neared the other end.

Over the next half hour or so he crashed a few more times, though never as spectacularly as that first one. He needed to be very careful to point his hand straight down the center of the hallway, or else he'd drift to the side and end up scraping across the wall. He also had to be acutely aware of the device, as it was remarkably easy to flip the activation switch accidentally by brushing his hand against something.

He kept practicing, and was able to go back and forth for quite a while before the device stopped working. He lurched to a halt midflight, hanging in the center of the hallway.

He rested his feet on the ground and deactivated the device. The weight he'd been using had hit the bottom. That had lasted him quite a long time—though much of that time had been resetting and moving around. In actual free fall, he probably wouldn't have longer than a few minutes of flight. But if he controlled the weight, using it in short bursts, he could make good use of those minutes.

He wouldn't be soaring about fighting Heavenly Ones in swooping battles with this. But he *could* get an extra burst of speed in a fight, and maybe move in an unexpected direction. Navani intended him to use it as a lift. It would work for that, certainly. And he intended to practice going up and down outside once it was dark.

But Kaladin also saw martial applications. And all in all, the device worked better than he'd expected. So he walked to the end of the hallway to set up again.

"More?" Syl asked.

"You have an appointment or something?" Kaladin asked.

"Just a little bored."

"I could crash into another wall, if you like."

"Only if you promise to be amusing when you do it."

"What? You want me to break more fingers?"

"No." She zipped around him as a ribbon of light. "Breaking your hands isn't very funny. Try a different body part. A funny one."

"I'm going to stop trying to imagine how to manage that," he said, "and get back to work."

"And how long are we going to be doing this decidedly unfunny crashing?"

"Until we don't crash, obviously," Kaladin said. "I had months to train with my Lashings, and longer to prepare for my first fight as a spearman. Judging by how quickly the Fused found the second node, I suspect I'll have only a few days to train on this device before I need to use it."

When the time came—assuming Navani or the Sibling could give him warning—he wanted to be ready. He knew of at least one way to quiet the nightmares, the mounting pressure, and the mental exhaustion. He couldn't do much about his situation, or the cracks that were ever widening inside him.

But he *could* stay busy, and in so doing, not let those cracks define him.

The sand originated offworld. It is only one of such amazing wonders that come from other lands—I have recently obtained a chain from the lands of the dead, said to be able to anchor a person through Cognitive anomalies. I fail to see what use it could be to me, as I am unable to leave the Rosharan system. But it is a priceless object nonetheless.

—From *Rhythm of War*, page 13 undertext

Jasnah had never gone to war. Oh, she'd been *near* to war. She'd stayed behind in mobile warcamps. She'd walked battlefields. She'd fought and killed, and had been part of the Battle of Thaylen Field. But she'd never *gone to war.*

The other monarchs were baffled. Even the soldiers seemed confused as they parted, letting her stride forward among them in her Shardplate. Dalinar, though, had understood. *Until you stand in those lines, holding your sword and facing down the enemy force, you'll never understand. No book could prepare you, Jasnah. So yes, I think you should go.*

A thousand quotes from noted scholars leaped to her mind. Accounts of what it was like to be in war. She'd read hundreds; some so detailed, she'd been able to smell the blood in the air. Yet they all fled like shadows before sunlight as she reached the front of the coalition armies and looked out at the enemy.

Their numbers seemed endless. A fungus on the land ahead, black and white and red, weapons glistening in the sun.

Reports said there were about forty thousand singers here. That was a number she could comprehend, could analyze. But her eyes didn't see forty thousand, they saw *endless* ranks. Numbers on a page became meaningless. She hadn't come to fight forty thousand. She'd come to fight a *tide*.

On paper, this place was the Drunmu Basin in Emul. It was a vast ocean of shivering grass and towering pile-vines. In meetings, the Mink had insisted that a battle here favored the coalition side. If they let the enemy retreat to cities and forts, they could hunker down and make for tough shells to crack. Instead he'd pushed them to a place where they'd feel confident standing in a full battle, as they had a slight advantage in high ground and the sun to their backs. Here they would stand, and the Mink could leverage the coalition's greater numbers and skill to victory.

So logically she understood that this was a battle that her forces wanted. In person, she felt overwhelmed by the distance to the enemy—distance she, with the others, would have to cross under a barrage of enemy arrows and spears. It was hard not to feel small, even in her Plate.

The horns sounded, ordering the advance, and she noted two Edgedancers keeping close to her—likely at her uncle's request. Though she'd always imagined battles beginning with a grand charge, her force moved mechanically. Shields up, in formation, at a solid march that the veteran troops maintained as arrows started falling. Running would break the lines, not to mention leave the soldiers winded when they arrived.

She winced as the first arrows struck. They fell with an arrhythmic series of *snaps,* metal on wood, like hail. One bounced off her shoulder and another skimmed her helm. Fortunately, the arrows were soon interrupted as Azish light cavalry executed a raid on the enemy archers. She heard the hooves, saw the Windrunners soaring overhead, guarding the horsemen from the air. The enemy kept misjudging cavalry, which hadn't been available in significant numbers thousands of years ago.

Through it all, the Alethi troops kept marching forward, shields up. It took an excruciatingly long time, but since Jasnah's side was the aggressor, the enemy had no impetus to meet them. They maintained their position atop their shallow incline. She could see why the enemy would think it wise to stand here, as Jasnah's forces had to make their assault up this hillside.

The enemy resolved into a block of figures in carapace and steel armor, holding large shields and sprouting with pikes several lines deep. These singers did not fight like the Parshendi on the Shattered Plains; these were drilled troops, and the Fused had adapted quickly to modern warfare. They had a slight myopia when it came to cavalry, true, but they knew far better how to most effectively employ their Surgebinders.

By the time Jasnah's block of troops was in position, she felt exhausted from staying at a heightened level of alert during the march. She stopped with the others, grass retreating in a wave before her—as if it could sense the coming fight like it sensed a storm. She had ordered her Plate to intentionally dull its light, so it looked like that of an ordinary Shardbearer. The enemy would still single her out, but not recognize her as the queen. She would be safer this way.

The horns rang out. Jasnah started up the last part of the incline at not quite a run. It was too shallow to be called a hill, and if she'd been out on a walk, she wouldn't have remarked much on the slope. But now she felt it with each step. Her Plate urged her to move, as did the Stormlight she breathed in, but if she ran too far ahead of her block of troops she could be surrounded. The enemy would have Fused and Regals hiding among their ranks, waiting to ambush her. Other than the Heavenly Ones, few Fused chose to meet Shardbearers in direct combat.

Jasnah summoned Ivory as a Blade, the weapon falling into her waiting gauntlets. *Ready?* she asked.

Yes.

She charged the last few feet to the pike block and swept with Ivory. Her job was to break their lines; a full Shardbearer could cause entire formations to crumble around her.

To their credit, this singer formation did not break. It buckled backward, pikes scraping her armor as she tried to get in close and attack, but it held. Her honor guard—along with those two Edgedancers—came in behind to keep her from being surrounded. Nearby, another block of five thousand soldiers hit the enemy. Grunts and crunches sounded in the air.

Holding her Blade in a two-handed grip, Jasnah swept back and forth, cutting free pike heads and trying to strike inward at the enemy.

They moved with unexpected flexibility, singers dancing away, staying out of the range of her sword.

This is less effective, Ivory said to her. *Our other powers* are. *Use them?*

No. I want to know the real feeling of war, Jasnah thought. *Or as close to it as I can allow myself, in Plate with Blade.*

Ever the scholar, Ivory said with a long-suffering tone as Jasnah shouldered past some pikes—which were practically useless against her—and managed to ram her Blade into the chest of a singer. The singer's eyes burned as she fell, and Jasnah ripped the sword around, causing others to curse and shy back.

It wasn't only academics that drove her. If she was going to order soldiers into battle, she needed more than descriptions from books. She needed to *feel* what they felt. And yes, she could use her powers. Soulcasting had proven useful to her in fights before, but without Dalinar, she had limited Stormlight and wanted to conserve it.

She *would* escape to Shadesmar if things went poorly. She wasn't foolish. Yet this knowledge nagged at her as she swept through the formation, keeping the enemy busy. She couldn't ever *truly* feel what it was like to be an unfortunate spearman on the front lines.

She could hear them shouting as the two forces crashed together. The formations seemed so deliberate, and on the grand scale they were careful things. Positioned with a kind of terrible momentum that forced the men at the front to fight. So while the block remained firm, the front lines ground against one another, screaming like steel being bent.

That was a feeling Jasnah would never experience. The weight of a block of soldiers on each side crushing you between them—with no possible escape. Still, she wanted to know what she could. She swept around, forcing more singers back—but others began prodding her with pikes and spears, shoving her to the side, threatening to trip her.

She'd underestimated the effectiveness of those pikes; yes, they were useless for breaking her armor, but they *could* maneuver her like a chull being prodded with poles. She stumbled and felt her first true spike of fear.

Control it. Instead of trying to right herself, she turned her shoulder toward the enemy, turning her off-balance stumble into a rush, crashing out of the enemy ranks near her soldiers. She hadn't killed many of the enemy, but she didn't need to. Their ranks rippled and bowed from her efforts, and her soldiers exploited this. On either side of her, they matched pikes and spears with the enemy—the front row of her soldiers rotating to the back line of the block every ten minutes under the careful orders of the rank commander.

Engulfed by the sounds of war, Jasnah turned toward the enemy, and her honor guard formed up behind her. Then—sweat trickling down her brow—she charged in again. This time when the enemy parted around her, they revealed a hulking creature hidden in their ranks. A Fused with carapace that grew into large axelike protrusions around his hands: one of the Magnified Ones. Fused with the Surge of Progression, which let them grow carapace with extreme precision and speed.

The regular soldiers on both sides kept their distance, forming a pocket of space around the two. Jasnah resisted using her powers. With her Shards, she should be evenly matched against this creature—and her powers would quickly reveal who she was, as there were no other Surgebinders in the coalition army who had their own Plate.

There is another reason you fight, Ivory said, challenging her.

Yes, there was. Instead of confronting that, Jasnah threw herself into the duel, Stormlight raging in her veins. She sheared free one of the Fused's axe-hands, but the other slammed into her and sent her sprawling. She shook her head, resummoning her Blade and sweeping upward as the Fused rammed its hand down. She cut off the axe, but the trunk of the creature's arm slammed against her chest. Carapace grew over her like the roots of a tree, pinning her to the ground.

The Fused stepped away, snapping the carapace free at its elbow, leaving her immobilized. Then he turned as her honor guard distracted him.

Ah, we're getting so much wonderful experience, Ivory said to her. *Delightful.*

Other soldiers came in at Jasnah and began ramming thin pikes through her faceplate. One pierced her eye, making her scream. Stormlight healed her though, and her helm sealed the slit to prevent further attacks. With Stormlight, she didn't need it to breathe anyway. But this, like her quick summoning of her Blade, was a concession. It risked revealing what she was.

She ripped her hand free of the constricting carapace, then used Ivory as a dagger to cut her way out. She rolled free, tripping singers and kicking at their legs to send them sprawling. But as she came out of her roll, that storming Fused lunged in, slamming two axe-hands at her head, cracking the Plate. The helm howled in pain and annoyance, then lapped up her Stormlight to repair itself.

Such fun is, Ivory said. *But of course, Jasnah mustn't use her powers. She wants to play soldier.*

Jasnah growled, going to one knee and punching her fist at the Fused's knee—but it overgrew with carapace right before she connected. Her punch didn't even move the creature. Ivory became a short sword in her hand as she slashed at the Fused—but this exposed her to another hit in the helm, which laid her flat. She groaned, putting one hand against the rock.

Steady stone, a part of her mind thought. *Happy and pleased with its life on the plains.* No, it would resist her requests to change.

Ivory formed as a shield on her arm as the enemy began smashing. Blood on her cheek mixed with sweat; though her eye had healed, the regular soldiers were trying to get at her again, her honor guard doing their best to hold them back.

Fine.

She reached out to the air, which was stagnant and morose today. Draining Stormlight from the gemstones at her waist, she gave it a single command. *Change.* No begging, as she'd tried when younger. Only firmness.

The bored air accepted, and formed into oil all around them. It rained from the sky in a splash, and even appeared in the mouths of fighting soldiers. Her honor guard knew to withdraw at that sign, coughing and stumbling as they stepped back from the fight around her in a ten-yard circle. The enemy soldiers remained in place, cursing and coughing.

Jasnah slammed her fists together—one affixed with steel, the other with flint. Sparks erupted in front of her, and the entire section of the battlefield came alight.

The Magnified One stumbled in shock, and Jasnah leaped at him, forming Ivory into a needle-like Blade that she rammed directly into his chest. Her lunge was on target, and pierced the enemy's gemheart. The Fused toppled backward, eyes burning like the fires around her.

She finished off as many of the enemy soldiers as she could find in the flames. Her helm—transparent as glass from the inside—started to get covered in soot, and soon she had to retreat out of the fire.

Her vision was clear enough to see the horror of the nearby singers as they witnessed a burning Shardbearer explode from the fires, as if from the center of Damnation itself. That fear stunned them as she hit their line like a boulder, working death upon the collapsing ranks. Their corpses fell among the gleeful spren that writhed on the battlefield, exulting in the powerful emotions. Fearspren, painspren, anticipationspren.

She fought like a butcher. Hacking. Kicking. Throwing bodies into the lines to panic the others. Making waves that her soldiers exploited. At one point, something slammed into her from behind, and she assumed she'd have to face another Fused—but it was a dead Windrunner, dropped from the skies above by a passing Heavenly One.

She left the dead man on the bloody ground and returned to the battle. She didn't think of strategy. Strategy was for stuffy tents and calm conversations over wine. She simply killed. Striking until her arms were sluggish despite both armor and Stormlight. Though her troops rotated, she didn't give herself that luxury. How could she? They were struggling and bleeding in a foreign land, for stakes she promised them were important. If she rested, more of them died.

After what seemed like an eternity, she found herself gasping, wiping blood from her helm to see. The helm opened vents on the side, bringing in cool fresh air, and she stumbled, standing alone on the battlefield. Wondering why she'd started breathing again.

Running out of Stormlight, she thought, numb. She looked down at her gauntleted palm, which was stained with orange singer blood. How had she gotten so much on her? She vaguely remembered fighting another Fused, and some Regals, and . . .

And her block of troops was marching up toward the center of the battle, on trumpeted orders that echoed in her head. Horn blasts that meant . . . that meant . . .

Jasnah, Ivory said. *To the side, see what is.*

One of the Edgedancers moved among the fallen, searching for those they could heal. The second stepped up to Jasnah and pressed a large topaz into her hand. He then gestured toward the rear lines.

"I need to do more," Jasnah said.

"Continue in this state," the Edgedancer said, "and you will do more harm than good. More soldiers will die to protect you than you will cost the enemy. Do you want that, Your Majesty?"

That cut through the numbness, and she turned to where he pointed. Reserves formed up there, among standards proclaiming battle commanders and field medic stations.

"You need to rest," the Edgedancer said. "Go."

She nodded, accepting the wisdom and stumbling away from the battlefield. Her honor guard—reduced to half its former size—followed her in an exhausted clot. Shoulders slumped. Faces ashen. How long had it been? She checked the sun.

That can't be, she thought. *Not even two hours?*

The battle had moved away from this region, leaving corpses like fallen branches behind a storm. As she approached, a figure in black broke off from the reserves and hastened through the mess to meet her. What was Wit doing here?

He was trailed by a small group of servants. As they reached her, he snapped his fingers, and the servants rushed forward to towel down Jasnah's armor. She dismissed her helm, opening her face to the air—which felt cold, despite Emul's heat. She left the rest of her armor in place. She didn't dare remove it, in case enemies came hunting her.

Wit proffered a bowl of fruit.

"What is this?" she asked.

"Valet service."

"On the battlefield?"

"A place without much Wit, I agree. Or, I should say, a place that only exists when Wit has failed. Still, I should think I would be welcome. To offer a little perspective."

She sighed, but didn't object further. Most Shardbearers had crews to help keep them fighting. She did need a drink and some more Stormlight.

She found herself staring, however. At . . . well, all of it.

Wit remained quiet. He was expert at knowing when to do that, though admittedly he rarely employed the knowledge.

"I've read about it, you know," she eventually said. "The feeling you get out there. The focus that you need to adopt to cope with it, to keep moving. Simply doing your job. I don't have their training, Wit. I kept getting distracted, or frightened, or confused."

He tapped her hand. The closed left gauntlet, where she held the

Edgedancer's topaz. She stared at it, then drew in the Light. That made her feel better, but not all of her fatigue was physical.

"I'm not the unstoppable force I imagined myself to be," she said. "They know how to deal with Shardbearers; I couldn't bring down a Fused in a fair fight."

"There are no fair fights, Jasnah," Wit said. "There's never been such a thing. The term is a lie used to impose imaginary order on something chaotic. Two men of the same height, age, and weapon will not fight one another fairly, for one will always have the advantage in training, talent, or simple luck."

She grunted. Dalinar wouldn't think much of that statement.

"I know you feel you need to show the soldiers you can fight," Wit said softly. "Prove to them, maybe to yourself, that you are as capable on a battlefield as Dalinar is becoming with a book. This is good, it breaks down barriers—and there will be those wrongheaded men who would not follow you otherwise.

"But take care, Jasnah. Talented or not, you cannot conjure for yourself a lifetime of experienced butchery through force of will. There is no shame in using the powers you have developed. It is not unfair—or rather, it is no more unfair when the most skilled swordsman on the battlefield falls to a stray arrow. Use what you have."

He was right. She sighed, then took a piece of fruit—gripping it delicately between two gauntleted fingers—and took a bite. The cool sweetness shocked her. It belonged to another world. It washed away the taste of ash, renewing her mouth and awakening her hunger. She'd grown that numb after just two hours of fighting? Her uncle had, on campaign, fought for hours on end—day after day.

And he bore those scars, she supposed.

"How goes the battle?" she asked.

"Not sure," Wit said. "But the generals were right; the enemy is determined to stand here. They must think they can win, and so let us perpetuate this pitched battle, rather than forcing us into temperamental skirmishes."

"So why do you sneer?"

"It's not a sneer," he said. "Merely my natural charisma coming through." He nodded to the side, to where a distant hill—small but steep-sided—flashed with light. Thunder cracked the air despite the open sky. Men tried to rush the position, and died by the dozens.

"I think we're coming to the end of traditional battlefield formations," Wit said.

"They served us well today."

"And perhaps will for a time yet," Wit said. "But not forever. Once upon a time, military tactics could depend on breaking enemy positions with enough work. Enough lives. But what do you do when no rush—no number of brave charges—will claim the position you need?"

"I don't know," she said. "But the infantry block has been a stable part of warfare for millennia, Wit. It has adapted with each advance in technology. I don't see it becoming obsolete any time soon."

"We will see. You think your powers are unfair because you slay dozens, and they cannot resist? What happens when a single individual can kill *tens of thousands* in moments—assuming the enemy will kindly bunch up in a neat little pike block. Things will change rapidly when such powers become common."

"They're hardly common."

"I didn't say they were," he said. "Yet."

She took a drink, and finally thought to order her honor guard to rest. Their captain would send in fresh men.

Wit offered to massage her sword hand, but she shook her head. She instead ate another piece of fruit, then some ration sticks he gave her to balance the meal. She accepted a few pouches of spheres as well. But as soon as her fresh honor guard arrived, she marched out in search of a field commander who would know where to best position her.

⁘

Seven hours later, Jasnah tromped across a quiet battlefield, searching for Wit. He'd visited her several times during the fighting, but it had been hours since their last encounter.

She hiked through the remnants of the battle, feeling an odd solitude. As darkness smothered the land, she could almost pretend the scattered lumps were rockbuds, not bodies. The scents, unfortunately, did not go away with the light. And they remained a signal, defiant as any banner, of what had happened here. Blood. The stench of burning bodies.

In the end, loss and victory smelled the same.

They sounded different though. Cheers drifted on the wind. Human voices, with an edge to them. These weren't cheers of joy, more cheers of relief.

She made for a particular beacon of light, the tent with an illuminated set of coalition flags flying at the same height, one for each kingdom. Inside, she'd be welcomed as a hero. When she arrived, however, she didn't feel like entering. So she settled down on a stone outside within sight of the guards, who were wise enough not to run and fetch anyone. She sat for some time and stared out at the battlefield, figuring Wit would locate her eventually.

"Daunting, isn't it?" a voice asked from the darkness.

She narrowed her eyes, and searched around until she found the source: a small man sitting nearby, throwing sparks from his Herdazian sparkflicker in the night. Each burst of light illuminated the Mink's fingers and face.

"Yes," Jasnah said. "'Daunting' is the right word. More so than I'd anticipated."

"You made a wise choice, going out there," the Mink said. "Regardless of what the others said. It's too easy to forget the cost. Not only to the boys who die, but to the ones who live. Every commander should be reminded periodically."

"How did we do?"

"We broke the core of their strength," he said. "Which is what we wanted—though it wasn't a rout. We'll need another battle or two on nearly this scale before I can tell you if we've really won or not. But today was a step forward. Do that often enough, and you'll inevitably cross the finish line."

"Casualties?"

"Never take casualty reports on the night of the battle, Brightness," he said. "Give yourself a little time to enjoy the meal before you look at the bill."

"*You* don't seem to be enjoying yourself."

"Ah, but I am," he said. "I am staring at the open sky, and wearing no chains." He stood up, a shadow against the darkness. "I'll tell the others I've seen you, and that you are well, if you'd rather retreat to your tent. Your Wit is there, and unless I misunderstand, something has disturbed him."

She gave the Mink her thanks and stood. Wit was disturbed? The implications of that harried her as she marched through the frontline warcamp to her tent. Inside, Wit sat at her travel table, scribbling furiously. So far, she'd caught him writing in what she thought were five different alien scripts, though he didn't often answer questions about where they had originated.

Today, he snapped his notebook closed and plastered a smile on his face.

She trusted him, mostly. And he her, mostly. Other aspects of their relationship were more complicated.

"What is it, Wit?" she said.

"My dear, you should rest before—"

"*Wit.*"

He sighed, then leaned back in his seat. He was immaculate, as always, with his perfectly styled hair and sharp black suit. For all his talk of frivolity, he knew exactly how to present himself. It was something they'd bonded over.

"I have failed you," he said. "I thought I'd taken all necessary precautions, but I found a pen in my writing case that did not work."

"So . . . what? Is this a trick, Wit?"

"One played on me, I'm afraid," he said. "The pen was *not* a pen, but a creature designed to appear like a pen. A cremling, you'd call it, cleverly grown to the shape of something innocent."

She grew cold, and stepped forward, her Plate clinking. "One of the Sleepless?"

He nodded.

"How much do you think it heard?"

"I'm uncertain. I don't know when it replaced my real pen, and I'm baffled how my protections—which are supposed to warn me of entities like this—were circumvented."

"Then we have to assume they know everything," Jasnah said. "All of our secrets."

"Unfortunately," Wit said. He sighed, then pushed his notebook toward her. "I'm writing warnings to those I communicated with. The bright side is that I don't *think* any of the Sleepless are working with Odium."

Jasnah had only recently learned that the Sleepless were anything other than a myth. It had taken meeting a friendly one—seeing with her own eyes that an entity could somehow be made up of thousands of cremlings working in concert—for her to accept their existence.

"If it's not working for the enemy, then who?" she asked.

"Well, I've written to my contacts among them, to ask if it is one of theirs keeping a friendly eye on amiable allies. But . . . Jasnah, I know at least one of them has thrown their lot in with the Ghostbloods."

"Damnation."

"I believe it is time," Wit said, "that I told you about Thaidakar."

"I know of him," Jasnah said.

"Oh, you think you do," he said. "But I've *met* him, several times. On other planets, Jasnah. The Ghostbloods are not a Rosharan organization, and I don't think you appreciate the danger they present. . . ."

As we dig further into this project, I am left questioning the very nature of God. How can a God exist in all things, yet have a substance that can be destroyed?

—From *Rhythm of War*, page 21

L ight was far more interesting than Navani had realized.

It constantly surrounded them, flooding in through windows and beaming from gemstones. A second ocean, white and pure, so omnipresent it became invisible.

Navani was able to order texts brought from Kholinar, ones she'd presumed lost to the conquest. She was able to get others from around the tower, and there were even a few with relevant chapters already here in the library room. All were collected at Raboniel's order and delivered, without question, to Navani for study.

She consumed the words. Locked away as she was, she couldn't do much else. Each day she wrote mundane instructions to her scholars— and hid ciphered messages within them that equated to nonsense. Rushu would know what she was doing from context, but the Fused? Well, let them waste their time trying to figure out a reason to the figgldygrak she wrote. Their confusion might help her slip through important messages later.

That didn't take much time, and she spent the rest of her days studying light. Surely there could be no *harm* in her learning, as Raboniel wanted. And the topic was so fascinating.

What *was* light? Not just Stormlight, but all light. Some of the ancient scholars claimed you could measure it. They said it had a *weight* to it. Others disagreed, saying instead that it was the *force* by which light moved that one could measure.

Both ideas fascinated her. She'd never thought of light as a thing. It simply . . . was.

Excited, she performed an old experiment from her books: splitting apart light into a rainbow of colors. All you had to do was put a candle in a box, use a hole to focus the light, then direct it through a prism. Then, curious, she extrapolated and—after several attempts—was able to use *another* prism to recombine the component colors into a beam of pure white light.

Next, she used a diamond infused with Stormlight instead of a candle. It worked the same, splitting into components of light, but with a larger band of blue. Voidlight did the same, though the band of violet was enormous, and the other colors mere blips. That was strange, as her research indicated different colors of light should only make bands brighter or weaker, not increase their size.

The most interesting result happened when she tried the experiment on the Towerlight Raboniel had collected. It wasn't Stormlight *or* Lifelight, but a combination of the two. When she tried the prism experiment with this light, *two separate* rainbows of colors—distinct from one another—split out of the prism.

She couldn't recombine them. When she tried sending the colors through another prism, she ended up with one beam of white-blue light and a separate beam of white-green light, overlapping but not combined as Towerlight was.

She sat at the table, staring at the two dots of light on the white paper. That green one. Could it be Lifelight? She likely couldn't have told the difference between it and Stormlight, without the two to compare—it was only next to one another that Stormlight looked faintly blue, and Lifelight faintly green.

She stood up and dug through the trunk of personal articles she'd had Raboniel's people fetch for her, looking for her journals. The day of

Gavilar's death was still painful to remember, fraught with a dozen different conflicting emotions. She'd recorded her impressions of that day's events six separate times, in differing emotional states. Sometimes she missed him. At least the man he had once been, when they'd all schemed together as youths, planning to conquer the world.

That was the face he'd continued to show most everyone else after he'd started to change. And so, for the good of the kingdom, Navani had played along. She'd created a grand charade after his death, writing about Gavilar the king, the unifier, the mighty—but just—man. The ideal monarch. She'd given him exactly what he'd wanted, exactly what she'd threatened to withhold. She'd given him a legacy.

Navani closed the journal around her finger to hold her place, then took a few deep breaths. She couldn't afford to become distracted by that tangled mess of emotions. She reopened the journal and turned to the account she'd made of her encounter with Gavilar in her study on the day of his death.

He had spheres on the table, she had written. *Some twenty or thirty of them. He'd been showing them to his uncommon visitors—most of whom have vanished, never to be seen again.*

There was something off about those spheres. My eyes were drawn to several distinctive ones: spheres that glowed with a distinctly alien light, almost negative. Both violet and black, somehow shining, yet feeling like they should extinguish illumination instead of promote it.

Navani reread the passages, then inspected the pale green light she had split out of the Towerlight. Lifelight, the Light of Cultivation. Could Gavilar have had this Light too? Could she have mistaken Lifelight diamonds for emeralds? Or, would Lifelight in a gemstone appear identical to a Stormlight one at a casual glance?

"Why wouldn't you *talk* to me, Gavilar?" she whispered. "Why wasn't I worth trusting. . . ." She braced herself, then read further in her account—right up to the point where Gavilar plunged the knife in the deepest.

You aren't worthy. That's why, she read. *You claim to be a scholar, but where are your discoveries? You study light, but you are its opposite. A thing that destroys light. You spend your time wallowing in the muck of the kitchens and obsessing about whether or not some lighteyes recognizes the correct lines on a map.*

Storms. That was so painful.

She forced herself to linger on his words. *You are its opposite. A thing that destroys light* . . .

Gavilar had spoken of the same concept as Raboniel, of light and its opposite. Coincidence? Did it have to do with that sphere that bent the air?

The guard at her door began humming, then stepped to the side. Navani could guess what that meant. Indeed, Raboniel soon entered, followed by that other Fused who was so often nearby. The femalen with a similar topknot and skin pattern, but a blank stare. Raboniel seemed to like to keep her near, though Navani wasn't certain if it was for protection or for some other reason. The second Fused was one of the more . . . unhinged that Navani had seen. Perhaps the more sane ones purposely kept an eye on specific insane ones, to prevent them from hurting themselves or others.

The insane Fused walked over to the wall and stared at it. Raboniel walked toward the desk, so Navani rose and bowed to her. "Ancient One. Is something wrong?"

"Merely checking on your progress," Raboniel said. Navani made room so Raboniel could bend down, the orange-red hair of her topknot brushing the table as she inspected Navani's experiment: a box letting out the illumination from a Towerlight gemstone, which was split through a prism, then recombined through another into two separate streams of light.

"Incredible," Raboniel said. "This is what you do when you experiment, instead of fighting against me? Look, Stormlight *and* Lifelight. As I said."

"Yes, Ancient One," Navani said. "I've been reading about light. The illumination that comes from the sun or candles cannot be stored in gemstones, but Stormlight can. So what *is* Stormlight? It is not simply illumination, as it gives *off* illumination.

"It's as if Stormlight is at times a liquid. It behaves like one when you draw it from a full gemstone into an empty one, mimicking osmosis. While captured, the illumination given off by Stormlight behaves like sunlight: it can be split by a prism, and diffuses the farther it gets from its source. But the Stormlight must be different from the illumination it radiates. Otherwise, how could we hold it in a gemstone?"

"Can you combine them?" Raboniel asked. "Stormlight and Void-light, can they be mixed?"

"To prove that humans and singers can be unified," Navani said.

"Yes, of course. For that reason."

She's lying, Navani thought. She couldn't be certain, as singers often acted in strange ways, but Navani suspected more here.

The strange insane Fused began saying something in their language. She stared up at the wall, then said it louder.

Raboniel glanced at her, hummed softly, then looked at Navani. "Have you discovered anything more?"

"That's about it," Navani said. "I couldn't get Lifelight and Stormlight to recombine, but I don't know if this counts as truly splitting them apart—as I've only split their radiation, not the pooled Light itself."

"I've thought about your mixing of oil and water, and I am intrigued. We need to know. Can Stormlight and Voidlight be mixed? What would happen if they were combined?"

"You are quite focused on that idea, Ancient One," Navani said, thoughtfully leaning back. "Why?"

"It's why I came here," Raboniel said.

"Not to conquer? You talk of peace between us. What would that alliance be like, to you, if we could achieve it?"

Raboniel hummed a rhythm and opened Navani's box, taking out the sphere of Towerlight. "The war has stretched so long, I've seen this kind of tactic play out dozens of times. We have never held the tower before, true, but we've seized Oathgates, taken command posts, and held the capital of Alethela a couple of times. All part of an eternal, endless slog of a war. I want to end it. I *need* to find the tools to *truly* end it, for all of our . . . sanity."

"End how?" Navani pressed. "If we work together like you want, what happens to my people?"

Raboniel turned the Towerlight sphere over in her fingers, ignoring the question. "We've known about this new Light ever since the tower was created—but I am the one who theorized it was Stormlight and Lifelight combined. You have confirmed this. This *is* proof. Proof that what I want to do is possible."

"Have you ever heard of spheres that *warp* the air around them?" Navani asked. "Like they were extremely hot?"

Raboniel's rhythm cut off. She turned toward Navani. "Where did you hear of such a thing?"

"I remembered a conversation about it," Navani lied, "from long ago—with someone who claimed to have seen one."

"There are theories," Raboniel said. "Matter has its opposite: negative axi that destroy positive axi when combined. This is known, and confirmed by the Shards Odium *and* Honor. So some have thought . . . is there a negative to light? An anti-light? I had discarded this idea. After all, I assumed that if there was an opposite to Stormlight, it would be Voidlight."

"Except," Navani said, "we have no reason to believe that Stormlight and Voidlight are opposites. Tell me, what would happen if this theoretical negative light were to combine with its positive?"

"Destruction," Raboniel said. "Instantaneous annihilation."

Navani felt cold. She'd told her scholars—the ones to whom she'd entrusted Szeth's strange sphere—to experiment with the air-warping light. To move it to different gemstones, to try using it in fabrials. Could it be that . . . they'd somehow mixed that sphere's contents with ordinary Voidlight?

"Continue your experiments," Raboniel said, putting down the sphere. "Anything you need for your science shall be yours. If you can combine Voidlight and Stormlight without destroying them—therefore proving they are *not* opposites . . . well, I should like to know this. It will require me to discard years upon years of theories."

"I have no idea where to begin," Navani protested. "If you let me have my team back . . ."

"Write them instructions and put them to work," Raboniel said. "You have them still."

"Fine," Navani said, "but I have *no idea* what I'm doing. If I were trying to do this with liquids, I'd use an emulsifier—but what kind of emulsifier does one use on *light*? It defies reason."

"Try anyway," Raboniel said. "Do this, and I'll free your tower. I'll take my troops and walk away. This knowledge is worth more than any one location, no matter how strategic."

I'm sure, Navani thought. She didn't believe for a single heartbeat that Raboniel would do so—but at the same time, this knowledge would obviously give Navani an edge. Why did Raboniel want to prove, or disprove, that the two Lights were opposites? What *was* her game here?

She wants a weapon, perhaps? That explosion I inadvertently caused? Is that what Raboniel is hunting?

The Fused by the wall started talking again, louder this time. Again Raboniel hummed and glanced over.

"What does she say?" Navani asked.

"She . . . asks if anyone has seen her mother. She's trying to get the wall to talk."

"Her mother?" Navani thought, cocking her head. She hadn't thought that the Fused would have parents—but of course they did. The creatures had been born mortal, thousands of years ago. "What happened to her mother?"

"She's right here," Raboniel said softly, gesturing to herself. "That was another hypothesis of mine that was disproven. Long ago. The thought that a mother and daughter, serving together, might help one another retain their sanity."

Raboniel walked to her daughter and turned her to steer her out the door. And while singers tended not to show emotion on their faces, Navani thought for sure she could read pain in Raboniel's expression—a wince—as the daughter continued to ask for her mother. All the while staring unseeingly past her.

BEARER OF AGONIES

I am not convinced any of the gods can be destroyed, so perhaps I misspoke. They can change state however, like a spren—or like the various Lights. This is what we seek.

—From *Rhythm of War*, page 21 undertext

Dalinar touched his finger to the young soldier's forehead, then closed his eyes and concentrated.

He could see something extending from the soldier, radiating into the darkness. Pure white lines, thin as a hair. Some moved, though one end remained affixed to the central point: the place where Dalinar's finger touched the soldier's skin.

"I see them," he whispered. "Finally."

The Stormfather rumbled in the back of his mind. *I was not certain it could be done,* he said. *The power of Bondsmiths was tempered by Honor, for the good of all. Ever since the destruction of Ashyn.*

"How did you know about this ability?" Dalinar said, eyes still closed.

I heard it described before I fully lived. Melishi saw these lines.

"The last Bondsmith," Dalinar said. "Before the Recreance."

The same. Honor was dying, possibly mad.

"What can I do with these?" Dalinar asked.

I don't know. You see the Connections all people have: to others, to spren, to time and reality itself. Everything is Connected, Dalinar, by a vast web of interactions, passions, thoughts, fates.

The more Dalinar watched the quivering white lines, the more details he could pick out. Some were brighter than others, for example. He reached out and tried to touch one, but his fingers went through it.

Spren have these too, the Stormfather said. *And the bond that makes Radiants is similar, but far stronger. I don't think these little ones are particularly useful.*

"Surely these mean something," Dalinar said.

Yes, the Stormfather said. *But that doesn't mean they can be exploited. I heard Melishi say something once. Imagine you had two pieces of cloth, one red, one yellow. Before you and your brother parted, you each reached into a bag and selected one—but kept it hidden, putting it away in a box, unseen.*

You parted, traveling to distant quarters of the land. Then, by agreement, let us say that on the same day at the same time you each opened your box and took out your cloth. Upon finding the red one, you'd instantly know your brother had found the yellow one. You shared something, that bond of knowledge—the Connection exists, but isn't something that can necessarily be exploited. At least not by most people. A Bondsmith though . . .

Dalinar removed his finger and opened his eyes, then thanked the young soldier—who seemed nervous as he returned to his place near the front of the building, joining the still-disguised Szeth. Dalinar checked his arm fabrial. Jasnah and the others should be returning from the front lines soon. The battle won, the celebrations completed. All without Dalinar.

It felt so strange. Here he was, worried about Navani and the tower—but unable to do anything until he had more information. Worried about Adolin off in Shadesmar—separated from him, like the two brothers in the Stormfather's story. Shared destinies, shared fates, yet Dalinar felt powerless to help either his son or his wife.

You do have a part in this, he told himself firmly. *A duty. Master these powers. Best Odium. Think on a scale bigger than one battle, or even one war.* It was difficult, with how slowly his skills seemed to be progressing. So much time wasted. Was this what Jasnah had experienced all those years, chasing secrets when nobody else had believed her?

He had another duty today, in addition to his practice. He'd been putting it off, but he knew he should delay no longer. So, he collected Szeth and walked through the camp, turning his path toward the prison.

He needed to talk to Taravangian in person.

The building that housed the former king was not a true prison. They hadn't planned for one of those in the temporary warcamp here in Emul. A stockade, yes. But military discipline was by necessity quick. Anything demanding more than a week or two in confinement usually resulted in a discharge or—for more serious infractions—an execution.

Taravangian required something more permanent and more delicate. So they'd blocked off the windows on a sturdy home, reinforced the door, and set guards from among Dalinar's best soldiers. As Dalinar approached, he noted how the upper-floor windows were now filled with stark crem bricks, mortared into place. It had felt wrong to give Taravangian a home instead of a cell—but seeing those windows, it also felt wrong to leave him without sunlight.

Dalinar nodded to the salutes at the door, then waited for the guards to undo the locks and pull the door open for him. Nobody worried about his safety or made a comment about his single guard. They all thought the precautions were to prevent Taravangian from being rescued, and would never have wondered whether the Blackthorn could handle himself against an elderly statesman.

They didn't have any inkling, even now, how dangerous Taravangian was. He sat on a stool near the far wall of the main room. He'd put a ruby into the corner and was staring at it. He turned when Dalinar entered, and actually smiled. Storming man.

Dalinar waved for Szeth to remain right inside the door as the guards closed and locked it behind them. Then Dalinar approached the corner, wary. He'd charged into many a battle with less trepidation than he now felt.

"I had wondered if you would come," Taravangian said. "It has been nearly two weeks since my betrayal."

"I wanted to be certain I wasn't somehow being manipulated," Dalinar said, honestly. "So I waited until certain tasks were accomplished before coming to you, and risking letting you influence me."

Though, deep down, Dalinar admitted that was mostly an excuse. Seeing this man was painful. Perhaps he should have let Jasnah interrogate Taravangian, as she'd suggested. But that seemed the coward's route.

"Ah, certain tasks are accomplished, then?" the old man asked. "By now you've surely recovered from the betrayal of the Veden armies. You've clashed with Odium's forces in Emul? I warned Odium that we should have moved earlier, but he was adamant, you see. This was the way he wanted it to happen."

The frankness of it felt like a boot directly to Dalinar's gut. He steeled himself. "That stool is too uncomfortable for a man of your years. You should be given a chair. I thought they'd left the building furnished. Do you have a bed? And surely they gave you more than a single sphere for light."

"Dalinar, Dalinar," Taravangian whispered. "If you wish me to have comfort, don't ask after the chair or the light. Answer my questions and talk to me. I need that more than—"

"Why?" Dalinar interrupted. He held Taravangian's gaze, and was shocked at how much asking the question *hurt*. He'd known the betrayal was coming. He'd known what this man was. Nevertheless, the words were *agonizing* as they slipped from his lips again. "Why? *Why* did you do it?"

"Because, Dalinar, you're going to lose. I'm sorry, my friend. It is unavoidable."

"You can't know that."

"Yet I do." He sagged in his seat, turning toward the corner and the glowing sphere. "Such a poor imitation of our comfortable sitting room in Urithiru. Even that was a poor imitation of a real hearth, crackling with true flames, alive and beautiful. An imitation of an imitation.

"That's what we are, Dalinar. A painting made from another painting of something great. Perhaps the ancient Radiants could have won this fight, when Honor lived. They didn't. They barely *survived*. Now we face a god. Alone. There is no victory awaiting us."

Dalinar felt . . . cold. Not shocked. Not surprised. He supposed he could have figured out Taravangian's reasoning; they'd talked often about what it meant to be a king. The discussions had grown more intense, more meaningful, once Dalinar had realized what Taravangian had done to acquire the throne of Jah Keved. Once he'd known that—instead of chatting with a kindly old man with strange ideals—he had been talking to another murderer. A man like Dalinar himself.

Now he felt disappointed. Because in the end, Taravangian had let that side of him rule. No longer on the edge. His friend—yes, they were friends—had stepped off the cliff.

"We *can* defeat him, Taravangian," Dalinar said. "You are not nearly so smart as you think."

"I agree. I was once, though." He clarified, perhaps noticing Dalinar's confusion. "I visited the Old Magic, Dalinar. I saw her. Not just the Nightwatcher, I suspect, but the other one. The one you saw."

"Cultivation," he said. "There *is* one who can face Odium. There were *three* gods."

"She won't fight him," Taravangian said. "She knows. How do you think I found out we'd lose?"

"She told you that?" Dalinar strode forward, squatting down beside Taravangian, coming to eye level with the aged man. "She *said* Odium would win?"

"I asked her for the capacity to stop what was coming," Taravangian said. "And she made me brilliant, Dalinar. Transcendently brilliant, but just once. For a day. I vary, you know. Some days I'm smart, but my emotions seem stunted—I don't feel anything but annoyance. Other days I'm stupid, but the tiniest bit of sentimentality sends me into tears. Most days I'm like I am today. Some shade of average.

"Only one day of brilliance. One *single* day. I've often wished I'd get another, but I guess that was all that Cultivation wanted me to have. She wanted me to see for myself. There *was* no way to save Roshar."

"You saw no possible out?" Dalinar said. "Tell me honestly. Was there absolutely no way to win?"

Taravangian fell silent.

"Nobody can see the future perfectly," Dalinar said. "Not even Odium. I find it impossible to believe that you, no matter how smart, could have been *absolutely* certain there was no path to victory."

"Let's say you were in my place," Taravangian said. "You saw a shadow of the future, the best anyone has ever seen it. Better, in fact, than any mortal could achieve. And you saw a path to saving Alethkar—everyone you love, everything you know. You saw a very plausible, very reasonable opportunity to accomplish this goal.

"But you also saw that to do more—to save the world itself—you would have to rely on such wild bets as to be ludicrous. And if you failed at those very, very, *very* long odds, you'd lose everything. Tell *me* honestly, Dalinar. Would you not consider doing what I did, taking the rational choice of saving the few?" Taravangian's eyes glistened. "Isn't that the way of the soldier? Accept your losses, and do what you can?"

"So you sold us out? You helped *hasten* our destruction?"

"For a price, Dalinar," Taravangian said, staring again at the ruby that was the room's hearth. "I *did* preserve Kharbranth. I tried, I promise you, to protect more. But it is as the Radiants say. Life before death. I saved the lives of as many as I could—"

"Don't use that phrase," Dalinar said. "Don't sully it, Taravangian, with your crass justifications."

"Still standing on your high tower, Dalinar?" Taravangian asked. "Proud of how far you can see, when you won't look past your own feet? Yes, you're very noble. How *wonderful* you are, fighting until the end, dragging every human to death with you. They can all die knowing you never compromised."

"I made an oath," Dalinar said, "to protect the people of Alethkar. It was my oath as a highprince. After that, a greater oath—the oath of a Radiant."

"And is that how you protected the Alethi years ago, Dalinar? When you burned them alive in their cities?"

Dalinar drew in a sharp breath, but refused to rise to that barb. "I'm not that man any longer. I changed. I take the next step, Taravangian."

"I suppose that is true, and my statement was a useless gibe. I wish you *were* that man who would burn one city to preserve the kingdom. I could work with that man, Dalinar. Make him see."

"See that I should turn traitor?"

"Yes. As you live now, *protecting* people isn't your true ideal. If that were the case, you'd surrender. No, your *true* ideal is never giving up. No matter the cost. You realize the pride in that sentiment?"

"I refuse to accept that we've lost," Dalinar said. "That's the problem with *your* worldview, Taravangian. You gave up before the battle started. You think you're smart enough to know the future, but I repeat: *Nobody* knows for certain what will happen."

Strangely, the older man nodded. "Yes, yes perhaps. I could be wrong. That would be wonderful, wouldn't it, Dalinar? I'd die happy, knowing I was wrong."

"Would you?" Dalinar said.

Taravangian considered. Then he turned abruptly—a motion that caused Szeth to jump, stepping forward, hand on his sword. Taravangian, however, was just turning to point at a nearby stool for Dalinar to sit.

Taravangian glanced at Szeth briefly and hesitated. Dalinar thought he caught a narrowing of the man's eyes. Damnation. He'd figured it out.

The moment was over in a second. "That stool," Taravangian said, pointing again. "I carried it down from upstairs. In case you visited. Would you join me here, sitting as we once did? For old times' sake?"

Dalinar frowned. He didn't want to take the seat out of principle, but that *was* prideful. He would sit with this man one last time. Taravangian was one of the few people who truly understood what it felt like to make the choices that Dalinar had. Dalinar pulled over the stool and settled down.

"I *would* die happily," Taravangian said, "if I could see that I was wrong. If you won."

"I don't think you would. I don't think you could stand not being the one who saved us."

"How little you know me, despite it all."

"You didn't come to me, or any of us," Dalinar said. "You say you were extremely smart? You figured out what was going to happen? What was your response? It wasn't to form a coalition; it wasn't to refound the Radiants. It was to send out an assassin, then seize the throne of Jah Keved."

"So I would be in a position to negotiate with Odium."

"That argument is crem, Taravangian. You didn't need to murder people—you didn't need to be king of Jah Keved—to accomplish any of this. You *wanted* to be an emperor. You made a play for Alethkar too. You sent Szeth to kill me, instead of talking to me."

"Pardon, Blackthorn, but please remember the man you were when I began this. He would not have listened to me."

"You're so smart you can predict who will win a war before it begins, but you couldn't see that I was changing? You couldn't see that I'd be more valuable as an ally than as a corpse?"

"I thought you would fall, Dalinar. I predicted you would join Odium, if left alive. Either that or you would fight my every step. Odium thought the same."

"And you were both wrong," Dalinar said. "So your grand plan, your masterful 'vision' of the future was simply *wrong*."

"I . . . I . . ." Taravangian rubbed his brow. "I don't have the intelligence right now to explain it to you. Odium will arrange things so that no matter what choice you make, he will win. Knowing that, I made the difficult decision to save at least one city."

"I think you saw a chance to be an emperor, and you took it," Dalinar said. "You wanted power, Taravangian—so you could give it up. You wanted to be the glorious king who sacrificed himself to protect everyone else. You have always seen yourself as the man who must bear the *burden* of leading."

"Because it's true."

"Because you like it."

"If so, why did I let go? Why am I captured here?"

"Because you want to be known as the one who saved us."

"No," Taravangian said. "It's because I knew my friends and family could escape if I let you take me. I knew that your wrath would come upon me, not Kharbranth. And as I'm sure you've discovered, those who knew what I was doing are no longer involved in the city's government. If you were to attack Kharbranth, you would attack innocents."

"I'd never do that."

"Because you have me. Admit it."

Storm him, it was true—and it made Dalinar angry enough to draw a single boiling angerspren at his feet. He had no interest in retribution against Kharbranth. They, like the Vedens—like Dalinar himself—had all been pawns in Taravangian's schemes.

"I know it is difficult to accept," Taravangian said. "But my goal has never been power. It has always *only* been about saving whomever I could save."

"I can't debate that, as I don't know your heart, Taravangian," Dalinar said. "So instead I'll tell you something I know for certain. It *could* have gone differently. You could have truly joined with us. Storms . . . I can imagine a world where you said the oaths. I imagine you as a better leader than I ever could have been. I feel like you were so close."

"No, my friend," Taravangian said. "A monarch cannot make such oaths and expect to be able to keep them. He must realize that a greater need might arise at any time."

"If so, it's impossible for a king to be a moral man."

"Or perhaps you can be moral and still break oaths."

"No," Dalinar said. "No, oaths are part of what *define* morality, Taravangian. A good man must strive to accomplish the things he's committed to do."

"Spoken like a true son of Tanavast," Taravangian said, clasping his hands. "And I believe you, Dalinar. I believe you think exactly what you say. You *are* a man of Honor, raised to it through a life of his religion— which you might be upending, but it retains its grip on your mind.

"I wish I could commend that. Perhaps there *was* another way out of this. Perhaps there *was* another solution. But it wouldn't be found in your oaths, my friend. And it would not involve a coalition of noble leaders. It would involve the sort of business with which you were once so familiar."

"No," Dalinar said. "There is a *just* way to victory. The methods must match the ideal to be obtained."

Taravangian nodded, as if this were the inevitable response. Dalinar sat back on his seat, and they sat in silence together for a time, watching the tiny ruby. He hated how this had gone, how the argument forced him into the most dogmatic version of his beliefs. He knew there was nuance in every position, yet . . .

Aligning his methods and his goals was at the very soul of what he'd learned. What he was trying to become. He had to believe there was a way to lead while still being moral.

He stared at that ruby, that glimmer of red light, reminiscent of an Everstorm's lightning. Dalinar had come here expecting a fight, but was surprised to realize he felt more sorrow than he did anger. He felt Taravangian's pain, his regret for what had occurred. What they had both lost.

Dalinar finally stood up. "You always said that to be a king was to accept pain."

"To accept that you must do what others cannot," Taravangian agreed. "To bear the agonies of the decisions you *had* to make, so that others may live pure lives. You should know that I have said my good-byes and intentionally made myself worthless to Odium and my former compatriots. You will not be able to use my life to bargain with anyone."

"Why tell me this?" Dalinar said. "You would make it worthless to keep you prisoner. Do you *want* to be executed?"

"I simply want to be clear with you," Taravangian said. "There is no further reason for me to try to manipulate you, Dalinar. I have achieved what I wanted. You may kill me."

"No, Taravangian," Dalinar said. "You have lived your convictions, however misguided they may be. Now I'm going to live mine. And at the end, when I face Odium and win, you will be there. I'll give you this gift."

"The pain of knowing I was wrong?"

"You told me earlier that you *wished* to be proven wrong. If you're sincere—and this was never about being right or about gaining power—then on that day we can embrace, knowing it is all over. Old friend."

Taravangian looked at him, and there were tears in his eyes. "To that day, then," he whispered. "And to that embrace."

Dalinar nodded and withdrew, collecting Szeth at the door. He paused briefly to tell the guards to bring Taravangian some more light and a comfortable chair.

As they walked away, Szeth spoke from behind him. "Do not trust his lies. He pretends to be done plotting, but there is more to him. There is *always* more to that one."

Dalinar glanced at the stoic bodyguard. Szeth so rarely offered opinions.

"I don't trust him," Dalinar said. "I can't walk away from any conversation with that man, no matter how innocent, without going over and over what he said. That's part of why I was so hesitant to go in there."

"You are wise," Szeth said, and seemed to consider the conversation finished.

> *Do not mourn for what has happened. This notebook was a dream we shared, which is itself a beautiful thing. Proof of the truth of my intent, even if the project was ultimately doomed.*
>
> —From *Rhythm of War*, page 27

Venli scrambled through the hallways of Urithiru. She shoved past a group of humans who were too slow to get out of the way, then pulled to a halt, breathing heavily as she looked out onto the balcony.

That song . . . That song reminded her of her mother's voice.

But it wasn't her, of course. The femalen who sat by the balcony—weaving a mat and singing to Peace—was not Jaxlim. Her red skin pattern was wrong, her hairstrands too short. Venli leaned against the stone doorway as others on the balcony noticed her, and the femalen's voice cut off. She glanced toward Venli and began to hum to Anxiety.

Venli turned and walked away, attuning Disappointment. Hopefully she hadn't frightened the people. A Regal looking so wild must have given them a scare.

Timbre pulsed inside her.

"I keep hearing her songs," Venli said. "In the voices of people I pass.

I keep remembering those days when I sang with her. I miss those days, Timbre. Life was so simple then."

Timbre pulsed to the Lost.

"She didn't have much sense left when my betrayal came," Venli explained to the spren's question. "Part of me thinks that a mercy, as she never knew. About me . . . Anyway it was the storms that eventually killed her. She was with the group that escaped, but they fled into the chasms. And then . . . we did what we did. The flood that came upon the Plains that day . . . Timbre, she drowned down there. Dead by my hand as surely as if I'd stabbed her."

The little spren pulsed again, consoling. She felt Venli couldn't *completely* be blamed for what she'd done, as the forms had influenced her mind. But Venli had *chosen* those forms.

She often thought back to those early days, after releasing Ulim. Yes, her emotions had changed. She'd pursued her ambition more and more. But at the same time, she hadn't responded like Eshonai, who had seemed to become a different person entirely when adopting a form of power. Venli seemed more resistant somehow. More herself, regardless of form.

That should have made her attune Joy, for she could only guess this had helped her escape Odium's grip. But it also made her responsible for what she'd done. She couldn't blame it on spren or forms. She'd been there, giving those orders.

Timbre pulsed. *I helped.* And . . . yes, she had. When she'd first appeared, Venli had grown stronger, more able to resist.

"Thank you," Venli said. "For that, and for what you continue to do. I'm not worthy of your faith. But thank you."

Timbre pulsed. Today was the day. Raboniel was spending all her time with Navani, and seemed to be thoroughly enjoying the difficulty of manipulating the former queen. That left Venli free. She'd secured a small sack of gemstones, some with Voidlight, some with Stormlight.

Today she was going to see what it *really* meant to be on this path of Radiance.

She'd already selected an area in which to practice. During morning reports, Venli had learned the Pursuer's scouts were carefully combing the fifteenth floor. The majority of Raboniel's soldiers were busy watching the humans, and didn't often venture to the higher floors. So Venli had chosen a place on the eighth floor—a place that the Pursuer had already searched, but that was far from population centers.

The tower up here was silent, and oddly reminded her of the chasms in the Shattered Plains. Those stone pits had also been a place where the sun was difficult to remember—and also a place resplendent with beautiful stone.

She ran her fingers across a wall, expecting to feel bumps from the vibrant strata lines, but it was smooth. Like the walls of the chasms, actually. Her mother had died in those pits. Likely terrified, unable to understand what was happening as the water rushed in and . . .

Venli attuned the Lost and put down her small sack of spheres. She took out a Stormlight one first, then glimpsed into Shadesmar. She hadn't again seen the Voidspren she'd spotted near Rlain's cell, though she'd watched carefully these last few days. She'd eventually put Rlain together with the surgeon and his wife, and delivered all three of them to help care for the fallen Radiants.

Shadesmar revealed no Voidspren hiding in cremlings, so she hesitantly returned her vision to the Physical Realm and drew in a breath of Stormlight. That she could do, as she'd practiced it together with Timbre over the months.

Stormlight didn't work like Voidlight did. Rather than going into her gemheart, it infused her entire body. She could feel it raging—an odd feeling more than an unpleasant one.

She pressed her hand to the stone wall. "Do you remember how we did this last time?" she asked Timbre.

The little spren pulsed uncertainly. That had been many months ago, and had drawn the attention of secretspren, so they had stopped quickly. It seemed, though, that all Venli had needed to do was press her hand against the wall, and her powers had started activating.

Timbre pulsed. She wasn't convinced it would work with Stormlight, not with the tower's defenses in place. Indeed, as Venli tried to do . . . well, anything with the Stormlight, she felt as if there were some invisible wall blocking her.

She couldn't push the Stormlight into her gemheart to store it there—not with the Voidspren trapped inside. So Venli let the Light burn off on its own, breathing out to hasten the process. Then she took out a Voidlight sphere. She could get these without too much trouble—but she didn't dare sing the Song of Prayer to create them herself. She worried about drawing Odium's attention; he seemed to be ignoring her these days, and she'd rather it remain that way.

Timbre pulsed encouragingly.

"You sure?" Venli said. "It doesn't seem right, for some reason, to use his power to fuel our abilities."

Timbre's pulsed reply was pragmatic. Indeed, they used Voidlight every day—a little of it, stored in their gemheart—to power Venli's translation abilities. She wasn't certain if her ability to use Voidlight for Radiant powers came from the fact that she was Regal, or if any singer who managed a bond would be able to do the same.

Today, she drew the Voidlight in like Stormlight, and it infused her gemheart fully. The Voidlight didn't push her to move or act, like the Stormlight had. Instead it enflamed her emotions, in this case making her more paranoid, so she checked Shadesmar again. Still nothing there to be alarmed about.

She pressed her hand to the wall again, and tried to feel the stone. Not with her fingers. With her soul.

The stone responded. It seemed to stir like a person awaking from a deep slumber. *Hello*, it said, though the sounds were drawn out. She didn't hear the word so much as feel it. *You are . . . familiar.*

"I am Venli," she said. "Of the listeners."

The stones trembled. They spoke with one voice, but she felt as if it was also many voices overlapping. Not the voice of the tower, but the voices of the many different sections of stones around her. The walls, the ceiling, the floor.

Radiant, the stones said. *We have . . . missed your touch, Radiant. But what is this? What is that sound, that tone?*

"Voidlight," Venli admitted.

That sound is familiar, the stones said. *A child of the ancient ones. Our friend, you have returned to sing our song again?*

"What song?" Venli asked.

The stone near her hand began to undulate, like ripples on the surface of a pond. A tone surged through her, then it began to pulse with the song of a rhythm she'd never heard, but somehow always known. A profound, sonorous rhythm, ancient as the core of Roshar.

The entire wall followed suit, then the ceiling and the floor, surrounding her with a beautiful rhythm set to a pure tone. Timbre, with glee, joined in—and so Venli's body aligned with the rhythm, and she felt it humming through her, vibrating her from carapace to bones.

She gasped, then pressed her other hand to the rock, aching to feel the song against her skin. There was a rightness about this, a perfection. *Oh, storms,* she thought. *Oh, rhythms ancient and new. I belong here.*

She *belonged* here.

So far, everything she'd done with Timbre had been accidental. There had been a momentum to it. She'd made choices along the way, but it had never felt like something she deserved. Rather, it was a path she had fallen into, and then taken because it was better than her other options.

But here . . . she *belonged* here.

Remember, the stones said. The ground in front of her stopped rippling and formed shapes. Little homes made of stone, with figures standing beside them. Shaping them. She heard them humming.

She *saw* them. Ancient people, the Dawnsingers, working the stone. Creating cities, tools. They didn't need Soulcasting or forges. They'd dip lengths of wood into the stone, and come out with axes. They'd shape bowls with their fingers. All the while, the stone would sing to them.

Feel me, shaper. Create from me. We are one. The stone shapes your life as you shape the stone.

Welcome home, child of the ancients.

"How?" Venli asked. "Radiants didn't exist then. Spren didn't bond us . . . did they?"

Things are new, the stones hummed, *but new things are made from old things, and old peoples give birth to new ones. Old stones remember.*

The vibrations quieted, falling from powerful thrummings, to tiny ripples, to stillness. The homes and the people melted back to ordinary stone floor, though the strata of this place had changed. As if to echo the former vibrations.

Venli knelt. After several minutes, breathing in gasps, she realized she was completely out of Voidlight. She searched her sack, and found all of her spheres drained save for a single mark. She'd gone through those spheres with frightening speed. But that moment of song, that moment of connection, had certainly been worth the cost.

She drew in this mark, then hesitantly placed her hand to the wall again. She felt the stone, willing and pliable, encouraging her and calling her "shaper." She drew out the Voidlight and it infused her hand, making it glow violet-on-black. When she pressed her thumb into the stone, the rock molded beneath her touch, as if it had become crem clay.

Venli pressed her entire hand into the stone, making a print there and feeling the soft—but still present—rhythm. Then she pulled off a piece of the rock and molded it in her fingers. She rolled it into a ball, and the viscosity seemed to match what she needed—for when she held her hand forward and imagined it doing so, the stone ball melted into a puddle. She dropped it then, and it clicked when it hit the ground—hard, but imprinted by her fingers.

She picked it up and pressed it back into the wall, where it melded with the stone there as if it had never been removed.

Once she was done, she considered. "I want this, Timbre," she whispered, wiping her eyes. "I *need* this."

Timbre thrummed excitedly.

"What do you mean, 'them'?" Venli asked. She looked up, noticing lights in the hallway. She attuned Anxiety, but then the lights drew closer. The three little spren were like Timbre: in the shape of comets with rings of light pulsing around them.

"This is dangerous," Venli hissed to Reprimand. "They shouldn't be here. If they're seen, the Voidspren will destroy them."

Timbre pulsed that spren couldn't be destroyed. Cut them with a Shardblade, and they'd re-form. Venli, however, wasn't so confident. Surely the Fused could do something. Trap them in a jar? Lock them away?

Timbre insisted they'd simply fade into Shadesmar in that case, and be free. Well, it was risky, no matter what she said. These spren seemed more . . . awake than she'd expected though. They hovered around her, curious.

"Didn't you say spren like you need a bond to be aware in the Physical Realm? An anchor?"

Timbre's explanation was slightly ashamed. These were eager to bond Venli's friends, her squires. That had given these spren access to thoughts and stability in the Physical Realm. Venli *was* the anchor.

She nodded. "Tell them to get out of the tower for now. If my friends start suddenly manifesting Radiant powers—and the stone starts singing in a place others could see—we could find ourselves in serious trouble."

Timbre pulsed, defiant. How long?

"Until I find a way out of this mess," Venli said. She pressed her hand to the wall, listening to the soft, contented hum of the stones. "I'm like a baby taking her first steps. But this might be the answer we need. If I can sculpt us an exit through the collapsed tunnels below, I should be able to sneak us out. Maybe we can even make it seem like we died in a further cave-in, covering our escape."

Timbre pulsed encouragingly.

"You're correct," Venli said. "*We* can do this. But we need to take it slowly, carefully. I rushed to find new forms, and that proved a disaster. This time we'll do things the right way."

ONE FAMILY

EIGHT YEARS AGO

Eshonai accompanied her mother into the storm.

Together they struck out into the electric darkness, Eshonai carrying a large wooden shield to buffer the wind for her mother, who cradled the bright orange glowing gemstone. Powerful gusts tried to rip the shield out of Eshonai's hand, and windspren soared past, giggling.

Eshonai and her mother passed others, notable for the similar gemstones they carried. Little bursts of light in the tempest. Like the souls of the dead said to wander the storms, searching for gemhearts to inhabit.

Eshonai attuned the Rhythm of the Terrors: sharp, each beat puncturing her mind. She wasn't afraid for herself, but her mother had been so frail lately.

Though many of the others stood out in the open, Eshonai led her mother to the hollow she'd picked out earlier. Even here, the pelting rain felt like it was trying to burrow through her skin. Rainspren along the top of the ridge seemed to dance as they waved along with the furious tempest.

Eshonai huddled down beside her mother, unable to hear the rhythm the femalen was humming. The light of the gemstone, however, revealed a grin on Jaxlim's face.

A grin?

"Reminds me of when your father and I came out together!" Jaxlim shouted at Eshonai over the stormwinds. "We'd decided not to leave it to fate, where one of us might be taken and the other not! I still remember the strange feelings of passion when I first changed. You're too afraid of that, Eshonai! I do want grandchildren, you realize."

"Do we have to talk about this now?" Eshonai asked. "Hold that stone. Adopt the new form! Think about it, *not* mateform."

Wouldn't *that* be an embarrassment.

"The lifespren aren't interested in someone my age," her mother said. "It simply feels nice to be out here again! I'd been beginning to think I would waste away!"

Together they huddled against the rock, Eshonai using her shield as an improvised roof to block the rain. She wasn't certain how long it would take the transformation to begin. Eshonai herself had only adopted a new form once, as a child—when her father had helped her adopt workform, since the time of changes had come to her.

Children needed no form, and were vibrant without one—but if they didn't adopt a form upon puberty in their seventh or eighth year, they would be trapped in dullform instead. That form was, essentially, an inferior version of mateform.

Today, the storm stretched long, and Eshonai's arm began to ache from holding the shield in place. "Anything?" she asked of her mother.

"Not yet! I don't know the proper mindset."

"Attune a bold rhythm!" Eshonai said. That was what Venli had told them. "Confidence or Excitement!"

"I'm trying! I—"

Whatever else her mother said was lost in the sound of thunder washing across them, vibrating the very stones, making Eshonai's teeth chatter. Or perhaps that was the cold. Normally chill weather didn't bother her—workform was well suited to it—but the icy rainwater had leaked through her oiled coat, sneaking down along her spine.

She attuned Resolve, keeping the shield in place. She *would* protect her mother. Jaxlim often complained that Eshonai was unreliable, prone to fancy, but that wasn't true. Her exploration was difficult work. It was *valuable* work. She *wasn't* unreliable or lazy.

Let her mother see this. Eshonai holding her shield in defiance of the rain—in defiance of the Rider of Storms himself. Holding her mother close, warming her. Not weak. Solid. Dependable. *Determined.*

The gemstone in her mother's hands began to glow brighter. *Finally,* Eshonai thought, shifting to give her mother more space to enact the transformation, the recasting of her soul, the ultimate connection between listener and Roshar itself.

Eshonai shouldn't have been surprised when the light burst from the gemstone and was absorbed—like water rushing to fill an empty vessel—into her *own* gemheart. Yet she was. Eshonai gasped, the rhythms disrupting and vanishing—all but one, an overwhelming sound she'd never heard before. A stately, steady tone. Not a rhythm. A pure note.

Proud, louder than the thunder. The sound became everything to her as her previous spren—a tiny gravitationspren—was ejected from her gemheart.

The pure tone of Honor pounding in her ears, she dropped the shield—which flew away into the dark sky. She wasn't supposed to have been taken, but in the moment she didn't care. This transformation was wonderful. In it, a vital piece of the listeners returned to her.

They needed more than they had. They needed *this.*

This . . . this was *right.* She embraced the change.

While it happened, it seemed to her that all of Roshar paused to sing Honor's long-lost note.

∴

Eshonai came to, lying in a puddle of rainwater cloudy with crem. A single rainspren undulated beside her, its form rippling and its eye staring straight upward toward the clouds, little feet curling and uncurling.

She sat up and surveyed her tattered clothing. Her mother had left Eshonai at some point during the storm, shouting that she needed to get under cover. Eshonai had been too absorbed by the tone and the new transformation to go with her.

She held up her hand and found the fingers thick, meaty, with carapace as grand as human armor along the back of the hand and up the arm. It covered her entire body, from her feet up to her head. No hairstrands. Simply a solid piece of carapace.

The change had shredded her shirt and coat, leaving only her skirt—and that had snapped at the waist, so it barely hung on her body. She stood up, and even that simple act felt different than it had before. She was *propelled* to her feet by unexpected strength. She stumbled, then gasped, attuning Awe.

"Eshonai!" an unfamiliar voice said.

She frowned as a monstrous figure in reddish-orange carapace stepped over some rubble from the highstorm. He had tied his wrap on awkwardly, plainly having suffered a similar disrobing. She attuned Amusement, though it didn't look silly. It seemed impossible that such a dynamic, muscular figure could *ever* look silly. She wished there were a rhythm more majestic than Awe. Was that what *she* looked like too?

"Eshonai," the malen said with his deep voice. "Can you believe this? I feel like I could leap up and touch the clouds!"

She didn't recognize the voice . . . but that pattern of marbled skin *was* familiar. And the features, though now covered by a carapace skull-cap, were reminiscent of . . .

"Thude?" she said, then gasped again. "My voice!"

"I know," he said. "If you've ever wished to sing the low tones, Eshonai, it seems we've found the perfect form for it!"

She searched around to see several other listeners in powerful armor standing and attuning Awe. There were a good dozen of them. Though Venli had provided around two dozen gemstones, it seemed not all of the volunteers had taken to the new form. Unsurprising. It would take them time and practice to determine the proper mindset.

"Were you overwhelmed too?" Dianil said, striding over. Her voice was as deep as Eshonai's now, but that curl of black marbling along her brow was distinctive. "I felt an overpowering need to stand in the storm basking in the tone."

"There are songs of those who first adopted workform," Eshonai said. "I believe they mention a similar experience: an outpouring of power, an amazing tone that belonged purely to Cultivation."

"The tones of Roshar," Thude said, "welcoming us home."

The twelve of them gathered, and though she knew some better than others, there seemed to be an instant . . . connection between them. A comradery. They took turns jumping, seeing who could get the highest, singing to Joy, as silly as a bunch of children with a new toy. Eshonai hefted a rock and hurled it, then watched it soar an incredible distance.

She even drew a gloryspren—with flowing tails and long wings.

As the others selected their own rocks to try beating her throw, she heard an incongruous sound. The drums? Yes, those *were* the battle drums. A raid was happening at the city.

The others gathered around her, humming to Confusion. An attack by one of the other families? *Now?*

Eshonai wanted to laugh.

"Are they *insane*?" Thude asked.

"They don't know what we've done," Eshonai said, looking around at the flat expanse of rock outside the city where they'd engaged the highstorm. Many listeners were only now making their way out of the sheltered cracks in the ground.

Their best warriors, however, would have stayed at the city in the small, strong structures built there. More than one family had claimed a city right after a storm. It was one of the best times to attack, assuming you could muster your numbers quickly enough.

"This is going to be fun," Melu said to Excitement.

"I don't know if that's the correct way to think of it," Eshonai said, though she felt the same eagerness. A desire to charge in. "Though . . . if we can arrive before the boasts are done . . ."

The others began attuning Amusement or Excitement, grinning. Eshonai led the way, ignoring the calls of those leaving the stormshelter. There was a more urgent matter to attend to.

As they approached the city, she could see the rival family mustered outside the gateway, lifting spears and making challenges and taunts. They wore white, of course. It was how one knew an attack was happening, rather than a request for trade or other interaction.

As long as the boasts were continuing, the actual battle hadn't yet begun. She'd participated in several fights for cities during her family's years trying to claim one, and they'd always been nasty affairs—the worst one leaving over a *dozen* people dead on each side.

Well, today they'd see about . . .

She stopped, holding up her hand to make the others pause. They did so—though a part of Eshonai wondered why she had decided to take charge. It simply felt natural.

They'd been approaching a fissure in the wall surrounding the city. That wall might once have been grand, but mere hints of its former majesty remained. Most of it had worn low, split by large gaps.

Here, a figure moved in the shadows. It looked ominous, dangerous—but then Venli emerged into the light, waving them forward. How had she gotten to the city so quickly?

Eshonai approached, and Venli looked her up and down with a slow, deliberate gaze. The drums beat in the background, urging Eshonai forward. Yet that look in her sister's eyes . . .

"So it worked," Venli said. "Praise the ancient storms for that. You look good, sister. All bulked up and ready to serve."

"This isn't who I am," Eshonai said, gesturing to the form. "But there is a certain . . . thrill to holding it."

"Go visit Sharefel," Venli said. "He's waiting for you."

"The drums . . ." Eshonai said.

"The enemy will continue howling insults for a little while yet," Venli said. "Visit Sharefel."

Sharefel. The family's Shardbearer. Upon obtaining this city, by tradition the defeated family had given up the city's Shards for her family to protect and keep.

"Venli," Eshonai said. "We do *not* use Shards upon other listeners. Those are for hunts alone."

"Oh, sister," Venli said to Amusement, walking around her, then inspecting Thude and the others. "If we're going to *ever* stand a hope of resisting the humans—when they inevitably turn against us—we must be ready to bear the weapons with which we were blessed."

Eshonai wanted to attune Reprimand at the suggestion, but she remembered the things Dalinar Kholin had said to her. If the listeners weren't unified, they *would* be easy pickings.

"I want to get to the fight," Melu said to Excitement, an anticipation-spren—like a long streamer connected to a round sphere below—bouncing around behind her.

"I think it's worth trying not to kill anyone," Thude said to Consideration. "With this form . . . I feel it would be unfair."

"Bear the Shards," Venli urged. "Show them the dangers of approaching us to demand battle."

Eshonai pushed past her sister, and the others followed. Venli trailed along behind as well. Eshonai didn't intend to use the Shards against her people, but perhaps there *was* a purpose to visiting Sharefel. She wound through the city, passing crem-filled puddles and vines stretching out from rockbuds to lap up the moisture.

The Shardbearer's hut was by the front wall, near the drums. It was one of the strongest structures in the city, one they always kept well-maintained. Today the door was open, welcoming. Eshonai stepped into the doorway.

"Ah . . ." a soft voice said to the Rhythm of the Lost. "So it is true. We have warriors once more."

Eshonai stepped forward, finding the elderly listener sitting in his seat, light from the doorway illuminating his pattern of mostly black skin. Feeling it appropriate, even if she didn't quite know why, she knelt before him.

"I have long sung the old songs," Sharefel said, "dreaming of this day. I always thought I would be the one to find it. How? What spren?"

"Painspren," Eshonai said.

"They flee during storms."

"We captured them," Eshonai said as a couple of others entered the chamber, striking dangerous silhouettes. "Using a human method."

"Ahh . . ." he said. "I shall try it myself then, at the next storm. But this is a new era, and deserves a new Shardbearer. Which of you will take my Shards? Which of you can bear this burden, and this glory?"

The group became still. Not all families had Shardbearers; there were only eight sets among all the listeners. Those who held the proper eight cities were blessed with them, to be wielded only in hunts against greatshells. Those were rare events, where many families would band together to harvest a gemheart for growing crops, then feast upon the slain beast.

That . . . did not seem the future of their Shards anymore. *If the humans discover we have these,* Eshonai thought, *it* will *be war.*

"Give the Shards to me," Melu said to Excitement. She stepped forward, though Thude put his hand upon her breastplate as if to restrain her. She hummed to Betrayal, and he hummed to Irritation. A challenge from both.

This could get ugly *very* quickly.

"No!" Eshonai said. "No, none of us will take them. None of us are ready." She looked to the elderly Shardbearer. "You keep them. With Plate, you are as firm as any warrior, Sharefel. I merely ask that you stand with us today."

The drums stopped sounding.

"I will not lift the Blade against other listeners," Sharefel said to Skepticism.

"You will not need to," Eshonai said. "Our goal today will not be to win a battle, but to promise a new beginning."

◈

A short time later, they stepped out of the city. Once, gates had likely stood in this opening, but the listeners could not create wooden marvels on that scale. Not yet.

The battle had already started, though it hadn't moved to close combat yet. Her family's warriors would step forward and throw their spears, and the other family would dodge. Then the attacking family would return spears. If someone was hit, one side might withdraw and give up the battle. If not, eventually one side might rush the other.

Spren of all varieties had been drawn to the event, and spun or hovered around the perimeters. Eshonai's family's archers hung back, their numbers a show of strength, though they wouldn't use their weapons here. Bows were too deadly—and too accurate—to be used in harming others.

There . . . *had* been times, unfortunately, when in the heat of fighting, traditions had been broken. Normal battles had become horrific massacres. Eshonai had never been part of one of those, but she'd seen the aftereffects during her childhood, when passing a failed assault on another city.

Today, both sides stopped as the warforms emerged—accompanied by a full Shardbearer in glistening Plate. Eshonai's family parted, humming to Awe or Excitement.

Eshonai picked up a spear, as did several of the others. They came to a halt in the center of the field. The opposing family scrambled back, their warriors brandishing spears. Their postures—and the few sounds of humming Eshonai could make out—were terrified.

"We have found warform," Eshonai shouted to Joy. An inviting rhythm, not an angry one. "Come, join us. Enter our city, live with us. We will share our knowledge with you."

The others shied away further. One of them shouted, to Reprimand,

"You'll consume us! Make us slaves. We won't be our own family any longer."

"We are all *one* family!" Eshonai said. "You fear being made slaves? Did you see the poor slaveforms the humans had? Did you see the armor of the humans, their weapons? Did you see the fineness of their clothing, the wagons they created?

"You cannot fight that. I cannot fight that. But together, *we* could fight that. There are tens of thousands of listeners around the Plains. When the humans return, let us show them a united *nation,* not a bunch of squabbling tribes." She gestured to the other warforms, then let her gaze linger on Sharefel in his Shardplate.

"We won't fight you today," Eshonai said, turning back to the enemy family. "*None* of this family will fight you today. But if any of you persist, you will *personally* discover the true might of this form. We are going to approach the Living-Songs family next. You may choose to be the first to join with our new nation, and be recognized for your wisdom for generations. Or you can be left until the end, to come groveling for membership, once our union is nearly complete."

She hefted her spear and threw it—shocking herself with the power behind that throw. It soared over the enemy family and disappeared far into the distance. She heard more than one of them humming to the Rhythm of the Terrors.

She nodded to the others, and they joined her, marching into the city. A few seemed annoyed. They wanted a battle to test their abilities. She'd never known listeners to be bloodthirsty, and she didn't feel this form had changed her that much—but she did admit she felt a certain eagerness.

"We should train," she said to the others. "Work out some of our aggression."

"That sounds wonderful," Thude said.

"As long as we can do it in front of everyone else," Melu said to Irritation. "I'd like them to understand how easily I could have cracked their skulls." She looked to Eshonai. "But . . . that was well done. I guess I'm glad I didn't have to rip anyone apart."

"How did you learn to give speeches?" one of the others asked from behind. "Did you learn that talking to those trees, out in the wilderness?"

"I'm not a hermit, Dolimid," she said to Irritation. "I just like the idea of being free. Of not being locked into one location. As long as we don't know what is out there, we're likely to be surprised. Tell me, would we be scrambling now to get our people in order if we'd simply *explored* our surroundings? We could have been preparing to face the humans for generations, if we hadn't been so afraid."

The others hummed to Consolation, understanding. Why had Eshonai had so much trouble persuading people before? Was her present ease because of the connection she felt with these listeners, the first warforms?

There was so much to learn from this form, so much to experiment with. She felt a spring in her step. Perhaps this would be a better form for exploration—she could leap obstacles, run faster. There was so much *possibility*.

They entered the city, her family's warriors—those who had been throwing their spears outside—trotting in with them, immediately accepting the authority of the warforms. As they passed Sharefel's hut, she saw Venli again, lurking in the shadows. This was *her* victory, after a fashion.

Eshonai probably should have gone to congratulate her, but couldn't bring herself to do it. Venli didn't need more songs praising her. She already had a big enough ego.

Instead, Eshonai led the group to the stormshelter, where the rest of their family was emerging. Each and every one deserved to see the new form up close.

PURE TONES
OF ROSHAR

I leave you now to your own company.

—From *Rhythm of War*, page 27

Navani hit the tuning fork and touched it to a glowing diamond. When she pulled it away from the gemstone, a tiny line of Stormlight followed behind it—and when she touched the fork to an empty diamond, the Stormlight flowed into it. The transfer would continue as long as the fork made the second diamond vibrate.

Sometimes I think of it like a gas, she thought, taking notes on the speed of the flow. *And sometimes a liquid. I keep wavering between the two, trying to define it, but it must be neither one. Stormlight is something else, with some of the properties of both a liquid and a gas.*

After completing this control experiment—and timing how quickly the Stormlight flowed—she set up the real experiment. She did this inside a large steel box her scholars had created for dangerous experiments, Soulcast into shape with a thick glass window at one end. She'd forced the enemy to drag it in from the hallway outside, then place it on top of her desk.

She wasn't certain if this would save her from a potential explosion, but since the box didn't have a top, the force of the destruction *should* go upward—and as long as she stayed low and watched through the window, it should shield her.

It was the best she could do in these difficult circumstances. She told the singers she was taking normal precautions, and tried not to indicate to them that she expected an explosion. And indeed she didn't—the sphere that had killed her scholars had *not* been Voidlight, but something else. Something Navani didn't yet understand. She was convinced that mixing Voidlight and Stormlight wouldn't create an explosion, but a new kind of Light. Like Towerlight.

She began this next experiment the same way as the previous one, drawing out Stormlight and sending it toward another diamond. Then she reached into the box with tongs and placed a Voidlight diamond in the center of the flow, between the Stormlight diamond and the tuning fork.

The Stormlight didn't react to the Voidlight diamond at all. It simply streamed around the dark gemstone and continued to the vessel diamond. As the tuning fork's tone quieted, the stream weakened. When the fork fell silent, the Stormlight hanging in the air between the two diamonds puffed away and vanished.

Well, she hadn't expected that to do anything. Now for a better test. She'd spent several days working under a singular hypothesis: that if Stormlight reacted to a tone, Voidlight and Towerlight would as well. She'd needed to take a crash course in music theory to properly test the idea.

The Alethi traditionally used a ten-note scale—though it was more accurately two five-note quintaves. This was right and orderly, and the greatest and most famous compositions were all in this scale. However, it wasn't the *only* scale in use around the world. There were dozens. The Thaylens, for example, preferred a twelve-note scale. A strange number, but the twelve steps *were* mathematically pleasing.

In researching the tone the tuning fork created, she'd discovered something incredible. Anciently, people had used a *three-note* scale, and a few of the compositions remained. The tone that drew Stormlight was the first of the three notes from this ancient scale. With some effort—it had required sending Fused to Kholinar through the Oathgate to raid the royal music conservatory—she'd obtained tuning forks for the other two notes in this scale. To her delight, Voidlight responded to the third of the three notes.

She hadn't been able to find any indication in her reading that people had once known these three notes correlated to the three ancient gods. No Alethi scholars seemed to know that one of these tones could prompt a reaction in Stormlight, though Raboniel had—upon questioning—said she'd known. Indeed, she'd been surprised to learn that Navani had only recently discovered the "pure tones of Roshar," as she called them.

Navani had tried singing the proper tones, but hadn't been able to make the light respond. Perhaps she couldn't match the pitch well enough, because Raboniel had been able to do it—singing and touching one gemstone, then moving her finger to another while holding the note. The Stormlight had followed her finger just as it did a tuning fork.

Today Raboniel was off tending to other tasks, but Navani could use the tuning forks to replicate her singing ability. Three tones: a note for Honor, a note for Odium, and a note for Cultivation. Yet Vorinism only worshipped the Almighty. Honor.

Theology would have to wait for another time. For now, she set up her next experiment. She created streams of Stormlight and Voidlight—drawing each out from a diamond in a corner of her box—and crossed the streams at the center. The two lights pushed upon one another and swirled as they met, but then separated and streamed to their separate forks.

"All right," Navani said, writing in her notebook. "What about this?" She picked up the partially empty Voidlight diamond and then brought out a fresh Stormlight diamond, fully infused.

In fabrial science, you captured a spren by creating a gemstone with a kind of vacuum in it—you drew out the Stormlight, leaving a sphere with a void or suction inside. It would then pull in a nearby spren, which was made of Light. It was like any pressure differential.

She hoped to be able to refill the Voidlight sphere with Stormlight, now that a portion of the Voidlight had been removed. She hit the tuning fork, started the Stormlight streaming out of its diamond, then tried to get it to go into the Voidlight diamond by making it vibrate to the fork's tone.

Unfortunately, when she touched the tuning fork to the Voidlight diamond, it immediately stopped vibrating and the tone died. Extinguished like a candle doused with water. She was able to get the Stormlight to bunch up against the Voidlight diamond, by putting the fork next to it, but when she got the Voidlight to stream out toward the side of the table—theoretically creating an active pressure differential in that diamond—she couldn't get it to suck Stormlight in. Only once all of the Voidlight was out could she infuse the diamond with Stormlight.

"Like oil and water indeed," she said, making notes. Yet the way the streams didn't repel one another when touching felt like proof they weren't opposites.

She rose and—after noting the results of this experiment—went to talk to the Sibling. Navani could easily fool the guards into thinking she was simply strolling among the bookshelves to read a passage or two, as she often did this. Today, she began picking through the books on the back shelf while resting her hand on the Sibling's vein in the wall.

"Are we being watched?" Navani asked.

I've told you, the Sibling said. *Voidspren can't be invisible in the tower. That protection is different from the one suppressing enemy Surgebinders, and Raboniel hasn't corrupted it yet.*

"You also told me you could sense if a Voidspren was near."

Yes.

"So . . . are any near?"

No, the Sibling said. *You do not trust my word?*

"Let's just call it a healthy paranoia on my part," Navani said. "Tell me again of—"

You continue to experiment with fabrials, the Sibling interrupted. *We need to talk more about that. I do not like what you've been doing.*

"I haven't captured any more spren," Navani whispered. "I've been working with Stormlight and Voidlight."

Dangerous work. The man who forges weapons can claim he's never killed, but he still prepares for the slaughter.

"If we're going to restore your abilities, I need to understand how Light works. So unless you have a better idea for me to do this, I'm going to have to continue to use gemstones and—yes—fabrials."

The Sibling fell silent.

"Tell me again about Towerlight," Navani said.

This is growing tedious.

"Do you want to be saved, or not?"

. . . Fine. Towerlight is my Light, the Light I could create.

"Did you need a Bondsmith to make it?"

No. I could make it on my own. And my Bondsmith could create it, through their bond with me.

"And that Light, in turn, powered the tower's defenses."

Not only the defenses. Everything.

"Why does it no longer work?"

I already explained that!

"This is a common investigative method," Navani said calmly, flipping through her book with her left hand. "My goal is to make you restate facts in different ways, leading you to explain things differently—or to remember details you forgot."

I haven't forgotten anything. The defenses no longer work because I don't have the Light for them. I lost most of my strength when I lost the ability to hear the two pure tones of Roshar. I can make only a tiny amount of Light, enough to power a few of the tower's basic fabrials.

"Two tones of Roshar?" Navani said. "There are three."

No, there are two. One from my mother, one from my father. The tone of Odium is an interloper. False.

"Could part of the reason you lost your abilities relate to that tone *becoming* a pure tone of Roshar? Odium truly becoming one of the three gods?"

I . . . don't know, the Sibling admitted.

Navani noted this hypothesis.

We need to find a way to restore my Towerlight, the Sibling said, *and remove the Voidlight from my system.*

"And that," Navani said, "is exactly what I'm working on." If she could figure out how to combine two Lights, then it would be the first step toward creating Towerlight.

She clearly needed an emulsifier, a facilitator. What kind of emulsifier could "stick" to Stormlight and make it mix with Voidlight? She shook her head, taking her hand off the vein on the wall. She'd been here too long, so she took a book and strolled to the front of the room, lost in thought. However, as she reached her desk, she found a small box waiting for her.

She glanced at the guard by the door, who nodded. Raboniel had sent it. Navani opened the box, breathless, and found a brightly glowing diamond. At first glance, it seemed to be another Stormlight sphere. But as she held it up and placed it next to a true one, she could see the green tinge to the one Raboniel had sent.

Lifelight. She'd promised to get some for Navani.

"Did she say how she acquired this?" Navani asked.

The guard shook his head.

Navani had a guess. The Sibling had lost sight of Lift, but had explained something was odd about that girl. Something Navani held as a hope that might get them out of this.

Hands steady—though anticipationspren shot up around her—Navani used the middle tuning fork on this new diamond. And it worked: she was able to draw Lifelight out and send it streaming into a gemstone.

Towerlight was Lifelight and Stormlight combined. So perhaps Lifelight—the Light of Cultivation—had some property that allowed it to mix with other Lights. Holding her breath, Navani repeated her earlier experiments, except with Lifelight instead of Voidlight.

She failed.

She couldn't get Stormlight and Lifelight to mix. No use of tuning forks, no touching of the streams or clever use of gemstone differentials, worked.

She tried mixing Voidlight and Lifelight. She tried mixing all three. She tried every experiment she'd listed in her brainstorming sessions earlier. Then she did them all again, until—because each experiment allowed a little Lifelight to vanish into the air—she'd used it all up.

Shooing away exhaustionspren, she stood, frustrated. Another dead end. This was as bad as the morning's experiments, when she'd tried everything she could think of—including using two tuning forks at once—to make Towerlight move from its gemstone. She'd failed at that as well.

She gathered all the used diamonds and deposited them by the door guard to be picked up and reinfused—there was a highstorm coming today. After that, she paced, frustrated. She knew she shouldn't let the lack of results bother her. Real scientists understood that experiments like this weren't failures; they were necessary steps on the way to discovery. In fact, it would have been remarkable—and completely unconventional—to find a good result so early in the process.

The problem was, scientists didn't have to work under such terrible deadlines or pressures. She was isolated, each moment ticking them closer to disaster. The only lead she had was in trying to mix the Lights, in the hope that she could eventually create more Towerlight to help the Sibling.

She wandered the room, pretending to inspect the spines of books on the shelves. *If I make my discovery, Raboniel will know, since a guard is always watching. She'll force the answer out of me, and so even in these attempts to escape, I'm furthering her goals—whatever those are.*

Navani was on the cusp of something important. The revelations she'd been given about Stormlight fundamentally changed their understanding of it and the world at large. Three types of power. The possibility they could be blended. And . . . possibly something else, judging by that strange sphere that warped the air around it.

Her instincts said that this knowledge would come out eventually. And the ones who controlled it, exploited it, would be the ones who won the war.

I need another plan, she decided. If she did discover how to make Towerlight, and if the shield did fall, Navani needed a way to isolate the crystal pillar for a short time. To defend it, perhaps to work on it.

Navani gripped her notebook in her safehand, to appear as if she were writing down the titles of books. Instead she quickly took notes on an idea. She'd been told she could have anything she needed, so long as it was relevant to her experiments. They also let her store equipment out in the hallway.

So, what if she created some fabrial weapons, then stored them in the hallway? Innocent-looking fabrials that, once activated, could be used to immobilize guards or Fused coming to stop her from working on the pillar? She sketched out some ideas: traps she could create using seemingly innocent fabrial parts. Painrials to administer agony and cause the muscles to lock up. Heating fabrials to burn and scald.

Yes . . . she could create a series of defenses in the form of failed experiments, then store them "haphazardly" in crates along the hallway. She could even arm them by using Voidspren gems, as she could demand those for use in her experiments.

These plans soothed her; this was something meaningful she could do. However, the experiments, and their potential, still itched at her. What was Raboniel's true goal? Was it to make a weapon herself—like the one that had destroyed the room and Navani's two scientists?

A few hours had passed, so it wouldn't look strange if she went to the back of the stacks again. She picked up a book and settled down in a chair she'd placed nearby. Although she wasn't directly visible to the guard, she pretended to read as she reached her hand to the wall and touched the vein.

"Any spren nearby?" Navani asked.

I cannot feel any, the Sibling said with a resigned tone.

"Good. Tell me, do you know anything of the explosion that happened on the day of the invasion? It involved two of my scientists in a room on the fifth floor."

I felt it. But I do not know what caused it.

"Have you ever heard of a sphere, or a Light, that *warps* the air around it? One that appears to be Voidlight unless you look at it long enough to notice the warping effect?"

No, the Sibling said. *I've never heard or seen anything like that—though it sounds dangerous.*

Navani considered, tapping her finger against the wall. "I haven't been able to get any of the Lights to mix. Do you know of any potential binding agent that could make them stick together? Do you know how Towerlight is mixed from Stormlight and Lifelight?"

They don't mix, the Sibling said. *They come together, as one. Like I am a product of my mother and father, so Towerlight is a product of me. And stop asking me the same questions. I don't care about your "investigative methods." I've told you what I know. Stop making me repeat myself.*

Navani took a deep breath, calming herself with effort. "Fine. Have you been able to eavesdrop on Raboniel at all?"

Not much. I can only hear things near a few people that are relevant. I can see the Windrunner. I think the Edgedancer has been surrounded by ralkalest, which is why she's invisible. Also, I can see one particular Regal.

"Any ideas on why that is?"

No. Regals weren't often in the tower in the past, and never this variety. She can speak all languages; perhaps this is why I can see near her. Though she vanishes sometimes, so I cannot see all she does. I can also see near the crystal pillar, but with the field set up, I hear mere echoes of what is happening outside.

"Tell me those, then."

It's nothing relevant. Raboniel is trying her own experiments with the Light—and she hasn't gotten as far as you have. This seems to frustrate her.

Curious. That did a little for Navani's self-esteem. "She really wants this hybrid Light. I wonder . . . maybe fabrials made with a hybrid Stormlight-Voidlight would work in the tower, even if the protections were turned against her again. Maybe that is why she wants it."

You are foolish to presume to know what one of the Fused wants. She is thousands of years old. You can't outthink her.

"You'd better hope that I can." Navani flipped a few pages in her notebook. "I've been thinking of other ways out of this. What if we found you someone to bond, to make them Radiant? We could—"

No. Never again.

"Hear me out," Navani said. "You've said you'll never bond a human again, because of the things we do to spren. But what about a singer? Could you theoretically bond one of them?"

We are talking of resisting them, and now you suggest I bond *one? That seems insane.*

"Maybe not," Navani said. "There's a Parshendi in Bridge Four. I've met him, and Kaladin has vouched for him. He claims that his people rejected the Fused long ago. What about him? Not a human. Not someone who has ever created a fabrial—someone who knows the rhythms of Roshar."

The Sibling was silent, and Navani wondered if the conversation was over. "Sibling?" she asked.

I had not considered this, they said. *A singer who does not serve Odium? I will need to think. It would certainly surprise Raboniel, who thinks that I am dead or sleeping.*

In any case, I cannot form a bond now, with the protections up. I would need him to touch my pillar.

"What if I had him here?" Navani said. "Ready to try when the shield falls? And with some distractions in place to give you time to talk to him."

I cannot form a bond with just anyone, the Sibling said. *In the past I spent years evaluating Bondsmith squires to select one who fit me exactly. Even they eventually betrayed me, though not as badly as other humans.*

"Can we really afford pickiness right now?"

It's not pickiness. It is the nature of spren and the bond. The person must be willing to swear the correct oaths, to unite instead of divide. They must mean it, and the oaths must be accepted. It is not simply a matter of throwing the first person you find at me.

Beyond that, since I cannot create Towerlight, they will not be able to either. A bond would do nothing unless we solve the problems with my powers. It would be better if you focused on that problem instead.

"Fine," Navani said, sensing an opening. "But I need time to research all of this. It is difficult to work while feeling I have a knife to my neck. If I knew the nodes were being defended, that would take the pressure off me. Tell me where one of them is. I have a list here of plans to protect it. I can read them off to you."

The Sibling was silent, so Navani continued.

"We can have Kaladin start searching—loudly and obviously—on a different level, leading the enemy on a chase in the wrong direction. In the meantime, while they're distracted, we could sneak up to the node and reinforce its defenses.

"We have some crem that hasn't hardened yet, kept wet in the tower stores. We could seal up the node location entirely. Maybe run the crem through with some training sheaths for Shardblades, so it would be extra difficult to cut. That could earn us hours to get troops in to defend it, if it does get discovered.

"Or, if I knew where one of the nodes was, I might be able to have Kaladin begin infusing it with more Stormlight. That might counteract the Voidlight that Raboniel has used on you. If she can corrupt you through a node, could we not perhaps cleanse you through one? I think it's worth trying, because my efforts to create Towerlight are stalled."

She waited, gripping her pad tightly. Her other ideas were sketchier than those. She wouldn't use them unless these arguments didn't work.

So good with words. Humans are like persuasionspren. I can't speak with one of you without being changed.

Navani continued to wait. Silence was best now.

Fine, the Sibling said. *One of the two remaining nodes is in the well at the center of the place you call the Breakaway market. It is near other fabrials there. One hidden among many.*

"On the first floor?" Navani asked. "That's such a populated area!"

All of the nodes are down low. There was talk of installing others farther away, but my Bondsmith did not have the resources—my falling-out with the humans was driving them away. The project wasn't completed. Only the four on the first few floors were completed.

Navani frowned—though the well was a clever place to hide a fabrial. Many of the workings of the tower remained mysterious to modern scholars, so a cluster of gemstones working as pumps might indeed camouflage another fabrial. In fact, Navani had studied drawings of those pumps herself. Had this mechanism been there, unnoticed, all along?

This is a good node for your agent to visit, the Sibling said. *Because it can be reached from the back ways. Have your Windrunner visit it through the aquifers, and we will see if—by infusing it with Stormlight—he can counteract the corruption. It might not work, as I am not simply of Honor or of Cultivation. But . . . it could help.*

"And the final node?" Navani asked.

Is mine alone, the Sibling replied. *Show me that your work on this one helps, human, and then we can speak further.*

"A fair compromise," Navani said. "I *am* willing to listen, Sibling."

She left the wall and grabbed some books to read, to cover what she'd been doing. And she did need to study more, after all. She'd have loved to have more books on music theory, but this archive didn't have anything more specific on the topic. She did have Kalami's notes about the gemstones they'd discovered that used certain buzzing vibrations as substitutes for letters. Perhaps those would help.

She was browsing through those notes, walking idly among the stacks, when she saw the Sibling's light flashing. She hurried over, nervous about how bright the light was. She glanced at the guard, hoping he hadn't seen, and put her hand to the wall.

"You need to—"

They've found the node in the well. We're too late.

"What? *Already?*"

I am as good as dead.

"Contact Kaladin."

They already have the node, and he's too far away. We—

"Contact Kaladin," Navani said. "*Now.* I'll find a way to distract Raboniel."

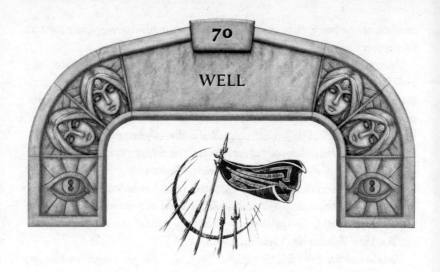

WELL

Opposites. Opposites of sounds. Sound has no opposite. It's merely overlapped vibration, the same sound, but sound has meaning. This sound does, at least. These sounds. The voices of gods.

—From *Rhythm of War*, final page

Kaladin awoke to something dark attacking him.

He screamed, struggling against the clinging shadows. They'd been assaulting him for an eternity, wrapping around him, constricting him. Voices that never relented, fingers of shadow that drilled into his brain.

He was in a dark place full of red light, and the shadows laughed and danced around him. They tormented him, flayed him, stabbed him again and again and wouldn't let him die. He fought back the hands that gripped, then he crawled across the floor, pulling up against the wall and breathing shallowly. The rushing sounds of his own blood in his ears drowned out the laughter.

One shadow continued watching him. One terrible shadow. It stared at him, then turned and took something from beside the wall before vanishing. Vanishing . . . out the door.

Kaladin blinked, and the shadows melted from his mind. The terrible laughter, the phantom pain, the whispers. His mind always interpreted those as Moash's voice.

A nightmare. Another nightmare.

"Kaladin?" Syl asked. She sat on the floor in front of him. He blinked, glancing sharply one way, then the other. The room seemed to settle into place. Teft sleeping on the stone bench. A few chips set out for light. Fearspren, like globs of goo, undulating in the corners.

"I . . ." He swallowed, his mouth dry. "I had a nightmare."

"I know."

He carefully relaxed his posture, embarrassed at how he must appear huddled up by the wall. Like a child frightened of the dark. He couldn't afford to be a child. Too much depended on him. He stood up, his clothing sweaty. "What time is it?"

"Midday," she said.

"My schedule is completely off." He tried to pull himself together as he stepped over to get a drink, but he stumbled and caught himself on the ledge. He had to grip it tightly as the nightmare threatened to resurface. Stormfather. This was the most oppressive one yet.

"Kaladin . . ." Syl said.

He took a long drink, then froze.

His spear was gone from beside the door.

"What happened?" he demanded, slamming the tin cup down harder than he'd intended. "Where is my spear!"

"The Sibling contacted us," she said, still sitting on the floor. "That's why Dabbid tried to wake you. Another node has been found—*inside* the well in the market. The enemy is there already."

"Storms!" Kaladin said. "We need to go." He reached for Navani's fabrial and his pouch of gems. He found the latter, but the fabrial was gone.

"Dabbid?" Kaladin demanded.

"You were huddled there muttering," Syl said, finally lifting into the air. "And you didn't seem to be able to see me. The Sibling is terrified. I could hear them while sitting on Dabbid's shoulder. And so . . ."

Kaladin grabbed the bag of gems and dashed out of the room, Syl following as a ribbon of light. He caught up with Dabbid at the first stairwell—just two hallways over. The shorter bridgeman stood with the spear and fabrial held close to his chest, staring down with a panicked expression.

He jumped as he saw Kaladin, then let out a loud relieved sigh. Kaladin took the fabrial.

"You were going to go try to stop the Fused," Kaladin said. "Because I didn't get up."

Dabbid nodded.

"Dabbid, you barely know how to use a spear," Kaladin said, quickly strapping on the fabrial. He'd had only four days of practice with the device. It would have to be enough.

Dabbid didn't respond, of course. He helped Kaladin strap the fabrial on, then held out the spear.

Kaladin took it, then gave the Bridge Four salute.

Dabbid returned it. Then, remarkably, said something, in a voice soft and gravelly. "Life. Before. Death."

Storms. Those were the first words Kaladin had ever heard from the man. He grinned, gripping Dabbid by the shoulder. "Life before death, Dabbid."

Dabbid nodded. There wasn't time for more; Kaladin turned away from the stairwell and began running again. Screams from the nightmare echoed in his head, but he didn't have time for weakness. He had to stop the corruption of that gemstone—and barring that, he had to destroy the node. That was the only way to buy Navani the time she needed.

He had to get there quickly, which meant he couldn't use the stairs. He'd have to go straight down through the atrium.

※

"I need to see the Lady of Wishes immediately!" Navani proclaimed to the guard. "I've made a discovery of incalculable value! It cannot wait for—"

The guard—a Regal stormform—simply started walking and gestured for her to follow. He didn't even need the full explanation.

"Excellent," Navani said, joining him in the hallway. "I'm glad you see the urgency."

The guard walked her to the large stairwell that led up to the ground floor. A Deepest One stood here, her fingers laced before her. "What is it?" she asked in heavily accented Alethi. "A sudden illness?"

"No," Navani said, taken aback. "A discovery. I think I've found what the Lady of Wishes was searching for."

"But of course you can't share it with anyone but Raboniel herself," the Fused said, a faintly amused rhythm to her voice.

"Well, I mean . . ." Navani trailed off.

"I'll see if I can reach her via spanreed," the Fused said. "I'll tell her it is *most* urgent."

Storms. They were *expecting* an attempted distraction from Navani. That thought was reinforced as the Fused glided to a cabinet that had been set up by the wall. She carefully, but slowly, selected a spanreed from the collection stored there.

It was a reverse distraction. They'd *known* Navani would attempt something like this. But how had they known that *she* would know that . . .

She stepped back, her eyes widening as the terrible implications struck her. Kaladin was in serious danger.

※

Barefoot and armed with a spear, Kaladin burst out onto the walkway around the atrium, then hurled himself out into the open space eleven stories in the air. Full of Stormlight—hoping it would save him in case this didn't work—he pointed his hand directly beneath him and engaged Navani's fabrial.

As soon as it was activated, he lurched to a halt in the air, hovering—his muscles straining as he was basically doing a handstand with one hand. But as long as the counterweight in the distant shaft was held motionless, Kaladin would be as well.

He gripped the bar across his left hand and began to fall downward, almost as if he were Lashed. In fact, he was counting on it seeming like nothing was wrong with his powers—that he was a full Windrunner ready for battle. He wouldn't be able to keep up such a facade for long, but perhaps it would gain him an advantage.

His descent—at a speed a notch below insane—gave him a view out the enormous atrium window, running all the way up the wall to his right. Strangely, it was dark outside, though Syl had said it was midday. He didn't have to ask for clarification, as a flash of lightning bespoke the truth. A highstorm. He still found it incredible that he could be so deep within a tower that one could be going on without him realizing it. Even in the best stormshelters, you usually felt the rumbles of thunder or the anger of the wind.

His fall certainly drew attention. Heavenly Ones dressed in long robes turned from their midair meditations. Shouts rose from Regals or singers along the various levels. He wasn't certain if Leshwi was among them or not, as he passed too quickly.

Using the fabrial, he slowed himself before he hit the ground, then deactivated the device entirely and fell the last five feet or so. Stormlight absorbed that drop, and he startled dozens of people—many of them human—who hadn't heard the disturbance above. Commerce was now allowed and encouraged by the Fused, and the atrium floor had become a secondary market—though a more transient one than the Breakaway a short distance off. That was where he would find the well.

Kaladin's luminescence would be starkly visible against the dark window, lit in flashes. The shouts of alarm above were swallowed in the voluminous atrium as Kaladin oriented himself, then ran for a stack of crates. He took a few steps up them to launch into the air some ten feet high, then he pointed his left hand and engaged Navani's device.

He flew like a Windrunner, his body upright, left arm held at chest height, elbow bent. It *might* look like he was using Lashings. Though Windrunners sometimes dove and flew headfirst like they were swimming, just as often they would fly "standing" up straight—like he did now.

He did tuck his legs up as he went soaring over the heads of the people, who ducked. Syl zipped along beside him, imitating a stormcloud. People cried out, surprised—but also excited—and Kaladin worried about what he was showing them. He didn't want to inspire a revolt that would get hundreds killed.

The best he could hope for was to get in, destroy the fabrial, and get out alive. That goal whispered of a much larger problem. Navani had said there were four nodes. Today, he'd try to destroy the third. At this rate, the last one would fall in a few days, and then what?

He pushed that thought out of his mind as he flew along the top of a corridor, inches from the textured stone ceiling. He didn't have time for second-guessing, or for dwelling on the crippling darkness and anxiety that continued to scratch at his mind. He had to ignore that, then deal with the effects later. Exactly as he'd been doing far too long now.

"Watch for an ambush," he told Syl as they burst from the corridor and into the Breakaway market. This large room, truly cavernous, was four stories high and packed with shops along the ground. Many were along roadways that Navani—reluctantly adapting to the will of the people—had laid out in the way they wanted. Other parts were snarls of tents and semipermanent wooden structures.

Central to the layout was the enormous well. Kaladin wasn't high enough to see over the buildings and make it out, but he knew the location. The Edgedancer clinic was nearby, though it was now staffed by ordinary surgeons. He hoped his parents and little brother had made it safely there, where the other surgeons would hide them. They'd checked a few days back and found his father's clinic empty.

Storms. If he lost his family . . .

"The Pursuer!" Syl said. "He was waiting by the other entrance."

Kaladin reacted just in time, deactivating the fabrial and dropping to the ground, where he tucked and rolled. The relentless Fused appeared from his ribbon of light and dropped to the ground too, but Kaladin rolled to his feet out of the creature's reach.

"Your death," the creature growled, crouched among terrified marketgoers, "is growing tedious, Windrunner. How is it you recovered all of your Lashings?"

Kaladin launched himself into the air, activating the device and shooting upward. It jerked his arm painfully, but he'd grown used to that—and Stormlight worked to heal the soreness. He'd also practiced his old one-handed spear grips. Hopefully that training would serve him today.

He wasn't nearly as maneuverable with this device as he was with Lashings. Indeed, as the Pursuer gave chase as a ribbon, Kaladin's only real recourse was to cut the device and drop past him. Near the ground, Kaladin pointed his hand to the side and reengaged the device, then went shooting out across the crowd in the general direction of the well. Maybe—

He lurched to a stop as the first of the device's weights bottomed out.

A heartbeat later the Pursuer slammed into him, grabbing him around the neck and hanging on.

"Kaladin!" Syl shouted. "Heavenly Ones! Over a dozen of them! They're streaming in through the tunnels."

"Good," Kaladin said with a grunt, dropping his spear and grappling against the Pursuer with the hand he could move.

"*Good?*" she asked.

He couldn't both grapple and twist the dial on his fabrial—the one that would activate the second weight. But he *could* deactivate the device using one hand, so he did that, dropping them ten feet to the ground. The Pursuer hit first with a grunt. He hung on though, rolling Kaladin to try to pin him.

"Turn . . . the dial," Kaladin said to Syl, using both hands to struggle with the Pursuer.

"When you die," the creature said in his ear, "I will find the next Radiant your spren bonds and kill *them* too. As payment for the trouble you have given me."

Syl zipped down to his left wrist and took the shape of an eel, pushing against the raised section at the center of the dial. She could turn a page, lift a leaf. Would she be strong enough to—

Click.

Kaladin twisted in the Pursuer's grip, barely managing to press his left hand to the creature's armored chest. Activating the device sent them both moving upward—but slowly. Storms, Kaladin hadn't thought this through. He'd only be able to lift as much as the counterweight. Apparently he and the Pursuer together were about that heavy.

Fortunately, rather than taking advantage of the slow movement, the Pursuer paused and glanced at Kaladin's hand, trying to figure out what was happening. So, as they inched upward, Kaladin was able to rip his right hand free. He reached for the scalpel he'd affixed in a makeshift sheath at his belt, then brought it up and rammed it into the Pursuer's wrist, slicing the tendons there.

The creature immediately let go, vanishing, leaving a husk behind. Once that dropped off of Kaladin, he immediately went darting up into the sky, pulled by his hand in an awkward motion that nearly ripped his arm from its socket.

"This . . . isn't that effective, is it?" Syl asked.

"No," Kaladin said, slowing himself by relaxing his grip. He went to draw in more Stormlight, but realized he still had plenty raging in his veins. That was one advantage of the fabrial; he didn't use up Light nearly as quickly.

The Heavenly Ones circled him in the air, but kept their distance. Kaladin searched for the Pursuer—the creature had used two bodies. He had a third one to waste before the fight became dangerous for him, so he wouldn't retreat yet.

There, Kaladin thought, noting the red ribbon weaving between Heavenly Ones. The motions looked timid, uncommitted, and Kaladin took a moment to figure out why. The Pursuer was trying to delay Kaladin; each moment wasted was another one that might lead to the Sibling being corrupted.

Below, the market streets were quickly emptying of people. Kaladin's fears about them revolting weren't being realized, fortunately—but he couldn't spend forever in a standoff with the Pursuer. So he disengaged the device and started falling.

This finally made the Pursuer dart for him, and Kaladin quickly re-engaged the device—lurching to a halt. He twisted—though he couldn't move his left arm—and prepared his knife. This sudden motion made the Pursuer back off, however. Could the creature . . . be afraid? That seemed implausible.

Kaladin didn't have time to reflect, as he needed to engage the Pursuer a third time for his plan to work. So he turned away, inviting the attack—and receiving it as the Pursuer committed, darting in and forming a body that grabbed for Kaladin. Despite trying to speed away, Kaladin wasn't quite able to evade the creature's grip.

Kaladin was forced to let the Pursuer grab him around the neck as he stabbed the creature in the arm between two plates of carapace, trying to sever the tendons. The monster grunted, his arm around Kaladin's throat. They continued to soar about thirty feet off the ground. Kaladin ignored the tight grip and maneuvered the scalpel. Perhaps if he could force the Pursuer to waste Voidlight healing . . .

Yes. Cut enough times to be worried, the Pursuer let go and flew away, seeking a place to recover. Panting, Kaladin used the device to drop to the ground. He landed on an empty street between two tents. People huddled inside both, crowding them.

Kaladin forced himself to jog to where he'd dropped his spear. Heavenly Ones circled above, preparing to attack. Syl moved up beside him, watching them. Two dozen now. Kaladin searched them, hoping . . .

There. He raised his spear toward Leshwi, who hovered apart from the others, wearing clothing too long for practical battle—even in the air. This event had caught her unaware.

Please, he thought. *Accept the fight.*

That was his best hope. He couldn't fight them all at once; he could barely face the Pursuer. If he wanted any chance of getting to the node, he'd need to fight a single opponent—one who wasn't as relentless as the Pursuer.

He worried he'd already wasted too much time. But if he could get Leshwi to agree to a duel . . .

She raised her spear toward him.

"Syl," he said, "go to the well and find the fabrial of the node. It's probably a sapphire, and should have a glass sphere nearby like the one we saw before."

"Right," she said. "It will probably be underwater. That's what the Sibling said. Near the pump mechanisms. Can . . . can you swim?"

"Won't need to, with Stormlight to sustain me and the fabrial to move me," Kaladin said, lifting his hand and rising into the air above the market. "But the well is likely under heavy guard. Our best chance to destroy the fabrial will be for me to break from this fight and fly straight down to it, then hit the device in one blow before anyone realizes what I'm doing. I'll need you to guide me."

"Sounds good." She hesitated, looking toward him.

"I'll be all right," he promised.

She flew off to do as he requested. He might be too late already. He could feel something changing. A greater oppression, a heaviness, was settling upon him. He could only assume it was the result of the Fused corrupting the Sibling.

Well, he couldn't move in that direction until Syl had the way prepared for him, so this would have to do. He leveled out in the air opposite Leshwi, his hand still held upward above him. The pose made him look overly dramatic, but he tried to appear confident anyway.

Leshwi wore the same body as last time, muscular, tall, wrapped in flowing black and white clothing. Her lance was shorter than normal, perhaps intended for indoor fighting.

Right. Well, he hoped to give a good showing in this fight, long enough to give Syl time to scout for him. So he cut the fabrial and dropped in the air, spinning and giving himself a few seconds of free fall. He felt almost like a real Windrunner—which was dangerous, as he almost tried to sculpt his fall with his hands in the wind. Fortunately, he remembered to engage the device as he neared the rooftops.

He lurched to a stop with a painful *jolt*, his arm bent, his elbow held close to his side. He had the most stability this way, his muscles keeping him as if he were standing upright with his left arm tucked in to keep his center of gravity close and tight.

He gripped the device's bar and his left hand tugged him forward, zooming over the roofs of the shops. It made for a pitiful approximation of a true Windrunner maneuver, but Leshwi dove after him anyway, echoing their previous contests.

Eyes watering from the pain in his arm, Kaladin dropped to a rooftop and spun to raise his spear toward Leshwi, gripping it firmly in his right hand—a classic formation grip, with the spear up beside his head. *Heal!* he thought at his arm as Leshwi slowed above, holding her lance in one hand and hovering.

She was plainly cautious, so Kaladin infused a patch of the rooftop with a Reverse Lashing, picturing it pulling on tassels of clothing. Leshwi's robes rippled and were pulled toward Kaladin, but she took a knife from her belt and cut them, dropping her train and much of the excess clothing to flutter down to affix itself to the rooftop.

Kaladin raised himself into the air again, wincing at the pain in his shoulder.

"What is wrong, Windrunner?" Leshwi asked in heavily accented Alethi, coming closer. "Your powers fail you."

"Fight me anyway," Kaladin called up at her. As he did, he caught a glimpse of the Pursuer's bloodred ribbon weaving out of a building below.

Leshwi followed his gaze and seemed to understand, for she raised her lance toward him in an attack posture. Kaladin took a deep breath and returned his spear to the overhand grip, weapon up by his head, his elbow cocked. He'd been trained in this grip for shield and spear combat. It was best with a group of friends each with shields up—but what combat wasn't?

He waited for her to get close, then stabbed at her, causing her to dodge away. The Pursuer's ribbon fluttered around nearby, weaving between watching Heavenly Ones.

Leshwi made a few more token attempts to engage him, and for a moment the fight seemed almost fair. Then Leshwi rose into the air and passed overhead, while Kaladin was left to twist—then disengage his device and drop a few feet before lurching into a hanging position, facing her. She cocked her head, then flew to the side and attacked him from that direction.

He tried to deflect, but he was too immobile. Her spear bit him in the left arm, causing him to grunt in pain. Blood spread from the wound, and—as before—it didn't heal immediately. In fact, his Stormlight seemed to be responding slower than it had earlier in this fight.

Storms, this had been a mistake. He couldn't duel Leshwi like this. He'd be better off on the ground; he'd be outmatched against opponents with the high ground, but at least he wouldn't be frozen in place. If Navani ever wanted these devices to be useful in aerial combat, she had a lot of work to do.

So he fled, engaging the device and sending himself flying between a couple of Heavenly Ones who moved dutifully to the sides to let Leshwi follow. Even the Pursuer seemed to respect the duel, as his ribbon stopped following and vanished below.

At least that part of Kaladin's plan had worked. Unfortunately, Leshwi had clearly put together that he couldn't veer to either side— and that his acceleration was limited to a single Lashing, the maximum from one falling weight. So while he crossed the vast room in seconds, the moment he slowed to prevent himself from hitting the wall, she slammed into him from behind. The force of the hit made him grip the speed-control bar by accident, and he was rammed into the wall by his own fist, Leshwi pressing him from behind.

She put a knife to his neck. "This is a sham, Stormblessed," she said in his ear. "This is no contest."

He squeezed his eyes shut, fighting off the pain of the hit and the cut to his arm—though that finally appeared to be healing. Slowly, but at least it was happening.

"We could drop to the ground," he said through gritted teeth. "Fight a duel without Surges."

"Would you actually do that?" Leshwi said. "I think you cannot spare the time. You're here to interfere with whatever the Lady of Wishes is doing."

Kaladin grunted his reply, not wanting to waste Stormlight by speaking.

Leshwi, however, pulled away in the air, leaving him to turn around awkwardly as he'd done before, with a dropping lurch. She drifted down to eye level with him. Past her, he spotted Syl rising into the air and coming toward him. She made a quick glyph in the air. *Ready.*

As Leshwi started talking, he fixed his attention on her so she wouldn't think anything was amiss.

"Surrender," she said. "If you give your weapon to me now, I might be able to get the Lady of Wishes to turn aside the Pursuer. Together we could start to work toward a true government and peace for Roshar."

"A true government and peace?" Kaladin demanded. "Your people are in the middle of *conquering* mine!"

"And did your leader not conquer his way to the throne?" she asked, sounding genuinely confused. "This is the way of your people as well as mine. Besides, you must admit my people govern better. The humans under our control have not been treated unfairly. Certainly they live better than the singers fared under your domination."

"And your god?" Kaladin asked. "You can promise me that once humankind has been subdued, he won't have us exterminated?"

Leshwi didn't respond, though she hummed to a rhythm he couldn't distinguish.

"I know the kind of men who follow Odium," Kaladin said softly. "I've known them all my life. I bear their brands on my forehead, Leshwi. I could almost trust you for the honor you've shown me—if it didn't mean trusting him as well."

She nodded, and seemed to accept this as a valid argument. She began lowering, perhaps to engage in that fight he'd suggested, without powers.

"Leshwi," he called after she had lowered partway. "I feel the need to point out that I didn't *agree* to fight you below. I simply noted it was an option."

"What is the distinction?" she called up.

"I'd rather you not see this as a broken oath," he said, then disengaged the fabrial and pointed it right at Syl before launching himself that direction—straight over Leshwi's head.

He didn't wait to see if she gave chase. Syl streaked ahead of him, leading him straight across the room toward the blue pool of water at the center. Guards were there, pushing people into buildings, but the way was open. The other Heavenly Ones kept their distance from him, assuming he was still dueling with Leshwi.

He cut the fabrial right as he passed over the well, then pointed his hand down and engaged it. His aim was true, and he sucked in more Stormlight as he splashed into the water. It *hurt* to hit, far more than he'd expected from something soft like water. His arm kept pulling him downward though, despite the resistance.

It quickly grew dark, and a part of him panicked at never having been this far beneath water before. His ears reacted oddly, painfully. Fortunately, his Stormlight sustained him in the chill depth. It also gave him light to see a figure below, swimming beside a group of glowing gemstones on the wall, secured here deep beneath the surface.

The figure turned toward him, her topknot swirling in the water—lit from the side by a variety of gemstone hues. It was her, the one who had been so fascinated with him last time. This time she seemed surprised, drawing a dagger from her belt and swinging it at him.

However, Kaladin found that Navani's fabrial worked far better in this environment. He could easily disengage it and swing it in another direction without dropping or lurching—and the added pull meant he easily outmaneuvered this Fused.

He spun around her and moved lower in the water. The well's shaft was only about ten feet wide, so when she pushed off a wall, she could reach him—but behind her, Syl highlighted the correct gemstone.

He engaged his own fabrial, which towed him past the Fused, letting her get a clean cut across his chest with her dagger. Blood clouded the water, but Kaladin connected his fist against the sapphire, knocking it free. He spun his spear in the water and jabbed it at the wires of the fabrial cage, then pried loose the glass sphere. That should do it.

Now to get out. He looked upward through the red water, and began to feel dizzy. Healing was coming so slowly.

Syl soared ahead of him as he used the fabrial to rise up, leaving the annoyed Fused behind. Syl's light was encouraging, as it seemed to be getting darker in here.

My Stormlight is running out. Storms. How was he going to get away? Dozens of Fused awaited him above. He . . . he might have to surrender, as Leshwi had insisted. Would they let him, now?

What was that rumbling? He saw light shimmering above, but it was *shrinking.* Syl made it out, but she didn't seem to have realized he was lagging behind her. And the light was vanishing.

A lid, he realized with panic. *They're putting a lid over the top of the well.* As he neared, in the last sliver of light he saw the hulking form of the Pursuer. Smiling.

The lid thumped in place right before Kaladin arrived. He burst into the small section of air between the top of the well's water level and the lid, gasping for breath.

But he was trapped. He slammed against the wood, trying to use the power of Navani's device to lift it—but he heard thumping as weights, likely stones, were set on top of it. More and more of them.

The Pursuer had been ready for this. He knew that even if Kaladin's gravitational Lashings worked, enough weight would keep the lid in place. In fact, it felt like the weights were alive. People, dozens of them, climbing on top of the lid. Of course. Why use stone when humans were heavy enough and far easier to move?

Kaladin pounded on the wood as he felt Syl panicking, unable to reach him. His Stormlight was fading, and it seemed the walls and the lid were closing in on him. He'd die in here, and it wouldn't take long. All the Pursuer had to do was wait. They could seal it above, denying him fresh air. . . .

In that moment of pure terror, Kaladin was in one of his nightmares again.

Blackness.

Encircled by hateful shadows.

Trapped.

Anxiety mounted inside him, and he began to thrash in the water, screaming, letting out the rest of his Stormlight. In that moment of panic, he didn't care. But as he fell hoarse from shouting, he heard—strangely enough—Hav's voice. Kaladin's old sergeant, from his days as a recruit.

Panic on the battlefield kills more men than enemy spears. Never run. Always retreat.

This water came from somewhere. There was another way out.

Kaladin took a deep breath and dove beneath the black water, feeling it surround him. His panic returned. He didn't know which way was up and which was down. How could you forget which way the *sky* was? But all was blackness. He fished in his pouch, finally managing to think clearly. He got out a glowing gemstone, but it slipped from his fingers.

And sank.

That way.

He pointed his fist toward the falling light and engaged Navani's device. He was in no state for delicacy, so he squeezed as tight as he could and lurched, towed by his arm farther into the darkness. He plunged past the fabrials and the Fused—she was swimming upward, and didn't seem concerned with him.

His ears screamed with a strange pain the deeper he went. He started to breathe in more Stormlight, but stopped himself. Underwater, he risked getting a lungful of liquid. But . . . he had no idea how to get Light when submerged. How had they never thought about this?

It was good that the device kept pulling him, because he might not have had the presence of mind to keep moving on his own. That was proven as he reached the gemstone he'd dropped, a garnet, and found it sitting on the bottom of the tube. A bright sapphire glowed here too, the one he'd knocked free. He grabbed it and disengaged the gauntlet fabrial, but it took him precious seconds to think and search around.

The tunnel turned level here. He moved in that direction, engaging the device, letting it pull him.

His lungs started to burn. He was still surviving on the breath he'd taken above, and didn't know how to get more Stormlight. He was still trailing blood as well.

Was that light ahead, or was his vision getting so bad that he was seeing stars?

He chose to believe it was light. When he reached it—more fabrial pumps—he shut off his fabrial, pointed his hand upward, and engaged the device again. Nightmares chased him, manifestations of his anxiety, and it was as if the world were crushing him. Everything became blackness once more.

The only thing he felt was Syl, so distant now, terrified. He thought that would be his last sensation.

Then he broke out of the water into the air. He gasped—a raw and primal action. A physiological response rather than conscious choice. Indeed, he must have blacked out anyway, for when he blinked and his senses returned, he found himself hanging by his aching arm from the ceiling in a reservoir beneath the tower.

He shook his head, and looked at his hand. He'd dropped the sapphire, and when he tried to breathe in Stormlight, nothing came. His pouch was empty of it. He must have fed off it while drifting in and out of consciousness. He was tempted to let himself sleep again. . . .

No! They'll be coming for you!

He forced his eyes open. If the enemy had explored the tower enough to know about this reservoir, they would come looking to be certain he was dead.

He disengaged the fabrial and dropped into the water. The cold shocked him awake, and he was able to use the fabrial to tug himself to the side of the reservoir. He crawled out onto dry stone. Amusingly, he was enough a surgeon to worry about how he'd contaminated this drinking water. Of all the things to think about right now . . .

He wanted to sleep, but could see blood dripping from his chest and arm, the wounds there not fully healed. So he stumbled to the side of the chamber and sucked the Stormlight from the two lamps there. Yes, the enemy knew about this place. If he hadn't been so addled, he'd have put together earlier that the light meant someone was changing the gemstones.

He stumbled, sodden and exhausted, down the hallway. There would be an exit. He vaguely remembered news of Navani's scouts finding this reservoir. They'd only known about it by having Thaylen free divers inspect the fabrials in the well.

Keep thinking. Keep walking. Don't drift off.

Where was Syl? How far was he from her now? He'd traveled quite a way in the darkness of that water.

He reached steps, but couldn't force himself to climb them. He just stood, numb, staring at them. So he used the fabrial. Slow, easy climbs with it tugging him up at one angle, then another. Back and forth. Again and again.

He knew he was close when he heard rumbling. The highstorm. It was still blowing, so he hadn't been in that blackness for an eternity. He let it call to him as he continued half-flying, half-trudging upward.

Finally he staggered out of a room on the ground floor of the tower. He emerged right into the middle of a group of singer troops shouting for people to go to their quarters.

The storm rumbled in the near distance. Several of the soldiers turned toward him. Kaladin had a moment of profound disconnect, as if he couldn't believe he was still alive. As if he'd thought that trudge up the stairwell had been his climb to the Tranquiline Halls.

Then one of the guards leveled a spear at him, and Kaladin's body knew what to do. Exhausted, wounded, nerves worn all the way to Damnation, Kaladin grabbed that spear and twisted it out of the man's hands, then swept the legs of the next soldier.

A few Regals not far off shouted, and he caught sight of a Heavenly One—not Leshwi—rising into the air and pointing a lance at him. They weren't through with him yet.

He turned and ran, holding that stolen spear, drawing in Stormlight from lanterns—but feeling it do nothing at all to heal him. Even the slow healing from before had apparently stopped working. Either he'd further undermined his powers somehow by destroying the fabrial, or—more likely—the Sibling was too far gone toward corruption.

Chased by dozens of soldiers, Kaladin ran for the storm. Though it was dangerous outside, at least the enemy would have difficulty finding him in the tempest. He couldn't fight them—the only way to escape was to do something truly desperate.

He reached the front entryway of the tower, where winds coursed in through a portal that might once have held a wooden gate. They'd never taken the time to put in a new one. Why would they? The storms rarely reached this high.

Today they had.

Today, Kaladin reached the winds.

And like everything else today, they tried their best to kill him.

Voice of Lights. Voice for Lights. If I speak for the Lights, then I must express their desires. If Light is Investiture, and all Investiture is deity, and deity has Intent, then Light must have Intent.

—From *Rhythm of War*, final page

Dalinar no longer feared highstorms.

It had been some time now since he'd worried that he was mad. Yet—as a poorly treated horse learned to flinch at the mere sound of a whip—something had persisted inside of Dalinar. A learned response that a storm meant losing control.

So it was with a deep and satisfying sense of relief that today, Dalinar realized he didn't fear the storm. Indeed, when Elthebar listed the time of today's storm, Dalinar felt a little surge of *excitement*. He realized he felt more awake on highstorm days. More capable.

Is that you? he asked of the Stormfather.

It is us, the Stormfather replied. *Me and you. I enjoy passing over the continent, as it gives me much to see—but it also tires me as it energizes you.*

Dalinar stepped away from the table and dismissed his attendants and scribes, who had finished briefing him on the latest intelligence regarding Urithiru. He could barely control his mounting concern about Navani and the tower. Something was wrong. He could feel it in his bones.

So he'd begun looking for options. The current plan was for him to lead an expedition into Shadesmar, sail to the tower, then open up a perpendicularity to let spies in. Unfortunately, they didn't know if it would work. Would he even be able to activate a perpendicularity in the area?

He had to try *something*. The latest letters from Navani, although they did contain her passcodes, felt unlike her. Too many delays, too many assurances she was fine. He'd ordered a team of workers to begin clearing the rubble that prevented his scouts from entering through the basement. That would reportedly take weeks, and Shardblades couldn't be summoned in the region, being suppressed like fabrials and Radiant powers.

He pressed his palm flat against the table, gritting his teeth. He ignored the stack of reports from the front lines. Jasnah and the others were handling the war, and he could see their victory approaching. It wasn't inevitable, but it was highly likely.

He should be focusing on his Bondsmith training. But how could he? He wanted to find a set of Plate, borrow a Blade, and go march to the battlefront and find someone to attack. The idea was so tempting, he had to acknowledge how much he'd come to depend on emotional support from the Thrill of battle. Storms, sometimes he longed so *powerfully* for the way he'd felt alive when killing. Such emotions were remarkably similar to what he'd felt upon giving up the drink. A quiet, anxious yearning that struck at unexpected moments—seeking the pleasure, the *reward*.

He couldn't blame everything he'd done on the Thrill. That had been Dalinar in those boots, holding that weapon and glorying in destruction. That had been Dalinar lusting to kill. If he let himself go out and fight again, he knew he'd realize a part of him still loved it.

And so, he had to remain here. Find other ways of solving his problems. He stepped out of his personal dwelling, another small stone hut in Laqqi, their command city.

He took a deep breath, hoping the fresh air would clear his mind. The village was now fully fortified against both storms and attacks, with high-flying scout posts watching the land all around and Windrunners darting in to deliver reports.

I must get better with my powers, Dalinar thought. *If I had access to the map I could make with Shallan, we might be able to see exactly what is happening at Urithiru.*

It would not help, the Stormfather said in his mind, a sound like distant thunder. *I cannot see the tower. Whatever weakens the Windrunners when they draw close weakens me too, so the map would not reveal the location. However, I could show it to you. Perhaps you can see better than I.*

"Show me?" Dalinar asked, causing Szeth—his omnipresent shadow—to glance at him. "How?"

You can ride the storm with me, the Stormfather said. *I have given others this privilege on occasion.*

"Ride the storm with you?" Dalinar said.

It is like the visions that Honor instructed me to grant, only it is now. Come. See.

"Martra," Dalinar said, looking to the scribe who had been assigned to him today. "I might act odd for a short time. Nothing is wrong, but if I am not myself when my next appointment begins, please make them wait."

"Um . . . yes, Brightlord," she said, hugging her ledger, eyes wide. "Should I, um, get you a chair?"

"That would be a good idea," Dalinar said. He didn't feel like being closed up inside. He liked the scent of the air, even if it was too muggy here, and the sight of the open sky.

Martra returned with a chair and Dalinar settled himself, facing eastward. Toward the Origin, toward the storms—though his view was blocked by the large stone stormbreak.

"Stormfather," he said. "I'm—"

He became the storm.

Dalinar soared along the front of the stormwall, like a piece of debris. No . . . like a gust of wind blowing with the advent of the storm. He could see—comprehend—far more than when he'd flown under Windrunner power.

It was a great deal to take in. He surged across rolling hills with plants growing in the valleys between them. From up high it looked like a network of brown islands surrounded by greenery—each and every lowland portion filled to the brim with a snarl of underbrush. He'd never seen anything quite like it, the plants unfamiliar to him, though their density did faintly remind him of the Valley where he had met Cultivation.

He didn't have a body, but he turned and saw that he towed a long shadow. The storm itself.

When the Windrunner flew on my winds, he zipped about, the Stormfather said, and Dalinar felt the sounds all around him. *You simply think. You complain about meetings, but you are well suited to them.*

"I grow," Dalinar said. "I change. It is the mark of humanity, Stormfather, to change. A prime tenet of our religion. When I was Kaladin's age, I suspect I would have acted as he."

We approach the mountains, the Stormfather said. *Urithiru will come soon. Be ready to watch.*

A mountain range started to grow up to Dalinar's right, and he realized where they must be—blowing through Triax or Tu Fallia, countries with which he had little experience. These weren't the mountains where he'd find Urithiru, not yet. So he experimented with motion, soaring closer to the overgrown valleys.

Yes . . . this landscape was alien to him, the way the underbrush snarled together so *green*. Full of grass, broad leaves, and other stalks, all woven together with vines and bobbing with lifespren. The vines were a netting tying it all together, tight against storms.

He saw curious animals with long tentacles for arms and leathery skin instead of chitin. Malleable, they easily squeezed through holes in the underbrush and found tight pockets in which to hide as the stormwall hit. Strange that everything would be so different when it wasn't that far from Alethkar. Only a little trip across the Tarat Sea.

He tried to hang back to inspect one of the animals.

No, the Stormfather said. *Forward. Ever forward.*

Dalinar let himself be encouraged onward, sweeping across the hills until he reached a place where the underbrush had been hollowed out to build homes. These valleys weren't so narrow or deep that flooding would be a danger, and the buildings were built on stilts a few feet high anyway. They were grown over by the same vine netting, the edges of the buildings melding with the underbrush to borrow its strength.

Once, this village had likely been in an enviable location—protected by the surrounding plants. Unfortunately, as he blew past, he noted multiple burned-out buildings, the rest of the village in shambles.

The Everstorm. Dalinar's people had adapted to it; large cities already had walls on all sides, and small villages had been able to rely upon their government's stockpiles to help them survive this change in climate. But small, isolated villages like this had taken the brunt of the new storm with nobody to help. How many such places existed on Roshar, hovering on the edge of extinction?

Dalinar was past the place in a few heartbeats, but the memory lingered. Over the last two years, what cities and towns hadn't been broken by the sudden departure of the parshmen had been relentlessly attacked by storm or battle. If they won—*when* they won—the war, they would have a great deal of work to do in rebuilding the world.

As he continued his flight, he saw something else discouraging: a pair of foragers trapped while making their way back toward their home. The ragged men huddled together in a too-shallow ravine. They wore clothing of thick woven fibers that looked like the rug material that came out of Marat, and their spears weren't even metal.

"Take mercy upon them," Dalinar said. "Temper your fury, Stormfather."

It is not fury. It is me.

"Then protect them," Dalinar said as the stormwall hit, plunging the ill-fated men into darkness.

Should I protect all who venture out into me?

"Yes."

Then do I stop being a storm, stop being me?

"You can be a storm with mercy."

That defies the definition and soul of a storm, the Stormfather said. *I must blow. I make this land exist. I carry seeds; I birth plants; I make the landscape permanent with crem. I provide Light. Without me, Roshar withers.*

"I'm not asking you to abandon Roshar, but to protect those men. Right here. Right now."

I . . . the Stormfather rumbled. *It is too late. They did not survive the stormwall. A large boulder crushed them soon after we began speaking.*

Dalinar cursed, an action that translated as crackling lightning in the nearby air. "How can a being so close to divinity be so *utterly* lacking in honor?"

I am a storm. I cannot—

You are not merely a storm! Dalinar bellowed, his voice changing to rumbles of thunder. *You are capable of choice! You hide from that, and in so doing, you are a COWARD!*

The Stormfather did not respond. Dalinar felt him there, subdued—like a petulant child scolded for their foolishness. Good. Both Dalinar and the Stormfather were different from what they once had been. They had to be better. The world *demanded* that they be better.

Dalinar soared up higher, no longer wanting to see specifics—in case he was to witness more of the Stormfather's unthinking brutality. Eventually they reached snow-dusted mountains, and Dalinar soared to the very top of the storm. Lately the storms had been creeping higher and higher in the sky—something people wouldn't normally notice, but which was quite obvious in Urithiru.

It is natural, the Stormfather said. *A cycle. I will go higher and higher until I am taller than the tower, then the next few storms will lower. The highstorm did this before the tower existed.*

There seemed to be a timidity to the words, uncharacteristic of the Stormfather. Perhaps Dalinar had rattled him.

Soon he saw the tower approaching.

You can see it? the Stormfather said. *The details?*

"Yes," Dalinar said.

Look quickly. We will pass rapidly.

Dalinar steered himself as a gust of wind, fixating upon Urithiru. Nothing seemed overtly wrong with it. There wasn't anyone up on the Cloudwalk level, but with the storms growing higher, that wouldn't be advisable anyway.

"Can we go inside?" Dalinar asked as they approached.

You may, the Stormfather said. *I cannot go inside, just as I cannot infuse spheres indoors. When a piece splits off, it is no longer me. You will need to quickly rejoin, or the vision will end.*

Dalinar picked the lowest accessible balcony in the tower's east-jutting lobes, up on the fourth tier, and lowered himself until he was right on target. As the storm passed, he soared in through the open balcony into the quiet hallway beyond.

It was over too swiftly. A rush through a dark hallway until he found the southern diagonal corridor, where he tried to reach the ground floor, but Dalinar was suddenly pulled out another balcony without having seen any signs of life. The stormwall passed by to crest the mountains and continue on toward Azir and his body.

"No," Dalinar said. "We need to look again."

You must continue forward. Momentum, Dalinar.

"Momentum kept me doing terrible things, Stormfather. Momentum *alone* is not a virtue."

We cannot do what you ask.

"Stop making excuses and *try* for once!" Dalinar said, provoking lightning around him. He resisted the push to continue at the front and—though it caused the Stormfather to groan with fits of thunder—Dalinar moved into the inner portions of the storm. The black chaos behind the stormwall.

He was wind blowing against wind, a man swimming against a tide, but he pushed all the way back to Urithiru. The Stormfather grumbled, but Dalinar didn't sense pain from the spren. Just . . . surprise. As if the Stormfather were genuinely curious about what Dalinar had managed to do.

It was difficult to stay in place, but he hovered outside the first tier, searching for anything alarming. The fury of the wind tugged at him. The Stormfather rumbled, and lightning flashed.

There. Dalinar felt something. A . . . faint Connection, like when he learned someone's language. His Surgebinding, his powers, drew him through the wind around the outside base of the tower—until he found something remarkable. A single figure, almost invisible in the darkness, clinging to the outside of the tower on the eighth level.

Kaladin Stormblessed.

Dalinar could not fathom what had brought the Windrunner to expose himself like this in a storm, but here he was. Holding on tightly to a ledge. His clothing was ragged, and he was wounded—bleeding from numerous cuts.

"Blood of my fathers," Dalinar whispered. "Stormfather, do you see him?"

I . . . feel him, the Stormfather said. *Through you. He seems to be waiting for the center of the storm, where his spheres and Stormlight will renew.*

Dalinar drew close to the young man, who had buried his head into his shoulder for protection. He was soaked through, a piece of his shirt slapping against the stone over and over.

"Kaladin?" Dalinar shouted. "Kaladin, what has happened?"

The young man didn't move. Dalinar calmed himself, resisting the furious winds, and drew power from the soul of the storm.

KALADIN, he said.

Kaladin shifted, turning his head. His skin had gone pale, his hair matted and whipped into rain-drenched knots. Storms . . . he looked like a dead man.

WHAT HAS HAPPENED? Dalinar demanded as the storm.

"Singer invasion," Kaladin whispered into the wind. "Navani captured. The tower on lockdown. Other Radiants are all unconscious."

I WILL FIND HELP.

"Radiant powers don't work. Except mine. Maybe those of a Bondsmith. I'm fighting. I'm . . . trying."

LIFE BEFORE DEATH.

"Life . . ." Kaladin whispered. "Life . . . before . . ." The man's eyes fluttered closed. He sagged, going limp, and dropped off the wall, unconscious.

NO. Dalinar gathered the winds, and with a surge of strength, used them to hurl Kaladin up and over the ledge of the balcony, onto the eighth floor of the tower.

That strained his abilities, and at last the tide grabbed Dalinar and *forced* him toward the front of the storm. As it happened, he was ejected from the vision and found himself in Emul, sitting in his chair. An honor guard of soldiers had arrived, forming a circle around him so people couldn't gawk. Though it had been a long time since Dalinar had been taken involuntarily in a vision, he appreciated the gesture.

He shook himself, rising to stand. Nearby, Martra held up her notebook. "I wrote down everything you said and did! Like Brightness Navani used to. Did I do it right?"

"Thank you," Dalinar said, scanning what she'd written. It seemed he had spoken out loud, like when in one of the old visions. Only, Martra hadn't heard the parts where he'd spoken as the storm.

One of the guards coughed, and Dalinar noticed one of the others gawking at him. The youth turned away immediately, blushing.

Because I was reading, Dalinar thought, handing back the notebook. He looked at the sky, expecting to see stormclouds—though here the highstorm would still be hours away from this region.

Stormfather, he thought. *The tower was invaded. Our worst fears are confirmed. The enemy controls Urithiru.* Storms, that felt painful to acknowledge. First Alethkar, then the tower? And Navani captured?

Now he knew why the enemy had thrown away Taravangian. Maybe even the entire army here in Emul. They'd been sacrificed to keep Dalinar occupied.

"Go to Teshav," Dalinar said to Martra. "Have her gather the monarchs and my highlords. I need to call an emergency meeting. Cancel everything else I was to do today."

The young woman yelped, perhaps at being given such an important task. She ran on his orders immediately. The soldiers parted at Dalinar's request, and he looked toward the sky again.

Stormfather, did you hear me?

You have hurt me, Dalinar. This is the second time you have done so. You push against our bond, forcing me to do things that are not right.

I push you to stretch, Dalinar said. *That is always painful. Did you hear what Stormblessed told me?*

Yes, he said. *But he is wrong. Your powers will not work at Urithiru. It seems . . . they have turned the tower's protections against us. If that is true, you would need to be orders of magnitude stronger, more experienced than you are, to open a perpendicularity there. You'd have to be strong enough to overwhelm the Sibling.*

I need to say more oaths, Dalinar said. *I need to better understand what I can do. My training goes too slowly. We need to find a way to speed it up.*

I cannot help you. Honor is dead. He was the only one who knew what you could do, in full. He was the only one that could have trained you.

Dalinar growled in frustration. He began to pace the unworked stone in front of his warcamp house.

Kaladin, Shallan, Jasnah, Lift . . . all of them picked up on their powers naturally, Dalinar said. *But here I am, many months after our Bonding, and I have barely progressed.*

You are something different from them, the Stormfather replied. *Something greater, more dangerous. But also more complicated. There has never been another like you.*

Distant thunder. Drawing closer.

Except . . . the Stormfather said.

Dalinar looked up as a thought struck him. Likely the same one that had occurred to the Stormfather.

There was another Bondsmith.

⸪

A short time later, an out-of-breath Dalinar arrived at a small building in the far northern part of the camp. People raced about, preparing for the imminent storm, but he ignored them. Instead he burst into the small building, surprising a woman tending to a hulking man seated on the floor, bent forward, muttering to himself.

The woman leaped to her feet, reaching for the sword she wore at her side. She was of a difficult race to distinguish—maybe Azish, with that dark skin tone. But her eyes were wrong—like a Shin person. These two were beings trapped outside of time. Creatures almost as ancient as Roshar. The Heralds Shalash and Talenelat.

Dalinar ignored the woman's threatening pose and strode forward, seizing her by the shoulders. "There were ten of you. Ten Heralds. All were members of an order of Knights Radiant."

"No," Shalash said. "We were before the Radiants. They were modeled upon us, but we were not in their ranks. Except for Nale."

"But there was one of you who was a Bondsmith," Dalinar said. "Ishi, Herald of Luck, Herald of Mysteries, Binder of Gods."

"Creator of the Oathpact," Shalash said, forcing herself out of Dalinar's grip. "Yes, yes. We all have names like that. Useless names. You should stop talking about us. Stop worshipping us. Stop *painting* us."

"He's still alive," Dalinar said. "He was unchained by the oaths. He would understand what I can learn to do."

"I'm sure," Shalash said. "If any—except me—are still sane, it would be him."

"He's near here," Dalinar said, in awe. "In Tukar. Not more than a short flight southeast of this very town."

"Isn't there an army in the way?" Shalash said. "Isn't pushing the enemy back—crushing them into Ishar's army—our *main* goal right now?"

"That's what Jasnah and our army are doing," Dalinar said. "But I have another task. I need to find a way to speak to the god-priest, then convince him to help me rescue Urithiru."

Intent matters. Intent is king. You cannot do what I attempt by accident. You must mean it. This seems a much greater law than we've ever before understood.

—From *Rhythm of War,* endnotes

Navani sat quietly in her cell of a library room, waiting. Hours passed. She requested food and was given it, but neither the guard nor the Deepest One watching her answered when she asked questions. So she waited. Too nervous to study. Too sick to her stomach to dare try speaking to the Sibling.

After all her assurances and promises, Navani had proven untrustworthy after all.

Raboniel finally arrived, wearing a simple outfit of trousers, a blouse, and a Thaylen vest. She'd previously said she found their designs fascinating. She'd chosen traditionally male clothing, but likely didn't mind the distinction.

The Lady of Wishes observed Navani from the doorway, then shooed the guards away. Navani gritted her teeth, then stood up and bowed. She'd been hurt, outmatched, and defeated. But she couldn't let anger and humiliation rule. She *needed* information.

"You didn't persist in trying to contact me," Raboniel said. "I assume you realized what had happened."

"How long were you listening in on my conversations with the Sibling, Ancient One?" Navani said.

"Always," Raboniel said. "When I could not be listening in, I had another Fused doing it."

Navani closed her eyes. *I gave them the secret to the third node. I pried it out of the Sibling, walking directly into the enemy's plan.*

"You shouldn't be too hard on yourself," Raboniel said. "The Sibling is truly to blame—they always *have* been so innocent. And unaware of their own naiveness. When I touched the pillar, I knew the Sibling was awake—but pretending to be dead. So I let the ruse continue, and I listened. I couldn't know that decision would bear fruit, but that is why you nurture nine seeds and watch for the one that begins growing."

"The Sibling told me . . ." Navani said. "They said we couldn't outthink you."

"Yes, I heard that," Raboniel said. "It made me worry that you'd spotted my surveillance. It seemed too obvious a line said to distract me."

"How?" Navani asked, opening her eyes. "How did you do it, Ancient One? Surely the Sibling would have known if their communication could be compromised."

Raboniel hummed a rhythm, then walked over and tapped Navani's stacks of notes. "Study. Find us answers about Light, Navani. Stop trying to fight me; help me end this war instead. That was *always* your purpose here."

Navani felt nausea stirring her insides. She'd thrown up once already from the sick feeling of what she'd done. What she'd cost the Sibling. She forced it down this time, and as Raboniel left, she managed to ask one more question.

"Kaladin," she said. "The Windrunner. Did you kill him, Ancient One?"

"I didn't," she said. "Though I did land a fine cut on him. You have likely realized that he succeeded in destroying the node, as the shield is still up. However, when the Windrunner was spotted fleeing the tower a good half hour after, his wound hadn't healed—so I think the Sibling's transformation is almost complete. This makes your Windrunner's powers quite unreliable. I find it unlikely he survived after running out into the storm."

"Into the *storm*?" Navani asked.

"Yes. A pity. Perhaps the Sibling can tell you if he is dead or not—if so, I should very much like to study his corpse."

Raboniel left. Navani pushed through her sickness to write, then burn, a prayer of protection for Kaladin. It was all she could do.

Then she rested her head on the table to think about the profound scope of her failure.

THE END OF

Part Three

İNTERLUDES

SZETH • CHIRI-CHIRI • TARAVANGIAN

Highspren are enigmatic beings in the best of circumstances. In Shadesmar, their forms are as solid as any of the other spren, although they appear as human-shaped holes in reality, spaces that look out onto unfamiliar starry skies

Distinguishing individual highspren is incredibly difficult, unless they happen to have a distinct silhouette. However, highspren seem to have no difficulty in identifying one another.

When they move, the stars do not move with them. Watching these beings walk is like looking through a moving window onto an alternate reality.

In the Physical Realm, they appear as a tear or hole, hanging in the air.

Szeth-son-Honor tried to slouch.

Dalinar said that slouching a little would help him imitate an ordinary soldier on a boring guard duty. Dalinar said Szeth prowled when he walked, and was too intense when standing at watch. Like a fire burning high when it should be smoldering.

How did one *stop* being intense? Szeth tried to understand this as he forced himself to lean against a tree, folding his arms as Dalinar had suggested. In front of him, the Blackthorn played with his grand-nephew, the child of Elhokar. Szeth carefully checked the perimeter of the small clearing. Watching for shadows. Or for people suspiciously lingering in the nearby camp—visible through the trees.

He saw nothing, which troubled him. But he tried to relax anyway.

The cloudy sky and muggy weather today were reminiscent of the coast of Shinovar, where Szeth's father had worked as a shepherd in his youth. With this thick grass, Szeth could almost imagine he was home. Near the beautiful white cliffs, listening to lambs bleat as he carried water.

He heard his father's gentle words. *The best and truest duty of a person is to add to the world. To create, and not destroy.*

But no. Szeth was not home. He was standing on profane stone in a forest clearing outside a small town in Emul. Dalinar knelt down, showing Gavinor—a child not yet five—how to hold his practice sword.

It had been a few minutes, so Szeth left the tree and made a circuit of the clearing, inspecting a few suspicious bundles of vines. "Do you see anything dangerous, sword-nimi?" he asked softly.

Nope, the sword said. *I think you should draw me. I can see better when I'm drawn.*

"When you are drawn, sword-nimi, you attempt to drain my life."

Nonsense. I like you. I wouldn't try to kill you.

The weapon projected its pleasant voice into Szeth's mind. Dalinar didn't like the sensation, so the sword now spoke only to Szeth.

"I see nothing dangerous," Szeth said, returning to his place beside the tree, then tried to at least *appear* relaxed. It was difficult, requiring vigilance and dedication, but he did not want to be chastised by Dalinar again.

That's good, right? Nothing dangerous?

"No, sword-nimi," Szeth said. "It is not good. It is concerning. Dalinar has so many enemies; they will be sending assassins, spies. If I do not see them, perhaps I am too lax or too unskilled."

Or maybe they aren't here to find, the sword said. *Vasher was always paranoid too. And he could* sense *if people were near. I told him to stop worrying so much. Like you. Worry, worry, worry.*

"I have been given a duty," Szeth said. "I will do it well."

Dalinar laughed as the young boy held his toy sword high and proclaimed himself a Windrunner. The child had been through a horrifying experience back in Kholinar, and he was quiet much of the time. Haunted. He'd been tortured by Voidspren, manipulated by the Unmade, neglected by his mother. Though Szeth's sufferings had been different, he couldn't help but feel a kinship with the child.

Dalinar clearly enjoyed seeing the child become more expressive and enthusiastic as they played. Szeth was reminded again of his own childhood spent playing with the sheep. A simple time, before his family had been given to the Honorblades. Before his gentle father had been taught to kill. To subtract.

His father was still alive, in Shinovar. Bearer of a different sword, a different burden. Szeth's entire family was there. His sister, his mother. It had been long since he'd considered them. He let himself do so now because he'd decided he wasn't Truthless. Before, he hadn't wanted to sully their images with his mind.

Time to make another round of the clearing. The child's laughter grew louder, but Szeth found it *painful* to hear. He winced as the boy jumped up on a rock, then leaped for his granduncle to catch him. And Szeth . . . if Szeth moved too quickly, he could catch sight of his own frail soul, attached incorrectly to his body, trailing his motions like a glowing afterimage.

Why do you hurt? the sword asked.

"I am afraid for the child," Szeth whispered. "He begins to laugh happily. That will eventually be stolen from him again."

I like to try to understand laughter, the sword said. *I think I can feel it. Happy. Ha! HA! Vivenna always liked my jokes. Even the bad ones.*

"The boy's laughter frightens me," Szeth said. "Because I am near. And I am . . . not well."

He should not guard this child, but he could not bring himself to tell Dalinar, for fear the Blackthorn would send him away. Szeth had found purpose here in following an Ideal. In trusting Dalinar Kholin. He could not afford to have that Ideal shaken. He could not.

Except . . . Dalinar spoke uncertainly sometimes. Concerned that he wasn't doing the right thing. Szeth wished he didn't hear Dalinar's weakness, his worries. The Blackthorn needed to be a moral rock, unshakable, always certain.

Dalinar was better than most. He *was* confident. Most of the time. Szeth had only ever met *one* man more confident than Dalinar in his own morality. Taravangian. The tyrant. The destroyer. The man who had followed Szeth here to this remote part of the world. Szeth was certain that, when he'd been visiting Taravangian with Dalinar the other day, the old man had seen through his illusory disguise.

The man would not let go. Szeth could feel him . . . *feel* him . . . plotting.

When Szeth returned to his tree, the air split, showing a blackness speckled faintly with stars beyond. Szeth immediately set down his sword by the trunk of the tree.

"Watch," he said, "and shout for me if danger comes."

Oh! All right! the sword said. *I can do that. Yes, I can. You might want to leave me drawn though. You know, so that if someone bad comes along, I can really* get *'em.*

Szeth walked around the rear of the tree, following the rift in the air.

It was as if someone had pried back the fabric of reality, like splitting skin to look at the flesh underneath.

He knelt before the highspren.

"You do well, my acolyte," the spren said, its tone formal. "You are vigilant and dedicated."

"I am," Szeth said.

"We need to discuss your crusade. You are a year into your current oath, and I am pleased and impressed with your dedication. You are among the most vigilant and worthy of men. I would have you earn your Plate. You still wish to cleanse your homeland?"

Szeth nodded. Behind, Dalinar laughed. He didn't seem to have noticed Szeth's momentary departure.

"Tell me more of this proposed crusade," the highspren said. It had not blessed Szeth with its name, though Szeth was its bonded Radiant.

"Long ago, my people rejected my warnings," Szeth said. "They did not believe me when I said the enemy would soon return. They cast me out, deemed me Truthless."

"I find inconsistencies to the stories you tell of those days, Szeth," the highspren said. "I fear that your memory, like those of many mortals, is incomplete or corrupted by the passage of time. I will accompany you on your crusade to judge the truth."

"Thank you," Szeth said softly.

"You may need to fight and destroy those who have broken their own laws. Can you do this?"

"I . . . would need to ask Dalinar. He is my Ideal."

"If you progress as a Skybreaker," the highspren said, "you will need to *become* the law. To reach your ultimate potential, you must know the truth yourself, rather than relying on the crutch presented by the Third Ideal. Be aware of this."

"I will."

"Continue your duty for now. But remember, the time will soon come when you must abandon it for something greater."

Szeth stood as the spren made itself invisible again. It was always nearby, watching and judging his worthiness. He entered the clearing and found Dalinar chatting quietly with a woman in a messenger uniform.

Immediately Szeth came alert, seizing the sword and striding over to stand behind Dalinar, prepared to protect him.

I hope it's all right that I didn't call for you! the sword said. *I could sense her, although I couldn't see her, and she seemed to be not evil. Even if she didn't come over to pick me up. Isn't that rude? But rude people can be not evil, right?*

Szeth watched the woman carefully. If someone wanted to kill Dalinar, they'd surely send an assassin who seemed innocent.

"I'm not sure about some of the things on this list," she was saying. "A pen and paper? For a man?"

"Taravangian has long since abandoned the pretense of being unable to read," Dalinar said.

"Then paper will let him plot against us."

"Perhaps," Dalinar said. "It could also simply be a mercy, giving him the companionship of words. Fulfill that request. What else?"

"He wishes to be given fresh food more often," she said. "And more light."

"I asked for the light already," Dalinar said. "Why hasn't the order been fulfilled?"

Szeth watched keenly. Taravangian was making demands? They should give him nothing. He was *dangerous*. He . . .

Szeth froze as the little boy, Gavinor, stepped up to him. He raised a wooden sword hilt-first toward Szeth. The boy should fear him, yet instead he smiled and waggled the sword.

Szeth took it, hesitant.

"The stone is the oddest request," the messenger woman said. "Why would he have need of a perfectly round, smooth stone? And why would he specify one with a vein of quartz?"

Szeth's heart nearly stopped. A round stone. With quartz inclusions?

"An odd request indeed," Dalinar said, thoughtful. "Ask him why he wants this before fulfilling the request."

A round stone.

With quartz inclusions.

An Oathstone.

For years, Szeth had obeyed the law of the Oathstone. The centuries-old tradition among his people dictated the way to treat someone who was Truthless. An object, no longer a man. Something to own.

Taravangian wanted an Oathstone. Why?

WHY?

As the messenger trotted away, Dalinar asked if Szeth would like to join sword practice, but he could barely mumble an excuse. Szeth returned to his spot by the tree, clutching the little wooden sword.

He *had* to know what Taravangian was planning.

He had to stop the man. Before he killed Dalinar.

C hiri-Chiri tried to hide in her grass. Unfortunately, she was growing too big. She wasn't like a regular cremling, those that scuttled around, tiny and insignificant. She was something grander. She could think. She could grow. And she could fly.

None of that helped as she tumbled out of the grass of the pot onto the desktop. She rolled over and clicked in annoyance, then looked toward Rysn, who sat making noises with another soft one. Chiri-Chiri did not always understand the mouth noises of the soft ones. They did not click, and there was no rhythm to them. So the sounds were sometimes just noises.

Sometimes they were not. There *was* a pattern to them that she was growing better at understanding. And there was a *mood* at times to their tones, almost like a rhythm. She crawled closer along the desk, trying to listen.

It was difficult. Chiri-Chiri did not like listening. She liked to do what felt right. Sleeping felt right. Eating felt right. Saying she was happy, or hungry, or sad felt right.

Communication should be about moods, desires, needs. Not all these flapping, flapping, sloppy wet noises.

Like the ones Rysn made now, talking to the old soft one who was like a parent. Chiri-Chiri crawled over the desk and into her box. It didn't smell as alive as the grass, but it was nice, stuffed with soft things and covered over with some vines. She clicked for it. Contentment. Contentment felt right.

"I do not understand half of what you explain, Rysn," the old soft one said as the two sat in chairs beside the table. Chiri-Chiri understood some of the words. And his hushed tone, yet tense. Confused. That was confusion. Like when you are bitten on the tail by one you thought was happy. "You're saying these things . . . these Sleepless . . . are all around us? Moving among us? But they aren't . . . human?"

"They are as far from human as a being can get, I should guess," Rysn said, sipping her tea. Chiri-Chiri understood her better. Rysn wasn't confused. More thoughtful. She'd been that way ever since . . . the event at the homeland.

"This is not what I thought I was preparing you for," the old soft one said, "with your training in negotiation."

"Well, you always liked to travel paths others thought too difficult," Rysn said. "And you relished trading with people ignored by your competition. You saw opportunity in what others discarded. This is somewhat the same."

"Pardon, Rysn—dear child—but this feels *very* different."

The two fell silent, but it wasn't the contented silence of having just eaten. Chiri-Chiri turned to snuggle back into her blankets, but felt a vibration coming up through the ground. A kind of call, a kind of warning. One of the rhythms of Roshar.

It reminded her of the carapace of the dead ones she had seen in the homeland. Their hollow skull chitin, their gaping emptiness, so still and noiseless. A silence of having eaten all, and having then been consumed.

Chiri-Chiri could not hide. The rhythm whispered that she could not do only easy things. Dark times were coming, the hollow skulls warned. And the vibrations of that place. Encouraging. Demanding. *Be better. You must be better.*

And so, Chiri-Chiri climbed out of her box and crawled up onto the arm of Rysn's chair. Rysn scooped her up, assuming she wanted scratches at the part along her head where carapace met skin. And it did feel nice. Nice enough that Chiri-Chiri forgot about hollow skulls and warning rhythms.

"Why do I feel," the old soft one said, "that you shouldn't have told me about any of this? The more people who know what you've done, Rysn, the more dangerous it will be for you."

"I realize this," she said. "But . . . Babsk . . . I had to tell *someone*. I need your wisdom, now more than ever."

"My wisdom does not extend to the dealings of gods, Rysn," he said. "I am just an old man who thought himself clever . . . until his self-indulgences nearly destroyed the life and career of his most promising apprentice."

Rysn sat up sharply, causing Chiri-Chiri to start and nip at her fingers. Why did she stop scratching?

Oh. Emotions. Chiri-Chiri could nearly feel them thrumming through Rysn, like rhythms. She was sad? Why sad? They had enough to eat. It was warm and safe.

Was it about the hollowness? The danger?

"Babsk," Rysn said. "You *still* blame yourself for my foolishness? My follies were *mine* alone."

"Ah, but I knew of your brashness," he said. "And it was my duty to check it." He took her hands, so Chiri-Chiri nipped at them a little— until Rysn glared at her. They didn't taste good anyway.

The two soft ones shared something. Almost like they *could* project emotions with a vibration or a buzz, instead of flapping their lips and squishing their too-melty faces. Those really were odd. Why didn't all their skin flop off, without carapace to hold it in? Why didn't they hurt themselves on everything they bumped?

But yes, they shared thoughts. And finally the old one nodded, standing. "I will help you bear this, Rysn. Yes, I should not complain about my own deficiencies. You have come to me, and show me great honor in doing so."

"But you mustn't tell anyone," she said to him. "Not even the queen. I'm sorry."

"I understand," he said. "I will ponder what you've told me, then see what advice—if any—I can have on this unique situation." He took his hat and moved to leave, but hesitated and said a single word. "Dawnshards." He imbued it with meaning somehow. Disbelief and wonder.

After he'd left, a few nips got Rysn to start scratching again. But she felt distracted, and soon Chiri-Chiri was unable to enjoy the scratches. Not with the hollow eyes speaking to her. Warning her.

To enjoy easy days, sometimes you had to first do difficult things. Rysn activated her chair—which flew a few inches off the ground, though it didn't have any wings. Chiri-Chiri jumped off onto the desk.

"I need something to eat," Rysn said. And Chiri-Chiri concentrated on the sounds, not the tired cadence.

Eat. Food.

"Eeeaaat." Chiri-Chiri tried to get her mandibles to click the sounds, blowing through her throat and making her carapace vibrate.

Rysn smiled. "I'm too tired. That almost sounded . . ."

"Rrrrrizzznn," Chiri-Chiri said. "Eeeeaat. Voood." Yes, that seemed right. Those were good mouth noises. At least, Rysn dropped her cup of tea and made a shocked vibration.

Perhaps doing it this way *would* be better. Not just because of the hollow skulls. But because, if the soft ones could be made to understand, it would be far easier to get scratches when they were required.

THE SWORD

Taravangian awoke hurting. Lately, each morning was a bitter contest. Did it hurt more to move or to stay in bed? Moving meant more pain. Staying in bed meant more anguish. Eventually he chose pain.

After dressing himself with some difficulty, he rested at the edge of the bed, exhausted. He glanced at the notes scratched on the side of an open drawer. Should he hide that? He should. The words appeared jumbled to him today. He had to stare at them a long time to get them to make sense.

Dumb. How dumb was he? Too . . . too dumb. He recognized the sensation, his thoughts moving as if through thick syrup. He stood. Was that light? Yes, sunlight.

He shuffled into the main room of his prison. Sunlight, through an open window. Strange. He hadn't left a window open.

Windows were all boarded up, he thought. *Someone broke one. Maybe a storm?*

No. He slowly realized that Dalinar must have ordered one opened. Kindly Dalinar. He liked that man.

Taravangian made his way to the sunlight. Guards outside. Yes, they would watch. They knew he was a murderer. He smiled at them anyway, then opened the small bundle on the windowsill. A notebook, a pen, and some ink. Had he asked for that? He tried to remember.

Storms. He wanted to sleep. But he couldn't sleep through another day. He'd done that too often.

He returned to his room and sat—then realized he had forgotten what he'd intended to do. He retraced his steps, looked down at the pen and paper again, and only then remembered. He went back into his bedroom. Unhooked the drawer with the instructions. Slowly read them.

Then again.

He laboriously copied them into the notebook. They were a list of things he needed to say if he could meet Szeth alone. Several times, the words "Don't talk to Dalinar" were underlined. In his current state, Taravangian was uncertain about that. Why not talk to him?

Smarter him was convinced they needed to do this themselves. Dalinar Kholin could *not* be entrusted with Taravangian's plans. For Dalinar Kholin would do what was right. Not what was needed.

Taravangian forced himself to get food. He had some in the other room, bread that had gone stale. He should have asked for better food. Only after chewing on it did he think to go look at the table right inside his door where they delivered his meals. Today was the day new food came. And there it was. Fresh bread. Dried meat. No jam.

He felt like a fool. Why not look for fresh food *before* forcing yourself to choke down the old stuff? It was difficult to live like this. Making easy mistakes. Forgetting what he was doing and why.

At least he was alone. Before he'd gotten good staff, people had always been so angry at him when he was stupid. And since he got emotional when stupid, he often cried. Didn't they understand? He made their lives difficult. But he *lived* the difficulty. He wasn't trying to be a problem.

People took their minds for granted. They thought themselves wonderful because of how they'd been born.

"Traitor!" a voice called into the room. "You have a visitor!"

Taravangian felt a spike of alarm, his fingers shaking as he closed and gripped the notebook. A visitor? Szeth had come? Taravangian's planted seed bore fruit?

He breathed in and out, trying to sort through his thoughts. They were a jumble, and the shouting guard made him jump, then scramble toward the sound. He prepared himself for the sight of Szeth. That haunted stare. Those dead eyes. Instead, at the window, Taravangian saw a young man with black hair peppered blond. The Blackthorn's son Renarin.

Taravangian hesitated, though the guards waved for Taravangian to come speak to the youth.

He hadn't prepared for this. Renarin. Their quiet salvation. Why had he come? Taravangian hadn't prepared responses in his notebook for *this* meeting.

Taravangian stepped up to the window, and the guards retreated to give them privacy. Here Taravangian waited, expecting Renarin to speak first. Yet the boy stood silent, keeping his distance from the window—as if he thought Taravangian would reach out and grab him.

Taravangian's hands were cold. His stomach churned.

"Something changed," Renarin finally said, looking away as he spoke. He avoided meeting people's eyes. Why? "About you. Recently. Why?"

"I do not know, Brightlord," Taravangian said—though he felt sweat on his brow at the lie.

"You've hurt my father," Renarin said. "I believe he thought, up until recently, that he could change you. I don't know that I've seen him as morose as when he speaks of you."

"I would . . ." Taravangian tried to think. Words. What words? "I would that he had changed me, Brightlord. I would that I could have been changed."

"I believe that is true," Renarin said. "I see your future, Taravangian. It is dark. Not like anything I've seen before. Except there's a point of light flickering in the darkness. I worry what it will mean if that goes out."

"I would worry too."

"I can be wrong," Renarin said. He hesitated, then closed his eyes—as if carefully thinking through his next words. "You are in darkness, Taravangian, and my father thinks you are lost. I lived through his return, and it taught me that no man is ever so far lost that he cannot find his way back. You are not alone."

The young man opened his eyes, stepped forward, then lifted his hand and presented it toward Taravangian. The gesture felt awkward. As if Renarin wasn't quite sure what he was doing.

He wants me to take his hand.

Taravangian didn't. Seeing it made him want to break into tears, but he contained himself.

Renarin withdrew his hand and nodded. "I'll let you know if I see something that could help you decide." With that the boy left, accompanied by one of the guards—the man who had yelled at Taravangian earlier.

That left one other guard: a short, nondescript Alethi man who walked up to the window to eye Taravangian. Taravangian watched Renarin walking away, wishing he had the courage to call after the boy.

Foolish emotions. Taravangian was not lost in darkness. He had chosen this path, and he knew precisely where he was going. Didn't he?

"He is wrong," the guard said. "We can't all return from the dark. There are some acts that, once committed, will always taint a man."

Taravangian frowned. That guard had a strange accent. He must have lived in Shinovar.

"Why did you ask for an Oathstone?" the guard demanded. "What is your purpose? Do you wish to tempt or trick me?"

"I don't even know you."

The man stared at him with unblinking eyes. Eyes like one of the dead . . . and Taravangian finally understood what on any other day he would have seen immediately. The guard wore a different illusion today.

"Szeth," Taravangian whispered.

"Why? Why do you seek an Oathstone? I will *not* follow your orders again. I am becoming my own man."

"Do you have the sword?" Taravangian asked. He reached out, foolish though it was, and tried to grab Szeth. The man stepped away in an easy motion, leaving Taravangian grasping at air. "The sword. *Did you bring it?*"

"I *will not serve you*," Szeth said.

"Listen to me," Taravangian said. "You have to . . . the sword . . . Wait a moment." He furiously began flipping through the notebook for the words he'd copied from the desk drawer.

"'The sword,'" he read, "'is something we didn't anticipate. It was nowhere in the Diagram. But Odium fears it. Do you understand? He *fears* it. I think it might be able to harm him. We attack him with it.'"

"I will not serve you," Szeth said. "I will not be manipulated by you again. My stone . . . was always only a stone. . . . My father said . . ."

"Your father is dead, Szeth," Taravangian said. "Listen to me. Listen." He read from the notebook. "'Fortunately, I believe his ability to see us here is limited. Therefore, we may talk freely. I doubt you can harm Odium directly unless you are in one of his visions. You must get into one of those visions. Can you do this?'"

There were more notes in the book about how to manipulate Szeth. Taravangian read them, and the words made him hurt. Hadn't this man been through enough?

He rejected those manipulations and looked up at Szeth. "Please," Taravangian whispered. "Please help me."

Szeth didn't appear to have heard. He turned to go.

No! "Listen," Taravangian said, going off script, ignoring the orders of his smarter self. "Give *Dalinar* the sword. Dalinar is taken to Odium's vision sometimes. It should travel with him. Do you understand? Odium thinks the sword is in Urithiru. He *doesn't realize you're here*. He can't see it because of Renarin."

Smarter Taravangian claimed he didn't want to work with Dalinar because it was too dangerous, or because Dalinar wouldn't believe. Those lies made dumb Taravangian want to pound his fists at his own face out of shame. But the truth was more shameful.

Szeth did not care which Taravangian he was speaking to. "I don't understand your manipulations," the man said as he walked away. "I should have realized I wouldn't be able to understand the way your mind works. All I can do is refuse."

He left, sending the other guard back to watch Taravangian—who stood gripping his little notebook, crying.

FOUR

A Knowledge

ADOLIN • SHALLAN • NAVANI •
VENLI • ESHONAI • BRIDGE FOUR

The Calligraphic Phonemes

A	I	M	SH				
B	F	N	T				
V	P	O	TH				
CH	G	U	Y				
K	H	R	J				
D	L	S	Z				
E							

The Hybrid Phonemes (below) have gained popularity recently and incorporate shortcuts experienced calligraphers have used for decades. In a hundred years, I suspect this set will supersede the others and be the basis for a more streamlined Alethi glyph system.

A	I	M	SH				
B	F	N	T				
V	P	O	TH				
CH	G	U	Y				
K	H	R	J				
D	L	S	Z				
E							

Now, on to different things! (Finally.) You know my tendency towards boredom, and I suspect your giving me this latest errand was less to collect information and more for your own amusement, to see if you could interest me in something other than smuggling artifacts, covertly collecting strange weapons, and drawing in those secret sketchbooks you've endlessly chided me about since you discovered them. (For the record, I also enjoy learning rude phrases in other languages, thank you very much. I'm not entirely uncultured.)

I regret to inform you that your clever scheme to make a scholar of me might have, unfortunately, worked. For, while I hope to never return to the Calligraphers Guild, I did discover something intriguing.

The instructors in the guild, especially the self-proclaimed calligro-cartographer Isasik Shulin, have repeatedly told us it is futile to pick apart the phonemes from old glyphs. Nobody tells me what not to do (except for you, though I don't always listen), so picking apart old glyphs is exactly what I've done, dissecting them like little biology projects. My rebellion yielded very little until I teased out some bits from the ancient glyph for Roshar, which oddly looks a lot like the ancient symbol for the Knights Radiant, but the phonemes in the glyph don't say "Roshar." If you separate out its components, this emerges:

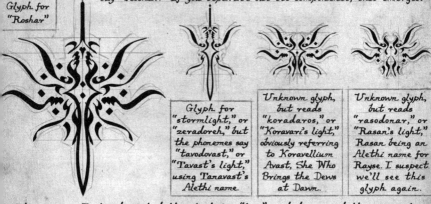

Glyph for "Roshar"

Glyph for "stormlight," or "zeradoreh," but the phonemes say "tavodovast," or "Tavast's light," using Tanavast's Alethi name.

Unknown glyph, but reads "koradaros," or "Koravari's light," obviously referring to Koravellium Avast, She Who Brings the Dews at Dawn.

Unknown glyph, but reads "rasodonar," or "Rasan's light," Rasan being an Alethi name for Rayse. I suspect we'll see this glyph again.

Then again, I also dissected the glyph for "love" and discovered the principle phonemes for "friendly cremling," so I could be, as they say, seeing shades in the mist, unless we're looking for a new name for our little organization.

Next page: How to swear like a Horneater. Oo'kali'laa'e!

EIGHT YEARS AGO

Venli could hear new rhythms. She tried to hide this fact, attuning the old, boring rhythms around others. It was so *difficult.* The new rhythms were her majesty, the proof that she was
special. She wanted to shout them, *flaunt* them.

Quiet, Ulim said from her gemheart. *Quiet for now, Venli. There will be
time enough later to enjoy the Rhythm of Praise.*

She attuned Exultation, but did not hum it as she walked through the
room where her scholars worked. Ulim had given her hints about finding another form, nimbleform. He wouldn't tell her the exact process
yet, so she'd gathered these scholars and set them to work.

Over time, she intended to use them as an excuse to reveal many important discoveries. Including ones that Ulim had promised her. Greater
forms than these. Power.

You are special, Ulim whispered as she idled near a pair of her scholars
who were trying to trap a windspren that had flown in to tease them. *I
could sense you from far away, Venli. You were chosen by our god, the true god
of all singers. He sent me to explain how wonderful you are.*

The words comforted her. Yes. That was right. She *would* wear forms
of power. Only . . . hadn't she once wanted those . . . for her mother?
Wasn't that the point?

You will be great, he said within her gemheart. *Everyone will recognize your majesty.*

"Well, I want nimbleform soon," she whispered to Ulim, stepping out of the chamber. "It has been too long since warform. My sister and her sycophants get to tromp around the cities on display like heroes."

Let them. Those are your grunts, who will be sent to die fighting the humans once our plot is accomplished. You should take time "finding" nimbleform. It will be too suspicious for you to find another so soon.

She folded her arms, listening to the new rhythm praise her. The city buzzed with activity, thousands of listeners from a dozen families passing by. Eshonai and the others had made great strides toward true unity, and the elders of the various families were talking to one another.

Who would get the glory for that? Venli had orchestrated this grand convergence, but everyone *ignored* her.

Perhaps she should have taken warform. Ulim had urged her to be one of the first, but she'd hesitated. She hadn't been frightened, no, but she'd assumed she could manipulate better without taking the form.

That had been a mistake, and this was her reward: Eshonai taking all the credit. Next time, Venli would do it herself.

"Ulim," she whispered, "when will the other Voidspren be ready?"

Can't say for certain, he replied. *That stupid Herald is still standing strong all these years later. We have to work around him.*

"The new storm," Venli whispered.

Yes. It's been building in Shadesmar for centuries. We need to get our agents close enough to it on this side—a place that is out in the ocean, mind you—so they can use gemstones to pull my brothers and sisters across. Then those stones have to be physically transported here. You have no idea how much of a pain it all is.

"I'm well acquainted by now," she said to Derision. "You never shut up about it."

Hey, you're the only one I get to talk to. And I like to talk. So . . .

"Nimbleform. When?"

We have bigger problems. Your people aren't ready to accept forms of power. At all. They're far too timid. And the way they fight . . .

"What's wrong with the way we fight?" Venli asked to Conceit. "Our warriors are powerful and intimidating."

Please, Ulim replied. *The humans have remembered how to make good steel all these centuries, and even figured out some things we never learned. Meanwhile, your people throw spears at each other like primitives. They yell and dance more than they fight. It's embarrassing.*

"Maybe you should have gone to the humans then."

Don't be childish, Ulim said. *You need to know what you're facing. Imagine a hundred thousand men in glistening armor, moving in coordinated blocks, lifting a wall of interlocking shields—broken only by the spears coming out to bite your flesh.*

Imagine thousands upon thousands of archers loosing waves of arrows that sweep in a deadly rain. Imagine men on horseback charging—thunder without lightning—and riding down anyone in their path. You think you can face that with a few semicoherent boasts?

Venli's confidence wavered. She looked out toward the Shattered Plains, where their warforms trained on a nearby plateau. She'd nudged them toward that, following Ulim's suggestions. He knew a lot about manipulating people; with his help she could get the others to do pretty much anything.

A part of her thought she should be concerned about that. But when she tried to think along those lines, her mind grew fuzzy. And she ended up circling back to whatever she'd been thinking about before.

"Eshonai guesses that the humans are bluffing about how many cities they have," she said. "But if they have dozens like they told us, then our numbers would be roughly equal. If we can get all the families to listen to us."

Roughly equal? Ulim said, then started laughing. An outrageous sound, uproarious. It made her gemheart vibrate. *You and them? Even? Oh, you blessed little idiot.*

Venli felt herself attune Agony. She *hated* the way he made her feel sometimes. He'd whisper about how great she was, but then they'd get deep into a conversation and he'd speak more freely. More derogatorily.

"Well," she said, "maybe we don't have to fight them. Maybe we can find another way."

Kid, you're not gonna have a choice on that one, Ulim said. *They will make sure of it. You know what they've done to all the other singers in the world? They're slaves.*

"Yes," Venli said. "Proof that my ancestors were wise in leaving."

Yeah, please don't say that around any of my friends, Ulim said. *You'll*

*make me look bad. Your ancestors were traitors. And no matter what
you do, the humans will make you fight. Trust me. It's what they always
do.*

*Your primitive little paradise here is doomed. Best you can do is train
some soldiers, practice using the terrain to your advantage, and prepare to get
some actual forms. You don't get to choose to be free, Venli. Just which master
to follow.*

Venli pushed off from the wall and began walking through the city.
Something was wrong about Ulim. About her. About the way she
thought now . . .

You have no idea the power that awaits you, Venli, Ulim said to the
Rhythm of Craving. *In the old days, forms of power were reserved for the
most special. The most valuable. They were strong, capable of amazing feats.*

"Then how did we ever lose?" she asked.

*Bah, it was a fluke. We couldn't break the last Herald, and the humans
found some way to pin the whole Oathpact on him. So we got stuck on Braize.
Eventually the Unmade decided to start a war without us. That turned out
to be exceedingly stupid. In the past, Odium granted forms of power, but Ba-
Ado-Mishram thought she could do it. Ended up handing out forms of power
as easily as Fused give each other titles, Connected herself to the entire singer
species. Became a little god. Too little.*

"I . . . don't understand."

*I'll bet you don't. Basically, everyone relied way too much on an oversized
spren. Trouble is, spren can get stuck in gemstones, and the humans figured this
out. End result: Ba-Ado-Mishram got a really cramped prison, and everyone's
souls got seriously messed up.*

*It will take something big to restore the minds of the singers around the
world. So we're going to prime the pump, so to speak, with your people. Get
them into stormform and pull the big storm over from Shadesmar. Odium
thinks it will work, and considering he's anything but a* little *god, we are
going to do what he says. It's better than the alternative, which generally involves a lot of pain and the occasional flavorful dismemberment.*

Venli nodded to some listeners passing by. Members of another family; she could tell by the colors of the bands on their braids and the type
of gemstone bits in the men's beards. Venli deliberately hummed one of
the weak old rhythms for them to hear, but these newcomers didn't give
her a second glance despite her importance.

Patience, Ulim said. *Once the Return arrives, you will be proclaimed as the one who initiated it—and you will be given everything you deserve as the most important of all listeners.*

"You say my ancestors were traitors," Venli whispered. "But you need us. If they hadn't split off, you wouldn't have us to use in your plot. You should bless what they did."

They got lucky. Doesn't mean they weren't traitors.

"Perhaps they knew what Ba-Ado-Mishram was going to do, and so they attuned Wisdom, not Betrayal, in their actions."

She knew the name, of course. As a keeper of songs, she knew the names of all nine Unmade—who were among the gods her people swore to never follow again. But the more she talked with Ulim, the less regard she gave the songs. The old listeners had memorized the wrong things. How could they retain the names of the Unmade, but forget something as simple as how to adopt workform?

Anyway, who cares what your ancestors did? Ulim said. *We need to prepare your people for forms of power, then get them to summon Odium's storm. Everything will take care of itself after that.*

"That might be harder than you think, spren," Venli said to Derision. She quieted her voice as another group of listeners passed. The city was so packed these days, you could barely find any peace to think.

Forms of power, Venli. The ability to reshape the world. Strength beyond anything you've ever dreamed of having.

She stuffed her hands into the pockets of her robe as she reached the heart of the city. She hadn't realized she was coming this way, to her family's home. She stepped inside, and found her mother picking apart a rug she had woven. Jaxlim glanced up at Venli, jumping.

"It's only me," Venli said to Peace.

"I got it wrong again," Jaxlim said, huddling over her rug. "Wrong every time . . ."

Venli tried to attune Indifference, one of the new rhythms, but she couldn't find it. Not here, not with her mother. She instead settled down on the floor, cross-legged, like she'd sat as a child when learning the songs.

"Mother?" Venli asked to Praise. "Everyone makes mistakes."

"Why can't I do anything *right* anymore?"

"Mother, can you tell me the first song?" Venli whispered.

Jaxlim kept picking at the rug.

"You know it," Venli said. "Days we sing. Days we once knew? Days of—"

"Days of pain," Jaxlim said, to the Rhythm of Memories. "Days of loss. Days of glory."

Venli nodded as Jaxlim continued. This song was more of a chant, the original recitation of her people leaving the war. Leaving their gods. Striking out on their own.

This is painful to hear, Ulim noted. *Your people had no idea what they were doing.*

Venli ignored him, listening, feeling the Rhythm of Memories. Feeling . . . like herself. This *had* all been about finding a way to help her mother, hadn't it? At the start?

No, she admitted. *That's what you told yourself. But you want more. You've always wanted more.*

She knew forms changed the way a person thought. But was she in a new form now? Ulim had been dodgy in explaining it. Evidently she had a normal spren in her gemheart to give her workform—but Ulim was there too, crowding in. And he could speak to her, even hear what she was thinking.

You single-handedly delivered warform to your people, Ulim whispered. *Once you give them additional forms, they will revere you. Worship you.*

She wanted that respect. She wanted it so *badly.* But she forced herself to listen to what her ancestors had done, four hundred of them striking out alone, wearing dullform.

The fools were inbred, then, Ulim said. *No wonder . . .*

"These people created us," she whispered. Her mother continued singing, and didn't seem to have heard the interruption. "They were *not* fools. They were heroes. Their *primary* teaching, preserved in everything we do, is to *never* let our gods rule us again. To never take up forms of power. To never serve Odium."

Then don't serve him, Ulim said. *Deal with him. You have something he needs—you can approach him from a place of power. Your ancestors were lowly things; that was why they wanted to leave. If they'd been at the top, like your people will be, they'd have never wanted such a thing.*

Venli nodded. But she was more persuaded by other arguments. War *was* coming with the humans. She could feel it in the way their soldiers eyed her people's weapons. They had enslaved those parshmen. They'd do the same to Venli's people.

The ancient songs had become irrelevant the moment Eshonai had led the humans to the Shattered Plains. The listeners could no longer hide. Conflict *would* find them. It was no longer a choice between their gods or freedom. It was a choice between their gods and human slaving brands.

How do we proceed? Ulim asked.

Venli closed her eyes, listening to her mother's words. Her ancestors had been desperate. "We will need to be equally desperate," Venli whispered. "My people need to see what I have seen: that we can no longer remain as we have been."

The humans will *destroy them.*

"Yes. Help me prove it."

I am your servant in this, Ulim said to Subservience. *What do you propose?*

Venli listened. Jaxlim's voice cracked and she trailed off. Jaxlim had forgotten the song again. The older femalen turned away and cried softly.

It broke Venli's heart.

"You have agents among the humans, Ulim?" Venli whispered.

We do.

"Can you communicate with them?"

I have ways of doing so.

"Have your agents influence those at the palace," Venli said. "Get the Alethi to invite us to visit. Their king spoke of it before he left; he's considering it already. We must bring our people there, then show them how powerful the humans are. We must overwhelm my people with our own insignificance."

She stood up, then went to comfort her mother.

We must make them afraid, Ulim, Venli thought. *We must make them sing to the Terrors long into the night. Only then will they listen to our promises.*

It shall be done, he replied.

Words.
I used to be good with words.
I used to be good at a lot of things.

Venli tried to attune the Rhythm of Conceit as she walked the halls of Urithiru. She kept finding the Rhythm of Anxiety instead. It was difficult to attune an emotion she didn't feel; doing so felt like a worse kind of lie than she normally told. Not a lie to others, or to herself. A lie to Roshar.

Timbre pulsed comfortingly. These were dangerous times, requiring dangerous choices.

"That sounds an awful lot like the things Ulim told me," Venli whispered.

Timbre pulsed again. The little spren was of the opinion that Venli couldn't be blamed for what she'd done, that the Voidspren had manipulated her mind, her emotions, her goals.

Timbre, for all her wisdom, was wrong in this. Ulim had heightened Venli's ambitions, her arrogance, but *she'd* given him the tools to work with. A part of her continued to feel some of those things. Worse, Ulim had occasionally left her gemheart during those days, and she'd still gone through with those plans, without his influence.

She might not bear *full* blame for what had happened. But she'd been a willing part of it. Now she had to do her best to make up for it. So she kept her head high, walking as if she owned the tower, trailed by Rlain, who carried the large crate as if on her orders. Everyone needed to see her treating him as a servant; hopefully that would quash some of the rumors about the two of them.

He hurried closer as they entered a less populated section of the tower. "The tower *does* feel darker now, Venli," he said to the Rhythm of Anxiety—which didn't help her own mood. "Ever since . . ."

"Hush," she said. She knew what he'd been about to say: Ever since the fight in the market.

The whole tower knew by now that Kaladin Stormblessed, Windrunner and champion, fought. That his powers still functioned. The Fused had worked hard to spread a different narrative—that he'd been faking Radiant powers with fabrials, that he'd been killed during a cruel attack on innocent singer civilians in the market.

Venli found that story far-fetched, and she knew Stormblessed only by reputation. She doubted the propaganda would fool many humans. If Raboniel had been behind it, the message would have been more subtle. Unfortunately, the Lady of Wishes spent most of her time with her research, and instead let the Pursuer lead.

His personal troops dominated the tower. Already there had been a half dozen instances of singers beating humans near to death. This place was a simmering cauldron, waiting for the added bit of fuel that would bring it to a boil. Venli needed to be ready to get her people out when that happened. Hopefully the crate Rlain carried would help with that.

Head high. Hum to Conceit. Walk slowly but deliberately.

By the time they reached the Radiant infirmary, Venli's nerves were so tight she could have played a rhythm on them. She shut the door after Rlain—they'd recently had it installed by some human workers— and finally attuned Joy.

Inside the infirmary, the human surgeon and his wife cared for the comatose Radiants. They did a far better job of it than Venli's staff; the surgeon knew how to minimize the formation of sores on the humans' bodies and how to spot signs of dehydration.

When Venli and Rlain entered, the surgeon's wife—Hesina—hurried over. "Is this them?" she asked Rlain, helping him with the crate.

"Nah, it's my laundry," he said to Amusement. "Figured Venli here is so mighty and important, she might be able to get someone to wash it for me."

Joking? *Now?* How could he act so indifferent? If they were discovered, it would mean their executions—or worse.

The human woman laughed. They carried the box to the back of the room, away from the door. Hesina's son put down the shoestrings he'd been playing with and toddled over. Rlain ruffled his hair, then opened the crate. He moved the decoy papers on top, revealing a group of map cases.

Hesina breathed out in a human approximation of the Rhythm of Awe.

"After Kal and I parted," Rlain explained, "and the queen surrendered, I realized I could go anywhere in the tower. A little black ash mixed with water covered my tattoo, blending it into my pattern. Humans were confined to quarters, and so long as I looked like I was doing something important, the singers ignored me.

"So I thought to myself, 'What can I do to best undermine the occupation?' I figured I had a day at most before the singers got organized and people started asking who I was. I thought about sabotaging the wells, but realized that would hurt too many innocents. I settled on this."

He waved his hand over the round tubes filling the crate. Hesina took one out and unrolled the map inside. It depicted the thirty-seventh floor of the tower, meticulously mapped.

"So far as I know," Rlain said, "guard posts and master-servant quarters just contain maps of the lower floors. The upper-level maps were kept in two places: the queen's information vault and the map room. I stopped by the map room and found it burned out, likely at the queen's order. The vault was on the ground floor, far from where her troops could have reached. I figured it might still be intact."

Rlain shrugged a human shrug. "It was shockingly easy to get in," he continued to Resolve. "The human guards had been killed or removed, but the singers didn't know the value of the place yet. I walked right through a checkpoint, stuffed everything I could into a sack, and wandered out. I said I was on a search detail sent to collect any form of human writing."

"It was brave," Lirin the surgeon said, stepping over and folding his arms. "But I don't know how useful it will be, Rlain. There's not much they'd want on the upper floors."

"It might help Kaladin stay hidden," Rlain said.

"Maybe," Lirin said. "I worry you put yourself through an awful lot of effort and danger to accomplish what might add up to a mild inconvenience for the occupation."

The man was a pragmatist, which Venli appreciated. She, however, was interested in other matters. "The tunnel complex," she said. "Is there a map here of the tunnels under the tower?"

Rlain dug for a moment, then pulled out a map. "Here," he said. "Why?"

Venli took it reverently. "It's one of the few paths of escape, Rlain. I came in through those tunnels—they're a complicated maze. Raboniel knew her way through, but I doubt I could get us out on my own. But with this . . ."

"Didn't the enemy collapse those tunnels?" Lirin asked.

"Yes," Venli said. "But I might have a way around that."

"Even if you do," Lirin said, "we'd have to travel through the most heavily guarded section of the tower—where the Fused are doing their research on the tower fabrials."

Yes, but could she use her powers to form a tunnel through the stone? One that bypassed Raboniel's workstation and the shield, then intersected with these caverns below?

Perhaps. Though there was still the greater problem. Before they could run, she had to ensure the Fused wouldn't give chase. Escaping the tower only to die by a Heavenly One's hand in the mountains would accomplish nothing.

"Rlain," Hesina said. "These are wonderful. You did more than anyone could have expected of you."

"I might have been able to do more, if I hadn't messed up," Rlain said to Reconciliation. "I was stopped in the hallway, asked to give the name of the Fused I was operating under. I should have played dumb instead of using the name of one I'd heard earlier in the day. Turns out that Fused doesn't *keep* a staff. She's one of the lost ones."

"You could have locked yourself in a cell the moment the tower fell," Lirin said, "and pretended to be a prisoner. That way, the Fused could have liberated you, and no one would be suspicious."

"Every human in the tower knows about me, Lirin," Rlain said. "The 'tame' Parshendi your son 'keeps.' If I'd tried a ploy like that, the singers would have found me eventually, and I'd have ended up in a cell for real." He shrugged again. "Did anyway though."

He and Hesina began digging through the maps, Rlain chatting with them as they did. He seemed to like these humans, and looked more comfortable around them than he was with her. Beyond that, the way he used human mannerisms to exaggerate his emotions—the way the rhythms were a subtle accent to his words, rather than the driving power behind them—it all seemed a little . . . pathetic.

Lirin returned to his work tending the unconscious. Venli strolled over to him, attuning Curiosity. "You don't like what they're doing," Venli said, nodding toward the other two.

"I'm undecided," Lirin said. "My gut says that stealing a few maps won't hurt the occupation. But perhaps if we turned the maps *in* and claimed we found them in a forgotten room, there's a good chance it would earn us favor with the Fused. Perhaps it would prove Hesina and I aren't malcontents, so we could come out of hiding."

"It isn't the hiding that protects you," Venli said, "it is Lady Leshwi's favor. Without it, the Pursuer would kill you, no matter what you did to prove yourself. He'd kill other Fused, if he thought it would let him fulfill his tradition. And the others would applaud him."

Lirin grunted—a human version of Derision, she thought—as he knelt beside a Radiant and lifted her eyelids to check her eyes. "Nice to know your government has its idiocies too."

"You really don't want to resist, do you?" Venli said to Awe. "You truly want to live with the occupation."

"I resist by controlling my situation," Lirin said. "And by working with those in power, rather than giving them reason to hurt me and mine. It's a lesson I learned very painfully. Fetch me some water."

Venli was halfway to the water station before she realized she'd done what he said, despite telling him—*several* times—that he needed to show her more respect. What a strange man. His attitude was so commanding and in charge, but he used it to reinforce his own subservience.

Timbre thrummed as Venli returned to him with the water. She needed to practice her powers some more—particularly if she might be required to tunnel them down through many feet of rock to reach an exit. She took the tunnel map and gave it to Jial, one of her loyalists. Jial folded it and placed it into her pocket as a knock sounded at the door.

Venli glanced toward Rlain and Hesina, but they'd apparently heard, for they covered up the crate of maps. It still looked suspicious to Venli, but she went to the door anyway. Fused wouldn't knock.

Accordingly, she opened the door and let in a group of humans who bore water jugs on poles across their shoulders. Six workers—the same ones as always. That was good, for although Venli had permission from Raboniel to bring a human surgeon in to care for the fallen Radiants, she had lied in saying she'd gone to the clinic to recruit him.

Eventually, Lirin and Hesina would be recognized—but best to limit their exposure to as few people as possible. The water carriers delivered their burdens to the room's large troughs, then helped with the daily watering of the patients. It demanded near-constant work to give broth and drink to so many unconscious people.

Venli checked the time by the Rhythm of Peace. She needed to visit Raboniel for translation duty soon—there were books in Thaylen that the Lady of Wishes wanted read to her.

She doesn't care about anything other than her research, Venli thought. *What could be so important?*

"You there," Lirin said. "What is that on your head?"

Venli turned to find the surgeon confronting one of the water bearers. Lirin pushed back the hair on the man's head and pointed. She hummed to Irritation—the surgeon was generally calm, but once in a while something set him off. She strode over to settle the situation, to find that the water bearer—a short man with far too much hair on his body—had painted his forehead with some kind of ink.

"What is that?" Venli asked.

"Nothing, Brightness," the man said, pulling out of Lirin's grip. "Just a little reminder." He moved on, but one of the other water carriers—a female this time—had a similar marking on her forehead.

"It's a *shash* glyph," Lirin said.

As soon as Venli knew it was writing, her powers interpreted it. "Dangerous? Why do they think they're dangerous?"

"They don't," Lirin said—wearing his upset emotions on his face. "They're fools."

He turned to go, but Venli caught him by the arm and hummed to

Craving. Which of course he couldn't understand. So she asked, "What does it *mean*?"

"It's the brand on . . . on the forehead of Kaladin Stormblessed."

Ah . . . "He gives them hope."

"That hope is going to get them killed," Lirin said, lowering his voice. "This isn't the way to fight, not with how brutal the Regals in the tower have started acting. My son may have gotten himself killed resisting them. Heralds send it isn't true, but his example *is* going to cause trouble. Some of these might get the terrible idea of following in his steps, and that will inevitably provoke a massacre."

"Maybe," Venli said, letting him go. Timbre pulsed to an unfamiliar rhythm that echoed in her mind. What *was* it? She could swear she'd never heard it before. "Or maybe they simply need something to keep them going, surgeon. A symbol they can trust when they can't trust their own hearts."

The surgeon shook his head and turned away from the water carriers, instead focusing on his patients.

like many other spren in Shadesmar,
peakspren wear human clothing.

Peakspren fashion,
and to some degree
their textures, remind
me of the Unkalaki

The cracks in their skin
don't appear to affect
them in any way.

Some of these
cracks almost
seem to form
glyphs or symbols.

There is as much variety in color and texture to their stone
forms as could be imagined by any geologist. They can be as
smooth as polished marble or as rough as porous basalt.

In the Physical Realm, peakspren can disappear into
stone to stay hidden. To reappear, they break out of
other nearby stone, even if it's as small as a pebble.

75

THE MIDDLE STEP

There was a time when others would approach me for help with a problem. A time when I was decisive. Capable. Even authoritative.

I t was a crystalline day in Shadesmar as Adolin—guarded as always by two honorspren soldiers—climbed to the top of the walls of Lasting Integrity. During his weeks incarcerated in the fortress, he'd discovered that there *were* weather patterns in Shadesmar. They just weren't the same type as in the Physical Realm.

When he reached the top of the wall, he could see a faint shimmer in the air. It was only visible if you could look a long distance. A kind of violet-pink haze. Crystalline, they called it. On days like these, plants in Shadesmar grew quickly enough to see the change with your eyes.

Other types of "weather" involved spren feeling invigorated or dreary, or certain types of smaller spren getting more agitated. It was never about temperature or precipitation.

From the top of the wall, he could really get a sense of the fortress's size. Lasting Integrity was enormous, several hundred feet tall. It was also hollow, and had no roof. Rectangular and resting on the small side, all four of its walls were perfectly sheer, without windows. No human city would ever have been built this way; even Urithiru needed fields at its base and windows to keep the people from going mad.

But Lasting Integrity didn't follow normal laws of nature. You could walk on the interior walls. Indeed, to reach the top, Adolin had strolled vertically up the inside of the fortress wall. His body thought he had been walking on the ground. However, at the end of the path, he'd reached the battlements. Getting onto them had required stepping off what seemed to be the edge of the ground.

As he'd done so, gravity had caught his foot, then propelled him over so he was now standing at the very top of the fortress. He felt vertigo as he glanced *down* along a wall he'd recently treated as the ground. In fact, he could see all the way to the floor hundreds of feet below.

Thinking about it gave him a headache. So he looked outward across the landscape. And the view . . . the view was spectacular. Lasting Integrity overlooked a sea of churning beads lit by the cold sun so they shimmered and sparkled, an entire ocean of captured stars. Huge swells washed through the bay and broke into crashing falls of tumbling beads.

It was mesmerizing, made all the more interesting by the lights that congregated and moved in the near distance. Tukar and the people who lived there, reflected in the Cognitive Realm.

The other direction had its own less dramatic charms. Rocky obsidian shores gave way to growing forests of glass, lifespren bobbing among the trees. Lifespren were larger here, though still small enough that he wouldn't have been able to see them save for the bright green glow they gave off.

These lights blinked off and on, a behavior that seemed unique to this region of Shadesmar. Watching, Adolin could swear there was a coordination to their glows. They'd blink in rippling waves, synchronized. As if to a beat.

He took it in for a moment. The view wasn't why he'd come, however. Not fully. Once he'd spent time drinking in the beauty, he scanned the nearby coast.

Their camp was still there, tucked away a short walk into the highlands, nearer the trees. Godeke, Felt, and Malli waited for the results of his trial. With some persuasion, the honorspren had allowed Godeke to come in, given him a little Stormlight, and let him heal Adolin's wound. The honorspren had expelled Godeke soon after, but permitted Adolin to communicate with his team via letters.

They'd traded—with his permission—a few of his swords to a passing caravan of Reachers for more food and water. Non-manifested weapons were worth a lot in Shadesmar. The Stump, Zu, and the rest of Adolin's soldiers had left to bring word to his father. Though Adolin had initially anticipated a quick and dramatic end to his incarceration, the honorspren hadn't wanted an immediate trial. He should have realized the punctilious spren would want time to prepare.

Though aspects of the delay were frustrating, the wait favored him. The longer he spent among the honorspren, the more chance he had to persuade them. Theoretically. So far, the spren of this fortress seemed about as easy to persuade as rocks.

One other oddity was visible from this high perch. Gathering on the coast nearby was an unusual group of spren. It had begun about two weeks ago as a few scattered individuals, but those numbers grew each day. At this point, there had to be two hundred of them. They stood on the coast all hours of the day, motionless, speechless.

Deadeyes.

"Storms," said Vaiu. "There are so many."

Vaiu was Adolin's primary jailer for excursions like this. He was a shorter honorspren and wore a full beard, squared like that of an ardent. Unlike many others, Vaiu preferred to go about bare-chested, wearing only an old-style skirt a little like an Alethi takama. With his winged spear, he seemed like a depiction of a Herald from some ancient painting.

"What happened to the ones you let in?" Adolin asked.

"We put them with the others," Vaiu explained. "Everything about them seems normal, for deadeyes. Though we don't have space left for more. We never expected . . ." He shook his head. There were no lights of souls near those deadeyes; this wasn't a gathering of Shardbearers in the Physical Realm. The deadeyes were moving of their own accord, coming up from the depths to stand out here. Silent. Watching.

The fortress had quarters for deadeyes. Though Adolin had little love for these honorspren and their stubbornness, he had to admit there *was* honor in the way they treated fallen spren. The honorspren had dedicated themselves to finding and caring for as many as they could. Though they'd taken Maya and put her in with the others, they let Adolin visit her each morning to do their exercises together. While they wouldn't let her wander free, she was treated quite well.

But what would they do with so many? The honorspren had taken in the first group, but as more and more deadeyes arrived, the fortress had reluctantly shut its gates to them.

"It doesn't make any sense," Vaiu said. "They should all be wandering the oceans, not congregating here. What provoked this behavior?"

"Has anyone tried asking them?" Adolin asked.

"Deadeyes can't talk."

Adolin leaned forward. Around his hands on the railing, pink crystal fuzz began to grow: the Shadesmar version of moss, spreading because of the crystalline day.

The distance was too great for him to distinguish one scratched-out face from another. However, he did notice when one vanished into mist. Those spren were Shardblades—hundreds of them, more than he'd known existed. When their owners summoned them, their bodies evaporated from Shadesmar. Why were they here? Deadeyes usually tried to keep close to their owners, wandering through the ocean of beads.

"There is a Connection happening," Vaiu said. "Deadeyes cannot think, but they are still spren—bound to the spiritweb of Roshar herself. They can feel what is happening in this keep, that justice will finally be administered."

"If you can call it justice," Adolin said, "to punish a man for what his ancestors did."

"*You* are the one who suggested this course, human," Vaiu said. "You took their sins upon you. This trial cannot possibly make remediation for the thousands murdered, but the deadeyes sense what is happening here."

Adolin glanced at his other guard, Alvettaren. She wore a breastplate and a steel cap—both formed from her substance, of course—above close-cropped hair. As usual she stared forward, her lips closed. She rarely had anything to add.

"It is time for today's legal training," Vaiu said. "You have very little time until the High Judge returns and your trial begins. You had best spend it studying instead of staring at the deadeyes. Let's go."

Veil was really starting to hate this fortress. Lasting Integrity was built like a storming monolith, a stupid brick of a building with *no windows*. It was impossible to feel anything other than *trapped* while inside these walls.

But that wasn't the worst of it. The worst was how honorspren had no respect whatsoever for the laws of nature. Veil opened the door from the small building she shared with Adolin, looking out at what seemed to be an ordinary street. A walkway of worked stone led from her front door and passed by several other small buildings before dead-ending at a wall.

However, as soon as she stepped out, her brain started to panic. Another flat surface of stone hung in the air *above* her, instead of the sky. It was clustered with its own buildings—and people, mostly honorspren, walked along its pathways. To her left and right were two other surfaces, much the same.

The actual sky was *behind* her. She was walking on the inside surface of one of the walls of the fortress. It squeezed her mind, making her tremble. *Shallan,* Veil thought, *you should be leading. You'd like the way this place looks.*

Shallan did not respond. She huddled deep within, refusing to emerge. Ever since they'd discovered that Pattern had been lying to them, probably for years, she had become increasingly reclusive. Veil was able to coax her out now and then, but lately something . . . dangerous had come with her. Something they were calling Formless.

Veil wasn't certain it was a new persona. If it wasn't, would that be even worse?

Veil let Radiant take over. Radiant wasn't so bothered by the strange geometry, and she took off down the path without feeling vertigo— though even she had trouble sometimes. The worst parts were the strange halfway zones at the corners where each plane met, where you had to step from one wall to another. The honorspren did it easily, but Radiant's stomach did somersaults every time she had to.

Shallan, Radiant thought, *you should sketch this place. We should carry drawings with us when we leave.*

Nothing.

Honorspren liked to keep the hour exactly, so the bells told Radiant she was on time as she turned up the side of the wall toward the sky, passing various groups of spren going about their business. This wall of the fortress—the southern plane—was the most beautified, with gardens of crystalline plants of a hundred different varieties.

Fountains somehow flowed here, the only free water Radiant had seen in Shadesmar. She passed one fountain that surged and fell in powerful spouts; if a spray got beyond about fifteen feet high, the water would suddenly break off the top and stream down toward the *actual* ground rather than back toward the wall plane. Storms, this place didn't make any kind of sense.

Radiant turned away from the fountain and tried to focus on the people she was passing. She hadn't expected to find anyone other than honorspren in here, considering how strict the fortress was, but apparently its xenophobic policy had only been instituted a year ago. Any other people then living inside the fortress were allowed to stay, though they'd be forbidden reentry if they left.

That meant ambassadorial delegations from the other spren nations—as well as some tradespeople and random wanderers—had been grandfathered into the honorspren lockdown. Most importantly, seventeen humans lived here.

Without direction from Shallan, and with the honorspren taking their time preparing their trial, Radiant and Veil had reached a compromise. They'd find Restares, the person Mraize had sent them to locate. They wouldn't take any actions against him unless they could get Shallan to decide, but Radiant was perfectly willing to locate him. This man, the phantom leader of the Sons of Honor, was a key part of this entire puzzle—and she was intensely curious why Mraize wanted him so badly.

Restares was, according to Mraize, a human male. Radiant carried a description of the man in her pocket, though none of the honorspren Veil had asked knew the name. And unfortunately, the description was rather vague. A shorter human with thinning hair. Mraize said Restares was a secretive type, and would likely be using an alias and perhaps a disguise.

He was supposedly paranoid, which made perfect sense to Radiant. Restares led a group of people who had worked to restore the singers and the Fused. The coming of the Everstorm had led to the fall of multiple kingdoms, the deaths of thousands, and the enslavement of millions. The Sons of Honor were deplorable for seeking these things. True, it wasn't clear their efforts had in fact influenced the Return, but she could understand why they wanted to hide.

Upon first entering the fortress, she'd asked to be introduced to the other humans residing in the place. In response, the honorspren had given her the full list of all humans living here. With limited locations to search, she'd assumed her task would be easy. Indeed, it had started out that way. She'd started with the largest group of people: a caravan of traders from a kingdom called Nalthis, a place out in the darkness beyond the edges of the map. Veil had chatted with them at length, discovering that Azure—who had moved on from the fortress by now—was from the same land.

Radiant had trouble conceptualizing what it meant for there to be kingdoms out away from the continent. Did Azure's people live on islands in the ocean?

No, Veil thought. *We're avoiding the truth, Radiant. It means something else. Like Mraize told us. Those people came from another land. Another world.*

Radiant's mind reeled at the thought. She took a deep breath, slowing near a group of trees—real ones from the Physical Realm, kept alive with Stormlight instead of sunlight—that were the centerpieces of this park. The tops were so high that when leaves fell off, they drifted down toward the real ground, through the middle of the fortress.

Shallan, Radiant thought. *You could come and talk to people from other worlds. This is too big for Veil and me.*

Shallan stirred, but as she did, that darkness moved with her. She quickly retreated.

Let's focus on today's mission, Radiant, Veil said.

Radiant agreed, and forced Veil to emerge. She could handle the strange geography; she had to. She put her head down and continued. None of the travelers from Nalthis looked like Restares, or seemed likely to be him in disguise. The next handful on her list had been Horneaters; apparently there was a clan of them who lived in Shadesmar. She'd doubted any were Restares, but she'd interviewed each of them just in case.

That done, Veil had been left with five people. Four turned out to be wanderers. None had been open about their pasts, but over the weeks she'd met with them one by one. After conversing with each, she had reported on them to Mraize. He had eliminated each of those as possibilities.

Now, only a single name remained on her list. This person was the most reclusive of them all—but was male, and the descriptions of him from the honorspren indicated that he was probably her quarry. Today she would finally catch a glimpse of him. With the subject confirmed she could call Mraize, find out what message she was supposed to deliver to Restares, then be done with this mission.

The target called himself "Sixteen." He supposedly came out of his home once every sixteen days exactly—the regularity of it amused the honorspren, who suffered the odd fellow because of the novelty. No one knew how he survived without food, and no one reported a terrible stench or anything like that from him—though he didn't ever seem to bathe or empty a chamber pot. Indeed, the more she'd learned about him, the more Veil was certain this mysterious man was her target.

His home was a small box built near the statue garden. Veil had made a habit of visiting this garden, where she tried to coax Shallan out by drawing. It worked occasionally, though Shallan usually retreated after a half hour or so of sketching.

Today, Veil curled up on a bench with a sketchpad, coat enveloping her, hat shading her eyes. Today was the day that Sixteen would emerge, assuming he followed his pattern. All she had to do was wait and not act suspicious.

Shallan, Veil said, opening the sketchbook. *See? It's time to draw.*

Shallan started to emerge. Unfortunately, a faint humming sound made her panic and Veil was thrust back into control. She sighed, glancing to the side—to where Pattern walked among the statues, which she'd been told were of honorspren killed in the Recreance. Tall men and women with heroic builds and clothing that—though made of stone—seemed to ripple in the wind. How odd that they'd made these; after all, the real individuals were still around, though deadeyed.

Pattern bobbed over to her. He was easy to tell from other Cryptics; he had an excitable spring to his step, while others slunk or crept, more furtive.

"I thought you were watching the Nalthians today," Veil said.

"I was!" he said, plopping down on the bench beside her. "But Veil, I do not think any of them are Restares. They do not look like him at all. They do not even look like people from Roshar. Why do you think

Azure appeared so much like an Alethi, when these have the wrong features?"

"Don't know," Veil said, pretending to sketch. "But this Restares could be using something like Lightweaving. I need you to watch them carefully."

"I am sorry," Pattern said, his pattern slowing, like a wilting plant. "I miss being with you."

You're worried you'll miss something important, traitor, Shallan thought. *And want an excuse to keep spying on me.*

Veil sighed again. She reached over and put her hand on Pattern's. He hummed softly.

We need to confront him, Radiant thought. *We need to find out exactly why he is lying.*

Veil wasn't so certain. It was all growing so messy. Pattern, Shallan's past, the mission they were on. She needed Shallan to remember. That would solve so much.

Wait, Radiant thought. *Veil, what do you know? What do you remember that I do not?*

"Veil?" Pattern asked. "Can I talk to Shallan?"

"I can't force her to emerge, Pattern," Veil said. Stormwinds; she suddenly felt so tired. "We can try later, if you want. For now, Sixteen is going to come out of that house in a few minutes. I need to be ready to intercept him in a way that reveals his face, but doesn't make him suspicious of me."

Pattern hummed. "Do you remember," he said softly, "when we first met on the boat? With Jasnah? Mmm . . . You jumped in the water. She was so shocked."

"Nothing shocks Jasnah."

"That did. I barely remember—I was so new to your realm."

"That wasn't the first time we met though," Radiant said, sitting up straighter. "Shallan had spoken oaths before, after all. She had a Shardblade."

"Yes." If he had been human, his posture would have been described as unnaturally still. Hands clasped, seated primly. His pattern moved, expanding, contracting, rotating upon itself. Like an explosion.

"I think," he finally said, "we have been doing this wrong, Radiant. I once tried to help Shallan remember, and that was painful for her. Too painful. So I started to think it was good for her not to remember. And the lies *were* delicious. Nothing is better than a lie with so much truth."

"The holes in her past," Radiant said. "Shallan doesn't want to remember them."

"She can't. At least not yet."

"When Shallan summoned you as a Blade," Radiant said, "and killed her mother, were you surprised? Did you know she was going to do something that drastic?"

"I . . . don't remember," Pattern said.

"How can you not remember?" Radiant pressed.

He remained quiet. Radiant frowned, considering the lies she'd caught him in during the last few weeks.

"Why did you want to bond a human, Pattern?" Radiant found herself asking. "In the past, you've seemed so certain that Shallan would kill you. Yet you bonded her anyway. Why?"

This is a dangerous line of questioning, Radiant, Veil warned. *Be careful.*

"Mmm . . ." Pattern said, humming to himself. "Why. So many answers to a why. You want the truest one, but any such truth is also a lie, as it pretends to be the only answer." He tipped his head to the right, looking toward the sky—though so far as she knew, he didn't "see" forward, as he didn't have eyes. He seemed to sense all around him.

She glanced in the same direction. Colors shimmered in the sky. It was a crystalline day.

"You and the others," Pattern said, "refer to Shadesmar as the world of the spren, and the Physical Realm as 'your' world. Or the 'real' world. That is not true. We are not two worlds, but one. And we are not two peoples, but one. Humans. Spren. Two halves. Neither complete.

"I wanted to be in the other realm. See that part of our world. And I knew danger was coming. All spren could sense it. The Oathpact was no longer working correctly. Voidspren were sneaking onto Roshar, using some kind of back door. Two halves cannot fight this enemy. We need to be whole."

"And if Shallan killed you?"

"Mmm. I was sure you would. But together, we Cryptics thought we needed to try. And I volunteered. I thought, maybe even if I die it will be the step other spren need. You cannot reach the end of a proof without many steps in the middle, Shallan. I was to be the middle step."

He turned toward her. "I no longer believe you will kill me. Or perhaps I wish to no longer believe you will kill me. Ha ha."

Radiant wanted to believe. She wanted to know.

This will lead to pain, Veil warned.

"Can I trust you, Pattern?" Radiant asked.

"Any answer will be a lie," he said. "I cannot see the future like our friend Renarin. Ha ha."

"Pattern, have you lied to us?"

His pattern wilted. ". . . Yes."

Radiant took a deep breath. "And have you been spying on us? Have you been using the cube Mraize gave us, in secret?"

"I'm sorry, Radiant," he said softly. "I couldn't think of another way."

"Please answer the questions."

"I have," he said, his pattern growing even smaller.

There, Radiant thought. *Was that so hard? We should have asked him right away, Veil.*

It was only then that she noticed, deep inside, that Shallan was seething. Twisting about herself, trembling, fuming, alternating between terror and anger.

That . . . didn't seem good.

Pattern's pattern swirled small and tight. "I try to be worthy of trust. That is not a lie. But I have brought someone for Shallan to meet. I think it is important."

He stood with a smooth inhuman motion, then gestured behind him with one long-fingered hand. Radiant frowned and glanced over her shoulder. Leaves from the trees farther up the plane lazily drifted down the central corridor. A faint shimmer dusted the air, and a small crystal tree started to grow in miniature on the bench beside her hand.

Standing near a statue behind them was a dark figure wearing a stiff robe. Like Pattern's, but dustier. And a head trapped in shadow. Twisted and wrong.

Damnation, Veil thought.

Shallan emerged. She grabbed Radiant, shoved her away someplace dark and small, and slammed the door shut.

Shallan . . . Veil thought, then her voice crumpled. She should remain sectioned away. In the past, they hadn't talked to one another this way. They'd simply taken turns being in control, as they were needed.

Shallan was in control. The other two became whispers. "No," she said to Pattern. "We are not doing this."

"But—" he said.

"*NO*," she said. "I want *nothing* from you, Pattern. You are a traitor and a liar. You have betrayed my trust."

He wilted, flopping onto the bench. Shallan saw movement from the corner of her eye and spun, her heart thundering in her ears. The small building she'd come here to watch—Sixteen's home—had opened, and a furtive figure had emerged. Hunched over, face hidden in the cowl of a cloak, the figure hurried through the statue park.

Excellent. It was time to fulfill Mraize's mission.

Shallan . . . Veil whispered.

She ignored the voice and settled down on the bench, acting nonchalant as she opened her notebook. Veil's plan had included wandering through the statue park, idly flipping through her notebook, then bumping into Sixteen—hopefully getting a good look at his face.

Unfortunately, Shallan wasn't in position yet to do that. She'd been distracted by Pattern and his lies. She stood and meandered toward the statue garden, trying to appear nonthreatening. She needed to determine for certain that Sixteen was her target. Then . . .

Then what.

Kill him.

What are you doing? Veil thought. Such a distant, annoying voice. Couldn't she quiet it entirely?

You were the one who wanted to go forward with Mraize's plan, Shallan thought. *Well, I agree. So two of us have decided.*

I wanted to gather information, Veil thought. *I wanted to use it against him. Why are you suddenly so aggressive?*

Because this was exactly who Shallan was. Who she'd always been. She stalked toward the statue garden. Radiant was, of course, screaming and railing at her—but she was outvoted.

Shallan had been watching and learning these last months, and she'd picked up some things from Veil. She knew to get into Sixteen's blind spot, then stop and appear like she was sketching a statue—so when he turned to glance around, she seemed unremarkable.

She knew to glide forward when he turned away. She knew to step carefully, putting the heel of her foot down first and rolling toward the toe. She knew to walk on the sides of her feet as much as possible, not letting the flats slap.

She got right up behind Sixteen as he hunched over, fiddling with some notes. She grabbed him by the shoulder, then spun him around. His hood fell, revealing his face.

He was Shin; there was no mistaking that pale, almost sickly skin and those childlike eyes. Restares was a short Alethi man with wispy hair. This man was short, yes, but completely bald, and was not Alethi. So unless Mraize was wrong and Restares was a Lightweaver, this was not her man.

He shouted and said something to her in a language she didn't recognize. She released him, and he fled toward his home. Her heart thumping in her chest, she pulled her hand out of the satchel. She hadn't even realized she'd reached into that, for a weapon.

She didn't need it. This wasn't him.

Pattern walked up, having recovered some of his characteristic perkiness. There was no sign of the other spren he'd wanted her to meet.

"Well!" he said. "That was exciting. But this is not him, is it?"

"No," Shallan said. "It's not."

"Shallan, I need to explain to you. What I've been doing."

"No," Shallan said, covering her pain. "It is done. Let's move forward instead."

"Mmm . . ." Pattern said. "I . . . What has happened to you? Something has changed. Are you . . . Veil?"

"No," Shallan said. "I'm me. And I've finally made a difficult decision that was a long time coming. Come on, we need to report to Mraize. His intel was wrong—Restares is not in this fortress."

76

HARMONY

Such skills, like my honor itself, are now lost to time. Weathered away, crushed to dust, and scattered to the ends of the cosmere. I am a barren tree of a human being. I am the hollow that once was a mighty peak.

The Sibling refused to speak to Navani.

She lowered her hand and stared at the garnet vein in the wall. Such a wonderful secret. In plain sight, surrounding her all this time. So common your eyes passed over it, and if you noticed it at all, you remarked only briefly. Simply another pattern in the strata.

The soul of Urithiru had been watching her all along. Perhaps if Navani had discovered it sooner, they could have achieved a different result.

She replaced her hand on the vein. "I'm sorry," she whispered. "Please know that I'm sorry. Truly."

For the briefest moment, she thought the Sibling would respond this time. Navani felt something, faint as the movement of a shadow deep within the ocean. No words came.

With a sigh, Navani left the crystal vein and wound her way through the shelves of the small library to reach her desk beside the door. Today, in addition to the guard, Raboniel's daughter—with the topknot and the vacant eyes—sat on the floor right inside.

Navani settled onto her seat, trying to ignore the insane Fused. Notes and half-finished experiments cluttered her desk. She didn't have the least bit of interest in continuing them. Why would she? Everything she'd attempted so far had been a sham. She wrote out her daily instructions to the scholars—she was having them perform tests on Voidspren fabrials, which Raboniel had delivered before everything went wrong. She gave this to a messenger, then sat there staring.

Eventually Raboniel herself made an appearance, wearing an Alethi havah that fit her surprisingly well. Clearly a good dressmaker had tailored it to the Fused's taller, more broad-shouldered frame. One might have thought her form would make her unfeminine, particularly with the unpronounced bust common to most singer femalens. Instead—with the excellent cut and the confidence of her stride—Raboniel wore the dress as if it had always been designed to accentuate someone of height, power, and poise. She had made this fashion her own. Adolin would have approved.

At least he was safe. Adolin, Renarin, Jasnah, Dalinar, and little Gav. Her entire family safe from the invasion and the mess Navani had made. It was one small blessing she could thank the Almighty for sending her.

Raboniel had brought a stool—a low one, so that when she sat on it, she was at eye level with Navani. The Fused set a basket on the floor, then pulled out a bottle of burgundy wine. A Shin vintage, sweeter than traditional Alethi wines, known as an amosztha—a Shin wine made from grapes.

"Your journals," Raboniel said, "indicate you are fond of this vintage."

"You read my journals?" Navani said.

"Of course," Raboniel said, setting out two glasses. "You would have wisely done the same in my position." She uncorked the bottle and poured half a cup for Navani.

She didn't drink. Raboniel didn't force her, instead inspecting the wine with an expert eye, then taking a sip. "Ah, yes," she said. "*That* is a taste infused with *memory*. Grapes. Your ancestors never could get them to live outside Shinovar. Too cold, I believe. Or perhaps it was the lack of soil. I found that explanation odd, as grapevines seem similar to many of our native plants.

"I wasn't there when your kind came to our world. My grandmother, however, always mentioned the smoke. At first she thought you had strange skin patterns—but that was because so many human faces had been burned or marked by soot from the destruction of the world they left behind.

"She talked about the way your livestock moaned and cried from their burns. The result of humans Surgebinding without oaths, without checks. Of course, that was before *any* of us understood the Surges. Before the spren left us for you, before the war started."

Navani felt the hair go up on the back of her neck as she listened. Storms. This creature . . . she had lived during the shadowdays, the time before history. They had no primary accounts of those days. Yet one sat before her, drinking wine from Navani's secret stash, musing about the origins of humanity.

"So long ago," Raboniel said, with a soft, almost indistinguishable cadence to her words. "So very, very long ago. What has it been? Seven *thousand* years? I don't think you can comprehend how tired I am of this war, Navani. How tired all of us are. Your Heralds too."

"Then let's end it," Navani said. "Declare peace. Withdraw from the tower and I will convince Dalinar to engage in talks."

Raboniel turned her wine cup around, as if trying to see the liquid within from different angles. "You think talks haven't been tried? We are born to fight one another, Navani. Opposites. At least so I thought. I always assumed that if Stormlight and Voidlight could be forced to truly mix, then . . . poof, they'd annihilate one another. Much as we're doing to one another in this endless war . . ."

"Is that what this is all about?" Navani asked. "Why you want me to combine the Lights so badly?"

"I need to know if you're right," Raboniel said. "If you are, then so much of what I've planned will collapse. I wonder . . . whether sometimes I can't see clearly anymore. Whether I assume what I *want* to be true *is* true. You live long enough, Navani, and you forget to be careful. You forget to question."

Raboniel nodded toward Navani's desk. "No luck today?"

"No interest," Navani said. "I think it is time for me to accept your initial offer and start carrying water."

"Why waste yourself like that?" Raboniel asked, her rhythm becoming intense. "Navani, you *can* still defeat me. If it wasn't possible for humans to outthink the Fused, you'd have fallen during the first few

Returns. The first few Desolations, as you call them.

"Instead you always pushed us back. You fought with *stones*, and you beat us. My kind pretends we know so much, but during many Returns, we'd find ourselves struggling to *catch up* to your kind. That is our terrible secret. We hear the rhythms, we understand Roshar and the spren. But the rhythms don't change. The spren don't change.

"If you and I discover this secret together, you'll be able to use it better than I will. Watch and see. At the very least, prove me wrong. *Show* me that our two Lights can meld and mix as you theorize."

Navani considered it, though storms, she knew she shouldn't have. It was another trick—another catalyst added to the system to push the reaction forward. Yet Navani couldn't lie to herself. She *did* want to know. As always, questions teased her. Questions were disorder awaiting organization. The more you understood, the more the world aligned. The more the chaos made sense, as all things should.

"I've run into a problem," Navani said, finally taking a sip from her cup. "I can make the two Lights intersect—I can get them to pool around the same gemstone, swirling out like smoke caught in a current of air. But they won't mix."

"Opposites," Raboniel said, leaning forward to look at the diagrams and notes Navani had made on each failed attempt.

"No, merely inert substances," Navani said. "The vast majority of elements, when combined, produce no reaction. I'd have long ago named these two things immiscible if I hadn't seen Towerlight."

"It is what gave me the original idea," Raboniel said. "I decided if there was a hybrid between Honor's Light and Cultivation's, there must be a *reason* no one had mixed Odium's Light with either."

"Questions are the soul of science," Navani said, sipping her wine. "But assumptions must be proven, Ancient One. From my research I believe these two aren't opposites, but it isn't *proven* to me yet."

"And to prove it?"

"We need an emulsifier," Navani said. "Something that causes them to mix. Unfortunately, I can't fathom what such an emulsifier would be, though it might be related to sound. I only recently learned that Stormlight responds to tones."

"Yes," Raboniel said, taking a sphere off the desk. "The sounds of Roshar."

"Can you hear the Light?" Navani asked.

Raboniel hummed—then thought to nod—her response. She held up a diamond, crystalline and pure, filled with Stormlight from the highstorm the day before. "You have to concentrate, and know what you're seeking, to hear it from a sphere. A pure tone, extremely soft."

Navani hit the proper tuning fork, letting the tone ring in the room. Raboniel nodded. "Yes, that is it. Exactly the same. Only . . ."

Navani sat up. "Only?"

"The sphere's tone has a rhythm to it," Raboniel explained, eyes closed as she held the sphere. "Each Light has a rhythm. Honor's is stately. Cultivation's is stark and staccato, but builds."

"And Odium's?"

"Chaos," she said, "but with a certain strange logic to it. The longer you listen, the more sense it makes."

Navani sat back, sipping her wine, wishing she had access to Rushu and the other scholars. Raboniel had forbidden her from drawing on their expertise in this matter, giving the problem to Navani alone. Navani, who wasn't a scholar.

What would Jasnah do in this situation? Well, other than find a way to kill Raboniel?

Navani felt the answers were right in front of her. So often, that was the case with science. The ancient humans had fought with stone weapons, but the secrets to metallurgy had been within their grasp. . . .

"Does Towerlight have a tone?" Navani asked.

"Two tones," Raboniel said, opening her eyes and setting down the Stormlight sphere. "But they aren't simply the tones of Cultivation and of Honor. They are . . . different, changed so that they are in harmony with one another."

"Curious," Navani said. "And is there a rhythm to it?"

"Yes," Raboniel said. "Both tones adopt it, harmonizing as they play the same rhythm. A symphony combining Honor's control and Cultivation's ever-building majesty."

Their Towerlight spheres had all run out by now, and Raboniel had no way to restore them, so there was nothing for them to check.

"Plants grow by Stormlight," Navani said, "if you beat the proper rhythm in their presence."

"An old agricultural trick," Raboniel said. "It works better with Lifelight, if you can find some."

"*Why*, though?" Navani asked. "Why does Light respond to tones? Why is there a rhythm that makes plants grow?" Navani dug in her materials and began setting up an experiment.

"I have asked myself this question many times," Raboniel said. "But it seems like asking why gravity pulls. Must we not accept some fundamentals of science as baselines? That some things in this world simply work?"

"No, we don't have to," Navani said. "Even gravity has a mechanism driving it. There are proofs to show why the most basic addition problems work. Everything has an explanation."

"I have heard," Raboniel said, "that the Lights respond to sound because it is reminiscent of the voice of the Shards commanding them to obey."

Navani hit the tuning forks, touched them to their respective gemstones, then put them in place. A thin stream of Stormlight ran from one gemstone, a thin stream of Voidlight from the other. They met together at the center—swirling around an empty gemstone. Neither Light entered it.

"Voidlight and Stormlight," Navani said. "The voices of gods." Or perhaps something older than that. The reason the beings called gods spoke the way they did.

Raboniel came in close, shoulder-to-shoulder with Navani as they observed the streams of Light.

"You said that Stormlight and Lifelight make a rhythm together when they mix," she said. "So, if you could imagine a rhythm that mixed Stormlight and *Voidlight*, what would it be like?"

"Those two?" Raboniel said. "It wouldn't work, Navani. They are opposites. One orderly, organized. The other . . ."

Her words drifted off, and her eyes narrowed.

". . . the other chaotic," Raboniel whispered, "but with a *logic* to it. An understandable logic. Could we perhaps contrast it? Chaos always seems more powerful when displayed against an organized background. . . ." Finally she pursed her lips. "No, I cannot imagine it."

Navani tapped the rim of her cup, inspecting the failed experiment.

"If you could hear the rhythms," Raboniel said, "you'd understand. But that is beyond humans."

"Sing one for me," Navani said. "Honor's tone and rhythm."

Raboniel complied, singing a pure, vibrant note—the tone of Stormlight, the same as made by the tuning fork. Then she made the tone waver, vibrate, pulse in a stately rhythm. Navani hummed along, matching the tone, trying to affix it into her mind. Raboniel was obviously overemphasizing the rhythm, making it easier for her to recognize.

"Change now," Navani said, "to Odium's rhythm."

Raboniel did so, singing a discordant tone with a violent, chaotic rhythm. Navani tried to match it with Honor's tone. She had vocal training, like any lighteyed woman of her dahn. However, it hadn't been an area of express study for her. Though she tried to hold the tone against Raboniel's forceful rhythm, she quickly lost the note.

Raboniel cut off, then softly hummed a different rhythm. "That was a fine attempt," Raboniel said. "Better than I've heard from other humans, but we must admit you simply aren't built for this kind of work."

Navani took a drink, then swirled the wine in her cup.

"Why did you want me to sing those rhythms?" Raboniel asked. "What were you hoping to accomplish?"

"I thought that perhaps if we melded the two songs, we could find the proper harmony that would come from a combination of Stormlight and Voidlight."

"It won't be that easy," Raboniel said. "The tones would need to change to find a harmony. I've tried this many times, Navani, and always failed. The songs of Honor and Odium do not mesh."

"Have you tried it with a human before?" Navani asked.

"Of course not. Humans—as we just proved—can't hold to a tone or rhythm."

"We proved nothing," Navani said. "We had a single failed experiment." She set her cup on the table, then crossed the room and dug through her things. She emerged with one of her arm sheaths, in which she'd embedded a clock and other devices. Like other Stormlight fabrials in the tower, it didn't work any longer. But it *was* rigged to hold a long sequence of gemstones.

Navani ripped off the interior leather of the sheath, then settled at the table and fiddled with the screws and set new gemstones—full of Stormlight—into it.

"What is this?" Raboniel said.

"You can hear the songs and rhythms of Roshar," Navani said. "Perhaps it's merely because you have better hearing."

Raboniel hummed a skeptical rhythm, but Navani continued setting the gemstones.

"We can hear them because we are the children of Roshar," Raboniel said. "You are not."

"I've lived here all my life," Navani said. "I'm as much a child of this planet as you are."

"Your ancestors were from another realm."

"I'm not speaking of my ancestors," Navani said, strapping the sheath on so the flats of the gemstones touched her arm. "I'm speaking of myself." She reset her experiment on the table, sending new lines of Stormlight and Voidlight out of gemstones, making them swirl at the center around an empty one.

"Sing Honor's tone and rhythm again, Ancient One," Navani asked.

Raboniel sat back on her stool, but complied. Navani closed her eyes, tightening her arm sheath. It had been built as a fabrial, but she wasn't interested in that function. All she wanted was something that would hold large gemstones and press them against her skin.

She could feel them now, cool but warming to her touch. Infused gemstones always had a tempest inside. Was there a sound to them too? A vibration . . .

Could she hear it in there? The tone, the rhythm? With Raboniel singing, she thought she could. She matched that tone, and felt something on her arm. The gemstones reacting—or rather the Stormlight inside reacting.

There *was* a beat to it. One that Raboniel's rhythm only hinted at. Navani could sing the tone and feel the gemstones respond. It was like having a stronger singer beside her—she could adapt her voice to match. The Stormlight itself guided her—providing a control, with a beat and rhythm.

Navani added that rhythm to her tone, tapping her foot, concentrating. She imagined a phantom song to give it structure.

"Yes!" Raboniel said, cutting off. "Yes, that's it!"

"Odium's rhythm now," Navani said to Honor's tone and beat.

Raboniel did so, and it struck Navani like a wave, making her tone falter. She almost lost it, but the gemstones were her guide. Navani sang louder, trying to hold that tone.

In turn, Raboniel sang more forcefully.

No, Navani thought, taking a breath then continuing to sing. *No, we can't fight.* She took Raboniel's hand, singing the tone, but softer. Raboniel quieted as well. Holding the Fused's hand, Navani felt as if she were reaching for something. Her tone changed slightly.

Raboniel responded, their two tones moving toward one another, step by step, until . . .

Harmony.

The rhythms snapped into alignment, a burst of chaotic notes from Raboniel—bounded by a regular, orderly pulse from Navani.

Heartbeats. Drumbeats. Signals. *Together.*

Navani reached over and placed their clasped hands on the empty gemstone at the center of the experiment, holding them there as they sang for an extended moment in concert. In tandem, a pure harmony where neither took control.

The two of them looked at each other, then fell silent. Carefully, they removed their hands to reveal a diamond glowing a vibrant black-blue. An impossible color.

Raboniel trembled as she picked the gemstone out of its place, then held it up, humming a reverential rhythm. "They did not annihilate one another, as I assumed. Indeed, as part of me hoped. You were right, Navani. Remarkably, I have been proven wrong." She turned the gemstone in her fingers. "I can name this rhythm: the Rhythm of War. Odium and Honor mixed together. I had not known it before today, but I recognize its name; I know this as surely as I know my own. Each rhythm carries with it an understanding of its meaning."

The sphere they had created was different from Szeth's—blue instead of violet, and lacking the strange distortion. Navani couldn't be certain, but it seemed to her *that* was what Raboniel had been seeking.

"Ancient One," Navani said. "Something confuses me. Why would you have preferred that these two annihilate one another?" Navani had an inkling why. But she wanted to see what she could prompt the Fused to reveal.

Raboniel sat for a long time, humming softly to herself as she inspected the gemstone. She seemed fascinated by the motion within, the

Stormlight and the Voidlight mixed to form something that surged in brilliant raging storms, then fell still—peaceful and quiet—between.

"Do you know," the Fused finally asked, "how Honor was killed?"

"I . . . am not certain I accept that he was."

"Oh, he was. At least the being you call the Almighty—the being who controlled the Shard of power that was Honor—is dead. Long dead. Do you know *how*?"

"No."

"Neither do I," Raboniel said. "But I wonder."

Navani sat back in her seat. "Surely, *if* it is true—and my husband says it is, so I accept the possibility—then the mechanisms of the deaths of gods are far beyond the understanding of humans and Fused alike."

"And did you not tell me earlier that *everything* has a mechanism? The gods give us powers. What are those powers? Gravitation, Division, Transformation . . . the fundamental Surges that govern all things. You said that nothing simply *is*. I accept that, and your wisdom. But by that same logic, the gods—the Shards—must work not by mystery, but by knowledge."

She turned the gemstone in her fingers, then met Navani's eyes. "Honor was killed using some process we do not yet understand. I assume, from things I have been told, that some *opposite* was used to tear his power apart. I thought if I could discover this opposite Light, then we would have power over the gods themselves. Would that not be the power to end a war?"

Storms. *That* was what he'd wanted. *That* was what Gavilar had been doing.

Gemstones. Voidlight. A strange sphere that *exploded* when affixed to a fabrial . . . when mixed with another Light . . .

Gavilar Kholin—king, husband, occasional monster—had been searching for a way to kill a god.

Suddenly, the extent of his arrogance—and his magnificent planning—snapped together for Navani. She knew something Raboniel did not. There *was* an opposite to Voidlight. It wasn't Stormlight. Nor was it this new mixed Light they'd created. But Navani *had* seen it. Held it. Her husband had given it to Szeth, who had given it to her.

By the holiest name of the Almighty . . . she thought. *It makes sense*. But like all great revelations, it led to a multitude of new questions. Why? How?

Raboniel stood up, completely oblivious to Navani's epiphany. The Fused tucked away the gemstone, and Navani forced herself to focus on this moment. This discovery.

"I thought for certain it was something about the nature of Odium's power contrasting Honor's power that led to the destruction," Raboniel said. "I was wrong, and you have proven exceedingly helpful in leading me to this proof. Now, I must abandon this line of reasoning and focus on my actual duty—the securing of the tower."

"And your promise that you would leave if I helped you find this Light?"

"I'm sorry," Raboniel said. "Next time, try not to be so trusting."

"In the end," Navani whispered, "you are his, and I am Honor's."

"Unfortunately," Raboniel said. "You may remain here and continue whatever other research you wish. You have earned that, and my gratitude. If you would like to seek a simple job in the tower instead, I will arrange it. Consider your options, then tell me your wishes." Raboniel hesitated. "It is rare for a Fused to be in the debt of a human."

With that, she left. Navani, in turn, downed the rest of the cup of wine, her head abuzz with implications.

77

THE PROPER LEGALITY

SEVEN AND A HALF YEARS AGO

Venli ducked out of the way of a patrol of human guards. As she hid in the doorway, she attuned Peace in an attempt to calm her emotions. She'd come with her people to sign the treaty, but that—and the feast to mark the occasion—was still hours away. While her people prepared, Venli crept through forbidden hallways in their palace.

The pair of guards, chatting in the Alethi tongue, continued on their patrol. She breathed quietly, trying hard not to let the majesty of this human building overwhelm her. Ulim assured her that her people had built equally grand structures once, and they would again. They would build such amazing creations, this palace of Kholinar would look like a hut by comparison.

Would that she could skip this middle part, where she was required to be in such danger. Planning with Ulim, that she liked. Being famous for revealing warform, that she loved. This creeping about though . . . She'd expressly disobeyed human rules, slipping into forbidden sections of the palace. If she were caught . . .

She closed her eyes and listened to the Rhythm of Peace. *Only a little longer,* she thought. *Just until Ulim's companions reach us. Then this will all be over.*

However, she found herself questioning more now that Ulim had left her gemheart. Ulim spoke of a hidden storm and a coming war, with figures of legend returning to fight. That talk spun in her head—and things that seemed so rational a day ago now confused her. Was this really the best way to convince her people to explore forms of power? Wasn't she toying with war and destruction? Why *was* Ulim so eager?

As soon as they'd reached the palace, he'd insisted that she help him gather a bag of gemstones left by his agent here. More spren, like him, ready to be delivered to Venli's scholars. That hadn't been part of the original plan. She'd merely wanted to show her people how dangerous the humans were.

But what was she to do? She'd started this boulder rolling down the cliff. If she tried to stop it now, she'd be crushed. So she continued doing as he said. Even if, without him in her gemheart, she felt old and dull. Without him, she couldn't hear the new rhythms. She craved them. The world made more sense when she listened to those.

"There you are," Ulim said, zipping down the hallway. He moved like lightning, crawling along the top of the stone—and he could vanish, making only certain people able to see him. "Why are you cringing like a child? Come on. We must be moving."

She glanced around the corner. The guards had long since moved on. "I shouldn't have to do this," Venli hissed at him. "I shouldn't have to expose myself."

"Someone needs to carry the gemstones," Ulim said. "So unless you want me to find someone *else* to be the greatest among your people, do what I say."

Fine. She crept after him, though she'd lately found Ulim's tone increasingly annoying. She disliked his crass, dismissive attitude. He'd better not abandon her again. He had claimed he needed to scout the way, but she was half convinced he wanted her to be discovered.

He led her up a stairwell. The Rhythm of Fortune blessed her, and she emerged onto the top floor without meeting any humans—though she did have to hide in the stairwell as more guards passed.

"Why must we come all the way up here!" she hissed after they passed. "Couldn't your friend have brought the gemstones into the basement, where all the other listeners are?"

"I . . . lost contact with her," Ulim admitted.

"You *what*?" Venli said.

He whirled on the floor, then the lightning rose up to form his little humanlike figure. "I haven't heard from Axindweth in a few days. I'm certain it's all right. We have a meeting point where she leaves things for me. The gemstones will be there."

Venli hummed to Betrayal. How could he leave out such an important detail? She was sneaking through the human palace—jeopardizing the treaty—based on flawed information? Before she could demand more answers, however, Ulim turned back into a patch of energy on the floor and shot forward.

She had no choice but to scramble after him across the hallway, feeling terribly exposed. They should have brought Demid. She liked how he listened to what she said, and he always had a ready compliment. He'd enjoy sneaking about, and she'd feel braver with him along.

She wove through the hallways, certain she'd be discovered at any moment. Yet by some miracle, Ulim got her through to a small room with chamber pots scattered across the floor. She pulled out a gemstone and noted a hole in the floor on one side of the room—it looked like they dumped waste in here, pouring it into some foul cesspit several stories below.

This was her goal? A privy? She gagged, and was forced to start breathing through her mouth.

"Here," Ulim said, crackling on the side of one of the chamber pots.

"So help me," Venli said to Skepticism, "if I find human waste inside . . ."

She removed the lid. Fortunately, the interior was clean and empty save for a folded piece of paper.

Ulim pulsed to Exultation. He'd been worried, it seemed. Venli unfolded the paper, and knew the Alethi script well enough to figure out it was a list of cleaning instructions.

"It's ciphered," Ulim said. "Do you think we'd be so stupid as to leave notes in the open where anyone could read them? Let me interpret. . . ."

He formed into the shape of a human, standing on a table full of pots. She hated that he took a human form rather than that of a listener. He leaned forward, his eyes narrow.

"Bother," he said.

"What?"

"Let me think, femalen," he snapped.

"*What does it say?*"

"Axindweth says she's been discovered," he said. "She's a very specific and rare kind of specialist—the details need not concern you—but there is apparently another of her kind in the palace. An agent for someone else. They found her and turned the human king against her. She's decided to pull out."

". . . Pull out?" Venli said. "I don't understand that phrasing."

"She's leaving! Or left. Perhaps days ago."

"Left the palace?"

"The *planet*, you idiot."

Ulim blurred, carapace-like barbs breaking his skin and jabbing out, then retracting. It seemed to happen to the beat of one of the new rhythms, perhaps Fury.

Ulim told her so little. Venli knew there was a way to travel from this world to the place the humans called Damnation. The land of the Voidspren. Many thousands of spren waited there to help her people, but they couldn't get free without some Surge or power. Something to . . . pull them across the void between worlds.

So what did this mean? Had his agent returned to the world Ulim had come from? Or had she gone someplace else? Was she gone for good? How were they going to transfer spren across to this land, to build power for the storm?

Most importantly, did Venli *want* that to happen? He'd promised her forms of power, but she'd assumed that she'd bring this to the Five after frightening them with how powerful the humans were. Everything was moving so quickly, slipping out of her control. She almost demanded answers, but the way those spikes broke Ulim's skin—the way he pulsed—made her remain quiet. He was a force of nature come alive. And the particular force he exhibited now was destructive.

Eventually his pulsing subsided. The spikes settled beneath his skin. He remained standing on the table, staring at the sheet of paper with the offending words.

"What do we do?" Venli finally asked.

"I don't know. There is nothing here for us. I . . . I have to leave, see if I can find answers elsewhere."

"Leave?" Venli said. "What about your promises? What about our plans?"

"We *have no plans*!" Ulim said, spinning on her. "You said coming here would *intimidate* your people. Is that happening? Because from what *I've* seen, they seem to be enjoying themselves! Planning to feast and laugh, maybe get into storming bed with the humans!"

Venli attuned Determination, and then it faded to Reconciliation. She had to admit it; her people *weren't* intimidated, not like she was. Even Eshonai had grown more relaxed—not more worried—as they'd interacted with the humans. These days, Venli's sister didn't even wear warform.

Venli wanted to blame her alone, but the problems with the listeners were far bigger than Eshonai. No one else seemed to see what Venli did. They should have been terrified by all the parshmen—the enslaved singers—in the palace. Instead, Venli's people seemed *curious*.

No one saw the threat Venli did. She didn't understand, or believe, some of the things Ulim said. But in coming here, Venli realized for herself that the humans could not be trusted. If she didn't do anything, it would be her people—her *mother*—enslaved to the humans.

Ulim formed into crackling lightning and zipped down the table leg and along the floor. She took a step after him, attuning the Terrors—but he was gone, out under the door. By the time she looked into the hall, he'd vanished.

She closed the door and found herself breathing heavily. She was alone in the enemy's stronghold, having snuck into forbidden hallways. What should she do? What *could* she do?

Wait. Ulim would come back.

He didn't though. And each moment she stood there attuned to the Terrors was more excruciating than the last. She had to strike out on her own. Perhaps she could sneak back the way she'd come? She ripped up the note, then dumped it out the shaft with the waste. She attuned Determination and slipped from the room.

"You there!"

She cringed, attuning Mourning. One hallway. She hadn't been able to cross even *one hallway*.

A human soldier in a glistening breastplate marched up, a long, wicked weapon in his hand—a spear, but with an axe's head.

"Why are you here?" he asked her in the Alethi tongue.

She played dumb, speaking in her own language. She pointed toward the steps. Perhaps if he thought she couldn't speak Alethi, he'd simply let her go?

Instead he took her roughly by the arm and marched her along the hallway. Each time she tried to pull away he yanked harder, leading her down the steps and through this maze of a palace. He eventually deposited her in a room where several women were writing with spanreeds—Venli still wished her people knew how to make those. A gruff older soldier with a proper beard took reports.

"Found this one on the top floor," the guard said, pushing Venli into a seat. "She was poking around in a suspicious way."

"Does she speak Alethi?" asked the man with the beard.

"No, sir," the man said. He saluted, then returned to his post.

Venli sat quietly, trying not to attune rhythms with too much dread. Surely this wouldn't look *too* bad. She could complain she got lost. And wandered up several flights of stairs . . . And snuck past guards . . . When they'd been told several times to stay away . . .

When I find Ulim again, she thought, attuning Betrayal, *I will* . . . What? What could she do to a spren? What was she without him and his promises? She suddenly felt very, very small. She *hated* that feeling.

"You look like one of their scholars," the older man said, his arms folded. "You really can't speak Alethi? Or were you playing dumb?"

"I . . . was playing dumb." She immediately regretted speaking. Why had she exposed herself?

The man grunted. Their version of attuning Amusement, she thought. "And what were you doing?"

"Looking for the privy."

Dead flat stare. The human version of attuning Skepticism.

"I found it," she said to Reconciliation. "Eventually. Room with all the pots."

"I'm going to note this," he said, nodding to one of the scribes, who began writing. "Your name?"

"Venli," she said.

"If you were a human, I'd lock you up until someone came for you—or I'd give you to someone who could get me answers. But that treaty is being signed tonight. I don't want to cause any incidents. Do you?"

"No, sir," she said.

"Then how about this? You sit here, in this room with us, for the next four hours. Once the feast happens and the treaty is signed, we'll see. Everything happens without a problem, and you can go in for the after-feast. Something goes wrong . . . well, then we'll have another conversation, won't we?"

Venli attuned Disappointment, but nothing was going to happen. She'd probably suffer nothing more than a talking-to from her sister. Part of her would rather be locked up.

She nodded anyway. In truth, she found the man's actions surprisingly rational. Keeping her close would stop anything she might have planned—and if she truly was a lost guest, he wouldn't be in any real trouble for holding her for a few hours.

She contemplated insisting she was too important for this. She discarded that idea. Caught so quickly after being abandoned by Ulim . . . Well, it was hard to keep pretending she was strong. The feeling of smallness persisted.

The soldier left her to go talk quietly to the women, and Venli made out some of their conversation. He had them report to other guard stations in the palace, informing them he'd picked up a wandering "Parshendi" and asking if anyone else had seen individuals entering forbidden or suspicious locations.

Venli found herself attuning *Praise* unexpectedly. It was . . . nice to be alone. Lately, Ulim had always been around. She began thinking about how she could clean this up. Go talk to the Five. Maybe—despite how much it hurt to admit it—go ask Eshonai for advice.

Unfortunately, Ulim soon zipped in through the open door as a trail of red lightning. She hummed Confusion, then Betrayal, as he moved up her chair leg and formed into a person on her armrest.

"We have a big problem," Ulim said to her.

She hummed a little louder.

"Oh, get over yourself, girl," he said. "Listen, there are *Heralds* in the palace tonight."

"Heralds?" she whispered. "Here? They're dead!"

"Hush!" he said, glancing over his shoulder at the humans. "They're not dead. You have no idea how royally, colossally, *incredibly* ruined we are. I saw Shalash first and followed her—then ran across not only

Kalak, but *Nale*. I think he saw me. He shouldn't have been able to, but—"

A figure darkened the doorway to the guard post. The bearded soldier looked up. Venli turned slowly, attuning Anxiety. The newcomer was an imposing figure with deep brown skin and a pale mark on his cheek, almost like a listener might have as part of their skin pattern. He was in uniform, though it wasn't of the cut the Alethi wore.

He looked at Venli, then pointedly at Ulim—who groaned. Then the man finally looked over at the soldier.

"Ambassador?" the guardsman asked. "What do you need?"

"I heard a report that you are holding one of the thinking parshmen here," the newcomer said. "Is this her?"

"Yes," the guardsman said. "But—"

"I request," the man said, "to have this prisoner released into my care."

"I don't think I can do that, Ambassador," the guardsman said, glancing at the scribes for confirmation. "You . . . I mean, that is a *very* unusual request."

"This femalen is important to this night's activities," the man said. He stepped forward, placing something on the nearest scribe's desk. "This is a seal of deputation. I have legal jurisdiction in this land, as granted by your king. You will authenticate it."

"I'm not sure . . ." the scribe woman said.

"You will authenticate it," the man repeated. Perfectly void of emotion or rhythm. He made Venli feel cold. Particularly as he turned toward her.

Behind him, the scribes began scribbling with their spanreeds. The newcomer blocked most of Venli's view of them.

"Hello, Ulim," the man said in a soft, steady voice.

"Um . . . hello, Nale," the spren said. "I . . . um. I didn't expect to see you here. Um, today. Anytime, actually . . . Ever . . . How is, ah, Shalash?"

"Small talk is unnecessary, Ulim," Nale said. "We are not friends. You persist only because I cannot destroy spren." The strange man affixed his unblinking gaze on Venli. "Listener. Do you know what this is?"

"Just another spren," she said.

"You are wise," Nale said. "He *is* just another spren, isn't he? How long have you known him?"

Venli didn't reply—and she saw Ulim pulse to Satisfaction. He did not want her speaking.

"Brightlord," one of the scribes called. "It appears you are correct. You may requisition this prisoner. We were simply going to hold her until—"

"Thank you," Nale said, taking his seal from the scribe, then walked out into the hall. "Follow, listener."

Ulim hopped onto her shoulder and grabbed hold of her hair. "Go ahead," he whispered. "But don't tell him anything. I am in so much trouble. . . ."

Venli followed the strange man from the guard room. She'd never seen a human that shade before, though it wasn't a true onyx like a listener pattern. This was more the color of a rockbud shell.

"How many are there?" Nale asked her. "Spren like him? How many have returned?"

"We—" Ulim began.

"I would hear the listener," Nale said.

She'd rarely known Ulim to be quiet, and he rarely did as she asked. At *this* man's rebuke, however, Ulim fell immediately silent. Ulim was *frightened* of this being. So did that mean the songs about them were true?

A Herald. Alive.

Ulim was right. The Return had begun. The humans would soon be marching to destroy her people. It was the only conclusion she could come to, based on her knowledge of the songs. And based on meeting this man.

Storms. Her people *needed* forms of power.

And to get them, she somehow had to navigate this conversation without being murdered by this creature.

"Answer my question," the Herald said. "How many spren like him are there? How many Voidspren have returned?"

"I have seen only this one," Venli said.

"It is impossible that he has remained on Roshar all these years," Nale said. "It has been . . . a long time, I believe. Generations perhaps, since the last true Desolation?"

How could this creature not remember how long it had been since the Returns ended? Perhaps he was so far above mortals that he didn't measure time the same way.

"I thought it impossible for them to cross the distance between worlds," Nale said. "Could it have been . . . No. Impossible. I've been vigilant. I've been careful. You must tell me! How did you accomplish his return?"

So cold. A voice with no rhythms, and no human emotions. Yet those words . . . He was raving. Perhaps it wasn't that he measured time differently, but that he was addled? Though she'd been considering telling him the truth, that instinct retreated before his dead words.

She might not trust Ulim completely, but she *certainly* couldn't turn to this Herald instead.

"We didn't do anything to return them," she said, taking a gamble based on what he'd said earlier. "It was what *you* did."

"Impossible," Nale repeated. "Ishar said only a Connection between the worlds could cause a bridge to open. And Taln has not given in. I would know if he had. . . ."

"Do not blame us," Venli said, "for your failure."

Nale kept his eyes forward. "So, Gavilar's plan is working. The fool. He will destroy us all." Nale sneered, a sudden and unexpected burst of emotion. "That foolish idiot of a man. He lures us with promises, then breaks them by seeking that which I *told* him was forbidden! Yes. I heard it tonight. The proof I need. I know. I know. . . ."

Storms, Venli thought. *He really is mad.*

"I have been vigilant," the man ranted. "But not vigilant enough. I must take care. If the bonds start forming again . . . if we let the pathway open . . ." He suddenly stopped in the hallway, making her halt beside him. His face became flat again. Emotionless. "I believe I must offer you a service, listener. The king is planning to betray your people."

"What?" she said.

"You can prevent disaster," Nale said. "There is a man here in the city tonight. I have been tracking him due to his unusual circumstances. He possesses an artifact that belonged to a friend of mine. I have sworn not to touch said artifact, for . . . reasons that are unimportant to you."

Confusion thrummed in Venli's ears. But on her shoulder, Ulim had perked up.

"I have legal jurisdiction here to act on behalf of the king," Nale said. "I cannot, however, take specific action *against* him. Tonight I found reason to have him killed, but it will take me months of planning to achieve the proper legality.

"Fortunately, I have read your treaty. There is a provision allowing one party to legally break it and attack the other—should they have proof the other is conspiring against them. I know for a fact that Gavilar is planning to use this very provision to assault your people in the near future. I give you this knowledge, sworn by a Herald of the Almighty. You have proof that he is conspiring against you, and may act.

"The man who can help you is a slave for sale in the market. The person who owns him is hoping some of the king's wealthy visitors will want to pick up new servants before the feast. You have little time remaining. The slave you want is the sole Shin man among the crowd. The gemstones your people wear as ornaments will be enough to buy him."

"I don't understand," Venli said.

Nale looked at Ulim on her shoulder. "This Shin man bears Jezrien's Blade. And he is expertly trained in its employ." He looked back to Venli. "I judge you innocent of any crime, using provision eighty-seven of the Alethi code—pardon of a criminal who has a more vital task to perform for the good of the whole."

He then strode away, leaving them in the hall.

"That was . . ." Ulim said. "Wow. He's far gone. As bad as some of the Fused. But that was well done, Venli. I'm trying not to sound too surprised. I think you may have fooled someone who is basically a god."

"It's an old trick, Ulim," she said. "Everyone—humans, listeners, and apparently gods—deep down suspects that every failure is their own. If you reflect blame on them, most people will assume they are responsible."

"Maybe I gave up on you too easily," he said. "Old Jezrien's Blade is here, is it? Curious . . ."

"What does that mean?"

"Let's say," Ulim told her, "your people were to start a war with the humans. Would that lead your people to the desperation we want? Would they take the forms we offer?"

"Attack the humans?" Venli said to Confusion. They stood alone in the hallway, but she still hushed her voice. "Why would we do what that Herald said? We're not here to *start* a war, Ulim. I merely want to get my people ready to face one, should the humans try to destroy us!"

Ulim crackled with lightning, then moved up her arm, toward her gemheart. She hesitated to let him in. He worked in strange ways, not according to the rules. He could move in and out of her without a highstorm to facilitate the transformation.

He began to vibrate energy through her. *You were so clever, Venli, tricking Nale. This is going to work. You and me. This bond.*

"But . . . a war?"

I don't care why Nale thought we should attack the king, Ulim said. *It has given me a seed of an idea. It's not his plan, but* your *plan we're following. We came here to make your people see how dangerous the humans are. But they are foolish, and you are wise. You can see how much of a threat they are. You need to show them.*

"Yes," Venli said. That *was* her plan.

Ulim slipped into her gemheart.

The humans are planning to betray you, Ulim said. *A Herald confirmed it. We* must *strike at them first.*

"And in so doing, make our people desperate," Venli said. "When the humans retaliate, it will threaten our destruction. Yes . . . Then I could persuade the listeners they need forms of power. They must accept our help, or be annihilated."

Exactly.

"A war would . . . likely mean the deaths of thousands," Venli said, attuning Anxiety. The rhythm felt small and weak. Distant. "On both sides."

Your people will be restored to their true place as rulers of this entire land, Ulim said. *Yes, blood will spill first. But in the end you will rule, Venli. Can you pay this small price now, for untold glories in the future?*

If it meant being strong enough to never again be weak? Never again feeling as small as she had today?

"Yes," she said, attuning Destruction. "What do we do?"

Inkspren weapons may or may not be sheathed, and sometimes hang in the air at their sides or backs, not needing to be attached physically to remain with them.

They do not wear armor. Instead, the armor is a part of their form and sometimes defies human concepts of anatomy.

It reminds me less of steel and more of shell or carapace.

Each surface has an iridescent sheen, a rainbow shimmer that moves independently of the surrounding lights.

In the Physical Realm, inkspren can change their size, but not their shape. They can be as large as a human, or as small as a speck of dust, but they will always look like themselves.

So, words. Why words, now? Why do I write?

Shallan hurried into the room she shared with Adolin, putting the strange experience with Sixteen behind her. No need to think about . . . that other spren. The Cryptic deadeye. *Stay focused, and don't let Radiant slip out again.*

Pattern shadowed her, closing the door with a click. "Aren't you supposed to be meeting with Adolin right now?"

"Yes," Shallan said, kneeling beside the bed and pulling out her trunk. "That makes this the best time to contact Mraize, as we don't risk Adolin walking in on us."

"He will wonder where you are."

"I'll make it up to him later," Shallan said, unlocking the trunk and looking in.

"Veil?" Pattern said, walking up.

"No, I'm Shallan."

"Are you? You feel wrong, Shallan. Mmm. You must listen. I did use the cube. I have a copy of the key to your trunk. Wit helped me."

"It's no matter," Shallan said. "Done. Over. Don't care. Let's move on and—"

Pattern took her hands, kneeling beside her. His pattern, once so alien to her eyes, was now familiar. She felt as if by staring at its shifting lines, she could see secrets about how the world worked. Maybe even about how she worked.

"Please," Pattern said. "Let me tell you. We don't have to talk about your past; I was wrong to try to force you. Yes, I did take the cube. To talk to Wit. He has a cube like it too, Shallan! He told me.

"I was so worried about you. I didn't know what to do. So I went to him, and he said we could talk with the cube, if I was worried. Mmm . . . About what was happening with you. He said I was very funny! But when I talked to him last, he warned me. He's been spied on by the Ghostbloods. The things I told him, another heard. That was how Mraize knew things."

"You talked to Wit," Shallan whispered. "And a spy overheard? That . . . That means . . ."

"None of your friends are traitors," Pattern said. "Except me! Only a little though! I am sorry."

No spy. And Pattern . . .

Was this another lie? Was she getting so wrapped up in them that she couldn't see what was true? She gripped his too-long hands. She wanted so badly to trust again.

Your trust kills, Shallan, the dark part of her thought. The part she named Formless. Except it wasn't formless. She knew exactly what it was.

For now, she retreated—and released Veil and Radiant. Veil immediately took control and gasped, putting her hand to her head. "Storms," she whispered. "That was a . . . strange experience."

"I have made things worse," Pattern said. "I am very foolish."

"You tried to help," Veil said. "But you should have come to me. I'm Veil, by the way. I could have helped you."

Pattern hummed softly. Veil got the sense that he didn't trust her completely. Well, she wasn't certain she trusted her own mind completely, so there was that.

"There's a lot to think about in what you said," Veil said. "For now, please don't keep anything more from us. All right?"

Pattern's pattern slowed, then quickened, and he nodded.

"Great." Veil took a deep breath. Well, that was over.

Who killed Ialai? Shallan whispered from inside.

Veil hesitated.

Perhaps Pattern was *the one who moved the cube all those times,* Shallan said. *And he's the reason Mraize knew about the seed we planted about the corrupted spren. But someone killed Ialai. Who was it?*

Storms. There was more to this mess. A lot more. Veil, however, needed time to digest it. So for now, she put all of that aside and picked up the communication cube. She repeated the incantation. "Deliver to me Mraize, cube, and transfer my voice to him."

It took longer this time than others; she didn't know what the difference was. She sat there some ten minutes before Mraize finally spoke.

"I trust you have only good news to report, little knife," his voice said.

"It's bad news—but you're getting it anyway," she said. "This is Veil, with Pattern here. We've eliminated the final human in Lasting Integrity from consideration. Either Restares has learned to disguise himself beyond my ability to spot him, or he's not here."

"How certain are you of this?" Mraize said, calm. She'd never seen him get upset at bad news.

"Depends," she said. "Like I said, he *could* have disguised himself. Or maybe your intel is wrong."

"It's possible," Mraize admitted. "Communication between realms is difficult, and information travels slowly. Have you asked if any humans left the fortress recently?"

"They claim the last human who left was five months ago," she said. "But that was Azure, not Restares. I know her. I've described our quarry to several honorspren, but they say the description is too vague, and that many humans look alike to them. I'm inclined to think they're telling the truth. They completely neglected to mention that Sixteen—the person I've spent the last few days planning to intercept—was Shin."

"Troubling," Mraize said.

"You've been vague in your answers to me," Veil said. "Let me ask clearly. Could Restares have become a Lightweaver? Cryptics have different requirements for bonding than most Radiants."

"I highly doubt Restares would have joined any Radiant order," Mraize said. "It's not in his nature. I suppose, however, that we can't discount the possibility. There are variations on Lightweaving in the cosmere that do not require a spren—plus the Honorblades exist and are poorly tracked these days, even by our agents."

"I thought they were all in Shinovar, except the one Moash wields."

"They were." Mraize said it simply, directly, with an implication: She wasn't getting any more information on that topic. Not unless she finished this mission, whereupon he had promised to answer all her questions.

"You should equip yourself with Stormlight," Mraize suggested. "If you have not found Restares, there is a chance he knows you are there—and that could be dangerous. He is not the type to fight unless cornered, but once pushed, there are few beings as dangerous on this planet."

"Great, wonderful," Veil said. "Nice to know I have to start sleeping with one eye open. You could have warned me."

"Considering your paranoia, would you have done anything differently?" Mraize sounded amused.

"You're probably right about the Stormlight," Veil said. "The honorspren do have a store of it; they let us use it to heal Adolin. Makes me wonder where they obtained all the perfect gemstones to hold it for so long."

"They've had millennia to gather them, little knife," Mraize said. "And they love gemstones, perhaps for the same reason we admire swords. During the days of the Radiants, some even believed the stories of the Stone of Ten Dawns, and spent lifetimes hunting it. How will you obtain Stormlight from these honorspren?"

"I'll begin working on a plan," she said.

"Excellent. And how is your . . . stability, little knife?"

She thought about Shallan taking control, locking Veil and Radiant away somehow. "Could be better," she admitted.

"Answers will help free you," Mraize said. "Once you've earned them."

"Perhaps," Veil said. "Or perhaps you'll be surprised at what I already know." The trouble wasn't getting answers. It was finding the presence of mind to accept them.

Now, was there a way she could confirm what Pattern had said? About Wit, and the Ghostbloods spying on him? She toyed with the idea, but decided not to say anything. She didn't want to tell Mraize too much.

Her musings were interrupted by the sound of people shouting. That was uncommon here in honorspren territory.

"I need to go," she told Mraize. "Something's happening."

The honorspren had a multitude of reasons for delaying Adolin's trial. Their first and most obvious excuse was the need to wait for the "High Judge," a spren who was out on patrol. Adolin had spent weeks assuming this was the Stormfather, because of things they'd said. Yet when he'd mentioned that the other day, the honorspren had laughed.

So now he had no idea who or what the High Judge was, and their answers to him were strange. The High Judge was some kind of spren, that seemed clear. But not an honorspren. The judge was of a variety that was very rare.

In any case, waiting for the High Judge to return gave the honorspren time to prepare documentation, notes, and testimonies. Had that all been ready, though, they wouldn't have allowed the trial to proceed yet. Because Adolin, they explained, was an idiot.

Well, they didn't say it in so many words. Still, he couldn't help but suspect that was how they felt. He was woefully ignorant of what they considered proper trial procedure. Thus he found himself in today's meeting. Every two days he had an appointment for instruction. The honorspren were quite clear: His offer, worded as it had been, let them condemn him as a traitor and murderer. Though that hadn't completely been his intent, this trial would let them pin the sins of the ancient Radiants on him. Before they did so, they wanted him to understand proper trial procedure. What strange beings.

He stepped softly through the library, a long flat building on the northern plane of Lasting Integrity. Honorspren liked their books, judging by the extensive collection—but he rarely saw them in here. They seemed to enjoy owning the books, treating them like relics to be hoarded.

His tutor, on the other hand, was a different story. She stood on a step stool, counting through books on an upper shelf. Her clothing, made of her substance, was reminiscent of a Thaylen tradeswoman's attire: a knee-length skirt with blouse and shawl. Unlike an honorspren, her coloring was an ebony black, with a certain sheen in the right light. Like the variegated colors oil made on a sword blade.

She was an inkspren; Jasnah had bonded one, though Adolin had never seen him. This one called herself Blended—a name that felt peculiar to him.

"Ah, Highprince," she said, noting him. "You *are*."

"I am," he said. During their weeks talking together, he'd grown mostly accustomed to her distinctive style of speaking.

"Good, good," she said, climbing down the steps. "Our time nearly is not. Come, we must talk."

"Our time nearly is not?" Adolin said, hurrying alongside her. She was shorter than most honorspren, and wore her hair—pure black like the rest of her—pinned up in something that wasn't quite a braid. Though her skin was mostly monochrome black, faint variations outlined her features, making her round face and small nose more visible.

"Yes," she said. "The honorspren have set the date for your trial. It is."

"When?"

"Three days."

"The High Judge is here, then?" Adolin asked as they reached their study table.

"He must be returning soon," she said. "Perhaps he already *is* in this place. So, we must make decisions." She sat without ceasing her torrent of words. "You are not ready. Your progress is not, Highprince Adolin. I do not say this to be insulting. It simply is."

"I know," he said, sitting down. "Honorspren law is . . . complex. I wish you could speak for me."

"It is not their way."

"It seems designed to be frustrating."

"Yes," she agreed. "This is unsurprising, as it was devised by a stuck-up bunch of prim, overly polished buttons."

There was no love lost between inkspren and honorspren. And Blended was supposedly among the more diplomatic of her type—she was the official inkspren emissary to Lasting Integrity.

"I know an honorspren in my realm," Adolin said. "She can be . . . interesting at times, but I wouldn't call her prim."

"The Ancient Daughter?" Blended asked. "She's not the only one whose personality *is* as you speak. Many honorspren used to be like that. Others still are. But Lasting Integrity, and those who here are, have had a strong effect on many honorspren. They preach isolation. Others listen."

"It's so extreme," Adolin said. "They must see there is a better way of dealing with their anger at humans."

"Agreed. A better solution is. I would simply kill you."

Adolin started. ". . . Excuse me?"

"If a human tries to bond me," Blended said, flipping through the books in her stack, "I will attack him and kill him. This better solution is."

"I don't think Radiants *force* bonds," Adolin said.

"They would coerce. I would strike first. Your kind are not trustworthy." She set aside one of her books, shaking her head. "Regardless, I am worried about your training. It is weak, through no fault of yours. The honorspren will use the intricacies of their laws against you, to your detriment. You will be as a child trying to fight a duel. I believe trials among your kind are more direct?"

"Basically, you go before the lighteyes in charge and plead your case," Adolin said. "He listens, maybe confers with witnesses or experts, then renders judgment."

"Brief, simple," she said. "Very flawed, but simple. The honorspren of this region like their rules. But perhaps a better solution is." She held up one of the books she'd been looking through when he arrived. "We can motion for a trial by witness. A variety more akin to what you know already."

"That sounds great," Adolin said, relaxing. If he had to listen to one more lecture including terms like "exculpatory evidence" and "compensatory restitution," he would ask them to execute him and be done with it.

Blended took notes as she spoke. "It is well I spent these weeks training you in basics. This will prepare you for your best hope of victory, which is this format. Therefore, before I explain, recite to me your general trial strategy."

They'd gone over this dozens of times, to the point that Adolin could have said it backward. He didn't mind; you drilled your soldiers in battle formations until they could do maneuvers in their sleep. And this trial would be like a battle; Blended had repeatedly warned him to be wary of verbal ambushes.

"I need to persuade them that I cannot be held accountable for the actions of the ancient Radiants," Adolin said. "That they cannot shun me or my father because of things done by ancient humans. In order to accomplish this, I will prove my character, I will prove that the modern

Radiants are unconnected to the old orders, and I will prove that our actions in the face of the current crisis are proof of the honor men display."

Blended nodded. "We will choose a trial by witness. Assuming your motion is accepted, the trial will happen in three phases over three days. The first day, the High Judge is presented with three testimonies against your cause. The next day, you give your testimony. The final day, accusers are allowed one rebuttal, then judgment is requested. This format is not often chosen, because it allows so much weight of testimony against you. However, factoring in how weak your grasp of legal systems is, well . . . this choice is best."

Adolin felt a tremble deep inside. He wished for a fight he could face with sword in hand—but that was the trouble. Any given Radiant could do better than he at such a fight, so his expertise with the sword was effectively obsolete. He could not train himself to the level of a Radiant; they could heal from wounds and strike with supernatural grace and strength. The world had entered an era where simply being good at swordplay was not enough.

That left him to find a new place. Father always complained about being unsuited for diplomacy; Adolin was determined not to make the same complaint. "If I may plead my case on the second day," he said, "then I'm for it. The other methods you suggested would require me to understand too much of their law."

"Yes," Blended said. "Though I worry that in giving testimony, you will incriminate yourself. Worse, you risk asking questions of the audience, presenting an opening for their condemnations. You could end up one man facing a crowd of experts in the law and rhetoric."

"I *have* to speak for myself though," Adolin said. "I fail to see how I can achieve what I want without talking to them. I need to prove myself and appeal to their honor."

Blended flipped through pages of notes. He'd noticed that when she wouldn't look at him, it meant she had something difficult to say.

"What?" Adolin asked her.

"You believe much in their honor, Prince Adolin. Your sense of justice . . . is."

"They are honorspren," he said. "Don't they basically *have* to be honorable?"

"A conundrum is in this thing," Blended said. "Yes, they *are* honors-pren. But honor . . . isn't something that . . . that *is*."

"What do you mean?"

"Men define honor," Blended said. "And no god can enforce it, no longer. Beyond that, spren like us are not mindless things. Our will is strong. Our perceptions mold our definitions of concepts such as honor and right and wrong. Just as with humans."

"You're saying that what they perceive as honorable might not be what I perceive as honorable. Syl warned me as much."

"Yes," she said. "What they *are* defines honor to them. *Whatever* they are."

"That's . . . frightening," Adolin admitted. "But there is goodness to them. They care for the deadeyes, even Maya, with great concern and attention."

"Hmmm, yes," Blended said. "That one. Did another spren tell you her name?"

"No, she told me herself."

"Deadeyes don't speak. This is."

"You all keep saying that, but you're wrong," Adolin said. "I heard her in my mind. Only once, true, but she said her name. Mayalaran. She's my friend."

Blended cocked her head. "Curious. Very curious . . ."

"Deep down, the honorspren must want to help. Surely they'll listen to me. Surely I can make them see."

"I will give you the best chance I can," she said. "But please understand. Spren—all spren—fear you with *good* reason. In order to prove you wrong, they need only prove that bonding men *is* a risk. That past failings of men *justify* wariness."

"Everything is a risk," Adolin said.

"Yes. Which is why this trial . . . is not strong for you. This truth *is,* Prince Adolin."

"To hear you say it like that," he said, trying to laugh about it, "it sounds like I have no chance!"

She closed her book. And did not respond.

He took a deep breath. "All right. How do we proceed?" he asked.

"I suspect the best thing is to discover if the High Judge's return is." Blended stood up, leaving the books on the table as she strode toward the doors. Adolin was expected to keep up. She claimed to hate the honorspren because of an ancient rivalry, but she sure did act like them. Neither gave much deference to human titles, for example. Adolin didn't consider himself stuck-up, but couldn't they treat him with a little more respect?

Outside, as always, he had that moment of jarring disconnect—his brain trying to reconcile that down wasn't down and up wasn't up. That people walked along all four faces inside the rectangular tower.

He doubted he could ever feel at ease in this place. The spren claimed it was not Surgebinding that let them walk on the walls here; the long-standing presence of the honorspren instead allowed the tower to choose a different type of natural law. Perhaps that sort of talk made sense to Shallan. Where was she anyway? She was often late to these tutoring meetings, but she usually showed up.

Blended led him across to the corner where the northern plane met the western plane; most of the official buildings were on the western one. Adolin always found this part curious; he had to step out and put one leg on the wall. He followed that by leaning back as he lifted his other leg, feeling like he was about to fall. Instead everything seemed to rotate, and he found himself standing on another plane.

"You do that better than most humans," Blended noted. "They often seem nauseated by the process."

He shrugged, then followed as she walked him toward a row of short buildings clustered near the base of the tower. Most buildings in Lasting Integrity were only one story. He wasn't certain what happened if they got too tall; were you in danger of falling off?

They passed groups of honorspren, and he thought about what Blended had said regarding their natures. Not simply of honor—of honor as defined by the spren themselves. Well, maybe they weren't all as stuffy as they seemed. He'd catch laughter or a hint of a mischievous grin. Then an older uniformed honorspren would walk past—and everyone would grow solemn again. These creatures seemed trapped between an instinct for playfulness and their natures as the spren of oaths.

He anticipated another tedious discussion with the honorspren who managed his case—but before Adolin and Blended entered the building of justice, she stopped and cocked her head. She waved for him to follow in another direction, and he soon saw why. A disturbance was occurring on the ground plane, near the gates into the city. A moment of panic made him wonder if his friends had decided to rescue him against his wishes—followed by a deeper worry that all those deadeyes outside had snapped and decided to rush the fortress.

It was neither. A group of spren crowded around a newly arrived figure. "The High Judge?" Adolin guessed.

"Yes," Blended said. "Excellent. You can make your petition to him." She walked that direction, down along the face of the western plane.

Adolin followed until he saw the details of the figure everyone was making such a fuss over.

The High Judge, it appeared, was human.

·•·

"Human?" Veil said, stopping in place. "That's impossible."

She squinted at the figure below, and didn't need to get close to see what her gut was already telling her. A short Alethi man with thinning hair. That was him, the one she'd been hunting. The High Judge was Restares.

"Mmm . . ." Pattern said. "They *did* say the High Judge was a spren. Perhaps the honorspren lied? Mmm . . ."

Veil stepped up to a small crowd of honorspren who had gathered on the southern plane to gawk at the newcomer. One was Lusintia, the honorspren assigned to show Veil around on her first day in the fortress. She was a shorter spren, with hair kept about level with the point of her chin. She didn't wear a uniform, but the stiff jacket and trousers she preferred might as well have been one.

Veil elbowed her way over to Lusintia, earning shocked glances from the honorspren, who generally didn't crowd in such a way. Pattern followed in her wake.

"That can't be the High Judge," Veil said, pointing. "I *specifically* asked if the High Judge was human."

"He's not," Lusintia said.

"But—"

"He might have the form of a man," Lusintia said. "But he is an eternal and immortal spren who blesses us with his presence. That is Kalak, called Kelek'Elin among your people. Herald of the Almighty. He commanded us not to tell people he was here—and ordered us specifically to not speak of him to humans, so we were not allowed to answer your questions until you saw him for yourself."

One of the Heralds. Damnation.

The man Mraize had sent her to find—and, she suspected, the man he wanted her to kill—was one of the *Heralds*.

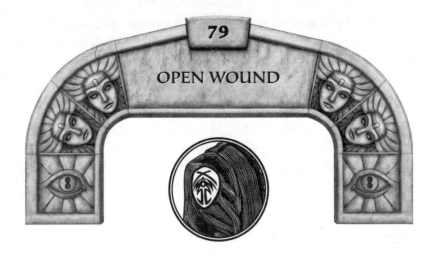

Jezrien is gone. Despite being all the way out here in Lasting Integrity, I felt him being ripped away. The Oathpact was broken already, but the Connection remained. Each of us can sense the others, to an extent. And with further investigation, I know the truth of what happened to him. It felt like death at first, and I think that is what it ultimately became.

Rlain stepped into the laundry room, and felt every single *storming* head in the place turn to look at him. The singer guards at the door perked up, one nudging the other and humming to Curiosity. Human women working the large tubs of sudsy water turned as they scrubbed. Men who were toiling at bleaching vats—with long poles to move the cloth inside—stopped and wiped brows. Chatter became whispers.

Rlain. Traitor. Reject. Oddity.

He kept his head high—he hadn't lived through Bridge Four to be intimidated by a quiet room and staring eyes—but he couldn't help feeling like he was the one gemstone in the pile that didn't glow. Somehow, with the singers invading Urithiru, he'd become *more* of an outsider.

He strode past the vats and tubs to the drying station. Some of the tower's original fabrials—the lifts, the main wells, the air vents—had been altered to work with Voidlight. That meant the workers here could set out large racks for drying in this room where the vents blew a little stronger. There was talk that the Fused would get other fabrials in the tower working soon, but Rlain wasn't privy to their timelines.

Near the drying racks he found a small cart waiting for him, filled with clean bedding. He counted the sheets as the foreman—a lighteyed human who always seemed to be standing around when Rlain visited—leaned against the wall nearby, folding his arms.

"So," he said to Rlain, "what's it like? Roaming the tower. Ruling the place. Pretty good, eh?"

"I don't rule anything," Rlain said.

"Sure, sure. Must feel good though, being in charge of all those people who used to own you."

"I'm a listener," Rlain said to Irritation. "I was never an Alethi slave, just a spy pretending to be one." Well, except for Bridge Four. That had felt like *true* slavery.

"But your people are in charge now," the man prodded, completely unable to take a hint.

"They aren't my people," Rlain said. "I'm a listener—I come from an *entirely* different country. I'm as much one of them as *you* are an Iriali."

The man scratched his head at that. Rlain sighed and wheeled the cart over to pick up some pillows. The women there didn't usually talk to him, so he was able to pile up the pillows without getting more than a few scowls.

He *could* hear their whispers, unfortunately. Better than they probably thought he could.

". . . Don't speak too loudly," one was saying. "He'll report you to them."

"He was here all along," another hissed. "Watching the Windrunners, planning when best to strike. He's the one who poisoned them."

"Hovers over them like a vengeful spren," a third said. "Watching to kill any who wake up. Any who—"

She squealed as Rlain spun toward the three women. Their eyes opened wide and they drew back. Rlain could *feel* their tension as he walked up to them.

"I like cards," he said.

The three stared at him in horror.

"Cards," Rlain said to Longing. "I'm best at towers, but I like run-around too. I'm pretty good, you know. Bisig says it's because I'm good at bluffing. I find it fun. I *like* it."

The three women exchanged looks, obviously confused.

"I thought you should know something about me," Rlain said. "I figured maybe if you did, you would stop making things up." He nodded to them, then forcibly attuned Peace as he went back to tie the pillows into place on the top of his cart. As he began wheeling it away, the whispers started again.

"You heard him," the first woman hissed. "He's a gambler! Of course. *Those* kind can see the *future*, you know. Foul powers of the Void. He likes to take advantage of those unwise enough to bet against him. . . ."

Rlain sighed, but kept going. At the door, he knew to step to the side as one of the singer guards tried to trip him. They hadn't tired of that same old terrible trick—no matter how many times he visited. He shoved his way out the door quickly, but not before one of them called, "See you tomorrow, traitor!" to the Rhythm of Reprimand.

Rlain pushed the cart through the halls of Urithiru. There were a lot of people out, both human and singer. Bringing water from the wells was a full-time duty for many hundreds of workers. A lot of the population had moved away from the perimeter, which was growing too cold. Instead they crowded together into these interior rooms.

Humans gave way for him. Most of the singers didn't glance at him, but those who did usually noticed his tattoo. Their rhythms changed, and their eyes followed him. Some hated him for the treason of his ancestors. Others had been told the listeners were a brave frontrunner group who had prepared for Odium's return. These treated Rlain with reverence.

In the face of it all—the frightened humans, the mistrusting Regals, the occasionally awed ordinary singers—he wished he could simply be *Rlain*. He hated that to every one of them, he was some kind of representation of an entire people. He wanted to be seen as a person, not a symbol.

The closest he'd come had been among the men of Bridge Four. Even though they'd named him "Shen," of all things. That was like naming one of their children "Human." But for all their faults, they had succeeded in giving him a home. Because they'd been willing to try to see him for himself.

As he pushed his cart, he caught sight of that cremling again. The nondescript brown one that would scuttle along walls near the ceiling, blending in with the stonework. They were still watching him.

Venli had warned him about this. Voidspren invisibility didn't work properly in the tower. So it appeared that, to keep an eye on someone here, they'd begun entering an animal's gemheart. He tried to pretend he hadn't seen it. Eventually, it turned and scuttled down a different hallway. Voidspren weren't fully able to control the animals they bonded; though apparently the dumber the animal, the easier they were to influence. So there was no way of telling if the Voidspren had decided it had seen enough for the day, or if its host was merely distracted.

Rlain eventually reached the atrium, and like many people, he briefly basked in the light coming through the large eastern window. There was always a lot of traffic in here these days. Though only the privileged among the singers were allowed to use the lifts, people of both species came here for light.

He crossed the atrium with his cart, then pushed it through into the Radiant infirmary. He still couldn't relax—as a surprising number of humans moved through the room among the unconscious Radiants.

Ostensibly they all had a reason to be there. Water carriers, people to change the bedpans, others recruited to help feed broth to the Radiants. There were always new volunteers—the men and women of the tower were turning coming here into some kind of pilgrimage. Look in on the Radiants. Care for them. Then go burn prayers for them to recover. None of the people working in here seemed bothered by the fact that—not two years ago—they would have cursed by the Lost Radiants.

Eyes chased Rlain as he—forcing himself to walk to the beat of the Rhythm of Peace—delivered the cart of freshly laundered sheets and pillows to those changing them. A man with one arm and haunted eyes was overseeing this work today. Like most of the others in the room, he'd painted his forehead with the *shash* glyph. That baffled Rlain.

A few days ago, Lezian the Pursuer had ordered his men to beat those who wore the forehead mark—though only a day later, that order had been reversed by Raboniel. Still seemed strange that so many humans would wear the thing. They had to realize they were singling themselves out.

Though he'd been forced to rein in his men, and there had been fewer incidents recently, the Pursuer continued to push for more brutality in the tower. Unnervingly, he'd placed a few guards here in the infirmary: two stormform Regals currently, on rotation with several other Regals, who stood watch at all hours.

Rlain felt their stares on him as he walked to the back of the room where Lirin and Hesina had used hanging sheets to section off a part as a kind of office and living quarters for themselves. Rlain forced himself to attune Confidence until he could step between the sheets.

Inside he found Lirin peeking out at the stormforms. A small surgery station was set up behind him, where Lirin could see patients—because of course he needed to do that. Kaladin had spoken of his father, and Rlain felt he knew Lirin and Hesina, though he'd interacted with them in person for only a few weeks.

"Well?" Rlain asked.

"The stormforms have seen me and Hesina," Lirin whispered. "We couldn't stay hidden all the time. But I don't think it matters. By this point, *someone* must have recognized us. I wouldn't be surprised if those Regals were sent here in the first place because this 'Pursuer' discovered we were here."

"Maybe you should remain quiet," Rlain said, searching the ceiling for cremlings. "Or maybe we should get you out."

"We've been watching for cremlings," Lirin said. "And haven't seen any. Nothing so far. As for the Pursuer, Venli says that we should be safe from him, so long as that Heavenly One, Leshwi, protects us."

"I don't know how much I trust any of them, Lirin," Rlain said. "Particularly Fused."

"Agreed," Lirin said. "What games are they playing? Leshwi didn't even ask after my son. Do you have any idea why they are acting this way?"

"Sorry," Rlain said. "I'm baffled. Our songs barely mention the Fused except to say to avoid them."

Lirin grunted. Like the others, he seemed to expect Rlain to understand the Fused and Regals more than he did—but to the surgeon's credit, he and Hesina had accepted Rlain without suspicion, despite his race. For all that Lirin complained about Kaladin, it seemed he considered someone his son called a friend to be worthy of trust.

"And Venli?" Lirin asked. "She wears a Regal form. Can we trust her?"

"Venli could have left me in prison," Rlain said. "I think she's proven herself."

"Unless it's a long con of some sort," Lirin said, his eyes narrowing.

Rlain hummed to Reconciliation. "I'm surprised to hear of your suspicion. Kaladin said you always saw the best in people."

"My son doesn't know me nearly as well as he presumes," Lirin said. He continued standing by the drapes.

Rlain made his way past the surgery table to where Hesina had set out one of his stolen maps on the floor. There, he hummed to Anxiety. "Maybe we shouldn't have these out," he whispered. "With those Regals around."

"We can't live our lives terrified of enemies at every corner, Rlain," Hesina said. "If they wanted to take us, they'd have done it already. We have to assume we're safe, for now."

Rlain hummed to Anxiety. But . . . there was wisdom in her words. He forced himself to calm. He had seen that cremling, yes, but didn't *know* it had a Voidspren. Perhaps he *was* jumping at shadows. Likely, he was just on edge because of the way everyone treated him during his trips through the tower.

"I keep thinking," Hesina said, looking over the map, "that if we could get this to Kal, it might help."

Rlain glanced at Lirin, humming to Curiosity. Hesina wouldn't catch the rhythm, but she clearly understood his body language.

"Lirin's dispute is not mine," Hesina said. "He can play the stoic pacifist all he wants—and I'll love him for it. But I'm not going to leave Kal out there alone with no help. You think if he had exact maps of the tower, he might have a better chance?"

"Couldn't hurt," Rlain said, kneeling beside her. They'd all heard about what Kaladin had done the other day—appearing spectacularly in the Breakaway market, engaging the Fused, fighting in the air.

The Fused were obviously frightened. They had immediately started publicizing that they'd killed him. Too quickly, and too forcefully, without a body to show. The people of the tower weren't buying it, and neither was Rlain. He'd joined Bridge Four later than most, but he'd been there for Kaladin's most dramatic transformations. Stormblessed was alive in the tower somewhere, planning his next move.

Hesina continued to pore over the map of the tower's sixth floor—but Rlain noticed something else. Hesina had set another map aside, one of the Shattered Plains. Rlain unrolled it fully and found himself attuning the Rhythm of the Lost. He'd never seen a full map, this detailed, of the entire Plains.

The immensity didn't surprise him. He'd been out there as both listener and bridgeman. He'd flown with the Windrunners. He understood the scope of the Shattered Plains, and was prepared for Narak to seem diminutive when compared to the expanse of plateaus stretching in all directions. But he wasn't prepared for how *symmetrical* it all was, now that he could see it all at once.

Yes, the Plains had most definitely been broken in a pattern. He hummed to Curiosity as he peered closer, and he picked out some cramped writing on the far eastern side of the Plains—where the plateaus were worn smaller by the winds. That was the direction the chasmfiends migrated after breeding or pupating. A dangerous area full of greatshells, herd animals, and predators as large as buildings.

"Hesina?" Rlain said, turning the map in her direction. "Can you read this part to me?"

She leaned over. "Scout report," she said. "They found a camp out there, it seems. Some kind of large caravan or nomadic group. Maybe they're Natans? A lot of this area is unexplored, Rlain."

He hummed to himself, wondering if he should learn to read. Sigzil was always talking about how useful it was, though Rlain didn't like the idea of relying on written words that had no life, instead of on songs. A piece of paper could be burned, lost, destroyed in a storm—but an entire people and their songs could not be so easily . . .

He trailed off. An entire people. It struck him anew that he was alone.

No, Venli is here, he thought. There were two of them. He'd never particularly liked Venli, but at least he wasn't the sole listener. It made him wonder. Should they . . . try to rebuild? The idea nauseated him for multiple reasons. For one, the times he'd tried mateform himself, things hadn't gone the way he—or anyone really—had expected.

Lirin abruptly pulled back from the curtains. His motion was so sudden that Hesina took it as a warning and immediately grabbed a sheet and pulled it over the maps. Then she laid out some bandages—to appear as if she'd spread the sheet onto the floor to keep the bandages clean as she rolled them. It was an excellent cover-up—one Rlain ruined by belatedly moving to tuck away his map of the Shattered Plains.

"It's not that," Lirin said, grabbing Rlain by the shoulder. "Come look. I think I recognize one of the workers."

Lirin pointed out through the drapes, directing Rlain toward a short man. He had a mark on his forehead, but it wasn't an inked *shash* glyph. It was a Bridge Four tattoo like Rlain's own. Dabbid kept his eyes down, walking with his characteristic sense of mute subservience.

"I think that man was one of Kaladin's friends," Lirin said. "Am I right?"

Rlain nodded, then hummed softly to Anxiety and stepped out into the main room. He and Dabbid had often been set to work together as the only two members of Bridge Four who hadn't gained Windrunner abilities. Seeing him opened that wound again for Rlain, and he hummed forcibly to Peace.

It wasn't his fault that spren were as racist as humans. Or as singers. As people.

He quietly took Dabbid by the arm, steering him away from the Regals. "Storms, I'm glad to see you," Rlain whispered. "I was worried about you, Dabbid. Where have you been? Were you frightened? Here, come help me bring some water to the others. Like the work we used to do, remember?"

He could imagine the poor mute hiding in a corner, crying as enemies flooded the tower. Dabbid had become kind of a mascot for Bridge Four. One of the first men Kaladin had saved. Dabbid represented what had been done to them, and the fact that they'd survived it. Wounded, but still alive.

Dabbid resisted as Rlain tugged him toward the water trough. The shorter bridgeman leaned in, then—remarkably—*spoke*.

"Rlain," Dabbid said. "Please help. Kaladin is asleep, and he won't wake up. I think . . . I think he's dying."

80

THE DOG
AND THE DRAGON

The singers first put Jezrien into a gemstone. They think they are clever, discovering they can trap us in those. It only took them seven thousand years.

Kaladin existed in a place where the wind hated him.

He remembered fighting in the market, then swimming through the well. He vaguely remembered running out into the storm—wanting to let go and drop away.

But no, he couldn't give up. He'd climbed the outside of the tower. Because he'd known that if he fled, he'd leave Dabbid and Teft alone. If he fled, he'd leave Syl—maybe forever. So he'd climbed and . . .

And the Stormfather's voice?

No, *Dalinar's* voice.

That had been . . . days ago? Weeks? He didn't know what had happened to him. He walked a place of constant winds. The faces of those he loved appeared in haunting shadows, each one begging for help. Flashes of light burned his skin, blinded him. The light was *angry*. And though Kaladin longed to escape the darkness, each new flash trained him to be more afraid of the light.

The worst part was the wind. The wind that hated him. It flayed him, slamming him against the rocks as he tried to find a hiding place to escape it.

Hate, it whispered. *Hate. Hate hate.*

Each time the wind spoke, it broke something inside Kal. Ever since he could remember—since childhood—he had loved the wind. The feel of it on his skin meant he was free. Meant he was alive. It brought new scents, clean and fresh. The wind had always been there, his friend, his companion, his ally. Until one day it had come to life and started talking to him.

Its hatred crushed him. Left him trembling. He screamed for Syl, then remembered that he'd abandoned her. He couldn't remember how he'd come to this terrible place, but he remembered *that.* Plain as a dagger in his chest.

He'd left Syl alone, to lose herself because he'd gotten too far away. He'd abandoned the wind.

The wind crashed into him, pressing him against something hard. A rock formation? He was . . . somewhere barren. No sign of rockbuds or vines in the flashes of terrifying light. Only endless windswept, rocky crags. It reminded him of the Shattered Plains, but with far more variation to the elevations. Peaks and precipices, red and grey.

So many holes and tunnels. Surely there was a place to hide. *Please. Just let me rest. For a minute.*

He pushed forward, holding to the rock wall, trying not to stumble. He had to fight the wind. The terrible wind.

Hate. Hate. Hate.

Lightning flashed, blinding him. He huddled beside the rock as the wind blew stronger. When he started moving, he could see a bit better. Sometimes it was pure darkness. Sometimes he could see a little, though there was no light source he could locate. Merely a persistent direction-less illumination. Like . . . like another place he couldn't remember.

Hide. He had to hide.

Kal pushed off the wall, struggling against the wind. Figures appeared. Teft begging to know why Kal hadn't rescued him. Moash pleading for help protecting his grandparents. Lirin dying as Roshone executed him.

Kal tried to ignore them, but if he squeezed his eyes shut, their cries became louder. So he forced himself forward, searching for shelter. He struggled up a short incline—but as soon as he reached the top, the wind reversed and blew him from behind, casting him down the other side. He landed on his shoulder, scraping up his arm as he slid across the stone.

Hate. Hate. Hate.

Kal forced himself to his knees. He . . . he didn't give up. He . . . wasn't a person who was allowed to give up. Was that right? It was hard . . . hard to remember.

He got to his feet, his arm hanging limp at his side, and kept walking. Against the wind again. *Keep moving. Don't let it stop you. Find a place. A place to hide.*

He staggered forward, exhausted. How long had it been since he'd slept? Truly slept? For years, Kal had stumbled from one nightmare to another. He lived on willpower alone. But what would happen when he ran out of strength? What would happen when he simply . . . couldn't?

"Syl?" he croaked. "Syl?"

The wind slammed into him and knocked him off balance, shoving him right up to the rim of a chasm. He teetered on the edge, terrified of the darkness below—but the wind didn't give him a choice. It pushed him straight into the void.

He tumbled and fell, slamming into rocks along the chasm wall, denied peace even while falling. He hit the bottom with a solid *crack* to his head and a flash of light.

Hate. Hate. Hate.

He lay there. Letting it rail. Letting it pummel him. Was it time? Time to finally let go?

He forced himself to look up. And there—in the distance along the bottom of the chasm—he saw something beautiful. A pure white light. A longing warmth. The sight of it made him weep and cry out, reaching for it.

Something real. Something that didn't hate him.

He *needed* to get to that light.

The fall had broken him. One arm didn't work, and his legs were a mess of agony. He began crawling, dragging himself along with his working arm.

The wind redoubled its efforts, trying to force him back, but now that

Kaladin had seen the light, he *had* to keep going. He gritted his teeth against the pain and hauled himself forward. Inch after inch. Defying the screaming wind, ignoring the shadows of dying friends.

Keep. Moving.

The light drew closer, and he longed to enter it. That place of warmth, that place of peace. He heard . . . a sound. A serene tone that wasn't spiteful wind or whispered accusations.

Closer. Closer.

A little . . . farther . . .

He was just ten feet away. He could . . .

Suddenly, Kaladin began to *sink*. He felt the ground change, becoming *liquid*. Crem. The rock had somehow become crem, and it was sucking him down, collapsing beneath him.

He shouted, stretching his good arm toward the glowing pool of light. There was nothing to climb on, nothing to hold on to. He panicked, sinking deeper. The crem covered him, filling his mouth as he screamed—begging—reaching a trembling hand toward the light.

Until he slipped under the surface and was again in the suffocating darkness. As he sank away, Kal realized that the light had never been there for him to reach. It had been a lie, meant to give him a moment of hope in this awful, *horrible* place. So that hope could be taken. So that he could finally.

Be.

Broken.

A glowing arm plunged into the crem, burning it away like vapor. A hand seized Kaladin by the front of his vest, then heaved him up out of the pool. A glowing white figure pulled him close, sheltering him from the wind as it hauled him the last few feet toward the light.

Kaladin clung to the figure, feeling cloth, warmth, living breath. Another person among the shadows and lies. Was this . . . was this Honor? The Almighty himself?

The figure pulled him into the light, and the rest of the crem vanished, leaving a hint of a taste in Kaladin's mouth. The figure deposited Kaladin on a small rock situated like a seat. As it stepped back, the figure drew in color, the light fading away, revealing . . .

Wit.

Kaladin blinked, glancing around. He was at the bottom of a chasm, yes, but inside a bubble of light. Outside, the wind still raged—but it couldn't affect this place, this moment of peace.

He put a hand to his head, realizing he didn't hurt any longer. In fact, he could see now that he was in a nightmare. He was *asleep*. He must have fallen unconscious after fleeing into the tempest.

Storms . . . What kind of fever did he have to prompt such terrible dreams? And why could he see it all so clearly now?

Wit looked up at the tumultuous sky far above, beyond the chasm rims. "This isn't playing fair. Not fair at all . . ."

"Wit?" Kaladin asked. "How are you here?"

"I'm not," Wit said. "And neither are you. This is another planet, or it looks like one—and not a pleasant one, mind you. The kind without lights. No Stormlight ones, gaseous ones, or even electric ones. Damn place barely has an atmosphere."

He glanced at Kaladin, then smiled. "You're asleep. The enemy is sending you a vision, similar to those the Stormfather sent Dalinar. I'm not certain how Odium isolated you though. It's hard for Shards to invade minds like this except in a specific set of circumstances."

He shook his head, hands on his hips, as if he were regarding a sloppy painting. Then he settled down on a stool beside a fire that Kaladin only now saw. A warm, inviting fire that completely banished the chill, radiating straight through Kaladin's bones to his soul. A pot of simmering stew sat on top, and Wit stirred it, sending spiced fragrances into the air.

"Rock's stew," Kaladin said.

"Old Horneater recipe."

"Take everything you have, and put him in pot," Kaladin said, smiling as Wit handed him a bowl of steaming stew. "But it's not real. You just told me."

"Nothing is real," Wit said. "At least by one measure of philosophy. So enjoy what you seem to be able to eat and don't complain."

Kaladin did so, taking the most wonderful bite of stew he'd ever tasted. It was hard to avoid glancing out past the glowing barrier of light at the storm outside.

"How long can I stay with you?" Kaladin asked.

"Not long, I fear," Wit said, serving himself a bowl of stew. "Twenty minutes or so."

"I have to go back out into that?"

Wit nodded. "I'm afraid it's going to get worse, Kaladin. I'm sorry."

"Worse than this?"

"Unfortunately."

"I'm not strong enough, Wit," Kaladin whispered. "It has all been a lie. I've never been strong enough."

Wit took a bite of his stew, then nodded.

"You . . . agree?" Kaladin asked.

"You know better than I what your limits are," Wit said. "It's not such a terrible thing, to be too weak. Makes us need one another. I should never complain if someone recognizes their failings, though it might put me out of a job if too many share your wisdom, young bridgeman."

"And if all of this is too much for me?" Kaladin asked. "If I can't keep fighting? If I just . . . stop? Give up?"

"Are you close to that?"

"Yes," Kaladin whispered.

"Then best eat your stew," Wit said, pointing with his spoon. "A man shouldn't lie down and die on an empty stomach."

Kaladin waited for more, some insight or encouragement. Wit merely ate, and so Kaladin tried to do the same. Though the stew was perfect, he couldn't enjoy it. Not while knowing that the storm awaited him. That he wasn't free of it, that it *was* going to get worse.

"Wit?" Kaladin finally said. "Do you . . . maybe have a story you could tell me?"

Wit froze, spoon in his mouth. He stared at Kaladin, lowering his hand, leaving the spoon between his lips—before eventually opening his mouth to stare slack-jawed, the spoon falling into his waiting hand.

"What?" Kaladin asked. "Why are you so surprised?"

"Well," Wit said, recovering. "It's simply that . . . I've been waiting for someone to actually *ask*. They never seem to." He grinned, then leaned forward and lowered his voice. "There is an inn," he whispered, "that you cannot find on your own. You must stumble across it on a misty street, late at night, lost and uncertain in a strange city.

"The door has a wheel on it, but the sign bears no name. If you find the place and wander inside, you'll meet a young man behind the bar. He has no name. He cannot tell it to you, should he want to—it's been taken from him. But he'll know you, as he knows everyone who enters the inn. He'll listen to everything you want to tell him—and you *will* want to talk to him. And if you ask him for a story, he'll share one. Like he shared with me. I will now share it with you."

"All right . . ." Kaladin said.

"Hush. This isn't the part where you talk," Wit said. He settled in, then turned his hand to the side with a curt gesture, palm up. A Cryptic appeared beside him, forming as if from mist. This one wore a stiff robe like they did in Shadesmar, the head a lacy and intricate pattern somehow more . . . fine and graceful than that of Shallan's Pattern.

The Cryptic waved eagerly. Kaladin had heard that Wit was a Lightweaver now, but he hadn't been surprised. He felt he'd seen Wit Lightweave long ago. Regardless, he didn't act like he was in one of the Radiant orders. He was just . . . well, Wit.

"This story," Wit said, "is a meaningless one. You must not search for a moral. It isn't *that* kind of story, you see. It's the *other* kind of story."

The Cryptic held up a flute, and Kaladin recognized it. "Your flute!" he said. "You found it?"

"This is a dream, idiot," Wit said. "It's not real."

"Oh," Kaladin said. "Right."

"I'm real!" the Cryptic said with a musical, feminine voice. "Not imaginary at all! Unfortunately, I *am* irrational! Ha ha!" She began to play the flute, moving her fingers along it—and while soft music came out, Kaladin wasn't certain what she was doing to produce the sounds. She didn't have lips.

"This story," Wit said, "is called 'The Dog and the Dragon.'"

"The . . . what and the what?" Kaladin said. "Or is this not the part where I speak yet?"

"You people," Wit said. "A dog is a hound, like an axehound." He held up his palm, and a creature appeared in it, four-legged and furry, like a mink—only larger, and with a different face shape.

"It is funny, you can't realize," Wit said. "Humans will selectively breed for the same traits regardless of the planet they're on. But you can't be amazed at the convergent examples of domestication across the cosmere. You can't know any of this, because you live on a giant ball of rock full of slime where everything is wet and cold all the time. This is a dog, Kaladin. They're fluffy and loyal and wonderful. This, on the other hand, is a dragon."

A large beast appeared in his other hand, like a chasmfiend—except with enormous outstretched wings and only four legs. It was a brilliant pearlescent color, with silver running along the contours of its body. It also had smaller chitinous bits than a chasmfiend—in fact, its body was covered with little pieces of carapace that looked smooth to the touch. It stood proud, with a prominent chest and a regal bearing.

"I know of just one on Roshar," Wit noted, "and she prefers to hide her true form. This story isn't about her, however, or any of the dragons I've met. In fact, the dragon is barely in the story, and I'd kindly ask you not to complain about that part, because there's really nothing I can do about it and you'll only annoy Design."

The Cryptic waved again. "I get annoyed easily!" she said. "It's endearing."

"No it's not," Wit said.

"It's endearing!" Design said. "To everyone but him! I drew up a proof of it!" The music continued playing as she spoke, and the way she moved her fingers on the flute seemed completely random.

"One day, the dog saw the dragon flying overhead," Wit continued, sending the illusory dragon soaring above his hand.

Kaladin was glad for the story. Anything to keep his attention off the hateful wind, which he could faintly hear outside, howling as if eager to rush into the bubble of light and assault him.

"The dog marveled," Wit said, "as one might expect. He had never *seen* anything so majestic or grand. The dragon soared in the sky, shimmering with iridescent colors in the sunlight. When it curved around and passed above the dog, it called out a mighty challenge, demanding in the human tongue that all acknowledge its beauty.

"The dog watched this from atop a hill. Now, he wasn't particularly large, even for a dog. He was white, with brown spots and floppy ears. Not of any specific breed or lineage, and small enough that the other dogs often mocked him. He was a common variety of a common species of a common animal that most people would rightfully ignore.

"But when this dog stared at the dragon and heard the mighty boast, he came to a realization. Today, he had encountered something he'd always wished for but never known. Today he'd seen perfection, and had been presented with a goal. From today, nothing else mattered.

"He was going to become a dragon."

"Hint," Design whispered to Kaladin, "that's impossible. A dog can't become a dragon."

"Design!" Wit said, turning on her. "What did I *tell* you about spoiling the ending of stories!"

"Something stupid, so I forgot it!" she said, her pattern bursting outward like a blooming flower.

"Don't *spoil stories!*" Wit said.

"That's stupid. The story is really long. He needs to hear the ending so he'll know it's worth listening all the way."

"That's *not* how this works," Wit said. "It needs drama. Suspense. *Surprise.*"

"Surprises are dumb," she said. "He should be informed if a product is good or not before being asked to commit. Would you like a similar surprise at the market? Oh, you can't buy a *specific* food. You have to carry a sack home, cut it open, *then* find out what you bought. Drama. Suspense!"

Wit gave Kaladin a beleaguered look. "I have bonded," he said, "a *literal* monster." He made a flourish, and a Lightweaving appeared between them again, showing the dog on a hilltop covered in grass that looked dead, since it didn't move. The dog was staring upward at the dragon, which was growing smaller and smaller as it flew away.

"The dog," Wit continued, "sat upon that hilltop through an entire night and day, staring. Thinking. Dreaming. Finally, he returned to the farm where he lived among others of his kind. These farm dogs all had jobs, chasing livestock or guarding the perimeter, but he—as the smallest—was seldom given any duty. Perhaps to another this would be liberating. To him it had always been humiliating.

"As any problem to overcome is merely a set of *smaller* problems to overcome in a sequence, he divided his goal of becoming a dragon into three steps. First, he would find a way to have colorful scales like the dragon. Second, he would learn to speak the language of men like the dragon. Third, he would learn to *fly* like the dragon."

Wit made the scene unfold in front of Kaladin. A colorful land, with thick green grass that wasn't dead after all—it simply didn't move except in the wind. Creatures unlike any Kaladin had ever seen, furry and strange. Exotic.

The little dog walked into a wooden structure—a barn, though it hadn't been built with stone on the east side to withstand storms. It barely looked waterproof. How would they keep the grain from spoiling? Kaladin cocked his head at this oddity as the dog encountered a tall man in work clothing sorting through bags of seeds.

"The dog chose the scales first," Wit continued, accompanied by the quiet flute music, "as it seemed the easiest, and he wanted to begin his transformation with an early victory. He knew the farmer owned many seeds in a variety of colors, and they were the shape of little scales. Because he was not a thief, the dog did not take these—but he asked the other animals where the farmer obtained new ones.

"It turns out, the farmer could *make* seeds by putting them in the ground, waiting for plants to grow, then taking more seeds from the stalks. Knowing this, the dog borrowed some seeds and did the same, accompanying the farmer's eldest son on his daily work. As the youth worked, the dog moved alongside him, digging holes for seeds with his paws and planting them carefully with his mouth."

It was an amusing scene, watching the dog work. Not only because the animal did all this with feet and snout—but because the ground *parted* when the dog pawed at it. It wasn't made of stone, but something else.

"This is in Shinovar, isn't it?" Kaladin asked. "Sigzil told me about ground like that."

"Hush," Wit said. "This isn't the part where you talk. The farmer's eldest son found the dog's actions quite amusing—then incredible as the dog went out each day, gripping a watering can in his teeth. The little dog watered each seed, just as the farmer did. He learned to weed and fertilize. And eventually the dog was rewarded with his own small crop of colorful seeds.

"After replacing what he'd borrowed from the farmer, the dog got himself wet and rolled in his seeds, sticking them all over his body. He then presented himself to the other dogs.

"'Do you admire my wonderful new scales?' he asked his fellow animals. 'Do I not look like a dragon?'

"They, in turn, laughed at him. 'Those are not scales!' they said. 'You look stupid and silly. Go back to being a dog.'"

Kaladin put a spoonful of stew into his mouth, staring at the illusion. The way the colors worked was mesmerizing, though he had to admit the dog did look silly covered in seeds.

"The dog slunk away, feeling foolish and hurt. He had failed at his first task, to have scales like a dragon. The dog, however, was not daunted. Surely if he could *speak* with the grand voice of a dragon, they would all see. And so, the dog spent his free time watching the children of the farmer. There were three. The eldest son, who helped in the fields. The middle daughter, who helped with the animals, and the toddler—who was too young to help, but was learning to speak."

Wit made the family appear, working in the yard—the farmer's wife, who was taller than the farmer. A youth, lanky and assiduous. A daughter who would someday share her mother's height. A baby who toddled around the yard, tended by them all as they did their chores.

"This," Wit noted, "is almost too easy."

"Too easy?" Kaladin asked, absently taking another bite of stew.

"For years, I've had to make do with *hints* of illusions. *Suggesting* scenes. Leaving most to the imagination. Now, having the power to do more, I find it less satisfying.

"Anyway, the dog figured that the best way to learn the language of men was to study their youngest child. So the dog played with the baby, stayed with him, and listened as he began to form words. The dog played with the daughter too, helped her with yard work. He soon found he could understand her, if he tried hard. But he couldn't form words.

"He tried *so hard* to speak as they did, but his mouth could not make that kind of speech. His tongue did not work like a human tongue. Eventually, while watching the tall and serious daughter, he noticed she could make the words of humans on paper.

"The dog was overjoyed by this. It was a way to speak without having a human tongue! The dog joined her at the table where she studied, inspecting the letters as she made them. He failed many times, but eventually learned to scratch the letters in the dirt himself.

"The farmer and his family thought this an amazing trick. The dog was sure he had found a way to prove he was becoming a dragon. He returned to the other dogs in the field and showed them his writing ability by writing their names in the dirt.

"They, however, could not read the words. When the dog explained what writing was, they laughed. 'This is not the loud and majestic voice of a dragon!' the dogs said. 'This is speaking so quietly, nobody can hear it! You look silly and stupid. Go back to being a dog.'

"They left the dog to stare at his writing as rain began to fall, washing the words away. He realized they were correct. He had failed to speak with the proud and powerful voice of the dragon."

The image of the dog in the rain felt far too familiar to Kaladin. Far too *personal.*

"But there was still hope," Wit said. "If the dog could just *fly*. If he could achieve this feat, the dogs would *have* to acknowledge his transformation.

"This task seemed even harder than the previous two. However, the dog had seen a curious device in the barn. The farmer would tie bales of hay with a rope, then raise or lower them using a pulley in the rafters.

"This was essentially flying, was it not? The bales of hay soared in the air. And so, the dog practiced pulling on the rope himself, and learned the mechanics of the device. He found that the pulley could be balanced with a weight on the other side, which made the bales of hay lower slowly and safely.

"The dog took his leash and tied it around him to make a harness, like the ones that wrapped up the hay. Then he tied a sack slightly lighter than he was to the rope, creating a weight to balance him. After using his mouth to tie the rope to his harness, he climbed to the top of the barn's loft, and called for the other dogs to come in. When they arrived, he leaped gracefully off the loft.

"It worked! The dog lowered down slowly, striking a magnificent pose in the air. He was *flying*! He soared like the dragon had! He felt the air around him, and knew the sensation of being up high, with everything below him. When he landed, he felt so proud and so free.

"Then the other dogs laughed the loudest they had ever laughed. 'That is not flying like a dragon!' they said. 'You fell slowly. You looked so stupid and silly. Go back to being a dog.'

"This, at long last, crushed the dog's hopes. He realized the truth. A dog like him simply could not become a dragon. He was too small, too quiet, too silly."

Frankly, the sight of the dog being lowered on the rope *had* looked a bit silly. "They were right," Kaladin said. "That wasn't flying."

Wit nodded.

"Oh, is this the place where I talk?" Kaladin said.

"If you wish."

"I don't wish. Get on with the story."

Wit grinned, then leaned forward, waving in the air and making the sounds of shouting come from a distant part of the illusion, not yet visible. "What was that? The dog looked up, confused. He heard noises. Sudden shouting? Yells of panic?

"The dog raced out of the barn to find the farmer and his family huddled around the small farmyard well, which was barely wide enough for the bucket. The dog put his paws up on the edge of the well and looked down. Far below, in the deep darkness of the hole, he heard crying and splashing."

Kaladin leaned forward, staring into the darkness. A pitiful, gurgling cry was barely audible over the splashing.

"The littlest child of the farmer and his wife had fallen into the well," Wit whispered, "and was *drowning*. The family screamed and wept. There was nothing to be done. Or . . . was there?

"In a flash, the dog knew what to do. He bit the bucket off the well's rope, then had the eldest son tie the rope to his harness. He wrote 'lower me' in the dirt, then hopped up onto the rim of the well. Finally, he threw himself into the well as the farmer grabbed the crank.

"Lowered down on this rope, the dog 'flew' into the darkness. He found the baby all the way underwater, but shoved his snout in and took hold of the baby's clothing with his teeth. A short time later, when the family pulled him back up, the dog appeared holding the littlest child: wet, crying, but very much alive.

"That night, the family set a place for the little dog at their table and gave him a sweater to keep him warm, his name written across the front with letters he could read. They served a feast with food the dog had helped grow. They gave him some of the cake celebrating the birthday of the child whose life he had saved.

"That night, it rained on the other dogs, who slept outside in the cold barn, which leaked. But the little dog snuggled into a warm bed beside the fire, hugged by the farmer's children, his belly full. And as he did, the dog sadly thought to himself, 'I could not become a dragon. I am an utter and complete failure.'

"The end."

Wit clapped his hands, and the images vanished. He gave a seated bow. Design lowered her flute and flared out her pattern again, as if to give her own bow.

Then Wit picked up his bowl of stew and continued eating.

"Wait," Kaladin said, standing. "That's *it*?"

"Did you miss 'the end' at the end?" Design said. "It indicates that is the end."

"What kind of ending is that?" Kaladin said. "The dog decides he's a failure?"

"Endings are an art," Wit said loftily. "A precise and *unquestionable* art, bridgeman. Yes, that is the ending."

"Why did you tell me this?" Kaladin demanded.

"You asked for a story."

"I wanted a *useful* story!" he said, waving his hand. "Like the story of the emperor on the island, or of Fleet who kept running."

"You didn't specify that," Wit said. "You said you wanted a story. I provided one. That is all."

"That's the wrong ending," Kaladin said. "That dog was *incredible*. He learned to write. How many animals can write, on any world?"

"Not many, I should say," Wit noted.

"He learned to farm and to use tools," Kaladin said. "He saved a child's *life*. That dog is a storming hero."

"The story wasn't about him trying to be a hero," Wit said. "It was about him trying to be a dragon. In which, pointedly, he *failed*."

"I told you!" Design said happily. "Dogs can't be dragons!"

"Who cares?" Kaladin said, stalking back and forth. "By looking up at the dragon, and by trying to become better, he outgrew the other dogs. He achieved something truly special." Kaladin stopped, then narrowed his eyes at Wit, feeling his anger turn to annoyance. "This story is about me, isn't it? I said I'm not good enough. You think I have impossible goals, and I'm *intentionally* ignoring the things I've accomplished."

Wit pointed with his spoon. "I *told* you this story has no meaning. You promised not to assign it one."

"As a matter of fact," Design said, "you didn't give him a chance to promise! You simply kept talking."

Wit glared at her.

"Blah blah blah blah blah!" she said, rocking her pattern head back and forth at each word.

"Your stories always have a point," Kaladin said.

"I am an *artist*," Wit said. "I should thank you not to demean me by insisting my art must be trying to *accomplish* something. In fact, you shouldn't enjoy art. You should simply admit that it exists, then move on. Anything else is patronizing."

Kaladin folded his arms, then sat. Wit, playing games again. Couldn't he ever be clear? Couldn't he ever say what he meant?

"Any meaning," Wit said softly, "is for you to assign, Kaladin. I merely tell the stories. Have you finished your stew?"

Kaladin realized he had—he'd eaten the entire bowl while listening.

"I can't keep this bubble up much longer, I'm afraid," Wit said. "He'll notice if I do—and then he'll destroy me. I have violated our agreement, which exposes me to his direct action. I'd rather not be killed, as I have seven more people I wanted to insult today."

Kaladin nodded, standing up again. He realized that somehow, the story fired him up. He felt stronger, less for the words and more for how annoyed he'd grown at Wit.

A little light, a little warmth, a little *fire* and he felt ready to walk out into the winds again. Yet he knew the darkness would return. It always did.

"Can you tell me the real ending?" Kaladin asked, his voice small. "Before I go back out?"

Wit stood and stepped over, then put his hand on Kaladin's back and leaned in. "That night," he said, "the little dog snuggled into a warm bed beside the fire, hugged by the farmer's children, his belly full. And as he did, the dog thought to himself, 'I doubt any dragon ever had it so good anyway.'"

He smiled and met Kaladin's eyes.

"It won't be like that for me," Kaladin said. "You told me it would get worse."

"It will," Wit said, "but then it will *get better*. Then it will get worse again. Then better. This is life, and I will not lie by saying every day will be sunshine. But there will be sunshine again, and that is a very different thing to say. That is truth. I promise you, Kaladin: *You will be warm again.*"

Kaladin nodded in thanks, then turned to the hateful winds. He felt a push against his back as Wit sent him forward—then the light vanished, along with all it contained.

81

TRAPPED

SEVEN YEARS AGO

Eshonai tipped her head back, feeling water stream off her carapace skullplate. Returning to warform after so long in workform felt like revisiting a familiar clearing hidden in the trees, rarely encountered but always waiting for her. She *did* like this form. She would *not* see it as a prison.

She met Thude and Rlain as they emerged from hollows in the stone where they too had returned to this form. Many of her friends had never left it. Warform was convenient for many reasons, though Eshonai didn't like it quite as well as workform. There was something about the aggression this form provoked in her. She worried she would seek excuses to fight.

Thude stretched, humming to Joy. "Feels good," he said. "I feel alive in this form."

"Too alive," Rlain said. "Do the rhythms sound louder to you?"

"Not to me," Thude said.

Eshonai shook her head. She didn't hear the rhythms any differently. Indeed, she'd been wondering if—upon adopting this form again—she'd hear the pure tone of Roshar as she did the first time. She hadn't.

"Shall we?" she asked, gesturing toward the spreading plateaus. Rlain started toward one of the bridges, but Thude sang loudly to Amusement and charged the nearby chasm, leaping and soaring over it with an incredible bound.

Eshonai dashed after him to do the same. Each form brought with it a certain level of instinctual understanding. When she reached the edge, her body knew what to do. She sprang in a powerful leap, the air whistling through the grooves in her carapace and flapping the loose robe she'd worn into the storm.

She landed with a solid crunch, her feet grinding stone as she slid to a stop. The Rhythm of Confidence thrummed in her ears, and she found herself grinning. She *had* missed that. Rlain landed next to her, a hulking figure with black and red skin patterns forming an intricate marbling. He hummed to Confidence as well.

"Come on!" Thude shouted from nearby. He leaped another chasm.

Attuning Joy, Eshonai ran after him. Together the three of them chased and dashed, climbed and soared—spanning chasms, climbing up and over rock formations, sprinting across plateaus. The Shattered Plains felt like a playground.

This must be what islands and oceans are like, she thought as she surveyed the Plains from up high. She'd heard about them in songs, and she'd always imagined an ocean as a huge network of streams moving between sections of land.

But no, she'd seen Gavilar's map. In that painting, the bodies of water had seemed as wide as countries. Water . . . with nothing to see but more water. She attuned Anxiety. And Awe. Complementary emotions, in her experience.

She dropped from the rock formation and landed on the plateau, then bounded after Thude. How far would she have to travel to find those oceans? Judging by the map, only a few weeks to the east. Once such a distance would have been daunting, but now she'd made the trek all the way to Kholinar and back. The trip to the Alethi capital had been one of the sweetest and most exhilarating experiences of her life. So many new places. So many wonderful people. So many strange plants, strange sights, strange foods to taste.

When they'd fled, the same wonders had become threats overnight. The entire trip home had been a blur of marching, sleeping, and foraging in human fields.

Eshonai reached another chasm and leaped, trying to recapture her excitement. She increased her pace, coming up even with Thude and eventually passing him—before the two of them pulled to a halt to wait for Rlain, who had slowed a few plateaus back. He had always been a careful one, and he seemed better able to control the inclinations of the new form.

Her heart racing, Eshonai reached out of habit to wipe her brow—but this form didn't have sweat on her forehead to drip into her eyes. Instead, the carapace armor trapped air from her forward motion, then pushed it up underneath to cool her skin.

The awesome energy of the form meant she could probably have kept running for hours before feeling any real strain. Perhaps longer. Indeed, the warforms during their flight from Alethkar had carried food for the others and *still* moved faster than the workforms.

At the same time, Eshonai was getting hungry. She remembered well how much food this form required at each meal.

Thude leaned against a high rock formation as they waited, watching some windspren play in the air. Eshonai wished she'd brought her book for drawing maps of the Plains. She'd found it in the human market of Kholinar—such a small, simple thing. It had been expensive by Alethi standards, but oh so cheap by her standards. An entire book of papers? All for a few little bits of emerald?

She'd seen steel weapons there too. Sitting in the market. *For sale.* The listeners protected, polished, and revered each weapon they'd found on the Plains—keeping them for generations, passed down from parent to child. The humans had entire stalls of them.

"This is going to go poorly for us, isn't it?" Thude asked.

Eshonai realized she'd been humming to the Lost. She stopped, but met his eyes and knew that he knew. Together they walked around the stone formation and looked westward, toward the cities that had for centuries been listener homes. Dark smoke filled the air—the Alethi burning wood as they set up enormous cookfires and settled into their camps.

They'd arrived in force. Tens of thousands of them. Swarms of soldiers, with dozens of Shardbearers. Come to exterminate her people.

"Maybe not," Eshonai said. "In warform, we're stronger than they are. They have equipment and skill, but we have strength and endurance. If we *have* to fight them, this terrain will heavily favor us."

"Did you really have to do it though?" Thude asked to Pleading. "Did you *need* to have him killed?"

She'd answered this before, but she didn't avoid the responsibility. She *had* voted for Gavilar to die. And she'd been the reason for the vote in the first place.

"He was going to bring them back, Thude," Eshonai said to Reprimand. "Our ancient gods. I *heard* him say it. He thought I'd be happy to hear of it."

"So you killed him?" Thude asked, to Agony. "Now they'll kill *us*, Eshonai. How is this any better?"

She attuned Tension. Thude, in turn, attuned Reconciliation. He seemed to recognize that bringing this up again and again was accomplishing nothing.

"It is done," Eshonai said. "So now, we need to hold out. We might not even have to fight them. We can harvest gemstones from the greatshells and speed crop growth. The humans can't leap these chasms, and so they'll have trouble ever getting to us. We'll be safe."

"We'll be trapped," Thude said. "In the center of these Plains. For months, perhaps years. You're fine with that, Eshonai?"

Rlain finally caught up to them, jogging over and humming to Amusement—perhaps he thought the two of them silly for speeding ahead.

Eshonai looked away from Thude and stared out across the Plains—not toward the humans, but toward the ocean, the Origin. Places she could have gone. Places she'd *planned* to go. Thude knew her too well. He understood how much it hurt to be trapped here.

They will strike inward, she thought. *The humans won't come all this way to turn around because of a few chasms. They have resources we can only imagine, and there are so many of them. They'll find a way to get to us.*

Escaping out the other side of the Plains wasn't an option either. If the chasmfiends there didn't get them, the humans eventually would. To flee would be to abandon the natural fortification of the Plains.

"I'll do what I have to, Thude," Eshonai said to Determination. "I'll do what is right whatever the cost. To us. To me."

"They have fought wars," Thude said. "They have generals. Great military thinkers. We've had warform for only a year."

"We'll learn," Eshonai said, "and create our own generals. Our ancestors paid with their very minds to bring us freedom. If the humans find a way to come for us in here, we *will* fight. Until we persuade the humans that the cost is too high. Until they realize we won't go meekly to slavery, like the poor beings they use as servants. Until they learn they cannot have us, our Blades, or our souls. We are a *free* people. Forever."

⁂

Venli gathered her friends around, humming softly to Craving as she revealed the gemstones in her hands. Voidspren. Five of them, trapped as Ulim had been when first brought to her.

Inside her gemheart, he hummed words of encouragement. Ever since the events at the human city, he'd treated her with far more respect. And he'd never again abandoned her. The longer he remained, the better she could hear the new rhythms. The rhythms of power.

She had claimed this section of Narak—the city at the center of the Plains—for her scholars. Friends who she and Ulim had determined, after careful discussion, shared her hunger for a better world. Trustworthy enough, she hoped. Once they had Voidspren in their gemhearts, she'd be far more confident in their discretion.

"What are they?" Demid asked, his hand resting on Venli's shoulder. He'd been the first and most eager to listen. He didn't know everything, naturally, but she was glad to have him. She felt stronger when he was around. Braver than Eshonai. After all, could Eshonai have ever taken *this* step?

"These hold spren," Venli explained. "When you accept one into your gemheart, they'll hold your current spren with them, keeping you in your current form—but you'll have a secret companion to help you. Guide you. Together, we're going to solve the greatest challenge our people have ever known."

"Which is?" Tusa asked to Skepticism.

"Our world is connected to another," Venli explained, handing one gemstone to each of her friends. "A place called Shadesmar. *Hundreds* of spren exist there who can grant us the ability to harness the power of the storms. They've traveled a long way, as part of a great storm. They've gone as far as they can on their own, however. Getting gemstones like these to our side takes enormous effort, and is impossible on a large scale.

"So we need another way to bring those spren across. We're going to figure it out, then we're going to persuade the rest of the listeners to join with us in adopting forms of power. We'll be smart; we won't be ruled by the spren this time around. We'll rule them.

"Eshonai and the others have foolishly thrown everyone into an unwanted war. So *we* have to take this step. We will be remembered as the ones who saved our people."

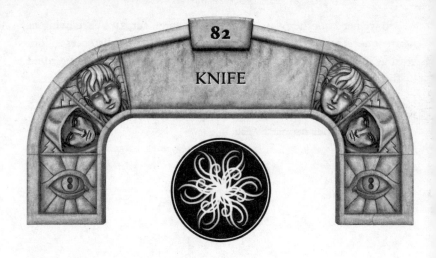

Oh ... Father ... Seven thousand years.

H ow could you not tell me this?" Radiant demanded as she knelt and shouted at the cube on the floor. "Restares is not only the honorspren's High Judge, he's one of the *storming* Heralds!"

"You didn't require the information at that time," Mraize's voice said. "Be Veil. She will understand."

"Veil is even *more* angry at you, Mraize," Radiant said, standing up. "You sent us into a dangerous situation without proper preparation! Withholding this information wasted *weeks* while the three of us searched the fortress like an idiot."

"We didn't want you asking after a Herald," Mraize said, his voice frustratingly calm. "That might have alerted him. So far as we're aware, he hasn't figured out that we know his true identity. Gavilar may have known, but no others in the Sons of Honor had an inkling that they served one of the very beings they were seeking—in their naive ignorance—to restore to Roshar. The irony is quite poetic."

"Mmm . . ." Pattern said from beside the door, where he was watching for Adolin.

"What?" Radiant asked him. "You like irony now too?"

"Irony tastes good. Like sausage."

"And have you ever tasted sausage?"

"I don't believe I have a sense of taste," Pattern said. "So irony tastes like what I imagine sausage would taste like when I'm imagining tastes."

Radiant rubbed her forehead, looking back at the cube. So unfair. She was accustomed to being able to stare down her troops, but one could not properly glare at a man who talked to you out of a box.

"You told us we'd know what to do when we found Restares," Radiant told Mraize. "Well, we are here now and we have *no* idea how to proceed."

"What did you do the moment you found out?" Mraize said.

"Cursed your name."

"Then?"

"Contacted you directly to curse at you some more."

"Which was the correct choice. See, you knew exactly what to do."

Radiant folded her arms, warm with anger. Frustration. And . . . admittedly . . . embarrassment. She bled into being Veil, and the anger returned.

"The time has come," she said, "for us to deal, Mraize."

"Deal? The deal has already been set. You do as I have requested, and you will receive the offered reward—in addition to the practice and training you are receiving under my hand."

"That is interesting," Veil said. "Because I see this differently. I have come all this way, through great hardship. Because of Adolin's sacrifice, I've gained access to one of the most remote fortresses on Roshar. I have succeeded where you explicitly told me your other agents have failed.

"Now that I'm here, instead of receiving 'training' or 'practice' as you say, I find that you've been withholding vital information from me. From my perspective, there is no incentive to continue this arrangement, as the promised reward is of little interest to me. Even Shallan is questioning its value.

"Your refusal to give me important information makes me question what else you held back. Now I'm questioning if what I'm to do here is possibly against my interests, and the interests of those I love. So let me ask plainly. Why am I really here? Why are you so interested in Kelek? And why—explicitly—should I continue on this path?"

Mraize did not respond immediately. "Hello, Veil," he finally said. "I'm glad you came out to speak with me."

"Answer my questions, Mraize."

"First, it is time to open the cube," Mraize said.

Veil frowned. "The communication cube? I thought you said that would ruin the thing."

"If you break into it, you *will* ruin it. Pick it up. Heft it. Listen for the side where my voice is weakest as I hum."

She knelt beside the cube again and picked it up, listening to Mraize's humming voice. Yes . . . the sound was weaker from one direction.

"I've found it," she said.

"Good," Mraize said. "Put your hand on that plane of the cube and twist it to the right."

She felt it click as she touched it. She suspected Mraize had done something to unlock the device from wherever he was. When she twisted that plane of the cube, it turned easily and came off, revealing a small compartment that contained an intricate metal dagger with a gemstone on the end of the grip.

"So you *do* want me to kill him," she said.

"One cannot kill a Herald," Mraize said. "They are immortal. Do not think of Kelek as a person. He is an ageless, eternal spren formed of Honor's substance and will. He is as gravity or light. Force, not man."

"And you want me to stab that force with this knife," Veil said, undoing the straps and prying it out from the cube. The cavity was only a small part of the hollow portion in the cube, and a layer of steel sectioned off the rest. Mraize's voice came from the sealed portion. How had he weighted the cube such that she didn't feel one end was heavier than the other?

"I want you," he said, "to collect the soul of Kelek, also known as Restares. The knife will trap his essence in that gemstone."

"That seems overly cruel," Veil said, looking over the knife.

"Cruel like the spanreeds you so eagerly use, despite the spren trapped inside? It is no different. The being called Kelek is a receptacle of incredible knowledge. Gemstone imprisonment will not hurt him, and we will be able to communicate with him."

"We have *two* other Heralds in the tower," Veil said. "I could ask them anything you want to know."

"You think they'd answer? How useful have they been, talking to Jasnah? Talenelat is completely insane, and Shalash is deceptively reticent. They talk of their Oathpact, yes, and fighting the Fused—but rarely reveal anything practical."

"This isn't very persuasive," Veil said. "Yes, I know what you want me to do—but I suspected it from the beginning. If you want me to do this, I need to know *why*. What *specifically* do you expect to learn from him?"

"Our master, Thaidakar, has an . . . affliction similar to that of the Heralds. He needs access to a Herald to learn more about his state so he might save himself from the worst of its effects."

"That's not good enough," Veil said. "Radiant and Shallan won't let me do your dirty work for such a petty reason." She put the dagger back in the cube. "I came here to report on Restares's location. Shallan specifically told you we wouldn't kill him—and yes, I count stabbing him with this device as the same thing."

"Little knife," Mraize said, his voice growing softer, "why did Sadeas need to die?"

She hesitated, her hand still on the dagger, which she was trying to reattach to the straps in the cube.

"This being," Mraize continued, "that they call Kelek is a monster. He, along with the other eight, abandoned their Oathpact and stranded Talenelat—the Bearer of Agonies—alone in Damnation, to withstand torture for thousands of years. The enemy has returned, but have the Heralds come to help? No. At best they hide. At worst, their madness leads them to hasten the world's destruction.

"Kelek has become indecisive to the point of madness. And like most of them, he is afraid. He wants to escape his duties. He worked with Gavilar knowing full well that doing so would cause the return of the Fused and the end of our peace, because he hoped to find a way to escape this world. A way to abandon us as he had already abandoned his oaths and his friends.

"He possesses knowledge essential to our fight against the invaders. However, he will not share it willingly. He hides himself away in the world's most remote fortress and tries to pretend there is no war, that he is not culpable. He *is*. The only way to make him do his duty is to bring him back by force—and the best and easiest way to do that is to trap his soul."

Storms. That was a longer speech than she usually got out of Mraize. There was passion, conviction to his voice. Veil almost felt persuaded.

"I can't move against him," she said. "He is set to judge Adolin in this trial. If Kelek vanished, that would throw all kinds of suspicion on us—and Adolin would most certainly be imprisoned. I can't risk it."

"Hmm . . ." Mraize said. "If only there were a way that someone—having locked away Kelek's soul—could take his place. Wear his face. Pass judgment, vindicating your husband and commanding the honorspren to join the war again. If *only* we had sent a person capable of single-handedly turning the tide of this war through the use of a targeted illusion."

In that moment, Veil lost control to Shallan. Because what Mraize said here . . . it made too much sense.

Oh storms, Shallan thought, growing cold. *Stormfather above and Nightwatcher below . . . He's right. That is a solution to this problem. A way to let Adolin win. A way to bring the honorspren back.*

So this was how he manipulated her this time. She wanted to buck him for that reason alone. If only what he said weren't so logical. It would be easy to replace Kelek, assuming she could get some Stormlight. . . .

No, Veil warned. *It's not that easy. We'd have a difficult time impersonating a Herald.*

We'd do the replacement at the last moment, Shallan thought. *On the final day of the trial—to reduce the amount of time we need to pretend, and to give us a few days to scout out his personality.*

"Killing Sadeas saved thousands of lives," Mraize continued in his soft, oily voice. "Delivering Kelek to us, sending the honorspren to bond Windrunners, could save *millions.*"

"Veil isn't certain we could imitate a Herald," Shallan said.

"The Herald is erratic," Mraize said. "All of them are now. With a few pointers, you could escape notice. Honorspren are not good at noticing subterfuge—or at distinguishing what is odd behavior for humans, or those who were once human. You can accomplish this. And after the trial, 'Kelek' could insist he has to visit Urithiru himself, leaving the spren completely ignorant of what you've done."

"It would be wrong, Mraize. It *feels* wrong."

"Earlier, Veil demanded a deal. Though I normally reject this sort of talk, I find it encouraging that she did not demand money, or power. She wanted information, to know why she was doing what she did. You three are worthy hunters.

"So I will revise the deal as requested. Perform as I ask here, and I will release you from your apprenticeship. You will become a full member of our organization—you will not only have access to the knowledge you seek, but also have a say in what we are doing. Our grand plans."

Inside, Veil perked up at this. But Shallan was surprised by how much *she* responded to that offer. A full Ghostblood? That was the way . . . The way to . . .

"Strike at a Herald," she said. "It sounds wrong, Mraize. Very wrong."

"You are weak," he said. "You know it."

She bowed her head.

"But part of you is not," he continued. "A part that *can be* that strong. Let that side of you do what needs to be done. Save your husband, your kingdom, and your world all at once. Become that hunter, Shallan.

"Become the knife."

⁘

The honorspren surrounding the High Judge made room for Adolin as he approached, Blended following behind. He didn't miss the glares that many of them gave her. No, there was no love lost between the two varieties of spren.

He should probably feel reverence for the High Judge. This was Kelek, though the spren called him Kalak for some reason. Either way, he was one of the Heralds—so Blended had explained. Many people back home thought of him as the Stormfather, and though that had never been true, he *was* one of the most ancient beings in all of creation. A god to many. An immortal soldier for justice and Honor.

He was also short, with thinning hair. He felt like the type of man you'd find administering some minor city in the backwater of Alethkar. And if he was anything like Ash or Taln, the two Heralds who now resided at Urithiru . . .

Well, his acquaintance with those two caused Adolin to lower his expectations in this particular case.

Kelek spoke with several honorspren leaders as they strolled up the lower portion of the western plane, entering a stone pathway made up of a multitude of colored cobblestones vaguely in the pattern of a gust of wind. The group paused as they saw Adolin ahead.

He removed his hand from his sword out of respect, then bowed to the Herald.

"Hmm? A human?" Kelek said. "Why is he here? He looks dangerous, Sekeir."

"He is," said the honorspren beside Kelek. Sekeir was a leader of the fortress, and appeared as an ancient honorspren with a long blue-white beard. "This is Adolin Kholin, son of Dalinar Kholin."

"The Bondsmith?" Kelek said, and *shied away* from Adolin. "Good heavens! Why have you let him in here?"

"I have come, great one," Adolin said, "to petition the honorspren for their aid in our current battle."

"Your current battle? Against Odium?" Kelek laughed. "Boy, you're doomed. You realize that, right? Tanavast is *dead*. Like, completely dead. The Oathpact is broken somehow. The only thing left is to try to get off the ship before it sinks."

"Holy Lord," Sekeir said, "we let this one in because he offered to stand trial in the stead of the humans, for the pain they have caused our people."

"You're going to try him for the *Recreance*?" Kelek asked, looking around uncertainly at the others near him. "Isn't that a bit extreme?"

"He offered, Holy Lord."

"Not a smart one, is he?" Kelek looked to Adolin, who hesitantly pulled up from his bow. "Huh. You've gotten yourself in deep, boy. They take this kind of thing *very* seriously around here."

"I hope to show them, great one, that we are not their enemies. That the best course forward is for them to join us in our fight. It is, one might say, the *honorable* choice."

"Honor is dead," Kelek snapped. "Aren't you paying attention? This world belongs to Odium now. He has his own storm, for heaven's sake."

Blended nudged Adolin. Right. He was so distracted by Kelek that he'd forgotten the purpose of meeting with him.

"Great one," Adolin said, "I've decided to petition for a trial by witness. Would you be willing to grant me this?"

"Trial by witness?" Kelek said. "Well, that would make this mess end faster. What do you think, Sekeir?"

"I don't think this would be a wise—"

"Hold on; I don't care what you think," Kelek said. "Here I am, years after joining you, and you *still* don't have a way for me to get off this cursed world. Fine, boy, trial by witness it is. We can start it . . . um, the day after tomorrow? Is that acceptable for everyone?"

No one objected.

"Great," Kelek said. "Day after tomorrow. Okay then. Um . . . let's have it at the forum, shall we? I guess everyone will want to watch, and that has the most seats."

"Object to this," Blended whispered to Adolin. "Do not let it be. You don't want to have to persuade the audience as well as the judge."

"Great one," Adolin said, "I had hoped this to be an intimate, personal discussion of—"

"Tough," Kelek said. "You should have thought of that before coming in here to create a storm. Everyone knows how this trial will end, so we might as well make a good time of it for them."

Adolin felt a sinking sensation as Kelek led the group of honorspren around him. Though few lighteyed judges were ever truly impartial, there was an expectation that they'd try to act with honor before the eyes of the Almighty. But this Herald basically told him the trial would be a sham. The man had made his judgment before hearing any arguments.

How on Roshar was that *ever considered a deity?* Adolin thought, in a daze. The Heralds had fallen so far.

Either that, or . . . perhaps these ten people had *always* been only that. People. After all, crowning a man a king or highprince didn't necessarily make him anything grander than he'd been. Adolin knew that firsthand.

"That could have gone better," Blended said, "but at least a trial by witness is. Come. I have one day, it seems, to prepare you to be thrown into the angerspren's den. . . ."

THE GAMES OF
MEN AND SINGERS

*I remember so few of those centuries. I am a blur. A smear on the
page. A gaunt stretch of ink, made all the more insubstantial with
each passing day.*

Venli knelt on the floor of a secluded hallway on the fifteenth
floor of Urithiru. The stones whispered to her that the place
had once been called Ur. The word meant "original" in the
Dawnchant. An ancient place, with ancient stones.

There was a spren that lived here. Not dead, as Raboniel had once
proclaimed. This spren was the veins of the tower, its inner metal and
crystal running through walls, ceilings, floors.

The stones had not been created by that spren, though a grand project
had reshaped them. Reshaped Ur, the original mountain that had been
here before. The stones *remembered* being that mountain. They remembered so many things, which they expressed to Venli. Not with words.
Rather as impressions, like those a hand left in crem before it dried.

Or the impression Venli's hands left in the floor as they sank into the
eager stone. *Remember,* the stones whispered. *Remember what you have
forgotten.*

She remembered sitting at her mother's feet as a child, listening to
the songs. The music had flowed like water, etching patterns in her

brain—memories—like the passage of time etched canals in stone.

Listeners were not like humans, who grew slow as trees. Listeners grew like vines, quick and eager. By age three, she'd been singing with her mother. By age ten, she'd been considered an adult. Venli remembered those years—looking up to Eshonai, who seemed so big, although just a year older than Venli. She had vague memories of holding her father's finger as he sang with her mother.

She remembered love. Family. Grandparents, cousins. How had she forgotten? As a child, ambition and love had been like two sides of her face, each with its own vibrant pattern. To the sound of Odium's rhythms, one side had shone, while the other withered. She had become a person who wanted only to achieve her goals—not because those goals would help others, but because of the goals themselves.

It was in that moment that Venli saw for herself the depth of his lies. He claimed to be of all Passions, and yet where was the love she'd once felt? The love for her mother? Her sister? Her friends? For a while, she'd even forgotten her love for Demid, though it had helped to awaken her.

It felt wrong to be using his Light to practice her Surgebinding, but the stones whispered that it was well. Odium and his tone had become part of Roshar, as Cultivation and Honor—who had not been created alongside the planet—had become part of it. His power was natural, and no more wrong or right than any other part of nature.

Venli searched for something else. The tone of Cultivation. Odium's song could suffuse her, fueling her powers and enflaming her emotions, but that tone . . . that tone had belonged to her people long before he'd arrived. While she searched for it, she listened to her mother's songs in her mind. Like chains, spiked into the stone so they'd remain strong during storms, they reached backward through time. Through generations.

To her people, leaving the battlefield. Walking away rather than continuing to squabble over the same ground over and over. They hadn't merely rejected the singer gods, they'd rejected the *conflict*. Holding to family, singing to Love despite their dull forms, they'd left the war and gone a new way.

The tone snapped into her mind, Cultivation and Odium mixing into a harmony, and it thrummed through Venli. She opened her eyes as power spread from her through the stones. They began to shake and vibrate to the sound of her rhythm, liquid, forming peaks and valleys in time with the music. The floor, ceiling, and walls before her rippled, and a trail of people formed from the stone. Moving, alive again, as they strode away from pain, and war, and killing.

Freedom. The stones whispered to her of freedom. Rock seemed so stable, so unchangeable, but if you saw it on the timescale of spren, it was always changing. *Deliberately.* Over centuries. She had never known her ancestors, but she knew their songs. She could sing those and imitate their courage. Their love. Their wisdom.

The power slipped from her, as it always did. The tone faded, and her control over the stone ended. She needed more practice and more Light. Still, she didn't need Timbre's encouraging thrum to keep her spirits high as she stood. For she had in front of her, in miniature, a sculpture of her ancestors striking out toward the unknown.

More, she had their songs. Because of her mother's diligent and insistent teaching, the songs had not died with the listeners.

❖

An hour later, Venli walked the hallways much lower in the tower, waiting for Leshwi.

She met with the Heavenly One almost every day. Raboniel knew the meetings were happening, of course. And Leshwi knew that Raboniel knew. Still, Venli and Leshwi met in secret; it was all part of the dance of politics between the Fused.

They met as if by happenstance. Leshwi hovered solemnly through a corridor at the right time, her long black train rustling against the stone. Venli fell into step beside her mistress.

"The Pursuer has found the Windrunner's parents, Ancient One," Venli said. "I'm certain of it. He posted two nightform Regals at the Radiant infirmary."

"Which ones?"

"Urialin and Nistar."

"'Light' and 'mystery,'" Leshwi said, translating their names from the ancient language. Like many of the Regals, they had taken new names for themselves upon their awakening. "Yes, this is a signal. But the Pursuer is not that subtle; if you look, I suspect that Raboniel is the one who suggested those two."

"What do we do?" Venli said to Anxiety.

"Nothing, for now. My authority extends far enough to protect them. This is merely a warning."

"Raboniel threatens to let the Pursuer have the humans," Venli said. "That is why she posted those two guards. To lord her advantage over us."

"Perhaps," Leshwi said, floating with her hands behind her back. "Perhaps not. Raboniel does not think like other Fused, Venli. She hears a much grander song. A skewed and twisted one, but one she seeks to sing without traditional regard for Odium's plans or those of Honor, now dead."

"She makes her own side then," Venli said. "She seeks to play both armies against one another and profit herself."

"Do not transpose your mortal ambitions upon Raboniel," Leshwi said to Ridicule. "You think too small, Venli, to understand her. *I* think too small to understand her. Regardless, you did well in bringing this to me. Watch for other signs like this."

They reached the atrium, the hallway they'd been following merging with it like a river flowing into a sea. Here, Heavenly Ones soared up and down, delivering supplies to the scouts and Masked Ones on the upper floors. Those continued to keep watch for Windrunners. The charade was wearing thin at this point; Raboniel was certain Dalinar Kholin had seen through it and knew something very wrong was happening at the tower.

The supplies to the upper floors could have been delivered via the lifts. However, Raboniel had put the Heavenly Ones to work, making it very clear that she had both the authority and the inclination to keep them busy.

This had driven off many of them, who preferred their sanctuaries in Kholinar. Perhaps that had been the point. Leshwi instead did as she was asked. She floated up and over the railing, her long train slipping over and then falling to drift in the open air beneath her. Another Heavenly One soared upward past them, trailing cloth of gold and red.

"Ancient One," Venli said to Craving, stepping up to the railing. "What are we watching Raboniel for, if not to understand how she's trying to gain advantage over us? What is the purpose of my spying?"

"We watch," Leshwi said, floating down to eye level with Venli, "because we are frightened. To Raboniel, the games of men and singers are petty things—but so are their *lives*. We watch her, Venli, because we want a world to remain when she is finished with her plots."

Venli felt a chill, attuning the Terrors. As Leshwi flew off, Venli took a lift, haunted by those words. *The games of men and singers are petty things . . . but so are their lives. . . .*

The ominous words pulled Venli down from her earlier optimism. After stepping off the lift, she decided to stop and check on Rlain and the others. She couldn't help attuning Agony at the idea of those Regals in the infirmary. At least the surgeon and his wife had the good sense to mostly stay out of sight.

Venli slipped into the draped-off section of the room, where Hesina was keeping watch today. She nodded as Venli entered, then grimaced and glanced toward the others inside. There was a new human here, one Venli didn't recognize, who stood with his eyes down, not speaking.

A tension in the room was coming entirely from Lirin and Rlain, who faced off at the rear, Rlain humming softly to Betrayal. What on Roshar?

"I can't believe I'm hearing this," Rlain said. "I *can't* believe it. He's your *son*."

"My son is long dead, bridgeman," Lirin said, quickly packing a small bag full of surgical implements. "Kaladin kept trying to explain this, and I only recently started understanding. He doesn't want to be my son anymore. If that's the case, it's difficult for me to see him as anything other than a killer and an agitator. Someone who recklessly endangered not just my family, but the lives of every human in the tower, while pursuing a vengeful grudge."

"So you're going to leave him to die?" Rlain demanded.

"I didn't say that," Lirin snapped. "Do *not* put words in my mouth. I'll go as I would for anyone wounded."

"And afterward?" he demanded. "You said—"

"I *said* we'd see," Lirin said. "It's possible I'll need to bring him down here to give him long-term care."

"You would give him up for execution!"

"If that's what is required, then so be it. I'll do my job as a surgeon, then let Kaladin deal with the consequences of his actions. I'm finished being a pawn in games of death. For *either* side."

Rlain threw up his hands. "What is the point of trying to save him if you're intending to have him killed!"

"Quiet!" Venli hissed, glancing out the flimsy drapes toward the others in the room outside. "What is going on here?"

Lirin glared at Rlain, who again hummed to Betrayal.

"Our son survived the events of the other day," Hesina said to Venli. "This is one of his friends. He says Kaladin's powers aren't working properly, and his wounds aren't healing. He's in a coma and is slowly dying of what sounds like internal bleeding."

"That or an infection," Lirin said, stuffing a few more things into his bag. "Can't tell from the description."

"We're not taking you to him," Rlain said, "unless you *promise* not to give him and Teft up to the enemy." He looked to the other man in the room, the newcomer, who nodded in agreement.

"Then he'll die for certain," Lirin snapped. "Blood on *your* hands."

The two glared at each other, and Venli attuned Irritation. As if she didn't have enough to worry about.

"I'll go," Hesina said, walking over and taking the surgery bag off the table.

"Hesina—"

"He's my son too," she said. "Let's be on with this, Rlain. I can show you how to treat the fever and give him some anti-inflammatories, along with something to fight the infection."

"And if it *is* internal bleeding?" Lirin asked. "He will need surgery. You can't perform an operation like that in the field, Hesina."

He sounded angry, but those were *fearspren* at his feet. Not angerspren. The surgeon turned away and pretended to arrange his instruments. But humans were so full of emotion, it spilled out of them. He couldn't hide what he was feeling from Venli. Frustration. Worry.

He could say what he wanted. But he loved his son.

"He needs to be brought here," Lirin said, his voice laden with pain as plain as any rhythm. "I will go with you to help him. Then . . . I want you to listen to my suggestion. If he's in a coma, he *will* need long-term care. We can put him in this room and pretend he's unconscious like the others. It's the best way."

"He'd rather die," the newcomer whispered. There was something odd about his voice that Venli couldn't place. He slurred his words.

The chamber fell silent. Save for one thing.

Timbre vibrated with excitement inside Venli. The little spren was at it so loudly, Venli was certain the others would hear. How could they not?

"It was going to catch up to Kal eventually," Lirin said, his tone morose. "Most soldiers don't die on the battlefield, you know. Far more die from wounds days later. My son taught you about triage, didn't he? What did he say about people with wounds like his?"

The two former bridgemen glanced at each other.

"Make them comfortable," the human with the slurred words said. "Give them drink. Pain medication, if you can spare it. So they are peaceful when they . . . when they die."

Again the room grew quiet. All save for Timbre, practically bursting with sound.

It's time. It's time. It's time!

When Venli spoke, she almost believed it was Timbre saying the words and not her.

"What if," she said, "I knew about an Edgedancer whose powers still seem to work? One who I think we can rescue?"

⁘

It didn't take much time to explain the plan. Venli had been thinking about this for days now; she'd only needed some practice with her powers, and a little help from Rlain.

The Edgedancer was kept in the same cell Rlain had occupied not long ago. Venli could get through that wall with ease; she was in control of her powers enough for that. The real trick would be pulling off the rescue without revealing or implicating herself.

Timbre pulsed in annoyance as Venli and Rlain hurried toward the cell. The human, Dabbid, was taking another route. Venli didn't want to be seen walking with him.

"How did you get a Shardblade?" Rlain asked softly, to Curiosity. "And how do they not know you have one?"

"It's a long story," Venli said. Mostly because she hadn't thought of a proper lie yet.

"It's Eshonai's, isn't it? Do you know what happened to her? I know you said she's dead . . . but how?"

She died controlled by a Voidspren, Venli thought, *because I tricked her into inviting one into her gemheart. She fell into a chasm after fighting a human Shardbearer, then drowned. Alone. I found her corpse, and—under the direction of a Voidspren—desecrated it by stealing her Shards. But I don't have them.*

There was a lot she *could* say. "No. I got it from a dead human. I bonded it while traveling to Kholinar, before the Fused found me and the others."

"That was when they . . . they . . ." Rlain attuned the Rhythm of the Lost.

"Yes," Venli said to the same rhythm. "When they took the rest of our friends. They left me because Odium wanted me to travel around, telling lies about our people to 'inspire' the newly awakened singers."

"I'm sorry," Rlain said. "That must have been difficult for you, Venli."

"I survived," Venli said. "But if we're going to save this Radiant, we *need* to be certain the Fused can't trace this break-in to us. You can't intervene, Rlain. The human has to manage the distraction himself."

Rlain hummed to Consideration.

"What?" Venli asked.

"Dabbid isn't the person I'd put in charge of something like this," he said. "Until today, I thought he was completely mute."

"Is he trustworthy?"

"Absolutely," Rlain said. "He's Bridge Four. But . . . well, I'd like to know why he spent so long without talking. The bridge runs hit him hard, I know, but there's something else." He hummed to Determination. "I won't intervene unless something goes wrong."

"If you do, we *all* have to go into hiding," Venli said to Skepticism. "So make *sure* before you do anything."

He nodded, still humming to Determination, and they split up at the next intersection. Venli found her way to a particular quiet section of hallway, lit only by her held sphere. Most humans stayed away from this area; the Pursuer's troops were housed nearby. Raboniel's occasional orders for peace to be maintained in the tower were barely enough to restrain those soldiers.

She attuned Peace—sometimes used by listeners for measuring time.

Beyond this wall was the cell. As the fourth movement of the rhythm approached, Venli pressed her hand against the stone and drew in Voidlight, requisitioned just earlier to replace what she'd used. Storms, she hoped news of her taking so much didn't reach Raboniel.

Timbre pulsed reassuringly. This stone, like the one earlier today, responded to Venli's touch. It shivered and rippled, as if it were getting a good back-scratching.

The stone whispered to her. *Move to the side.* It guided her to the correct spot to breach the cell. Timbre's rhythms pulsed through the rock, making it vibrate with the Rhythm of Hope. The fourth movement of Peace arrived—the moment when Rlain would signal Dabbid to go in to the guards, bringing food for their lunch. Merely another servant doing his job. Nothing unusual, even if lunch came early today.

Timbre exulted in the Rhythm of Hope as Venli pushed her hand into the stone. It felt good, warm and enveloping. Unlike what happened with the Deepest Ones, Venli displaced the rock. It became as crem in her fingers, soft to the touch.

She wasn't expert enough to get it to move on its own into the shapes she wanted. It usually did what it wanted in those cases, such as forming the tiny statues on the floor above. So for now, she simply pushed her hand forward until it hit air on the other side. Then she pressed with her other hand and pulled the two apart, forming an opening straight through the stone—the normally hard rock curling and bunching up before her touch.

A surprised set of human eyes appeared at the other end of the foot-long hole, looking through at her.

"I'm going to get you out," Venli whispered to the Rhythm of Pleading, "but you have to *promise* you won't tell anyone what I've done. You won't tell them about the powers I'm using. Not even other Radiants. They think I'm cutting you out with a Shardblade."

"What are you?" the human whispered in Alethi.

"Promise me."

"Fine, promised. Done. Hurry. The guards are eating, and they didn't even share none of it."

Venli continued shoving aside the stone. It took a ton of Light, and Timbre pulsed to Consolation—apparently she thought Venli's efforts crude, lacking finesse and skill.

Well, it did the job. She managed to form a hole big enough for the human girl. When Venli let go of the stone, it hardened instantly—she had to shake a few chips of it free of her fingers. The girl poked it, then hopped through.

Hopefully the guards would assume a human Stoneward had survived and saved the girl. Venli gestured for the Edgedancer to follow her—but the girl wavered. She seemed as if she was going to bolt away in another direction.

"Please," Venli said. "We need you. To save a life. If you run now, he'll die."

"Who?"

"Stormblessed," Venli said. "Please, hurry with me."

"You're one of them," the girl said. "How'd you get Radiant powers?"

"I . . . am not Radiant," Venli said. "I have powers from the Fused that are like Radiant powers. I'm a friend of Rlain. The listener who was a bridgeman? Please. I wouldn't free you only to put you in danger, but we *need* to go, now!"

The girl cocked her head, then nodded for Venli to go first. The Edgedancer followed on silent feet, sticking to the shadows.

Eshonai used to walk like that, Venli thought. *Quietly in the wilderness, to not disturb the wildlife.* This girl didn't have that same air about her though.

Timbre was pulsing contentedly to Hope. Venli couldn't feel the same yet, not until she was certain Rlain and Dabbid hadn't been caught. She led the little Radiant girl to a room nearby to wait.

"You're a traitor to them, then?" the girl asked her.

"I don't know what I am," Venli said. "Other than someone who didn't want to see a child kept in a cage."

Venli jumped almost to the ceiling when Rlain finally strode in with Dabbid. The quiet bridgeman ran over and hugged the human girl, who grinned.

"Eh, moolie," she said. "Strange friends ya got these days. You seen a chicken around here? Big red one? I lost 'im when I was running away."

Dabbid shook his head, then knelt before the girl. "Healing. It works?"

"Eh!" she said. "You can talk!"

He nodded.

"Say 'buttress,'" she told him. "It's my favorite word."

"Healing?" he asked.

"Yeah, I can still heal," she said. "I think. I should be able to help him."

He took her hand, insistent.

"I'll go with you," Rlain said. He glanced at Venli and she hummed to Skepticism, indicating she wouldn't go. She had to attend Raboniel.

"I won't stay away too long," Rlain promised her. "I don't want to draw suspicion." The other two left, but he lingered, then hummed to Appreciation. "I'm sorry about what I said when you first saw me in the cell. You're not selfish, Venli."

"I am," she said. "A lot of things are confusing to me these days—but of that fact I'm certain."

"No," he said. "Today you're a hero. I know you've been through rough times, but today . . ." He grinned and hummed to Appreciation again, then ducked out after the others.

If only he knew the whole story. Still, she felt upbeat as she headed toward the scholar rooms below.

"Can I say the words now?" she asked Timbre.

The pulse indicated the negative. Not yet.

"When?" Venli asked.

A simple, straightforward pulse was her answer.

You'll know.

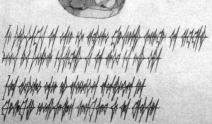
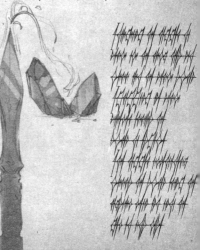

*Midius once told me ... told me we could use Investiture ... to
enhance our minds, our memories, so we wouldn't forget so much.*

Raboniel made good on her promise to leave Navani to her
own designs. The Fused studied the shield that protected the
Sibling—but without Navani to accidentally act as a spy, Raboniel's progress wasn't nearly as rapid as before. Occasionally—when
pacing so she could glance out past the guard—Navani would catch Raboniel sitting on the floor beside the blue shield, holding up the sphere
full of Warlight and staring at it.

Navani found herself in a curious situation. Forbidden to take part
in the administration of the tower, forbidden direct contact with her
scholars, she had only her research to occupy her. In a way, she had been
given the gift she'd always wished for: a chance to *truly* see if she could
become a scholar.

Something had always prevented her from full dedication. After
Gavilar's death, she'd been too busy guiding Elhokar and then Aesudan.
Perhaps Navani could have focused on scholarship when she'd first come
to the Shattered Plains—but there had been a Blackthorn to seduce and
then a new kingdom to forge. For all she complained about politics and
the distractions of administering a kingdom, she certainly did find her

way into the middle of both with frightful regularity.

Perhaps Navani *should* go do menial labor. At least that way she'd be among the people. And wouldn't risk doing any more damage. Except . . . Raboniel would certainly never let her go around unsupervised. Plus, the lure of unknown secrets called to Navani. She had information Raboniel did not. Navani had *seen* a sphere that warped air, filled with what seemed to be some kind of anti-Voidlight. She knew about the explosion.

The thing Raboniel wanted to create was possible. So . . . why not try to find out how to make it? Why not see what she could *actually* do? *The power to destroy a god. Negative Light. Can I crack the secret?*

What if Navani was thinking too small in trying to save the tower? What if there was a way to end the war once and for all? What if Navani really *could* find a way to destroy Odium?

She needed to try. But how to even start? Well . . . the best way to encourage discoveries from her scholars was usually to cultivate the proper environment and attitude. Keep them studying, keep them experimenting. Oftentimes the greatest discoveries came not because a woman was looking for them, but because she was so engrossed in some other topic that she started making connections she never would have otherwise.

So, over the next few days, Navani tried to replicate this state in herself. She ordered parts, supplies, fabrial mechanisms—some all the way from Kholinar—and they were delivered without a word of complaint. That included, most importantly, many gemstones bearing corrupted spren to power fabrials.

To warm up, she spent time creating weapons that wouldn't look like weapons. Traps she could use, if she grew truly desperate, to defend her room or the pillar room. She wasn't certain how she would deploy them—or if she would need to. For now, it was something scholarly to do, something familiar, and she threw herself wholeheartedly into the work.

She hid painrials inside other fabrials, constructed to appear innocuous. She made alarms to distract, using technology they'd discovered from the gemstones left by the old Radiants in Urithiru. She used conjoined rubies to make spring traps that would release spikes.

She put Voidlight spheres in her fabrial traps, then set them to be armed by a simple trick. A magnet against the side of the cube, in precisely the right place, would move a metal lever and arm the traps. This way they wouldn't activate until she needed them. She had these boxes stored out in the hallway, as if they were half-completed experiments she intended to return to in a few days. The space was already lined with boxes from the other scholars, so Navani's additions didn't feel out of place.

Afterward, she had Raboniel help her make more Warlight for experiments. Navani couldn't create it by herself, unfortunately. No combination of tuning forks or instruments replicated Raboniel's presence—but so far as Navani could tell, the Fused also couldn't create it without a human's help.

Navani got better at humming the tone, mastering the rhythm. In those moments, she felt as if she could hear the very soul of Roshar speaking to her. She'd never been particularly interested in music, but—like her growing obsession with Light—she found it increasingly fascinating. Waves, sounds, and what they meant for science.

Underlying all the work she did was a singular question: How would one make the *opposite* of Voidlight? What had been in that sphere of Gavilar's?

In Vorinism, pure things were said to be symmetrical. And all things had an opposite. It was easy to see why Raboniel had assumed the dark Light of the Void would be the opposite of Stormlight, but darkness *wasn't* truly an opposite of light. It was simply the absence of light.

She needed some way to measure Investiture, the power in a gemstone. And she needed some kind of model, a form of energy that she knew had an opposite. What things in nature had a *provable*, measurable opposite?

"Magnets," she said, pushing aside her chair and standing up from her notes. She walked up to the guard at her chamber door. "I need more magnets. Stronger ones this time. We kept some in the chemical supplies storehouse on the second floor."

The guard hummed a tone, and accompanied it with a long-suffering sigh for Navani's benefit. He glanced around for support, but the only other singer nearby was Raboniel's daughter, who sat outside the room with her back to the wall, holding a sword across her lap and staring off into the distance while humming. It wasn't a rhythm, Navani realized, but a tune she recognized—a human one sung sometimes at taverns. How did the Fused know it?

"I suppose I can see it done," the guard said to Navani. "Though some of our people are growing annoyed by your persistent demands."

"Take it up with Raboniel," Navani said, walking to her seat. "Oh, and the Fused use some kind of weapon that draws Stormlight out of Radiants they stab. Get me some of that metal."

"I'll need the Lady of Wishes to approve *that*," the guard said.

"Then ask her. Go on. I'm not going to run off. Where do you think I'd go?"

The guard—a stormform Regal—grumbled and moved off to do as she asked. Navani had teased out a few things about him during her incarceration. He'd been a parshman slave in the palace at Kholinar. He thought she should recognize him, and . . . well, perhaps she should. Parshmen had always been so invisible though.

She tried a different experiment while she waited. She had two halves of a conjoined ruby on the desk. That meant a split gemstone—and a split spren, divided right through the center. She was trying to see if she could use the tuning fork method to draw out the halves of the spren and rejoin them in a larger ruby. She thought that might please the Sibling, who still wouldn't talk to her.

She put a magnifying lens on one half of the gemstone and watched as the spren within reacted to the tuning fork. This was a corrupted flamespren; that shouldn't change the nature of the experiment, or so she hoped.

It *was* moving in there, trying to reach the sound. It pressed against the wall of the gemstone, but couldn't escape. *Stormlight can leak through micro-holes in the structure,* Navani thought. *But the spren is too large.*

A short time later, someone stepped up to the doorway; Navani noticed the darkening light of someone moving in front of the lamp. "My magnets?" Navani asked, holding out her hand while still peering at the spren. "Bring them here."

"Not the magnets," Raboniel said.

"Lady of Wishes," Navani said, turning and bowing from her seat. "I apologize for not recognizing you."

Raboniel hummed a rhythm Navani couldn't distinguish, then walked over to inspect the experiment.

"I'm trying to rejoin a split spren," Navani explained. "Past experience shows that breaking a gemstone in half lets the flamespren go—but in that case, the two halves grow into separate flamespren. I'm trying to see if I can merge them back together."

Raboniel placed something on the desk—a small dagger, ornate, with an intricately carved wooden handle and a large ruby set at the base. Navani picked it up, noting that the center of the blade—running like a vein from tip to hilt—was a different kind of metal than the rest.

"We use these for collecting the souls of Heralds," Raboniel noted. "Or that was the plan. We've taken a single one so far, and . . . there have been complications with that capture. I had hoped to harvest the two you reportedly had here, but they left with your expeditionary force."

Navani flipped the weapon over, feeling cold.

"We've used this metal for several Returns to drain Stormlight from Radiants," Raboniel said. "It conducts Investiture, drawing it from a source and pulling it inward. We used it to fill gemstones, but didn't realize until the fall of Ba-Ado-Mishram that capturing spren in gemstones was possible. It was then that one of us—She Who Dreams—realized it might be possible to trap a Herald's soul in the same way."

Navani licked her lips. So it was true. Shalash had told them Jezerezeh'Elin had fallen. They hadn't realized how. This was better than absolute destruction though. Could he be recovered this way?

"What will you do with their souls?" Navani asked. "Once you have them?"

"Same thing you've done with the soul of Nergaoul," Raboniel said. "Put them somewhere safe, so they can never be released again. Why did you want this metal? The guard told me you'd asked after it."

"I thought," Navani said, "this might be a better way to conduct Stormlight and Voidlight—to transfer it out of gemstones."

"It would work," Raboniel said. "But it isn't terribly practical. Raysium is exceptionally difficult to obtain." She nodded to the dagger she'd given Navani. "That specific weapon, you should know, contains only a small amount of the metal—not enough to harvest a Herald's soul. It would not, therefore, be of any danger to me—should you consider trying such an act."

"Understood, Ancient One," Navani said. "I want it only for my experiments. Thank you." She touched the tip of the dagger—with the white-gold metal—to one half of the divided ruby. Nothing happened.

"Generally, you need to stab someone with it for it to work," Raboniel said. "You need to touch the soul."

Navani nodded absently, resetting her equipment with the tuning fork and the magnifying lens, then watching the spren inside move to the sound. She set the tip of the dagger against it again, watching for any different behavior.

"You seem to be enjoying yourself," Raboniel noted.

"I would enjoy myself more if my people were free, Lady of Wishes," Navani said. "But I intend to use this time to some advantage."

Their defense of the tower, frail though it was, had utterly collapsed. She couldn't reach Kaladin, hear the Sibling, or plan with her scholars. There was only one node left to protect the heart of the tower from corruption.

Navani had a solitary hope remaining: that she could imitate a scholar well enough to build a new weapon. A weapon to kill a god.

In her experiment, nothing happened. The spren couldn't get out of the ruby, even with the tone calling it. The spren was vivid blue, as it was corrupted, and appeared as *half* a spren: one arm, one leg. Why continue to manifest that way? Flamespren often changed forms—and they were infamous for noticing they were being watched. Navani had read some very interesting essays on the topic.

She picked up a small jeweler's hammer. Carefully, she cracked the half ruby, letting the spren escape. It sprang free, but was immediately captured by the dagger. Light traveled along the blade, then the ruby at the base began to glow. Navani confirmed that the half spren was inside.

Interesting, Navani thought. *So, what if I break the other half of the ruby and capture that half in the same gemstone?* Excited, she reached to grab the other half of the ruby—but when she moved it, the dagger skidded across the table.

Navani froze. The two halves of the spren were still conjoined? She'd expected that to end once the original imprisonment did. Curious, she moved the dagger. The other half of the ruby flew out several feet toward the center of the room.

Too far. *Much* too far. She'd moved the dagger half a foot, while the paired ruby had moved three times as far. Navani stared at the hovering ruby, her eyes wide.

Raboniel hummed a loud rhythm, looking just as startled. "How?" she asked. "Is it because the spren is corrupted?"

"Possibly," Navani said. "Though I've been experimenting with conjoined spren, and corrupted ones seem to generally behave the same as uncorrupted ones." She eyed the dagger. "The gemstone on the dagger is larger than the one it was in before. Always before, you had to split a gemstone in two equal halves to conjoin them. Perhaps by moving one half to a larger gemstone, I have created something new. . . ."

"Force multiplication?" Raboniel asked. "Move a large gemstone a short distance, and cause the small gemstone to go a very long one?"

"Energy will be conserved, if our understanding of fabrial laws is correct," Navani said. "Greater Light will be required, and moving the larger gemstone will be more difficult in equivalency to the work done by the smaller gemstone. But storms . . . the implications . . ."

"Write this down," Raboniel said. "Record your observations. I will do the same."

"Why?" Navani asked.

"The Rhythm of War, Navani," Raboniel said as an explanation—though it didn't seem one to Navani. "Do it. And continue your experiments."

"I will," she said. "But Lady of Wishes, I'm running into another problem. I need a way to measure the strength of Stormlight in a gemstone."

Raboniel didn't press for details. "There is sand that does this," she said.

"Sand?"

"It is black naturally, but turns white in the presence of Stormlight. It can, therefore, be used to measure the strength of Investiture—the more powerful the source of power nearby, the quicker the sand changes. I will get some for you." She hummed loudly. "This is amazing, Navani. I don't think I've known a scholar so capable, not in many Returns."

"I'm not a . . ." Navani trailed off. "Thank you," she said instead.

Why would I want *to remember?*

Dabbid had been different all his life.

That was the word his mother had used. "Different." He liked that word. It didn't try to pretend. Something *was* different about him. He had been six when he started talking. He still couldn't do adding in his head. He could follow instructions, but he forgot steps if they were too long.

He was different.

The surgeons hadn't been able to say the reason. They said some people are just different. He was always going to be like this. The midwife, when she heard about him later, said the cord was wrapped around his neck when he was born. Maybe that was why.

When he'd been young, Dabbid had tried putting a rope around his neck to see how it felt. He hadn't jumped off a ledge. He hadn't tied the other end to anything. He hadn't tried to die. He'd just tightened it a little, so he could know what baby Dabbid had felt.

When someone saw, everyone had panicked. They called him stupid. They took ropes away from him for years. They thought he was too dumb to know it would hurt him. He often got into trouble like that. Doing things others wouldn't do. Not understanding it would make people panic. He had to be very careful not to make regular people frightened. They liked to be scared of him. He did not know why. He was different. But not scary different.

It had gotten worse when his mother died. People had become meaner on that day. It wasn't his fault. He hadn't even been there. But suddenly, everyone was meaner. He ended up at war, serving a lighteyes. Washing his clothing.

When a darkeyed baby was born to the man's wife, everyone had gotten angry at Dabbid. He'd explained that they were wrong. Everybody was wrong sometimes.

It hadn't been until much later that he'd realized the brightlady had lied. To punish someone other than her secret lover. He *could* understand things, if he had time to think about them. Sometimes.

He'd ended up running bridges. Dabbid didn't remember much from that time. He'd lost track of the days. He'd barely spoken back then. He had been confused. He had been frightened. He had been angry. But he didn't let people know he was angry. People got scared and hurt him when he was angry.

He'd done his job, terrified more each day, certain he would die. In fact, he'd figured he must already be dead. So when a horse—from one of Sadeas's own soldiers—had all but trampled him, shoving him and hurling him to the ground, his arm broken, he'd curled up and waited to die.

Then . . . Kaladin. Kaladin Stormblessed. He hadn't cared that Dabbid was different. He hadn't cared that Dabbid had given up. Kaladin hauled him out of Damnation and gave him another family.

Dabbid couldn't quite recall when he'd started to come out of his battle shock. He hadn't ever *really* lost it. Who could? People clapping sounded like bowstrings snapping. Footfalls sounded like hooves. Or he'd hear singing, like the Parshendi, and he was there again. Dying.

Still, he had started to feel better. Somewhere along the way, he'd started to feel like his old self. Except he'd had a new family. He'd had *friends.*

And none of them had known he was different.

Well, they thought he was another kind of different. They thought he had been hurt by the battle, like all of them. He was *one* of them. They hadn't known about his mind. How he'd been born.

He didn't like it when people used the word "stupid" for the way he was. People called one another stupid when they made mistakes. Dabbid wasn't a mistake. He could *make* mistakes. Then he was stupid. But not always. He couldn't think fast like others. But that made him different, not stupid. Stupid was a choice.

In the past, his speech had told people he was different. He'd figured that out when he was moving from job to job after his mother died. When he'd spoken, they'd known. So . . . with Bridge Four . . . he'd just kept on not speaking.

That way they wouldn't know. That way they wouldn't realize he was Dabbid different. He could just be Bridge Four different.

Then everyone had started getting spren. Except him. And then the tower had started talking to him. And . . . he still wasn't certain if he'd done something stupid or not. But going to Rlain, that *hadn't* been stupid. He was certain of it.

So today, he tried not to think about his mistakes. He tried not to think about how if he'd been stronger, he could have helped Kaladin fight. He tried not to think about how he'd lied to the others by pretending he couldn't speak. He tried to focus on what he could do to help.

He led Rlain up through the tunnels. They met singers a couple of times. Rlain talked, his voice calm with rhythms, and the singers let them go. They went up and up, and Dabbid showed him a hidden stairwell. They snuck past the guard patrols on the sixth floor.

Up and up. Dabbid's heart thumped. Worrying. Would Lift meet them, like she'd promised? Lift knew the tower better than they did. She said she could make it on her own. But would she run away?

When they reached the meeting place on the tenth floor, they found her waiting. She sat on the ground, eating some curry and bread.

"Where did you get *that*?" Rlain asked.

"Fused," she said, gesturing. "Funny. They need to eat. Suppose that means they poop, right?"

"I suppose," Rlain said, sounding disapproving.

"Ain't that a kick in the bits?" Lift asked. "You get made immortal; you can live through the centuries. You can fly, or walk through rock, or something like that. But you still gotta piss like everyone else."

"I don't see the point of this conversation," Rlain said. "Hurry. We need to get to Kaladin."

Lift rolled her eyes in an exaggerated way, then stood up and handed Dabbid some flatbread. He nodded in thanks and tucked it away for later.

"When didya start talkin'?" Lift asked him.

"I was six," he said. "Mom said."

"No, I mean . . ." She gestured at him.

Dabbid felt himself blush, and he looked at his feet. "I could for a long time. Just didn't."

"Didn't want to talk? I've *never* felt like that. Except this once, when I ate the queen's dinner, but it had been sitting *out*, see, and she didn't put it away like she should have. It's her fault, I told her, because it's like leavin' a sword out where a baby could step on it and cut up her foot or somethin'."

"Can we please keep moving?" Rlain demanded.

Dabbid led them the rest of the way. He felt more anxious now. Was he too late? Had Kaladin died while he was gone? Was he too slow to help? Too different to have realized earlier what he should have done?

Dabbid led them to the place on the eleventh floor, but the door had stopped working. It had been too long since Kaladin infused it. They had Lift though, and when she pressed her hand to the gemstone, the door opened.

It smelled of sweat and blood in there. Dabbid hurried past the place where Teft lay unconscious, reaching Kaladin. On the floor, wrapped in blankets. Thrashing. Still alive.

Still alive.

"Storms," Lift said, stepping over. Kaladin's face was coated in sweat. His teeth were gritted, his eyes squeezed shut. He flailed in his blankets, growling softly. Dabbid had cut off his shirt to look for wounds. While there were scabs all along Kaladin's side, the worst part was the infection. It spread across the skin from the cut. A violent redness. Hateful, covered in little rotspren.

Lift stepped back, wrapping her arms around herself. "Storms."

"I've . . . never seen a fever like that," Rlain said, towering over the two of them. Did he know how large he was in warform? "Have you?"

Lift shook her head.

"Please," Dabbid said. "Please help."

Lift held out her hand, palm forward, and burst alight with power. Stormlight rose from her skin like white smoke, and she knelt. She shied away as Kaladin thrashed again, then she lunged forward and pressed her hand to his chest.

The redness immediately retreated, and the rotspren fled, as if they couldn't stand the presence of her touch. Kaladin's back arched. He was hurting!

Then he collapsed into the blankets. Lift pressed her other hand against his side, and the wound continued to heal, the redness fleeing. She furrowed her brow and bit her lip. Dabbid did the same. Maybe it would help.

She pushed so much Stormlight into Kaladin he started glowing himself. When she sat back, the scabs flaked off his side, leaving smooth new skin.

"That . . . was hard," she whispered. "Even harder than when I saved Gawx." She wiped her brow. "I'm sweating."

"Thank you," Dabbid said, taking her hand.

"Ew," she said. Oh. It was the hand she'd just used to wipe her head.

"*Thank you*," he said.

She shrugged. "My awesomeness—the slippery part—doesn't work anymore. But this does. Wonder why."

Rlain went to close the door. Dabbid tried to make Kaladin comfortable, bunching up a blanket to make a pillow. His friend was still unconscious, but sleeping peacefully now.

"I have a lot of questions, Dabbid," Rlain said. "First off, why have you been keeping quiet when you could speak?"

"I . . ."

"He don't gotta say nothin' if he don't wanna," Lift said. She'd found their rations already, and was eating. Wow.

"He's Bridge Four," Rlain said. "We're family. Family doesn't lie to one another."

"I'm sorry," Dabbid said softly. "I just . . . didn't want you to know I'm . . . different."

"We're all different," Rlain said, folding his arms. Storms, he was so frightening in carapace armor.

"I'm more different," Dabbid said. "I . . . I was born different."

"You mean born . . . you know . . . an idiot?" Rlain said.

Dabbid winced. He hated that word, though Rlain didn't use it hatefully. It was just a word to him.

"Touched," Lift said. "I've known lotsa kids like him on the street. They don't think the same way as everyone else. It happens."

"It happens," Dabbid agreed. "It happened to me. But you didn't know. So you couldn't treat me like I was . . . wrong. You know about being extra different, right Rlain?"

"I guess I do," he said. "You shouldn't feel that you have to hide what you are though."

"I will be fixed," Dabbid said, "when I get a spren. Becoming Radiant will heal me, because my brain isn't supposed to be like this. I was hurt after I was born. The tower said so."

"The tower?" Rlain asked.

"The tower can talk," Lift said. "It's a spren."

"And it promised to heal you, Dabbid?"

He nodded. Though it hadn't said that in so many words. He wondered now if it had been lying.

The queen hadn't been pleased by how he'd snuck around, doing tasks for the Sibling. Maybe he should be more suspicious. Even of spren.

But someday . . . when he was Radiant . . .

Rlain dug out a new set of blankets for Kaladin from the pile. Dabbid had washed those earlier, as he'd wanted something to do. They got Kaladin untangled from the sweaty ones, then wrapped him in—

"What in storming Damnation are you fools doing?" a gruff voice said from behind them.

Dabbid froze. Then turned around slowly. Lift was perched on the end of Teft's shelf, absently munching on a ration bar—Soulcast grain, cooked and pressed. She was pulling her hand back from Teft's exposed foot, Stormlight curling off her body.

Teft, in turn, was pushing himself up to sit.

Teft was *awake*.

Dabbid let out a whoop and leaped up. Rlain just started humming like he did sometimes.

"What?" Lift said. "Wasn't I supposed to heal the stinky one too?"

"Stinky?" Teft said, looking under his blanket. "Where in Damnation are my clothes? What happened to me? We were at the tavern, right? Storms, my *head*."

"You can wake the Radiants?" Rlain asked, rushing over and seizing Lift by the arms. "Why didn't you say something?"

"Huh?" she said. "Look, shellhead, I've been in a stormin' *cage*. My spren vanished, said he was going to try to get help, and I ain't heard from him since. Bet he joined the Voidbringers, storming traitor. I don't know what's been goin' on in the tower. What's wrong with the others?"

"In a cage?" Teft said. "Why? And where are my *storming* clothes?"

"There's a lot to explain, Teft," Rlain said. "The tower is occupied by the enemy and . . ." He stopped, then frowned, glancing toward Kaladin.

Kaladin . . . Kaladin was *stirring*. They all hushed. Even Teft. Kaladin blinked and *opened his eyes*. He grew tense, then saw Rlain and Dabbid and relaxed, taking a deep breath.

"Is this a dream?" he whispered. "Or am I finally awake?"

"You're awake, Kal," Rlain said, kneeling to take Kaladin by the shoulder. "Thank the purest tones. You're awake. It worked."

Dabbid stepped back as Teft said something, causing Kaladin to sit up—then laugh in joy. It had worked.

Dabbid wasn't Radiant. He wasn't brave. He wasn't smart. But today he hadn't been stupid either.

Once, Kaladin had pulled Dabbid out of Damnation itself. It felt good to return that act of heroism with a small one of his own.

THE SONG OF MORNINGS

A YEAR AND A HALF AGO

As the war with the humans progressed, Venli became increasingly certain she'd made the correct decision.

How could her people, after generations of stagnation, hope to stand by themselves in the world? If recent reports were true, the humans had *Surgebinders* again, like those spoken of in the songs. Ulim was right. A bigger war than this was coming. Venli's people needed to be prepared.

Venli stood with folded arms, attuned to Confidence as she watched a listener warband return from a raid. Eshonai and her soldiers had won the day, and they brought a large gemheart with them. Eshonai herself delivered it up to Denshil, their head of farming.

Her warriors didn't look like victors. Bloody, wounded, their ancient weapons sagging in their grips as if weighted by groundspren. More than a few of the soldiers walked alone. Warpairs who had lost a member.

Venli watched with hidden glee. Surely they were close to breaking. If she could bring them a form of power . . . would they accept it? Venli remembered her hesitance, and weakness, when she'd started along this path years ago. She'd been technically a youth then, though fully grown. Now she was an adult. She saw as an adult did.

She turned and cut through a side street of the ancient city, passing large crem-covered walls like tall ridges of natural stone. You'd have to cut deep with a Shardblade to find the worked stone at the heart.

This was the more direct way, so she was waiting as Denshil walked past with the gemstone. He was scrawny even when wearing workform, and had a pattern of black and red skin that looked like true marble-work, all rough and coarse. He jumped as he saw Venli.

"What are you doing," he hissed to Anxiety as she walked along beside him.

"Acting naturally," she said. "I'm head of our scholars. It's normal for me to visit our farmers and see how their work is progressing."

He still acted nervous, but at least he attuned Peace as they walked. It didn't matter. They passed few listeners on the streets. All who weren't absolutely needed as farmers, caretakers, or other essential workers had joined Eshonai.

In a perfect bit of poetry, this ensured that the bravest of the listeners—those most likely to resist Venli when she brought them stormform—fought on the front lines each day, dying. Each corpse brought Venli one step closer to her goal.

She'd stopped pretending this was *only* about protecting her people. As she'd grown into herself and become more confident, she'd decided what she truly wanted. True freedom—with the power to make certain she'd never have to be dependent upon anyone else, listener or spren. True freedom couldn't exist while someone else had power over you.

So yes, her work was about helping her people, in part. But deep within her—where the rhythms began—Venli promised herself that *she* would be the one who obtained the most freedom.

"How goes your work?" Venli asked to Confidence.

Denshil's rhythm slipped to Anxiety again. Foolish farmer. He'd better not give them away.

"The others believe me," he said softly, "and they should. I'm not saying anything that's a *lie*, really. If we cut these gemhearts like the humans do, they hold more Stormlight. But I don't mention the extra bits I cut off before delivering the faceted stone to the fields. . . ."

"How much have you saved?"

"Several hundred gemstones."

"I need more," Venli said.

He blatantly attuned Irritation. "More? What crazy rhythm are you listening to?"

"We need one for every listener in the city."

"I can't," he said. "If you—"

"You *can*," Venli said to Reprimand. "And you will. Cut the gemstones smaller. Give less to the fields."

"And if we end up starving because of it? Gemstones break, you know, when you sing to them. We *will* run out."

"We won't live long enough to starve, Denshil. Not if the humans get here. Not if they find your children and take away their songs . . ."

The malen attuned Longing immediately. The listeners had few children these days. Most had stopped taking mateform years ago, and they had never been as fecund a people as the humans apparently were.

"Think how you could improve," Venli said. "For them, Denshil. For your daughter."

"We should bring this to the Five," he said.

"We will. You can watch me bring the proposal to them. This will be done properly—you and I are simply preparing the way."

He nodded, and Venli let him rush on ahead to the ancient building where he practiced gem cutting—an art Ulim had taught him.

Say a name on the breeze and it will return, she thought, noting a red light glowing from within an old abandoned building. They'd had to cut the window out to get to the structure inside. She strolled over, and Ulim stepped out onto the windowsill—invisible to everyone but those he chose.

"You've learned to lie very well," he said to Subservience.

"I have," she said. "Are we ready?"

"Close," he said. "I feel the storm on the other side. I think it's nearly here."

"You think?" Venli demanded.

"I can't see into Shadesmar," he snapped to Derision.

She didn't quite understand his explanations of what was happening. But she knew a storm was mounting in Shadesmar. In fact, the storm had been building for generations—growing in fury, intensity. It barred the way to Damnation.

That storm was where Ulim had originally come from. There were also thousands of another kind of spren in the storm: stormspren. Mindless things like windspren or flamespren.

Venli had to find a way to pull those stormspren across and capture them. To that end, a large portion of the roiling storm had been broken off by the god of gods, the ancient one called Odium. This storm was his strength, his essence. Over painful months, he'd moved the storm across the landscape—unseen—until it arrived here. Kind of. Almost.

"What will happen," Venli asked to Curiosity, "when my storm comes to this world?"

"Your storm?"

"I am the one who summons it, spren," she said. "It is *mine*."

"Sure, sure," he said. A little too quickly, and with too many hand gestures. He had grown obsequious over the last few years—and liked to pretend that his betrayal of her in the Kholinar palace had never happened.

"When this storm comes, you *will* serve me," Venli said.

"I serve you now."

"Barely. Promise it. You'll serve me."

"I will serve," he said. "I promise it, Venli. But we have to *bring* the stormspren to this side first. And persuade the listeners to take the forms."

"The second will not be a problem."

"You're too certain about that," he said. "Remember, they killed the Alethi king to *prevent* this from happening. Traitors."

He got hung up on that idea. Though he'd been the one to whisper about the location of the slave with the Honorblade—and he'd agreed to help start a war to make her people desperate—he *could not* get over the reasoning her people had used. Ulim hadn't found out about Eshonai's experience with King Gavilar until weeks later, and he'd been livid. How dare the listeners do exactly what he wanted, but for the wrong reason!

Foolish little spren. Venli attuned Skepticism—and *almost* felt something different, something more. A better rhythm. Right outside her reach.

"Focus less on that," Venli said. "And more on your duties."

"Yes, Venli," he said, voice cooing as he spoke to Subservience. "You're going to be amazed by the power you get from stormform. And the massive storm you'll bring through? It will be unlike *anything* the world has ever seen. Odium's raw power, blowing across the world in the wrong direction. It will devastate the humans, leave them broken and easily conquered. Ripe for your domination, Venli."

"Enough," she said. "Don't sell it so hard, Ulim. I'm not the child you found when you first arrived here. Do your job, and get the storm into position. I'll capture the stormspren."

"How, though?"

How. "They are the spren of storms, right?"

"Well, *a* storm," Ulim said. "In the past, they mostly spent their time inside gemhearts. Odium would directly bless the singer, making them a kind of royalty. They didn't really wander about much."

Royalty? She liked the sound of that. She smiled, imagining how Eshonai would act toward her *then*.

"My scholars are confident," Venli said. "From what you've told them, and the experiments we've done with other kinds of spren, we think if we can gather a small collection of stormspren in gemstones, others will get pulled through more easily."

"But we need that initial seed!" Ulim said. "How?"

She nodded to the sky, where her imaginings had brought forth a gloryspren. An enormous brilliant sphere, with wings along the sides. "Those pop in when we think the proper thoughts. Feel the right things. So, what brings stormspren?"

"A storm . . ." Ulim said. "It might work. Worth trying."

They'd have to experiment. Even with his help, it had taken several tries to figure out nimbleform—and that was a relatively easy form. Still, she was pleased with their progress. Yes, it had taken far, far longer than she'd anticipated. But over those many years, she'd become the person she was now. Confident, like her younger self had never been.

She turned to make her way toward where her scholars studied the songs, written in the script she'd devised. Unfortunately, she soon spotted a tall, armored figure heading her direction. Venli immediately turned down a side road, but Eshonai called to her. Venli attuned Irritation. Eshonai would follow her if she hurried on, so she slowed and turned.

Venli's sister looked so strange in Shardplate. It . . . well, it *fit* her. It supernaturally molded to her form, making space for her carapace, shaping itself to her figure, but it was more than that. To Venli, some of the warforms seemed like they were playing pretend—their faces didn't match their new shape. Not Eshonai. Eshonai *looked* like a soldier, with a wider neck, powerful jaw and head, and enormous hands.

Venli regretted encouraging Eshonai to visit the former Shardbearer. She hadn't expected that years later, she'd feel dwarfed by her sister. Though much about Venli's life was enviable now—she had position, friends, and responsibility—there was a part of her that wished she'd been able to obtain this without Eshonai *also* gaining high station.

"What?" Venli asked to Irritation. "I have work to do today, Eshonai, and—"

"It's Mother," Eshonai said.

Venli immediately attuned the Terrors. "What about her? What's wrong?"

Eshonai attuned Resolve and led Venli quietly to their mother's home on the outskirts of town. A small structure, but solitary, with plenty of room for gardening projects.

Their mother wasn't in the garden, working on her shalebark. She was inside lying on a hard cot, her head wrapped in a bandage. One of Venli's scholars—Mikaim, who was their surgeon—stepped away from the cot. "It's not bad," she said. "Head wounds can be frightful, but it was little more than a scrape. The bigger worry is how afraid she was. I gave her something to help her sleep."

Venli hummed to Appreciation and Mikaim withdrew. Eshonai stood opposite Venli over the cot, her helmet under her arm, and for a time the two of them hummed together to the Lost. A rare moment when they both heard the same rhythm.

"Do you know what happened?" Venli finally asked.

"She was found wandering one of the outer plateaus. Frightened, acting like a little child. She didn't respond to her own name at first, though by the time she got here she had recovered enough to begin answering questions about her childhood. She didn't remember how she hurt herself."

Venli breathed deeply, and listened to the haunting Rhythm of the Lost, a violent beat with staccato notes.

"We might need to confine her to her house," Eshonai said.

"No!" Venli said. "Never. We can't do that to her, Eshonai. Imprisonment *on top* of her ailment?"

Eshonai attuned Reconciliation, settling down on the floor, her Shardplate scraping softly. "You're right, of course. She must be allowed to see the sky, look to the horizon. We can get her a servant perhaps. Someone to keep watch over her."

"An acceptable accommodation," Venli said, lingering beside the cot. She really should check on her scholars.

Eshonai leaned—gingerly, because her Plate was so heavy—against the wall. She closed her eyes, humming to Peace. It was forced, a little loud. She was trying to override other rhythms.

She looks more like herself sitting like that, Venli thought idly, remembering Eshonai as a child. The sister who would pick Venli up when she scraped her knee, or who would chase cremlings with her. Eshonai had always seemed so vibrant—so alive. As if she'd been trying to burst out, her soul straining against the confines of a flawed body.

"You always led me toward the horizon," Venli found herself saying. "Even as children. Always running to the next hill to see what was on the other side . . ."

"Would that we could return," Eshonai said to the Lost.

"To those ignorant days?"

"To that joy. That innocence."

"Innocence is more false a god than the ones in our songs," Venli said, sitting beside her sister. "People who chase it will find themselves enslaved."

Venli felt tired, she realized. She'd been spending far too many nights thinking of plans. And it would only get worse, as she needed to start going out into storms to trap stormspren.

"I'm sorry I brought us to this," Eshonai whispered to Reconciliation. "We've lost so many. How far will it go? All because I made a snap decision in a moment of tension."

"That sphere," Venli said. "The one King Gavilar gave you . . ." They'd all seen it, though it had faded several months later.

"Yes. A dark power. And he claimed to be seeking to return our gods."

Ulim had been nervous about Gavilar's sphere. The little spren said Gavilar hadn't been working with him, or any of Odium's agents—indeed, he'd been hostile to them. So Ulim had no idea how he'd obtained Odium's Light.

"Maybe," Venli said, "if the humans are seeking to contact our gods, perhaps we should explore the option too. Perhaps the things from our songs are—"

"Stop," Eshonai said to Reprimand. "Venli, what are you saying? You better than most should know the foolishness of what you say."

I'm always a fool to you, aren't I? Venli attuned Irritation. Unfortunately, this was the Eshonai she'd come to know. Not the child who encouraged her. The adult who held her back, ridiculed her.

"Sing the song with me," Eshonai said. "'Terrible and great they were, but—'"

"Please don't turn this into another lecture, Eshonai," Venli said. "Just . . . stop, all right?"

Eshonai trailed off, then hummed to Reconciliation. The two of them sat for a time, the light outside dimming as the sun drifted toward the horizon. Venli found herself humming to Reconciliation as well. She explored the rhythm, finding a complementary tone to Eshonai's, seeking again—for a brief moment—to be in tune with her sister.

Eshonai quietly changed to Longing, and Venli followed. And then, cautiously, Venli switched to Joy. Eshonai followed her this time. Together they made a song, and Venli began singing. It had been . . . well, years since she'd practiced the songs. She'd long ago stopped thinking of herself as the apprentice song keeper; they had plenty of others to uphold their traditions, now that they'd united the families.

She still remembered the songs though. This was the Song of Mornings. A teaching song, meant to train a young child for more complex rhythms and songs. There was something satisfying about a simple song you could sing well. You could add your own complexity. And you could sing the song's soul—rather than struggle with missed lyrics or failed notes.

She let her voice drift off at the end, and Eshonai's humming quieted. Dusk fell outside. The perfectly wrong time for the Song of Mornings. She loved that it had worked so well anyway.

"Thank you, Venli," Eshonai said. "For all that you do. You don't get enough credit for having brought us these forms. Without warform, we wouldn't stand a chance of resisting the humans. We'd probably be their slaves."

"I . . ." Venli tried to attune Confidence, but it slipped away from her. "As long as you and Demid know what I did, I suppose it doesn't sting so much when others pass me over."

"Do you think you could find me a different form?" Eshonai said.

"A form that would let me talk better, more diplomatically? I could go to the humans and explain what happened. Maybe I could speak with Dalinar Kholin. I feel like . . . like he might listen, if I could find him. If I could make my tongue work. They don't hear the rhythms, and it's so difficult to explain to them. . . ."

"I can try," Venli said, Pleading sounding in her ears. Why Pleading? She hadn't attuned that.

"Then maybe I could talk to you," Eshonai said quietly, drooping from fatigue. "Without sounding like I'm trying to lecture. You'd know how I really feel. Mother would understand that I don't try to run away. I just want to see . . ."

"You'll see it someday," Venli promised. "You'll see the whole world. Every vibrant color. Every singing wind. Every land and people."

Eshonai didn't respond.

"I . . . I've been doing things you might not like," Venli whispered. "I should tell you. You'll explain that what I'm doing is wrong though, and you're always right. That's part of what I hate about you."

But her sister had already drifted off. The stiff Shardplate kept her in a seated position, slumped against the wall, breathing softly. Venli climbed to her feet and left.

That night, she went into the storm to hunt stormspren for the first time.

*Maybe if I remembered my life, I'd be capable of being confident like
I once was. Maybe I'd stop vacillating when even the most simple of
decisions is presented to me.*

The weather turned energetic by the time Adolin's trial arrived.
The honorspren he passed chatted more, and seemed to have
more of a spring to their steps as they flowed toward the forum
on the southern plane of Lasting Integrity.

He couldn't feel the weather, though Blended said it was like a faint
drumming in the back of her mind, upbeat and peppy. Indeed, the inkspren seemed chattier.

He felt more nervous than at his first ranked duel—and far less prepared. Legal terms, strategies, even the details of his political training
all seemed distant as he walked down the steps to the amphitheater
floor. As Blended had feared, the place was packed with honorspren.
Many wore uniforms or other formal attire, though some wore loose,
flowing outfits that trailed behind them as they walked. These seemed
more free-spirited. Perhaps their presence would help the crowd turn to
his side.

Blended said that was important. The High Judge—being who he
was—would likely listen to the mood of the crowd and judge accordingly.

Adolin wished someone had explained to him earlier how fickle his judge would be. That might favor Adolin, fortunately: he could depend on some level of erratic behavior from Kelek, whereas the honorspren were basically all against him from the start.

They didn't boo as he reached the floor of the forum; they had too much decorum. They hushed instead. He found Shallan seated next to Pattern over on the left side. She pumped her fist toward him, and he had the impression she was Radiant at the moment.

Kelek sat upon a thronelike seat with a bench before it, both built in among the forum's tiers. The Herald seemed imposing, and Adolin was reminded that—despite the man's odd behavior—Kelek was thousands of years old. Perhaps he would listen.

"All right, all right," Kelek said. "Human, get over there on the podium and stand there until this show finishes and we can execute you."

"Holy One," an honorspren said from his side. "We do *not* execute people."

"What else are you going to do?" Kelek said. "You don't have prisons, and I doubt he'll care if you exile him. Hell, half the people in this place would regard escaping your presence to be a *reward*."

"We are building a proper holding cell," the honorspren said, looking toward Adolin. "So he can be kept healthy and on display for years to come."

Wonderful, Adolin thought, stepping into the place indicated. The consequences of failure, however, had always been far bigger than his own life. The war needed Radiants, and Radiants needed spren. If Adolin failed, it meant leaving thousands of troops to die without proper support.

He needed to stand here, tall and confident, and *win* this challenge. Somehow.

He turned to face the crowd. According to Blended, today would be the worst of the days. Three witnesses against him. Tomorrow he'd get to have his say.

"Very well," Kelek said. "I suppose you need to give trial terms, Sekeir?"

The bearded honorspren stood up. "Indeed, Honored One."

"Make it fast," Kelek said.

Adolin took a moment of enjoyment from the affronted way Sekeir received that injunction. The honorspren had likely planned a lengthy speech.

"As you wish, Honored One," Sekeir said. "Today, we enter a trial as demanded by this human, Adolin Kholin, to determine if he can bear the sins of the Recreance—where men killed their spren. Since this event happened, which no one disputes, then we must simply prove that we are wise to stay away from all humans as a result."

"Right, then," Kelek said. "Human, this works for you?"

"Not exactly, Honored One," Adolin said, using the opening statement Blended had helped him prepare. "I did not agree to be tried for my ancestors. I agreed to be tried for myself. I told the honorspren I personally bear no blame for what humans did in the past. Because of that, I contend that the honorspren are acting dishonorably by ignoring my people's pleas for help."

Kelek rubbed his forehead. "So we're arguing over even the definitions? This doesn't bode well."

"There is no argument," Sekeir said. "Honored One, he says he wishes to bear no sins of his ancestors, and we should instead prove why he specifically can't be trusted. But the Recreance is a large portion of why we cannot trust his kind! We set the terms when he entered: He would have to stand trial for all humankind. He can dissemble if he wishes, but he *did* enter our fortress, and therefore agreed to our terms."

Kelek grunted. "That makes sense. Human, you're going to have to stand trial as he wishes. That said, I'll keep your arguments in mind when I finally judge."

"I suppose I must agree," Adolin said. Blended had warned him not to push too hard here.

"So . . . trial by witness, right?" Kelek said. "I'm to listen to the arguments presented, then decide. Either the honorspren are being selfish, denying honor, and I should command them to go to the battlefield. Or I decide they've been wise, that humans are not worthy of trust—and we throw this man in a prison as an example?"

"Yes, Honored One," Sekeir said.

"Great," Kelek said. "I assume you had no lack of volunteers, Sekeir. Who is first?"

"Amuna," said the honorspren. "Come, and bear your witness."

The audience whispered quietly as a female spren rose from her spot on the front row. She wore a warrior's pleated skirt and a stiff shirt. She was slender and willowy, and when she stepped she was as graceful as a leaf in the wind. Adolin recognized her; this was the spren to whom he'd been forced to surrender Maya on their first day in Lasting Integrity. He'd occasionally seen Amuna again during his daily visits to Maya.

The two honorspren sitting beside her bore ragged clothing and scratched-out eyes like Maya's. On a glowing honorspren's face, the scratches made a stark contrast.

"You all know me," said the spren in the pleated skirt, "so I will speak for the benefit of Highprince Adolin. I am Amuna, and my duty is to care for the deadeyes in Lasting Integrity. We take their care very seriously."

"And the ones watching outside?" Adolin asked. He was allowed to talk during testimonies, though Blended had warned him to be careful. If he was too belligerent, the High Judge could order him gagged. And he had to be careful not to address the audience in a way that invited them to interrogate him.

"We . . . cannot accept them all in, unfortunately," Amuna said. "We had not thought to see so many. We *have* tried to invite in all of the honorspren deadeyes."

"Are there many?" Adolin asked.

"In total? We have some twenty deadeyed honorspren in the fortress now, though there were some *two thousand* honorspren alive at the time of your betrayal. A single one survived."

"Syl," Adolin said.

"The Ancient Daughter was in a catatonic state," Amuna said, "and was spared. But every other honorspren—every *single* one—had answered the call of the Radiants during the False Desolation. Can you understand the magnitude of that tragedy, Highprince Adolin? The murder of an entire species, all in one day? Absolute extermination, performed by the most intimate of friends?

"We often encounter deadeyes wandering aimlessly in the barrens, or standing in the shallows of the ocean. We bring them here, give them Stormlight, care for them the best we can. Frequently, we can do only a little before they are summoned away to your world—where their corpses are used to continue your brutal murders!"

She turned, gesturing toward the two deadeyes on the bench—and though she faced Adolin, her words were obviously for the crowd. They, not the High Judge, were the true adjudicators.

"This is what you'd have us return to?" she demanded. "You say you aren't the same people who lived so long ago, but do you honestly think you're any better than them? I'd contend you are worse! You pillage, and murder, and burn. You spare no expense nor effort when given an opportunity to ruin another man's life. If the ancient Radiants were not trustworthy, then how can you *possibly* say that you are?"

Murmurs of assent washed through the crowd. They didn't jeer or call as a human audience might—he'd suffered that during many a dueling bout. Blended had warned him not to say too much by way of defense today, but they seemed to want *something* from him.

"Every man fails his own ideals," Adolin said. "You are right. I am not the honorable man I wish that I were. But my father is. Can you deny that the Stormfather himself was willing to take a chance upon a man from this epoch?"

"This is a good point," Kelek said, leaning forward. "The Stormfather is all we have left of old Tanavast. I would not have thought to find his Bondsmith again, no indeed."

Amuna spun toward Adolin. "Do you know what would happen, Prince Adolin, if the Stormfather were to be killed?"

Adolin paused, then shook his head.

"A wise answer," she said. "As no one knows. We were fortunate that no Bondsmiths existed at the time of the Recreance, though how the Sibling knew to end their bond early is a matter of dispute. I can only imagine the catastrophe that awaits us when your father kills his spren."

"He won't," Adolin said. "My father is no common man."

"Such could be said of all the Radiants in times past," Amuna said, stepping toward him. "But now, *I* am the one who cares for the betrayed. I hear their voiceless sorrow; I see their sightless pain. I would have Lasting Integrity pulled down, stone by stone, before I agree to send a single honorspren to suffer a similar fate."

She bowed to Kelek, then turned and sat between the two deadeyes. They continued to sit, faces forward, motionless.

Adolin ground his teeth and glanced to Shallan for support. At least there was one friendly face out in that crowd. He forced himself to re-main standing, hands clasped behind him in the posture his father used when he wanted to appear commanding. He'd worn his best coat. For all it mattered. Storms, he felt exposed here on the floor, surrounded by all the glowing figures. This was worse than when he'd been alone in the dueling arena facing four Shardbearers. At least then he'd had his Blade in hand and Plate on his back.

They waited for Kelek to call the next witness. The High Judge, instead, spent a good twenty minutes writing in his notebook. He was a divine being, like a kind of ardent, if magnified a thousand times. It wasn't surprising to see him writing. Adolin just hoped the notes he was taking related to the testimony. He half expected that the Herald was solving word puzzles like the ones Jasnah enjoyed.

Eventually, the Herald dug something out of his pocket—fruit it seemed, though it was bright green and it crunched when Kelek took a bite.

"Looks good," Kelek said. "Nothing too unexpected, though I have to say he *does* have a good point. An unchained Bondsmith is dangerous, but the Stormfather *did* choose one anyway. . . ."

"You know how erratic the Stormfather has been lately," said an elderly female honorspren at Kelek's side. "His wisdom is no longer something to trust."

"Valid, valid," Kelek said. "Well then, next witness."

"Next to speak will be Blended," Sekeir said. "Inkspren emissary to Lasting Integrity."

What? Adolin thought as his tutor stood up from the crowd and walked to the floor of the arena. The watching honorspren murmured together quietly at the sight.

"Wait," Adolin said. "What is this?"

"They asked me to witness against you," she said. "So a spren who is not an honorspren would have a chance to weigh in on this proceeding."

"But . . . you're my tutor. Didn't you volunteer to train me?"

"I wanted you well-trained," she said, "so the trial could be as fair as possible. This thing is. But my hatred of what your kind did also is." She turned to Kelek. "Honored One, I was alive when men betrayed us. Unlike the honorspren, my kind were not so foolish as to assign *all* as Radiant spren. We lost over half our numbers, but some of us watched from outside."

She eyed Adolin. "We knew men as they were and are. Untrustworthy.

Changeable. Spren find it difficult to break a bond. Some say it is impossible for us. Men, however, barely last a day without betraying some Ideal.

"Why should we beings of innate honor have been surprised when the event happened? It is not the fault of men that they are as fickle as the falling rain. This thing is. They should not be trusted, and the shame of doing so is our fault. Never again should spren and men bond. It is unnatural."

"Unnatural?" Adolin said. "Spren and skyeels bond to fly. Spren and greatshells bond to grow. Spren and singers bond to create new forms. This is as natural as the changing seasons."

And thank you, Shallan, he thought, glancing at her, *for your interest in all this.*

"Humans are not from this land," Blended said. "You are invaders, and bonds with you are *not* natural. Be careful what you say—you will encourage us to return to the singers. They betrayed us long ago, but never on the scale of the humans. Perhaps the highspren have the correct idea in joining with the armies of the Fused."

"You'd side with them?" Adolin said. "Our *enemies?*"

"Why not?" she said, strolling across the stage. "They are the rightful heirs of this land. They have been pushed to desperation by your kind, but they are no less reasonable or logical. Perhaps your kind would do better to acknowledge their rule."

"They serve Odium," Adolin said, noticing many of the honorspren shifting in their seats, uncomfortable. "Men might be changeable, yes. We might be corrupt at times, and weak always. But I know evil when I see it. Odium is *evil.* I will never serve him."

Blended eyed the crowd, who nodded at Adolin's words. She gave him a little nod herself, as if in acknowledgment of a point earned.

"This tangent is irrelevant," she said, turning to Kelek. "I can say, with some ease, that a good relationship between honorspren and inkspren is not. Any would acknowledge this. My testimony's value is, then, of extra import.

"I *lived through* the pain and chaos of the Recreance. I saw my siblings, beloved, dead. I saw families ripped apart, and pain flowing like blood. We might be enemies, but in one thing unification *is.* Men should *never again* be trusted with our bonds. If this one wishes to accept punishment for the thousands who escaped it, I say let him. Lock him away. Be done with him and any who, like him, wish to repeat the massacre of the past." She looked directly at Adolin. "This truth is."

Adolin felt at a loss to say anything. What defense could he offer? "We are not the same as the ones before," he said.

"Can you promise you will be different," she demanded. "Absolutely promise it? Promise that *no* further spren will be killed from bonds, if allowed to be?"

"Of course not," Adolin said.

"Well, I *can* promise that none will die so long as no more bonds are made. The solution *is* easy."

She turned and walked back to her place.

Adolin looked to Kelek. "There are no promises in life. Nothing is sure. She says spren won't die without bonds, but can you say what will happen if Odium reigns?"

"I find it most curious she'd prefer that possibility, young man," Kelek said. He started writing in his notebook again. "But it is seriously damning of you that an inkspren would be willing to testify alongside an honorspren. Damning indeed . . ." Kelek took another bite of his fruit, leaving only the core, which he absently set on the table in front of him.

Frustrated, Adolin forced himself to calm. The trial was proceeding well on at least one axis. The honorspren weren't trying to force the actual sins of the Recreance on him; they were taking a more honorable approach of proving that men hadn't changed, and bonds were too risky.

Blended and he had decided this tactic was safer for Adolin; Kelek could very well decide that there was no reason to imprison him for things the ancients did. At the same time, Adolin was losing the hearts of the watching spren. What would it matter if he "won" the trial if the spren were even more strongly convinced they shouldn't help in the conflict?

He searched the crowd, but found mostly resentful expressions. Storms. Did he really think he could prove anything to them? Which of the ten fools *was* he for starting all this?

No, I'm not a fool, he told himself. *Just an optimist. How can they not see? How can they sit here and judge me, when men are dying and other spren fight?*

The same way, he realized, that the highprinces had spent so long playing games with the lives of soldiers on the Shattered Plains. The same way any man could turn his back on an atrocity if he could persuade himself it wasn't his business.

Men and spren were not different. Blended had tried to tell him this, and now he saw it firsthand.

"The third and final witness," the honorspren officiator said, "is Notum, once captain of the ship *Honor's Path*."

Adolin felt his stomach turn as Notum—looking much improved from the last time Adolin had seen him—emerged from the top of the forum, where a group of standing honorspren had obscured him from Adolin's view. Still, Adolin was shocked. Notum had been forbidden to enter Lasting Integrity despite his wounds, and had stayed with the others outside the walls—though the honorspren of the tower had delivered him some Stormlight to aid in his healing. Messages from Godeke had indicated that Notum had eventually returned to patrol.

Now he was here—and in uniform, which was telling. He also wouldn't meet Adolin's eyes as he stepped down onto the floor of the forum. Spren might claim the moral high ground; they claimed to be made of honor. But they also *defined* honor for themselves. As men did.

"Offered to end your exile, did they, Notum?" Adolin asked softly. "In exchange for a little backstabbing?"

Notum continued to avoid his gaze, instead bowing to Kelek, then unfolding a sheet of paper from his pocket. He began to read. "I have been asked," he said, "to relate the erratic behavior I witnessed in this man and his companions. As many of you know, I first encountered this group when they fled the Fused in Celebrant over one year ago. They used subterfuge to . . ."

Notum trailed off and looked toward Adolin.

Give him Father's stare, Adolin thought. The stern one that made you want to shrivel up inside, thinking of everything you'd done wrong. A general's stare.

Adolin had never been good at that stare.

"Go ahead," he said instead. "We got you in trouble, Notum. It's only fair that you get a chance to tell your side. I can't ask anything of you other than honesty."

"I . . ." Notum met his eyes.

"Go on."

Notum lowered his sheet, then said in a loud voice, "Honor is not dead so long as he lives in the hearts of men!"

Adolin had never heard the statement before, but it seemed a trigger to the honorspren crowd, who began standing up and shouting in outrage—or even in support. Adolin stepped back, amazed by the sudden burst of emotion from the normally stoic spren.

Several officials rushed the floor of the forum, pulling Notum away as he bellowed the words. "Honor is not dead so long as he lives in the hearts of men! Honor is not—"

They dragged him out of the forum, but the commotion continued. Adolin put his hand on his sword, uncertain. Would this turn ugly?

Kelek shrank down in his seat, looking panicked as he put his hands to his ears. He let out a low whine, pathetic and piteous, and began to shake. The honorspren near him called for order among the crowd, shouting that they were causing pain to the Holy One.

Many seemed outraged at Notum's words, but a sizable number took up his cry—and these were pushed physically out of the forum. There was a tension to this society Adolin hadn't seen before. The honorspren were no monolith; disagreement and tension swam in deep waters here—far below the surface, but still powerful.

The officiators cleared the forum—even Shallan and Pattern were forced out. Everyone basically ignored Adolin. As the place finally settled down, and only a few officials remained, Adolin walked up the few forum steps to the High Judge's seat. Kelek lounged in his seat, ignoring the fact that he'd been curled up on the floor trembling mere moments earlier.

"What was that?" Adolin asked him.

"Hmmm?" Kelek said. "Oh, nothing of note. An old spren argument. Your coming has opened centuries-old wounds, young man. Amusing, isn't it?"

"Amusing? That's all?"

Kelek started whistling as he wrote in his notebook.

They're all insane, Adolin thought. *Ash said so. This is what thousands of years of torture does to a mind.*

Perhaps it was best not to push on the raw wound.

"That went well for me today, wouldn't you say?" Adolin asked him.

"Hmm?" Kelek said.

"One witness could not refute my point about my father," Adolin said. "Another made my argument for me by pointing out that siding against the Radiants is practically serving Odium. Then Notum put his honor before his own well-being. It went well for me."

"Does it matter?" Kelek asked.

"Of course it does. That's why I'm here."

"I see," Kelek said. "Did the ancient Radiants betray their spren, killing them?"

"Well, yes," Adolin said. "But that's not the question. The question is whether modern humans can be blamed."

Kelek continued writing.

"Honored One?" Adolin asked.

"Do you know how old I am, young man?" Kelek looked up and met Adolin's eyes, and there was *something* in them. A depth that made him, for the first time, seem distinctly inhuman. Those eyes seemed like eternal holes. Bored through time.

"I," Kelek said softly, "have known many, *many* men. I've known some of the best who ever lived. They are now broken or dead. The best of us inevitably cracked. Storms . . . I ran when the Return came this time, because I knew what it meant. Even Taln . . . Even Taln . . ."

"He didn't break," Adolin said.

"The enemy is here, so he did," Kelek said firmly. He waved toward the honorspren. "They deserve better than you, son. They deserve better than *me*. I could never judge them for refusing to bond men. How could I? I could *never* order them back into that war, back into that hole. To do so would be to . . . to abandon what little honor I have left. . . ."

Adolin took a deep breath. Then he nodded.

"I just told you that your cause is hopeless," Kelek said, turning to his writing. "You do not seem concerned."

"Well, Honored One," Adolin said. "I agreed to this trial—even with Sekeir's insistence I be blamed for what my ancestors did—because it was the only way to get a chance to talk to the honorspren. Maybe you will judge against me—but so long as I get a chance to have my say, then that will be enough. If I persuade even one or two to join the battle, I'll have won."

"Optimism," Kelek said. "Hope. I remember those things. But I don't think you understand the stakes of this trial, child—nor do you understand what you've stumbled into. The things that inkspren said—about joining Odium's side—are on the minds of many spren. Including many in this very fortress."

That hit Adolin like a gut punch. "Honorspren would *join* the enemy?" Adolin said. "That would make them no better than the highspren!"

"Indeed; I suspect their dislike of highspren is part of why they hesitate. The honorspren in favor of joining the enemy worried how such a suggestion would be received. But here you are, giving them a chance to make their arguments, acting as a magnet for all of their frustration and hatred.

"Many are listening. If honorspren start joining the enemy . . . well, many other varieties of spren would soon follow. I dare think they'd go in large numbers." Kelek didn't look up. "You came here to recruit. But I suspect you will end up tipping these finely balanced scales, and not in the direction you desire."

⁘

About an hour after the first stage of the trial—an hour she'd spent consoling Adolin in his sudden terror that he would accidentally cause a mass defection of spren to the side of the enemy—Shallan climbed a tree.

She stretched high, clinging to a branch near the top. It was a normal tree, one of the real ones the honorspren managed to grow here. It felt good to feel bark beneath her fingers.

She reached with one arm into the open space above the tree, but couldn't feel anything different. Had she hit the barrier yet? Maybe a little farther . . .

She shimmied a little higher, then reached out, and thought she felt an oddity as she got exactly high enough. An invisible tugging on the tips of her fingers.

Then her foot slipped.

In a second she was tumbling through the air. She didn't fall all the way to the base of the structure, merely to the floor of her plane. She hit with a loud *crack,* then lay dazed before letting out a loud groan.

Lusintia the honorspren was at her side a moment later.

As I suspected . . . Veil thought. *She always seems to be nearby.* She'd clearly been assigned to watch Shallan.

"Human!" she said, her short hair hanging along the sides of her white-blue face. "Human, are you hurt?"

Shallan groaned, blinking.

"Mmm . . ." Pattern said, stepping over. "Rapid eye blinks. This is serious. She could die."

"Die?" Lusintia said. "I had no idea they were so *fragile!*"

"That was a long fall," Pattern said. "Ah, and she hit her head when she landed on the stones here. Not good, not good."

Other honorspren were gathering, muttering to themselves. Shallan groaned again, then tried to focus on Pattern and Lusintia, but let her eyes slip shut.

"We must act quickly," Pattern said. "Quickly!"

"What do we do!" Lusintia said.

"You have no hospital here?"

"Of course we don't have a hospital!" Lusintia said. "There are only a couple dozen humans here."

"Mmm . . . but you won't let them come back in if they leave, so they are basically caged here. You should feel bad. Very bad. Yes."

Storms, Veil thought. *Is that the best he can do? How did we ever let him fool us?*

"Tell me what to do!" Lusintia said. "Do we carry her out to that Edgedancer?"

"It will take too long. She will die. Poor human whom I love very much. It will be tragic for her to die here, in the center of honorspren power and protection. Unless, of course, she were to be given Stormlight."

"Wait . . . Stormlight?"

"Yes, she *is* Radiant," Pattern said. "It would heal her."

Shallan suppressed a smile. Pattern *was* a tad transparent, but the honorspren here plainly had little experience with humans. They swallowed the bait without question, and soon Shallan was being carried by a team of four. She tucked away the piece of cloth-wrapped stone she'd used to smack the ground as she landed, giving the impression that she'd hit her head.

In reality, her arm *did* ache. She had undoubtedly bruised it when she hit, though this wasn't the worst self-inflicted wound she'd sustained in the name of science. At least this time her scheme hadn't involved deliberately embarrassing herself in front of several attractive men.

She made sure to groan occasionally, and Pattern kept exclaiming how worried he was. That kept Lusintia and the other honorspren motivated as they hauled Shallan to a specific building, their footfalls echoing against enclosing stone.

They had a hushed but urgent conversation with a guard. Shallan made a particularly poignant whimper of pain at exactly the right moment, and then she was in. Light surrounded her as she was brought someplace brilliant. They hadn't let her in here last time, when they retrieved Stormlight for Adolin's healing.

She let her eyes flutter open and found that most of the Stormlight was contained in a large construction at the center of the room. A kind of vat, or tall jar. This was technology Shallan hadn't heard of before coming to Shadesmar, and apparently not even the honorspren knew how it worked. They could be purchased from a group of strange traveling merchants called the Eyree.

Shelves nearby held a collection of loose gemstones, each glowing brightly. The wealth of Lasting Integrity: gemstones—gathered over millennia—so flawless, so perfect, that they didn't leak. She'd been told a gemstone like this could, with repeated exposures to storms, absorb far more Stormlight than its size should be able to contain.

She tested this, reaching out with a weak hand toward one of them and sucking in a breath of Stormlight—which streamed to her as a glowing, misty white light.

She immediately felt better: invigorated, alert. Storms, how she'd missed that. Simply *holding* Stormlight was stimulating. She grinned—not part of the act—then decided to leap to her feet. The ache in her arm vanished; she felt like dancing with joy.

Instead she let Veil take over. This next part needed her—Shallan remained the better actress, but Veil was better at most other espionage skills.

Veil made a show of touching her head where she'd been "wounded." "What happened?" she asked. "I don't remember. I was trying to see if I could reach the barrier where the gravity of the plane ran out."

"You were very foolish, human," Lusintia said. "You are so fragile!

How could you endanger yourself in such a manner? Do you not realize that mortals die if broken?"

"It was in the name of science," Veil said, reaching to her waist where she'd secured her notebook before climbing. She yanked it out and dropped it in a flurry. At the same time she swept her safehand to the side and dropped a dun emerald in place of a brightly glowing one.

The sleight of hand—performed hundreds of times beneath Tyn's watch, then perfected on her own—was covered as she stumbled and brushed the shelf, disturbing the many gems and shaking their light. She was able to slip the stolen emerald into her black leather glove.

This all happened in the moment the honorspren focused on her falling notebook. Veil quickly snatched it off the ground and held it to her chest, grinning sheepishly.

"Thank you," she said. "You saved my life."

"We would not have you die," Lusintia said. "Death is a terrible thing, and we . . ." She trailed off, looking at the shelf and the dun emerald it now contained. "Storms alight! You ate the *entire thing*? Human, how . . ."

Another spren, an angry male in uniform, began shoving Shallan out. "That was *years'* worth of stored Stormlight!" he exclaimed. "Get out! Go, before you eat anything more! If you fall again, I will have you turned away!"

Veil smothered her grin, apologizing as she stumbled out and met Pattern outside. An embarrassed Lusintia was forced to stay behind and fill out a report on the incident.

"Mmm . . ." Pattern said. "Thank you for letting me lie. Did it work?"

Veil nodded.

"Mmm. They are stupid."

"Stupidity and ignorance are not the same thing," Veil said. "They're just unaccustomed to both humans and subterfuge. Come on. Let's make ourselves scarce before someone thinks to search me."

A YEAR AND A HALF AGO

A banging came on the door, and Eshonai pulled it open and stared out into a tempest. Grand lightning flashes shattered the blackness in brief emotional bouts, revealing Venli, her eyes wide, grinning and soaked, clutching something in two hands before her.

She stumbled into the room, trailing water—which caused their mother to chide her. Jaxlim was in one of her . . . episodes where she saw the two of them as children.

Venli—seemingly oblivious to anything other than the gemstone—wandered past their mother. She rubbed her thumb on the gemstone, which was about a third the size of her fist.

"Storms," Eshonai said, pushing the door closed. "You did it?" She set the beam in place, then left it rattling in the wind as she stepped over to Venli.

But . . . no, the gemstone wasn't glowing. Was it? Eshonai leaned closer. It *was* glowing, but barely.

"It worked," Venli whispered to Awe, clutching the stone. "It *finally* worked. The secret *is* lightning, Eshonai! It pulls them through. When I drew close enough right after a strike, I found *hundreds* of them. I snagged this one before the others returned to the other side. . . ."

"The other side?" Eshonai asked.

Venli didn't respond. She seemed like a different person lately, always exhausted from working long nights—and from her insistence on going out in each and every storm to try to capture a stormspren. And now this. Venli cradled the gemstone, ignoring the water streaming from her clothing.

"Venli?" Eshonai said. "If you want my help in bringing this to the Five, you will need to let me see what you've done."

Venli stared at her, quiet, no rhythm at all. Then she stood tall and hummed to Confidence, proffering the gemstone. Eshonai attuned Curiosity and took it. Yes . . . it did have a spren inside, though it glowed with an odd light. Too dark, almost dusty. Smoky. It was difficult to tell its color through the green of the emerald, but it seemed shadowed, like lightning deep within the clouds.

"This spren is unlike any I've ever seen," Eshonai said.

"Stormform," Venli whispered. "Power."

"Dangerous power. This could destroy the listeners."

"Eshonai," Venli said to Reprimand, "our people are already *being* destroyed. Don't you think that this time, instead of making a snap decision based on songs from thousands of years ago, we should at least *try* a different solution?"

Rumbling thunder outside seemed to agree with Venli's words. Eshonai handed the gemstone back, then hummed to Betrayal to indicate what she thought of Venli's argument. But the rhythm didn't express how deeply the words cut.

Turning her back on her sister, Eshonai walked to the door again and threw aside the bar. Ignoring both Venli and her mother as they cried objections, Eshonai stepped out into the storm.

The wind hit her hard, but in warform's armor she barely felt the icy raindrops. She stood in the light spilling from the door until Venli pushed it closed, plunging Eshonai into darkness.

She attuned the Rhythm of Winds and started walking. Humans feared the storms. They always hid indoors. Eshonai respected the storms, and usually preferred to meet them with a stormshield. But she did not fear them.

She walked away from her mother's house, eastward into the wind. These days, her life had constantly been against the wind. It blew so hard, she barely felt she was making progress. Maybe she'd have been better off letting it steer her.

If she hadn't fought so much—if she hadn't spent so much time thinking about her explorations or her dreams—would she have settled into her role as general faster? If she'd doubled down on her raids at the start, would she have been able to shove the humans out of the warcamps before they got a foothold?

Like a rockbud, humans were. Soft at first, but capable of gripping onto the stone and growing into something practically immovable. In this—despite their lack of rhythms—they belonged to Roshar better than the listeners did. If she could truly travel the world, would she find them growing in every crevice?

She neared the edge of the plateau that made up the central heart of Narak, the city of exile. She walked carefully, letting flashes of lightning guide her way. She stepped right up to the edge of the chasm, facing into the wind.

"What do you want from us?" she shouted. "Answer me, Rider! Spren of the storm! You're a traitor like us, aren't you? Is that why you sent Venli those little spren?"

The wind blasted her, as if to push her off balance. Debris spun and sputtered in the wind, spiraling around her—the lightning making each piece seem frozen in the moment. A quick sequence of bolts struck nearby, and the thunder vibrated and rattled her carapace. Absolute darkness followed.

At first she thought maybe the Rider of Storms had chosen to appear to her. However, this darkness was ordinary. She could still feel the wind, rain, and debris.

"What kind of choice is this?" she demanded. "Either we let the humans destroy us, or we turn away from the *one* thing that defines us? The one value that matters?"

Darkness. Rain. Wind. But no reply.

What had she expected? An actual answer? Was this a prayer, then? Didn't make a lot of sense, considering that the very thing she resisted was a return to her people's old gods.

Those gods had never deserved reverence. What was a god who only made demands? Nothing but a tyrant with a different name.

"Everything I've done," she said into the wind, "has been to ensure we remain our own people. That's all I want. I gave up my dreams. But I will not give up our minds."

Brave words. Useless words. They would have to take Venli's discovery to the Five, and they would have to let her test it. Eshonai knew that as well as she knew the Rhythm of Peace. They couldn't reject a potential new form now.

She turned to go, then heard something. Rock scraping on rock? Was the plateau cracking? Though she could barely hear it, the noise must be quite loud to reach her over the din of the tempest.

Eshonai stepped backward—but her footing seemed unsteady, and she didn't want to move without a flash of lightning to guide her. What if—

Branching light flashed in the heavens far to the east. It lit the sky white, highlighting debris, illuminating the land around her. Everything except for an enormous shadow silhouetted in front of her.

Eshonai's breath caught. The rhythms froze in her head. That shape . . . sinuous, yet massive. Claws as thick as her body gripping the rim of the chasm mere feet in front of her. It couldn't be—

Lightning flashed again, and she saw its face. A chasmfiend snout, with jagged swords for teeth, head cocked to the side to watch her.

She didn't run. If it wanted her, she was already dead. Prey ran, and the beasts were known to play with things that acted like prey, even if they weren't hungry. Still, standing there in pitch-darkness—not daring to attune a rhythm—was the hardest thing she'd ever done.

When the lightning next flashed, the chasmfiend had lowered its incredible head toward her, its eye close enough that she could have stabbed it without needing to lunge.

Darkness fell. Then a small burst of light appeared directly ahead of her. A small spren made of white fire. It zipped forward, trailing an afterimage. Like a falling star. It moved closer, then spun around her.

By its light, she could see the chasmfiend slowly retreat into the chasm, its spikelike claws leaving scores on the stone. Her heart beating like thunder, Eshonai attuned Anxiety and hurried home. The strange little spren followed her.

Instead I think, if I were to remember my life in detail, I would be-
come even worse. Paralyzed by my terrible actions. I should not like
to remember all those I have failed.

Days passed. Navani barely noticed.

For the first time in her life, she let go completely. No worries about Dalinar or Jasnah. No worries about the tower. No thoughts about the million other things she should be doing.

This was what she should be doing.

Or so she allowed herself to believe. She let herself be free. In her little room of a laboratory, everything fit together. She'd met scholars who claimed they needed chaos to function. Perhaps that was true for some, but in her experience, good science wasn't about sloppy inspiration. It was about meticulous incrementalization.

With no distractions, she was able to draw up precise experiments—charts, careful measurements, *lines.* Science was all about lines, about imposing order on chaos. Navani reveled in her careful preparations, without anyone to tease her for keeping her charts so neat or for refusing to skip any steps.

Sometimes Raboniel visited and joined in the research, writing her own musings alongside Navani's in their notebook. Two opposing forces in harmony, focused on a single goal.

Raboniel gave her the strange black sand, explaining the difference between static and kinetic Investiture. Navani observed and measured, learning for herself. The sand slowly turned white when exposed to Stormlight or Voidlight. However, if a fabrial was *using* the Light, the sand changed faster.

You could wet the sand to reset it to black, though it had to be dry again before it could turn white. It was a useful way to measure how much Light a given fabrial was using. She noticed that it also changed colors in the presence of spren. This was a slow change too, but she *could* measure it.

Anything you could measure was useful to science. But for these few blessed days, it seemed like time was *not* properly measurable—for hours passed like minutes. And Navani, despite the circumstances, found herself *loving* the experience.

❖

"I don't know exactly where the sand comes from," Raboniel said, settled on her stool beside the wall, flipping through Navani's latest set of charts. "Offworld somewhere."

"Offworld?" Navani asked, looking up from the fabrial she'd been housing. "As in . . . another . . . planet?"

Raboniel hummed absently. A confirmation? Navani felt she could tell what this rhythm meant.

"I wanted to go, for years," Raboniel said. "Visit the place myself. Unfortunately, I learned it wasn't possible. I'm trapped in this system, my soul bound to Braize—you call it Damnation—a planet farther out in orbit around the sun."

To hear her speak of such things so casually amazed Navani. Other worlds. The best telescopes couldn't do more than confirm the existence of other celestial bodies, but here she was, speaking to someone who had *visited* one of them.

We came from another, Navani reminded herself. *Humans, migrating to Roshar.* It was so strange for her to think about, to align the mythos of the Tranquiline Halls with an actual location.

"Could . . . I visit them?" Navani asked. "These other worlds?"

"Likely—though I'd stay away from Braize. You'd have to get through the storm to travel there anyway."

"The Everstorm?"

Raboniel hummed to an amused rhythm. "No, no, Navani. You can't travel to Braize in the Physical Realm. That would take . . . well, I have no idea how long. Plus there's no air in the space between planets. We sent Heavenly Ones to try it once. No air, and worse, the strange pressures required them to carry a large supply of Voidlight for healing. Even so prepared, they died within hours.

"One instead travels to other worlds through Shadesmar. But again, stay away from Braize. Even if you could get through the barrier storm, the place is barren, devoid of life. Merely a dark sky, endless windswept crags, and a broken landscape. And a lot of souls. A lot of not particularly sane souls."

"I'll . . . remember that."

Other worlds. It seemed too vast a concept for her to grasp right now—and that was saying something, as she was presently contemplating the death of a god. She turned to her experiment. "Ready."

"Excellent," Raboniel said, closing the book. "Mizthla?"

Navani's stormform guard entered the room, seeming somewhat annoyed. Though that was common for him. "Mizthla" was his singer name; he said the Alethi had called him Dah. A simple glyph instead of a true name, because it was easier to remember. Perhaps if she had lived her entire life called something because of its utility, Navani would have shared his disposition.

She presented him with the fabrial, which was . . . well, not a true fabrial. The housing was a mere coil of copper wires around some gemstones. Raboniel knew a method of *changing* the polarity of a magnet, a process involving the lightning channeled from a stormform. Captive lightning seemed to have boundless potential applications, but Navani kept herself focused—maybe the polarity-swapping process would also work on gemstones filled with Voidlight.

Navani and Raboniel left the room, as the lightning could be unpredictable. "Remember," Navani said on her way out, "only a *tiny* release of energy. Don't melt the coils this time."

"I'm not an idiot," the Regal said to her. "Anymore."

Outside, Navani glanced down the hallway—lined with boxes of equipment, some hiding her traps—toward the shield around the Sibling. It seemed darker inside than before.

She and Raboniel avoided the topic. Working closely together did not make them allies, and both recognized it. In fact, Navani had been trying to find a way to hide future discoveries from Raboniel, if she made any.

Lightning flashed in the room, then Mizthla called for them. They hurried in as he set the coiled-up fabrial on the desk. It was likely still hot to the touch, so Navani gave it a few minutes, despite wanting to rip the gemstones out immediately to inspect the result.

"I have noticed something in your journals," Raboniel said as the two of them waited. "You often remark that you are not a scholar. Why?"

"I've always been too busy to engage in true scholarship, Ancient One," Navani said. "Plus, I don't know that I have the mind for it; I'm not the genius my daughter is. So I've always seen it as my duty to grant patronage to true scholars, to publicize their creations and see them properly encouraged."

Raboniel hummed a rhythm, then picked up the fabrial with the copper coiling it. The metal burned her fingers, but she healed from it. "If you are not a scholar, Navani," she said, "then I have never met one."

"I admit that I have trouble accepting that, Ancient One. Though I'm pleased to have fooled you."

"Humility," Raboniel said. "It's not a Passion my kind often promote. Would it help you believe if I told you that you no longer have to use titles when speaking to me? Your discoveries so far are enough to recommend you as my equal."

This seemed an uncommon privilege. "It does help, Raboniel," Navani said. "Thank you."

"Thanks need not be provided for something self-evident," Raboniel said, holding up the fabrial. "Are you ready?"

Navani nodded. Raboniel pulled the gemstones out from within the coil, then inspected them. "The Voidlight seems unchanged to me," she said.

Navani hadn't expressly told Raboniel she was hunting for anti-Voidlight. She shrouded her quest in many different kinds of experiments—like this one, where she explained she simply wanted to see if Light responded to exposure to lightning. She suspected that Raboniel suspected, however, that Navani was at least still intrigued by the idea of anti-Light.

Navani sprinkled some of the black sand on the tabletop, then placed the gemstone in the center, measuring the strength of the Investiture inside. But because the air didn't warp around this gemstone, she secretly knew her experiment had failed. This was not anti-Voidlight. She made a note in her log. Another failed experiment.

Raboniel hummed a rhythm. A regretful one? Yes, that was what it seemed to be. "I should return to my duties," she said, and Navani could pick out the same rhythm in her voice. "The Deepest Ones are close to finding the final node."

"How?" Navani asked.

"You know I can't tell you that, Navani." Though she had spoken of leaving, she remained sitting. "I'm so tired of this war. So tired of capturing, killing, losing, dying."

"We should end it then."

"Not while Odium lives."

"You'd actually kill him?" Navani asked. "If you had the chance?"

Raboniel hummed, but looked away. *That humming is . . . embarrassment?* Navani thought. *She recognizes she's lied to me, at least by implication. She doesn't truly want to kill Odium.*

"When you were hunting the opposite of Voidlight, you didn't want to use it against him," Navani guessed. "You teased me with the idea, but you have another purpose."

"You learn to read rhythms," Raboniel said, standing up.

"Or I simply understand logic." Navani stood, and took Raboniel's hands. The Fused allowed it. "You don't have to kill the Sibling. Let's find another path."

"I'm not killing the Sibling," Raboniel said. "I'm . . . doing something worse. I'm unmaking the Sibling."

"Then let's *find another path.*"

"You think I haven't searched for one already?" She removed her hands from Navani's, then picked up and proffered their notebook, the one where they logged their experiments. *Rhythm of War,* they called it. Odium and Honor working together, if only for a short time.

"I've run some experiments on the conjoined rubies you created—the ones of different sizes," Raboniel said. "I think you'll like the implications of what I've discovered; I wrote them in here earlier. This might make moving your enormous sky platforms easier."

"Raboniel," Navani said, taking the notebook. "Negotiate with me, help me. Let's join forces. Let's make a treaty, you and I, ignoring Odium."

"I'm sorry," the Fused said. "But the best chance we have of ending this war—barring a discovery between us—is for my kind to control Urithiru. I *will* finish my work with the Sibling. Ultimately, we are still enemies. And I would not be where I am—able to contemplate a different solution—if I were not fully willing to do what has been asked of me. Regardless of the cost, and regardless of the pain it causes."

Navani steeled herself. "I had not thought otherwise, Lady of Wishes. Though it leaves me sorrowful." On a whim, she tried humming to the Rhythm of War. It didn't work—the rhythm required two people in concert with one another.

In return, however, Raboniel smiled. "I would give you something," she said, then left.

Confused, Navani sat at the table, feeling tired. These days of furious study were catching up to her. Had it been selfish to spend so much time pretending to be a scholar? Didn't Urithiru beg for a queen? Yes, it would be wonderful to find a power to use against Odium, but . . . did she really think *she* could solve such a complex problem?

Navani tried to return to her experiments. After an hour, she conceded that the spark wasn't there. For all her talk of control and organization, she now found herself subject to the whims of emotion. She couldn't work because she didn't "feel" it. She would have called that nonsense—though of course not to their face—if one of her scholars had told her something similar.

She stood abruptly, her chair clattering to the ground. She'd picked up a habit of pacing from Dalinar, and found herself prowling back and forth in the small chamber. Eventually Raboniel appeared in the doorway, accompanied by two nimbleform singers.

The Fused waved, and the femalens hurried into the room. They carried odd equipment, including two thin metal plates perhaps a foot and a half square and a fraction of an inch thick, with some odd ridges and crenellations cut into them. The nimbleforms attached them to Navani's desk with clamps, so the metal plates spread flat, one on each side—like additions to the desk's workspace.

"This is an ancient form of music among my kind," Raboniel said. "A way to revel in the rhythms. As a gift, I have decided to share the songs with you."

She gestured and hummed to the two young singers, who jumped to obey, each pulling out a long bow—like one might use on a stringed instrument. They drew these along the sides of the metal plates, and the metal began to vibrate with deep tones, though they had a *rougher* texture to them. Full and resonant.

Those are Honor's and Odium's tones, Navani thought. Only these were the shifted versions that worked in harmony with one another.

Raboniel stepped up beside Navani. In accompaniment to the two tones, she played a loud rhythm with two sticks on a small drum. The sequence of beats grew loud and stately, then soft and fast, alternating. It wasn't exactly the Rhythm of War, but it was as close as music could likely get. It vibrated through Navani, loud and triumphant.

They continued at it for an extended time, before Raboniel called a stop and the two young singers—sweating from the work of vigorously making the tones—quickly gathered the plates, unclamping them from the sides of the desk.

"Did you like it?" Raboniel asked her.

"I did," Navani said. "The tones were a terrible cacophony when combined, but somehow beautiful at the same time."

"Like the two of us?" Raboniel asked.

"Like the two of us."

"By this music," Raboniel said, "I give you the title Voice of Lights, Navani Kholin. As is my right."

Raboniel hummed curtly, then *bowed* to Navani. With no other words, she waved for the singers to take their equipment and go. Raboniel retreated with them.

Feeling overwhelmed, Navani walked up to the open notebook on her desk. Inside, Raboniel had written about their experiments in the women's script—and her handwriting was growing quite practiced.

Navani understood the honor in what she'd just been given. At the same time, she found it difficult to feel proud. What did a title, or the respect of one of the Fused, mean if the tower was still being corrupted, her people still dominated?

This is why I worked so hard these last few days, Navani admitted to herself, sitting at the desk. *To prove myself to her.* But . . . what good was that if it didn't lead to peace?

The Rhythm of War vibrated through her, proof that there *could* be harmony. At the same time, the nearly clashing tones told another story. Harmony could be reached, but it was exceedingly difficult.

What kind of emulsifier could you use with people, to make *them* mix? She closed the notebook, then made her way to the back of the room and rested her hand on the Sibling's crystal vein.

"I have tried to find a way to merge spren who were split by fabrial creation," she whispered. "I thought it might please you."

No response came.

"Please," Navani said, closing her eyes and resting her forehead against the wall. "Please forgive me. We need you."

I . . . The voice came into her mind, making Navani look up. She couldn't see the spark of the Sibling's light in the vein, however. Either it wasn't there, or . . . or it had grown too dim to see in the light of the room.

"Sibling?" she asked.

I am cold, the voice said, small, almost imperceptible. *They are killing . . . killing me.*

"Raboniel said she is . . . unmaking you."

If that is true I . . . I will . . . I will die.

"Spren can't die," Navani said.

Gods can die . . . Fused can . . . can die . . . Spren can . . . die. If I am made into someone else, that is death. It is dark. The singer you promised me though . . . I can see him sometimes. I like watching him. He is with the Radiants. He would have made . . . a good . . . a good bond. . . .

"Then bond him!" Navani said.

Can't. Can't see. Can't act through the barrier.

"What if I brought you Stormlight?" Navani said. "Infused you the same way they've been infusing you with Voidlight? Would that slow the process?"

Cold. They listen. I'm afraid, Navani.

"Sibling?"

I don't . . . want . . . to die. . . .

And then silence. Navani was left with that haunting word, *die,* echoing in her mind. At the moment, the Sibling's fear seemed far more powerful than the Rhythm of War.

Navani had to do *something.* Something more than sitting around daydreaming. She stalked back to her desk to write down ideas—any ideas, no matter how silly—about what she could do to help. But as she sat, she noticed something. Her previous experiment rested there, mostly forgotten. A gemstone amid sand. When the singers had set up their plates, they hadn't disturbed Navani's work.

The music of the plates had caused the entire desktop to vibrate. And that had made the sand vibrate—and it had therefore made patterns on her desktop. One pattern on the right, a different on the left, and a third where the two mixed.

Stormlight and Voidlight weren't merely types of illumination. They weren't merely strange kinds of fluid. They were *sounds. Vibrations.*

And in vibration, she'd find their opposites.

90

ONE CHANCE

Regardless, I write now. Because I know they are coming for me. They got Jezrien. They'll inevitably claim me, even here in the honorspren stronghold.

Adolin stepped onto his podium at the honorspren forum. The circular disc had been pulled out to the center of the arena. Today, he would have the stage all to himself.

He'd arrived early, so he wouldn't have to push his way through the crowd. He wanted to appear in control, awaiting their scorn rather than taking the long walk down the steps with everyone watching. One felt like the action of a man who had orchestrated his situation. The other felt like a prisoner being led to execution.

Shallan and Pattern seated themselves as others began to arrive. The forum could hold a couple hundred spren, and as the honorspren—all glowing faintly white-blue—settled, he noted that far more of them wore uniforms today. The ones who had seemed sympathetic to Notum's proclamation were conspicuously absent from the seats. Adolin found that frustrating, though he did notice some spren from yesterday crowding around the top, where they could stand and watch.

The honorspren seemed determined to seed the seated positions with those who were predisposed against him. *No reason to sweat,* Adolin thought, standing with his hands clasped behind his back. *It's just your one chance to speak for yourself. Your one chance to turn all this around.*

Ideally, this would be the day that went best for him. He could explain his case and answer questions from the audience. Kelek's words from the day before weighed heavily upon him; this wasn't merely about the honorspren and whether some would join the Windrunners. It was a much larger argument.

Was humankind worth fighting for? Adolin somehow had to make that argument today. Blended had warned him he'd need to fend off questions and keep the argument on topic. He couldn't afford to engage the crowd too directly, couldn't afford to let them control the conversation.

That done, the trial would convene for one final meeting, where the honorspren could present a single last witness, whom Adolin could question, to rebut his arguments.

He bowed to Kelek as the Herald arrived. He'd changed into official-looking violet robes, a marked difference from yesterday. Did that mean he was taking this more seriously?

Adolin waited respectfully for the High Judge to seat himself among the group of honorspren officials. Adolin had learned that six of them were among the "ten honored by storms." The ten oldest existing honorspren, other than Syl. Hierarchy was important to this group.

"All right," Kelek said. "Let's get this over with. You may speak."

"Thank you, Honored One," Adolin said, then turned toward the crowd. "I don't think my words today will surprise anyone. Yet I've staked my future on the opportunity to say them to you. In person. To look you in the eyes, and ask you if you *truly* think this is justice.

"Men hold grudges. It is one of our greatest failings. Sometimes families will continue a cycle of hatred for generations, all for some slight that no one remembers. While I won't compare your very real pain and betrayal to something so insignificant, I hope to find in you—immortal pieces of Honor—a more perfect way of—"

"Did you know," a spren in the front row interrupted, "that your father almost killed the Stormfather?"

Adolin stumbled in his speech. "I will answer questions at the end," he said. "As I was saying, I had hoped to find—"

"Did you know about it?" the honorspren demanded, shouting. "Did you know he *almost killed the Stormfather?*"

"I find that difficult to believe," Adolin said. He glanced up at the top of the forum, where the standing spren were shuffling and whispering to one another. The audience fell quiet, waiting for Adolin. A question had been asked, but he didn't have to answer it, not yet. He controlled the floor.

So he remained focused as Blended had taught him, then purposefully continued his statement. "In *you*," Adolin said to the crowd, "I had hoped to find *honor*. Ancient spren bonded with us because they believed that together, we became something stronger, something *better* than we were alone.

"I admit to human weakness. I will not hide it. But I have not seen you admit to *your* weakness. You claim to be creations of honor. That you are better than men. Yet you refuse to prove it, to show it.

"I know of spren who do. Brave spren, who have come to the battle to join with men. In so doing, they have become *stronger*. They grow, like the people who bond them. Why do we need Radiants? Because they represent our best selves. We are of Honor and Cultivation. Honor, for an ideal. Cultivation, for the power to reach *toward* that ideal.

"The Stormfather himself agrees that this is the correct choice. People may not be perfect, but they're worth helping strive *for* perfection. And *you* are worth more than you can ever be sitting alone and refusing to grow."

That went over well. The honorspren liked a good speech, he'd learned—and those at the top in particular seemed swayed. He took a breath, preparing to move to his next point. Unfortunately, in the pause, that same honorspren from before leaped to his feet.

"The Stormfather made his choice," the spren said loudly, "and in so doing, put himself in danger—he nearly died. Did you *know about this*?"

Kelek leaned forward in his judge's seat. That was dangerously close to a statement, which the audience was not allowed to make. Trial by witness allowed Adolin to make declarations, but the audience could only question.

"I did not know of this event," Adolin told the spren. "So I cannot offer insight into why it happened, or what the circumstances were."

"How could you not know?" a different spren, in the second row, demanded. "If you've come to persuade us to become Radiant spren, shouldn't you know the cost of what you're asking? I think—"

"Enough of that," Kelek snapped. "Do you want to be ejected, Veratorim?"

The spren quieted immediately.

"Proceed, human," Kelek said, settling back and lacing his fingers before himself.

"My second argument," Adolin said, "is to show to you that the kingdoms of the world have put aside their differences to unite together to face this challenge. I brought a letter from my cousin, Jasnah, which was torn up. Fortunately, I can quote parts to you. She proves that the modern kingdoms are—"

"Has she tried to kill *her* spren?" the spren in the first row asked.

"She proves," Adolin continued, "that our modern kingdoms are united in ways that—"

"Yes, but has she tried to kill her spren?"

"Look," Adolin snapped, "do you want me to talk or not? Do you want to hear my testimony, like you've offered, or do you just want to take shots at me?"

The spren smiled. And Adolin realized what he'd done. By asking a question, Adolin had invited an answer.

"I think," the spren said, standing up, "that the most relevant question is if these new Radiants can be trusted. *That's* what you need to prove. The Stormfather *told* us that Dalinar Kholin forced him to physically manifest. Dalinar Kholin, your father, using the *Stormfather's essence* to work one of the Oathgates!"

"That's against his oath!" another one exclaimed. "Did you know about your father's actions?"

"I'm sure he had good reasons," Adolin said. "If you would—"

"Good reasons?" the standing honorspren said. "He was *running away*. Does this seem like the kind of behavior we should trust in a Bondsmith? From the man *you* said was ideal, that *you* promised would never betray us. How do you respond to this?"

Adolin looked to Kelek. "Can I please continue my witness?"

"You invited this discussion, son," Kelek said. "You need to engage him now." Kelek nodded toward the crowd at the top of the forum. Those who had joined with Notum yesterday waited quietly, wanting answers.

Adolin sighed, glancing to Shallan for strength before continuing.

"I cannot speak for my father. You'll have to ask him. I trust him; the Stormfather trusts him; that should be enough."

"He is a walking disaster," the spren said. "He is a murderer by his own testimony. This is *no* Bondsmith."

Adolin ignored that, as it wasn't a question. And theoretically, he could let this subject die and continue.

"Jasnah's letter," he began, "is—"

"Kaladin Stormblessed almost killed *his* spren too," a completely different honorspren said. "The Ancient Daughter, most precious of children. Did you know that?"

Adolin ground his teeth. "I do know what happened between Kaladin and Syl. It was a difficult time for all of us, a point of transition. Kaladin didn't know he was breaking his oaths—he was merely having a difficult time navigating conflicting loyalties."

"So you're ignorant *and* dangerous," the spren in the second row said. "Your Radiants barely know what they're doing! You could kill your spren by accident!"

Kelek waved, and the spren was grabbed by attendants and carried up and out of the forum. But Adolin saw this for what it was. A coordinated attack, and the ejection a calculated risk to get the words out.

"We're *not* killing our spren," Adolin said to the crowd. "These incidents are isolated, and we don't have proper context to discuss them."

"Is that so?" yet another honorspren said. "You can *swear* that none of your Radiants have killed their spren?"

"Yes! None of them have. They . . ." He trailed off.

Damnation. He'd met one, hadn't he? Killed recently—that Cryptic in the market.

"They what?" the spren demanded.

If he answered the question truthfully, it could be the end. Adolin took a deep breath, and did what Blended had warned him against. He engaged the audience. "I could answer, but you don't care, do you? You obviously planned together how to attack me today. This is an ambush. You don't care about honor, and you don't care what I have to say. You simply want to throw things at me."

He stepped forward and lifted his hands to the sides. "All right. Go ahead! But know this! You say that spren don't lie, that spren are not changeable like men? Next time you try to pretend that is true, remember this day! Remember how you lied when you said I'd have a fair trial. Remember how you treated the man who came to you in good faith!"

The crowd fell silent. Even his most vocal challengers sat.

"You were warned about this trial multiple times, human," Kelek said from behind. "They have made their choice."

"Not all of them," Adolin said. "I *thought* I'd find rational people inside these gates. Honorable spren. But you know what? I'm happy I didn't. Because now I know you for what you are. You're people, like any of us. Some of you are scared. It makes you afraid to commit. It makes you consider things you would once have thought irrational.

"I understand that. I am *glad* to find you are like humans, because I know what it means. It means you question—that you're afraid, you're uncertain. Believe me, I feel these things too. But you can't sit here and pretend that all humans are the same, that all humans deserve to be thrown away, when you yourselves are as flawed as we are. This trial proves it. Your hearts prove it."

He stared out at them. Daring them. Challenging them.

Finally, looking uncomfortable, the spren in the first row cleared his throat and stood. "Did you know—"

"Oh, cut the act," Adolin said to him. "You want to continue this farce? Fine. Do what you're going to do. I'll make it legal and ask—what is it you've *obviously* planned next to try to discredit me?"

The spren searched about the audience, uncertain. "I . . . Well, did you know about this?" He waved toward the top of the forum. The spren there parted, and everyone turned, looking up at someone being led down the steps by Amuna, the limber honorspren who kept the deadeyes. Today she led a Cryptic—one with a broken pattern, the head wilted.

Damnation. It was as he'd feared.

"Do you know this Cryptic?" Amuna demanded from the steps.

"If it's the same one I saw when I first landed on these shores," Adolin said, "then no. I just saw them once, in the market where the caravans cross."

"You know her story?"

"I . . . Yes, I was told it by a shopkeeper."

"She was killed only a few years ago," Amuna said. "This is proof of your lies. Modern Radiants cannot be trusted."

"There is no evidence that a Radiant did this," Adolin said. "We encountered humans—who have nothing to do with my people—who attacked Notum. Perhaps *they* attacked her."

"That kind of attack leaves a spren who can eventually be healed, with enough Stormlight," Amuna said. "The only *true* death for a spren—the only way to create a deadeye—is through broken Radiant oaths." Amuna gestured toward the deadeye. "This Cryptic didn't fall during the days of the Recreance. She was killed less than a decade ago. By one of your Radiants."

"Likely someone new, untested," Adolin said. "Someone we don't know about. Not one of ours; a poor new Radiant who didn't understand what they were doing. If you'd simply . . ."

But he knew he'd lost them. The crowds shifted, pulling away from the Cryptic, scooting in their seats. Another spren from the first row stood up and shouted questions at Adolin, joined by a dozen others, their words piling atop one another. How many spren would have to die before he admitted Radiants were a bad idea? Did he know the old Radiants had killed their spren because they worried about something *more* dangerous?

Adolin lowered his arms before the assault. Blended had tried to prepare him as best she could, but Adolin was no expert in legal defenses. He'd let himself be maneuvered, like being backed into unfavorable footing in a duel.

The reveal of the Cryptic overshadowed anything else he might say, any other arguments he could make. He looked to Kelek, who nodded, then gestured for him to go. Angry questions battered Adolin as he walked up the steps with as much dignity as he could manage. He knew when a duel was rigged. They'd been *telling* him from the beginning that it would be. And still he'd believed he could convince them.

Idiot.

⁘

Some hours after Adolin's second day of trial, Shallan closed her eyes, resting her head against his bare chest, listening to his heartbeat.

She would never have thought she'd find that sound so comforting. For most of her life, she'd never considered what it would mean to be this close to someone. It would have been alien for her to imagine the blissful warmth of skin against skin, her safehand reaching alongside his face, fingers curled into his hair. How could she possibly have anticipated the wonderful intimacy of feeling his breath on her hair, of listening to his heartbeat, louder to her than her own. The rhythm of his life.

Lying there, everything seemed—for a moment—perfect.

Adolin rested his arm across her bare back. The room was dark, their drapes drawn closed. She wasn't accustomed to darkness; usually you had a chip sitting out to give at least a little light. But here they had no spheres.

Except what she had hidden in the trunk. Sequestered with the cube that spoke between realms. And a very special knife.

"I love you," Adolin whispered in the dark. "What did I do to deserve you?"

"Blaspheme, perhaps," she said. "Or play pranks on your brother. I'm not sure what a person might do to make the Almighty curse them with me. Perhaps you were simply too slow to run away."

He trailed his hand up her bare spine, making her shiver as he finally rested it on the back of her head. "You're brilliant," he whispered. "Determined. Funny."

"Sometimes."

"Sometimes," he admitted, and she could hear the smile on his lips. "But always beautiful."

He thought that. He actually did. She tried to believe she deserved it, but it was difficult. She was so wrapped up in lies, she literally didn't know who she was anymore.

What if he found out? What if he knew what she *really* was?

"Your terrible taste in women," Shallan whispered, "is one of the things I love most about you." She pressed her head to his chest again, feeling the blond hairs tickle her cheek. "And I do love you. That's the only thing I've figured out about my life."

"After today, I have to agree with you on this trial idea of mine. It was a terrible plan."

"I'd be the world's biggest hypocrite if I couldn't love you despite your occasional stupid idea."

He rubbed the back of her head through her hair. "They're going to imprison me," he said. "They're already building the cell. I will be a symbol to them, a display for other spren to come and see."

"I'll break you out," Shallan said.

"How?"

"I stole some Stormlight," she said. "I'll grab my agents and Godeke, and we'll stage a rescue. I doubt the honorspren will give chase; they're too paranoid for that."

Adolin breathed out in the darkness.

"Not going to forbid me?" Shallan asked.

"I . . . don't know," he said. "There are some here who want to listen to me, Shallan. Some I can persuade. But they're afraid of dying, and I find myself uncertain. Not everyone is suited to war, and that's what I'm recruiting them for. I can't truthfully promise them they'll live, that their Radiants won't betray them. Maybe it's not right to demand they join us."

"Kelek told you their leaders were considering going to the enemy's side," Shallan said. "If that happens, those spren will end up bonding people anyway, regardless of what they think now. And the people they'll bond aren't the type to worry about the safety of their spren."

"True," Adolin said. "Storms, I wish I could get through to everyone here. Maybe tomorrow. I have a chance to rebut their witness, ask my own questions. . . ."

"Adolin? You said this is a terrible plan. Will the last day change that?"

"Maybe not," he said. "But at least it's a terrible plan that lets me engage with them. It lets them see a human trying to be honorable. Even if he's terrible at it."

"You're not terrible at being honorable."

He grimaced. "Someone smarter could have won this," he said softly. "Jasnah could have made them see. Instead it's just me. I wish . . . I wish I *knew*, Shallan. What to do. How to make them see."

She squeezed her eyes shut, attempting to return to that earlier moment of perfection. She couldn't. There was too much pain in his voice. His heartbeat had sped up. His breathing no longer felt serene to her, but frustrated.

It tore her apart to hear him like this. This was the man who had kept them all together when Kholinar fell, the man who was normally so optimistic. He'd come here determined to prove to his father—and maybe to himself—that he was still valuable. This stupid trial was going to take that from him.

Unless.

No, Radiant thought. *We can't fulfill Mraize's plan. He's manipulating you.*

We do what two of us agree to, Shallan said. *And I agree it is time to do as Mraize wants. We will take Kelek's soul, and we will imitate him at the trial. Veil and I will—*

No, Veil thought.

Shallan's breath caught. What?

I change my mind, Veil said. *I side with Radiant. I will* not *go kill Kelek. Two against one, Shallan.*

Something stirred deep inside of Shallan.

"I . . ." Adolin whispered. "I wish I could find out who killed that poor Cryptic. That's what ruined it today. Ruined it all."

It is time.

"This trial is not ruined," Formless said to Adolin. "You know, the more I contemplate it, the more I think maybe this trial *wasn't* such a bad idea. You're right. At least you're getting a chance to show them what an honorable man looks like."

"For all the good it's doing," Adolin said.

"I don't know," Formless said. "The High Judge *is* one of the Heralds. Maybe he'll end up surprising you. . . ."

91

WORTH SAVING

And so, I'll die.

Yes, die. If you're reading this and wondering what went wrong— why my soul evaporated soon after being claimed by the gemstone in your knife—then I name you idiot for playing with powers you only presume to understand.

Teft felt like a wet sack of socks that had been left out in a storm. The honest-by-Kelek's-own-breath truth was that he'd figured he'd done it again. When he'd woken up naked and sickly, he'd assumed he'd gone back to the moss. In that moment, he'd hated himself.

Then he'd seen Dabbid and Rlain. When he saw their joy—more heard it in Rlain's case—Teft knew he couldn't truly hate himself. This was where the oaths had brought him. His self-loathing was, day by day, fading away. Sometimes it surged again. But he was stronger than it was.

The others loved him. So, whatever he'd done, he would get up and make it right. That was the oath he'd taken, and by the Almighty's tenth name, he would keep it.

For them.

Then he'd found out the truth. He *hadn't* broken. He *hadn't* taken up the moss. It *wasn't* his fault. For once in his storming excuse for a life, he had been kicked to the gutter and woken up with a headache—and it *hadn't* been due to his own weakness.

A few days of healing later, he still found it remarkable. His streak held strong. Almost seven months with no moss. Damnation. He had an urge for some moss now, honestly. It would take the edge off his pounding headache.

But *Damnation. Seven months.* That was the longest he'd gone without touching the stuff since . . . well, since joining the army. Thirty years.

Never count those years, Teft, he told himself as Dabbid brought him some soup. *Count the ones you've been with friends.*

The soup had some meat in it, finally. What did they think would happen if he ate something proper? He'd been out for a few days, not a few years. That wasn't enough time to turn into some kind of invalid.

In fact, he seemed to have weathered it better than Kaladin. Storm-blessed sat on the floor—refused to take the bench because it was "Teft's." Had a haunted look to him and was a little shrunken, like he'd been hollowed out with a spoon. Whatever he'd seen when suffering those fevers, it hadn't done him any good.

Teft had felt that way before. Right now he was mostly aches, but he'd felt that way too.

"And we were supposed to be off storming duty," Teft grumbled, eating the cold soup. "Civvies. This is how we end up? Fate can be a bastard, eh, Kal?"

"I'm just glad to hear your voice," Kaladin said, taking a bowl of soup from Dabbid. "Wish I could hear hers . . ."

His spren. He'd lost her somehow, in the fighting when he'd gotten wounded.

Teft glanced to the side, to where Phendorana sat primly on the edge of his bench. He'd needed to reach to summon her, and she said she didn't remember anything that had happened since he went unconscious. She'd been . . . sort of unconscious herself.

Phendorana manifested as an older human woman, with mature features and no-nonsense Thaylen-style clothing, a skirt and a blouse. Her hair blew free as if in a phantom wind. Unlike Syl or some of the other honorspren, Phendorana preferred to manifest at the same size as a human.

She glanced at Teft, and he nodded toward Kaladin. Phendorana drew in a breath and sighed pointedly. Then—judging by how Kaladin's spoon paused halfway to his mouth—she let the others in the room see her.

"Your Surgebinding still works?" Phendorana asked Kaladin.

"Not as well as it did before the last fight," Kaladin said. "But I can draw in Stormlight, stick things together."

It was the same for Teft, but they'd found that if Lift didn't show up and do her little Regrowth thing to him every ten hours or so, he'd start to slip back into a coma. Something was *definitely* strange about that kid.

"If you can Surgebind," Phendorana said, "your bond is intact. The Ancient Daughter might have lost herself through separation—it is difficult for us to exist fully in this realm. However, I suspect she will stay close by instinct. If you can get to where you lost her, you should be fine."

"Should be," Kaladin said softly, then started eating again. He nodded in thanks as Dabbid brought him a drink.

They hadn't pushed Dabbid too hard on the fact that he could talk. It wasn't a lie, keeping quiet like he had. Not a betrayal. They each fought their own personal Voidbringers, and they each chose their own weapons. When it had come time to face the storm, Dabbid had done right by Teft and Kaladin. That was what mattered. That was what it meant to be Bridge Four.

A man could choose not to talk if he didn't want to. Wasn't no law against it. Teft knew a handful of people who should maybe try a similar tactic.

They continued eating in silence. After their initial joy at reuniting, their enthusiasm had dampened. Each thing Teft heard about their situation seemed worse than the one before. Fused in the tower. The queen captive. Radiants fallen. The tower spren slowly being corrupted, to the point that it was almost dead. Kaladin couldn't get it to talk to him anymore, and neither could Dabbid.

Grim days he'd awakened to. Almost wished they'd left him in a storming coma. What good was he at fixing any of this?

Phendorana glanced at him, sensing his emotions. He pointed his spoon at her and winked in thanks. No, he wasn't going to be down on himself. He'd sworn an Ideal.

Regardless. Grim days. Grim storming days.

The door opened a short time later, and Rlain entered with Lift, who scuttled forward and sniffed at the pot of soup. She wrinkled her nose.

"Be glad we have anything," Kaladin said. "That ardent in the monastery deserves credit. More than we gave him when we visited, Teft."

"Most people want to be helpful," Teft said. "Even if they need a nudge now and then. Kelek knows I do."

Lift hopped up onto his bench and stepped around Phendorana, then touched Teft, infusing him with Stormlight. He took a deep breath. And storm him, the air felt a little warmer. At least now he wouldn't fall asleep in his soup.

Rlain closed the door, then settled on the ground in the tight confines, his back to the stone wall, bits of his carapace scraping the stone.

"No news from the queen," Rlain said. "Lift managed to talk to one of the scholars, and she says Navani has been isolated for over two weeks now. She's imprisoned, forced to sleep in the scholars' rooms by herself."

"We're all basically imprisoned," Teft said. "Every storming one of us."

"No," Kaladin said. "We five are free."

"So what do we do?" Rlain asked. "We don't know where the last node is, the one keeping that shield up on the Sibling. If we did, it's not like we could protect it."

Kaladin had told them, in disheartening detail, about how difficult it had been to get in and destroy the previous two. Protecting one against the entire might of Odium's forces? Impossible. Teft agreed on that.

"If we break this last one," Teft said, "that's it. Tower's finished. But if we wait, the Fused will find a way to break it themselves. Tower's finished."

"We can't fight an entire army on our own," Kaladin said. "Teft and I have barely recovered, and our powers are temperamental at best. Two of us have lost our spren."

"The girl can wake the other Radiants," Teft said.

"The other Radiants are guarded," Kaladin said.

"Guards can be distracted or dealt with," Rlain said. "We did something similar to get Lift out. Venli is on our side. Or at least she's not on the other side—and she's Voice to the head Fused leading the occupation. We have resources."

Kaladin tipped his head back, his eyes closed.

"Lad?" Teft asked.

"I don't want any of you to take this the wrong way," Kaladin said, not opening his eyes. "I'm not giving up. I'm not broken. No more than usual. But I'm tired. Extremely tired. And I have to wonder. I *have* to ask myself. Should we keep fighting? What do we want to accomplish?"

"We want to win," Rlain said. "Free the tower. Restore the Radiants."

"And if we can't plausibly do that?" Kaladin leaned his head forward and opened his eyes. They'd gone dark again, of course, now that he'd been days without his Blade. The longer you kept your spren bonded, the more slowly the color faded. "I have to at least ask. Is it possible my father is correct? I'm starting to worry about what we might cause people to do if we keep fighting."

They grew quiet. And storm Teft if it wasn't a valid question. One not enough soldiers asked themselves. Right here, right now, should I be fighting? Is there a better way?

Teft took a spoonful of soup. "Did Sigzil ever explain to you boys how I got my father killed?"

The other occupants of the room turned to stare at him with slack jaws. He knew the rumors of what he'd done had moved through Bridge Four—and in the past he'd snapped at people who'd asked him about it. Storming fools.

"What?" Teft said. "It happened a long time ago. I'm over it, mostly. And a man shouldn't hide from what he's done. Gotta air things like this." He dug into his soup, but found his appetite waning. He set the bowl aside, and Phendorana put her hand on his.

"You were . . . young, weren't you?" Kaladin asked, carefully.

"I was eight when my father died," Teft said. "But the problems all started far earlier. It was some travelers, I think, who introduced the idea to the people of my hometown. Not quite a city. You might know it. Talinar? No? Nice place. Smells like flowers. Least in my memory it does. Anyway, the people of the town started meeting secretly. Talking about things they shouldn't have. The return of the Lost Radiants."

"How do you think they knew?" Kaladin asked. "You gave me Stormlight when I was dying, all the way back when *I* didn't know what I was doing. You recognized that it would heal me."

"Teft and I used to think," Phendorana said, "that the group who visited Teft's hometown—the Envisagers, they called themselves—were servants of some important lighteyes in Kholinar. Maybe they overheard what people like Amaram were planning, and ran with it. Only . . ."

". . . Only that was forty-five years ago," Teft said. "And when I asked Brightness Shallan about the group Amaram was part of, everything *she'd* found indicated they'd started less than ten years ago. But that's beside the point. I mean, I only met the leaders once, when my parents brought me to the initiation ceremony."

He shivered, remembering. The blasphemous things they'd chanted— shrouded in dark robes, with spheres affixed to masks to represent glowing eyes—had terrified the boy he'd been. But that hadn't been the worst. The worst had been what they'd done to try to become Radiants. The things they'd pushed their members to do. His mother had been one of those. . . .

"It turned dark," Teft said. "The things my people—my family— did . . . Well, I was around eight when I went to the citylord. I told him, thinking he'd run the worst of the troublemakers out of town. I didn't realize . . ."

"What nahn was your family?" Kaladin asked.

"Sixth," Teft said. "Should have been high enough to avoid execution. My mother was already dead by then, and my father . . ." He glanced up at the rest of them, and felt their sympathy. Well, he didn't want any storming sympathy. "Don't look at me like that. It was a long time ago, like I said. I eventually joined the military to get away from that town.

"It haunted me for a long time. But ultimately, you know what? You know Kelek's own *storming* truth? Because of what my parents did and taught me, I was able to save *you*, Kal. They won in the end. They were *right* in the end." He picked up his soup and forced himself to begin eating it. "We can't storming see the future, like Renarin can. We've gotta do what we think is best, and be fine with that. It's all a man can do."

"You think we should keep fighting?" Rlain said.

"I think," Teft said, "that we need to rescue those Radiants. Maybe we don't need to fight, but we've *got* to get *them* out. I don't like the smell of what you've been telling me. Lined up like that, watched over? The enemy is planning something for our friends."

"I can wake them," Lift said. "But they ain't gonna be in fightin' shape. And I'll need a whole bunch of food. Like . . . an entire chull's worth."

"If we can wake them," Rlain said, "we don't need to fight. We can have them run. Escape."

"How?" Kaladin asked. "We can't possibly hope to get all the way to the Oathgates."

"There's a window," Rlain said. "In the infirmary room. We can break it maybe, and escape out that way."

"To fall hundreds of feet," Kaladin said.

"That might take the Windrunners out of the influence of the tower," Teft said with a grunt. He thought about dropping hundreds of feet, not knowing if his powers would reactivate before he hit bottom. "I'd try it, and prove it can be done. The rest of you could watch and see if I fly up in the distance. If I do, you could follow."

Kaladin rubbed his forehead. "Assuming we could break the glass. Assuming we could get enough Stormlight to infuse the Windrunners. Assuming they're strong enough, after being incapacitated for so long, to try something that insane. Look, I like that we're exploring ideas . . . but we need to take time to consider all our options."

Teft nodded. "You're the officer. I leave the decision to you."

"I'm not an officer any longer, Teft," Kaladin said.

Teft let the objection slide, though it was completely wrong. One thing a good sergeant knew was when to let the officer be wrong. And Kaladin *was* an officer. He'd acted like one even when he'd been a slave. Like he'd been raised by a bunch of lighteyes or something. His official status or rank couldn't change what he was.

"For now," Kaladin said, "we wait. If we have to, we will break in and rescue the Radiants. But first we need to recover, we need to plan, and we need to find a way to contact the queen. I'd like her input."

"I might be able to get in to see her," Rlain said. "They have servants cart food and water to her and her scholars. Venli's people are often assigned that detail, and I could hide my tattoo and substitute for one of them."

"Good," Kaladin said. "That would be great. And while we wait, we don't do anything too rash. Agreed?"

The others nodded, even Lift and Dabbid. Teft too, though this wasn't the sort of situation where you had luxuries like time to come up with the perfect plan. Teft determined he'd just have to be ready to act. Take that next storming step. You couldn't change the past, only the future.

He ate his soup as the conversation turned to lighter topics, and found himself smiling. Smiling because they were still together. Smiling because he'd made the right decision to stay in the tower when Kal needed him. Smiling because he had survived so long without moss or drink, and was able to wake up and see color to the world.

Smiling because, for how bad everything could be, some things were still good.

He shifted as Phendorana poked him. He looked over and caught her grinning as well.

"Fine," he muttered. "You were storming right. You have always been right."

Teft *was* worth saving.

The bond is what keeps us alive. You sever that, and we will slowly decompose into ordinary souls—with no valid Connection to the Physical or Spiritual Realms. Capture one of us with your knives, and you won't be left with a spren in a jar, foolish ones. You'll be left with a being that eventually fades away into the Beyond.

Venli stood dutifully beside Raboniel, acting as her Voice as daily reports were delivered. Mostly Venli was here to interpret. While Raboniel had learned Alethi quite well—she claimed to have always been talented at languages—many of their current group of Regals spoke Azish, having been parshmen in that region.

Today Raboniel took the reports while sitting on a throne at the mouth of the hallway with the murals. This meant they were at the bottom of the stairwell leading upward to the ground floor. Venli couldn't help but be reminded of the humans who had died in the last hopeless push to reach the crystal pillar. Those memories were laced with the scents of burning flesh and the sounds of bodies hitting the ground.

Venli glanced at the freshly built portion of steps, hastily constructed with scaffolding underneath to replace the part broken during the fighting. Then she attuned Indifference—a rhythm of Odium. She had to be certain those rhythms continued to punctuate her words, though lately they made her mouth feel coated in oil.

"The Lady of Wishes hears your report," Venli said to the current Regal, who stood bowed before them. "And commends you on your Passion for the search—but you are wrong, she says. The Windrunner *is* alive. You are to redouble your efforts."

The Regal—wearing a sleek form known as relayform, often worn by scouts—bowed lower. Then she retreated up the steps.

"I believe that is the last of them, Ancient One," Venli said to Raboniel.

Raboniel nodded and rose from her throne, then walked into the hallway leading to the two scholar rooms. Her specially tailored Alethi-style dress fluttered as she walked, accentuating the lean, thin pieces of carapace armor along her arms and chest.

Venli followed; the Fused hadn't indicated she should withdraw. Though Raboniel had a workstation and desk set up at the end of the hallway, she always preferred to take reports out near the stairwell. It was as if Raboniel lived two separate lives here. The commander-general of the singer armies seemed so different from the scholar who cared nothing for the war. The second Raboniel was the truer one, Venli thought.

"Last Listener," Raboniel mused. "Last no more. Your people were the only group of singers to successfully reject Fused rule and make their own kingdom."

"Were there . . . unsuccessful attempts?" Venli dared ask, to Craving.

"Many," Raboniel said. She hummed to Ridicule. "Do not make the same mistake as the humans, assuming that the singers have always been of one mind. Yes, forms change our thinking at times, but they merely enhance what's inside. They bring out different aspects of our personalities.

"Humans have always tried to claim that we are nothing but drones controlled by Odium. They like that lie because it makes them feel better about killing us. I wonder if it assuaged their guilt on the day they stole the minds of those they enslaved."

Raboniel's desk was nestled right up against the shield—which, once a bright blue, had grown dark and violet.

Raboniel sat and began looking through her notes. "Do you regret what you personally did, Last Listener?" she asked to Spite. "Do you hate yourself for your betrayal of your people?"

Timbre pulsed. Venli should have lied.

Instead she said, "Yes, Ancient One."

"That is well," Raboniel said. "We all pay dearly for our choices, and the pain lingers, when one is immortal. I suspect you still crave the chance to become a Fused. But I have found in you a second soul, a regretful soul.

"I am pleased to discover it. Not because I admire one who regrets their service—and you should know Odium does not look favorably upon second-guessing. Nevertheless, I had thought you to be like so many others. Abject in your cravings, ambitious to a fault."

"I was that femalen," Venli whispered. "Once."

Raboniel glanced at her sharply, and Venli realized her mistake. She'd said it to the Lost. One of the old rhythms that Regals weren't supposed to be able to hear.

Raboniel narrowed her eyes and hummed to Spite. "And what are you now?"

"Confused," Venli said, also to Spite. "Ashamed. I used to know what I wanted, and it seemed so simple. And then . . ."

"Then?"

"They all died, Ancient One. People I . . . loved dearly, without realizing the depth of my feelings. My sister. My once-mate. My mother. All just . . . gone. Because of me."

Timbre pulsed reassuringly. But Venli didn't want reassurance or forgiveness at that moment.

"I understand," Raboniel said.

Venli stepped closer, then knelt beside the table. "Why do we fight?" she asked to Craving. "Ancient One, if it costs so much, *why* fight? Why suffer so much to secure a land we will not be able to enjoy, because all those we love will be gone?"

"It is not for *us* that we fight," Raboniel said. "It is not for *our* comfort that we destroy, but for the comfort of those who come after. We sing rhythms of Pain so they may know rhythms of Peace."

"And will he ever let *us* sing to Peace?"

Raboniel did not respond. She shuffled through a few papers on her table. "You have served me well," she said. "A little distractedly, perhaps.

I ascribe that to your true allegiance being to Leshwi, and your reports to her interfering with your duties to me."

"I am sorry, Ancient One."

Raboniel hummed to Indifference. "I should have arranged for a regular meeting for you to give her your spy reports. Maybe I could have written them for you, to save time. At any rate, I cannot fault you for loyalty to her."

"She . . . doesn't like you very much, Ancient One."

"She is afraid of me because she is shortsighted," Raboniel said. "But Leshwi is among the best we have, for she has managed to not only remember why we fight, but to *feel* it. I am fond of Leshwi. She makes me think that once we win, there will be some Fused who can rule effectively. Even if she is too softhearted for the brutalities we now must perpetuate."

Raboniel selected a paper off the desk and handed it to Venli. "Here. Payment for your services. My time in the tower runs short; I will finish unmaking the Sibling, and then will be on to other tasks. So I will now dismiss you. If you survive what comes next, there is a chance you may find some peace of your own, Venli."

Venli took the paper, humming to Craving. "Ancient One," she said, "I am a weak servant. Because I am so confused about what I want, I do not deserve your praise."

"In part, this is true," Raboniel said. "But I like confusion. Too often we belittle it as a lesser Passion. But confusion leads a scholar to study further and push for secrets. No great discovery was ever made by a femalen or malen who was confident they knew everything.

"Confusion can mean you have realized your weaknesses. I forget its value sometimes. Yes, it can lead to paralysis, but also to truth and better Passions. We imagine that great people were always great, never questioning. I think they would hum to Ridicule at that idea. Regardless, take that gift and be off with you. I have much to do in the coming hours."

Venli nodded, scanning the paper as she rose. She expected a writ of authority—given by Fused to favored servants, granting them extra privileges or requisitions. Indeed, there was exactly that on the front. But on the back was a hastily sketched map. What was this?

"I had hoped to find good maps of the tower," Raboniel noted to Fury.

"But Navani had some burned, and disposed of the others—though she feigns ignorance. This, however, is a report from a human scout who was flying along the eastern rim of the Shattered Plains."

Upon closer inspection, the page read in the human femalen writing system, *it appears the group we assumed were Natan migrants are instead Parshendi. A group of a few thousand, with a large number of children.*

Venli read it again.

"Did some of your kind leave?" Raboniel asked absently. "Before the coming of the Everstorm?"

"Yes. Rebels who did not want the new forms, along with the children and the elderly. They . . . escaped into the chasms. Shortly before the storms met, and the floodwaters came. They . . . they should have been completely destroyed. . . ."

"Should have. What a hateful phrase. It has caused me more grief than you could know." She began writing in one of her notebooks. "Perhaps it has treated you with kindness."

Venli clutched the paper and ran, not giving Raboniel a proper farewell.

I felt it happen to Jezrien. You think you captured him, but our god is Splintered, our Oathpact severed. He faded over the weeks, and is gone now. Beyond your touch at long last.

I should welcome the same. I do not. I fear you.

Formless awoke early on the day of Adolin's final judgment. It was time. She slipped from the bed and began dressing. Unfortunately, she'd moved a little too quickly, as Adolin stirred and yawned.

"Veil's clothing," he noted.

Formless didn't respond, still dressing.

"Thank you," Adolin said, "for Shallan's support last night. I needed her."

"There are some things only she can do," Formless said. Would that be a problem, now that Shallan no longer existed?

"What's wrong, Veil?" Adolin said, sitting up in bed. "You seem different."

Formless pulled on her coat. "Nothing's different. I'm the same old Veil."

Don't you use my name, Veil thought deep inside. *Don't you dare lie to him like that.*

Formless stopped. She'd thought Veil locked away.

"No," Adolin said. "Something *is* different. Become Shallan for a moment. I could use her optimism today."

"Shallan is too weak," Formless said.

"Is she?"

"You know how troubled her emotions are. She suffers *every day* from a traitorous mind." She put on her hat.

"I knew a one-armed swordsman once," Adolin said, yawning. "He had trouble in duels because he couldn't hold a shield, or two-hand a sword."

"Obviously," Formless said, turning and rummaging in her trunk.

"But I tell you," Adolin said, "no one could arm-wrestle like Dorolin. *No one.*"

"What is your point?"

"Who do you think is stronger?" Adolin asked. "The man who has walked easily his entire life, or the man with no legs? The man who must pull himself by his arms?"

She didn't reply, fiddling with the communication cube, then tucking Mraize's knife into her pocket along with her gemstone of Stormlight.

"We don't always see strength the right way," Adolin said. "Like, who is the better swimmer? The sailor who drowns—giving in at long last to the current after hours of fighting—or the scribe who has never stepped into the water?"

"Do you have a point with these questions?" Formless snapped, slamming her trunk closed. "Because I don't see one."

"I know. I'm sorry." Adolin grimaced. "I'm not explaining it well. I just . . . I don't think Shallan is as weak as you say. Weakness doesn't make someone weak, you see. It's the opposite."

"That is foolishness," she said. "Return to sleep. Your trial is in a couple of hours, and you shouldn't be fatigued for it."

Formless stalked out into the living room. There she hid by the side of the door and waited to see if Adolin followed. Pattern perked up from where he'd been sitting at the desk, and Formless quieted him with a glare.

Adolin didn't come out. She heard him sigh loudly, but he remained in bed.

Good. She had to act quickly. Formless needed to give him this last gift, the gift of winning here in Lasting Integrity. She owed the memory of Shallan that much.

I know what you're doing, Veil whispered. *I've finally figured it out.*

Formless froze. She checked on Radiant—tucked into the prison of her mind, trying to break free but unable to speak. So why could Veil?

Well, she could ignore a voice or two. Formless sat at the desk and sketched the layout of the judge's home. They'd paced it off yesterday, and peeked in windows. With her talent for spatial awareness, this floor plan should be accurate.

You aren't a new persona, Veil thought. *If you were, you couldn't draw like that. You can lie to yourself, but not me.*

Formless froze again. Was this what she wanted? What she *really* wanted? She wasn't sure of anything anymore.

There were so many questions. Why was Veil able to talk? Who had killed Ialai? How would she extricate herself from Adolin, from the Radiants? Was that the life she desired?

Formless steeled herself, quieting the questions. She placed a hand on her forehead, breathing deeply.

Pattern stepped over, so Formless closed the sketchbook and slid it into her satchel.

". . . Veil?" Pattern asked. "What are you doing?"

"It has to happen today," Formless said. She checked the clock. "Soon. Before the judge leaves his quarters." She gripped the gemstone she'd hidden in her pocket.

"Veil," Pattern said. "This is not a good idea."

He is right, Veil thought. *He is right, Shallan.*

I am Formless, she thought back.

No you're not, Shallan.

"I wouldn't be so quick to tell me what is right and wrong, Pattern," Formless said to him. "We still haven't dealt with your betrayal and your lies. Perhaps you aren't the best judge of morality, and should leave that to me."

His pattern slowed and his shoulders slumped, and he stepped backward as if he wanted to vanish into the shadows.

Formless drew out a little Stormlight, savoring the sensation of it inside her veins. Then she performed a Lightweaving.

It worked. Formless was a composite of the three—a single person with Shallan's drawing and Lightweaving abilities, Radiant's determination and ability to get things done, and Veil's ability to push aside the pain. Veil's ability to see the *truth*.

The best of all three of them.

Lies, Shallan, Veil thought. *Storms. I should have seen this. I should have known. . . .*

She glanced at herself in the mirror, and found the Lightweaving to be perfect. She looked exactly like Lusintia, the honorspren woman. She even gave off the same faint glow. This was going to be so easy.

Formless packed her drawing tools in case she needed to quickly sketch a new face. A Lightweaving disguised her satchel as a cloth bag like the ones the honorspren used.

Bells from below announced that it was about an hour until the trial. She crossed the room, passing Pattern, who had withdrawn to the corner. He stood in the shadows, his pattern moving lethargically.

"What's happening?" he said. "Something is very wrong with you, Shallan. I have handled this so poorly. I talked to Wit yesterday, and he—"

"You're *still* doing that?" Formless said. "You're still *disobeying* me?"

Pattern pulled away further.

"I've had enough of you," Formless hissed. "Stay here and cover for me with Adolin. We'll talk about this at length after the trial."

She took a deep breath and peeked out to make sure no one was watching—they might wonder why Lusintia had been in Shallan's house—then slipped out and began crossing the southern plane. The fortress was quiet. Spren didn't sleep, but they did have less active periods. They would congregate at "night" in the homes of friends, leaving the walkways of the fortress relatively unwatched.

A few leaves fluttered through the open air between the four sides. Formless tried not to look at the other three planes, three cities making an impossible box around her. She wasn't good at—

"Veil," a voice said behind her. "I need to explain. I must tell you the truth. Mmm . . ."

She groaned and turned. Pattern was following her like a barely weaned axehound pup.

"You'll give away my disguise!" she snapped at him.

He stopped, his pattern slowing.

"You must know what Wit said," Pattern replied. "He is so wise. He seems to like you and hate everyone else. Ha ha. He made fun of me. It was very funny. I am like a chicken. Ha ha."

Formless closed her eyes and sighed.

"He said to tell you that we trust you," Pattern said. "And love you. He said I should tell you that you deserve trust and love. And you do. I'm sorry I've been lying. For a very long time. I'm so sorry. I didn't think you could handle it."

"Shallan couldn't," she said. "Go to the room and wait. I'll deal with you *later*."

She strode away, and fortunately he didn't follow. It was time to become the woman she'd been building toward ever since she left her home to steal from Jasnah. Formless could finally join the Ghostbloods. She didn't care about Shallan's past. Let it sleep. She could be like Veil, who didn't have to worry about such things.

You're pretending to be like me, Veil thought. *But Wit is right. You deserve to be loved, Shallan. You do.*

The High Judge's quarters were all the way at the top of the plane, near the battlements. It was difficult to ignore the strange geometry up here, past the parks and the trees, because the sky was so close. She wanted to spend time drawing it, but of course she wasn't like that anymore. She needed to find all this disorienting and strange. Like Veil.

It helped to focus on the target: a small building near the corner of the wall. She passed several honorspren, but not many. She waved to those who waved to her, but mostly strode forward with a sense of purpose.

Once Formless arrived, she loitered near the house, glancing around until she could be reasonably certain no one was looking. That was difficult, with multiple planes to watch. At least the plan was simple. Step up to the door. Soulcast the doorknob into smoke to get past the lock. Sneak in and make her way to the back room, which was the High Judge's study. Knife him before he could react, then take his place for the trial.

This was her last step. This was the end.

I . . . Radiant said, her voice distant. *I killed Ialai.*

Formless froze in place.

I saw . . . Radiant whispered, *that you were about to do it. That you had poison secreted in your satchel. So I stepped in. To protect you. So you* . . . *didn't have to do it. To prevent* . . . *what is happening to you now* . . . *Shallan* . . .

She squeezed her eyes shut. No. No, she wouldn't back down. She *had* to do this. To end it. To end the wavering.

She opened her eyes, strode up to the door, and grabbed the knob with her freehand. It vanished beneath her touch. Soulcasting really *was* easier on this side. The knob barely cared that she asked it to change.

She pushed open the door. The room inside was packed. Pieces of furniture stacked atop one another. Rolled tapestries. Knickknacks and mementos, like a small glass chicken on the windowsill and a pile of dusty letters on a table.

Formless shut the door with a quiet motion. The windows provided enough light to see by, and she could see the glow of candlelight beneath the room's other door, the one that led into the High Judge's study. Kelek was here. She revealed Mraize's knife, then stepped forward.

As she did so, she felt a coldness—like a sharp breeze. Stormlight left her in a rush. Formless paused, then glanced over her shoulder.

Veil stood behind her.

"I know why you're doing this, Shallan," Veil said. "There's no fourth persona. Not yet. You've given yourself another name, so you can tuck away the pain. You take that step though, and it will be real."

"This is who I want to be," Formless said. "Let me go."

"You're running again," Veil said. "You think you don't deserve Adolin, or your place as a Radiant. You're terrified that if your friends knew what you truly were, they'd turn away from you. Leave you. So you're going to leave them first.

"That's why you kept spending time with the Ghostbloods. That's why you're here. You see this as an out from your life. You figure if you *become* the despicable person the darkness whispers that you have been, then it will all be decided. No going back. Decision's made."

Formless . . . Formless . . .

Was just Shallan.

And Shallan wanted to do this. She wanted to show them what she truly was. So it would be over.

"I can't be Shallan," she whispered. "Shallan is weak."

Shallan put her hands to her eyes and trembled. Veil felt her emotions in a sudden wave of pain, frustration, shame, and confusion. It made her shake as well.

"Who is a better swimmer?" Veil whispered. "It's the sailor who has swum his entire life, even if he encounters rough seas that challenge him. Who is the stronger man? It *is* the man who must pull himself by his arms. And that swordsman with one arm . . . He was probably the best in raw skill. He couldn't win because of his disadvantages, but he wasn't weaker than the others."

Shallan stilled.

"Adolin is right," Veil said. "He's always been right about you. Tell me. Who is the strongest of mind? The woman whose emotions are always on her side? Or the woman whose own thoughts betray her? You have fought this fight every day of your life, Shallan. And *you are not weak.*"

"Aren't I?" Shallan demanded, spinning. "I killed my own father! I strangled him with my own hands!"

The words cut deep, like a spike through the heart. Veil winced visibly. But that cut to the heart somehow let warmth bleed out, flowing through her. "You have borne that truth for a year and a half, Shallan," Veil said, stepping forward. "You kept going. You *were* strong enough. You made the oath."

"And Mother?" Shallan snapped. "Do you remember the feel of the Blade forming in our hands for the first time, Veil? I do. Do you remember the *horror* I felt at the strike, which I never meant to make?"

Her mother, with stark red hair—a length of metal in her chest as her beautiful green eyes turned to coal. Burning out of her face. Shallan's voice, screaming at what she'd done. Screaming, *begging* to take it back. Wishing she were dead. Wishing . . . Wishing . . .

Another spike to the heart. More warmth bleeding out, blood flowing with thunderous heartbeats. Veil always felt so cold, but today she felt warm. Warm with pain. Warm with life.

"You can bear it," Veil whispered. She stepped forward, eye-to-eye with Shallan. "You can remember it. Our weakness doesn't make us weak. Our weakness makes us strong. For we had to carry it all these years."

"No," Shallan said, her voice growing soft. "No. I can't . . ."

"You can," Veil whispered. "I've protected you all these years, but it's time for me to leave. It's time for me to be done."

"I can't," Shallan said. "I'm *too weak!*"

"I don't think you are. Take the memories." Veil reached out her hand. "Take them back, Shallan."

Shallan wavered. Formless had vanished like a puff of smoke, revealing all her lies. And there was Veil's hand. Inviting. Offering to *prove* that Shallan was strong.

Shallan took her hand.

Memories flooded her. Playing in the gardens as a child, meeting a Cryptic. A beautiful, spiraling spren that dimpled the stone. Wonderful times, spent hidden among the foliage in their special place. The Cryptic encouraged her to become strong enough to help her family, to stand against the terrible darkness spreading through it.

Such a blessed time, full of hope, and joy, and truths spoken easily with the solemnity and wonder of a child. That companion had been a true friend to an isolated child, a girl who suffered parents who constantly fought over her future.

Her spren. A spren who could talk. A spren she could confide in. A companion.

And that companion had not been Pattern. It had been a different Cryptic. One who . . . One who . . .

Shallan fell to her knees, arms wrapped around herself, trembling. "Oh storms . . . Oh, God of Oaths . . ."

She felt a hand on her shoulder. "It's all right, Shallan," Veil whispered. "It's all right."

"I know what you are," Shallan whispered. "You're the blankness upon my memories. The part of me that looks away. The part of my mind that protects me from my past."

"Of course I am," Veil said. "I'm your *veil,* Shallan." She squeezed Shallan's shoulder, then turned toward the closed door. Had Kelek heard them talking . . . or . . . had they even spoken out loud?

Shallan surged to her feet. No. It hurt *too much.* Didn't it make more sense to become what Mraize wanted? Adolin would hate her for what she did. Dalinar would hate her. Shallan represented the very thing they all said they would never do. The thing they blamed for all of their problems. The thing that had doomed humankind.

She . . . she was worthless. She reached for the doorknob.

You can bear it, Radiant whispered.

No. She could become Formless and join the Ghostbloods whole-heartedly. Become the woman she'd created for herself, the strong spy who lived a double life without it bothering her. She could be confident and collected and painless and perfect.

Strength before weakness, Radiant said.

Not a woman who had . . . who had . . .

Be strong.

Shallan turned, breathing out, and Stormlight exploded from her like her life's own blood. It painted the room before her, coloring it, changing it to a lush garden. Covered in bright green vines and shalebark of pink and red.

Within it, a hidden place where a girl cried. The girl wept, then screamed, then said the terrible words.

"I don't *want* you! I hate you! I'm done! You never existed. You are nothing. And I am *finished*!"

Shallan didn't turn away. She *wouldn't*. She felt the ripping sensation again. The terrible pain, and the awful horror.

She hadn't known what she was doing, not truly. But she *had* done it.

"I killed her," Shallan whispered. "I killed my spren. My wonderful, beautiful, kindly spren. I broke my oaths, and I killed her."

Veil stood with her hands clasped before her. "It's going to hurt," Veil warned. "I'm sorry for the pain, Shallan. I did what I could—but I did it for too long."

"I know," Shallan said.

"But I have no strength that you do not, Shallan," Veil said. "You are me. We are me."

Veil became Stormlight, glowing brightly. The color faded from her, becoming pure white. Her memories integrated into Shallan's. Her skills became Shallan's. And Shallan recognized everything she had done.

She remembered preparing the needle hidden in her satchel to kill Ialai. She saw her past, and her growing worry in all its self-destructive horror. Saw herself growing into the lie that she could never belong with Adolin and the Radiants, so she began searching for another escape.

But that escape wasn't strength. *This* was strength. She closed her eyes, bearing the burden of those memories. Not only of what she'd done recently, but what she'd done in the garden that day. Terrible memories.

Her memories.

As there was nothing left for Veil to protect Shallan from feeling, she began to fade. But as she faded, one last question surfaced: *Did I do well?*

"Yes," Shallan whispered. "Thank you. Thank you *so* much."

And then, like any other illusion that was no longer needed, Veil puffed away.

Shallan took a deep breath, her pain settling in. Storms . . . Pattern was here. Not her new Pattern, the first one. The deadeye. Shallan needed to find her.

Later. For now, she had a job to do. As she gathered herself, the door to the study clicked open, and light spilled around a figure. An Alethi man with wispy hair and weary eyes. Shallan knew that expression well.

"I see," Kelek said. "So you are the one sent to kill me?"

"I was sent for that purpose," she said, holding up the knife. She set it on a nearby table. "Sent by someone who didn't realize I'd be strong enough to say no. You're safe from me, Kelek."

He walked over and picked up the knife in timid fingers. "So this is like the one they used on Jezrien?"

"I don't know," Shallan said honestly. "A group called the Ghostbloods wanted me to use that on you."

"Old Thaidakar has always wanted my secrets," Kelek said. "I thought it would be the man, your husband, who came for me. I wonder if he knows I've had trouble fighting these days. It's so hard to decide. To do anything really . . ."

"Is that why you've been so hard on Adolin?" Shallan asked. "At the trial?"

Kelek shook his head. "You two stumbled into a little war of ideologies. The older honorspren—they're so frightened of what happened to their predecessors. But the young ones want to go fight."

"I can tell you about the people who sent me," Shallan said. "We can share information. But first I have a request. You're about to convict my husband in this sham of a trial. I'd like you to reconsider."

Kelek wiped his brow with a handkerchief from his pocket. "So many questions," he said, as if he hadn't heard her request. "Who else knows I'm here? I feel like I'm close to finding a way offworld. Maybe . . . Maybe I should wait. . . ."

"I have information that could help you," Shallan said. "But I want to trade. There isn't much time for us to—"

She was interrupted as the door slammed open, revealing several honorspren—including Lusintia, the one Shallan had impersonated. She gestured aggressively at Shallan, who stepped back, reaching into her pocket for her gemstone.

It was dun. Somehow, in what she'd done with Veil, she'd used it all up.

"Attempting to influence the course of the trial?" Lusintia demanded. "Colluding with the judge?"

"She was . . . doing nothing of the sort," Kelek said, stepping up beside Shallan. "She was bringing me news from the Physical Realm. And I'd have you *not* barge into my quarters, thank you very much."

Lusintia stopped, but then looked over her shoulder toward a bearded male honorspren. Shallan recognized him as Sekeir, the one who had acted as prosecutor against Adolin on the first day of the trial. An important spren, perhaps the most important in the fortress. And one of the oldest ones.

"I think, Honored One," Sekeir said softly, "that you might be having another bout of your weakness. We shall have to sequester you, I'm afraid. For your own good . . ."

94

SACRIFICE

Nevertheless, I'm writing answers for you here, because something glimmers deep within me. A fragment of a memory of what I once was.

I was there when Ba-Ado-Mishram was captured. I know the truth of the Radiants, the Recreance, and the Nahel spren.

Adolin made no effort to arrive early to the last day of the trial. Indeed, each footstep felt leaden as he trudged toward the forum. He could see from a distance that the place was crowded—with even more spren gathered at the top of the steps than yesterday. Nearly every honorspren in the fortress had come to watch him be judged.

Though he didn't relish facing them, he also couldn't give up this opportunity. It was his last chance to speak for himself, for his people. He had to believe that some of them were listening.

And if he lost? If he was condemned to imprisonment? Would he let Shallan rescue him, as she'd offered?

If I did, he thought, *I would prove what the leaders of the honorspren have been saying all along: Men aren't worthy of trust.* What if the only way to win here was to accept their judgment? To spend years in a cell?

After all, what else are you good for, Adolin? The world needed Radiants, not princes—particularly not ones who had refused the throne. Perhaps the best thing he could do for humanity was become a living testimony of their honor.

That thought troubled him as he reached the crowd. They parted for him, nudging one another, falling silent as he descended.

Storms, I wasn't built for problems like this, Adolin thought. He hadn't slept well—and he worried about the way Shallan had been acting lately. She wasn't sitting in her spot, and neither was Pattern. Was she going to skip this most important day of the trial?

He was about halfway down the steps when he noticed another oddity: Kelek wasn't there. Sekeir—the aged honorspren with the long beard—had taken his place. He waved for Adolin to continue.

Adolin reached the floor of the forum and walked over to the judge's seat. "Where is Kelek?"

"The Holy One is indisposed," Sekeir said. "Your wife went to him in secret and tried to influence the course of the trial."

Adolin felt a spike of joy. So *that* was what she'd been up to.

"Do not smile," Sekeir said. "We discovered a weapon of curious design, perhaps used to intimidate the Holy One. Your wife is being held, and the Holy One is . . . suffering from his long time as a Herald.

"We have relieved him as High Judge, and I will sit in his place. You will find the documentation on your seat, to be read to you if you wish. The trial will continue under my direction. I am a far lesser being, but I will not be as . . . lax as he was."

Great, Adolin thought. *Wonderful.* He tried to find a way to use this to his advantage. Could he stall? Make some kind of plea? He looked at the audience and saw trouble, division. Perhaps he was a fool, but it seemed like some of them *wanted* to listen. *Wanted* to believe him. Those felt fewer than yesterday; so many others watched him with outright hostility.

So how could Adolin reach them?

Sekeir started the trial by calling for silence, something Kelek had never bothered to do. Apparently the hush that fell over the crowd wasn't enough, for Sekeir had three different spren ejected for whispering to one another.

That done, the overstuffed spren stood up and read off a prepared speech. And storms, did it go on. Windy passages about how Adolin had brought this upon himself, about how it was good that humans finally had a chance to pay for their sins.

"Do we need this?" Adolin interrupted as Sekeir paused for effect. "We all know what you're going to do. Be on with it."

The new High Judge waved to the side. A spren stepped up beside Adolin, a white cloth in her hands. A gag. She pulled it tight between her hands, as if *itching* for a chance.

"You may speak during the questioning of the witness," Sekeir said. "The defendant is not allowed to interrupt the judge."

Fine. Adolin settled into parade rest. He didn't have an enlisted man's experience with standing at attention, but Zahel had forced him to learn this stance anyway. He could hold it. Let them see him bear their lashes without complaint.

His determination in that regard lasted until Sekeir, at long last, finished his speech and called for the final witness to be revealed.

It was Maya.

Amuna led her by the hand, forcing back the watching honorspren. Though Adolin had gone to see Maya each morning—and they'd let him do his exercises with her—bars had separated them. They hadn't otherwise allowed him to interact with her, claiming deadeyes did best when it was quiet.

If so, why were they dragging her into the middle of a crowd? Adolin stepped forward, but the honorspren at his side snapped the gag in warning. He forced himself back into parade rest and clenched his jaw. Maya didn't *seem* any worse for the attention. She walked with that customary sightless stare, completely oblivious to the whispering crowd.

Sekeir didn't hush them this time. The bearded honorspren smiled as he regarded the stir Amuna and Maya made. They placed Maya on her podium, and she turned and seemed to notice Adolin, for she cocked her head. Then, as if only now aware of it, she regarded the crowded audience. She shrank down, hunching her shoulders, and glanced around with quick, jerky motions.

He tried to catch her gaze and reassure her with a smile, but she was too distracted. Damnation. Adolin hadn't hated the honorspren, despite their tricks, but this started him seething. How *dare* they use Maya as part of their spectacle?

Not all of them, he reminded himself, reading the mood of the crowd.

Some sat quietly, others whispered. And more than a few near the top wore stormy expressions. No, they didn't care for this move either.

"You may speak now, prisoner," Sekeir said to Adolin. "Do you recognize this deadeye?"

"Why are you questioning me?" Adolin said. "She is supposed to give witness, and I'm supposed to question her. Yet you've chosen a witness who cannot answer your questions."

"I will guide this discussion," Sekeir said. "As is my right as judge in the case of a witness too young or otherwise incapable of a traditional examination."

Adolin sought out Blended, a single black figure in a sea of glowing white ones. She nodded. This was legal. There were so many laws she hadn't had time to explain—but it wasn't her fault. He suspected he couldn't have understood every detail of the law even with years of preparation.

"Now," Sekeir said, "do you know this spren?"

"You know I do," Adolin snapped. "That is Mayalaran. She is my friend."

"Your 'friend,' you say?" Sekeir asked. "And what does this friendship entail? Do you perhaps have dinner together? Participate in friendly chats around the campfire?"

"We exercise together."

"Exercise?" Sekeir said, standing from his seat behind the judge's table. "You made a weapon of her. She is not your friend, but a convenient tool. A weapon by which you slay other men. Your kind never asks permission of Shardblades; you take them as prizes won in battle, then apply them as you wish. She is not your friend, Adolin Kholin. She is your *slave*."

"Yes," Adolin admitted. He looked to Maya, then turned away. "*Yes*, storm you. We didn't know they were spren at first, but even now that we do . . . we use them. We need to."

"Because you *need* to *kill*," Sekeir said, walking up to Adolin. "Humans are monsters, with a lust for death that can never be sated. You thrive upon the terrible emotions of the Unmade. You don't fight Odium. You *are* Odium."

"Your point is made," Adolin said more softly. "Let Maya go. Pass your judgment."

Sekeir stepped up to him, meeting his eyes.

"Look at her," Adolin said, gesturing. "She's terrified."

Indeed, Maya had shrunk down further and was twisting about, as if to try to watch all the members of the audience at once. She turned so violently, in fact, that Amuna and another honorspren stepped up to take her arms, perhaps to prevent her from fleeing.

"You want this to be easy, do you?" Sekeir asked Adolin, speaking in a softer voice. "You don't *deserve* easy. I had this fortress working in an orderly, organized manner before you arrived. You have no idea the frustration you have caused me, human." The honorspren stepped away from Adolin and faced the crowd, thrusting his hand toward Maya.

"Behold this spren!" Sekeir commanded. "See what was done to her by humans. This Kholin asks us to offer ourselves for bonds again. He asks us to trust again. It is vital, then, that we examine carefully the results of our last time trusting men!"

Maya began to thrash, a low growl rising in her throat. She did *not* like being constrained.

"This is a trial by witness!" Adolin shouted at Sekeir. "You are interfering, and go too far."

Blended nodded, and other honorspren in the crowd had stood up at the objection. They agreed. Whatever the law was, Sekeir was stretching it here.

"This witness," Sekeir said, pointing at Maya again, "lost her voice because of what *your people* did. I must speak for her."

"She doesn't want you to speak for her!" Adolin shouted. "She doesn't want to *be* here!"

Maya continued to push against her captors, increasingly violent. Some of the crowd responded with jeers toward Adolin. Others muttered and gestured toward Maya.

"Does it make you uncomfortable?" Sekeir demanded of Adolin. "Convenient, now, for you to care about what she wants. Well, *I* can read her emotions. That thrashing? It is the pain of someone who remembers what was done to her. She condemns you, Adolin Kholin."

Maya's cries grew louder. Frantic, guttural, they weren't proper shouts. They were the pained anguish of someone who had forgotten how to speak, but still needed to give voice to her agony.

"This poor creature," Sekeir shouted over the increasing din, "condemns you with each groan. She is our final witness, for hers is the pain we must never forget. Listen to her demand your punishment, Adolin Kholin! She was innocent, and your kind murdered her. Listen to her cry for blood!"

Maya's shouts grew louder and more *raw*. Some honorspren in the crowd pulled back, and others covered their ears, wincing. Adolin had heard that scream before, the time he'd tried to summon her as a Blade while in Shadesmar.

"She's in pain!" Adolin shouted, lunging forward. The spren watching him, however, had been waiting for this. They grabbed him and held him tight. "Let her go, you bastard! Your point is made!"

"My point cannot be made strongly enough," Sekeir shouted. "It must be repeated over and over. You will not be the only traitor who comes with a smile, begging to exploit us. My people must stay firm, must remember this moment, for their own good. They need to *see* what humans did!"

Maya's voice grew louder, gasping breaths punctuated by ragged howls. And in that moment, Adolin . . . *felt* her pain somehow. A deep agony. And . . . anger?

Anger at the honorspren.

"They trusted you," Sekeir said, "and you murdered them!"

She clawed at the hands, trying to free herself, her teeth flashing as she twisted her scratched-out eyes one way, then the other. Yes, Adolin could feel that agony as if it were his own. He didn't know how, but he *could*.

"Listen to her!" Sekeir said. "Accept her condemnation!"

"LET HER GO!" Adolin shouted. He struggled, then went limp. "Storms. Just let her go."

"I refuse judgment!" Sekeir said. "I don't need to give it. In the end, her testimony is the only one needed. Her *condemnation* is all we ever needed. Listen to her shouts; remember them as you rot, Adolin Kholin. Remember what your kind did to her. Her screams *are* your judgment!"

Maya's howls came to a crescendo of anguish, then she fell silent, gasping for breath. Weak. Too weak.

Take it, Adolin thought to her. *Take some of my strength.*

She looked right at him, and despite her scratched-out eyes, she *saw* him. Adolin felt something, a warmth deep within him. Maya drew in air, filling her lungs. Her expression livid as she gathered all of her strength, she prepared to shout again. Adolin braced himself for the screech. Her mouth opened.

And she spoke.

"*We! CHOSE!*"

The two words rang through the forum, silencing the agitated honorspren. Sekeir, standing with his back to her, hesitated. He turned to see who had interrupted his dramatic speech.

Panting, hunched forward in the grip of her captors, Maya managed to repeat her words. "We . . . We chose. . . ."

Sekeir stumbled away. The hands holding Adolin went slack as the honorspren stared in shock.

Adolin pulled free and crossed the stage. He shoved aside the startled Amuna and supported Maya, putting her arm across his shoulder to hold her up as he would a wounded soldier. She clung to him, stumbling as she struggled to remain upright.

Even as she did, however, she whispered it again. "We chose," she said, her voice ragged as if she had been shouting for hours. "Adolin, we *chose*."

"Blood of my fathers . . ." Adolin whispered.

"What is this?" Sekeir said. "What have you done to her? The sight of you has caused her to rave in madness and—"

He cut off as Maya pointed at him and released a terrifying screech, her jaw lowering farther than it should. Sekeir put his hand to his chest, eyes wide as her screech transformed into words.

"You. Cannot. Have. My. *SACRIFICE!*" she shouted. "Mine. My sacrifice. Not yours." She pointed at the crowd. "Not theirs." She pointed at Adolin. "Not his. Mine. *MY SACRIFICE.*"

"You knew what was going to happen when the Radiants broke their oaths," Adolin said. "They didn't murder you. You decided together."

She nodded vigorously.

"All this time," Adolin said, his voice louder—for the audience. "Everyone *assumed* you were victims. We didn't accept that you were partners with the Radiants."

"We chose," she hissed. Then, belting it loud as an anthem, "*WE CHOSE.*"

Adolin helped her step over to the first row of benches, and the honorspren sitting there scrambled out of the way. She sat, trembling, but her grip on his arm was fierce. He didn't pull away; she seemed to need the reassurance.

He looked around at the crowd. Then toward Sekeir and the other eldest honorspren seated near the judge's bench.

Adolin didn't speak, but he *dared* them to continue condemning him. He dared them to ignore the testimony of the witness they'd chosen, the one they'd pretended to give the power of judgment. He let them mull it over. He let them think.

Then they began to trail away. Haunted, perhaps confused, the honorspren began to leave. The elders gathered around Sekeir, who remained standing, dumbfounded, staring at Maya. They pulled him away, speaking in hushed, concerned tones.

They didn't touch Adolin. They stayed far from him, from Maya. Until eventually a single person remained in the stands. A female spren in a black suit, her skin faintly tinged with an oily rainbow. Blended stood up, then picked her way down the steps.

"I should like to take credit," she said, "for your victory in what everyone assumed was an unwinnable trial. But it was not my tutelage, or your boldness, that won this day."

Maya finally let go of Adolin's arm. She seemed stronger than before, though her eyes were still scratched out. He could feel her curiosity, her . . . awareness. She looked up at him and nodded.

He nodded back. "Thank you."

"Stren . . ." she whispered. "Stren. Be . . ."

"Strength before weakness."

She nodded again, then turned her scratched-out gaze toward the ground, exhausted.

"I don't intend to forget that you testified against me," Adolin said to Blended. "You played both sides of this game."

"It was the best way for me to win," she said, inspecting Maya. "But you should know that I suggested to the honorspren elders that they use your deadeye as a witness. They were unaware of the legal provision that allowed them to speak for her."

"Then her pain is *your* fault?" Adolin demanded.

"I did not suggest they treat her with such callousness," Blended said. "Their act *is* their own, as *is* their shame. But admittedly, I knew how they might act. I wanted to know if a truth exists—the one you said to me."

Adolin frowned, trying to remember.

"That she spoke," Blended reminded him. "To you. That friendship *exists* between you. I sought proof, and found that her name—recorded in old documents of spren treaties—*is* as you said. A curious fact to find. Indeed."

Blended strolled around Adolin and studied Maya's face. "Still scratched out . . ." she said. "Though a bond between you *is*."

"I'm . . . no Radiant," Adolin said.

"No. That is certain." Maya met Blended's gaze. "But something *is* happening. I must leave this place at last and return to the inkspren. If the words this deadeye spoke *are* . . ."

"If what she said is true," Adolin said, "then you have no further excuse for refusing humankind the bonds they need."

"Don't we?" Blended asked. "For centuries, my kind told ourselves an easy lie, yes. That humans had been selfish. That humans had murdered. But easy answers often *are*, so we can be excused.

"This truth, though, means a greater problem is. Thousands of spren *chose* death instead of letting the Radiants continue. Does this not worry you more? They truly believed that—as humans claimed at the time—Surgebinding would destroy the world. That the solution was to end the orders of Radiants. Suddenly, at the cost of many lives."

"Did you know the full cost, Maya?" Adolin asked, the question suddenly occurring to him. "Did you and your Radiants know that you would become deadeyes?"

Adolin felt Maya searching deep, pushing through her exhaustion, seeking . . . memories that were difficult for her to access. Eventually, she shook her head and whispered, "Pain. Yes. Death? No. Maybe."

Adolin sat beside her, letting her lean against him. "Why, Maya? Why were you willing to do it?"

"To save . . . save . . ." She sagged and shook her head.

"To save us from something worse," Adolin said, then looked to Blended. "What does it mean?"

"It means we've had all of this terribly wrong for much time, Highprince Adolin," she said. "And my own stupidity is. I have always thought myself smart." She shook her head as she stood before them, arms folded. "What an effective test. Very effective."

"This?" Adolin said, waving to the empty forum. "This was a complete and utter farce."

"I meant a different test," Blended said. "The *true* trial—the one you've been engaging in for the last few years: the test for this spren's loyalty. She was the only judge who ever mattered, and today was her chance to offer judgment." Blended leaned forward. "You passed."

With that she turned to go and strode up the steps—her stark onyx coloring making her seem a shadow with no accompanying body. "Easy answers no longer are," she said. "But if deadeyes can begin to return . . . this is grand news. Important news. I will convey this to my people.

"I do not know if making new Radiants is a good idea—but I must admit that your ancestors were not traitors. Something *did* frighten them enormously, to cause humans and spren to destroy their bonds. And if the spren did not know they would die . . . then pieces of this puzzle are still missing. The questions are more complicated, and more dangerous, than we ever knew."

With that, Blended left. Adolin let Maya rest for a few minutes. When he finally stood up, she joined him. She followed him as she normally did, expressionless and mild, but he could feel that she was not as insensate as she'd been. She was conserving energy.

She wasn't healed, but she was better. And when he had needed her, she had been willing to struggle through death itself to speak for him.

No, he thought. *She spoke for herself. Don't make the same mistake again.*

He needed to find Shallan and head to the Oathgate so they could share what he'd learned. Maybe the honorspren would swallow their pride and help. Maybe they would, as Blended said, find other reasons to fear.

Either way, he suspected the Radiant relationship would never be the same again.

95

WHAT SHE TRULY WAS

FOURTEEN MONTHS AGO

Venli scrambled through a nightmare of her own making.

Beneath a blackened sky, humans and listeners fought with steel and lightning. She heard screams more often than commands, and beneath it all, a new song. A song of summoning, joined by thousands of voices. The Everstorm was coming, building to a crescendo as the listeners called it.

She'd imagined this day as an organized effort by the listeners—led by her. Instead there was chaos, war, and death.

She did not join in the singing. She splashed through deep puddles, seeking to escape. The Weeping rains streamed down, soft but persistent. She passed listeners she recognized, all standing in a line, their eyes glowing red as they sang.

"Faridai," she said to one of them. "We have to get away. The humans are sweeping in this direction."

He glanced at her, but continued singing. The whole line seemed completely oblivious to the rain, and mostly oblivious to her words. She attuned Panic. They were overwhelmed by the new form, consumed by it.

She felt that same impulse, but was able to resist. Perhaps because of her long association with Ulim? She wasn't certain. Venli hurried away, looking over her shoulder. She couldn't make out much of what was happening on the battlefield. It stretched across multiple plateaus, veiled in mist and rain, shadowed by pitch-black clouds. Occasional bursts of red lightning showed that many of the new stormforms *were* fighting.

Hopefully they could control their powers better than Venli could. When she had released the energy of stormform—expecting grand attacks that smote her foes—the lightning had gone in wild directions, unpredictable. She didn't think she had hurt a single human, and now she felt limp, the glorious energy expended—and slow to renew.

She hid by a large lump of rock that might have been a building long ago. Behind her, humans attacked the line of listeners she'd left; she heard screams, felt a *crack* as lightning was released.

Their song did not start again, but she heard humans cursing and talking in their crude tongue, voices echoing over the sound of the rain. More dead. The storm was building, yes—nearly upon them. But how many listeners would be slaughtered before it arrived?

Surely the other battlefronts are doing better, she thought, squeezing her eyes closed and listening to the Rhythm of Panic. *Surely the listeners are winning.*

What of Ulim's promises? What of Venli's throne? She breathed in cold air, water streaming along the sides of her face, leaving her skin numb and her carapace chilled. She pressed against the rocks, trembling. It was all wrong. She wasn't supposed to be here. She was supposed to be safe.

The sound of boots scraping stone made her open her eyes in time to see a spear coming at her. She lunged to the side, but the weapon struck across the ridges on her cheek and nose, cutting only a thin slice in her skin—mostly deflecting off the carapace mask stormform had given her face.

She fell to the ground in a puddle and tried to pull away, one hand out and pleading. The human loomed over her, a terrible figure with his features completely lost in the shadow of his helm. He raised his spear.

"No, no," Venli said to Subservience in his language. "Please, no. I'm scholar. No weapon. Please, no."

He brandished his spear, but as she cringed—turning aside her face—no blow came. The man stepped away, then jogged off, joining some of his fellows who were forming up against an approaching group with glowing red eyes.

Venli felt at the scrape the spear had caused, amazed at how little it had wounded her. Then she felt at her skin, her clothing. He'd . . . he'd just left her alone. As she'd asked. She stared after the man, attuning Derision. The fool didn't know how important a listener he'd spared. He should have killed her.

Derision seemed to fade though, as she considered. Was . . . was that the proper rhythm, the proper feeling, she should feel upon being saved? What had happened to her these last few years? What had she let happen to her?

For a moment she heard the Rhythm of Appreciation instead. Part of her, it seemed, didn't want to bask in the glory of the new form. Part of her longed for the comforts of the familiar. When she'd been weak.

And this is strength? she thought as she picked herself up off the ground, listening to the thunder.

The new storm was approaching. It would save them, exterminating the humans and elevating the listeners who survived. She simply had to make certain she was one of them. She scurried away to search out a stronger group of listeners to protect her. She entered an open section of plateau, slick with water, near one of the chasms.

Bands of humans and listeners roamed along the edge of the chasm here, trying to get an upper hand against one another. If anything, the fighting in this area was more horrifying. She forcibly attuned Conceit and moved along the perimeter. Conceit. A good rhythm, a counterpart to Determination or Confidence—only grander. Conceit was a proud, strong rhythm with a surging fanfare of quick, complex, and bold beats.

That was how she needed to feel. This was her battlefield. She'd crafted this, she'd brought it all together. There was nothing to fear here. This was her victory celebration.

She passed one of the humans' dead horses, a Ryshadium by the size. It had been killed by lightning, so at least some of her people were capable of controlling their new abilities. Ahead—illuminated by scattered light through a patch of clouds—she saw two brilliant figures fighting along the edge of the chasm. Shardbearers.

Venli didn't know the human, but the listener was Eshonai. She was the last of their Shardbearers. The Plate was distinctive, even if the new form had . . . changed her. It was hard to associate the terrible warlord

Eshonai had become with the thoughtful femalen who had tried so hard to find a way out of the war.

Venli stopped beside a broken spire of rock and hunkered down, watching through the rain as the two clashed. Eshonai—particularly the enhanced Eshonai—could handle a duel on her own. Venli would just be in the way.

She was able to tell herself this, and believe it, right up until Eshonai was shoved off the rim of the chasm. One moment she was holding her own against the human. The next she was gone. Plunged into the abyss.

Venli watched her go with a feeling of disconnect. In Shardplate, Eshonai could survive that fall. Probably. Venli was the one in danger, with the human Shardbearer nearby. The new rhythms thrummed through her, whispering of power. Heightening her emotions. She was herself, not overly influenced by the form. In control. Not a slave.

Yet she felt . . . nothing. For a form that seemed so vibrant with emotions, that was wrong. Could the old Venli have watched her sister take a potentially deadly fall without so much as a sorrowful rhythm? Strange. Why no concern? What was happening to her?

Venli withdrew. She . . . she'd go find Eshonai later. Help get her out of the chasm. They could attune Amusement together as they thought of Venli—a simple scholar—doing *anything* to help in a fight between two Shardbearers.

The battlefield decayed further as Venli sought refuge. Screams. Lightning blasts. She saw in it something more terrible than just a clash over the future of their peoples. She saw something that *enjoyed* the killing. A force that seemed to be growing with the new storm, a force that loved passion, anger—any emotion, but especially those that came when people struggled.

Emotion was never stronger than when someone died. This force sought it, *craved* it. Venli felt its presence like a building miasma, more oppressive than the rainclouds or the storm. She crept among some large rock formations. Lumps that had been buildings, now blanketed by thick crem. She wasn't certain where she was in relation to the center of Narak.

Fortunately, she found a narrow fissure between the ancient buildings. She squeezed in, wet and overwhelmed by the building sensation. Something was coming, something incredible. Something terrible.

The new storm was here.

Venli allowed herself to attune the rhythm of her true emotions—the wild, frenetic beat of the Rhythm of Panic. A more virulent version of the Rhythm of the Terrors. Everything went black, the last few hints of sunlight consumed by the *weight* of this new storm. Then, red lightning. It electrified the sky, and Venli crouched. No. She was still too exposed.

She knew with a sudden, inexplicable confidence that if the storm saw her, it *would* destroy her.

Between bolts of lightning, she pushed out of the cavity of rock and felt her way along the side of the stone building. The winds began to howl. Something else . . . something else was coming. A highstorm too?

Panic almost overwhelmed her. Then—to her incredible relief—her fingers felt something. A hole cut into one of the crem-covered buildings. This was fresh, the cuts unnaturally smooth; a Shardbearer had been here.

She eagerly sought refuge inside, trying to banish the Rhythm of Panic, replace it with something else. Outside, the winds began to clash. She pressed against the rear wall of the small empty chamber, lit by the increasingly violent flashes of light outside. First red. Then white. Then the two tangled like fighting greatshells, crushing the land around them as they grappled.

Debris began to whip past the opening, lit by the rapid flashes, and the rhythms in her head went crazy. Breaking apart, movements of one melding with another. The ground trembled and groaned, and Venli sought to hide deeper in the building, away from the violence. As she passed a doorway, however, the floor undulated and she was cast to the ground.

With a sound so loud her whole body vibrated, an entire section of the stone building was ripped free—including the room she'd just left.

She was pelted by rain, exposed to the howling winds through the broken wall. This was the end. The end of the world. Tiny, terrified, she pressed herself between two solid-seeming chunks of rock and closed her eyes, unable to hear the rhythms over the sound of the tempest.

She knew what rhythm she'd hear if she could, though. For there, pressed between stones, Venli was forced to admit what she really was.

The truth that had always been there, covered over, encrusted with crem. Exposed only when the winds cut her to her soul.

She was no genius forging a new path for her people. Everything she'd "discovered" had been given or hinted at by Ulim.

She was no queen deserving of rule. She cared nothing for her people. Just for her own self.

She wasn't powerful. The winds and the storms reminded her that no matter what she did—no matter how hard she tried, no matter how much she pretended—she would always be small.

She had pretended she was those things, and would likely pretend them again as soon as she could lie to herself. As soon as she was safe. But here—with everything else flayed away and her soul stripped bare—Venli was forced to admit what she truly was. What she'd always been.

A coward.

I tell you; I write it. You must release the captive Unmade. She will not fade as I will. If you leave her as she is, she will remain imprisoned for eternity.

Rlain found her crying.

Venli could count on her fingers the number of times she could remember crying. Not merely attuning Mourning, but actually *crying*. Today she couldn't help herself. She knelt in the sectioned-off part of the infirmary room, overlooking the large map of the Shattered Plains that Rlain had stolen. She was alone. Lirin and Hesina were in the main room, seeing to the patients.

A note on the map hinted at what Raboniel had said: a group of nomads in the hills. Her people. They had *survived*.

She turned to Rlain, who—shocked—was humming to Awe at finding her like this.

"We're not the last," Venli whispered. "They are alive, Rlain. Thousands of them."

"Who?" He knelt. "What are you talking about?"

Venli wiped her eyes—she wouldn't have her tears destroying this glorious map. Venli handed him the note Raboniel had given her, but of course he couldn't read. So she read it out loud for him.

"You mean . . ." he said, attuning Awe. "Thousands of them?"

"It was Thude," Venli said. "He refused stormform. So did most of Eshonai's closest friends. I . . . I wasn't thinking back then. . . . I would have had them killed, but Eshonai separated them off and *let* them escape. Part of her fought, so she gave them a chance, and . . . And then . . ."

Storms, she was a mess. She wiped her eyes again.

"You would have had them *killed*?" Rlain asked. "Venli, I don't understand. What is it you're not telling me?"

"Everything," she whispered to Pleading. "A thousand lies, Rlain."

"Venli," he said, taking her hand. "Kaladin is awake. Teft is too. We have a plan. The start of one, at least. I came to explain it to Lirin and Hesina. We're going to try to wake the Radiants, but we need to get those stormforms out of the room. If you know something that might help, now would be a good time to talk."

"Help?" Venli whispered. "Nothing I do helps. It only hurts."

Rlain hummed to Confusion. At a gentle prompting from Timbre, Venli started talking. She began with the strange human woman who had given her the sphere, and went all the way up to when Thude and the others left.

She didn't hide her part in it. She didn't coat it with the Rhythm of Consolation. She gave it to him raw. The whole terrible story.

As she spoke, he pulled farther and farther away from her. His expression changed, his eyes widening, his rhythms moving from shocked to angry. As she might have expected. As she wanted.

When she finished, they sat in silence.

"You are a monster," he finally said. "*You* did this. You are responsible."

She hummed to Consolation.

"I suppose the enemy would have found another way," he said, "without your help. Regardless, Venli. You . . . I mean . . ."

"I need to find them," she said, rolling up the map. "There are daily transfers to Kholinar. Raboniel has released me from my duties here, and given me a writ allowing me to requisition whatever I need. I should be able to procure a spot in the next transfer, and from there go with some Heavenly Ones on a scouting mission out to the Shattered Plains."

"And in so doing, you'd lead the enemy directly to our people," Rlain said. "Venli, Raboniel obviously *wants* you to do this. She knows you're going to run to them. You're playing into whatever plot she has."

She'd considered that. She wasn't exactly in the most rational state of mind, however. "I have to do something, Rlain," she whispered. "I need to see them with my own eyes, even if I have to *walk* there."

"I agree, we should do that as soon as it's reasonable," Rlain said. He glanced toward the curtains, then spoke more quietly. "But now isn't the time. We have to save the Radiants."

"Do you *really* want me there when you do, Rlain? Do you want me around?"

He fell silent, then hummed to Betrayal.

"Smart," she said.

"I don't want you around right now, Venli," he said. "But storm me, we *need* you. And I think you're trustworthy. You told me this, after all. And who knows how much of what you did was influenced by your forms or those Voidspren?

"For now, let's work on saving the Radiants. If you're truly sorry for what you did, then this is the best way to prove it. After that, we can seek out our people *without* leading the Fused to them."

She looked away, then hummed to Betrayal herself. "No. This isn't my fight, Rlain. It never was. I have to go see if this map is true. I have to."

"Fine," he snapped. He stood to leave, then paused. "You know, all those months running bridges—then training with Kal and the others—I wondered. I wondered deep down if I was a traitor. I now realize I didn't have the first *notes* of understanding what it meant to be a traitor."

He ducked out between the curtains. Venli quietly tucked the map of the Shattered Plains into its case, then put it under her arm. It was time for her to go.

She found both Dul and Mazish caring for the fallen Radiants. Venli pulled them aside, and whispered, "The time has come. Are we ready to leave?"

"Finally," Dul said to Excitement. "We've siphoned away rations, canteens of water, blankets, and some extra clothing from what we were given to care for the Radiants. Harel has it all ready in packs, hidden among the other supplies in the storage room we were given."

"The people are ready," Mazish said. "Eager. We think we can survive in the cold up here for months."

"We'll need those supplies," Venli said, "but we might not have to survive in the mountains. Look." She showed them the writ of authority Raboniel had given her. "With this, we can get through the Oathgates, no questions asked."

"Maybe," Dul said to Appreciation. "So we go to Kholinar, but then what? We're back where we began."

"We take the supplies, and we use this writ to leave the city," Venli explained. "We hike out to the east and disappear into the wilderness to the east of Alethkar, like my ancestors did so many generations ago."

Then we make our way to the Shattered Plains, she thought. But . . . that would take too long. Could Venli find a way to scout ahead, using the aid of the Heavenly Ones? Perhaps get dropped off nearer the Unclaimed Hills, without revealing what she was truly seeking?

It seemed a lot to demand of this one writ. Plus, Raboniel knew about the listeners who had survived. Surely she'd eventually tell the other Fused.

For the moment, Venli didn't care. "Gather the others," she whispered. "The humans are going to attempt to rescue the Radiants here soon. The chaos should cover our escape. I want us to leave in the next day or two."

The other two attuned Resolve; they trusted her. More than she trusted herself. Venli doubted she would find redemption among the listeners who had escaped the Fused. In fact, she expected accusation, condemnation.

But . . . Venli *had* to try to reach them. For when they'd escaped, they'd taken her mother with them. Jaxlim might be dead—and if not, her mind would still be lost to age.

But she was also the last person—the *only* person—who might still love Venli, despite it all.

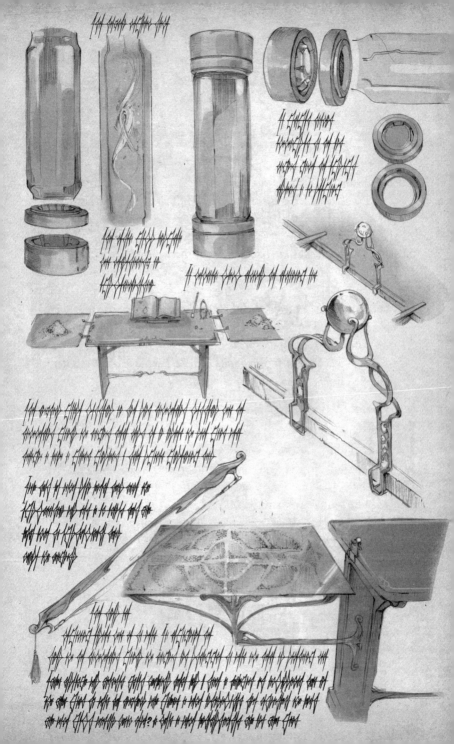

As one who has suffered for so many centuries . . . as one whom it broke . . . please find Mishram and release her. Not just for her own good. For the good of all spren.

For I believe that in confining her, we have caused a greater wound to Roshar than any ever realized.

Navani entered a feverish kind of study—a frantic near madness—as the work consumed her. Before, she had organized. Now she merely fed the beast. She barely slept.

The answer was here. The answer *meant* something. She couldn't explain why, but she *needed* this secret.

Food became a distraction. Time stopped mattering. She put her clocks away so they wouldn't remind her of human constructs like minutes and hours. She was searching for something deeper. More important.

These actions horrified a part of her. She *was* still herself, the type of woman who put her socks in the drawer so they all faced the same direction. She loved patterns, she loved order. But in this quest for meaning, she found she could appreciate something else entirely. The raw, *disorganized* chaos of a brain making connections paired with the single-minded order of a quest for one all-consuming answer.

Could she find the opposite to Voidlight?

Stormlight and Voidlight had their own kind of polarity. They were attracted to tones like iron shavings to a magnet. Therefore, she needed a tone that would push light *away*. She needed an opposite sound.

She wanted fluid tones, so she had a slide whistle delivered, along with a brass horn with a movable tube. However, she liked the sound of the plates best. They were difficult to increment, but she could order new ones cut and crafted quickly.

Her study morphed from music theory—where some philosophers said that the true opposite of sound was silence—to mathematics. Mathematics taught that there were numbers associated with tones—frequencies, wavelengths.

Music, at its most fundamental level, *was math.*

She played the tone that represented the sound of Voidlight again and again, embedding it into her mind. She dreamed it when she slept. She played it first thing when she arose, watching the patterns of sand it made on a metal plate. Dancing grains, bouncing up and down, settling into peaks and troughs.

The opposite of most numbers was a negative number. Could a tone be negative? Could there be a negative wavelength? Many such ideas couldn't exist in the real world, like negative numbers were an artificial construct. But those peaks and troughs . . . could she make a tone that produced the *opposite pattern*? Peaks where there were troughs, troughs where there were peaks?

During her feverish study into sound theory, she discovered the answer to this. A wave could be negated, its opposite created and presented in a way that *nullified* the original. Canceling it out. They called it destructive interference. Strangely, the theories said that a sound and its opposite *sounded exactly the same.*

This stumped her. She played the plates she'd created, indulging in their resonant tones. She put Voidlight spheres into her arm sheath and listened until she could hum that tone. She was delighted when—after hours of concerted practice—she could draw Voidlight out with a touch, like the Fused could do.

Humans *could* sing the correct tones. Humans *could* hear the music of Roshar. Her ancestors might have been aliens to this world, but she *was* its child.

That didn't solve the question though. If a tone and its destructive interference sounded the same, how could she sing one and not the other?

She played the tone on a plate, humming along. She next played a tuning fork, listened to the tones of the gemstones, then came back to the plate. It was wrong. *Barely* off. Even though the tones matched.

She asked for, and was given, a file. She tried to measure the notes the plate made, but eventually had to rely on her own ear. She worked on the plate, filing off small sections of the metal and then pulling the bow across it, getting the plate closer and closer.

She could *hear* the tone she wanted, she thought. Or was it madness? This desire to create an anti-sound?

It took hours. Maybe days. When it finally happened, she knelt bleary-eyed on the stone floor at some unholy hour. Holding a bow, testing her newest version of the plate. When she played this particular tone—bow on steel—something happened. Voidlight was shoved *out* of the sphere attached to the plate. It was pushed *away* from the source of the sound.

She tested it again, then a third time to be sure. Though she should have wanted to shout for joy, she simply sat there staring. She ran her hand through her hair, which she hadn't put up today. Then she laughed.

It worked.

·:·

The next day—washed and feeling *slightly* less insane—Navani incremented. She tested how loud the tone needed to be to produce the desired effect. She measured the tone on different sizes of gemstones and on a stream of Voidlight leaving a sphere to flow toward a tuning fork.

She did all of this in a way that—best she could—hid what she was doing from her watching guard. Hunched over her workspace, she was relatively certain the Regal there wouldn't be able to tell she'd made a breakthrough. The one last night hadn't watched keenly; he'd been dozing through much of it.

Confident that her tone worked, she began training herself to *hum* the tone the plate made. It did sound the same, but somehow it *wasn't* the same. As when measuring spren—which reacted to your thoughts about them—this tone needed *Intent* to be created. You had to know what you were trying to do.

Incredibly, it mattered that she *wanted* to hum the opposite tone to Odium's song. It sounded crazy, but it worked. It was repeatable and quantifiable. Inside the madness of these last few days, science still worked.

She had found Voidlight's opposite tone. But how could she create Light that expressed this tone? For answers, she looked to nature. A magnet could be made to change its polarity with some captive lightning, and another magnet could realign the pole. But Raboniel had mentioned they could *magnetize* an ordinary piece of metal that way too.

So were they really changing the polarity of the magnet? Or were they *blanking* the existing polarity—then rewriting it with something new? The idea intrigued her, and she made a few key requests of her jailers—some objects that would have to be fetched from one of the labs near the top of the tower.

Soon after, Raboniel came to check on her. Navani braced herself. She'd been planning for this.

"Navani?" the Fused asked. "This latest request is quite odd. I don't know what to make of it."

"It's just some esoteric lab equipment," Navani said from the desk. "Nothing of any real note, though it would be fun to use in some experiments. No bother if you can't find it."

"I authorized the request," Raboniel said. "If it is there, you shall have it."

That was a rhythm to express curiosity. She made a note in her book; she was trying to list them all.

"What are you working on?" Raboniel asked. "The guard tells me of a terrible sound you have been making, something discordant."

Damnation. The new tone *didn't* sound the same to a Regal. Could she explain it away? "I'm testing how atonal sounds influence Voidlight, if at all."

Raboniel lingered, looking over Navani's shoulder. Then she glanced at the floor, where a bucket of icy water, with snow from outside, held a submerged gemstone. It was an attempt to see if temperature could blank the tone of Voidlight.

"What are you not telling me?" Raboniel said to a musing rhythm. "I find your behavior . . . intriguing." She glanced to the side as her daughter trailed into the room.

The younger Fused was drooling today. Raboniel had a servant periodically put a cloth against the side of her daughter's mouth. It wasn't that her face was paralyzed; more that she didn't seem to notice or care that she was drooling.

"You write about something called 'axi' in our notebook," Navani said, trying to distract Raboniel. "What are these?"

"An axon is the smallest division of matter," Raboniel said. "Odium can see them. Theoretically, with a microscope powerful enough, we could see little balls of matter making up everything."

Navani had read many theories about such a smallest division of matter. It spoke to her state of mind that she barely considered it a curiosity to have such theories confirmed by a divine source.

"Do these axi have a polarity?" Navani asked, as she monitored the temperature of her experiment.

"They must," Raboniel said. "We theorize that axial interconnection is what holds things together. Certain Surges influence this. The forces between axi are fundamental to the way the cosmere works."

Navani grunted, writing another notation from the thermometer.

"What are you *doing*?" Raboniel asked.

"Seeing if a colder temperature changes the vibrations in a gemstone," Navani admitted. "Would you hold this one and tell me if the rhythm changes—or grows louder—as it warms up?"

"I can do that," Raboniel said, settling down on the floor beside the desk. Behind, her daughter mimicked her. The attendant—a singer in workform—knelt to dab at the daughter's lips.

Navani took the gemstone out with a pair of tongs and gave it to Raboniel. Though Navani could faintly hear the tones of gemstones if she pressed a lot of them to her skin, her skill wasn't fine-tuned enough to detect small changes in volume. She needed a singer to finish this experiment. But how to keep Raboniel from figuring out what she'd discovered?

Raboniel took the sphere and waited, her eyes closed. Finally she shook her head. "I can sense no change in the tone. Why does it matter?"

"I'm trying to determine if anything alters the tone," Navani said. "Creating Warlight requires a slight alteration of Odium's and Honor's tones, in order to put them into harmony. If I can find other things that alter Voidlight's tone, I might be able to create other hybrids."

It was a plausible enough explanation. It should explain her requests for plates and other devices, even the ice.

"A novel line of reasoning," Raboniel said to her curiosity rhythm.

"I had not thought you would take notice," Navani said. "I assumed you were busy with your . . . work." Unmaking the Sibling.

"I still need to bring down the final node," Raboniel said. "Last time I touched the Sibling, I thought I could sense it. Somewhere nearby . . . but it is very, very small. Smaller than the others . . ." She rose from the floor. "Let me know if you require further equipment."

"Thank you," Navani said from her desk. Raboniel lingered as Navani recorded her notes about the ice water experiment.

Navani managed to appear unconcerned right until she heard the plates being shifted. She turned to see Raboniel pulling out the new one, the one she'd hidden beneath several others. Damnation. How had she picked out that one? Perhaps it showed the most use.

Raboniel looked to Navani, who forced herself to turn away as if it were nothing. Then Raboniel played it.

Navani breathed out quietly, closing her eyes. She'd racked her mind for ways to hide what she was doing, taking every precaution she could . . . but she should have known. She was at such a severe disadvantage, watched at all times, with Raboniel always nearby. Navani opened her eyes and found Raboniel staring wide-eyed at the plate. She placed a sphere of Voidlight and played again, watching the Light eject from the sphere.

Raboniel spoke to a reverential rhythm. "A tone that *forces out* Voidlight?"

Navani kept her face impassive. Well, that answered one question. She'd wondered if the person playing the note needed the proper Intent to eject the Voidlight, but it seemed that creating the plate to align to her hummed tones was enough.

"Navani," Raboniel said, lowering the bow, "this is remarkable. And *dangerous*. I felt the Voidlight in my gemheart respond. It wasn't ejected, but my very *soul* cringed at the sound. I'm shocked. And . . . and *befuddled*. How did you create this?"

"Math," Navani admitted. "And inspiration."

"This could lead to . . ." Raboniel hummed to herself, then glanced at the bucket of ice water. "You're trying to find a way to dampen the vibrations of the Voidlight so you can rewrite it with a different tone. A different polarity. That's why you asked about axi." She hummed to an excited rhythm. And Damnation if a part of Navani wasn't caught up in that sound. In the thrill of discovery. Of being *so close*.

Careful, Navani, she reminded herself. She had to do her best to keep this knowledge from the enemy. There was a way, a plan she'd been making should Raboniel intrude as she had. A possible path to maintaining the secrets of anti-Voidlight.

For now, she needed to seem amenable. "Yes," Navani said. "I think what you wanted all along is possible, Raboniel. I have reason to believe there *is* an opposite Light to Voidlight."

"Have you written this down?"

"No, I've merely been toying with random ideas."

"A lie you must tell," Raboniel said. "I do not begrudge you it, Navani. But know that I *will* rip this room apart to find your notes, if I must."

Navani remained quiet, meeting Raboniel's gaze.

"Still you do not believe me," Raboniel said. "That we are so much stronger when working together."

"How could I trust your word, Raboniel?" Navani said. "You've already broken promises to me, and each time I've asked to negotiate for the benefit of my people or the Sibling, you've refused."

"Yes, but haven't I led you to a weapon?" she asked. "Haven't I given you the secrets you needed to make it this far? Within reach of something that could *kill a god*? All because we worked together. Let's take this last step as one."

Navani debated. She knew that Raboniel wasn't lying; the Fused *would* rip this room apart to find Navani's notes. Beyond that, she'd likely take away Navani's ability to requisition supplies—halting her progress.

And she was *so* close.

With a sigh, Navani crossed the room and took her notebook—the one they'd named *Rhythm of War*—from a hidden spot under one of the shelves. Perhaps Navani *should* have kept all of her discoveries in her head, but she'd been unable to resist writing them down. She'd needed to see her ideas on the page, to use notes, to get as far as she had.

Raboniel settled in to read, to learn what Navani had discovered about this new tone—humming a rhythm of curiosity to herself. A short time later, a servant arrived at the door carrying a large wooden box.

"At last." Navani stepped over, taking the box from the servant. Inside was a glass tube a little less than a foot in diameter, though it was several feet long, with thick metal caps on the ends.

"And that is?" Raboniel asked.

"A Thaylen vacuum tube," Navani said. "From the Royal Institute of Barometric Studies. We had this device near the top floor of the tower, where we were doing weather experiments."

She set the device down and took the notebook back from Raboniel, making a few notations to start her next experiment. The metal caps could be unscrewed to reveal chambers that, with the seals in place, wouldn't disturb the vacuum in the central glass chamber. She opened one end, then affixed an empty diamond into it. Next she used her jeweler's hammer to crack a gem full of Voidlight—which made it start to leak. She quickly affixed it into the berth on the other side of the vacuum tube. She redid the ends, then used a fabrial pump to remove the air from the side chambers.

Finally, she undid the clasps that sealed the side berths, opening them to the central vacuum. If she'd done everything correctly, little to no air would enter the central glass chamber—and she now had a gemstone on either end.

Raboniel loomed over Navani as she observed the Voidlight floating out into the vacuum. It didn't act as air would have—it wasn't pulled out, for example. Whatever Voidlight was, it didn't seem to be made up of axi. It was an energy, a power.

"What are we doing?" Raboniel asked softly.

"I believe this is the only way to completely separate Voidlight from the songs of Roshar," Navani explained. "There can be no sound in a vacuum, as there is no air to transfer the waves. So as this gemstone ejects Voidlight, I'm hoping the Light will not be able to 'hear' Odium's rhythm—for the first time in its existence."

"You think it doesn't emit the rhythm itself," Raboniel said, "but *echoes* it. Picks it up."

"Like spren pick up mannerisms from humans," Navani said. "Or how a piece of metal can be magnetized by touching a magnet over a long period of time."

"Ingenious," Raboniel whispered.

"We'll see," Navani said. She grabbed her bow, then pressed the plate against the side of the vacuum chamber and began playing her anti-Voidlight tone.

Raboniel winced at the sound. "The Light won't be able to hear," she said. "It's in a vacuum, as you said."

"Yes, but it's moving across, and will soon touch the empty diamond at the other side," Navani said. "I want this to be the first thing it hears when it touches matter."

They had to wait a good while as the Voidlight drifted in the vacuum, but Navani kept playing. In a way, this was the culmination of her days of fervor. The climax to the symphony of madness she'd been composing.

Voidlight eventually touched the empty diamond and was pulled inside. She waited until a good measure of it had been drawn in, then had Raboniel undo the clasp separating the diamond's enclosure from the vacuum. Navani opened this to a little *pop* of sound, then plucked out the diamond. It glowed faintly violet-black. She stared at it, looking closer, until . . .

Yes. A faint warping of the air around it. She felt a thrill as she handed it to Raboniel—who screamed.

Navani caught the diamond as Raboniel dropped it. The Fused pulled her hand to her breast, humming violently.

"I take it the sound wasn't pleasant," Navani said.

"It was like the tone that plate makes," Raboniel said, "but a thousand times worse. This is a *wrongness*. A vibration that *should not exist*."

"It sounds exactly the same as the tone of Odium to me," Navani said. She set the gemstone on her desk beside the dagger Raboniel had given her. The one that could channel and move Light.

Navani sat in the chair beside it. Raboniel joined her, moving a stool from beside the wall. Together, both of them stared at the little gemstone that seemed so wrong.

"Navani," Raboniel said. "This . . . This changes the world."

"I know," Navani said. She rubbed her forehead, sighing.

"You look exhausted," Raboniel noted.

"I've barely slept for days," Navani admitted. "Honestly, this is all so overwhelming. I need a break, Raboniel. To walk, to think, to gather my wits and get my blood moving again."

"Go ahead," Raboniel said. "I'll wait." She waved for the guard to go with Navani, though the Fused herself continued staring at the gemstone. In fact, Raboniel was so fixated on the diamond that she didn't notice Navani take *Rhythm of War* as she stepped out with the guard into the hallway.

She braced herself. Expecting . . .

An explosion.

It shook the corridor, striking with such physical force that Navani's guard jumped in shock. They both spun around to see smoke spewing from the room they'd left. The guard rushed back—grabbing Navani by the arm and hauling her along.

They found chaos. The desk had exploded, and Raboniel lay on the floor. The Fused's face was a mask of pain, and her front had been *shredded*—her havah ripped apart, the carapace scored and broken, the skin at her joints stuck with pieces of glass. Or diamond? She hadn't taken much shrapnel to the head, fortunately for her, though orange blood seeped from a thousand little wounds on her arms and chest.

At any rate, Raboniel was still alive, and Navani's scheme had failed. Navani had assumed that, in her absence, Raboniel would take the next step—to try mixing Voidlight with the new Light. Raboniel kept saying she expected the Lights to puff away when mixed, vanishing. She didn't expect the explosion.

Navani had hoped that if she died, it would delay Raboniel's corruption of the tower long enough for Navani to properly weaponize this new Light. That was not to be. The explosion had been smaller than the one that had destroyed the room with the scholars, and Raboniel was far tougher than a human.

A treasonous part of Navani was glad the Fused had not died. Raboniel sat up, then surveyed the room. Several of the bookshelves had collapsed, spilling their contents. Raboniel's daughter was still sitting where she'd been, as if she hadn't even noticed what had happened, despite the fact that she bore cuts on her face. Her attendant appeared to be dead, lying slumped on the ground, facedown. Navani felt a spike of legitimate sorrow for that.

"What did you do?" Navani said. "Lady of Wishes, what happened?"

Raboniel blinked as she stood. "I . . . put the diamond we created into the hilt of the dagger, then used the tip to draw Voidlight from another gemstone, to mix them. It seemed the best way to see if the two Lights would cancel one another out. I thought . . . I thought the reaction would be calm, like hot and cold water mixing. . . ."

"Hot and cold water don't immediately annihilate one another when they meet," Navani said. "Besides, heat under pressure—like Light in a gemstone—is another matter."

"Yes," Raboniel said, blinking several times, seeming dazed. "If you use the lightning of a stormform to ignite something under pressure, it always explodes. Perhaps if Voidlight and anti-Voidlight meet in open air, you'd get no more than a pop. But these were inside a gemstone. I have acted with supreme stupidity."

Other Fused—Deepest Ones—melded in through the walls to see what had happened. Raboniel waved them all off as her cuts healed under the power of her internal Voidlight. The Deepest Ones took the servant, who fortunately stirred as they carried him.

The desk was broken, the wall marked by a black scar. Navani smelled smoke—bits of desk still burned. So the explosion had involved heat, not pressure alone. Raboniel shooed away the guard and the other Fused, then picked through the rubble of the desk.

"No remnants of the dagger," Raboniel said. "Another embarrassment I must suffer, losing such a valuable weapon. I have others, but I'll need to eventually move you out of this room and have it scrubbed for every scrap of raysium. We might be able to melt it down and reforge the dagger."

Navani nodded.

"For now," Raboniel said, "I would like you to make me another gemstone filled with that anti-Voidlight."

"Now?" Navani asked.

"If you please."

"Don't you want to change?" Navani asked. "Have someone pick the shards of glass out of your skin . . ."

"No," Raboniel said. "I wish to see this process again. If you please, Navani."

It was said to a rhythm that indicated it would happen, regardless of what Navani "pleased." So she prepared the vacuum chamber—it had been behind Raboniel, sheltered from the brunt of the blast, fortunately. As Navani worked, Raboniel sent someone for another Herald-killing dagger. Why did she need that? Surely they weren't going to mix the Lights after what had happened.

Feeling an ominous cloud hanging over her, Navani repeated her experiment, this time filling the gemstone a little less—just in case—before removing it and holding it up.

Raboniel took it, and though she didn't drop it this time, she did flinch. "So strange," she said. She fitted it into her second dagger. Then she undid a screw and slipped out the piece of metal running through the center. She flipped it around—it had points on both ends, and a hole for the screw—before replacing it.

"To make the anti-Voidlight flow out of the gemstone along the blade?" Navani asked. "Instead of drawing in what it touches?"

"Indeed," Raboniel said. "You may wish to take cover." Then she turned, walked across the room, and stabbed her daughter in the chest.

Navani was too stunned to move. She stood there amid the rubble, gaping as Raboniel loomed over the other Fused, pushing the weapon in deeper. The younger Fused began to spasm, and Raboniel held her, ruthless as she pressed the weapon into her daughter's flesh.

There was no explosion. The Voidlight inside the Fused wasn't under pressure as it was in a gemstone, perhaps. There was a stench of burning flesh, and the skin blistered around the wound. The younger Fused trembled and screamed, clutching at her mother's arm with a clawed hand.

Then her eyes turned milky, like white marble. She went limp, and Navani thought she saw something escape her lips. Smoke? As if her entire insides had been burned away.

Raboniel pulled the dagger out, then tossed it away like a piece of rubbish. She cradled her daughter's body, pressing her forehead against that of the corpse, holding it close and rocking back and forth.

Navani walked over, listening to Raboniel's sorrowful rhythm. Though Raboniel's topknot of hair spilled around her face, Navani saw tears slipping down her red-and-black cheeks.

Navani wasn't certain she'd ever seen a singer cry before. This was not ruthlessness at all. This was something else.

"You killed her," Navani whispered.

Raboniel continued to rock the corpse, holding it tighter, shaking as she hummed.

"Elithanathile," Navani said, whispering the tenth name of the Almighty. "You killed her forever, didn't you?"

"No more rebirth," Raboniel whispered. "No more Returns. Free at last, my baby. *Free.*"

Navani pulled her hand up to her chest. That pain . . . she knew that pain. It was how she'd felt hearing of Elhokar's death at the hands of the bridgeman traitor.

Raboniel had done *this* killing though. Performed it herself! But . . . had the actual death happened long ago? Centuries ago? What had it been like, living with a child whose body constantly returned to life long after her mind had left her?

"This is why," Navani said, kneeling beside the two. "Your god hinted that anti-Voidlight was possible, and you suspected what it would do. You captured the tower, you imprisoned and pushed me, and possibly delayed the corruption of the Sibling. Because you hoped to find this anti-Voidlight. Not because you wanted a weapon against Odium. Because you wanted to show a mercy to your daughter."

"We could never create enough of this anti-Light to threaten Odium," Raboniel whispered. "That was another lie, Navani. I'm sorry. But you took my dream and you fulfilled it. After I had given up on it, you persisted. One might think the immortal being would be the one to continue pursuing an idea to its end, but it was you."

Navani knelt with her hands in her lap, feeling like she'd witnessed something too intimate. So she gave Raboniel time to grieve.

Fused grieved. The immortal destroyers, the mythical enemies of all life, grieved. Raboniel's grief looked identical to that of a human mother who had lost her child.

Eventually, Raboniel rested the body on the ground, then covered up the wound with a cloth from her pocket. She wiped her eyes and stood, calling for the guard to bring her some servants.

"What now?" Navani asked her.

"Now I make sure this death was truly permanent," Raboniel said, "by communicating with the souls on Braize. If Essu has indeed died a final death, then we'll know you and I have achieved our goal. And . . ." She trailed off, then hummed a rhythm.

"What?" Navani asked.

"Our notebook." Raboniel looked toward where it sat on the floor. Navani had placed it there while creating the second anti-Voidlight gemstone.

Raboniel hummed a different rhythm as servants entered, and she gave terse orders. She sent some to burn her daughter's corpse and send honors and the ashes to the family that had donated the body to her daughter. She had others gather the vacuum tube and metal plates from Navani's experiments.

Navani stepped forward to stop them, but Raboniel prevented her with a calm—but firm—hand. The Fused took the notebook from Navani's fingers.

"I will have a copy made for you," she promised Navani. "For now, I need this one to reconstruct your work."

"You saw how I did this, Raboniel."

"Yes, but I need to create a new plate, a new tone. For Stormlight."

Navani tried to pull free, but Raboniel's hold was firm. She hummed a dangerous rhythm, making Navani meet her eyes. Eyes that had been weeping were now firm and unyielding.

"So much for your words about working together," Navani said. "And you *dared* imply I was wrong to keep trying to hide things from you."

"I *will* end the war," Raboniel said. "That is the promise I will keep, for today we have discovered the means. Finally. A way to make certain that the Radiants can no longer fight. They function as Fused do, you see. If we kill the human, another Radiant will be born. The fight becomes eternal, both sides immortal. Today we end that. I have preserved the Radiants in the tower for a reason. Anti-Stormlight will need subjects for testing."

"You can't be implying . . ." Navani said. "You don't mean . . ."

"Today is a momentous day," Raboniel said, letting go and walking after the servants carrying Navani's equipment. "Today is the day we discovered a way to destroy Radiant spren. I will let you know the results of the test."

THE END OF

Part Four

INTERLUDES

HESINA • ADIN • TARAVANGIAN

HESINA

esina made a small notation in her notebook, kneeling above a map she'd rolled out on the floor. The cache Rlain had brought included five maps of Alethkar focused on different princedoms. Sadeas's was included, with notes about singer troop placements in certain cities and whatever else the scouts had seen while doing reconnaissance of the area.

It had taken her until now to realize she could check on Tomat. The city had several long paragraphs of attached observations, written by Kara the Windrunner. The singers had the city wall under repair, which was incredible on its own. That had been broken since . . . what, her *grandfather's* days? The infamous Gap would be gone if she ever visited again.

She couldn't find specifics about the people who had lived in the city, but that wasn't surprising. The Windrunners hadn't been able to get too close, after all. At least there were no reports of burnt-out houses, as in some other cities. It seemed the city had given in without too much of a fight, which boded well for local survival rates.

She wrote each detail in her notebook, then glanced up as Lirin slipped into their sectioned-off surgery chamber. He let the draped sheets fall closed, fabric rustling. He'd been studying the large model of Urithiru that was at the back of the infirmary room.

"You found Tomat?" he asked, adjusting his spectacles and leaning down beside her. "Huh. Anything useful?"

"Not much," she said. "Similar notes to other cities."

"Well, we'd probably know if your father died," Lirin said, straightening to gather some bandages from the counter.

"And how is that?"

"He'd be haunting me, obviously," Lirin said. "Living as a shade in the storms, calling for my blood. As I haven't heard a thing, I must assume the old monster is alive."

Hesina rolled up the map and gave her husband a flat glare, which he accepted with a smile and a twinkle to his eye.

"It's been twenty-five years," Hesina said. "He might have softened toward you by now."

"Stone doesn't soften with time, dear," Lirin replied. "It merely grows brittle. I think we'd sooner see a chull fly than see your father grow *soft*." He must have noticed that the topic legitimately worried her, because he turned away from the gibes. "I'd bet that he's fine, Hesina. Some men are too ornery to be bothered by something as mundane as an invasion."

"He wouldn't give up his business easily, Lirin. He's stubborn as a lighteyes—he'd order his guards to fight, even when everyone else had surrendered."

Lirin returned to his work, and after a short delay, said, "I'm sure he's fine."

"You are thinking that if he lifted a sword," Hesina said, "he deserved whatever he got."

And her father *would* use a sword. Under a special writ of forbearance from the citylord, who—even three decades ago—had been accustomed to doing whatever her father bullied him into doing. She'd met only one man who dared defy him.

"I'm thinking," Lirin said, "that my wife needs a supportive husband, not a self-righteous one."

"And our son?" she asked. "Which version of you does he deserve?"

Lirin stiffened, bandages held in front of him. She turned away, trying to contain her emotions. She hadn't planned to snap at him, but . . . well, she supposed she hadn't forgiven him for driving Kaladin away.

Lirin quietly stepped over, then settled down on the floor beside her, putting aside the bandages. Then he held up his hands. "What do you want of me, Hesina? Do you want me to abandon my convictions?"

"I want you," she said, "to appreciate your incredible son."

"He was supposed to be better than this. He was supposed to be better than . . . than I am."

"Lirin," she said softly. "You can't keep blaming yourself for Tien's death."

"Would he be dead if I hadn't spent all those years defying Roshone? If I hadn't picked a fight?"

"We can't change the past. But if you continue like this, you'll lose another son."

He looked up, then shifted his eyes away immediately at Hesina's cold glare. "I wouldn't have let him die," Lirin said. "If they hadn't decided to go get that Edgedancer, I'd have gone to Kaladin like they asked."

"I know that. But would you have insisted on bringing him here?"

"Maybe. He could have needed extended care, Hesina. Isn't it better to bring him here, where I can watch him? Better than letting him go on fighting an impossible battle, getting himself and others killed in this foolish war."

"And would you have done that to another soldier?" she pressed. "Say it wasn't your son who was wounded. Would you have brought *that* boy here and risked him being imprisoned, maybe executed? You've healed soldiers before, sending them back out to fight. That's always been your conviction. Treat anyone, no strings attached, no matter the circumstances."

"Maybe I need to rethink that policy," he said. "Besides, Kaladin has told me many times that he's not my son any longer."

"Great. I'm glad we could chat so I could persuade you to be *more* stubborn. I see that your thoughts and feelings are evolving on this topic—and because you're you, they're going the absolute *wrong* direction."

Lirin sighed. He stood and grabbed the stack of bandages, then turned to leave their little draped-off chamber.

Storm it, she wasn't done with him yet. Hesina rose, surprised at the depth of her frustration. "Don't you leave," she snapped, causing him to stop by the drapes.

"Hesina," he said, sounding tired. "What do you *want* from me?"

She stalked over to him, pointing. "I left everything for you, Lirin. Do you know why?"

"Because you believed in me?"

"Because I *loved* you. And I *still* love you."

"Love can't change the realities of our situation."

"No, but it *can* change people." She seized his hand, less a comforting gesture and more a demand that he remain there with her, so they could face this together. "I know how stressed you feel. I feel it too—feel like I'm going to get *crushed* by it. But I'm not going to let you continue to pretend Kaladin isn't your son."

"The son I raised would *never* have committed murder in my surgery room."

"Your *son* is a *soldier*, Lirin. A soldier who inherited his father's determination, skill, and compassion. You tell me honestly. Who would you rather have out there fighting? Some crazed killer who enjoys it, or the boy you trained to *care*?"

He hesitated, then opened his mouth.

"Before you say you don't want *anyone* fighting," Hesina interrupted, "know that I'll recognize that as a lie. We both know you've admitted that people need to fight sometimes. You simply don't want it to be your son, despite the fact that he's probably the *best* person we could have chosen."

"You obviously know the responses you want from me," Lirin said. "So why should I bother speaking?"

Hesina groaned, tipping her head back. "You can be so *storming frustrating*."

In return, he squeezed her hand gently. "I'm sorry," he said, his voice softer. "I'll try to listen better, Hesina. I promise."

"Don't just listen better," she said, pulling him out of the draped-off section and waving toward the larger room. "See better. Look. What do you see?"

The place was busy with humans who wanted to care for the Radiants. Hesina had instituted a rotation so that everyone got a chance. Beneath the gaze of two watching stormform Regals, people of all ethnicities—and wearing all kinds of clothing—moved among the comatose Radiants. Administering water, changing sheets, brushing hair.

Hesina and Lirin used a more carefully cultivated group—mostly ardents—to handle delicate matters like bathing the patients, but today's caregivers were common inhabitants of the tower. Darkeyes made up the majority of these, but each and every one wore a *shash* glyph like Kaladin's painted on their forehead.

"What do you see?" Hesina whispered again to Lirin.

"Honestly?" he asked.

"Yes."

"I see fools," he said, "refusing to accept the truth. Resisting, when they'll just get crushed."

She heard the words he left off: *Like I was.*

She towed him by his arm to one side of the room, where a man with only one arm sat on a stool, painting the glyph on a young girl's head. She ran off to her duty as Lirin and Hesina arrived. The man stood respectfully. Bearded, wearing a buttoned shirt and trousers, he had three moles on his cheek. He nodded to Hesina and Lirin. Almost a bow. As far as he could go without provoking a reaction from the watching Fused, who didn't like such signs of respect shown to other humans.

"I know you," Lirin said, narrowing his eyes at the man. "You're one of the refugees who came to Hearthstone."

"I'm Noril, sir," the man said. "You sent me to the ardents, on suicide watch. Thank you for trying to help."

"Well," Lirin said, "you seem to be doing better."

"Depends on the day, sir," Noril said. "But I'd say I'm better than I was when you met me."

Lirin glanced at Hesina, who squeezed his hand and gestured her chin toward Noril's forehead and the glyph.

"Why do you wear that glyph?" Lirin asked.

"To honor Stormblessed, who still fights." Noril nodded, as if to himself. "I'll be ready when he calls for me, sir."

"Don't you see the irony in that?" Lirin asked. "It was fighting in your homeland that made you flee, and therefore get into all the trouble you've faced. Fighting lost you everything. If people would stop with this nonsense, *I* would have to see far fewer men with battle shock like yours."

Noril settled down on his stool and used his hand to stir his cup of black paint, which he placed between his knees. "Suppose you're right, sir. Can't argue with a surgeon about the nonsense we do. But sir, do you know why I get up each day?"

Lirin shook his head.

"It's hard sometimes," Noril said, stirring. "Coming awake means leaving the nothingness, you know? Remembering the pain. But then I think, 'Well, *he* gets up.'"

"You mean Kaladin?" Lirin asked.

"Yes, sir," Noril said. "He's got the emptiness, bad as I do. I can see it in him. We all can. But he gets up anyway. We're trapped in here, and we all want to do something to help. We can't, but somehow he can.

"And you know, I've listened to ardents talk. I've been poked and prodded. I've been stuck in the dark. None of that worked as well as knowing this one thing, sir. He still gets up. He still fights. So I figure . . . I figure I can too."

Hesina squeezed Lirin's hand again, pulling him away as she thanked Noril with a smile.

"You want me to acknowledge," Lirin whispered, "that what Kaladin's doing is helping that man, while my surgeon's treatments could have done nothing."

"You said you'd listen," she said. "You asked what I *want* of you? I want you to talk to them, Lirin. The people in this room. Don't challenge them. Don't argue with them. Simply ask them why they wear that glyph. And *see* them, Lirin. Please."

She left him standing there and returned to her maps. Trusting in him, and the man she knew he was.

ADIN

Adin was going to be a Windrunner someday.

He had it all figured out. Yes, he was just a potter's son, and spent his days learning how to turn crem into plates. But the highmarshal himself had once been a darkeyed boy from an unknown village. The spren didn't *just* pick kings and queens. They watched everyone, looking for warriors.

So, as he followed his father through the halls of Urithiru, Adin found opportunities to glare at the invaders. Many might have said that at thirteen, he was too young to become a Radiant. But he knew for a fact there was a girl who had been chosen when she was younger than him. He had seen her leaving food out for old Gavam, the widow who sometimes forgot to collect her rations.

You had to be brave, even when you thought nobody was watching. That was what the spren wanted. They didn't care how old you were, if your eyes were dark, or if the bowls you made were lopsided. They wanted you to be *brave*.

Glaring at singers wasn't much. He knew he could—and would have to—do more. When the time was right. And he couldn't let the enemy catch him being unruly. So for now, he stepped to the side of the corridor with his father and let the large group of warforms pass. He dutifully stood there, his father's hand on his shoulder, their heads bowed.

But as soon as the warforms had passed, Adin looked up. And he glared after them, angry as he could be.

He wasn't the only one. He caught Shar, the seamstress's daughter, glaring too. Well, her uncle was a Windrunner, so maybe she figured she had a better chance than most—but surely the spren were more discerning than that. Shar was so bossy, you'd think she was lighteyed.

Doesn't matter, Adin reminded himself. *The spren don't care if you're bossy. They just want you to be brave.* Well, he could handle a little competition from Shar. And when he got his spren first, maybe he could give her a few tips.

Adin's father caught him glaring, unfortunately, and squeezed his shoulder. "Eyes down," he hissed.

Adin obeyed reluctantly, as another group of soldiers marched past— all heading for the atrium. Had there been some kind of disturbance? Adin had better not have missed another appearance by Stormblessed. He couldn't *believe* he'd spent the last fight napping.

He hoped the spren would look at people's parents when choosing their Radiants. Because Adin's father was extremely brave. Oh, he didn't glare at passing soldiers, but he didn't need to. Adin's father spent many afternoons tending the fallen Radiants. Directly beneath the gaze of the *Fused.* And every night he went out in secret, doing *something.*

Once the soldiers passed, everyone else continued on their way. Adin's ankle hurt a little, but it mostly felt better from when he'd hurt it. So he didn't even limp anymore. He didn't want a spren to see him acting weak.

What *was* going on? He went up on his toes, trying to look over the crowd, but his father didn't let him linger. Together they entered the market, then turned toward Master Liganor's shop. It felt strange to keep following their normal routine. How could they continue making pottery at a time like this? How could Master Liganor open the shop for business like nothing was happening? Well, that was part of their bravery. Adin had figured it out.

They entered the back of the shop and set up in the workroom. Adin got busy, knowing that they had to act normal—so the enemy wouldn't figure out something was up. You had to get them to feel secure, comfortable. Today, Adin did that by heaving out his bucket of crem, pouring off the water on top, and mixing it until it was a paste. Then he mashed it for his father until it was just the right consistency—a little more squishy than dough.

He worked the lump aggressively, showing those spren—who were undoubtedly watching him by now—that he had good strong arms. Windrunners needed strong arms, because they didn't use their legs much, on account of them flying around everywhere.

As he worked the crem—his arms starting to burn, the earthy scent of wet rock filling the air—he heard the front door shut. Master Liganor had arrived. The old man was nice, for a lighteyes. Once upon a time, he'd done all the glaze work on the pottery himself, but now it was all completed by Gub, the other journeyman besides Adin's father.

Adin mashed the crem to the proper consistency, then handed a chunk to his father, who had been cleaning and setting the wheel. Adin's father hefted it, pushed one finger in, then nodded approvingly. "Make another batch," he said, putting the chunk onto his wheel. "We'll practice your plates."

"I won't need to be able to make plates once I can fly," Adin said.

"And what if it takes you until your twenties to become a Windrunner?" his father asked. "You'll need to do something with your time until then. Might as well make plates."

"Spren don't care about plates."

"They must," his father said, spinning up the wheel by pumping his foot on the pedal. "Their Radiants have to eat, after all." He started shaping the crem. "Never underestimate the value of a job well done, Adin. You want a spren to notice you? Take pride in every job you do. Men who make sloppy plates will be sloppy fighting Fused."

Adin narrowed his eyes. How did his father know that? Was it merely another piece of wisdom drawn from his never-ending well of fatherly quips, or . . . was it from personal experience? Regardless, Adin dragged out another bucket of crem. They were running low. Where would they get more, now that traders weren't coming in from the Plains?

He was halfway through mixing the new batch when Master Liganor entered, wringing his hands. Short, bald, and tubby, he looked like a vase—the kind that had been made with too short a neck to really be useful. But he was nice.

"Something's happening, Alalan," the master said. "Something in the atrium. I don't like it. I think I'll close the shop today. Just in case."

Adin's father nodded calmly, still shaping his current pot. When he was on a pot, nothing could shake him. He kept sculpting, wetting his fingers absently.

"What do you think?" Master Liganor asked.

"A good idea," Adin's father replied. "Put out the glyph for lunch, and maybe we can reopen later."

"Good, good," the master said, bustling out of the workshop into the attached showroom. "I think . . . I think I'll head to my room for a while. You'll keep working? We're low on water pots. As always."

Master Liganor closed and latched the wooden windows at the front of the small shop, then locked the door. Then he went upstairs to his rooms.

As soon as he was gone, Adin's father stood up, leaving a pot *half-fin-ished* on the wheel. "Watch the shop, son," he said, washing his hands, then walked toward the back door.

Short, with curly hair and a quiet way about him, he was not the type someone would pick out of a crowd as a hero. Yet Adin knew exactly where he was going. Adin stood up, hands coated in crem. "You're going to go see what's happening, aren't you? In the atrium?"

His father hesitated, his hand on the doorknob. "Stay here and watch the shop."

"You're going to paint your head with the glyph," Adin said, "and go watch over the Radiants. Just in case. I want to go with you."

"Your ankle—"

"Is fine now," Adin said. "If something *does* go wrong, you'll need me to run home and tell Mother. Plus, if there's trouble, there could be looting here in the market. I'll be safer with you."

Adin's father debated, then sighed and waved him forward. Adin felt his heart thundering in his chest as he hurried to obey. He could feel it, an energy in the air. It would happen *today*.

Today, he'd pick up a spear and earn his spren.

VULNERABLE

Taravangian had given up on being smart.

It seemed that the longer he lived, the less his intelligence varied each day. And when it did vary, it seemed to move steadily downward. Toward stupidity. Toward sentimentality. His "smart" days lately would have been average just months ago.

He needed to act anyway.

He could not afford to wait upon intelligence. The *world* could not afford to wait upon the whims of his situation. Unfortunately, Taravangian had no idea how to proceed. He'd failed to recruit Szeth; Taravangian was too stupid to manipulate that man now. He'd started a dozen letters to Dalinar, and ripped them all up.

The right words. Dalinar would only respond to the *right* words. Plus, whatever Taravangian wrote seemed too much a risk to Kharbranth. He couldn't sacrifice his home. He *couldn't*.

Worse, each day he found time slipping away faster and faster. He'd wake from a nap in his chair and the entire day had passed. Usually it was the pain that woke him.

He wasn't simply old. He wasn't simply feeble. This was worse.

Today, Taravangian forced himself to move to keep from drifting off again. He hobbled through his prison of a house. Trying so hard to *think*. There had to be a solution!

Go to Dalinar, a part of him urged. *Don't write him. Talk to him.* Was

Taravangian actually waiting on the right words, or was there another reason he delayed? A willing disregard for the truth. The slightly smarter version of him didn't want to give this up to the Blackthorn.

He shuffled toward the small bathroom on the main floor, leafing through his notebook, looking over hundreds of crossed-out notes and ideas. The answer was here. He *felt* it. It was so frustrating, knowing how smart he *could* be, yet living below that capacity so much of the time. Other people didn't understand intelligence and stupidity. They assumed people who were stupid were somehow less human—less capable of making decisions or plans.

That wasn't it at all. He could plan, he merely needed time. He could remember things, given a chance to drill them into his brain. Part of being smart, in his experience, was about *speed* more than *capacity*. That and the ability to memorize. When he'd created problems to test his daily intelligence, they had taken these dynamics into account, measuring how quickly he could do problems and how well he could remember the equations and principles needed to do so.

He had none of that ability now, but he needed none of it. The answer *was* here, in the notebook. He settled down on the stool in his bathroom—too tired to move the seat elsewhere—as he flipped through the pages.

Taravangian had a huge advantage over almost everyone else. Others, stupid or smart, tended to overestimate their abilities. Not Taravangian. He knew exactly how it felt to be both smart and stupid. He could use that.

He *had* to. He needed to use every advantage he had. He had to create a plan as daring as the Diagram—and do so without the gifts Cultivation had given him.

The plan of a man, not a god.

He racked his brain for anything in the Diagram relating to Nightblood, the sword. But there was nothing. They hadn't anticipated the sword. Still, he had been given a report by agents he'd sent to research it by interviewing one of its former bearers. Taravangian pulled tidbits from that report from the recesses of his mind, then wrote them on a fresh page of his notebook.

The sword feeds on the essence that makes up all things, he wrote, scribbling by the light of a single ruby sphere. *It will draw out Stormlight*

eagerly, feasting. But if there is no Stormlight, it will feed on one's own soul.
The agent had noted that Nightblood worked like a larkin, the beasts that could feed on Investiture.

What else did he know? What other clues could he give himself?

Odium has greatly expanded intelligence, he wrote. *He can be in many places at once and can command the elements. But he feels the same way a man does. He can be tricked. And he seems to have a central . . . self, a core person.*

Szeth had refused to listen to Taravangian. However, the man *had* come when Taravangian seeded the proper incentive out into the world. So maybe he didn't need to make Szeth do anything other than arrive in the same place as Odium. The Shin assassin was reckless and unstable. Surely Szeth would strike out against Odium if he saw the god manifesting.

But how? How can I possibly make the timing work?

Taravangian sighed, his head thumping with pain. He looked across at the small hand mirror he'd set up on the counter. The ruby sphere he was using for light reflected in the mirror.

But his face did not reflect.

Instead he saw a shadowy figure, female, with long flowing black hair. The entire figure was a shadow, the eyes like white holes into nothingness. Taravangian blinked very slowly, then began to tremble with fear. Storms.

Storms.

He attempted to gather his wits and control his emotions. He probably would have run to hide if he had the strength. In this case, his weakening body served him, as it forced him to sit there until he could control himself.

"H . . . hello, Sja-anat," he finally managed to say. "I had not realized any of the Un . . . Unmade were here."

What is wrong with you? a voice said in his mind, warped and distorted, like a dozen voices overlapping. *What has happened to you?*

"This is how I am sometimes. It is . . . the Nightwatcher's fault."

No, the other one. The god. She touched three that I know. The child. The general. And you. The Old Magic . . . the Nightwatcher . . . I begin to wonder if it was all a cover, these many centuries. A way for her to secretly bring in people she wanted to touch. She has been playing a far more subtle game than Odium realized.

Why did you go to her? What did you ask?

"For the capacity to stop what was coming," he said. He was too frightened to lie. Even the smart him hadn't wanted to face one of these things.

She sows many seeds, Sja-anat said. *Can you do it? Can you stop what is coming?*

"I don't know," Taravangian whispered. "*Can* it be stopped? Can . . . *he* be stopped?"

I am uncertain. The power behind him is strong, but his mind is exposed. The mind and the power seek different goals. This leaves him . . . not weak, but vulnerable.

"I have wondered," Taravangian said, glancing down at his notebook, "if he is merely playing with me. I assume he looks over my shoulder at everything I write."

No. He is not everywhere. His power is, but he is not. There are limits, and his Voidspren eyes fear coming too close to a Bondsmith.

Something itched at Taravangian through the fear and confusion. Sja-anat . . . she spoke like she *wanted* Odium to fall. Wasn't there something in the Diagram about this? He tried to remember.

Storms. Was she tricking him into confessing? Should he stay quiet and not say anything?

No. He had to try.

"I need a way to lure Odium to me," Taravangian said. "At the right time."

I will arrange for you to be given gemstones with two of my children inside, she said. *Odium searches for them. He watches me, certain I will make a mistake and reveal my true intentions. We are Connected, so my children appearing will draw his attention.*

Good luck, human, when he does come. You are not protected from him as many on this world are. You have made deals that exempt you from such safety.

She faded from the mirror, and Taravangian hunched over, trembling as he continued to write.

PART
FIVE

Knowing a Home of Songs, Called Our Burden

THE KNIGHTS RADIANT • NAVANI •
BRIDGE FOUR • TARAVANGIAN •
VYRE • LEZIAN • WIT

I look forward to ruling the humans.

—Musings of El, on the first of the Final Ten Days

To Dalinar, the scent of smoke was inexorably tied to that of blood. He would have trouble counting how many times he'd performed this same long hike across a fresh battlefield. It had become a habit to perform a kind of autopsy of the fighting as he surveyed its aftermath. One could read the movements of troops by the way the dead had fallen.

Swaths of singers there indicated a line had broken and chaos had ruled. Human corpses bunched up against the wide river showed the enemy had used the waters—sluggish, since it had been a few days since the last storm—to push an entire company onto poor footing. Bodies stuck with arrows in the front indicated the first beats of the battle—and arrows in the back indicated the last ones, as soldiers broke and fled. He passed many corpses stuck with arrows bearing white "goosefeathers," a kind of fletching the Horneaters had delivered in batches to aid the war effort.

Blood flowed across the field, seeking little rifts in the stone, places where rainwater had left its mark. The blood here was more orange than red, but the two mixed to make an unwholesome shade, the off-red of a rotting methi fruit.

The smoke hung heavy in the air. On a battlefield this far afield, you burned the dead right here—sending only the officers home, already made into statues by the Soulcasters. Singer and human bodies smelled the same when they burned, a scent that would always bother him because of a specific battlefield. A specific city. A burned-out scar that was the mark of his greatest failure, and his greatest shame.

Charnel groups moved through the dead today, solemnly cutting patches from uniforms, as each was supposed to have the man's name inked on the back by the quartermaster scribe. Sometimes that didn't happen. Or sometimes the writing was ruined in the fighting. Those families would go without closure for the rest of their lives. Knowing, but wondering anyway.

Hoping.

Walking among the dead, he couldn't help but hear Taravangian's terrible—yet hauntingly logical—voice. There was a way to see the war ended. All Dalinar had to do was stop fighting. He wasn't ready yet, but the time might come. Every general knew there was a time to turn your sword point down and deliver it to your enemy with head bowed. Surrender was a valid tactic when your goal was the preservation of your people—at some point, continuing to fight worked contrary to that goal.

He could trust that the Fused were not intent on extinction. Odium, however . . . he could not trust. Something told Dalinar the ancient god of humankind, long abandoned, would not view this battlefield with the same regret Dalinar did.

He finished his grim survey, Szeth at his side as always. Several Azish generals, each newly decorated for their valor in this battle, also accompanied him. Along with two Emuli leaders, who were archers. Remarkably, the highest calling among the Emuli army was seen as *archery*. Dalinar knew his way around a bow, though he'd never considered it a particularly regal weapon, but here it was revered.

Dalinar walked a careful line for the local generals. He did not want them to see how much he reviled the deaths. A commander could not afford to revile the work in which he engaged. It did not make them bad men to be proud of their victory, or to enjoy tactics and strategy. Dalinar's forces would not get far employing pacifists as field generals.

But storms . . . ever since he'd conquered the Thrill and sent it to be sunk deep in the ocean, he'd found himself loathing these smells, these sights. That was becoming his deepest secret: the Blackthorn had finally become what men had been accusing him of for years. A soldier who had lost the will to kill.

He looped around, leaving the dead behind, instead passing victorious companies feasting in the very shadow of their butchery. He congratulated them, acted like the figurehead he'd made of himself. Of all those he saw, only the Mink seemed to notice the truth. That there was a reason Dalinar had worked so hard to find his replacement.

The short Herdazian man fell in behind Dalinar. "The war in Emul is done as of this battle," the Mink said. "The rest is cleanup. Unless the enemy infuses his troops here with serious resources—which would be incredibly wasteful at this point—we'll own Emul within the month."

"The enemy threw it away," Dalinar said.

"That's a stronger term than I'd use," the Mink said. "They fought. They wanted to hold. At the same time, they knew they couldn't move resources away from Jah Keved right now. That would risk destabilizing there, and perhaps lead us to claim it in the coming months.

"It is well the enemy wants to occupy and rule, not just destroy. They *could* have thrown enough at us here to end us on this front—but that would have left the rest of their war efforts in ruin. As it is, they knew exactly how many troops to put in Emul to lure us in with a large enough force—but they also knew to cut their losses if the battle turned against them."

"You've been extremely helpful," Dalinar said.

"Just remember your promise. Alethkar next, then Herdaz."

"Urithiru before both," Dalinar said. "But you have my word. No operations against the Iriali, no attempt to seize Jah Keved, until your people are free."

He likely didn't need the promise—the Mink was a wily man, and had easily recognized that if Dalinar were ever to recover Alethkar, it would be the best thing that could happen for an eventual recovery of the Mink's homeland. Once Jah Keved had gone to the enemy, Herdaz's tactical importance had soared.

The Mink departed to go enjoy the post-battle celebration with his personal unit of Herdazian freedom fighters. Dalinar ended up in the small battlefield command tent beside a goblet full of rubies. Couldn't they have been a different color?

Storms. It had been a long time since a battle had affected him like this.

It's like I'm drifting in the ocean, he thought. *We won today, but Navani is still trapped.* If he couldn't retake Urithiru, everything collapsed. Losing it was a huge setback in his *true* goal: pushing Odium to be frightened enough to make a deal.

So he sprang to his feet with relief when Sigzil the Windrunner entered, along with two of his team and Stargyle the Lightweaver—a handsome man with a soldier's build and a ready smile. The name was a little much; Dalinar doubted he'd had that one since birth, but he had a reputation for friendliness, and the lighteyed women of the court certainly seemed to think highly of him.

Like the other Lightweavers, the man refused to wear a uniform. Something about not feeling right wearing it again. Indeed, he bowed to Dalinar instead of saluting.

"Tell me good news, Radiant Sigzil," Dalinar said. "Please."

"Stargyle?" Sigzil asked.

"Sure thing," Stargyle said, breathing in Stormlight from a pouch at his belt. He began to paint with his fingers in the air. Each of them did it differently—Shallan had explained that they each needed some kind of focus to make their Surgebinding work. Hers was drawings. Stargyle appeared to have a different method, something more akin to painting.

The Lightweaving created a view from above, surveying a shoreline landscape. An army camped along the shore, though it didn't have much discipline. Large groups of men around campfires, no real uniforms. A variety of weapons. Ishar's troops seemed to have good numbers, however, and they were well-equipped. Their success on the battlefields in this region made Dalinar careful not to underestimate them. They might not have proper uniforms, but these were battle-hardened veterans.

"Here, Brightlord," Stargyle said—and the image began moving, as if in real life. "I can keep it all in my head, so long as I focus on the colors."

"The colors?" Dalinar said.

"I was a pigmenter's son growing up, Brightlord. I've always seen the world by its colors. Squint your eyes a little, and everything is really just color and shapes."

Dalinar inspected the moving illusion. It depicted the entire camp of people, and most interestingly a large pavilion at the center. It was colored in ringed patterns, like the bracelets he'd seen Tukari wear. He thought they had religious significance, though he didn't know much about the region. The Tukari were renowned for their mercenaries, their perfumes, and he believed their jewelry.

The illusion rippled as Dalinar walked closer. A single person stood in front of the pavilion. He wasn't wearing the same clothing as the soldiers, and wasn't holding a weapon.

"We get down closer in a second, sir," Sigzil said. "You should notice the person out front."

"I see him," Dalinar said, leaning forward.

Indeed, the image soon drew closer to the pavilion, and the figure became more distinct. An older man. Didn't seem Tukari, or Alethi. Yes . . . he was probably Shin, which was what Wit had said Ishar would appear to be. An older Shin man with a white beard and pale skin. Tukar was named after Tuk, their word for the Herald Talenelat—but it wasn't Taln who ruled them. Not now. It was a different Herald.

Ishar wore simple robes, deep blue. He spread his hands out to the sides, frost crystallizing on the stone around him, forming lines.

A glyph. The symbol for mystery, a question.

It seemed directed at Dalinar specifically. This was absolutely the right man. Dalinar didn't need to consult the drawings that Wit had provided.

He heard a hiss from beside him, and glanced with surprise to see that Szeth had left his post by the entrance to the tent. He'd joined Dalinar, standing very close to the illusion.

"One of my . . ." Szeth stopped himself, likely remembering that he wore the image of an Alethi man. "Blood of my fathers," he said instead, "that man is Shin?"

"Rather," Dalinar said, "he is from the people who long ago settled Shinovar and became the Shin. The Heralds existed before our nationalities were formed."

Szeth seemed transfixed, as if he'd never considered that one of the Heralds might be Shin. Dalinar understood; he'd seen many depictions of all ten Heralds, and they were usually all painted as Alethi. You had to search the masterworks of earlier ages to find depictions of the Heralds representing all the peoples of Roshar.

The illusion moved on from Ishar as the Windrunners finished their sweep of the area, bringing Stargyle higher, safely out of bowshot. The Lightweaving disintegrated.

"That's all we saw, Brightlord," Stargyle said. "I could show it again, if you want."

"No need," Dalinar said. "We've found him . . . and he's waiting for me."

"Waiting for you, sir?" Sigzil asked, glancing toward Lyn and Leyten.

"Yes," Dalinar said. "Do another scouting mission, and report back on what you find. I want to consult with Jasnah first—but we're going to go meet that man, Radiant Sigzil, and find out what he knows."

I had my title and my rhythms stripped from me for daring insist they should not be killed, but should instead be reconditioned. Repurposed.

—Musings of El, on the first of the Final Ten Days

Jasnah leaned back in her chair, lit by spherelight. The spanreed report had just arrived; today's conflict with the enemy armies had ended. The coalition forces had won. Emul was, essentially, now theirs.

She still ached from her part in earlier battles, though she'd sat this one out—Dalinar had been there, and they didn't want to put both of them on the same battlefield at once. Regardless, this particular offensive being finished checked one thing off her list, but there was so much to do, still, with Urithiru in enemy hands.

Her house here in their command camp was far nicer than the one Dalinar had picked for himself. She'd chosen it not for the luxury, or for the space, but because it had a second floor. Locked away in a central room on the second level—sharing no walls with the outside, alone save for Wit's company—she could finally let herself relax. If a Shardbearer broke in, or if a Skybreaker came through one of the upper windows, her fabrial traps would go off—sounding the alarm and giving her time to fight or escape into Shadesmar before she could be killed.

She had a boat waiting on the other side, as close to analogous to this location as Shadesmar would allow. She kept stores of Stormlight in the pockets of her dressing gown, which she now wore. She would never again be caught unaware. She would never again be left struggling in Shadesmar without proper resources, forced to spend weeks hunting a perpendicularity. It was only with these preparations that Jasnah felt safe enough to let herself become frustrated.

In her lifetime studying history, Jasnah had been guided by two principles. First, that she must cut through the biases of the historians in order to understand the past. Second, that only in understanding the past could she properly prepare for the future. She'd dedicated so much to this study. But a life's work could be shaken when history got up and started talking to you.

She leafed through papers more valuable than the purest emerald, filled with her interviews with the Heralds Ash and Taln. Living history. People who had *seen* the events she'd read about. In essence, years of her life had been wasted. What good were her theories now? They were halfway-reliable re-creations of what *might* have happened, pieced together from fragments of different manuscripts.

Well, now she could simply ask. The Challenge of Stormhold? Oh, Ash had been there. King Iyalid had been drunk. The treaty of four nights? A delaying tactic intended to position the enemy for a betrayal. All those debates, and Jochi was right while Jasnah was wrong. Settled as easily as that.

Of course, there were things the Heralds didn't know, things they wouldn't say, or—in Taln's case—things they *couldn't* say. Jasnah flipped through the pages, trying to piece together anything from her more recent interviews that would help with the situation at Urithiru. Even the Heralds knew little of this Sibling, the secretive tower spren.

She needed to present this to the other Veristitalians, see what they could tease from it all. Yet the words of the Heralds cast doubt on her second guiding principle—that the past was the best gauge of the future. There was another way. The enemy could see what would happen in the future. That terrified her. In relying on the past, Jasnah saw the future through occluded glass from within a chasm, if at all. Odium had a prime spot atop the watchtower.

She sighed, and Wit unfolded himself from the chair snug in the corner on the other side of the room. He stretched, then wandered over and knelt beside her before taking her unclothed safehand and kissing the tip of the index finger.

At that, Jasnah felt a little thrill of mystery. She'd come to realize, early in her youth, that she didn't approach relationships the same way everyone else seemed to. Her partners in the past had always complained that she was too cold, so academic. That had frustrated her. How was she to learn what others felt if she couldn't ask them?

She didn't have that problem with Wit. He presented an entire world of other problems, but he never was bothered by her questions. Even if he often dodged them.

"My dear," he said, "you pay me no heed. Be careful not to give undue attention only to the ravings of the mad. I warn you, without proper affection, your Wit will wilt."

She removed her hand from his grip and studied him. Keen eyes. A nose that was perhaps a bit too sharp. Most women, she suspected, would find him physically attractive. And indeed she appreciated his statuesque quality, with such interesting proportions and such an intense face. The nose humanized him, in her opinion, made him feel more real.

Curiously, he wasn't Alethi, but he had transformed himself to look like one. She'd been able to tease that much from him. He was something more ancient. He'd laughed when she'd asked, and said the Alethi hadn't *existed* when he'd been born, so he couldn't have been credited the honor of being one of her gifted people.

She found the way he spoke fascinating. After all this time—and all her worries—here was one who was her intellectual equal. Perhaps her *superior*. She didn't trust him, of course. But that was part of what intrigued her.

"How do we beat him, Wit?" she asked softly. "If he can truly see the future, then what possible chance do we have?"

"I once knew a man," Wit said, "who was the finest gambler in all his realm. Where he lived, you make your cards walk themselves around the table by breathing life into them. He was the best. Intelligent, skilled with the Breath of life, a shrewd gambler—he knew exactly how to bet and when. Everyone was *waiting* for the day when he lost. And eventually he did."

"That's different, Wit," Jasnah said. "He couldn't literally see the future."

"Ah, but you see, I was *rigging* the games. So I did know the future—as much as Odium does, anyway. I *shouldn't* have been able to lose. Yet I did."

"How?"

"Someone *else* rigged the game so that no matter what move I made, I could not win. The game was a tie, something I hadn't anticipated. I'd focused my cheating on making certain I didn't lose, but I'd bet on myself winning. And I bet it all, you see—if I'd have been more clever, I'd have let less be lost."

"So," she said, "how do we set it up so Odium doesn't win, even if he can't lose?"

Wit unfolded a paper from his pocket, still kneeling beside her. He seemed to genuinely like her, and she found his companionship invigorating. Full of questions, delights, and surprises. She could provide the intimacy he desired, though she knew he found her lack of excitement on that axis odd, perhaps unsatisfying. That was not a new experience for her; she'd always found it curious how others put their physical urges ahead of the more powerful emotions of bonding, relating, and engaging.

The chance to scheme, to *connect* with a being like Wit—*that* was exciting. She was curious how the relationship would develop, and that invigorated her. After so many failures, this was something new and interesting.

She cupped his face with her hand. She wished she could, deep down, truly trust him. He was something she, and this world, had never before known. That was electrifying. It was also so *extremely* dangerous.

Wit smiled at her, then smoothed out the paper on her writing desk. It was scribed in his own hand, of course. He came from a land where men had been encouraged to write, the same as women. He shot her a glance, then his smile became a grin. Yes, he *did* seem genuinely fond of their relationship, as much as she was. Indeed, he said it had taken him by surprise as it had her.

"A contract," she said, turning from him and reading the paper. "For Dalinar's contest with Odium." Wit had undoubtedly sculpted each word with precision. "If Dalinar wins, Odium retreats to Damnation for a thousand years. If Odium wins, he must remain in the system, but gets Roshar to do with as he pleases. The monarchs will submit to his rule—as will the Radiants who follow Dalinar."

"Perfect," Wit said. "Wouldn't you say?"

Jasnah sat back. "Perfect for you. If this is agreed to, you win no matter what. Odium remains contained in the Rosharan system either way."

Wit spread his hands before himself. "I've learned a few things since that challenge with the cards so many years ago. But Jasnah, this *is* for the best. If Dalinar wins, well, your people get what they want. But if Dalinar loses, Odium is contained. We're limiting our losses—making certain that at the boundaries of this planet, hell and hate must halt."

"It puts everything on this one contest of champions," Jasnah said. "I hate that tradition even when played for lower stakes."

"Says the woman who used me in a ploy to manipulate that very tradition not two weeks ago."

"Lower stakes," Jasnah repeated, "involving a meaningless loss such as your death."

"Jasnah!"

"Wit, you're immortal," she said. "You told me yourself."

"And you believed me?" he asked, aghast.

She paused and studied him.

He grinned, then kissed her hand again. He seemed to think that sort of thing would eventually spark passion in her. When in truth, physical stimulation was so inferior to mental stimulation.

"I told you I haven't died when killed—yet," he said. "Doesn't mean someone won't find a way someday, and I'd rather not give them an opportunity. Besides, even for me, being killed can confound."

"Don't distract me," she said. "Can we really risk the fate of the world on a simple *duel*?"

"Ah, but it's not a duel, Jasnah. That's the thing. It's not about the *contest*, but what *leads up* to the contest. I know Rayse. He is arrogant and enjoys being worshipped. He never does anything without delighting in how he can show off.

"He's also careful. Subtle. So to win, we need to make him certain he can't utterly lose. This contract does that. If his fail state is that he has to wait a thousand years to try again, well, that won't bother him. He has been here for thousands of years already. So he'll see another thousand as an acceptable loss. But to you and the budding Radiants, a thousand years is a *long* time. Long as a soulless star slumbers."

"A soulless star."

"Yes."

"Slumbers."

"As they do."

She stared at him flatly.

"Long as a rat rends rust?" he asked.

"Long as seasons see stories?"

"Oh, that's *delightful,* Jasnah. Pretend I was the one who could somehow stress said symphonion sounds."

She cocked an eyebrow at him.

"It means beautiful," he said.

"No it doesn't." She again studied the contract. "Sometimes I feel you aren't taking this as *seriously* as you should, Wit."

"It's a personal failing," he said. "The more serious something becomes, the more I find myself inappropriately involved. Indeedy."

Jasnah sighed.

"I'll stop," he said with a grin. "I promise. But look, Jasnah, Rayse—Odium—*is* someone we can defeat. If he has one great failing it's that he thinks he's smarter than he is. He tried exceptionally hard to make Dalinar into his champion. Why? Because he doesn't merely want to win, he wants to win in a way that *says* something. To everyone watching.

"He was so certain he could turn the Blackthorn that he bet almost everything on that singular gamble. Now he must be scared. While he pretends he has a dozen other plans, he's scrambling to locate a champion who can legitimately win. Because he knows—same as I'm telling you—that the contest *won't* only be about who can stab the hardest with their spear."

"What will it be about then?"

"Same thing it's always about, Jasnah," Wit said. "The hearts of men and women. Do you trust the hearts of those who fight on your side?"

She paused, and hoped he didn't read too much into it. Staring at the contract, she couldn't help but feel outmatched by all of this. She, who had been preparing for nearly two *decades* for these exact events, felt uncertain. Did she trust her *own* heart, when confronted with ancient troubles that had surely defeated better women than her?

"A wise answer," Wit whispered.

"I didn't give one."

"A wise answer." He squeezed her hand. "If you give Odium this contract—and get me the *assurance* that he *cannot* break free of this planetary system no matter what happens—then you won't have to trust the hearts of mortals, Jasnah. Because you'll have me. And everything I can give you."

"You've told me he would destroy you if he found you."

"We'll add a line to the contract," Wit said, "naming me as a contractual liaison for Honor—whom Dalinar represents. This will protect me from Odium's direct attacks for the life of the contract. He will *have* to abide by those terms, as they are part of the promise Rayse made by taking up the Shard of Odium. To fail that promise would give others an opening against him, and said failures have killed gods before. Odium knows it. So do this, and I can help you openly. As myself."

"And who is that, Wit?" she asked. "Who are you *really*?"

"Someone," he said, "who wisely turned down the power the others all took—and in so doing, gained freedoms they can never again have. I, Jasnah, am someone who *is not bound*."

She met his eyes—the eyes of something that wasn't a man. A thing that was eternal as a spren. Or, if he was to be believed, something even *older*.

"I feel," she said, "like I should be terrified by that statement."

"That's why I'm so fond of you," he said. "You are poised, you are smart, and you are always ready with a ploy; but when each of those things fails you, Jasnah, you are—above all else—*paranoid*."

Humans are weapons. We singers revere Passion, do we not? How can we throw away such an excellent channeling of it?

—Musings of El, on the first of the Final Ten Days

Kaladin woke with a start, ready to fight.

He struggled, his heart racing as he found his hands bound. Why? What was happening? He grunted, thrashing in the darkness, and . . .

He started to remember.

He'd tied his hands together on purpose, to prevent him from punching someone who woke him, like he'd done to Dabbid yesterday. He gasped, fighting the terror as he huddled against the wall. Kaladin told himself the visions were only nightmares, but he still wanted to claw at his own skull. Burrow into it, pull out all the terrible thoughts, the overwhelming darkness. Storms. He was . . . he was . . .

He was so *tired.*

Eventually he managed to calm himself enough to free his hands. He searched around the black chamber, but saw nothing. They hadn't left out any lights. Teft, however, was snoring softly.

Everything was all right. Kaladin was . . . was all right. . . .

He fumbled around his mat, looking for the canteen he'd placed there when going to sleep. What had awakened him? He remembered a . . . a song. A distant song.

He found the canteen, but then saw a light on the wall. Faint, almost invisible even in the darkness. Hesitant, he wiped the sweat from his brow, then reached out and touched the garnet. A voice, so very quiet, spoke in his mind.

. . . help . . . please . . .

Storms. The tower spren sounded frail.

"What is wrong? They found the last node?"

Yes . . . at . . . the model . . .

The model? Kaladin frowned, then remembered the large model of the tower in the infirmary room. In *there*? Near the Radiants?

Storms. That was where his parents were.

There is something else . . . so . . . much . . . worse. . . .

"What?" Kaladin demanded. "What could be worse?"

They will . . . soon kill . . . all the Radiants. . . .

"The Radiants?" Kaladin said. "The captive ones?"

. . . Please . . . send . . . me Rlain. . . .

The voice faded along with the light. Kaladin took a deep breath, trembling. Could he do this again? He took out a sphere, then woke Teft.

The other bridgeman came awake, grabbing Kaladin by the arm reflexively. His grip was weak. Despite what he said, the time in a coma had left him enervated.

I have to fight, Kaladin thought. *I'm the only one who can.*

"What is it?" Teft said.

"Something's happening," Kaladin said. "The tower's spren woke me, saying the final node has been located. The Sibling told me the Radiants are in danger, and asked me to send Rlain. I think they meant to send Rlain to Navani, like we'd been planning. Our hand seems to have been forced. We need to try to rescue the Radiants."

Teft nodded, groaning as he sat up.

"You don't seem surprised," Kaladin said.

"I'm not," Teft said, heaving himself to his feet. "This was coming, lad, no matter what we did. I'm sorry. Doesn't seem we have time to do it your father's way."

"Watchers at the rim," Kaladin said softly. "We'll need to move quickly. You get Lift ready to sneak in to the Radiants, so she can begin waking them up. I'll make a fuss outside to lure out the guards and distract the Pursuer. If the guards don't come out though, you'll have to neutralize them."

"All right then. Good enough." Teft pointed to the side, to where something lay folded on the ground. Bridge Four uniforms. Kaladin had asked Dabbid to get them changes of clothing. That was what he'd found? As they began to dress, Dabbid returned, frantic. He came up and grabbed Kaladin's arm.

"The tower spren talked to you too?" Kaladin asked.

Dabbid nodded. "They sounded so weak."

"Do you know where Rlain is?" Kaladin asked.

"I'm going to meet him," Dabbid said. "Fourth floor. Something's happened with Venli that has him really shaken. He didn't want to talk in the infirmary."

"Tell him the plan is a go," Kaladin said. "Someone needs to inform the queen. Do you think you two can get to her?"

"Rlain thinks he can," Dabbid said. "I will go with him. People ignore me."

"Go then," Kaladin said. "Tell her what we're doing, and that we're going to have to get the Radiants out. Then you two take up hiding in this room, and don't make any storms. We'll escape with the Radiants, get Dalinar, and return for you."

Dabbid wrung his hands, but nodded. "Bridge Four," he whispered.

"Bridge Four," Kaladin said. "I don't want to leave you two alone, Dabbid, but we *need* to move now—and I want the queen to be contacted. Plus . . . the Sibling said something. About sending Rlain to them."

"They said it to me too," Dabbid said. He gave the salute, which Kaladin returned, then moved off at a run.

"If something goes wrong," Kaladin said to Teft, continuing to dress in his uniform, "get out that window."

They'd practiced Kaladin's trick of infusing objects and his boots to climb down walls. In an emergency, someone might have to jump out the window and hope to regain their powers before they hit the ground—but that was an absolute last resort. The current plan was for the Windrunners to climb down the outside, each with another Radiant strapped to their backs.

It was far from a perfect plan, but it was better than letting the Fused murder the Radiants while they were in comas.

"Even if you only get yourself out," Kaladin said, "do it, rather than staying and making a hopeless stand. Take your spren and get to Dalinar."

"And you?" Teft said. "You'll follow, right?"

Kaladin hesitated.

"If I run, you run," Teft said. "Look, what happened the last two times a node was discovered?"

"The Pursuer was waiting for me," Kaladin admitted.

"He will be again," Teft said. "This is a trap, plain and simple. What the enemy *doesn't* know is that we don't care about the node. We're trying to free the Radiants. So distract him a little, yes, but then run and let them have their storming fabrial."

"I could try that."

"Give me an oath, lad. We can't do anything more in this tower. We need to reach Dalinar. I'm going to head that way with as many Radiants as I can rescue. You've got my back, right?"

"Always," Kaladin said, nodding. "I swear it. Get as many of the Radiants out as you can, and then run. Once you do, I'll follow."

I love their art. The way they depict us is divine, all red shades and black lines. We appear demonic and fearsome; they project all fear and terror upon us.

—Musings of El, on the first of the Final Ten Days

D alinar stepped into the Prime's warcamp home, and immediately felt as if he'd entered the wrong building. Surely this was a storage room where they were keeping extra furniture gathered from the surrounding abandoned towns.

But no, Dalinar was merely accustomed to austerity. It was an Alethi wartime virtue for a commander to eschew comfort. Dalinar had perhaps taken this idea too far on occasion—but he'd become comfortable with simple furniture, bare walls. Even his rooms in Urithiru had grown too cluttered for his taste.

Young Yanagawn came from a different tradition. This entry room was so full of rich furniture—painted bronze on every surface that wasn't of some plush material—that it created a maze Dalinar had to wind through to reach the other side. Adding to the difficulty, the room was *also* packed with a battalion's worth of servants. Twice Dalinar encountered someone in bright Azish patterns who had to physically climb onto a couch to let him pass.

Where had they found all of this? And those tapestries draping every visible space on the walls. Had they carried them all this way? He knew the Azish were more accustomed to long supply chains—they didn't have access to the number of food-making Soulcasters that the Alethi did—but this was excessive, wasn't it?

Though, he noted, turning back across the room as he reached the other side, *this would certainly slow an assassin or a force who tried to break in here and attack the Prime.*

In the next room he found an even greater oddity. The Prime—Yanagawn the First, Emperor of Makabak—sat in a throne at the head of a long table. Nobody else ate at the table, but it was stuffed with lit candelabras and plates of food. Yanagawn was finishing his breakfast, mostly pre-cut fruit. He wore a mantle of heavy cloth and an ornate headdress. He ate primly, spearing each bite of fruit with a long skewer, then raising it to his lips. He barely seemed to move, with one hand held crossed before his chest as he manipulated the skewer with the other.

A large rank of people stood to either side of him. They mostly seemed to be camp followers. Washwomen. Wheelwrights. Reshi chull keepers. Seamstresses. Dalinar picked out only a few uniforms.

Jasnah had already arrived for the meeting. She stood among the groups of people, and a servant ushered Dalinar in that direction as well, so he joined the bizarre display. Standing and watching the emperor eat his fruit one delicate bite at a time.

Dalinar liked the Azish—and they'd proven to be good allies with a shockingly effective military. But storms above and Damnation beyond, were they strange. Although curiously, he found their excess to be less nauseating than when an Alethi highprince indulged. In Alethkar this would be an expression of arrogance and a lack of self-restraint.

Here, there was a certain . . . cohesion to the display. Alethi servants of the highest order wore simple black and white, but the Azish ones were dressed almost as richly as the emperor. The overflowing table didn't seem to be *for* Yanagawn. He was merely another ornament. This was about the position of Prime, and the empire itself, more than an elevation of the individual man.

From what Dalinar had heard, they'd had trouble appointing this most recent Prime. The reason for that was, of course, standing directly behind Dalinar: Szeth, the Assassin in White, had killed the last two Primes.

At the same time, Dalinar couldn't imagine *anyone* wanting to be Prime. They had to deal with all this pomp, always on display. Maybe *that* was why their "scholarly republic" worked in a way Jasnah liked so much. They had accidentally made the position of emperor so awful, no sane person would want it—so they'd needed to find other ways to rule the country.

Dalinar had learned enough social grace to remain quiet until the display was complete. Each of the onlookers was then given a bronze plate full of food, which they accepted after bowing to the emperor. As they left one by one, other servants quickly made space at the table for Jasnah and Dalinar, though the clock he wore in his arm bracer told him he was still a few minutes early for the meeting.

Damnation's own device, that was. Had him hopping about like the Prime. Though admittedly, Dalinar was realizing how much less of his time was wasted now that everyone knew precisely when to meet together. Without ever saying a word, Navani was bringing order to his life.

Be safe. Please. My life's light, my gemheart.

He sent Szeth out, as neither of the other two monarchs had guards in the room. As they settled—the last of the observers leaving—Noura bowed to the Prime, then took a seat at the table deliberately positioned to be lower than the three of them. Some in the empire considered it a scandal that Dalinar, Jasnah, and Fen were always seated at the same height as the Prime, but Yanagawn had insisted.

"Dalinar, Jasnah," the youth said, relaxing as he removed his headdress and set it onto the table. Noura gave him a glance at that, but Dalinar smiled. She obviously thought the Prime should maintain decorum, but Dalinar liked seeing the youth grow more comfortable with his position and his fellow monarchs. "I'm sorry we didn't have plates of food for you as well," Yanagawn continued in Azish. "I should have known you'd both arrive early."

"It would have made a fine memento, Majesty," Jasnah said, laying out some papers on the table. "But we were not of the chosen today, so it wouldn't feel right to be so favored."

The boy looked to Noura. "I told you she understood."

"Your wisdom grows, Imperial Majesty," the older woman said. She was an Azish vizier—a high-level civil servant. Her own outfit had less gold on it than the Prime's, but it was nevertheless fantastically colored, with a cap and contrasting coat of a multitude of patterns and hues. Her long hair was greying and wound into a braid that emerged from her cap on one side.

"All right, Jasnah," Yanagawn said, leaning forward to inspect Jasnah's papers—though as far as Dalinar knew, he couldn't read Alethi. "Tell it to me straight."

Dalinar braced himself.

"We have practically no chance of recovering Urithiru," Jasnah said in Azish, her voice barely accented. "Our scouts confirm that fabrials don't work near it. That means if we were to re-create a smaller version of my mother's flying machine to deliver troops, it would drop the moment it drew too close.

"They've also blocked off the caverns. My uncle delivered a small force to the bottom, and that action seems to have informed the enemy that we know their ruse is up. They are no longer sending fake messages via spanreed, and we've seen singer troops on the balconies.

"With a Shardblade—which we discovered can be delivered into the protected area so long as it is not bound—our troops can cut through the blockage at the bottom. But while doing that the force would be exposed to archers on higher ground. And if we made it through that rubble, fighting all the way up through a contested tunnel system would be a nightmare.

"A march by soldiers along the tops of the mountains is impossible for a multitude of reasons. But if we *did* reach the tower, we'd lose. Our battlefields are a careful balance of Radiant against Fused, Shardbearer against Regal, soldier against soldier. At Urithiru, we'd have no Radiants—and the entire strategy would topple."

"We'd have Kaladin," Dalinar said. "His powers still work. The Stormfather thinks it's because he's far enough along in his oaths."

"With all due respect to him," Jasnah said, "Kaladin is just one man—and one you *relieved of duty* before we left."

She was correct, of course. Common sense dictated that one man was nothing against an army of Fused. Yet Dalinar wondered. Once, in the warcamps, he'd argued with Kaladin's soldiers who had set up a vigil for the young Windrunner—then presumed dead. Dalinar had been proven wrong that time. Now, he found himself possessing some of the same faith as those soldiers.

Beaten down, broken, surrounded by enemies, Kaladin continued to fight. He knew how to take the next step. They couldn't leave him to take it alone.

"Our best chance," Dalinar said to the others, "is to deliver me and a force through Shadesmar to the tower. I might be able to open a perpendicularity there, and we could surprise the enemy with an attack."

"You *might* be able to open one there, Uncle," Jasnah said. "What does the Stormfather think?"

"He isn't certain I am far enough along in my oaths or my skills to manage it yet," Dalinar admitted.

Jasnah tapped her notes. "An assault through Shadesmar would require a large number of ships—something we don't have on that side, and which I see no way of obtaining."

"We *need* to find a way to support Kaladin, Navani, and whatever resistance they are building," Dalinar said. "We might not need a large force of ships. A small group of trained soldiers might be able to sneak in, then disable the fabrial the enemy is using to stop Radiants."

"Undoubtedly," Jasnah said, "that is the method the enemy used to get *into* the tower. They will be guarding against this same tactic."

"So what?" Yanagawn said, chewing on some nuts he had hidden in a pocket of his oversized robes. "Jasnah, you argue against every point Dalinar makes. Are you saying we should give up *Urithiru* to the enemy?"

"Our entire war effort falls apart without it," Noura said. "It was the means by which we connected our disparate forces!"

"Not necessarily," Jasnah said, showing some small maps to the Prime. "As long as we have a stronger navy—and proper air support—we can control the southern half of Roshar. It will necessitate weeks or months of travel—but we can coordinate our battlefields as long as we have spanreeds."

"Still," Yanagawn said, glancing at Noura. The older woman nodded in agreement.

"This is a major blow," Dalinar said. "Jasnah, we *can't* simply abandon Urithiru. You yourself spent *years* trying to locate it."

"I'm not suggesting we do, Uncle," she said, her voice cold. "I'm merely presenting facts. For now, I think we need to act as if we will not soon retake the tower—which might mean moving against Ishar's forces in Tukar, so we can secure those positions. At any rate, we should be planning how to support our forces in southern Alethkar against the Vedens."

They were all valid points, the core of a cohesive and well-reasoned battle strategy. She was trying hard, and mostly succeeding, at learning to be a capable tactical commander. He couldn't blame her for feeling she had something to prove there; her entire life had been a series of people demanding she prove herself to them.

However, her quickness to abandon Urithiru smelled too similar to what Taravangian had done in abandoning Roshar. Give up quickly, once you think you're beaten.

"Jasnah," he said, "we *need* to try harder to liberate Urithiru."

"I'm not saying we shouldn't, only that such an action is going to be very difficult and costly. I'm trying to outline those costs so we're aware of them."

"The way you talk lacks hope."

"'Hope,'" she said, spreading her papers out on the table. "Have I ever told you how much I dislike that word? Think of what it means, what it implies. You have hope when you're outnumbered. You have hope when you lack options. Hope is always irrational, Uncle."

"Fortunately, we are not entirely rational beings."

"Nor should we want to be," she agreed. "At the same time, how often has 'hope' been the reason someone refuses to move on and accept a realistic attitude? How often has 'hope' caused more pain or delayed healing? How often has 'hope' prevented someone from standing up and doing what needs to be done, because they cling to a wish for everything to be different?"

"I would say," Yanagawn said, leaning forward, "that hope defines us, Jasnah. Without it, we are not human."

"Perhaps you are correct," Jasnah said, a phrase she often used when she wasn't convinced—but also didn't want to continue an argument. "Very well then, let us discuss Urithiru."

"Your powers will work," Dalinar said, "at least partially. You have said the Fourth Ideal."

"Yes," she said. "I have—though the Stormfather is uncertain whether the fourth oath will truly allow a Radiant to withstand the suppression. Am I correct?"

"You are," Dalinar said. "But if the enemy is resupplying via the Oathgates, there is only *one* way we can realistically do anything about this situation. We must destroy their suppression fabrial. And so my suggestion of a small team makes the most sense."

"And you are to lead it?" Jasnah said.

"Yes," Dalinar said.

"You are still far from mastering your powers. What if you *can't* open a perpendicularity at Urithiru?"

"I've been experimenting, practicing," Dalinar said. "But yes, I've a long way to go. So I've been considering another solution." He selected one of Jasnah's maps, then turned it for the others to see. "We came here to Emul to use a hammer-and-anvil tactic, shoving our enemy against an army here. The army of Ishar, the being the Azish call Tashi."

"Yes, and?" Jasnah asked.

"I have scouts surveying his position," Dalinar said, "and have visual confirmation—shown to me via Lightweaving—that the man himself is there. Wit's drawings confirm it. I have spoken with the Stormfather, and the two of us think this is our best solution. Ishar is a master with the Bondsmithing art. If I can recruit him, he could be the secret to saving Urithiru."

"Pardon," Noura said. "But haven't we determined that the Heralds are all . . . insane?" It was hard for her to say; their religion viewed the Heralds as deities. The Makabaki people worshipped *them*, and not the Almighty.

"Yes," Dalinar said, "but Ash indicates Ishar might have escaped with less damage than others. She trusts him."

"We've had letters from Ishar, Uncle," Jasnah said. "That are not encouraging."

"I want to try speaking with him anyway," Dalinar said. "We've been mostly ignoring his armies, other than to use them as our anvil. But if I were to approach with a flag of peace and parley, Ishar—"

"Wait," Yanagawn said. "You're going to go personally?"

"Yes," Dalinar said. "I need to see Ishar, ask him questions."

"Send your Radiants," Noura said. "Take this being captive. Bring him here. Then talk to him."

"I would rather go myself," Dalinar said.

"But . . . ." Yanagawn said, sounding utterly baffled. "You're a king.

This is even worse than when Jasnah went out in Plate and fought the enemy!"

"It's an old family tradition, Majesty," Jasnah said. "We are prone to putting ourselves into the thick of things. I blame long-standing Alethi conditioning that says the best general is the one who leads the charge."

"I suppose," Yanagawn said, "that a history of having excessive numbers of Shards might create a feeling of invincibility. But Dalinar, why do you raise this point now? To get our advice?"

"More to warn you," he said. "I've deliberately put the Mink in command of our military so I can step away to see to more . . . spiritual matters. Jasnah and Wit are preparing a contract for me to present to Odium, once we have pushed him to come speak to me again.

"Until we can make that work, I need to do something to help. I need to bring Ishar to our side—then see if he can teach me how to restore the Oathpact and help me rescue Urithiru."

"Well," Yanagawn said, looking to Noura. "Being allies with the Alethi is . . . interesting. Go with Yaezir's own speed then, I suppose."

Yaezir is dead, Dalinar thought, though he didn't say it.

Jasnah took the reins of the conversation next, explaining the contract she was preparing for Odium. She and Dalinar had already talked to Queen Fen earlier, via spanreed. Dalinar offered some explanations, but mostly let Jasnah do the persuading. She had an uphill battle, as getting the monarchs to agree to this contest would take some doing.

Jasnah could manage it; he was confident in her. His job, he was increasingly certain, involved his Bondsmithing, the Oathpact, and the Heralds.

Eventually the meeting came to an end. They agreed to meet again to talk over more points in the contract, but for now Yanagawn had to attend some religious ceremonies for his people. Dalinar needed to prepare for his trip to Tukar; he intended to go as soon as was reasonable.

As they rose to leave, Yanagawn replaced his headdress. "Dalinar," the youth said, "do we know anything of Lift? We left her at the tower."

"Kaladin said the other Radiants were unconscious," Dalinar said. "That probably includes her."

"Maybe," Yanagawn said. "She often does what she isn't supposed to. If you hear word, send to me, please?"

Dalinar nodded, joining Jasnah and withdrawing from Yanagawn's palace. The exterior might look as ordinary as every other building in the village, but a palace it was.

He collected Szeth, who was holding something for him. Dalinar took the large book—intimidating in size, though he knew it to be shorter than it appeared. The paper inside was covered with his own bulky letter-lines, larger and thicker than was proper, drawn deliberately with his fat fingers.

He held the book toward Jasnah. He'd allowed early drafts and portions of it to be shared—and they'd gotten out all over the coalition by now. However, he hadn't considered the book finished until he'd made some last changes earlier this week.

"*Oathbringer?*" she said, taking it eagerly. "It's complete?"

"No, but my part is done," Dalinar said. "This is the original, though the scribes have made copies following my last round of alterations. I wanted you to have the one I wrote."

"You should feel proud, Uncle. You make history with this volume."

"I fear you'll find it to be mostly religious drivel."

"Ideas are not useless simply because they involve religious thinking," Jasnah said. "Nearly all of the ancient scholars I revere were religious, and I appreciate how their faith shaped them, even if I do not appreciate the faith itself."

"The things you said about hope in the meeting," Dalinar said. "They bothered me, Jasnah. But perhaps in a good way. Who in the world would dispute an idea as fundamental as hope? Yet because we all accept it as vital, we don't think about it. What it really means. You do."

"I try," she said, glancing back toward the Prime's palace. "Tell me. Am I pushing too hard to establish myself as a military leader? I feel it's an important precedent, as your book here is, but . . . I hit the target a little too squarely, didn't I?"

Dalinar smiled, then put his hand on hers, which held up the book. "We are revealing a new world, Jasnah, and the way before us is dark until we bring it light. We will be forgiven if we stumble on unseen ground now and then." He squeezed her hand. "I would like you to do something for me. All of the great philosophical texts I've read have an undertext."

"Yes, about that . . ." He wasn't the only man who had been shaken to discover that for centuries, the women in their lives had been leaving commentaries for one another. Something dictated by a man would often have his wife's or scribe's thoughts underneath, never shared aloud. An entire world, hidden from those who thought they were ruling it.

"I would like you to write the undertext for *Oathbringer*," Dalinar said. "Openly. To be read and discovered by any who would like to read it."

"Uncle?" Jasnah said. "I'm not certain the tradition should continue. It was questionable to begin with."

"I find the insights offered in the undertexts to be essential," Dalinar said. "They change how I read. History is written by the victors, as many are fond of saying—but at least we have contrary insights by those who watched. I would like to know what you think of what I've said."

"I will not hold back, Uncle," Jasnah said. "If much of this *is* religious, I will be compelled to be honest. I will point out your confirmation biases, your fallacies. Perhaps it would be better if you gave the undertext task to my mother."

"I considered that," he said. "But I promised to unite instead of divide. I don't do that by giving my book only to those who agree with me.

"If we're revealing a new world, Jasnah, should we not do it together? Arguments and all? I feel like . . . like we are never going to agree on the details, you and I. This book though—it could show that we agree on the more important matters. After all, if an avowed atheist and a man starting his own religion can unite, then who can object that *their* personal differences are too large to surmount?"

"That's what you're doing, then?" she asked. "Creating a religion?"

"Revising the old one, at the very least," Dalinar said. "When the full text of this is released . . . I suspect it will create a larger schism among Vorinism."

"Me being involved won't help that."

"I want your thoughts nonetheless. If you are willing to give them."

She pulled the book close. "I consider it among the greatest honors I have ever been offered, Uncle. Be warned, however, I am not known for my brevity. This could take me years. I will be thorough, I will offer counterpoints, and I may undermine your entire argument. But I *will* be respectful."

"Whatever you need, Jasnah." He smiled. "I hope that in your additions, we will create something greater than I could have alone."

She smiled back. "Don't say it that way. You make it sound like the odds are against it being possible, where I should say that is the most reasonable outcome. Thank you, Uncle. For your trust."

HIGHSTORM COMING

> *To humans, our very visages become symbols. You find echoes of it*
> *even in the art from centuries before this Return.*

> —Musings of El, on the first of the Final Ten Days

There was a long line at the Oathgates today, but that was nothing new. Raboniel was certain the human kingdoms knew of the occupation by now, and so had authorized the Oathgates to be opened more frequently, allowing singer troops and servants occupying the tower to rotate out.

Venli's group of fifteen friends huddled behind her, holding their supplies—hopefully appearing to be merely another batch of workers given a chance to return to Kholinar for a break. Venli pulled her coat tight against the wind. Listeners didn't get as cold as humans seemed to, but she could still feel the bite of the wind—particularly since this form had carapace only as ornamentation, not true armor.

She wasn't completely certain what to do after reaching Kholinar. Raboniel's writ would certainly get her people out of the city, and even out of Alethkar. But Venli couldn't wait the weeks or months it would take for them to walk to the Shattered Plains. She *had* to find out if her mother was still alive.

How far would the power of the writ go? Raboniel was feared, respected. Could Venli get her entire team of fifteen flown to that scout post via Heavenly One? Her mind spun with lies about a secret mission from Raboniel at the Shattered Plains. Indeed, it wasn't too far from the truth. Raboniel had all but commanded her to go investigate the listener remnants.

And what then? Venli thought. *Raboniel knows about them. She knows I'm going. She's manipulating me. For what end?*

It didn't matter. Venli had to go. It was time.

Timbre pulsed softly as she stood in the line, map case over her shoulder, trying to ignore the wind.

"Are you disappointed in me?" Venli whispered to Conceit. "For leaving Rlain and the humans?"

Timbre pulsed. Yes, she was. The little spren was never afraid to be straight with Venli.

"What do you expect me to do?" she whispered, turning her head away from Dul so he wouldn't hear her talking. "Help with their insane plan? He'll get all those Radiants killed. Besides, you think I'd be any help to them?"

Timbre pulsed. Venli was doing well. Learning. She could help.

If I weren't a coward, Venli thought. "What if we got you a different host? A singer who cares, like Rlain."

Timbre pulsed.

"What do you mean?" Venli demanded. "You can't *want* me. I'm an accident. A mistake."

Another pulse.

"Mistakes can't be wonderful, Timbre. That's what *defines* them as mistakes."

She pulsed, more confident. How could she be *more* confident with each complaint? Stupid spren. And why wasn't this line moving? The transfers should be quick; they needed to exchange people and supplies before the highstorm arrived.

Venli told her people to wait, then stepped out of line. She marched to the front, where a couple of singers—formerly Azish, by their clothing— were arguing.

"What is it?" Venli demanded to Craving.

The two took in her Regal form, then the femalen answered. "We have to wait to perform the exchange, Chosen," she said, using an old formal singer term. "The human who works the Oathgates for us has run off."

"No one else has a living Blade, which is needed to operate the fabrial now," the other explained. "If you could find the one they call Vyre, and ask when he will return . . ."

Venli glanced toward the sky. She could feel the wind picking up. "The highstorm is nearly here. We should move everyone inside."

The two argued at first, but Venli spoke more firmly. Soon they started herding the frustrated singers toward the tower. Venli walked along the plateau, Timbre pulsing excitedly. She saw this as an opportunity.

"Why do you believe in me?" Venli whispered. "I've given you no reason. I've ruined everything I've touched. I'm a selfish, impotent, sorry excuse for a listener."

Timbre pulsed. Venli had saved her. Venli had saved Lift.

"Yes, but I had to be coaxed into both," Venli said. "I'm not a hero. I'm an accident."

Timbre was firm. Some people charged toward the goal, running for all they had. Others stumbled. But it wasn't the speed that mattered.

It was the direction they were going.

Venli lingered at the entrance to Urithiru. She hesitated, glancing over her shoulder. The previous highstorm had reached all the way past the sixth tier. This one would likely envelop nearly the entire tower, a rare occurrence, their scholars thought. She felt as if she could sense the power of it, the fury bearing down on them.

"What if," she whispered to Timbre, "I offered to use this writ to smuggle Stormblessed or his family out of Urithiru?"

Timbre pulsed uncertainly. Would the writ's authority extend that far? Venli thought perhaps it would. She wouldn't be able to get any of the unconscious Radiants out; they were too closely watched, and someone would send to Raboniel for confirmation. But a few "random" humans? That might work.

She found Dul and the others inside the front doors. Venli gathered them around, away from prying ears, and quickly handed her writ to Mazish. "Take this," Venli said. "If I don't return, you should be able to use it to get away."

"Without you?" Mazish said. "Venli . . ."

"I'll almost certainly return," Venli said. "But just in case, take the map too. You'll need it to find your way to the other listeners in secret."

"Where are you going?" Dul asked.

Venli hummed to the Lost. "I think we should offer to bring the surgeon and his family—including their son, the Windrunner—out with us. Help them escape the tower, take them to their own people at the Shattered Plains."

She watched them, expecting fear, perhaps condemnation. This would jeopardize their safety.

Instead, as a group, they hummed to Consideration.

"Having a Windrunner on our side could be useful," Mazish said. "He could certainly help us get to the Shattered Plains quicker."

"Yes!" said Shumin, the new recruit—still a little too eager for Venli's taste. "This is a *great* idea!"

"Would he help us though?" Dul asked.

"He treated Rlain well," Mazish said. "Even when he thought Rlain was only another parshman. I don't like what the humans did, but if we put this one in our debt, my gut says he won't betray us."

Venli scanned the other faces. Singers with a variety of skin patterns, now humming a variety of rhythms. None of them hummed to Betrayal, and they gave her encouraging nods.

"Very well," Venli said, "wait for me until the storm has passed. If I've not returned by then, take the next Oathgate transfer to Kholinar. I'll find you there."

They hummed at her words, so Venli started toward the atrium, hoping she'd be quick enough to stop Rlain from trying his desperate plan. She didn't know for certain if he'd take her offer. But this *was* the direction she should be moving.

⁂

Navani knelt on the floor of her office. It still smelled of smoke from the explosion the day before.

Despite Raboniel saying she wanted to scrape the chamber for broken pieces of the dagger, no one arrived to do that. They hadn't taken her to her rooms above. They hadn't brought her meals. They'd simply left her alone.

To contemplate her utter failure.

She felt numb. After her previous failure—when she'd exposed the node to her enemies—she'd picked herself up and moved on. This time she felt stuck. Worn. Like an old banner left too long exposed to the elements. Ripped by storms. Bleached by the sun. Now hanging in tatters, waiting to slip off the pole.

We can kill Radiant spren.

In the end, all Raboniel's talk of working together had been a lie. Of *course* it had. Navani had *known* it would be. She'd planned for it, and tried to hide what she knew. But had she really expected that to work? She'd repeatedly confirmed to herself that she couldn't outthink the Fused. They were ancient, capable beyond mortal understanding, beings outside of time and . . . And . . .

And she kept staring at the place where Raboniel's daughter had died. Where Raboniel had wept, holding the corpse of her child. Such a *human* moment.

Navani curled up on her pallet, though sleep had eluded her all night. She had spent the hours listening to the Fused in the hallway playing notes on metal plates and demanding new ones—until one final sound had echoed against the stone hallways. A chilling, *awful* sound that was wrong in all the right ways. Raboniel had found the tone.

The tone that could kill spren.

Should Navani feel pride? Even in that time of near madness, her research had been so meticulous and well annotated that Raboniel was able to follow it. What had taken Navani days, the Fused replicated in hours, breaking open a mystery that had stood for thousands of years. Evidence that Navani was a true scholar after all?

No, she thought, staring at the ceiling. *No, don't you dare take that distinction for yourself.* If she'd been a scholar, she'd have understood the implications of her work.

She was a child playing dress-up again. A farmer could stumble across a new plant in the wilderness. Did that make him a botanist?

She eventually forced herself up to do the only thing she was certain she couldn't ruin. She found ink and paper in the wreckage of the room, then knelt and began to paint prayers. It was partially for the comfort of familiarity. But storm her, she still *believed.* Perhaps that was as foolish as thinking herself a scholar. Who did she think was listening? Was she only praying because she was afraid?

Yes, she thought, continuing to paint. *I'm afraid. And I have to hope that someone, somewhere, is listening. That someone has a plan. That it all matters somehow.*

Jasnah took *comfort* in the idea that there was no plan, that everything was random. She said that a chaotic universe meant the only actions of actual importance were the ones they decided were important. That gave people autonomy.

Navani loved her daughter, but couldn't see it the same way. Organization and order existed in the very way the world worked. From the patterns on leaves to the system of compounds and chemical reactions. It all whispered to her.

Someone had known anti-Voidlight was possible.

Someone had known Navani would create it first.

Someone had seen all this, planned for it, and put her here. She had to believe that. She had to believe, therefore, that there was a way out.

Please, she prayed, painting the glyph for divine direction. *Please. I'm trying so hard to do what is right. Please guide me. What do I do?*

A voice sounded outside the room, and in her sleep-deprived state, she first mistook it for a voice speaking to her in answer. And then . . . then she heard what it was saying.

"The best way to distract the Bondsmith is to kill his wife," the voice said. Rough, cold. "I am therefore here to perform the act that you have so far refused to do."

Navani stood and walked to the door. Her femalen guard was someone new, but she didn't forbid Navani from peering down the hall toward Raboniel's workstation beside the Sibling's shield.

A man in a black uniform stood before Raboniel. Neat, close-cropped black hair, a narrow hawkish face with a prominent nose and sunken cheeks. Moash. The murderer.

"I continue to have use for the queen," Raboniel said.

"My orders are from Odium himself," Moash said. If a Fused's voice was overly ornamented with rhythms and meaning, his voice was the opposite. Dead. A voice like slate.

"He ordered you to come to me, Vyre," Raboniel said. "And I requested for you to be sent. So today, I need you to deal with my problems first. There is a worm in the tower. Eating his way through walls. He is increasingly an issue."

"I warned you about Stormblessed," Moash said. "I warned all of you. And you did not listen."

"You will kill him," Raboniel said.

"No enemy can kill Kaladin Stormblessed," Moash said.

"You promised that—"

"*No enemy* can kill Stormblessed," Moash said. "He is a force like the storms, and you cannot kill the storms, Fused."

Raboniel handed Moash something. A small dagger. "You speak foolishness. A man is merely a man, no matter how skilled. That dagger can destroy his spren. Spread that sand, and it will turn faintly white when an invisible spren flies overhead. Use it to locate his honorspren, then strike at it, depriving him of power."

"I can't kill him," Moash repeated a third time, tucking the dagger away. "But I promise something better. We make this a covenant, Fused: I ruin Stormblessed, leave him unable to interfere, and you deliver me the queen. Accepted?"

Navani felt herself grow cold. Raboniel didn't even glance in her direction. "Accepted," Raboniel said. "But do another thing for me. The Pursuer has been sent to destroy the final node, but I think he is delaying to encourage Stormblessed to show up and fight him for it. Break the node for me."

Moash nodded and accepted what seemed to be a small diagram explaining the location of the node. He turned on his heel with military precision and marched up the hallway. If he saw her, he made no comment, passing like a cold wind.

"Monster," Navani said, angerspren at her feet. "Traitor! You would attack your own friend?"

He stopped short. Staring straight ahead, he spoke. "Where were you, lighteyes, when your son condemned innocents to death?" He turned, affixing Navani with those lifeless eyes. "Where were you, *Queen*, when your son sent *Roshone* to Kaladin's hometown? A political outcast, a known murderer, exiled to a small village. Where he couldn't do any damage, right?

"Roshone killed Kaladin's brother. You could have stopped it. If any of you cared. You were never my queen; you are nothing to me. You are nothing to anyone. So don't speak to me of treason or friendship. You have no *idea* what this day will cost me."

He continued forward, bearing no visible weapon save the dagger tucked into his belt. A dagger designed to kill a spren. A dagger that Navani had, essentially, created. He reached the end of the hallway, burst alight with Stormlight—which somehow worked for him—and streaked into the air, rising through the open stairwell toward the ground floor.

Navani slumped in the doorway, objections withering in her throat. She knew he was wrong, but she couldn't find her voice. Something about that man unnerved her to the point of panic. He wasn't human. He was a Voidbringer. If that word had ever applied to any, it was Moash.

"What do you need?" her guard asked. "Have you been fed?"

"I . . ." Navani licked her lips. "I need a candle, please. For burning prayers."

Remarkably, she fetched it. Taking the candle, shivering, Navani cupped the flame and walked to her pallet. There, she knelt and began burning her glyphwards one at a time.

If there was a God, if the Almighty was still out there somewhere, had he created Moash? Why? Why bring such a thing into the world?

Please, she thought, begging as a ward shriveled, her prayers casting smoke into the air. *Please. Tell me what to do. Show me something. Let me know you're there.*

As the last prayer drifted toward the Tranquiline Halls, she sat back on her heels, numb, wanting to huddle down and forget about her problems. When she moved to do so, however, in the candlelight she caught sight of something glittering amid the wreckage of her desk. As if in a trance, Navani rose and walked over. The guard wasn't looking.

Navani brushed aside ash to find a metal dagger with a diamond affixed to the pommel. She stared at it, confused. It had exploded, hadn't it?

No, this is the second one. The one Raboniel used to kill her daughter. She tossed it aside, as if hating it, once the deed was done.

A precious, priceless weapon, and the Fused had discarded it. How long had Raboniel been awake? Did she feel like Navani, exhausted, pushed to the limit? Forgetting important details?

For there, glimmering violet-black in the gemstone, was a soft glow. Not completely used up in the previous killing.

A small charge of anti-Voidlight.

Kaladin took the steps down one at a time. Unhurried as he walked toward the trap.

A certain momentum pushed him forward. As if his next actions were Soulcast into stone, already unchangeable. A mountain seemed to fill in behind him, blocking his retreat.

Forward. Only forward. One step after another.

He emerged from the stairwell onto the ground floor. Two direform Regals had been guarding the path, but they backed off—hands on swords, humming frantically. Kaladin ignored them, turning toward the atrium. He set his spear to his shoulder and strode through this central corridor.

No more hiding. He was too tired to hide. Too wrung-out for tactics and strategy. The Pursuer wanted him? Well, he would have Kaladin, presented as he had always been seen. Dressed in his uniform, striding to the fight, his head high.

Humans and singers alike scattered before him. Kaladin saw many of the humans wearing the markings Rlain had described—*shash* glyphs drawn on their foreheads. Storm them, they believed in him. They wore the symbol of his shame, his failure, and his imprisonment. And they made it something better.

He couldn't help feeling that this was it. The last time he'd wear the uniform, his final act as a member of Bridge Four. One way or another, he had to move on from the life he'd been clinging to and the simple squad of soldiers who had formed the heart of that life.

All these people believed in a version of him who had already died. Highmarshal Kaladin Stormblessed. The valiant soldier, leader of the Windrunners, stalwart and unwavering. Like Kal the innocent youth, Squadleader Kaladin the soldier in Amaram's army, and Kaladin the slave . . . Highmarshal Stormblessed had passed. Kaladin had become someone new, someone who could not measure up to the legend.

But with all these people believing in him—falling in behind him, whispering with hope and anticipation—perhaps he could resurrect Stormblessed for one last battle.

He didn't worry about exposing himself. There was nowhere to run. Regals and singer soldiers gathered in bunches, tailing him and whispering harshly, but they would let a Fused deal with a Radiant.

Other Fused would know, though. Kaladin had been claimed already. He was Pursued.

As Kaladin drew near to the Breakaway—the hallway to his right would merge with the large open marketplace—he finally felt her. He stopped fast, looking that direction. The dozens of people following him hushed as he stared intently and raised his right hand in the direction of the market.

Syl, he thought. *I'm here. Find me.*

A line of light, barely visible, bounced around in the distance. It turned and spun toward him, picking up speed—its path growing straighter. She grew brighter, and awareness of her blossomed in his mind. They were not whole, either one, without the other.

She recovered herself with a gasp, then landed on his hand, wearing her girlish dress.

"Are you all right?" he whispered.

"No," she said. "No, not at all. That felt . . . felt like it did when I nearly died. Like it did when I drifted for centuries. I feel sad, Kaladin. And cold."

"I understand those feelings," he replied. "But the enemy, Syl . . . they're going to execute the Radiants. And they might have my parents."

She peered up at him. Then her shape fuzzed, and she was instantly in a uniform like his, colored Kholin blue.

Kaladin nodded, then turned and continued, shadowed by the hopes and prayers of hundreds. Shadowed by his own reputation. A man who would never cry in the night, huddled against the wall, terrified. A man he was determined to pretend to be. One last time.

He checked Navani's flying gauntlet, which he'd attached to his belt—easy to unhook, if needed—at his right side so it pointed behind him. Kaladin and Dabbid had reset its conjoined weights the other night. It hadn't worked so well for him in the previous fight, but now he understood its limitations. It was a device designed by engineers, not soldiers. He couldn't wear it on his hand, where it would interfere with his ability to hold a spear. But perhaps it could offer him an edge in another capacity.

With Syl flying as a ribbon of light beside his head, he strode into the atrium—with that endless wall of glass rising as a window in front of him. An equally endless hollow shaft in the stone rose up toward the pinnacle of the tower, surrounded by balconies on most levels. Heavenly Ones hovered in the air, though he didn't have time to search for Leshwi.

Syl moved out in front of him, then paused, hovering, seeming curious.

"What?" he asked.

Highstorm coming, she said in his head.

Of course there was. It was that kind of day.

People in the atrium began to scatter as they saw him, accompanied by anticipationspren. As the place emptied, he picked out a hulking figure standing in the dead center of the chamber, blocking the way to the room on the other side—the infirmary.

Kaladin brandished his spear in challenge. But the Pursuer cared nothing for honor. He was here for the kill, and he came streaking at Kaladin to claim it.

Watch them struggle. Witness their writhing, their refusal to surren-
der. Humans cling to the rocks with the vigor of any Rosharan vine.

—Musings of El, on the first of the Final Ten Days

T here he is," Teft said, ducking and moving with the crowd of
people in the atrium. With a cloak over his uniform, he didn't
draw attention. He'd found that was often the case. Kaladin
turned heads, even if he was dressed in rags. He was that kind of man.

But Teft? He looked forgettable. In this cloak he was simply another
worker, walking with his daughter through the atrium. Hopefully Lift
would keep her head down so the hood of her own cloak obscured her
features—otherwise someone might wonder why his "daughter" looked
an awful lot like a certain bothersome Radiant who was always making
trouble in the tower.

"What took him so long?" Lift whispered as the two of them sidled
over along the wall of the atrium, acting frightened of the sudden rush
of people who made way for Kaladin and the Pursuer.

"Boy likes to grandstand," Teft said. But storms, it was hard not to
feel inspired at the sight of Kaladin framed in the entryway like that in
a sharp blue uniform, his hair free, his scars bold and stark on his forehead. Eyes intense enough to pierce the darkest storm.

You did good with that one, Teft, he thought—giving himself permission to feel a little pride. *You ruined your own life something fierce, but you did good with that one.*

Phendorana whispered comfort in his ear. She'd shrunk, at his request, and rode on his shoulder. He nodded at the words. If his family hadn't gotten involved with the Envisagers, he wouldn't have known how to help Kaladin when he'd needed it. And then the Blackthorn probably would have died, and they wouldn't have found this tower. So . . . maybe it was time to let go of what he'd done.

Together, they inched along the wall toward the infirmary. Storm him if having his own personal spren wasn't the best thing that had happened to him, other than Bridge Four. She could be a little crusty at times, which made them a good match. She also refused to accept his excuses. Which made them an even better match.

Kaladin started fighting, and Teft couldn't spare him much more than a wish of goodwill. The lad would be fine. Teft simply had to do his part.

They waited to see if the guards in the infirmary came out at the ruckus, and blessedly they did. Unfortunately, one remained at the door, gaping at the battle but apparently determined to remain at his post.

Stormform Regal too, which was just Teft's luck. Still, he and Lift were able to work the press of the crowd to their advantage, pretending they were confused civilians. Maybe that stormform would let them "hide" in the infirmary.

Instead, the Regal at the door showed them an indifferent palm, gesturing for them to flee in another direction. He turned aside a number of other people who saw the infirmary as a convenient escape, so Teft and Lift didn't draw undue attention.

People in the atrium cried out as Kaladin and the Pursuer clashed. Heavenly Ones floated down to watch the battle, their long trains descending like curtains, adding to the surreal sight. In fact, *everybody's* eyes were fixed on the contest between Kaladin and the Pursuer. So, Teft took the Regal guard by the arm. These Regals had that captive lightning running through them, so touching the singer gave Teft a shock. He cried out and shook his hand, backing away as the stormform turned toward him in annoyance.

"Please, Brightlord," Teft said. "What is happening?"

As the Regal focused on him, Lift slipped around behind and cracked the door open.

"Be on with you," the Regal said. "Don't bother—"

Teft rushed the singer, tackling him around the waist and throwing him backward through the open door. The Regal's powers sent another shock through Teft, but in the confusion, Teft was able to get him to the ground and put him in a deadman's hold.

Lift shut the door with a click. She waited, anxious, as Teft struggled to keep pressure on the creature's throat. He pulled in all the Stormlight he had, but felt the stormform's power growing—the creature's skin crackling with red lightning.

"Healing!" Teft said.

Lift leapt over and pressed her hand against his leg as the stormform released a bolt of power straight through Teft into the floor. The *crack* it made was incredible. Teft felt a burning pain, like someone had decided to use his stomach as a convenient place to build their firepit.

But he held on, and Lift healed him. He even managed to roll to the side and use Stormlight to stick the Regal to the ground. That let him keep the pressure on and resist the shocks that followed—less powerful than the first.

Finally the Regal went limp, unconscious. Teft huffed and stood, though he first had to unstick his clothing from the floor. Storming Stormlight. He looked down and found the front of his shirt had been burned clean through.

He glanced to Phendorana, who had grown to full size. She folded her arms thoughtfully.

"What?" he asked.

"Your hair is standing up," she said, then grinned. She looked like a little kid when she did that, and he couldn't help returning the expression.

"Move!" she said to him. "Seal the door!"

"Right, right." He stepped over and infused the doorframe with Stormlight. Someone would have heard that lightning bolt. "Lift," he shouted as he worked, "get to it! I want these Radiants up and taking orders faster than an arrow falls." He glanced to Phendorana, standing beside him and meeting his eyes. "We *can* do this. Get them up, grab Kal's family, get out."

"Through the window?" she asked.

Outside the east-facing window was a sheer drop of hundreds of feet. He felt moderately good about his ability to climb down it. How far would everyone have to get before their Radiant powers returned? He feared the Heavenly Ones would find out before then and come after them.

Well, he'd see what the others said, once they were awake. Teft turned from the now-sealed door to inspect the room and Lift's progress. Where was that surgeon and his—

Lift screamed.

She leaped back as one of the bodies on the floor nearby emerged from beneath the sheet. The figure—dressed all in black—swung a *Shardblade* at her. She nearly managed to get away, but the Blade caught her in the thighs, cutting with the grace of an eel through the air.

Lift collapsed, her legs ruined by the Blade.

The figure in the black uniform turned from Lift and—blazing with Stormlight—focused on Teft. Sunken cheeks, prominent nose, glowing eyes.

Moash.

⁂

Kaladin didn't run.

He knew what the Pursuer would do.

Indeed, the creature acted as he had each time before—dropping a husk and streaking toward Kaladin to grapple him. That was one husk spent. The Pursuer had two others before he would be trapped in his form and had to either flee, or face Kaladin and risk dying.

Kaladin stepped directly into the Pursuer's path and dropped his spear, willingly entering the grapple. Turning at the last moment, he caught the Pursuer's hands as they reached for him. Thrumming with Stormlight, Kaladin held the Pursuer's wrists. Storms, the creature was stronger than he was. But Kaladin wouldn't run or hide. Not this time. This time he only had to give Teft and Lift enough space to work.

And Kaladin had discovered something during their last fight. This creature was *not* a soldier.

"Give in, little man," the Pursuer said. "I am as unavoidable as the coming storm. I will chase you forever."

"Good," Kaladin said.

"Bravado!" the Pursuer said, laughing. He managed to hook Kaladin's foot, then used his superior strength to shove Kaladin to the ground. Best Kaladin could do was hang on and pull him down as well. The Pursuer kneed Kaladin in the gut, then twisted to get him in a hold. "So foolish!"

Kaladin writhed, barely able to keep from being immobilized. Syl flitted around them. As the Pursuer tried for a lock, Kaladin twisted around and met the Pursuer's eyes, then smiled.

The Pursuer growled and repositioned to press Kaladin against the ground by his shoulders.

"I'm not afraid of you," Kaladin said. "But you're going to be afraid of me."

"Madness," the Pursuer said. "Your inevitable fate has caused madness in your frail mind."

Kaladin grunted, back to the cold stone, using both hands to push the Pursuer's right hand away. He kept his eyes locked on to the Pursuer's.

"I killed you," Kaladin said. "And I'll kill you now. Then every time you return for me, I'll kill you *again*."

"I'm immortal," the Pursuer growled. But his rhythm had changed. Not so confident.

"Doesn't matter," Kaladin said. "I've heard what people say about you. Your life isn't the blood in your veins, but the legend you live. Each death kills that legend a little more. Each time I defeat you, it will rip you apart. Until you're no longer known as the Pursuer. You'll be known as the Defeated. The creature who, no matter how hard he tries, *can't ever beat ME*."

Kaladin reached down and activated Navani's device at his belt, then pressed the grip that dropped the weight. It was as if someone had suddenly tied a rope to his waist, and then pulled him out of the Pursuer's grip, sliding him across the floor of the atrium.

He deactivated the device, then rolled to his feet, looking across the short distance at his enemy. Syl fell in beside him, glaring at the Pursuer in a perfect mimic of his posture. Then, together, they smiled as Kaladin pulled out his scalpel.

Moash kicked Lift toward the wall, sending her limp and tumbling. She lay still and didn't move after that. Moash floated forward, blade out, attention affixed solely on Teft.

Teft cursed himself for a fool. He'd focused on taking care of the Regal at the door; he should have known to check for irregularities. Now that he looked, he could see Kal's parents and brother bound and gagged, visible through a gap in the cloth of the draped-off section at the rear.

The real trap wasn't outside with the Pursuer. It was in here, with a much deadlier foe: a man who had been trained for war by Kaladin himself.

"Hello, Teft," Moash said softly, landing in front of the rows of unconscious people on the floor. "How are the men?"

"Safe from you," Teft said, pushing aside his cloak and unsheathing the long knife he had hidden underneath. Couldn't move through a crowd unseen with a spear, unfortunately.

"Not all of them, Teft," Moash said. There was a shadow on his face, despite the room's many lit spheres.

Moash lunged forward and Teft danced back, stepping carefully over the body of the unconscious Regal. He had space here in front of the door with no fallen Radiants to upset his footing. All Moash did at first was open a sack and throw something out across the floor nearby. Black sand? What on Roshar?

Teft held out his weapon, Phendorana at his side, but the knife seemed tiny compared to Moash's weapon: the assassin's Honorblade. The one that had killed old Gavilar.

It looked wicked in Moash's hand, shorter than most Blades—but in a lithe, deliberate way. This wasn't a weapon for slaying great monsters of stone.

It was a weapon for killing men.

Humans are a poem. A song.

—Musings of El, on the first of the Final Ten Days

"Hey," someone said to the Rhythm of Reprimand, "what are you doing?"

Rlain turned, shifting the barrel of water from one shoulder to the other. Dabbid pulled in close to him, frightened at the challenge. The two of them were in a nondescript passage of Urithiru, close to the steps down to the basement. This was the last guard post, and Rlain thought they had made it past.

"We're delivering water," Rlain said to Consolation, tapping his small water barrel. He wore makeup covering his tattoo, blending it into his skin pattern. "To the scholars."

"Why are you doing it?" the singer said. Not a Fused or Regal, merely an ordinary guard. She walked over and put a hand on Rlain's shoulder. "Let the human do that kind of work, friend. You are meant for greater things."

He glanced at Dabbid—who looked at the ground—and attuned Irritation. This wasn't the kind of resistance he'd anticipated.

"It's my job," Rlain said to the guard.

"Who assigned axehounds' work to a singer?" she demanded. "Come with me. You strike an imposing figure in warform. I'll teach you the sword. We're recruiting for our squad."

"I . . . I would rather do what I'm supposed to," he said to Consolation. He pulled free, and thankfully she let him go. He and Dabbid continued along the hallway.

"Can you believe it?" she said from behind. "How can so many keep on thinking like slaves? It's sad."

"Yeah," one of the other guards said. "I wouldn't expect it of that one most of all, considering."

Rlain attuned Anxiety.

"That one?" the femalen said, her voice echoing in the hallway.

"Yeah, he's that listener, isn't he? The one that was in prison until Raboniel's Voice pulled him out?"

Damnation. Rlain walked a little quicker, but it was no use, as he soon heard boots chasing him. The guard grabbed him by the elbow.

"Wait now," she said. "You're the listener?"

"I am," Rlain said to Consolation.

"Delivering water. You. A traitor?"

"We're not . . ." He attuned Determination and turned around. "We're not traitors. Venli is Raboniel's *Voice*."

"Yeah," the femalen said. "Well, you're not going down where the human queen is, not until I get confirmation that you're allowed. Come with me."

Dabbid pulled in closer to Rlain, trembling. Rlain looked toward the singer guards. Four of them.

No. He wasn't going to fight them. And not only because of the numbers. "Fine," he said. "Let's ask your superior, so I can get on with my duty."

They pulled him away, and Dabbid followed, whimpering softly as they were led—step by step—farther from their goal. Well, if the Sibling wanted him down there for some reason, they'd have to find a way to get him out of this.

⁛

The Pursuer lunged for Kaladin. Kaladin, however, was ready. He activated Navani's device, which was still attached to his belt. That tugged

Kaladin backward faster than a man could leap, and so he stayed out of the Pursuer's grip.

By this point, the singers had cleared most of the atrium of civilians. They'd lined the walls with soldiers—but not the flat side of the room with the window—though crowds continued to watch from the hallways and the balconies. Trusting in Kaladin.

Heavenly Ones hovered above the circular chamber, as if to judge the contest. In effect it was an arena. Kaladin projected as much strength and confidence as he could. He almost started to feel it, the worn-out, weathered fatigue retreating.

He needed the Pursuer to believe. To understand. That he had far more to lose from this contest than Kaladin did.

And he seemed to. For as Kaladin reached the other side of the room and disengaged Navani's device, the creature ejected his second body and shot toward Kaladin as a ribbon. He wanted to end this battle quickly.

The window had darkened from the approaching stormwall, which announced the highstorm. It hit with a fury that Kaladin could barely hear, and spheres became the room's only source of light.

Kaladin seized the Fused out of the air as he formed, and they clashed again. That was the Pursuer's third body. If he ejected this time, he'd have to go recharge, or risk forming a fourth body—and being killed.

They went to ground again, rolling as they wrestled, Kaladin trying to maneuver his knife. The Pursuer could heal with Voidlight, but the more of that he lost, the more likely he'd have to retreat.

This time the creature offered no taunts as he tried to get a grip on Kaladin's head. Likely to smash it into the ground, as he knew Kaladin's healing wasn't working properly. That gave Kaladin a chance to stab upward, forcing the Pursuer to grab his arm instead.

"You're no soldier," Kaladin said loudly, his voice echoing to all of those listening. "That's what I realized about you, Defeated One. You've never faced death."

"Silence," the Pursuer growled, twisting Kaladin's wrist.

Kaladin grunted, then rolled them both to the side, narrowly protecting his wrist from serious damage. He dropped the knife. Fortunately, he had found others.

"I've faced it every day of my life!" Kaladin shouted, rolling on top of the Fused. "You wonder why I don't fear you? I've *lived* with the knowledge that death is hounding me. You're nothing new."

"Be. *QUIET!*"

"But I'm something you *have never* known," Kaladin shouted, slamming the Pursuer down by his shoulders. "Thousands of years of life can't prepare you for something you've never met before, Defeated One! It can't prepare you for someone who *does not fear* you!"

Kaladin pulled out his boot knife and raised it. The Pursuer, seeing that coming, didn't do what he should have. He didn't try to grapple or knee Kaladin's stomach. He panicked and shot away as a ribbon of light, fleeing.

He materialized a short distance away in front of the watching soldiers. His fourth body. His last one. The one he was vulnerable in. He turned to look back at Kaladin, now standing atop his husk.

"I am death itself, Defeated One," Kaladin said. "And I've finally caught up to you."

⁖

Venli found a mob of people blocking the central corridor as she tried to reach the atrium. She attuned Anxiety and pushed through the press. Since she was a Regal, people did make way. Eventually she reached the front of the crowd, where a group of warforms stood in a line, blocking the way forward.

She suspected she knew what was happening. Rlain and his friends had already begun their rescue plan. She was too late.

"Make room," Venli demanded to Derision. "What is happening?"

One of the warforms turned. Venli didn't know him personally, but he was one of the Pursuer's soldiers. "Our master is fighting Stormblessed," he said. "We're to keep a perimeter, prevent people from interfering."

Venli craned her neck, tall enough to see that the room was being guarded by about a hundred of the Pursuer's troops, though she also saw some of Raboniel's personal guard—which she'd picked up from Leshwi.

Venli attuned the Terrors. What now? Could she help? She found, as she searched, that she genuinely *wanted* to. Not because Timbre was pushing her, and not because this was merely the path she was on. But because of the songs of the stones. And the whispers of those who had come before her.

"I'm the Voice of the Lady of Wishes," Venli said. "You think that your blockade applies to me? Step aside."

Reluctantly, the soldiers made way for her. And once she had a clear view, she couldn't help but pause. There *was* something about the way Stormblessed fought. Even grappling with the Pursuer, rolling across the ground, there was a certain determination to him. He freed himself from the grapple, then somehow leaped back twenty feet, though his powers shouldn't have been working that well.

The Pursuer became a ribbon and chased him, but Stormblessed didn't run. He reached out and *seized* the Pursuer right as he appeared. Fascinating. She could see why Leshwi found the human so interesting.

There was nothing Venli could do about this battle. She had to think about Rlain, and Lirin and his family. She searched the air and located Leshwi hovering nearby.

Venli made her way over to Leshwi as Stormblessed stood tall atop the Pursuer's husk. The lady floated down. She would not interfere in a duel such as this.

"This looks bad for Stormblessed," Venli whispered.

"No," Leshwi said to Exultation. "The Pursuer has used all of his husks. He will need to flee and renew."

"Why doesn't he?" Venli asked.

"Look," Leshwi said, and pointed at the silent atrium. A perimeter of soldiers with humans crowded behind them, peeking through. Fused in the air. All staring at the two combatants.

An incredible soldier, who seemed immortal and impervious, completely in control.

And a Fused, who somehow looked small by comparison.

∴

Teft dodged through the infirmary. He didn't dare engage Moash directly; instead he tried to stay out of reach. Buying time. For what though?

Moash drifted closer to them, eyes glowing.

"Stormblessed isn't going to come in and help, is he?" Phendorana asked softly, floating beside Teft.

"Kaladin can't be everywhere at once," Teft said. "He's just one man, though he often forgets that." He jumped backward over a body. Lift had stirred, and was quietly pulling herself across the ground toward one of the nearby Radiants, her legs dragging behind.

Good girl, Teft thought. He needed to keep Moash's attention.

"Never known a man to turn traitor as hard as you did," Teft called to Moash. "What was it that got you? What made you willing to kill your own?"

"Peace," Moash said, halting in the middle of the room. "It was peace, Teft."

"This is peace?" Teft said, gesturing. "Fighting your friends?"

"We're not fighting. You run like a coward."

"Every good sergeant is a coward! And proud of it! Someone needs to talk sense to the officers!"

Moash hovered in place, a black stain in the air. Before he could look and see Lift, Phendorana appeared to him, standing a short distance away. Moash glanced toward her sharply. Good, good. Distraction.

Moash, however, casually turned and slashed his Shardblade through the face of a Radiant beneath him. The unconscious woman's eyes burned and Lift cried out in horror, heaving herself forward to reach the body—as if she could do anything.

Moash glanced at Teft, then raised his Blade toward Lift.

"Fine!" Teft said, striding forward. "Bastard! You want me? Fine! Fight me! I'll show you who the better man is!"

Moash landed beside the body and walked straight toward Teft. "We both know who the better warrior is, Teft."

"I didn't say better warrior, you idiot," Teft said, lunging in with his knife. The stab was a feint, but Moash knew it. He sidestepped at precisely the right time, and tripped Teft as he tried to turn and swing again.

Teft went down with a grunt. He tried to roll, but Moash landed and kicked him in the side, hard. Something *crunched* in Teft's chest. A wound that blossomed with pain and didn't heal, despite his Stormlight.

Moash loomed overhead and raised his Blade, then swung it down without further comment. Teft dropped his knife—useless against a Blade—and raised his hands. He felt something from Phendorana. A harmony between them.

Teft was forgiven. Teft was *forgiven* and he was *close.*

Moash's Shardblade met something in the air—a phantom spear shaft, barely coalescing between Teft's hands—and *stopped*. It threw sparks, but it *stopped*. Teft gritted his teeth and held on as Moash finally showed an emotion. Surprise. He stumbled back, his eyes wide.

Teft let go, and Phendorana appeared beside him on the ground, puffing from exertion. He felt sweat trickling down his brow. Manifesting her like that—even a little—had been like trying to push an axehound through a keyhole. He wasn't certain he, or she, could do it a second time.

Best to try something else. Teft held his side, grimacing as he forced himself into a kneeling position. "All right, lad. I'm done. You got me. I surrender. Let's wait for Kaladin to show up, and you can continue this conversation with him."

"I'm not here for Kaladin, Teft," Moash said softly. "And I'm not here for your surrender."

Teft steeled himself. *Grapple him*, he thought. *Make that Blade a liability, too big to use*. His best hope.

Because Teft *did* have hope. That was what he'd recovered, these years in Bridge Four. The moss might take him again, but if it did . . . well, he would fight back again. The past could rot.

Teft, Windrunner, had *hope*.

He managed to get to his feet, prepared for Moash to lunge at him—but when Moash moved, it wasn't toward Teft. It was toward Phendorana.

What? Teft stood stunned as Moash pulled a strange dagger from his belt and slammed it down—right where Phendorana was kneeling.

She looked up with surprise and took the knife straight in the forehead. Then she screamed.

Teft leaped for her, howling, watching in horror as she *shrank*, writhing as Moash's dagger pinned her to the floor. Her essence *burned*, flaring outward like an explosion.

Something ripped inside Teft. Something deeper than his own heart. A part of his soul, his being, was torn away. He collapsed immediately, falling near the white spot in the sand that was all that remained of Phendorana.

No. No . . .

It hurt so much. Agony like a sudden terrible stillness. Nothingness. *Emptiness.*

It . . . it can't be. . . .

Moash tucked the dagger away methodically. "I can't feel sorrow anymore, Teft. For that I am grateful."

Moash turned Teft over with his foot. His broken ribs screamed, but felt like such an insignificant pain now.

"But you know what?" Moash said, standing over him. "There was *always* a part of me that resented how you were so eager to follow him. Right from the start, his little axehound. Licking his feet. He loves you. I thought I'd have to use his father. But I am . . . satisfied to have found something better."

"You are a monster," Teft whispered.

Moash took Teft calmly by the front of his burned shirt and hoisted him up. "I am no monster. I am merely silence. The quiet that eventually takes all men."

"Tell yourself that lie, Moash," Teft growled, gripping the hand that held him, his own hand clawlike from the horrible pain. "But know this. You can kill me, but you can't have what I have. You can *never* have it. Because *I* die knowing I'm loved."

Moash grunted and dropped him to the ground. Then he stabbed Teft directly through the neck with his Shardblade.

Confident, and somehow still full of hope, Teft died.

CHILDREN OF PASSIONS

For ones so soft, they are somehow strong.

—Musings of El, on the first of the Final Ten Days

The highstorm blowing outside the enormous window presented a view that Kaladin often saw, but others rarely knew. Flashing lightning, a swirling tempest, power raw and unchained.

Kaladin stepped off the Pursuer's decaying husk and walked forward. *Toward* the enemy.

The Pursuer searched around, likely realizing how large his audience was. Hundreds watching. He lived by lore, by reputation. He always killed anyone who killed him. He won each conflict eventually.

Now he saw that crumbling. Kaladin could hear it in the increasingly panicked rhythm the Pursuer hummed. Saw it in his eyes.

"Run," Kaladin told him. "Flee. I'll chase you. I will *never* stop. I am eternal. I am the storm."

The Pursuer stumbled back, but then encountered his soldiers holding the perimeter, humming an encouraging rhythm. Behind them humans gawked, their foreheads painted.

"Has it been long enough, do you think?" Syl whispered. "Are the others free?"

"Hopefully," Kaladin said. "But I don't think they'll be able to escape into that highstorm."

"Then they'll have to come out here, and we'll have to push for the crystal pillar room," she said, looking toward the infirmary. "Why haven't they appeared yet?"

"Once we defeat the Pursuer—when he breaks and runs—we'll find out," Kaladin said, unhooking Navani's device from his waist.

"Something's wrong," she said softly. "Something dark . . ."

Kaladin stepped to the very center of the atrium, marked by a swirling pattern of strata. He pointed his knife at the Pursuer. "Last body," Kaladin called. "Come fight, and we'll see who dies. We'll see if your reputation survives the hour."

The Pursuer, to his credit, came charging in. As he arrived, grabbing Kaladin, Kaladin pressed Navani's device against the Pursuer's chest and Lashed the bar down, binding it in place.

It launched backward, carrying the Pursuer with it. He slammed into the glass of the window, and his carapace cracked as he struck. He shook himself, recovering quickly—but didn't heal. He'd used up his Voidlight.

With effort, the Pursuer struggled to move the device, and managed to extricate himself from it—leaving it pressed to the window, which was smeared with his orange blood. More blood dripped from the cracked carapace at his chest.

Kaladin stalked toward him, holding the knife. "Flee."

The Pursuer's eyes widened and he stepped to the side, toward his soldiers.

"Flee!" Kaladin said.

The creature fell silent, no humming, no speaking.

"RUN FROM ME!" Kaladin demanded.

He did, dripping blood and shoving his way past the singer soldiers. He'd retreated from previous battles, but this time they both knew it meant something different.

This creature was no longer the Pursuer. He knew it. The singers knew it. And the humans watching behind knew it. They began to chant, gloryspren bursting in the air.

Stormblessed.

Stormblessed.

Stormblessed.

Trembling, Kaladin retrieved and deactivated Navani's device, then returned to the center of the room. He could feel their energy propelling him. A counter to the darkness.

He turned toward the infirmary. The door had been opened. When had that happened? He stepped toward it, but could see the Radiants in their lines on the floor, covered in sheets. Why weren't they up and awake? Were they feigning? That could work, pretending they were still asleep.

Something dropped from above. A body hit the ground in front of Kaladin with a callous *smack* of skull on stone. It rolled, and Kaladin saw burned-out eyes. A terribly familiar bearded face. A face that had smiled at him countless times, cursed at him an equal number, but had always been there when everything else went dark.

Teft.

Teft was dead.

⁙

Moash landed a short distance from where Kaladin knelt over Teft's body. Several of the watching soldiers stepped toward the Windrunner, but Moash raised his hand and stopped them.

"No," he said softly as Heavenly Ones hovered down around him. "Leave him be. This is how we win."

Moash knew exactly what Kaladin was feeling. That crushing sense of despair, that knowledge that nothing would be the same. Nothing could *ever* be the same. Light had left the world, and could never be rekindled.

Kaladin cradled Teft's corpse, letting out a low, piteous whine. He began to tremble and shake—becoming as insensate as he had when King Elhokar had died. As he had after Moash had killed Roshone. And if Kaladin responded that way to the deaths of his enemies . . .

Well, Teft dying would be worse. Far, far worse. Kaladin had been unraveling for years.

"That," Moash said to the Fused, "is how you break a storm. He'll be useless from here on out. Make sure nobody touches him. I have something to do."

He walked into the infirmary room. At the rear was the model of the tower, intricate in its detail, cut into a cross section with one half on either side. He knelt and peered at a copy of the room with the crystal pillar.

Beside it, produced in miniature, were a small crystal globe and gemstone. The fabrial glowed with a tiny light, barely visible. The final node of the tower's defenses, placed where anyone who looked would see it, but think nothing of it.

Raboniel had known though. How long? He suspected she'd figured it out days ago, and was stalling to continue her research here. That one was trouble. He summoned his Blade and used the tip to destroy the tiny fabrial.

Then he walked over to the sectioned-off portion of the room. The child Edgedancer lay here, tied up and unconscious, next to Kaladin's parents and brother. Odium was interested in the Edgedancer, and Moash had been forbidden to kill her. Hopefully he hadn't struck her head too hard. He didn't always control that as he should.

For now, he grabbed Lirin by his bound hands and dragged him—screaming through his gag—out of the infirmary. There Moash waited until the Pursuer came flying back as a shameful ribbon of light.

The Pursuer formed a body, and Moash pushed Lirin into the creature's hands. "This is Stormblessed's father," Moash whispered. "No! Don't say it loudly. Don't draw Kaladin's attention. His father is insurance; Kaladin has huge issues with the man. If Kaladin somehow regains his senses, *immediately* kill his father in front of him."

"This is nonsense," the Pursuer growled. "I could kill Stormblessed now."

"No," Moash said, grabbing the Pursuer and pointing at his face. "You know I have our master's blessing. You know I speak to Command. You *will not* touch Stormblessed. You can't hurt him; you can't kill him."

"He's . . . just a man. . . ."

"*Don't touch him,*" Moash said. "If you interfere, it will awaken him to vengeance. We don't want that yet. There are two paths open to him. One is to take the route I did, and give up his pain. The other is the route he *should* have taken long ago. The path where he raises the only hand that can kill Kaladin Stormblessed. His own."

The Pursuer didn't like it, judging by the rhythm he hummed. But he accepted Kaladin's bound and gagged father and seemed willing to stay put.

The guards had quieted the rowdy humans, and the atrium was falling still. Kaladin knelt before the storm, clinging to a dead man, shaking. Moash hesitated, searching inside himself. And . . . he felt nothing. Just coldness.

Good. He had reached his potential.

"Don't ruin this," he told the gathered Fused. "I need to go kill a queen."

⋄

Navani waited for her chance.

She had tried talking to the Sibling, but had heard only whimpers. So she had returned to the front of her room to wait for her chance to arrive.

It came when her door guard suddenly shouted, putting her hands to her head in disbelief. She ran down the hallway. When Navani peeked out, she saw what had caused the commotion: the field around the crystal pillar was gone. Someone had destroyed the final node. The Sibling was exposed.

Navani almost ran over to attack with the anti-Voidlight dagger. She hesitated though, eyeing her traps in the hallway.

A magnet. I need a magnet.

She'd seen one earlier, near the wreckage of her desk. She scrambled over and picked it up out of the rubble. Outside, she heard Raboniel's order echo with a clear voice.

"Run," she said to the guard. "Tell the Word of Deeds and the Night Known to attend me. We have work to do."

The guard dashed away. When Navani peeked out again, Raboniel was stepping into the chamber with the crystal pillar, alone.

A chance. Navani slipped into the hallway and moved quietly toward Raboniel. After passing the crates with her carefully prepared traps, she touched the magnet to a corner of the last crate and heard a *click*. She only dared take the time to arm one: a painrial that filled anyone who crossed this point in the hallway with immense agony.

That done, she moved to the end of the corridor. The room with the crystal pillar seemed darker than she remembered it. The Sibling had been almost fully corrupted.

Raboniel stood with her hand pressed against the pillar to finish the job. Navani forced herself forward, dagger held in a tight grip.

"You should run, Navani," Raboniel said to a calm rhythm, her voice echoing in the room. "There is a copy of our notebook on my desk in the hallway, along with your anti-Voidlight plate. Take them and make your escape."

Navani froze in place, holding the dagger's hilt so tightly, she thought she might never be able to uncurl her fingers.

She knows I'm here. She knows what she did in sending the guard away. Logic, Navani. What does it mean?

"You're letting me go on purpose?" she said.

"Since the final node has been destroyed," Raboniel said, "Vyre will soon return to claim his promised compensation. However, if you have escaped on your own . . . well, then I have not defaulted on my covenant with him."

"I can't leave the Sibling to you."

"What do you think to do?" Raboniel asked. "Fight me?" She turned, so calm and composed. Her eyes flickered to the dagger, then she hummed softly to a confused rhythm. She'd forgotten about it. She wasn't as in control as she pretended.

"Is this how you wish to end our association?" Raboniel asked. "Struggling like brutes in the wilderness? Scholars such as we, reduced to the exploitation of common blades? Run, Navani. You cannot defeat a Fused in battle."

She was right on that count. "I can't abandon the Sibling," Navani said. "My honor won't allow it."

"We're all children of Odium in the end," Raboniel said. "Children of our Passions."

"You just said we were scholars," Navani said. "Others might be controlled by their passions. We are something more. Something better." She took a deep breath, then turned the dagger in her hand, hilt out. "I'll give you this, then you and I can go back to my room to wait together. If Vyre *does* defeat Stormblessed, I will submit to him. If not, you will agree to leave the Sibling."

"A foolish gamble," Raboniel said.

"No, a compromise. We can discuss as we wait, and if we come to a more perfect accommodation, all the better." She proffered the dagger.

"Very well," Raboniel said. She took the dagger with a quick snap of her hand, showing that she didn't completely trust Navani. As well she shouldn't.

Raboniel strode down the hallway, Navani following several paces behind.

"Let's get to this quickly, Navani," Raboniel said. "I should think that the two of us—"

Then Raboniel stepped directly into Navani's fabrial trap.

For ones so varied, they are somehow intense.

—Musings of El, on the first of the Final Ten Days

K aladin clung to Teft's limp form and felt it all crumbling. The flimsy facade of confidence he had built to let himself fight. The way he pretended he was fine.

Syl landed on his shoulder, arms wrapped around herself, and said nothing. What was there to say?

It was over.

It was all just . . . over. What was there to life if he couldn't protect the people he loved?

Long ago, he'd promised himself he'd try one last time. He'd try to save the men of Bridge Four. And he'd failed.

Teft had been so vibrant, so alive. So sturdy and so constant. He'd finally defeated his own monsters, had really come into his own, claiming his Radiance. He had been a wonderful, loving, *amazing* man.

He'd depended on Kaladin. Like Tien. Like a hundred others. But he couldn't save them. He *couldn't* protect them.

Syl whimpered, shrinking in on herself. Kaladin wished he could shrink as well. Maybe if he'd lived as his father wanted, he could have avoided this. He said he fought to protect, but he didn't end up protecting anything, did he? He just destroyed. Killed.

Kaladin Stormblessed wasn't dead. He'd never existed.

Kaladin Stormblessed was a lie. He always had been.

The numbness claimed him. That hollow darkness that was so much worse than pain. He couldn't think. Didn't want to think. Didn't want anything.

This time, Adolin wasn't there to pull him out of it. To force him to keep walking. This time, Kaladin was given exactly what he deserved.

Nothing. And nothingness.

⁘

Navani froze in place. Raboniel—suddenly struck with incredible pain from Navani's trap—collapsed, dropping the dagger. Steeling herself, Navani went down on her hands and knees, then lunged forward to grab it.

The pain was excruciating. But Navani had tested these devices upon herself, and she knew what they did. She lost control of her legs, but managed to crawl forward and plunge the dagger into Raboniel's chest. She kept her weight on the weapon, pressing it down, smelling burned flesh.

Raboniel screamed, writhing, clawing at Navani. The painrial did its job however, and prevented her from fighting back effectively.

"I'm sorry," Navani said through gritted teeth. "I'm . . . sorry. But next time . . . try . . . not . . . to be . . . *so trusting.*"

The painrial soon ran out. Navani had set it up days ago, with a small Voidlight gemstone for power. It hadn't been intended to work for very long. She was pleased by the range though. She'd specifically worked on that feature.

Navani sat up, then wrapped her arms around herself, trying to fight off the phantom effects of the pain. Finally she looked toward Raboniel's corpse.

And found the Fused's eyes quivering, not glassy and white like her daughter's had been. Navani scrambled away.

Raboniel moved her arms limply, then turned her head toward Navani.

"How?" Navani demanded. "Why are you alive?"

"Not . . . enough . . . Light . . ." Raboniel croaked. She gripped the knife in her chest and pulled it free, letting out a sigh. "It hurts. I'm . . . I'm . . . not . . ." She closed her eyes, though she continued to breathe.

Navani inched forward, wary.

"You must take . . . the notebook . . ." Raboniel said. "And you must . . . run. Vyre . . . returns."

"You tell me to run, after I tried to kill you?"

"Not . . . tried . . ." Raboniel said. "I . . . cannot hear rhythms. . . . My soul . . . dying . . ." She pried open her eyes and fixed them on Navani. "You . . . tricked me well, Navani. Clever, clever. Well . . . done."

"How can you say that?" Navani said, glancing toward the desk and the papers on it.

"Live . . . as long as I . . . and you can appreciate . . . anything . . . that still surprises you. . . . Go, Navani. Run . . . The war must . . . end."

Navani felt sick, now that she'd gone through with it. An unexpected pain pricked her at the betrayal. Nevertheless, she moved to the desk and picked up the notebook.

I need to get this out of the tower, she realized. *It is perhaps even more important than the Sibling. A way to kill Fused permanently. A way to . . .*

To end the war. If both Radiant spren and Fused could die for good, it *could* stop, couldn't it?

"Stormfather," she whispered. "That's what it was all about." Raboniel wanted to end the war, one way or another. The notebook Navani held was a copy, and Navani realized that the original notebook would be in Kholinar, delivered to the leaders of the singer military—likely along with the vacuum chamber and the metal plates.

Navani walked over to Raboniel. "You wanted a way to end it," she said. "You don't care who wins."

"I care," Raboniel whispered. "I want . . . the singers to win. But your side . . . winning . . . is better than . . . than . . ."

"Than the war continuing forever," Navani said.

Raboniel nodded, her eyes closed. "Go. Run. Vyre will—"

Navani looked up as a blur flashed in the hallway, reflecting light. A *thump* hit her chest, and she grunted at the impact, stunned—briefly—before pain began to wash through her body. Sharp and alarming.

A knife, she thought, befuddled to see the hilt of a throwing knife sticking from the side of her torso, next to her right breast. When she took a breath, the pain sharpened with a sudden spike.

She looked up, pressing her hand to the wound, feeling warm blood spill out. At the far end of the hallway, a figure in a black uniform walked slowly forward. A Shardblade appeared in his hand. The assassin's Blade.

Moash had returned.

Highmarshal Kaladin was dead.

∴

Venli watched the human, so consumed by his grief that he knelt there, motionless, for minutes on end. And they all watched. Silent Heavenly Ones. Solemn guards. Disbelieving humans. No one seemed to want to speak, or even breathe.

That was how Venli should have felt upon losing her sister. Why didn't she have the emotions of a normal person? She'd been sad, but she didn't think she'd *ever* been so overcome by grief that she acted like Stormblessed.

Timbre pulsed comfortingly inside her. Everyone was different. And Venli *was* on the right path.

Except . . . there wasn't really a point in returning to help now, was there? It was over. Beside her, Leshwi descended until her feet touched the ground, then she bowed her head.

Show her, Timbre pulsed. *What you are.*

"What? Now?"

Show her.

Reveal what she was, in front of everyone? Venli shrank at the thought, attuning the Terrors.

One by one the other Heavenly Ones touched down, as if in respect. For an enemy.

"This is stupidity," the Pursuer said, shoving Lirin into Leshwi's hands. "I can't believe we're all just standing here."

Leshwi looked up from her vigil, humming to Spite. Then, amazingly, she pulled out a knife and cut Lirin's hands free.

"I have not forgotten how you tried to turn the Nine against me," the Pursuer said, pointing at Leshwi. "You seek to destroy my legacy."

"Your legacy is dead, Defeated One," Leshwi said. "It died when you ran from him."

"My legacy is untouched!" the Pursuer roared, causing Venli to stumble back, afraid. "And this is complete madness! I will prove myself and continue my tradition!"

"No!" Leshwi said, passing the still-gagged human to one of the other Heavenly Ones. She grabbed the Pursuer, but he left a husk in her hand, exploding out as a ribbon of light to cross the atrium floor.

"No . . ." Venli whispered.

The Pursuer appeared above Stormblessed. The Fused yanked a sharpened carapace spur off his arm, then—holding it like a dagger—he grabbed the kneeling man by one shoulder.

Kaladin Stormblessed looked up and let loose a howl that seemed to vibrate with a hundred discordant rhythms. Venli attuned the Lost in return.

The Pursuer stabbed, but Stormblessed grabbed his arm and turned, becoming a blur of motion. He somehow twisted around so he was behind the Pursuer, then found a knife somewhere on his person—moving with such speed that Venli had trouble tracking him. Stormblessed slammed the knife at the Pursuer's neck, who barely ejected from the husk in time.

He re-formed and tried to grab Stormblessed again. But there was no contest now. Kaladin moved like the wind, fast and flowing as he rammed his dagger through the Pursuer's arm, causing him to shout in pain. A knife toward the face followed, and the Pursuer ejected yet again. No one chanted or shouted this time, but when Stormblessed turned around, Venli saw his face—and she immediately attuned the Terrors.

His eyes were glowing like a Radiant's, his face a mask of pain and anguish, but the eyes . . . she *swore* the light had a yellowish-red cast to it. Like . . . like . . .

The Pursuer appeared near the soldiers at the perimeter by the wall. "Go!" he shouted to his men. "Attack him! Kill him, and then kill the other Radiants! Your orders are chaos and death!"

The Pursuer charged forward. The soldiers followed, then shied away. They wouldn't face Stormblessed and those eyes of his, so the Pursuer was left with no choice but to engage. Venli didn't know if he realized, but he was on his final body. Perhaps he knew he couldn't run this time, not and salvage any kind of reputation.

Stormblessed dashed to him, and they met near the vast window, flashing with lightning. The Pursuer tried to grab him, and Kaladin welcomed it, folding into the deadly embrace—then expertly slamming them both up against the window. Kaladin pressed the Pursuer to the glass—the storm outside flashed, shaking the tower, vibrating it and splashing it with light.

In that moment, Kaladin did something to the window. As he stepped back, he left the Pursuer stuck to the glass, immobilized and lacking the Voidlight to eject his soul. Kaladin didn't attack. Instead he reached down and infused the ground, but with power that didn't glow as strong as she thought it should.

The Pursuer's head . . . it was pulling forward against his neck, his eyes bulging. He groaned, and Venli realized that Stormblessed had infused the ground, then made it *pull* on the Pursuer's head. But his body was stuck to the wall.

Kaladin turned and strode toward the watching Heavenly Ones as the Pursuer's head *ripped* from his body and slammed to the floor with a crunch.

"Stormblessed," Leshwi said, stepping out to meet him. "You have fought and won. Your loss is powerful, I know, as mortals are—"

Kaladin shoved her aside. He was coming for Venli, she was sure of it. She braced herself, but he stalked past her, leaving her trembling to the Terrors. Instead Kaladin strode for the Heavenly One who was holding his father. Of course.

That Heavenly One panicked as any would. She shot off into the air, carrying the man. Two other Heavenly Ones followed.

Stormblessed looked up, then launched into the air using the strange fabrial that mimicked the Lashings.

Venli slumped to the ground, feeling worn out, though she hadn't done anything. At least it seemed to be over.

But not for the soldiers from the Pursuer's personal army, who gathered around his corpse. Dead a second time, to the same man. His reputation might be in shambles, but he *was* still Fused. He would return.

The soldiers turned toward the infirmary, remembering his last orders. They couldn't kill Stormblessed.

But they could finish off the invalid Radiants.

.˙.

Kaladin could barely see straight. He had only a vague memory of killing the Pursuer. He knew he'd done it, but remembering was hard. Thinking was hard.

He soared upward, chasing the creatures who had taken his father. He heard Lirin's shouts echoing from above, so he'd gotten his gag off. Each sound condemned Kaladin.

He didn't actually believe he could save his father. It was as if Lirin was already dead, and was screaming at Kaladin from Damnation. Kaladin wasn't exactly certain why he followed, but he had to get up high. Perhaps . . . perhaps he could see better from up high. . . .

Syl streaked ahead of him, entering the shafts that let lifts reach the final tiers of the tower. She landed on the topmost level of Urithiru. Kaladin arrived after activating a second weight halfway through the flight, then swung himself over the railing and deactivated the device in one move. He landed facing a Heavenly One who tried to block his path.

Kaladin . . .

He left that Heavenly One broken and dying, then tore through the upper chambers. Where?

The roof. They'd make for the roof to escape. Indeed, he found another Fused blocking the stairwell up, and Kaladin slammed Navani's device into the Fused's chest and locked it in place, sending him flying away, up through the stairwell and off into the sky.

Kaladin . . . I've forgotten. . . . Syl's voice. She was zipping around him, but he could barely hear her.

Kaladin burst out onto the top of the tower. The storm spread out around them, almost to the pinnacle, a dark ocean of black clouds rumbling with discontent.

The last of the Heavenly Ones was here, holding Kaladin's father. The Fused backed away, shouting something Kaladin couldn't understand.

Kaladin . . . I've forgotten . . . the Words. . . .

He advanced on the Heavenly One, and in a panic she threw his father. Out. Into the blackness. Kaladin saw Lirin's face for a brief moment before he vanished. Into the pit. The swirling storm and tempest.

Kaladin scrambled to the edge of the tower and looked down. Suddenly he knew why he'd come this high. He knew where he was going. He'd stood on this ledge before. Long ago in the rain.

This time he jumped.

107

UNITING

For ones so lost, they are somehow determined.

—Musings of El, on the first of the Final Ten Days

Navani managed to get to her feet, but after a few steps—fleeing toward the pillar, away from Moash—she was light-headed and woozy. Each breath was agony, and she was losing so much blood. She stumbled and pressed up against the wall—smearing blood across a mural of a comet-shaped spren—to keep from falling.

She glanced over her shoulder. Moash continued walking, an inevitable motion. Not rushed. His sword—with its elegant curve—held to the side so it left a small cut in the floor beside him.

"Lighteyes," Moash said. "Lying eyes. Rulers who fail to rule. Your son was a coward at the end, Queen. He begged me for his life, crying. Appropriate that he should die as he lived."

She saved her breath, not daring to respond despite her fury, and pressed on down the hallway, trailing blood.

"I killed a friend today," Moash said, his terrible voice growing softer. "I thought surely *that* would hurt. Remarkably, it didn't. I have become my best self. Free. No more pain. I bring you silence, Navani. Payment for what you've done. How you've lived. The way you—"

Navani hazarded a glance over her shoulder as he cut off suddenly.

Moash had stopped above Raboniel's body. The Fused had latched on to his foot with one hand. He cocked his head, seeming baffled.

Raboniel *launched* herself at him, clawing up his body. Her legs didn't work, but she gripped Moash with talonlike fingers, snarling, and stabbed him repeatedly with the dagger Navani had left.

The knife had no anti-Voidlight remaining—but it *was* draining his Stormlight. Raboniel had reversed the blade. Moash flinched at the attack, distracted, trying to maneuver his Shardblade to fight off the crazed Fused who grappled with him.

Move! Navani thought to herself. Raboniel was trying to buy time.

Even with renewed vigor, Navani didn't get far before the pain became too much. She stumbled into the room with the crystal pillar, abandoning thoughts of trying to escape into the tunnels beneath Urithiru.

Instead she forced herself forward to the pillar, then fell against it. "Sibling," she whispered, tasting blood on her lips. "Sibling?"

She expected to hear whimpering or weeping—the only response she'd received over the last few days. This time she heard a strange tone, both harmonious and discordant at once.

The Rhythm of War.

⁘

Dalinar flew through the air, Lashed by Lyn the Windrunner, on his way to find the Herald Ishar.

He felt something . . . rumbling. A distant storm. Everything was light around him up here, the sun shining, making it difficult to believe that somewhere it was dark and tempestuous. Somewhere, someone was lost in that blackness.

The Stormfather appeared beside him, moving in the air alongside Dalinar—a rare occurrence. The Stormfather never had features. Merely a vague impression of a figure the same size as Dalinar, yet extending into infinity.

Something was wrong.

"What?" Dalinar said.

The Son of Tanavast has entered the storm for the last time, the Stormfather said. *I feel him.*

"Kaladin?" Dalinar said, eager. "He's escaped?"

No. This is something far worse.

"Show me."

∴

Kaladin fell.

The wind tossed him and whipped at him. He was just rags. Just . . . rags for a person.

I've forgotten the Words, Kaladin, Syl said, weeping. *I see only darkness.* He felt something in his hand, her fingers somehow gripping his as they fell in the storm.

He couldn't save Teft.

He couldn't save his father.

He couldn't save himself.

He'd pushed too hard, used a grindstone on his soul until it had become paper thin. He'd failed anyway.

Those were the only Words that mattered. The only true Words.

"I'm not strong enough," he whispered to the angry winds, and closed his eyes, letting go of her hand.

∴

Dalinar was the storm around Kaladin. And at the same time he wasn't. The Stormfather didn't give Dalinar as much control as he had before, likely fearing that Dalinar would want to push him again. He was right.

Dalinar watched Kaladin tumble. Lost. No Stormlight. Eyes closed. It wasn't the bearing of a man who was fighting. Nor was it the bearing of someone who rode the winds.

It was the bearing of someone who had given up.

What do we do? Dalinar asked the Stormfather.

We witness. It is our duty.

We must help.

There is no help, Dalinar. He is too close to the tower's interference to use his powers, and you cannot blow him free of this.

Dalinar watched, pained, the rain his tears. There had to be something. *The moment between,* Dalinar said. *When you infuse spheres. You can stop time.*

Slow it greatly, the Stormfather said, *through Investiture and Connection to the Spiritual. But just briefly.*

Do it, Dalinar said. *Give him more time.*

⁘

Venli hummed to Agony as the slaughter began.

Not of the Radiants, not yet. Of the *civilians.* As soon as the Pursuer's soldiers started toward the helpless Radiants, the watching crowd of humans went insane. Led by a few determined souls—including a gruff-looking man with one arm—the humans started fighting. A full-on rebellion.

Of unarmed people against trained soldiers in warform.

Venli turned away as the killing began. The humans didn't give up though. They flooded the space between the warforms and the room with the Radiants, blocking the way with their own bodies.

"Can we prevent this?" Venli asked Leshwi, who had settled beside her after being pushed aside by Stormblessed.

"I will need the authority of Raboniel to countermand this particular order," Leshwi said to Abashment. "The Pursuer has command of law in the tower. I have already sent another of the Heavenly Ones to ask Raboniel."

Venli winced at the screams. "But Raboniel said these Radiants were to be preserved!"

"No longer," Leshwi said. "Something happened in the night. Raboniel had needed the Radiants for tests she intended to perform, but she had one of them brought to her, and afterward she said she needed no further tests. The rest are now a liability, possibly a danger, should they wake." She looked toward the dying humans, then shied away as some warforms ran past with bloody axes.

"It is . . . unfortunate," Leshwi said. "I do not sing to Joy in this type of conflict. But we have done it before, and will do it again, in the name of reclaiming our world."

"Can't we be better?" Venli begged to Disappointment. "Isn't there a way?"

Leshwi looked at her, cocking her head. Venli had again used one of the wrong rhythms.

Venli searched the room, past the angerspren and fearspren. Some of the singer troops weren't joining in the killing. She picked out Rothan and Malal, Leshwi's soldiers. They hesitated and did not join in. Leshwi picked better people than that.

Show her, Timbre pulsed. *Showhershowhershowher.*

Venli braced herself. Then she drew in Stormlight from the spheres in her pocket, and let herself begin glowing.

Leshwi hummed immediately to Destruction and grabbed Venli by the face in a powerful grip.

"What?" she said. "*What have you done?*"

⁂

Kaladin entered the place between moments.

He'd met the Stormfather here on that first horrible night when he'd been strung up in the storm. The night when Syl had fought so hard to protect him.

This time he drifted in the darkness. No wind tossed him, and the air became impossibly calm, impossibly quiet. As if he were floating alone in the ocean.

WHY WON'T YOU SAY THE WORDS? the Stormfather asked.

"I've forgotten them," Kaladin whispered.

YOU HAVE NOT.

"Will they mean anything if I don't feel them, Stormfather? Can I *lie* to swear an Ideal?"

Silence. Pure, incriminating silence.

"He wants me, as he wanted Moash," Kaladin said. "If he keeps pushing, he'll have me. So I have to go."

THAT IS A LIE, the Stormfather said. IT IS HIS ULTIMATE LIE, SON OF HONOR. THE LIE THAT SAYS YOU HAVE NO CHOICE. THE LIE THAT THERE IS NO MORE JOURNEY WORTH TAKING.

He was right. A tiny part of Kaladin—a part that could not lie to himself—knew it was true.

"What if I'm too tired?" Kaladin whispered. "What if there's nothing left to give? What if *that* is why I cannot say your Words, Stormfather? What if it's just too much?"

YOU WOULD CONSIGN MY DAUGHTER TO MISERY AGAIN?

Kaladin winced, but it was true. Could he do that to Syl?

He gritted his teeth as he began to struggle. Began to fight through the nothingness. Through the inability to think. He fought through the pain, the agony—still raw—of losing his friend.

He screamed, trembled, then sank inward.

"Too weak," he whispered.

There simply wasn't anything left for him to give.

⁘

It's not enough, Dalinar said. He couldn't see in this endless darkness, yet he could *feel* someone inside it. Two someones. Kaladin and his spren.

Storms. They hurt.

We need to give them more time, Dalinar said.

We cannot, the Stormfather said. *Respect his frailty, and don't force me on this, Dalinar! You could break things you do not understand, the consequences of which could be catastrophic.*

Have you no compassion? Dalinar demanded. *Have you no heart?*

I am a storm, the Stormfather said. *I chose the ways of a storm.*

Choose better, then! Dalinar searched in the darkness, the infinity. He was full of Stormlight in a place where that didn't matter.

In a place where all things Connected. A place beyond Shadesmar. A place beyond time. A place where . . .

What is that? Dalinar asked. *That warmth.*

I feel nothing.

Dalinar drew the warmth close, and understood. *This place is where you make the visions happen, isn't it?* Dalinar asked. *Time sometimes moved oddly in those.*

Yes, the Stormfather said. *But you must have Connection for a vision. You must have a reason for it. A meaning. It cannot be just anything.*

Good, Dalinar said, forging a bond.

What are you doing?

Connecting him, Dalinar said. Uniting him.

The Stormfather rumbled. *With what?*

108

MOMENTS

For ones so confused, they are somehow brilliant.

—Musings of El, on the first of the Final Ten Days

Kaladin jolted, opening his eyes in confusion. He was in a small tent. What on Roshar?

He blinked and sat up, finding himself beside a boy, maybe eleven or twelve years old, in an antiquated uniform. Leather skirt and cap? Kaladin was dressed similarly.

"What do you think, Dem?" the boy asked him. "Should we run?"

Kaladin scanned the small tent, baffled. Then he heard sounds outside. A battlefield? Yes, men yelling and dying. He stood up and stepped out into the light, blinking against it. A . . . hillside, with some stumpweight trees on it. This wasn't the Shattered Plains.

I know this place, Kaladin thought. *Amaram's colors. Men in leather armor.*

Storms, he was on a battlefield from his youth. The exhaustion had taken a toll on him. He was hallucinating. The surgeon in him was worried at that.

A young squadleader walked up, haggard. Storms, he couldn't be older than seventeen or eighteen. That seemed so young to Kaladin now, though he wasn't that much older. The squadleader was arguing with a shorter soldier beside him.

"We can't hold," the squadleader said. "It's impossible. Storms, they're gathering for another advance."

"The orders are clear," the other man said—barely out of his teens himself. "Brightlord Sheler says we're to hold here. No retreat."

"To Damnation with that man," the squadleader said, wiping his sweaty hair, surrounded by jets of exhaustionspren. Kaladin immediately felt a kinship with the poor fool. Given impossible orders and not enough resources? Looking along the ragged battle line, Kaladin guessed the man was in over his head, with all the higher-ranked soldiers dead. There were barely enough men to form three squads, and half of those were wounded.

"This is Amaram's fault," Kaladin said. "Playing with the lives of half-trained men in outdated equipment, all to make himself look good so he'll get moved to the Shattered Plains."

The young squadleader glanced at Kaladin, frowning. "You shouldn't talk like that, kid," the man said, running his hand through his hair again. "It could get you strung up, if the highmarshal hears." The man took a deep breath. "Form up the wounded men on that flank. Tell everyone to get ready to hold. And . . . you, messenger boy, grab your friend and get some spears. Gor, put them in front."

"In front?" the other man asked. "You certain, Varth?"

"You work with what you have . . ." the man said, hiking back the way he had come.

Work with what you have.

Everything spun around Kaladin, and he suddenly remembered this exact battlefield. He knew where he was. He knew that squadleader's face. How had he not seen it immediately?

Kaladin *had* been here. Rushing through the lines, searching for . . . Searching for . . .

He spun on his heel and found a young man—too young—approaching Varth. He had an open, inviting face and too much spring in his step as he approached the squadleader. "I'll go with them, sir," Tien said.

"Fine. Go."

Tien picked up a spear. He gathered the other messenger boy from the tent and started toward the place where he'd been told to stand.

"No, Tien," Kaladin said. "I can't watch this. Not again."

Tien came and took Kaladin's hand, then walked him forward. "It's all right," he said. "I know you're frightened. But here we can stand together, all of us. Three are stronger than one, right?" He held out his spear, and the other boy—who was crying—did the same.

"Tien," Kaladin said. "Why did you do it? You should have stayed safe."

Tien turned to him, then smiled. "They would have been alone. They needed someone to help them feel brave."

"They were slaughtered," Kaladin said. "So were you."

"So it was good someone was there, to help them not feel so alone as it happened."

"You were terrified. I saw your eyes."

"Of course I was." Tien looked at him as the charge began, and the enemy advanced up the hillside. "Who wouldn't be afraid? Doesn't change that I needed to be here. For them."

Kaladin remembered getting stabbed on this battlefield . . . killing a man. Then being forced to watch Tien die. He cringed, anticipating that death, but all went dark. The forest, the tent, the figures all vanished.

Except for Tien.

Kaladin fell to his knees. Then Tien, poor little Tien, wrapped his arms around Kaladin and held him. "It's all right," he whispered. "I'm here. To help you feel brave."

"I'm not the child you see," Kaladin whispered.

"I know who you are, Kal."

Kaladin looked up at his brother. Who somehow, in that moment, was full grown. And Kaladin was a child, clinging to him. Holding to him as the tears started to fall, as he let himself weep at Teft's death.

"This is wrong," Kaladin said. "I'm supposed to hold *you*. Protect *you*."

"And you did. As I helped you." He pulled Kaladin tight. "Why do we fight, Kal? Why do we keep going?"

"I don't know," Kaladin whispered. "I've forgotten."

"It's so we can be with each other."

"They all die, Tien. Everyone dies."

"So they do, don't they?"

"That means it doesn't matter," Kaladin said. "None of it *matters*."

"See, that's the wrong way of looking at it." Tien held him tighter. "Since we all go to the same place in the end, the moments we spent with each other are the only things that *do* matter. The times we helped each other."

Kaladin trembled.

"Look at it, Kal," Tien said softly. "See the colors. If you think letting Teft die is a failure—but all the times you supported him are meaningless—then *no wonder* it always hurts. Instead, if you think of how lucky you both were to be able to help each other when you *were* together, well, it looks a lot nicer, doesn't it?"

"I'm not strong enough," Kaladin whispered.

"You're strong enough for me."

"I'm not good enough."

"You're good enough *for me.*"

"I wasn't there."

Tien smiled. "You *are* here *for me,* Kal. You're here for all of us."

"And . . ." Kaladin said, tears on his cheeks, "if I fail again?"

"You can't. So long as you understand." He pulled Kaladin tight. Kaladin rested his head against Tien's chest, blotting his tears with the cloth of his shirt. "Teft believes in you. The enemy thinks he's won. But *I* want to see his face when he realizes the truth. Don't you? It's going to be *delightful.*"

Kaladin found himself smiling.

"If he kills us," Tien said, "he's simply dropped us off at a place we were going anyway. We shouldn't hasten it, and it *is* sad. But see, he *can't* take our moments, our Connection, Kaladin. And those are things that *really* matter."

Kaladin closed his eyes, letting himself enjoy *this* moment. "Is it real?" he finally asked. "Are *you* real? Or is this something made by the Stormfather, or Wit, or someone else?"

Tien smiled, then pressed something into Kaladin's hand. A small wooden horse. "Try to keep track of him this time, Kal. I worked hard on that."

Then Kaladin dropped suddenly, the wooden horse evaporating in his hand as he fell.

He searched around in the endless blackness. "Syl?" he called.

A pinprick of light, weaving around him. But that wasn't her.

"SYL!"

Another pinprick. And another.

But those weren't her. *That* was. He reached into the darkness and seized her hand, pulling her to him. She grabbed him, physical in this place and his own size.

She held to him, and shook as she spoke. "I've forgotten the Words. I'm supposed to help you, but I can't. I . . ."

"You are helping," Kaladin said, "by being here." He closed his eyes, feeling the storm as they broke through the moment between and entered the real world.

"Besides," he whispered, "I know the Words."

Say them, Tien whispered.

"I have always known these Words."

Say it, lad! Do it!

"I accept it, Stormfather! *I accept that there will be those I cannot protect!*"

The storm rumbled, and he felt warmth surrounding him, Light infusing him. He heard Syl gasp, and a familiar voice, not the Stormfather's.

THESE WORDS ARE ACCEPTED.

"We couldn't save Teft, Syl," Kaladin whispered. "We couldn't save Tien. But we *can* save my father."

And when he opened his eyes, the sky exploded with a thousand pure lights.

For ones so tarnished, they are somehow bright.

—Musings of El, on the first of the Final Ten Days

Leshwi fell to her knees before Venli, not flying, not hovering. On her *knees*. Venli knelt as well, as Leshwi still held to her face—but the grip softened.

A cool, beautiful light flooded in through the window behind. Like a frozen lightning bolt, brighter than any sphere. Bright as the sun.

"What have you done, Venli?" Leshwi said. "What have you *done*?"

"I . . . I swore the First Ideal of the Radiants," Venli said. "I'm sorry."

"Sorry . . ." Leshwi said. A joyspren burst around her, beautiful, like a blue storm. "*Sorry?* Venli, they've *come back* to us! They've *forgiven us*."

What?

"Please," Leshwi said to Longing, "ask your spren. Do they know of an honorspren named Riah? She was my friend once. Precious to me."

Leshwi . . . had friends? Among the *spren*?

Storms. Leshwi had lived *before* the war, when men and singers had been allies. Honor had been the god of the Dawnsingers.

Timbre pulsed.

"She . . . doesn't know Riah," Venli said. "But she doesn't know a lot of honorspren. She . . . doesn't think any of the old ones survived the human betrayal."

Leshwi nodded, humming softly to . . . to one of the old rhythms.

"My spren though," Venli said. "She . . . has friends, who are willing to maybe try again. With us."

"My soul is too long owned by someone else for that," Leshwi said.

Venli glanced toward the fighting. The sudden light hadn't halted them. If anything, it had made the Pursuer's soldiers more determined as they attacked. They seemed to enjoy the company of the angerspren and painspren. Some of the humans had wrestled away weapons, but most of them fought unarmed, trying desperately to keep the Radiants safe.

"I don't know what to do," Venli whispered. "I keep wavering between two worlds. I'm too weak, mistress."

Leshwi rose into the air, then ripped her side sword from its sheath. "It's all right, Voice. I know the answer."

She flew directly into the fight and began pulling away the soldiers, shouting for them to halt. When they didn't, Leshwi started swinging. And in seconds her troops had joined her, as singer fought singer.

❖

"Sibling," Navani whispered, clinging to the pillar. "What is happening? Why do you make that rhythm?"

Navani? The voice that responded was soft as a baby's breath on her skin. Almost imperceptible. *I hear this rhythm. I hear it in the darkness. Why?*

"Where is it coming from?"

There.

Navani was given an impression, a vision that overlaid her senses. A place in the tower . . . the atrium, dark from a storm blowing outside? Down here, deep within the basement, she hadn't realized one was going on.

Fighting. People were fighting, struggling, dying. Navani squinted at the vision. Her pain was fading—though a part of her felt that was a bad sign. But she could see . . . a Fused, flying a foot off the ground, fighting beside someone infused with Voidlight. A Regal? And those were humans with them, standing together. Side by side.

"What are they doing?" Navani asked.

Fighting other singers. I think. It's so dark. Why do they fight each other?

"What's in that room they defend?" Navani whispered.

That is where they put the fallen Radiants.

"Emulsifier," Navani whispered.

What?

"A joined purpose. Humans and singers. Honor and Odium. They're fighting to protect the helpless, Sibling."

The vision faded, but before it did, Navani spotted Rlain—the singer who worked with Bridge Four.

"He's there," Navani said, then found herself coughing. Each convulsion made the pain flare up again. "Sibling, he's there!"

Too far, they whispered. *Too late . . .*

Outside in the hallway, Moash hacked at Raboniel's left arm—making it fall limp. She clawed at him with her remaining arm, hissing, as the hand with the dagger dropped its weapon and dangled uselessly.

"Take me," Navani whispered to the Sibling. "Bond me."

No, the Sibling said, voice faint.

"Why?"

You aren't worthy, Navani.

⁘

Rlain heard the shouting long before they reached the atrium. The guards holding him attuned Anxiety and hurried him and Dabbid faster, though Rlain remained optimistic. That noise had to be from Kaladin's fight with the Pursuer.

Rlain was, therefore, utterly shocked when they walked into the atrium to find a full-on civil war. Singers fought against singers, and a group of humans stood side by side with one of the forces.

Rlain's guards went running—perhaps to find some kind of authority figure to sort out this nonsense—leaving him and Dabbid. But the fray ended quickly, and the side with the humans won. Few of the singers seemed to want to fight Fused, and so the troops fled, leaving the dead behind them.

"What?" Dabbid asked softly, the two of them hanging back in one of the side corridors where some human civilians—brave enough to watch, but not skilled enough to join—clustered.

Rlain made a quick assessment, then attuned the Rhythm of Hope. Five of the Heavenly Ones—and about twenty Regals under their command—had turned upon the soldiers of the Pursuer. The other Heavenly Ones seemed to have refused to join either side, and had retreated up higher into the atrium.

That was Leshwi, hovering near the front of the side that had won—holding a sword coated in orange singer blood. She seemed to be in charge.

A good number of people, both human and singer, were down and bleeding. It was a mess. "They need field surgeons," Rlain said. "Come on."

He and Dabbid raced in and—as Kaladin had trained them—started a quick triage. People began helping, and in minutes Rlain had them all binding wounds for both singers and humans, regardless of which side they'd fought on.

Lirin had supplies in the infirmary, fortunately—and when Dabbid returned with them, he brought Hesina, who seemed rattled by the fighting. It was a few minutes before Rlain got an explanation. Lirin had been taken? Kaladin had given chase?

Rlain attuned the Lost. No wonder Hesina looked like she'd been through a storm. Still, she seemed eager to have something to do, and took over leading the triage.

That let Rlain step away for a breather and wipe his hands. Some humans who had seen it all gave him scattered explanations. The Pursuer had ordered the slaughter of helpless Radiants, and both humans and singers had resisted his army. Before Rlain could go demand answers from Venli, several gruff human men approached him. He recognized them from the sessions Kaladin had been doing, helping them with trauma. They'd been forced to pick up weapons again, the poor cremlings.

"Yes?" Rlain asked.

They led him to a body placed reverently beside the wall, the eyes burned out. Teft.

Rlain fell to his knees as Dabbid joined him, letting out a quiet whimper, anguishspren surrounding them. They knelt together, heads bowed.

Rlain sang the Song of the Fallen, a song for a dead hero. It seemed the plan hadn't gone off too well for them either.

"Lift?" he asked.

"She's in the infirmary," Dabbid whispered. "Unconscious. Legs dead from a Blade. Looks like someone hit her hard on the head. She . . . is bleeding. I tried to give her Stormlight. Nothing happened."

Rlain attuned Mourning. Lift could heal others, but—like with Kaladin and Teft—her internal healing wasn't working. So much for waking the Radiants. He bowed his head for Teft, then left him there. Let the dead rest. It was their way, and he wished to be able to give the man a proper sky burial. Teft had been a good person. One of the best.

Behind him, other matters drew Rlain's attention. The humans and singers were already squabbling.

"You need to submit," Leshwi was saying, hovering above them in her imperious Fused way. "I will explain to Raboniel that the soldiers were uncontrolled and didn't obey my orders."

"And you think she'll let us walk?" one of the human women shouted. "We need to get out of here *right now*."

"If I let you go," Leshwi said, "it will seem that I am in rebellion. We can contain this if you submit."

"You're not in rebellion?" one of the men demanded. "What was *that* then?"

"We ain't obeying one of *you* again," another bellowed. "Ever!"

Shouts from both sides rose as singers ordered the people not to argue with one of the Fused. Rlain turned from one group to the other, then attuned Determination and wiped the makeup from his tattoo. He strode out between the groups. Field medicine wasn't the only thing Bridge Four had taught.

"Listen up!" he shouted to Confidence. "All of you!"

Remarkably, they fell silent. Rlain did his best Teft impersonation as he turned to the humans. "You all, you know me. I'm Bridge Four. I know you don't like me, but are you willing to trust me?"

The humans grumbled, but most of them nodded, prompted by Noril. Rlain turned toward the singers. "You all," he barked to Confidence, "*absolutely* committed treason. You acted against Odium's wishes, and he will seek retribution for that. You're as good as dead—and you Fused, you're in for an eternity of torture. Fortunately, you have *two people* here who can guide you—listeners from a people who escaped his control. So if you want to survive, you're going to *listen to me.*"

Leshwi folded her arms. But then muttered, "Fine." The other Heavenly Ones seemed willing to follow her lead.

Venli rushed over, and she was infused with the deep violet light of Voidlight. Far more so than an ordinary Regal. She glowed more, in fact, than a Fused.

"What are *you*?" Rlain demanded.

"A Radiant," she said to Consolation. "Kind of. I can use Voidlight to power my abilities, so they work in the tower."

"Figures," Rlain grumbled. "Kelek's breath . . . I wait years, then *you* of all people grab a spren first." Maybe that was too much Teft. "Anyway, it explains how you got Lift out. We need to get moving. Odium won't stand for a rebellion among his own. So you singers are going to come with us. We're going to grab the Radiants and we're going to carry them out onto the plateau, where we'll escape via the Oathgates to the Shattered Plains."

"That puts us in the humans' power," Leshwi said.

"I'll get you out of it," Rlain said. "*After* we're all safe. Understood? Gather up our wounded, grab those Radiants, and let's *get going.* Before Raboniel knows there was a rebellion, I want all involved parties—human and singer—out of this tower. Go!"

They started moving, trusting that he knew what he was saying. Which . . . he wasn't certain he did. Transporting a bunch of unconscious people would be slow, and there was a highstorm outside.

"Rlain," Venli said to Awe. "You gave orders to a *Fused.*"

He shrugged. "It's all about an air of authority."

"It's more than that," she said. "How?"

"I had good teachers," Rlain said, though he was a little surprised himself. He was a spy, used to staying back, letting others lead while he watched. Today, though, there hadn't been anyone else. And having been rejected by both sides, he figured he was an outsider—and therefore as close to a neutral party as there could be in this conflict.

Everyone worked together to move the unconscious Radiants and the wounded. Even Leshwi and the five other Heavenly Ones each carried a wounded soldier. Rlain spent the time checking the balconies up above. The dozens of Heavenly Ones who hadn't joined the battle had now vanished. Carrying word to Raboniel, undoubtedly. Or marshaling their personal forces to stop this rebellion.

Once everyone was together, Rlain waved for them to follow as he started the hike out. Venli hurried up beside him.

"How are we going to work the Oathgate?" she whispered.

"I know the mechanism," Rlain said. "I assume we can use your Blade to figure it out."

Venli hurried at his side as they entered a corridor. "My *Blade*?"

"You told me you cut Lift out of her cell with a Shardblade. I wondered why they let you have one instead of giving it to a Fused, but now I can piece it together. Yours is a living Radiant Blade—which can work the Oathgates. I guess your Voidlight lets you summon it?"

Venli hummed to Anxiety. "I don't have a Blade, Rlain."

"But—"

"I was lying! I used my powers to get her out. Timbre says I'm a long way from earning my own Blade!"

Damnation. "We'll figure something out," he said. "Right now, we need to keep moving."

Radiant.

—Musings of El, on the first of the Final Ten Days

A black storm.
   Black wind.
   Black rain.
Then, piercing the blackness like a spear, a lance of light.
Kaladin Stormblessed.
Reborn.

Kaladin exploded through the darkness, surrounded by a thousand joyful windspren, swirling like a vortex. "Go!" he shouted. "Find him!"

Though it felt like he'd been falling for hours, he had spent most of that time in the place between moments. If he was still falling through the sky, mere seconds had passed, and his father was falling somewhere below him.

Still alive.

Kaladin pointed downward, reaching out, preparing himself as hundreds of windspren met the storm and blew it back, creating an open path. A tunnel of light leading toward a single figure tumbling in the air, distant.

Still alive.

Kaladin's Lashings piled atop one another as Syl spun around him, laughing. Storms, how he'd missed her laughter. With his hand outstretched, Kaladin watched as a windspren slammed into it and flashed, outlining his hand with a glowing transparent gauntlet.

A dozen others slammed into him, joyful, exultant. Lines of light exploded around him as the spren transformed—being pulled into this realm and choosing to Connect to him.

He watched that tiny tumbling figure as it drew closer and closer. The ground, so near. They'd fallen the length of the tower and hundreds of feet below it in the storms.

The ground rose up to meet them.

Almost. *Almost.* Kaladin stretched out his hand, and—

⁘

Not worthy.

The words echoed against Navani's soul, and for the moment she forgot Moash. She forgot the tower. She was someplace else.

Not good enough.

Not a scholar.

Not a creator.

You have no fame, accomplishment, or capacity of your own. Everything that is distinctive about you came from someone else.

"Lies," she whispered. And they were.

They truly were.

She pressed her hand to the pillar. "Take me as your Bondsmith. I *am* worthy, Sibling. I say the Words. Life before death."

No. So soft. *We are . . . too different. . . . You capture spren.*

"Who better to work together than two who believe differently?" she said. "Strength before weakness. We can compromise. Isn't that the soul of building bonds? Of *uniting*?"

Moash kicked Raboniel away and she hit the wall, limp as a doll.

"We can find the answers!" Navani said, blood dribbling from her lips. "Together."

You . . . just want . . . to live.

"Don't you?"

The Sibling's voice grew too soft to hear. Moash looked down the hallway toward Navani.

So she closed her eyes and tried to hum. She tried to find Stormlight's tone, pure and vibrant. But she faltered. Navani couldn't hear that tone, not right now. Not with everything falling apart, not with her life seeping away.

She found herself humming a different tone instead. The one Raboniel had always given her, with its chaotic rhythm. Yes, this close to death, Navani could only hear that. His tone. Eager to claim her.

The Sibling whimpered.

And Navani inverted the tone.

All it took was Intent. Odium gave her the song, but she twisted it back upon him. She hummed the song of anti-Voidlight, her hand pressed to the pillar.

Navani! the Sibling said, voice growing stronger. *The darkness retreats ever so slightly. What are you doing?*

"I . . . created this for you . . ." Navani said. "I tried to . . ."

Navani? the Sibling said. *Navani, it's not enough. The song isn't loud enough. It seems to be hurting that man though. He has frozen in place. Navani?*

Her voice faltered. Her bloody hand slipped down to her side, leaving marks on the pillar.

I can hear my mother's tone, the Sibling said. *But not my tone. I think it's because my father is dead.*

"Honor . . ." Navani whispered. "Honor is not . . . dead. He lives inside the hearts . . . of his children. . . ."

Does he? Truly? It seemed a plea, not a challenge.

Does he? Navani searched deep. Was what she'd been doing honorable? Creating fabrials? Imprisoning spren? Could she really say that? Odium's tone rang in her ears, though she'd stopped humming its inverse.

Then, a pure song. Rising up from within her. Orderly, powerful. Had she done harm without realizing it? Possibly. Had she made mistakes? Certainly. But she'd been trying to help. That was *her* journey. A journey to discover, learn, and make the world better.

Honor's song welled up inside her, and she sang it. The pillar began to vibrate as the Sibling sang Cultivation's song. The pure sound of

Lifelight. The sound began to shift, and Navani modulated her tone, inching it closer and closer to . . .

The two snapped into harmony. The boundless energy of Cultivation, always growing and changing, and the calm solidity of Honor—organized, structured. They vibrated together. Structure and nature. Knowledge and wonder. Mixing.

The song of science itself.

That is it, the Sibling whispered to the Rhythm of the Tower. *My song.*

"Our emulsifier," Navani whispered to the Rhythm of the Tower.

The common ground, the Sibling said. *Between humans and spren. That is . . . that is why I was created, so long ago. . . .*

A rough hand grabbed Navani and spun her around, then pressed her against the pillar. Moash raised his Blade.

Navani, the Sibling said. *I accept your Words.*

Power flooded Navani. Infused her, making her pain evaporate like water on a hotplate. Together, she and the Sibling *created* Light. The energy surged through her so fully, she felt it bursting from her eyes and mouth as she looked up at Moash and spoke.

"Journey before destination, you bastard."

⁘

Lirin hung in the air, his eyes squeezed closed, trembling. He remembered falling, and the awful tempest. Darkness.

It had all vanished. Something had yanked on his arm—slowing him carefully enough to not rip his arm off, but jarringly enough that it ached.

Stillness. In a storm. Was he dead?

He opened his eyes and searched upward to find a column of radiant light stretching hundreds of feet in the air, holding back the storm. Windspren? Thousands upon thousands of them.

Lirin dangled from the gauntleted fist of a Shardbearer in resplendent Shardplate. Armor that seemed *alive* as it glowed a vibrant blue at the seams, Bridge Four glyphs emblazoned across the chest.

A flying Shardbearer. Storms. It was him.

Kaladin proved it by rotating so that they were right-side up—then hoisting Lirin into a tight embrace. Remarkably, as Lirin touched the

Plate, he couldn't feel it. It became completely transparent—barely visible, in fact, as a faint outline around Kaladin.

"I'm sorry, Father," Kaladin said.

"Sorry? For . . . for what?"

"I thought your way might be correct," Kaladin said. "And that I'd been wrong. But I don't think it's that simple. I think we're both correct. For us."

"I think perhaps I can accept that," Lirin said.

Kaladin leaned back—still holding him as they dangled barely twenty feet above the rocks. Storms. Was that how close they'd come? "Cutting it a little tight, don't you think, son?"

"A surgeon must be timely and precise."

"This is timely?" Lirin said.

"Well, you do hate it when people waste time," Kaladin said, grinning. Then he paused, letting go of Lirin with one arm—which was somewhat disconcerting, though Lirin now seemed to be floating on his own. Kaladin touched Lirin's forehead with fingers that felt normal, despite being faintly outlined by the gauntlet.

"What is this?" Kaladin asked.

Lirin remembered, with some embarrassment, what he'd finally let that one-armed fool Noril do to him. A painted *shash* glyph on Lirin's forehead.

"I figured," Lirin said, "that if an entire tower was going to show faith in my son, I could maybe try to do the same. I'm sorry, son. For my part." He reached up and brushed aside Kaladin's hair to see the brand there.

But as he did, he found scabs flaking away, the brands falling off to the stones below like a shell outgrown, discarded. Clean, smooth skin was left behind.

Kaladin reached to his forehead in shock. He prodded at the skin, as if amazed. Then he laughed, grabbing Lirin in a tighter embrace.

"Careful, son," Lirin said. "I'm not a Radiant. We mortals break."

"Radiants break too," Kaladin whispered. "But then, fortunately, we fill the cracks with something stronger. Come on. We need to protect the people in that tower. You in your way. Me in mine."

III

UNCHAINED

And so I am not at all dissatisfied with recent events.

—Musings of El, on the first of the Final Ten Days

D alinar returned from the Stormfather's vision and found himself still flying with the Windrunners—face mask in place, wrapped in several layers of protective clothing.

He felt clunky and slow after being the winds moments ago. But he reveled in what he'd heard and felt. What he'd said.

These Words are accepted.

Whatever was happening at Urithiru, Kaladin would face it standing up straight. God Beyond bless it to be enough, and that the Windrunner could reach Navani. For now, Dalinar had to focus on his current task.

He urged his speed to increase, but of course that did nothing. He had no control over this lesser flight; in it, Dalinar was little more than an arrow propelled through the air by someone else's power—buffeted by the jealous winds, which did not want him invading their sky.

A part of him acknowledged the puerile nature of these complaints. He was *flying*. Covering a hundred miles in less than half an hour. His current travel was a wonder, an incredible achievement. But for a brief time he'd known something better.

At least this particular flight was nearly finished. It was a relatively quick jump from the battlefields of Emul down to the border of Tukar, where Ishar's camp had been spotted. The main bulk of the god-priest's armies had repositioned during the coalition's campaign, fortifying positions in case the singers or Dalinar's army tried to advance into Tukar.

So as Dalinar's team reached the coast, they found several depopulated camps, marked by large bonfire scars on the stone. The region had been denuded—trees chopped for lumber, hills stripped of anything edible. An army could forage and hunt to stay alive here in the West, where plants grew more readily. In the Unclaimed Hills, that had never been possible.

Sigzil slowed their group of five Windrunners, Dalinar, and Szeth into a hovering position. Beneath them, Ishar's large pavilion remained, and some hundred soldiers stood in a ring in front. These wore similar clothing: hogshide battle leathers with hardened cuirasses painted a dark blue, closer to black than the Kholin shade. Not a true uniform, but in a theme at least. Considering their lack of Soulcasters and the prevalence of herdsmen in the area, the equipment made sense. They were armed mostly with spears, though some had steel swords.

"They're ready for us all right," the Azish Windrunner said, steadying Dalinar in the air so he didn't drift away. "Brightlord, I don't like this."

"We're all Radiant," Dalinar said, "with plenty of gemstones and a Bondsmith to renew our spheres. We're as prepared as anyone could be for whatever will happen below."

The companylord glanced toward Szeth, who had been ostensibly flown by Sigzil, but had actually used his own Stormlight. Dalinar had let Sigzil in on the secret, naturally—he wouldn't leave an officer ignorant of his team's capabilities.

"Let me at least send someone else down first," Sigzil said. "To talk, find out what they want."

Dalinar took a deep breath, then nodded. He was impatient, but one did not build good officers by ignoring their legitimate suggestions. "That would be wise."

Sigzil conferred with his Windrunners, then swooped toward the ground. Apparently "someone else" had meant him. Sigzil landed and was met by Ishar himself, who emerged from the pavilion. Dalinar could identify the Herald immediately. There was a bond between them. A Connection.

Sigzil was not attacked by the soldiers in the large ring. Talking to Shalash these last few days, Dalinar thought he had a good picture of the old Herald. He had always imagined Ishi as a wise, careful man, thoughtful. Really, Dalinar's image of him had always been similar to that of Nohadon, the author of *The Way of Kings*.

Shalash had disabused him of these notions. She presented Ishar as a confident, eager man. Energetic, more a battlefield commander than a wise old scholar. He was the man who had discovered how to travel between worlds, leading humans to Roshar in the first place.

One word that Shalash had never used was "crafty." Ishar was a bold thinker, a man who pulled others after him on seemingly crazed ideas that worked. But he was not a subtle man. Or at least he hadn't been. Shalash warned that all of them had changed over the millennia, their . . . personal quirks growing more and more pronounced.

Dalinar was not surprised that Sigzil was able to speak to the man, then fly back up safely. Ishar did not seem the type to plan an ambush.

"Sir," Sigzil said, floating up beside Dalinar. "I . . . don't think he's altogether sane, despite what Shalash says."

"That was expected," Dalinar said. "What did he say?"

"He claims to be the Almighty," Sigzil said. "God, born again, after being shattered. He says he's waiting for Odium's champion to come and fight him for the end of the world. I think he means you, sir."

Chilling words. "But he's willing to talk?"

"Yes, sir," Sigzil said. "Though I must warn you I don't like this entire situation."

"Understood. Take us down."

Sigzil gave the orders, and they made their way to the ground and landed in the center of the ring of soldiers. A few Windrunners summoned Shardblades; the others, not yet of the Third Ideal, carried spears. They surrounded Dalinar in a circular formation, but he patted Sigzil on the shoulder and made them part.

He walked toward Ishar, Szeth shadowing him on one side, Sigzil on the other. Dalinar had not expected the old Herald to look so strong. Dalinar was used to the frailty of men like Taravangian, but the person before him was a warrior. Though he was outfitted in robes and wearing an ardent's beard, his forearms and stance clearly indicated he was accustomed to holding a weapon.

"Champion of Odium," Ishar said in a loud, deep voice, speaking Azish. "It has been a long wait."

"I am not Odium's champion," Dalinar said. "I wish to be your ally in facing him, however."

"Your lies cannot fool me. I am Tezim, first man, aspect of the Almighty. I alone prepare for the end of the worlds. I should not have ignored your previous messages to me; I see now what you are. What you must be. Only a servant of my enemy could have captured Urithiru, my holy seat."

"Ishar," Dalinar said softly. "I know what you are."

"I am that man no longer," Ishar said. "I am Herald of Heralds, sole bearer of the Oathpact. I am more than I once was and I will become yet more. I shall absorb your power, Odium, and become a god among gods, Adonalsium reborn."

Dalinar took a tentative step forward, waving for the others to stay back. "I spoke to Ash," Dalinar said calmly. "She said to tell you that Taln has returned. He's hurt, and she pleads for your help in restoring him."

"Taln . . ." Ishar said. He adopted a far-off look. "Our sin. Bearer of our agonies . . ."

"Jezrien is dead, Ishar," Dalinar said. "Truly dead. You felt it. Ash felt it. He was captured, but his soul faded away after that. Her *father*, Ishar. She lost her father. She needs your counsel. Taln's madness terrifies her. She needs you."

"I prepared myself for your lies, champion of Odium," Ishar said. "I had not realized they would be so . . . reasonable. Yet you have already done too much to prove who you are. Taking my holy city. Summoning your evil storm. Sending your minions to torment my people. You have corrupted the spren to your side, so you can have false Radiants, but I have discovered your secrets." He held his hands as if to summon a Blade. "The time for the end is upon us. Let us begin the battle."

A weapon appeared from mist in his hands. A sinuous Shardblade lined with glyphs Dalinar did not recognize—though the Blade itself was vaguely familiar. Had he seen it before?

Szeth hissed loudly. "That Blade," he said. "The Bondsmith Honorblade. My *father's* sword. Where did you get it? What have you done to my father?"

Ishar stepped forward to strike at Dalinar.

While some humans left Rlain's band of rebels—returning to their rooms, hoping they hadn't been recognized—most of them stayed. Indeed, the numbers increased as many of the resisters fetched their families. Because Rlain had to let them go fetch families. What else could they do? Leave them to the Pursuer, who was known to target the loved ones of people he hunted?

All of this ate away at their time. They were also slowed by the need to carry both the wounded and the unconscious Radiants. Rlain did what he could to keep the main group moving, taking them through the Breakaway, avoiding the central corridor—where they'd be too easily exposed to Heavenly Ones from above.

However, he found himself attuning Despair. They were being watched—that cremling that harbored a Voidspren was following them along the wall. Rlain's band wasn't quite halfway through the market—still a fair distance from the front of the tower—when *cracks* broke the air, causing gawking marketgoers to flee. Stormform lightning strikes, used as a signal to empty the streets.

Rlain backed his haggard group against the wall of the large cavern and put their soldiers up front, the Heavenly Ones flying above. Deepest Ones began to emerge from the floor in front of them, and dozens of stormforms approached.

"You're right, listener," Leshwi said, lowering down beside him. "I couldn't have talked us out of this. *He* knows what we did. Those who approach are humming the Rhythm of Executions."

"Maybe we should have tried to reach the crystal pillar room," Rlain said. "And escaped through the tunnels beneath, as Venli suggested."

"No," Leshwi said. "Those tunnels are blocked. Our best hope was to escape out the front entrance of the tower, and perhaps cross the mountains. Unfortunately, judging by those rhythms, these who come aren't being sent by Raboniel. Odium wants me to know. I will be tortured like the Heralds once I return to Braize." She saluted Rlain. "So first, we fight."

Rlain nodded, then gripped his spear. "We fight," he said, then turned to Venli, who had stepped up by his side. "Are there any other spren like the one who bonded you? Would some want other willing singers? Someone like me?"

"Yes," Venli said to Mourning, "but I sent them away. The Fused would have seen them, hunted them." She paused, then her rhythm changed to Confusion. "And Timbre says . . . she says you're spoken for?"

"What?" he said. "By that honorspren who said he'd take me? I turned him down. I . . ."

The room went dark.

Then it shone as crystals grew out from his feet like . . . like stained glass windows, covering the floor. They showed a figure rising in blue-glowing Shardplate, and a tower coming alight.

Keep fighting, a voice said in his head. *Salvation will be, Rlain, listener. Bridger of Minds. I have been sent to you by my mother, at the request of Renarin, Son of Thorns. I have watched you and seen your worthiness.*

Speak the Words, and do not despair.

⁘

Sigzil blocked Ishar's attack using his Shardblade. The other Windrunners swarmed forward to protect Dalinar. Szeth, however, stumbled away. The sight of that Honorblade had plainly upset him.

The watching Tukari soldiers started to close their circle, but Ishar ordered them back. Then he danced away from Sigzil, shouting at Dalinar. "Fight me, champion! Face me alone!"

"I brought no weapon, Ishar," Dalinar said. "The time for the contest of champions has not yet come."

Ishar fought brilliantly as the other Windrunners tried to gang up on him. He was a blur with a flashing Blade, parrying, dodging, skepping his Blade—making it vanish for a brief moment to pass through a weapon trying to block it. The Windrunners had only recently started practicing the technique; Ishar performed the complex move with the grace of long familiarity.

He is a duelist, Dalinar thought. *Storms, and a good one.*

What did you expect? the Stormfather rumbled in his mind. *He defended mankind for millennia. The Heralds were not all warriors when they began, but all were by the end. Existing for three thousand years in a state of near-constant war changes men. Among the Heralds, Ishar was average in skill.*

Ishar faced all five Windrunners at once, and it seemed *easy* for him. He blocked one, then another, stepping away as a third tried to spear down from above, then swept around with his Blade, slicing the heads off two non-Shard spears.

Sigzil's Shardblade became a long dueling sword designed for lunges. He struck when Ishar's back was turned, but the Herald casually twisted and caught the Blade with one finger—touching it along the unsharpened side—and guided it past him. Sigzil stumbled as he drew too close, and Ishar lifted that same hand and slammed it against Sigzil's chest, sending him sprawling backward to the stones.

Ishar then turned and raised his Shardblade in one hand to deflect one of Lyn's strikes. Leyten came in, trying to flank, but he looked clumsy compared to the old Herald. Fortunately for the five, Ishar merely defended himself.

Despite earnestly trying, none could land a blow. It was as if . . . as if they were trying to hit where Ishar *was*, while he was able to move in anticipation of where they *would be*.

He is average among them? Dalinar asked. *Then . . . who was the best?*

Taln.

The one who sits in my camp? Dalinar thought. *Unable to do more than mumble?*

Yes, the Stormfather said. *There was no dispute. But take care; Ishar's skill as a duelist is a lesser danger. He has recovered his Honorblade. He is a Bondsmith unchained.*

Ishar suddenly dashed forward, rushing into one of Sigzil's attacks. The old man ducked the strike, then came up and touched Sigzil on the chest. When Ishar's hand withdrew, he trailed a line of Stormlight behind him. He touched his hand to the ground, and Sigzil stumbled, gasping as his glow started to fade. Ishar had apparently tethered Sigzil to the stones with some kind of glowing rope that drained the Stormlight out and into the ground.

The other four followed, almost faster than Dalinar could track. One after another, tethered to the stone. Not bound, not frozen, but their Light draining away—and all of them stumbled, slowing, as if their lives were being drained with it.

Dalinar glanced at Szeth, but the Shin man had fallen to his knees, wide eyed. Storms. Dalinar should have known better than to depend on the assassin as a bodyguard. Navani had warned him; Szeth was nearly as unstable as the Heralds.

Dalinar didn't want to see what happened when his troops ran out of Stormlight. He braced himself and thrust his hands between realms, then slammed them together as closed fists, knuckles meeting. In this, he united the three realms, opening a flash of power that washed away all color and infused the Radiants with Light.

Within the well of Light, Dalinar was nearly blinded—figures were mere lines, all shadows banished. Ishar, however, was distinct. Pale, eyes wide, whitened clothing rippling. He dropped his Blade and it turned to mist. Transfixed, he stepped toward Dalinar.

"How?" Ishar asked. The word sounded clear, an incongruity against the soundless rush of power surrounding them. "You . . . you open Honor's path. . . ."

"I have bonded the Stormfather," Dalinar said. "I need you, Ishar. I don't need the legend, the Herald of Mysteries. I need the man Ash says you once were. A man willing to risk his life, his work, and his very soul to save mankind."

Ishar strode closer. Holding the portal open was difficult, but Dalinar kept his hands pressed together. For the moment only he and Ishar existed here, in this place painted white. Ishar stopped a step or two from Dalinar. Yes, seeing another Bondsmith had shaken him.

I can reach him, Dalinar thought.

"I need a teacher," Dalinar said. "I don't know my true capabilities. Odium controls Urithiru, but I think with your help we could restore the Radiants there. Please."

"I see," Ishar said softly. He met Dalinar's eyes. "So. The enemy has corrupted the Stormfather too. I had hoped . . ."

He shook his head, then reached out and pressed his hand to Dalinar's chest. With the strain of keeping the perpendicularity open, Dalinar wasn't able to move away in time. He tried to drop the perpendicularity, but when he pulled his hands apart, it remained open—power roaring through.

Ishar touched his hand to his own chest, creating a line of light between him and Dalinar. "I will take this bond to the Stormfather. I will bear it myself. I sense . . . something odd in you. A Connection to Odium. He sees you as . . . as the one who will fight *against* him.

This cannot be right. I will take that Connection as well."

Dalinar gasped, falling to his knees as something was torn from him—it felt as if his very soul was being ripped out. The Stormfather screamed: a terrifying, agonized sound, like lightning that warped and broke.

No, Dalinar thought. *No. Please . . .*

A shadow appeared on the field of whiteness. A shape—the shape of a black sword. This single line of darkness swiped through the line connecting Dalinar to Ishar.

The white cord exploded and frayed, trailing wisps of darkness. Ishar was cast away, hitting the stone. The perpendicularity remained open, but its light dimmed to reveal Szeth standing between Dalinar and Ishar, brandishing his strange black Shardblade. His illusion melted off like paint in the rain, breaking into Light—which was sucked into the sword and consumed.

"Where," Szeth said to Ishar, his voice quiet, "did you get that Blade you bear?"

The Herald seemed not to have heard him. He was staring at Szeth's sword as it dripped black liquid smoke. Around it, the white light of the perpendicularity warped and was consumed, like water down a drain.

Szeth spun and stabbed the sword into the heart of the perpendicularity. The Stormfather shouted in anger as the perpendicularity collapsed, folding in upon itself.

In a flash, the world was full of color again. All five Windrunners lay on the ground, but they were stirring. Ishar scrambled to his feet before Szeth—who stood with one arm wreathed in black tendrils, gripping the sword that dripped nightmares and bled destruction.

"Answer me!" Szeth screamed. "Did you kill the man who held that Blade before you?"

"Of course not, foolish man," Ishar said, summoning his Blade. "The Shin serve the Heralds. They held my sword *for me.* They returned it when I revealed myself."

Dalinar wiped his brow, pulling himself to his feet. He felt numb, but at the same time . . . warm. Relieved. Whatever the Herald had begun, he had not been able to finish.

Are you all right? he asked the Stormfather.

Yes. He tried to steal our bond. It should not be possible, but Honor no longer lives to enforce his laws. . . .

The perpendicularity. Did Szeth . . . destroy it?

Don't be foolish, the Stormfather said. *No creation of mortal hands could destroy the power of a Shard of Adonalsium. He merely collapsed it. You could summon it again.*

Dalinar was not convinced that the thing Szeth bore was a simple "creation of mortal hands." But he said nothing as he forced himself to check on the Windrunners, whose Connections to the ground had vanished. Leyten had found his feet first and was helping Sigzil, who sat on the ground with a hand to his head.

"I think your worries about this meeting were well advised," Dalinar said, kneeling beside the Azish man. "Can you get us into the air?"

"Damnation," Sigzil whispered. "I feel like I spent last night drinking Horneater white." He burst alight with Stormlight, drawing it from the pouch at his belt. "*Storms.* The Light isn't washing away the pain."

"Yeah," Lyn said. The other three Windrunners were sitting up. "My head is pounding like a Parshendi drum, sir, but we should be able to Lash."

Dalinar glanced at Szeth, who was alight with Stormlight—though it was being drawn at a ferocious rate into his weapon. "My people," Szeth shouted, "were *not* going to return your weapons to you. We kept your secrets, but you lie if you say my father gave you that Blade!"

"Your father was barely a man when I found him," Ishar said. "The Shin had accepted the Unmade. Tried to make gods of them. *I* saved them. And your father *did* give me this Blade. He thanked me for letting him die."

Szeth screamed, charging Ishar—who raised his Blade to casually block him, as he had with the Windrunners. However, the meeting of the two Blades caused a burst of power, and the shock wave sent both men sprawling backward.

Ishar hit hard, dropping his Blade—and Dalinar was in position to see the length of the Honorblade as it hit and bounced, then came to a rest half stuck into the ground. There was a *chip* in its unearthly steel where it had met the black sword.

Dalinar, in all his life, had never seen a Shardblade marred in such a way, let alone one of the *Honorblades.*

Ishar looked up at Szeth, dazed, then grabbed his Blade and shouted an order. His soldiers—who had watched all this in silence—broke their circle, moving into a formation. Sigzil put his hand on Dalinar's shoulder, infusing him, preparing to Lash him.

"Wait," Dalinar said as Ishar stood and slammed his fists together. A perpendicularity opened, as it had before, releasing a powerful explosion of light.

Impossible . . . the Stormfather said in Dalinar's mind. *I didn't feel it happen. How does he do this?*

You're the one who warned me he was dangerous, Dalinar thought. *Who knows what he's capable of?*

Across the stone field, Szeth sheathed his sword just before it began feasting on his soul. Dalinar pointed Leyten that way. "Grab him. Get into the air. We're leaving. Sigzil, Lash me."

"Right, sir."

"Dalinar. Dalinar Kholin."

That . . . that was Ishar's voice.

"I can see clearly," the voice said from within the perpendicularity. "I do not know why. Has a Bondsmith been sworn? We have a Connection, all of us. . . . Nevertheless, I feel my sanity slipping. My mind is broken, and I do not know if it can be healed.

"Perhaps you can restore me for a short time after an Ideal is spoken near me. Everyone sees a little more clearly when a Radiant touches the Spiritual Realm. For now, listen well. I have the *answer,* a way to fix the problems that beset us. Come to me in Shinovar. I can reset the Oathpact, though I must be sane to do it. I must . . . have help . . . to . . ."

The voice stumbled, as if warping.

". . . to defeat you, champion of Odium! We will clash again, and I am ready for your wiles this time! You will not defeat me when next we meet, though you bear a corrupted Honorblade that bleeds black smoke! I *am ALMIGHTY.*"

Dalinar lurched, rising into the air as the Lashing took effect. The Windrunners darted up after him, including Leyten, who grabbed Szeth. As they left the column of light, Dalinar could see Ishar's soldiers stepping into the perpendicularity.

A short time later it vanished. The Herald, his men, and the Honorblade were gone. Transported into Shadesmar.

Together, Navani and the Sibling could *create* Light.

Light that drove the monster Moash back along the corridor, holding his arm before his eyes. Light that drove the knife from Navani's side as it healed her wound. Light that brought fabrials to life, Light that sang with the tones of Honor and Cultivation in tandem.

But her spren . . . The Sibling was so weak.

Navani grasped the pillar, pouring her power into it, but there was so much chaos muddying the system, like crem in a cistern of pure water. The Voidlight Raboniel had injected.

Navani couldn't destroy it, but maybe she could vent it somehow. She saw the tower now as an *entity*, with lines of garnet very like veins and arteries. And she *inhabited* that entity. It became her body. She saw thousands of closed doors the scouts had missed in mapping the tower. She saw brilliant mechanisms for controlling pressure, heat—

No, stay focused.

I think we need to vent the Voidlight, Navani said to the Sibling.

I . . . the Sibling said. *How?*

I can sing the proper tone, Navani said. *We fill the system with as much Towerlight as will fit, then we stop and vibrate these systems here, here, and here with the anti-Voidlight tone.*

I suppose, the Sibling said. *But how can we create the vibration?*

There's a plate on Raboniel's desk. I'll have my scholars play that. I'll need a model to sing it, but with that, I should be able to transfer the vibration through the system. That should force the enemy's corruption out through these broken gemstones in the pump mechanism. What do you think?

. . . Yes? the Sibling said softly. *I think . . . yes, that might work.*

With that done, we will need to restart the tower's protections, Navani said. *These are complex fabrials . . . made of the essence of spren. Of your essence?*

Yes, the Sibling said, their voice growing stronger. *But they are complicated, and took many years of—*

Pressure fabrial here, Navani said, inspecting it with her mind. *Ah, I see. A network of attractors to bring in air and create a bubble of pressure. Quite ingenious.*

Yes!

And the heating fabrials . . . not important now . . . but you've made hous-ings for them out of metals—you manifested physically as metal and crystal, like Shardblades manifest from smaller spren.

YES!

As she began working, Navani noticed an oddity. What was that moving through the tower? Highmarshal Kaladin? Flying quickly, his powers restored, wrapped in spren as armor. He had achieved his Fourth Ideal.

And he was going the wrong direction.

She could easily see his mistake. He'd decided the best way to protect the tower was to come here, to the pillar, and rescue Navani. But no, he was needed elsewhere.

She drew his attention with flashing lights on the wall.

Sibling? Kaladin's voice soon sounded through the system as he touched the crystal vein.

Yes and no, Highmarshal, Navani said. *The pillar is secure. Get to the Breakaway market. Tell the enemies you find there that they'd best retreat quickly.*

He obeyed immediately, changing the direction of his flight.

Navani, full of incredible awareness, got to work.

⁘

Dalinar persuaded the Windrunners to linger in the sky above Ishar's camp, rather than flying immediately back to the Emuli warcamp.

He worried about them though. The Radiants drooped like soldiers who had completed a full-day, double-time march. Ordinarily Storm-light would have perked them up, but they complained of headaches their powers couldn't heal.

The effects shouldn't be permanent, the Stormfather said. *But I cannot say for certain. Ishar Connected them to the ground. Essentially, their powers saw the stones as part of their body—and so tried to fill the ground with Stormlight as it fills their veins.*

I can barely make sense of what you said, Dalinar replied, hanging in the sky far above Ishar's camp. *How are such things possible?*

The powers of a Bondsmith are the powers of creation, the Stormfather said. *The powers of gods, including the ability to link souls. Always before,*

Honor was here to guard this power, to limit it. It seems that Ishar knows how to make full use of his new freedom.

The Stormfather paused, then rumbled more softly. *I never liked him. Though I was only a wind then—and not completely conscious—I remember him. Ishar was ambitious even before madness took him. He cannot bear sole blame for the destruction of Ashyn, humankind's first home, but he* was *the one Odium first tricked into experimenting with the Surges.*

You don't particularly like anyone, Dalinar noted.

Not true. There was a human who made me laugh once, long ago. I was somewhat fond of him.

It felt like a rare attempt at levity. Dared Dalinar hope it was progress in the ancient spren?

Below, Ishar's large pavilion waited, flapping in the gentle wind. Dalinar had seen no sign of servants or soldiers peeking out.

"Sir?" Sigzil said, floating over to Dalinar. "My troops need to rest."

"A few minutes longer," Dalinar said, narrowing his eyes.

"What are we waiting for, sir?"

"To see if Ishar returns. He fled to Shadesmar. He could return at any moment. If he does, we're leaving at speed. But if he doesn't . . ." Ishar hadn't been expecting to run. Szeth, and that strange Blade, had driven him away. "This could be a rare opportunity, Companylord. He was a scholar among Heralds; he might have written notes that give hints to applications of Bondsmith powers."

"Understood, sir," Sigzil said.

Dalinar glanced toward Szeth, who floated on his own away from the others, Lashed into the sky by his own power. Dalinar nodded toward him, and Sigzil—catching the meaning—gave Dalinar a brief Lashing that sent him over beside the assassin.

Szeth was muttering to himself. "How did he know? How did the old fool *know*?"

"Know what?" Dalinar said as he drifted near Szeth. "Ishar? How did he know about your people?"

Szeth blinked, then focused on Dalinar. It was odd to see him looking like himself with that too-pale skin and those wide eyes. Dalinar had grown accustomed to his Alethi illusions.

"I must begin preparing myself," Szeth said. "My next Ideal is my quest, my pilgrimage. I must return to my people, Blackthorn. I must face them."

"As you wish," Dalinar said. He wasn't certain he wanted to unleash this man upon anyone, least of all the one neutral kingdom of note in this conflict. But Jasnah had indicated it would happen, and besides, he doubted he could stop Szeth from doing anything he truly wanted to. "Your people. They have all of the Honorblades?"

"All but three," Szeth said. "The Blade of the Windrunners was mine for years. The Blade of the Skybreakers was reclaimed by Nin long ago. And of course the Blade of the Stonewards was never ours to protect. So there were seven, but if Ishar has his Blade . . ."

You don't need those other swords, a perky voice said in Dalinar's mind. *I am as good as ten swords. Did you see how great I was?*

"I saw," Dalinar said to the sword. "You . . . chipped a Shardblade. An *Honorblade.*"

I did? Wow. I am a great sword. We destroyed a lot of evil, right?

"You promised not to speak into the minds of others, sword-nimi," Szeth said softly. "Do you not remember?"

I remember. I just forgot.

"I will send a team with you to Shinovar," Dalinar said. "As soon as we return to our camp."

"No," Szeth said. "No. I must go alone, but not yet. I must prepare. I have . . . something important to do. He knew. He should not have known. . . ."

Storms. Dalinar wasn't certain who was more insane: Szeth or the sword. The combination was particularly unnerving.

Without them, you would be dead, the Stormfather said, *and I'd be bonded against my will. This Shin man is dangerous, but I fear Ishar more.*

"Sigzil," Dalinar called. "I don't think he's going to return anytime soon. Take us down. Let's see if he left anything of value in that tent."

⁜

Adin raised the spear he'd found in the atrium. People were crying, surrounded by fearspren, as the group of beleaguered humans and singers together made a circle around their wounded. They pushed the elderly and the children to the center, but Adin didn't go with those. The spren watching would see that he wasn't the type to hide. Even women had picked up weapons, including the surgeon's wife, who had given her son to one of the young girls at the center to hold. War was a masculine art, but when you started attacking women, you'd stopped engaging in war. You deserved anything that happened to you after that point.

Adin's father was among the wounded. Alive, bless the Heralds, but bleeding badly. He'd fought for the Radiants, when Adin . . . Adin had hidden in the hallway.

Storm him, he wasn't going to be a coward again. He . . . he wasn't. Adin fell into line beside a fearsome parshman in incredible carapace armor, then tried to position himself with his spear out, in that parshman's same posture.

The stormforms marched in, singing a terrible song. Adin found himself trembling, his hands slick on his spear.

Oh, storms.

In that moment, he didn't want to earn a spren. He didn't want to fight. He wanted to be home making plates, listening to his father hum. He didn't want to be standing here, knowing that they were all . . . all going to . . .

A hand took Adin by the shoulder and moved him backward. Not all the way back, but enough for the figure to stand in front of him. It was the quiet bridgeman, Dabbid. Adin didn't complain, not after seeing those stormforms. Felt good to have someone in front of him, though the bridgeman's spear shook. He was acting afraid to fool the enemy, right?

The stormforms didn't release lightning, which was good. The others had thought they might not, because of the marketplace. Their powers were too wild. Regardless, there seemed to be . . . be *hundreds* of them. A call came from somewhere behind, and they came charging in— rippling with red lightning that flashed when they touched something.

In seconds, everything was chaos. Adin screamed, squeezing his eyes shut, holding out his spear and shaking.

No, he had to fight. He had to—

Something knocked into him from behind, throwing him forward. The strike dazed him, and he lost his spear. When he rolled over, a Voidbringer with red eyes stood above him. The creature casually speared downward.

Adin didn't even have time to scream before—

Clink.

Clink?

The stormform cocked his head, humming an odd song. He stabbed at Adin's chest, but the spear stopped short again. Adin looked at his body as he lay prone on the floor.

His torso was surrounded by glittering blue armor. He raised his hands, and found them covered in gauntlets.

He was in Shardplate.

He was in SHARDPLATE.

"Ha!" he shouted, and kicked at the stormform. The creature went *flying,* soaring twenty feet and slamming into a wall. Adin had barely felt any resistance. It was like he'd always imagined. It . . .

The Shardplate vanished off him and turned into a group of *windspren,* which soared over to Dabbid, who was about to take an axe to the head.

Clink.

Both combatants—the human now shrouded in Shardplate, and the enemy who had hit him—froze in place, stunned. The enemy backed away, and the Plate flew off *again,* this time surrounding the lead Heavenly One. She'd been spearing at a stormform who released a flash of lightning that enveloped her.

When Adin's eyes cleared, he saw her floating in Shardplate, staring at her hands in obvious wonder. Confused, the stormforms began calling out, disengaging and re-forming into ranks.

The armor burst apart, forming those strange windspren who flew into the air overhead before latching on to a figure hovering above the buildings.

The Plate had fit everyone, but him it *matched.* A brilliant Knight Radiant in glowing armor, holding aloft an intricate Shardspear. He left the helmet off so they could all see. Kaladin Stormblessed, bright as the sun.

"I bring word from the Sibling!" he shouted. "They don't remember inviting you in. And considering that they aren't merely the master of this house, they literally are this house, your actions are quite the insult."

Brilliant lights suddenly began running up the walls, making the very core of the stones glow as if molten in the center. Similar lights burst to life in the ceiling.

The ground trembled, as if the entire mountain were shaking. Clanking sounds rang in the hallways, like distant machines, and *wind* began to blow in the vast chamber—which now was as bright as day. Most amazing, the lightning on the stormforms went *out*.

Deepest Ones, who had been clawing out of the ground and grabbing at the feet of soldiers, began screaming and going limp, trapped in the stone. The Heavenly Ones who had been helping dropped to the ground suddenly, then collapsed, unconscious.

Groans sounded from behind. The Radiants on the floor at the center of the circle began stirring. They were *awake*!

"You may turn in your weapons," Stormblessed said to the enemy. "And return to your kind unharmed, so long as you promise me one thing." He smiled. "Tell *him* that I'm *particularly* going to enjoy hearing what he looked like when he found out what happened here today."

⁘

A strange, unpleasant stench struck Dalinar as he stepped into Ishar's pavilion.

The odor was chemically harsh, and he felt a faint burning in his eyes. He blinked in the dim light, finding a large chamber filled with slab tables and sheets shrouding something atop them. Bodies? The Windrunners had gone in first, of course, but they were busy inspecting the recesses of the tent to check for an ambush.

Dalinar walked up to one of the slabs and yanked off the shroud. He simply found a body underneath, an incision in its abdomen made with clean surgical precision. Male, with the clothing cut off and lying beside the body. Very pale skin and stark white hair—in death, the hair and skin seemed almost the same color. That skin had a blue cast to it; probably a Natan person.

So Ishar was a butcher, a mad surgeon as well as a crazed theocrat. For some reason, that relieved Dalinar. It was disgusting, but this was an ordinary kind of evil. He'd expected something worse.

"Sir?" Mela the Windrunner called from across the room. "You should see this."

Dalinar walked over to Mela, who stood beside one of the other slabs. Szeth remained in the doorway to the pavilion, seated on the ground, holding his sheathed sword across his lap. He seemed not to care about the investigation.

Another corpse—half revealed by a drawn-back sheet—was on the slab in front of Mela, though this one was far stranger. The elongated body had a black shell covering most of it, from neck to feet. That had been cut free to open up the chest. Dalinar couldn't make sense of the shell. It looked like clothing, kind of, but was hard like singer carapace—and had apparently been attached to the skin.

The head was a soggy mass of black flesh, soft like intestines, with no visible eyes or features.

"What on Roshar . . ." Dalinar said. "The hands seem human, if too long, but the rest of it . . ."

"I have no idea," Mela said. She glanced away and shivered. "It's not human, sir. I don't know what it is."

In the back of Dalinar's mind, the Stormfather rumbled.

This . . . the spren said. *This is not possible.*

What? Dalinar asked.

That is a Cryptic, he said. *The Lightweaver spren. Only they don't have bodies in this realm. They can't.*

"Sir," Lyn said from a nearby slab. The corpse she'd uncovered was a pile of vines vaguely shaped like a person.

Cultivationspren . . . the Stormfather said. *Return to that first body you saw. Now.*

Dalinar did not object and walked toward the front of the pavilion. What he'd first dismissed as an ordinary body now seemed anything but. The white-blue hair, the pieces of clothing that were—he now recognized—the exact same color as the body. The Stormfather's thunder grew distant.

I knew him, the Stormfather said. *I could not see it at first. I did not want to see it. This is Vespan. Honorspren.*

"So they're not . . . some kind of attempt at making men into mimicries of spren," Dalinar said. "These are *actual* spren *corpses?*"

Spren don't have corpses, the Stormfather said. *Spren do not die like men. They are power that cannot be destroyed. They . . . This is* IMPOSSIBLE.

Dalinar searched through the chamber, where more and more

drawn-back sheets revealed different strange corpses. Several just skeletons, others piles of rock.

This place is evil, the Stormfather said. *Beyond evil. What has been done here is an abomination.*

Sigzil jogged over, holding some ledgers he'd found in the rear. Dalinar couldn't make sense of them, but Sigzil pointed at the Azish glyphs, reading them.

"This is a list of experiments, I think," the companylord said. "The first column is the name of a spren, the second column a date. The third is a time . . . maybe how long they lived? None seem to have survived longer than a few minutes."

"Blood of my fathers," Dalinar said, his hands trembling. "And this last column?"

"Notes, sir," Sigzil said. "Here, the last entry. 'Our first honorspren lived nearly fifteen minutes. A new record, and orders of magnitude longer than all previous attempts. Honorspren seem to have the most humanlike essences. When transferred, the organs and muscles form most naturally. We must capture more of them.

"'Cryptics and ashspren are impossible to bring over properly with our current knowledge. The process of creating bodies for them results in a physical form that collapses upon itself immediately. It appears their physiology works against the fundamental laws of the Physical Realm.'"

"Storms," Leyten said, running a hand through his short hair. "What does it mean?"

Leave this place immediately, the Stormfather said. *We must warn my children.*

"Agreed," Dalinar said. "Grab anything you think might be useful and meet me outside. We're leaving."

◆◆

Moash fled through the tower, using Lashing after Lashing, as he felt the structure rumble. Felt it come alive. Felt light begin to surround him.

Her light. The queen's light.

And before that, a terrible sound. It had pushed away his Connection to Odium, forcing Moash to feel pain for the things he'd done—pain he didn't want. Pain he'd given away.

That pain seethed and spread inside him. He'd killed Teft.

He'd. Killed. *TEFT.*

Get out, get out, get out! he thought as he tore through a hallway, uncaring whether he hit people with his Shardblade as he passed over their heads. He needed it ready. In case Kaladin found him. In case he hadn't broken.

The walls were glowing, and the light seemed *brighter* to Moash than it should have. He wasn't supposed to feel afraid! He'd given that away! He couldn't be the man he *needed* to be if he was afraid, or . . . Or.

The pain, the shame, the anger at himself was worse than the fear.

Get out. Go. Go!

The suffocating light surrounded him, burned him as he burst out the front gates of the tower. He *felt* more than saw what happened behind. Each level of the tower came alive, one at a time. The air warped with sudden warmth and pressure. So much light.

So much light!

Moash Lashed himself into the sky, darting out away from the tower. Soon after, however, he slammed into a hard surface. He dropped into something soft but cold, pained as his Stormlight kept him alive—barely. It ran out before it could fully heal him, so he lay there in the cold. Waiting for the numbness.

He wasn't supposed to have to *feel* anymore. That was what he'd been *promised*.

He couldn't blink. He didn't seem to have eyelids anymore. He couldn't see either—his vision had been burned away. He listened to distant cheers, distant sounds of exultation and joy, as he lay in the cold on the mountainside. The snow numbed his skin.

But not his soul. Not his wretched soul.

"Teft, I . . ." He couldn't say it. The words wouldn't form. He *wasn't* sorry for what he'd done. He was only sorry for how his actions made him feel.

He didn't want this pain. He deserved it, yes, but he didn't *want* it.

He should have died, but they found him. A few Heavenly Ones who had been in the air when the tower was restored. They'd awoken, it seemed, after falling from the sky and leaving the tower's protections.

They gave him Stormlight, then lifted him, carrying him away.

Odium's gift returned, and Moash breathed easier. Blissfully without his guilt. His spine healed. He could walk by the time they dropped him among a camp of a few others who had managed to flee the tower.

But he couldn't see them. No matter how much Stormlight he was given, his eyes didn't recover. He was blind.

Roshar will be united in its service of the greater war.

—Musings of El, on the first of the Final Ten Days

Exhausted and confused, Dalinar and the Windrunners eventually landed back at their Emuli warcamp, mere minutes before a highstorm was scheduled to arrive. He felt the weight of failure pulling him down, strong as gravity. He sagged as he dismissed the Windrunners to go rest.

He'd gone all that way for nothing. He was no closer to understanding his powers. No closer to doing something about the capture of Urithiru. No closer to rescuing Navani.

He probably should have gone to Jasnah to explain what they'd found, but he was so tired. He plodded through the camp, towing his failure like a cart behind him, populated by swirling exhaustionspren.

And that was when they found him: women running up with spanreeds to the tower that were suddenly working again. Messengers surrounded by gloryspren, bringing amazing news. Navani in contact, the tower and Oathgates functioning. Dalinar listened to it in a daze.

Good news. Finally, good news.

He wanted to immediately get flown to Azimir so he could go see Navani, but he recognized the foolishness in that. He needed at least a short rest before enduring another lengthy flight, and there was that imminent highstorm to worry about. He ordered a message sent to his wife, promising to come to her before the day was out. Then he asked Jasnah and the Prime if he could meet with them after the storm.

After that, they left him to at last approach the small building he made his base. It felt like coming home. Of course, he'd lived enough of his life out on campaign that "home" had acquired a loose definition. Any place with a soft bed usually counted.

Urithiru really is safe now, Dalinar, the Stormfather said in his mind. *I was so distracted by the dead spren that I didn't notice at first. The Sibling has fully awakened. Another Bondsmith? The implications of this . . .*

Dalinar was still trying to deal with those himself. Navani bonding a spren? That was wonderful, but he was so emotionally worn at the moment, he just wanted to sit and *think.* He pushed open the door to his house, stumbled through, and entered a vast golden field.

The ground shimmered as if infused with Stormlight. Dalinar pulled to a halt and turned around. The doorway was gone, the doorknob having vanished from his hand. The sky was a deep reddish orange, like a sunset.

He was in a vision. But he hadn't heard the highstorm hit.

And . . . no. This wasn't a highstorm vision. This was something else. He turned with trepidation, looking across the glimmering field to where a figure—clad in golden robes—stood on a nearby hilltop, facing away from Dalinar and staring out at the horizon.

Odium. *Storms within,* Dalinar thought, flagging. *Not now. I can't face him right now.*

Well, a soldier couldn't always pick his battlefield. This was the first time Odium had appeared to him in a year. Dalinar needed to use this.

He took a deep breath and pushed through his fatigue. He hiked up the hillside and eventually stopped beside the figure in gold. Odium held a small scepter like a cane, his hand resting on the ball at the top.

He appeared different from when Dalinar had last seen him. He still resembled a wise old man with a grey beard cut to medium length. A paternal air. Sagacious, knowing, understanding. Only now his skin was glowing in places, as if it had grown thin and a light inside was seeking to escape. The god's eyes had gone completely golden, as if they were chunks of metal set into a statue's face.

When Odium spoke, there was a harsh edge to his tone, his words clipped. Barely holding in his anger.

"Our Connection grows, Dalinar," Odium said. "Stronger by the day. I can reach you now as if you were one of my own. You should be."

"I will ever and always be *my* own," Dalinar said.

"I know you went to see Ishar. What did he tell you?"

Dalinar clasped his hands behind him and used the old commander's trick of remaining silent and staring in thought. Stiff back. Strong posture. Outwardly in control, even if you're one step from collapsing.

"You *were* supposed to be my champion, Dalinar," Odium said. "Now I see how you resisted me. You've been working with Ishar all along, haven't you? Is that how you learned to bind the realms?"

"You find it inconvenient, don't you?" Dalinar said. "That you cannot see my future. How does it feel to be human, Odium?"

"You think I fear humanity?" Odium said. "Humanity is *mine,* Dalinar. All emotions belong to me. This land, this realm, this people. They live for me. They always have. They always will."

And yet you come to me, Dalinar thought. *To berate me? You stayed away all these months. Why now?*

The answer struck him like the light of a rising sun. Odium had lost the tower—Urithiru was safe and there was another Bondsmith. He'd failed again. And now he thought Dalinar had been working with Ishar.

Cultivation's gift, though it had bled Dalinar, had given him the strength to defy Odium. All this time, he'd been asking what a god could possibly fear, but the answer was obvious. Odium feared men who would not obey him.

He feared Dalinar.

"Ishar told me some curious things this latest visit," Dalinar said. "He gave me a book with secrets in it. He is not as mad as I feared, Odium. He showed me my Connection to you, and explained how limited you are. Then he proved to me that a Bondsmith unchained is capable of incredible feats." He looked at the ancient being. "You are a god. You hold vast powers, yet they bind you as much as they free you. Tell me, what do you think of a human bearing the weight of a god's powers, but without that god's restrictions?"

"The power will bind you eventually, as it has me," Odium said. "You don't understand a fraction of the things you pretend to, Dalinar."

Yet you're afraid *of me,* Dalinar thought. *Of the idea that I might fully come into my power. That you're losing control of your plans.*

Perhaps Dalinar's errand to Tukar hadn't been a failure. He hadn't gained Ishar's wisdom, but so long as Odium *thought* he had . . .

Bless you, Renarin, Dalinar thought. *For making my life unpredictable to this being. For letting me bluff.*

"We made an agreement," Odium said. "A contest of champions. We never set terms."

"I have terms," Dalinar said. "On my desk. A single sheet of paper."

Odium waved his hand and the words began appearing—written as if in glowing golden ink—in the sky before them. Enormous, intimidating.

"You didn't write this," Odium said, his eyes narrowing. "Nor did that Elsecaller." The light grew more vibrant beneath Odium's skin, and Dalinar could feel its heat—like that of a sun—rising. Making his skin burn.

Anger. Deep anger, white hot. It was consuming Odium. His control was slipping.

"Cephandrius," Odium spat. "Ever the rat. No matter where I go, there he is, scratching in the wall. Burrowing into my strongholds. He could have been a god, yet he insists on living in the dirt."

"Do you accept these terms?" Dalinar asked.

"By this, if my champion wins," Odium said, "then Roshar is mine? Completely and utterly. And if yours wins, I withdraw for a millennium?"

"Yes. But what if you break your word? You've delayed longer than you should have. What if you refuse to send a champion?"

"I cannot break my word," Odium said, the heat increasing. "I basically am incapable of it."

"Basically?" Dalinar pressed. "What happens, Odium, if you *break your word.*"

"Then the contract is void, and I am in your power. Same, but reversed, if *you* break the contract. You would be in my power, and the restrictions Honor placed upon me—chaining me to the Rosharan system and preventing me from using my powers on most individuals—would be void. But that is not going to happen, and I am not going to break my word. Because if I *did,* it would create a hole in my soul—which would let Cultivation kill me.

"I am no fool, and you are a man of honor. We will both approach this contest in *good faith,* Dalinar. This isn't some deal with a Voidbringer from your myths, where one tricks the other with some silly twist of language. A willing champion from each of us and a fight to the death. They will meet on the top of Urithiru. No tricks, no lies."

"Very well," Dalinar said. "But as the terms state, if your champion is defeated, it isn't only you who must withdraw for a thousand years. The Fused must go with you, locked away again, as well as the spren that make Regals. No forms of power. No more Voidspren."

The light pulsed inside Odium and he turned his eyes back toward the horizon. "I . . . cannot agree to this."

"The terms are simple," Dalinar said. "If you—"

"I said I *cannot* agree," Odium said. "The Everstorm has changed everything, and Cephandrius should have realized this. Singers can adopt Regal forms powered by the Everstorm. The Fused are free now; they can be reborn without my intervention. The Oathpact could have imprisoned them, but it is now defunct. I am *literally* unable to do as you ask, not without destroying myself in the process."

"Then we cannot have an accommodation," Dalinar said. "Because I'm certainly not going to agree to anything less."

"And if I agreed to less?"

Dalinar frowned, uncertain, his mind muddled from fatigue. The creature was going to try to trick him. He was certain of it. So, he did what he thought best. He said nothing.

Odium chuckled softly, rotating his scepter beneath his hand so the butt ground against the golden stone at their feet. "Do you know why I make men fight, Dalinar? Why I created the Thrill? Why I encourage the wars?"

"To destroy us."

"Why would I want to destroy you? I am your *god,* Dalinar." Odium shook his head, staring into the infinite golden distance. "I need soldiers. For the true battle that is coming, not for one people or one miserable windswept continent. A battle of the gods. A battle for *everything.*

"Roshar is a training ground. The time will come that I unleash you upon the others who are not nearly as well trained. Not nearly as *hardened* as I have made you."

"Curious," Dalinar said. "I don't know if you've noticed, but your 'hardening' tactic has resulted in Fused who are going mad from the stress."

The light grew stronger inside Odium, seeming as if it might explode from his skin.

"If your champion wins, I will step away for a thousand years," he said. "I will retreat to Braize, and I will no longer speak to, contact, or influence the Fused or Voidspren. But I cannot contain them. And you will have to pray that your descendants are as lucky as you are, as I will be less . . . lenient when I return."

Dalinar started to speak, but Odium interrupted.

"Let me finish," he said. "In exchange for you giving up one thing you wanted, I will give up one in turn. If I win, I will give up my grand plans for Roshar. I will leave this planet for a thousand years, and abandon all I've worked for here. I give you and the singers freedom to make your own peace. Freedom for you, and freedom for me.

"This is all I ask for my victory: As you represent Honor, you can relax his prohibitions on me. No matter what happens in the contest, you never have to worry about me again. All I want is *away from this miserable system.*"

Of course it wouldn't be as easy as Wit had promised. Dalinar wavered. Wit looked out for himself, as he'd always said he would. The contract reinforced that idea. Odium offered a different, tempting prospect. To be rid of him, to fight this war as an ordinary war . . .

Two forces pulled at him. Which did he trust? He doubted that any mortal—Jasnah included—could construct a contract good enough to hold a god. But to simply give Wit what he desired?

Who do you trust more? Wit, or the god of anger?

It wasn't really in question. He didn't trust Wit much, but he didn't trust Odium at all. Besides, if Honor had died to trap this god here on Roshar, Dalinar had to believe the Almighty had done so for good reason.

So he turned to go. "Send me back, Odium," Dalinar said. "There will be no agreement today."

A flare of *heat* washed over him from behind. Dalinar spun, finding Odium glowing with a bright red-gold light, his eyes wide, his teeth clenched.

Stand firm, Dalinar thought to himself. *Wit says he can't hurt you. Not without breaking his word . . . not without inviting his own death . . .*

Wit hadn't included that last part. But Dalinar stood his ground, sweating, his heart racing. Until at last the power abated, the heat and light retreating.

"I would prefer," Odium said, "to make an agreement."

Why so eager? Dalinar thought. *It's the power, isn't it? It's ripping you apart for delaying. It wants out.*

"I've offered you an agreement," Dalinar said.

"I've told you that I *cannot* keep to these terms. I can seal myself away, but not my minions. I can demand that the Fused and the Unmade retreat—but not all currently obey my will. And I can do *nothing* about the Regals."

Dalinar took a deep breath. "Fine," he said, "but *I* cannot entertain an agreement that frees you from this world. So we should focus on our conflict, you and me. If I win, you are exiled to Damnation and withdraw from the conflict entirely. If you win, *I* will go into exile, and my people will have to fight without my aid."

"You offer a mortal life for that of a *god*?" Odium demanded. "No, Dalinar. If I win, I want the Knights Radiant. The forces of Alethkar and Urithiru will surrender to my Fused, and your Radiants will end this war. The other foolish kingdoms of men can keep fighting if they wish, but your people and mine will begin preparing for the *true* war: the one that will begin when the gods of other worlds discover the strength of Surgebinding. Your heirs will be bound to this, as you are."

"I cannot negotiate for people who are not yet born," Dalinar said. "Nor can I promise my Radiants will follow you, as you cannot promise the Fused will obey you. As I said, this must be between you and me. But . . . if you win, *I* will agree to order my armies to stand down and stop the fighting. I will give up the war, and those who wish to join you will be allowed to do so."

"Not good enough, Dalinar. Not nearly good enough." Odium took a long, suffering breath. That light pulsed inside of him, and Dalinar felt a kind of kinship to the ancient god then. Sensing *his* fatigue, which somehow mirrored Dalinar's own. "I want so much more than Roshar, so much more than one planet, one people. But my people . . . tire. I've worn them thin with this eternal battle. They seek endings, terrible endings. The entire war has changed, based on what your wife has done. You realize this."

"I do," Dalinar said.

"It is time for a true accommodation. A true ending. Do you not agree?"

"I . . . Yes. I realize it. What do you propose?"

Odium waved dismissively at the contract Wit had drawn up. "No more talk of *delays*, of sending me away. Of half measures. We have a contest of champions on the tenth of next month," Odium said. "At the tenth hour."

"So soon? The month ends tomorrow."

"Why delay?" Odium asked. "I know my champion. Do you know yours?"

"I do," Dalinar said.

"Then let us stop dancing and commit. On the tenth, our champions meet. If you win, I will withdraw to the kingdoms I currently hold— and I enforce an end to the war. I will even give up to you Alethkar, and restore your homeland to you."

"I must have Herdaz too."

"What?" Odium said. "That meaningless little plot of land? What are they to you?"

"It's the matter of an oath, Odium," Dalinar said. "You will restore to me Herdaz and Alethkar. Keep whatever other lands you've taken; they mostly followed you freely anyway. I can accept this, so long as you are still trapped on Roshar, as Honor wished."

"I will," Odium said, "though I will be able to focus my attentions on sending agents to the rest of the cosmere, using what I've conquered here as enough for now. However, if *I* win the contest of champions, I keep everything I've conquered—Herdaz and Alethkar included. And I want one other small thing. I want you, Dalinar."

"My life? Odium, I intend to be my own champion. I'll have died if you win."

"Yes," Odium said, eyes shining golden. "You will have. And you will give your soul to me. You, Dalinar, will join the Fused. You will become immortal, and will *personally* serve me. Bound by your oaths. *You* will be the one I send to the stars to serve my interests in the cosmere."

A cold shock ran through Dalinar. Like he'd felt the first time he'd been stabbed. Surprise, disbelief, terror.

You will join the Fused.

"Are we agreed?" Odium said, his skin now glowing so brightly that his features were difficult to make out. "You have gotten from me more than I ever thought I would give up. Either way, the war ends and you will have secured the safety of your allies. At the cost of gambling your own soul. How far does your honor extend, Blackthorn?"

Dalinar wavered. Stopping now, with Azir and Thaylenah safe—with a good portion of Roshar protected, and with a chance for more in Alethkar and Herdaz if he won—was truly more than he ever thought possible. A true end to the war.

Jasnah spoke of the need for councils. Groups of leaders. She thought putting too much power in the hands of one individual was dangerous. He could finally see her point, as he stood there on that field of golden light. This new deal would be good for his allies—they'd celebrate it, most likely. But he couldn't know for certain. He had to make a decision.

Dared he do that? Dared he risk his own soul?

I have *to contain him,* Dalinar thought. His people were celebrating their victory in Emul, but he knew—deep down—the enemy had given it away. He had preferred to secure his power elsewhere. The Mink had said it himself: If Odium had wanted to crush Azir, he could have. Instead, he'd secured what he had. Odium knew that in controlling Jah Keved, Alethkar, and Iri, he owned the strongest portion of Roshar.

Without this deal, Dalinar saw years of fighting ahead. Decades. Against an enemy whose Fused were constantly reborn. From years spent defending Alethkar, he knew exactly how difficult it would be to retake. Dalinar saw his people dying by the thousands, unsuccessfully trying to seize lands he himself had fortified.

Dalinar would lose this war in the long run. Honor had all but confirmed it. Renarin said victory in a traditional sense was nearly impossible as long as Odium drove his forces. And Taravangian, whom Dalinar didn't trust but *did* believe, had foreseen the same fact. The enemy *would* win, wearing them down over centuries if need be.

Their best chance was for Dalinar's champion to defeat Odium's. If that champion failed, then Dalinar's only reasonable option would be surrender anyway. He knew that, deep in his gut. Most importantly, this seemed his only *real* chance to free Alethkar.

He had to do it. He hadn't achieved what he had through indecision. He either trusted his instincts, and the promises of his god, or he had nothing.

He took a deep breath. "Final terms are these: A contest of champions to the death. On the tenth day of the month Palah, tenth hour. We each send a willing champion, allowed to meet at the top of Urithiru, otherwise unharmed by either side's forces. If I win that contest, you will remain bound to the system—but you will return Alethkar and Herdaz to me, with all of their occupants intact. You will vow to cease hostilities and maintain the peace, not working against my allies or our kingdoms in any way."

"Agreed," Odium said. "But if I win, I keep everything I've won—including your homeland. I still remain bound to this system, and will still cease hostilities as you said above. But I will have your soul. To serve me, immortal. Will you do this? Because I agree to these terms."

"And I," Dalinar whispered. "I agree to these terms."

"It is done."

EMOTION

And I will march proudly at the head of a human legion.

—Musings of El, on the first of the Final Ten Days

Disconnecting from the powers of the Sibling left Navani feeling small. Was this really what life had been like before? Before she'd blended her essence with the Sibling's—and gained awareness of the intricate motions of the thousands of fabrials that made up the Sibling's physical form?

She now felt so normal. Almost. She retained a hint of awareness in the back of her mind. A sense for the veins of crystal that permeated the tower; if she rested her hand against a wall she could sense its workings.

Heat. Pressure. Light. *Life.*

I swore I would never do this again, the Sibling said in her mind. *I swore I was done with humans.*

"Then it's good that spren, like humans, can change their minds," Navani said. She was a little surprised to find her body as she remembered it. With a cut in her havah, bloodstained where the knife had taken her.

Our bond is unusual, the Sibling said. *I still do not know what I think of what we've done.*

"If we meant our words, and keep them, does it matter?"

What of fabrials? the Sibling asked. *You did not promise to stop capturing spren.*

"We will find a compromise," Navani said, picking her way out of the room with the crystal pillar. "We will work together to find an acceptable path forward."

Will it be like your compromise with Raboniel, where you tricked her?

"That was the best compromise she and I could come to, and we both knew it," Navani said. "You and I can do better."

I wish to believe you, the Sibling said. *But as of yet, I do not. I am sorry.*

"Merely another problem to solve," Navani said, "through application of logic and hope, in equal measure."

She approached Raboniel's fallen body in the hallway, then knelt over it. "Thank you."

The eyes opened.

Navani gasped. "Raboniel?"

"You . . . lived. Good." One of her hands twitched; it seemed that Moash had cut her with his Blade low enough that it hadn't burned out her eyes, though one arm and both legs were obviously dead.

Navani raised her hand to her lips.

"Do . . . not . . . weep," Raboniel whispered. "I . . . would have killed . . . you . . . to accomplish . . . my goal."

"Instead, you saved me."

Raboniel breathed in a shallow breath, but said nothing.

"We'll meet again," Navani said. "You will be reborn."

"No. If I . . . die . . . I will return . . . mad. My soul . . . is burned . . . almost all away. . . . Do not . . . Please . . . Please . . ."

"What, then?" Navani said.

"This new Light . . . works. My daughter . . . is truly gone. So I made . . . more . . . anti . . . anti . . ."

"Anti-Voidlight. Where?"

Raboniel rocked her head to the side, toward her desk, situated in the hallway near the opening to the crystal pillar room. Navani rose and searched through the drawers, finding a black sack containing a diamond filled with the precious, terrible Light.

She returned and affixed the diamond to the dagger, which was wet with Moash's blood. After cleaning it and reversing the metal strip, she knelt beside Raboniel.

"Are you sure?" Navani asked.

Raboniel nodded. Her hand twitched, and Navani reached over and held it, which made the Fused relax.

"I . . . have done . . . what I wished. Odium . . . is worried. He may . . . allow . . . an ending. . . ."

"Thank you," Navani said softly.

"I never . . . thought . . . I would be sane . . . at the end. . . ."

Navani raised the dagger. And for the first time, she wondered if she was strong enough for this.

"I do wish . . ." Raboniel said, "I could hear . . . rhythms . . . again. . . ."

"Then sing with me," Navani said, and began to sing Honor's tone.

The Fused smiled, then managed a weak hum to Odium's tone. Navani modulated her tone, lowering her voice, until the two snapped together in harmony one last time.

Navani positioned the dagger above the wound in Raboniel's breast.

"End it . . . Navani . . ." Raboniel whispered, letting the song cease. "Make *sure* they let it all . . . end."

"I will," she whispered back, then—humming her best, holding the hand of a former immortal—Navani thrust the dagger in deep. Raboniel's nerves had mostly been severed, so she didn't spasm as her daughter had. Her eyes went a glassy marble white, and a breath escaped her lips—black smoke as her insides burned away. Navani kept humming until the smoke dissipated.

You have performed a kindness, the Sibling said in her head.

"I feel awful."

That is part of the kindness.

"I am sorry," Navani said, "for discovering this Light. It will let spren be killed."

It was coming to us, the Sibling said. *Consequences once chased only humans. With the Recreance, the consequences became ours as well. You have simply sealed that truth as eternal.*

Navani pressed her forehead against Raboniel's as the Fused had done for her daughter. Then she rose, surrounded by exhaustionspren. Storms. Without the Towerlight infusing her, her fatigue returned. How long had it been since she'd slept?

Too long. But today, she needed to be a queen. She tucked the dagger away—it was too valuable to simply leave lying around—and took her copy of *Rhythm of War* under her arm.

She left a note on Raboniel's corpse, just in case. *Do not dispose of this hero's body without first consulting the queen.*

Then she went to create order from the chaos of a tower suddenly set free.

* ❖ *

Taravangian awoke late in the day. He barely remembered falling asleep. He barely . . . could . . .

Could barely . . . think.

He was stupid. Stupider than he'd ever been before.

That made him weep. Stupid weeping. He cried and cried, overwhelmed by emotion and shamespren. A sense of failure. Of anger at himself. He lay there until hunger drove him to stand.

His thoughts were like crem. Thick. Slow. He stumbled down to the window, where they had left his basket of food. Trembling, he clutched it, weeping at his hunger. It seemed so *strong*. And storms, he drew so many spren when stupid.

He sat beside his fake hearth, and couldn't help wishing that Dalinar could be there with him. How grand that had been. To have a friend. A real *friend* who understood him. He trembled at the idea, then began digging in the basket.

He stopped as he found a note. Written by Renarin Kholin, sealed by his signet. Taravangian sounded out each glyph. It took forever—drawing a fleet of concentrationspren like ripples in the air—for him to figure out what it said.

Two words. *I'm sorry.* Two gemstones, glowing brightly, were included with the note. What were these?

I'm sorry. Why say that? What had the boy seen? He knew his future wasn't to be trusted. Other spren fled, and only fearspren attended him as he read those words. He needed to hide! He climbed off his chair and crawled to the corner.

He quivered there until he felt too hungry. He crawled over and began eating the flatbread in the basket. Then some kind of purple Azish vegetable mash, which he ate with his fingers. It tasted *so good*.

Had he ever eaten anything so wonderful? He cried over it.

The gemstones continued to glow. Large ones. With something moving in them. Hadn't . . . hadn't he been told to watch for something like that?

Thunder crackled in the sky, and Taravangian looked up. Was that the Everstorm? No. No, it was a highstorm. He hadn't realized it would come today. Thunder rattled the shutters, and he dropped the bread. He hid again in the corner with globs of trembling fearspren.

The thunder sounded angry.

He knows, Taravangian thought. *The enemy knows what I've done.* No. No, wrong storm.

He needed a way to *summon* Odium. Those gems. That was what they were for!

It would happen today.

Today he died.

Today it ended.

The door to his hut slammed open, broken at the hinges. Outside, guards scrambled away from a figure silhouetted against a darkening sky. The storm was almost here.

And Szeth had come with it.

Taravangian gasped, terrified, as this was not the death he had foreseen. He'd waited so long for a transcendent day when he would be supremely intelligent again. He'd never wondered about the opposite. A day when he was all emotion. A day when thoughts didn't move in his brain, and spren swarmed him, feeding gluttonously upon his passions.

Szeth stood quietly, his illusion gone, his bald head—freshly shaved—reflecting the light of the spheres that had spilled from the basket.

"How did you know?" the Shin finally asked. "And how long have you known?"

"Kn-known?" Taravangian forced out, crawling to the side through the fearspren.

"My father," Szeth said.

Taravangian blinked. He could barely understand the words, he was so stupid. Emotions fought inside him. Terror. *Relief* that it would soon be over.

"How did you know my father was dead?" Szeth demanded, striding into the room. "How did you know that Ishar reclaimed his sword? *How?*"

Szeth no longer wore white—he'd changed to an Alethi uniform. Why? Oh, disguise. Yes.

He wore the terrible sword at his side. It was too big. The tip of the sheath dragged against the wooden floor.

Taravangian hunched to the wall, trying to find the right words. "Szeth. The sword. You must . . ."

"I must do nothing," Szeth said, approaching steadily. "I ignore you as I ignore the voices in the shadows. You know the voices, Taravangian? The ones you gave me."

Taravangian huddled down, closing his eyes. Waiting, too overcome with emotion to do anything else.

"What are these?" Szeth said.

Taravangian opened his eyes. The gemstones. Szeth picked them up, frowning. He hadn't drawn that terrible sword.

Say something. What should he say? Szeth couldn't harm those. Taravangian needed them!

"Please," he cried, "don't break them."

Szeth scowled, then threw them—one after the other—at the stone wall, shattering them. Strange spren escaped, transparent windspren that trailed red light. They laughed, spinning around Szeth.

"Please," Taravangian said through the tears. "Your sword. Odium. You—"

"Ever you manipulate me," Szeth interrupted, watching the windspren. "Ever you seek to stain my hands with the blood of those *you* would kill. You brought all this upon us, Taravangian. The world would have been able to stand against the enemy if you hadn't made me murder half their monarchs."

"No!" Taravangian said. He stood up with effort, scattering the spren around him, his heart thundering in his chest. His vision immediately began to swim. He'd stood up too quickly. "We killed to *save* the world."

"Murders done to save lives," Szeth said softly, tracking Taravangian with eyes dark and shadowed from the room's poor light, now that the spheres were gone. "Idiocy. But I wasn't ever to object. I was Truthless. I simply followed orders. Tell me. Do you think that absolves a man?"

"No," Taravangian said, trembling with the weight of his guilt, shamespren bursting around him and floating, as petals of rockbud blossoms, to the ground.

"A good answer. You are wise for one so stupid."

Taravangian tried to dash away past Szeth. But of course his legs gave out. He got tripped and collapsed in a heap. He groaned, his heart thumping, his vision swimming.

A moment later, strong hands lifted him and slammed him back against the wall amid swarming exhaustionspren. Something *snapped* in Taravangian's shoulder, and pain spiked through his body.

He drooped in Szeth's grip, breathing out in wheezes.

The room started to grow golden.

"All this time," Szeth said, "I wanted to keep my honor. I tried *so hard*. You took advantage of that. You broke me, Taravangian."

Light. That golden light.

"Szeth," Taravangian said, feeling blood on his lips. Storms. "Szeth . . . He is here. . . ."

"I decide now," Szeth said, reaching toward his waist—not for the terrible sword, but for the small knife he was wearing beside it. "I *finally* decide. Me. No one else compelling me. Taravangian, know that in killing you, I make it *my choice*."

Rumbling thunder. A brilliant, terrible golden light. Odium appeared. When he did, his face was distorted, his eyes shining with angry power. Thunder broke the landscape, and Szeth began to fade.

You should not tempt me today, Taravangian! Odium thundered. *I have lost my champion* AGAIN, *and now I am bound by an agreement I do not want. How do they know how to move against me?* HAVE YOU BETRAYED ME, TARAVANGIAN? *Have you been speaking to Sja-anat?* WHAT HAVE YOU DONE?

The awe of that force—that transcendent power—left Taravangian quivering, spren of a dozen varieties swirling around him, fighting for his attention. So many *emotions*. He barely noticed Szeth pulling the knife free, for he was so overwhelmed—awed, frightened, excited all at once.

Fear won.

Taravangian cried out, his shoulder afire with pain, his body broken. His plans had been silly. How had he thought to outthink a god when stupid? He couldn't do that when smart. No wonder he'd failed.

Did you fail?

The sword is here.

Odium is here.

Cold steel bit Taravangian's skin as Szeth stabbed him right in the chest. At the same moment, Taravangian felt something pushing through his fear, his pain. An emotion he'd never thought to feel himself. Bravery.

Bravery surged through him, so powerfully he could not help but move. It was the dying courage of a man on the front lines charging an enemy army. The glory of a woman fighting for her child. The feeling of an old man on his last day of life stepping into darkness.

Bravery.

The Physical Realm faded as Odium pulled Taravangian into the place between worlds. Taravangian's body was not as weak here. This form was a manifestation of his mind and soul. And those were strong.

The sword at Szeth's waist—that strange, terrible sword—manifested here, in this realm where Odium brought Taravangian. The god looked down and saw the curling black darkness, and seemed surprised.

Taravangian seized the sword and pulled it free of its scabbard, hearing it scream for pleasure. He turned and thrust it upward—black smoke curling around his hands.

"Destroy!" the sword bellowed. "DESTROY!"

Taravangian *rammed* it up into Odium's chest.

The sword drank greedily of the god's essence, and as it did, Taravangian felt a *snap*. His body dying. Szeth finishing the job. He knew it immediately. Taravangian was dead. Anger rose in him like he had never known.

Szeth had *killed* him!

Odium screamed, and the golden place shattered, turning to darkness. The sword undulated in Taravangian's grip, pulling power from the god it had stabbed.

The figure that contained Odium's power—the *person* who controlled it—evaporated, taken by the sword. That alone was so much Investiture that Taravangian felt the sword grow dull in his fingers. Full, lethargic. As when a hot brand was shoved into a barrel of water, there was an initial hiss—but this power was too vast for the sword to drink.

It killed the person holding that power, however, which left a hole.

A *need*. A . . . vacuum, like a gemstone suddenly without Stormlight. It reached out, and Taravangian felt a distinct *Connection* to it.

Passion. Hatred. Today, Taravangian was *only* passion. Hatred, fear, anger, shame, awe. Bravery. The power loved these things, and it surged around him, enveloping him.

His soul vibrated.

Take me, the power pled, speaking not in words, but in emotion. *You are perfect. I am yours.*

Taravangian hesitated briefly, then thrust his hands into the well of power.

And Ascended to godhood, becoming Odium.

They should not be discarded, but helped to their potential. Their final Passions.

—Musings of El, on the first of the Final Ten Days

Rlain walked with Venli and his new friends—Dul, Mazish, and the others Venli had recruited—to the Oathgate, where Kaladin waited to transfer them to the Shattered Plains.

Rlain felt in a stupor, despite a day having passed since his revelation. Since speaking his first Words as a Truthwatcher.

The spren had been watching him, from the heart of a cremling. Rlain and Venli had mistaken Tumi for a Voidspren, but he wasn't exactly the same thing. Once an ordinary mistspren, Tumi had let Sja-anat touch him, and in so doing make him into something new. A spren of both Honor and Odium.

Tumi pulsed to a new rhythm. The Rhythm of War. Something he had learned recently. Something important for his siblings to hear.

Renarin knows? Rlain thought.

He suggested you, Tumi said. *And told our mother about you. He was right. Our bond will be strong, and you will be wondrous. We are awed by you, Rlain. The Bridger of Minds. We are honored.*

Honored. That felt good. To be chosen because of what *he'd* done.

Kaladin waited for them at the transfer room. He made the transfer with the Sylblade. The air of the Shattered Plains was wetter, and felt . . . familiar to Rlain as they stepped onto a platform outside Narak.

There they met with Leshwi and the other four Fused who, upon being transferred here earlier, had regained consciousness. Leshwi hovered over and tipped her head toward Kaladin in respect.

"You could stay here at Narak," Kaladin said to her. "We'd welcome your aid."

"We fought against our own to preserve lives," Leshwi said. "We do not wish that to continue. We will find a third option, outside this war. The path of the listeners."

"We'll find our way out here," Venli said to Confidence. "Somehow."

"Well, go with honor then," Kaladin said. "And with the queen's promise. If you change your minds, or if you and yours need refuge, we'll take you in."

The Heavenly Ones took to the air, humming to Praise. They began lowering the new listeners—and their supplies—down into the chasm for the hike eastward. With the highstorm passed, and with Fused to watch for chasmfiends from above, they should be able to make their way to the eastern flats where the other listeners had gone.

Rlain gave Venli a hug and hummed to Praise.

"I don't deserve any of this," she whispered to him. "I was weak, Rlain."

"Then start doing better," he told her, pulling back. "That is the path of Radiance, Venli. We're both on it now. Write me via spanreed once you find the others, and give my best to Thude and Harvo, if they made it."

She hummed to Appreciation. "You will come to us soon?"

"Soon," he promised, then watched her go.

Kaladin stepped up beside Rlain and rested a hand on his shoulder. Rlain couldn't feel the Plate, though it was apparently *always there*—invisible, but ready when needed. Like a Shardblade, but made up of many spren.

Kaladin didn't ask if Rlain wanted to leave with the others. Rlain had established that he needed to stay, at least until Renarin returned. Beyond that . . . well, there was something Rlain had started to fear. Something nebulous but—once it occurred to him—persistent. If the humans had a chance to win this war, but at the expense of taking the minds of all the singers as they'd done in the past, would they take it? Would they enslave an entire people again, if given the opportunity?

The thought disturbed him. He trusted Kaladin and his friends. But humankind? That was asking a lot. Someone needed to remain close, in order to watch and be certain.

He would visit the listeners. But he was a Radiant and he was Bridge Four. Urithiru was his home.

"Come on," Kaladin said. "It's time to go give Teft a proper send-off. Among friends."

∴

Taravangian's vision expanded, his mind expanded, his *essence* expanded. Time started to lose meaning. How long had he been like this?

He became the power. With it, he began to understand the cosmere on a fundamental level. He saw that his predecessor had been sliding toward oblivion for a long, long time. Weakened by his battles in the past, then deeply wounded by Honor, this being had been enslaved by the power. Failing to claim Dalinar, then losing the tower and Stormblessed, had left the being frail. Vulnerable.

But the *power* was anything but frail. It was the power of life and death, of creation and destruction. The power of gods. In his specific case, the power of emotion, passion, and—most deeply—the power of raw, untamed *fury*. Of hatred unbound.

In this new role, Taravangian had two sides. On one was his knowledge: ideas, understandings, truths, lies . . . Thousands upon thousands of possible futures opened up to him. Millions of potentials. So numerous that even his expanded godly mind was daunted by their variety.

On the other side was his fury. The terrible fury, like an unbridled storm, churned and burned within him. It too was so overwhelming he could barely control it.

He was aware of what he'd left behind in the mortal realm. Szeth had long since climbed to his feet and sheathed Nightblood. Beside him, the assassin had found a burned-out corpse, mostly eaten by the sword's attack. That was Rayse, Taravangian's predecessor, but Szeth wasn't able to tell. The sword had consumed clothing and most of the flesh, leaving bits of stone-grey bone.

They think that's me, Taravangian thought, reading the possible futures. *Szeth didn't see what happened to me spiritually. He doesn't know Odium was here.*

Almost all possible futures agreed. Szeth would confess that he'd gone to kill Taravangian, but somehow Taravangian had drawn Nightblood— and the weapon had consumed him.

They thought him dead. He was free. . . .

Free to destroy! To burn! To wreak havoc and terror upon those who had doubted him!

No. No, free to plan. To devise a way to save the world from itself. He could see so far! See so much! He needed to think.

To burn!

No, to plot!

To . . . To . . .

Taravangian was startled as he became aware of something else. A growing power nearby, visible only to one such as him. A godly power, infinite and verdant.

He was not alone.

⁘

They gave Teft a king's funeral, Soulcasting him to stone. A sculptor would be commissioned to create a depiction of Phendorana to erect next to him. The Sibling said there was a room, locked away, where the ancient Radiants stood forever as stone sentries. It would feel good to see Teft among them, in uniform and looking at them all with a scowl, despite the embalmer's best efforts.

It felt right.

All of Bridge Four came, except for Rock. Skar and Drehy had relayed the news after returning to the Shattered Plains—it seemed Kaladin wouldn't be seeing Rock again.

Together, the men and women of Bridge Four praised Teft, drank to him, and burned prayers for him in turn. Afterward, they sought a tavern to continue celebrating in a way Teft would have loved, even if he wouldn't have let himself participate.

Kaladin waited as they drifted away. They kept checking on him, of course, worried for his health. Worried about the darkness. He appreciated each and every one of them for it, but he didn't need that type of help today.

He was kind of all right. A good night's sleep, and finding peace restored to the tower, had helped. So he sat there, looking at the statue created from Teft's body. The others finally seemed to sense he needed to be alone. So they left him.

Syl landed beside him fully sized, in a Bridge Four uniform. He could faintly feel her when she rested her head on his shoulder.

"We won't stop missing him, will we?" she asked softly.

"No. But that's all right. So long as we cling to the moments we had."

"I can't believe you're taking this better than I am."

"I thought you said you were recovering."

"I am," she said. "This still hurts though." Once the tower had been restored, she'd mostly returned to herself. Some of what she'd felt had been gloom from what Raboniel had done.

Some of it wasn't.

"We could ask Dalinar," Kaladin said. "If maybe there's something wrong with you. A bond or something unnatural."

"He won't find one. I'm merely . . . alive. And this is part of being alive. So I'm grateful, even if part of it stinks."

He nodded.

"Really stinks," she added. Then for good measure, "Stinks like a human after . . . how long has it been since you had a bath?"

He smiled, and the two of them remained there, looking up at Teft. Kaladin didn't know if he believed in the Almighty, or in the Tranquiline Halls, or whether people lived after they died. Yes, he'd seen something in a vision. But Dalinar had seen many dead people in his visions, and that didn't mean they still lived somewhere. He didn't know why Tien had given the wooden horse to him, as if to prove the vision was real, only for it to immediately vanish.

That seemed to indicate Kaladin's mind had fabricated the meeting. He didn't let it prevent him from feeling that he'd accomplished something important. He'd laid down a heavy burden. The pain didn't go away, but most of the shame . . . that he let fall behind him.

Eventually, he stood up and embraced Teft's statue. Then he wiped his eyes and nodded to Syl.

They needed to keep moving forward. And that involved deciding what he was going to do with himself, now that the crisis had ended.

···

Taravangian grew more capable by the moment.

The power molded him as he bridled it. He stepped to the edge of infinity, studying endless possibilities as if they were a million rising suns and he were standing on the bank of an eternal ocean. It was beautiful.

A woman stepped up beside him. He recognized her full hair, black and tightly curled, along with her vibrant round face and dark skin. She had another shape as well. Many of them, but one deeper and truer than the others.

"Do you understand now?" she asked him.

"You needed someone who could tempt the power," Taravangian said, his light gleaming like gold. "But also someone who could control it. I asked for the capacity to save the world. I thought it was the intelligence, but later wondered if it was the ability to feel. In the end, it was both. You were preparing me for this."

"Odium's power is the most dangerous of the sixteen," she said. "It ruled Rayse, driving him to destroy. It will rule you too, if you let it."

"They showed you this possibility, I assume," Taravangian said, looking at infinity. "But this isn't nearly as . . . certain as I imagined it. It shows you things that can happen, but not the hearts of those who act. How did you *dare* try something like this? How did you know I'd be up to the challenge?"

"I didn't," she said. "I couldn't. You were heading this direction—all I could do was hope that if you succeeded, my gift would work. That I had changed you into someone who could bear this power with honor."

Such power. Such *incredible* power. Taravangian peered into infinity. He'd wanted to save his city, and had succeeded. After that, he'd wanted to save Roshar. He could do that now. He could end this war. Storms, Dalinar and Odium's contract—which bound Taravangian just as soundly—would do that already.

But . . . beyond that, what of the entire cosmere? He couldn't see that far yet. Perhaps he would eventually be able to. But he did know his predecessor's plans, and had access to some of his knowledge. So Taravangian knew the cosmere was in chaos. Ruled by fools. Presided over by broken gods.

There was so much to do. He sorted through Odium's previous plans and saw all their flaws. How had he let himself be maneuvered into this particular deal with Dalinar? How had he let himself rely so much upon a contest of champions? Didn't he know? The way to win was to make sure that, no matter the outcome, you were satisfied. Odium should never have entered a deal he could not absolutely control.

It can still be done, Taravangian realized, seeing the possibilities—so subtle—that his predecessor had missed. *Yes . . . Dalinar has set himself up . . . to fail. I* can *beat him.*

"Taravangian," Cultivation said, holding her hand out to him. "Come. Let me teach you about what you've been given. I realize the power is overwhelming, but you *can* control it. You can do better than Rayse ever did."

He smiled and took her hand. Inside, he exulted.

Oh, you wonderful creature, he thought. *You have no idea what you have done.*

He was finally free of the frailties of body and position that had always controlled and defined him. He *finally* had the freedom to do what he'd desired.

And now, Taravangian was going to save them all.

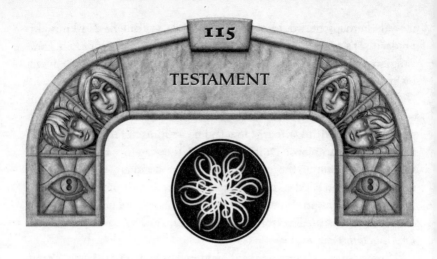

Yes, I look forward to ruling the humans.

—Musings of El, on the first of the Final Ten Days

Shallan sat by candlelight, writing quietly in her notebook. Adolin pulled his chair up beside her. "She looks better," he said, "than she did when I saw her in the market. But I don't know, Shallan."

Shallan put down the pen, then took his hands, glancing to the side where—in their little chamber in Lasting Integrity—her first spren sat on a chair, Pattern standing beside her and humming. Had the limp fibers of her head pattern straightened?

In talking with Pattern, they'd decided upon an Alethi name for Shallan's previous Cryptic. One that fit, best they could tell, with the meaning of her individual pattern.

"Testament does seem better, Adolin," Shallan said. "Thank you for speaking with her."

Maya sat on the floor, cross-legged, in a kind of warrior's pose. She hadn't recovered completely, but she *was* improved. And though she still didn't say much, Shallan doubted many beings—human or spren—had ever spoken words quite so valuable as Maya had at the trial. One might say, by simple economics, that Maya was one of the best orators who ever existed. If you aren't going to say much, then you might as well make what you *do* say mean something.

It gave them hope that whatever Shallan had done to Testament could also be repaired.

"I'll try to explain everything Maya and I have done," Adolin said as honorspren bells rang somewhere near. "But the truth is, I don't think either of us know. And I'm not exactly an expert on all this."

"Recent events considered? I think you're the *only* expert." Shallan reached up and cupped his face. "Thank you, Adolin."

"For?"

"Being you. I'm sorry for the secrets."

"You did tell me," he said. "Eventually." He nodded toward the knife with the gemstone, still unused, which rested beside her open notebook on one side of the table. The cube Mraize had sent rested on the other side. "The bells are ringing. Time?"

She removed her hand and situated herself at the desk. Adolin fell silent, waiting and watching as Shallan lifted the top of Mraize's cube. With help from Kelek, they'd gotten it open without harming the thing inside: a spren in the shape of a glowing ball of light, a strange symbol at the center. No one here recognized the variety of spren, but Wit called it a seon.

"Are you well, Ala?" Shallan asked. It was said like *A-lay.*

"Yes," the spren whispered.

"You can come out of the cube. You don't need to live in there anymore."

"I'm . . . supposed to stay. I'm not supposed to talk. To you. To anyone."

Shallan glanced at Adolin. The odd spren resisted attempts to get it free. It acted . . . like an abused child.

Another in the list of Mraize's crimes, Radiant thought.

Agreed, Shallan replied.

Radiant remained. They agreed that once they found the right path, she would eventually be absorbed as Veil had been. For now, Shallan's wounds were still fresh. Practically bleeding. But what she'd done would finally let her begin to heal. And she knew why Pattern had always been so certain she would kill him. And why he'd acted like a newly bonded spren when she'd begun noticing him on the ship with Jasnah. The simple answer was the true one. He *had* been newly bonded.

And Shallan had not one Shardblade, but two.

She still had questions. Things about her past didn't completely align yet, though her memory was no longer full of holes. There was much they didn't understand. For example, she was certain that, during the years between killing Testament and finding Pattern, her powers had still functioned in some small ways.

Some of this, Kelek said, had to do with the nature of deadeyes. Before the Recreance, they had never existed. Kelek said he thought this was why Mraize was hunting him. Something to do with the fall of the singers, and the Knights Radiant, so long ago—and the imprisoning of a specific spren.

"Contact Mraize please, spren," she whispered to the ball of light. "It is time."

The ball floated into the air, and the next part took barely a moment. The globe of light shifted to make a version of his face speaking to her. "Little knife," the face said in Mraize's voice. "I trust the deed has been done?"

"I did it," Shallan said. "It hurt so much. But she is gone."

"Excellent. That . . . *She*, little knife?"

"Veil and I are one now, Mraize," Shallan said, resting her hand on her notebook—which contained the fascinating things Kelek had told her about other worlds, other planets. Places he desperately wished to see.

Like the other Heralds, Kelek wasn't entirely stable. He was unable to commit to ideas or plans. However, to one thing he *had* committed: He wanted off Roshar. He was convinced that Odium would soon take over the world completely and restart torturing all the Heralds. Kelek would do practically anything to escape that fate.

There was a long pause from Mraize. "Shallan," he finally said, "we do *not* move against other Ghostbloods."

"I'm not one of the Ghostbloods," Shallan said. "None of us ever were, not fully. And now we are stepping away."

"Don't do this. Think of the cost."

"My brothers? Is that what you're referencing? You must know by now that they are no longer in the tower, Mraize. Pattern and Wit got them out before the occupation even occurred. Thank you for this seon, by the way. Wit says that unbound ones are difficult to come by—but they make for extremely handy communication across realms."

"You will never have your answers, Shallan."

"I have what I need, thank you very much," she said as Adolin put a comforting hand on hers. "I've been speaking to Kelek, the Herald. He seems to think the reason you're hunting him is because of an Unmade. Ba-Ado-Mishram? The one who Connected to the singers long ago, giving them forms of power? The one who, when trapped, stole the singers' minds and made them into parshmen?

"Why do you want the gemstone that holds Ba-Ado-Mishram, Mraize? What are you intending to do with it? What power do the Ghostbloods seek with a thing that can bind the minds of an entire people?"

Mraize didn't respond. The seon, imitating his face, hovered in place. Expressionless.

"I'll be returning to the tower soon," Shallan said. "Along with those honorspren who have decided—in light of recent revelations—to bond with humans. When I do, I expect to find you and yours gone. Perhaps if you cover yourself well, I won't be able to track you down. Either way, I *am* going to find that gemstone before you do. And if you get in my way . . . well, it will be a fun hunt. Wouldn't you say?"

"This will not end well for you, Shallan," Mraize said. "You make an enemy of the most powerful organization in all the cosmere."

"I think we can handle you."

"Perhaps. Can you handle my master? Can you handle *her* master?"

"Thaidakar?" Shallan guessed.

"Ah, so you've heard of him?"

"The Lord of Scars, Wit calls him. Well, when you next meet this Lord of Scars, give him a message from me."

"He comes here in avatar only," Mraize said. "We are too far beneath his level to be worthy of more."

"Then tell his *avatar* something for me. Tell him . . . we're done with his meddling. His influence over my people is finished." She hesitated, then sighed. Wit *had* asked nicely. "Also, Wit says to tell him, 'Deal with your own stupid planet, you idiot. Don't make me come over there and slap you around again.'"

"So it must be," Mraize said. "Know that in doing this, you have moved against the Ghostbloods in the most offensive of ways. We are now at war, Shallan."

"You've always been at war," Shallan said. "*I've* finally picked a side. Goodbye, Mraize. End contact."

The floating spren molded into a globe instead of Mraize's face. Shallan sat back, trying not to feel overwhelmed.

"Whoever they are," Adolin said, "we *can* handle them."

Ever optimistic. Well, he had good reason. With the leaders of the honorspren in disgrace, and Lasting Integrity open again to all who would visit, he had accomplished his mission. He'd been correct all along, both about the honorspren and about Shallan herself.

Shallan reached forward and flipped to the next page in her notebook, where she'd done a drawing using Kelek's descriptions. It showed a pattern of stars in the sky, and listed the many worlds among them.

Shallan had kept her head down too long. It was time to soar.

.•.

The listeners raised bows toward Venli as she walked up to their camp, alone, after insisting that the others stay back a few hundred feet.

She didn't blame the listeners for turning weapons against her. They assumed she had come to finish the job she'd started. So she raised her hands and hummed to Peace, waiting.

And waiting.

And waiting.

Finally, Thude himself emerged from behind their fortification of piled rocks. Storms, it was good to see him. By the counts they'd done from the air, almost all of them must have made it through the narrows and out this side. A thousand listener adults, along with many children.

Thude approached, wearing warform, but he stopped short of striking range. Venli continued to stand and hum, feeling a hundred bows focused on her. This eastern plain beyond the hills was a strange place—so open, and full of a surprising amount of grass.

"Storms. *Venli?*" Thude turned to dash back behind the fortifications.

She realized he must have just now seen her patterns. She was wearing a form he'd never known, so of course he hadn't recognized her from a distance. "Thude!" she called out, taking in enough Stormlight to glow in the daylight. "Thude, please!"

He stopped, seeing her Light.

"Did my mother make it?" she asked to Longing. "Is she alive?"

"She is," he called. "But her mind is gone."

"I think I might have a way to heal her."

"Traitor," he shouted. "You think I believe you? You would have had us killed!"

"I understand," she said softly to Consolation. "I deserve everything you can call me, and more. But I'm trying as I never did before. Please, listen to what I have to say."

He wavered, then crossed the stone to meet her. "Do the others know where we are? Does the enemy know?"

"I'm not sure," Venli said. "The humans found you. One Fused knew of you, but she is dead now. I don't know who she told."

"What is a Fused?"

"There's a lot you don't know," Venli said. "Our gods have returned, terrible as warned. I was largely responsible for this, even if Rlain says he's certain they would have found their way back anyway."

Thude perked up at Rlain's name.

"We're going to have to do something to protect ourselves," Venli said. "Something to make everyone leave us alone." She held out her hand, and a little spren in the shape of a comet flew up from the grass and started circling it. "She's new to this realm and a little confused. But she's seeking someone to bond and make into a Radiant. Like me and my friends."

"You came to us last time with a spren who wanted a bond," Thude said to Reprimand. "And what happened?"

"This will be different," Venli said, alight with Stormlight. "I've changed. I promise you all the time you need to test my words. To decide without being pushed. For now, please let me see my mother."

He hummed to Winds at last, a sign for her to follow, as he started walking back to camp. Venli attuned Joy.

"There are more of these spren that will make listeners into Radiants?" he asked.

"Yes," she said.

"How many?"

"Hundreds," she said.

The Rhythm of Joy grew loud inside Venli as she entered the camp—though many who saw her hummed to Anxiety. She cared for only one sight. An old singer woman sitting by a tent made from woven reeds.

Venli's heart leaped, and the rhythms sounded more pure. More vibrant. Jaxlim really was alive. Venli rushed forward, collapsing to her knees before Jaxlim, feeling as if she were again a child. In the good way.

"Mother?" she asked.

Jaxlim looked up at her. There was no recognition in the old listener's eyes.

"Without her," Thude said, stepping up beside Venli, "we're losing the songs. Nobody else who knew them escaped. . . ."

"It's all right," Venli said, wiping her tears. "It's going to be all right." Timbre, within Venli, let out a glorious song.

Venli held out her hand, and the little lightspren inched into the air, then began spinning around Venli's mother. The Reachers were searching for people who exemplified their Ideal: freedom. And the listeners were the perfect representation.

However, a Radiant bond required volition, and her mother couldn't speak Ideals—though the Reachers indicated that the start of the bonding process didn't require that. They also thought becoming Radiant would heal her mother, though they couldn't say for certain. Mental wounds were difficult, they explained, and healing depended greatly on the individual.

Jaxlim *could* still want this, couldn't she? She could still choose? "Listen, Mother," Venli pled to Peace. "Hear me. Please." Venli began singing the Song of Mornings. The first song she'd learned. Her mother's favorite. As she sang, listeners gathered around, lowering their weapons. They started humming rhythms to match hers.

When she finished, Thude knelt beside her. The little spren had slipped into Jaxlim's body to seek her gemheart, but no change had happened yet. Venli took out a Stormlight sphere, but her mother did not drink it in.

"It was beautiful," Thude said. "It's been too long since I heard one of the songs."

"I will restore them to you," Venli whispered, "if you'll have me. I understand completely if you won't—but I've brought other Radiants with me, my friends. Along with some of the enemy who have chosen to defect and become listeners."

Thude hummed to Skepticism.

"Again, if you turn me aside, that is understandable," Venli said. "But at least listen to my friends. You're going to need allies to survive in this new world, a world of Surgebinders. We can't go alone as we did before."

"We're not alone," Thude said. "I think you'll find that things have changed for us, as they have for you."

Venli hummed to Consideration. Then she heard a scraping sound, like rock on rock. Or . . . claws on rock?

A shadow fell over Venli, and she started, staring up at a powerful long neck with a wicked arrowhead face on the end. A chasmfiend. Here. And no one was panicking.

Storms. "That's . . ." she whispered. "That's how you got out of the chasms that night, during the storm?"

Thude hummed Confidence.

Before she could demand answers, something else interrupted her. A voice.

"Venli? Venli, is that you?"

Venli looked down to see that her mother's eyes had focused, *seeing* her.

Your Words, Venli, a distant femalen voice said in her mind, *are now accepted.*

116

MERCY

Nearly as much as I look forward to serving you, newest Odium. Who was so recently one of them. You understand. And you are the one I've been waiting to worship.

—Musings of El, on the first of the Final Ten Days

Around four hours after Teft's funeral, Kaladin went looking for Dalinar. The Blackthorn had returned the previous night, but Kaladin had been too exhausted that evening to do more than salute him, then find his bed.

So, he excused himself from the party at Jor's winehouse and soared up toward the top of the tower. It felt good to fly up all on his own. Here, as reported by the messenger who'd brought him the news, Kaladin and Syl found the Bondsmith . . . er, the Stormfather's Bondsmith . . . taking reports with Navani. The other Bondsmith. That was going to take some getting used to.

Kaladin and Syl intended to linger outside the small council room until Dalinar finished his current meeting, but as soon as he saw them, he broke it off and came trotting over.

"Kaladin," he said. "I've been meaning to speak with you."

"You've been busy, sir," Kaladin said. He glanced down at his uniform. "Maybe I shouldn't be wearing this."

Dalinar actually *blushed*. What a remarkable sight. "About that," he said. "I should have known I couldn't—and shouldn't—try to relieve someone like you from—"

"Sir," Kaladin interrupted. He glanced at Syl, who nodded. He turned back to Dalinar. "Sir, you were right. I have a lot of healing to do before I should be in command again."

"Even still?" Dalinar asked, glancing at Kaladin's forehead—and the missing brands. "After what you have accomplished? After swearing the Fourth Ideal?"

"The Ideals don't fix us, sir," Kaladin said. "You know that. We have to fix ourselves. Perhaps with a little help." He saluted. "We were on the correct path with me, sir. I *need* to take time away from the battle. Maybe so much time that I never return to full command. I have work to do, helping men like me and Dabbid. I'd like your permission to continue."

"Granted," Dalinar said. "You've grown, soldier. Few men have the wisdom to realize when they need help. Fewer still have the strength to go get it. Well done. Very well done."

"Thank you, sir," Kaladin said.

Dalinar hesitated—something seemed to be troubling him. He put his hands behind his back, watching Kaladin. Everyone else was celebrating. Not Dalinar.

"What is it, sir?" Kaladin asked.

"I haven't made it public knowledge yet, but Odium and I have set a time for our contest of champions."

"That's excellent," Kaladin said. "How long?"

"Ten days."

"Ten . . . *days?*"

Dalinar nodded.

Syl gasped, and Kaladin felt a spike of alarm. He'd always kind of thought . . . He'd spent this year assuming that . . .

"Sir," Kaladin said. "I can't . . ."

"I know, son," Dalinar said quietly. "You weren't right for the champion job anyway. This is the sort of thing a man must do himself."

Kaladin felt cold. Ten days. "The war . . . Does this mean . . . it will be over?"

"One way or another, it will end," Dalinar said. "The terms will enforce a treaty in ten days, following the contest. The contest will decide the fate of Alethkar, among . . . other items. Regardless, the hostilities will continue until that day, and so we must remain vigilant. I expect the enemy to make a play to capture what he can, before the treaty finalizes borders. I perhaps made a miscalculation there.

"Regardless, an end *is* in sight. But I'm going to need help from someone before this contest arrives. The fight won't simply be a swordfight— I can't explain what it *will* be. I don't know that I understand yet either, but I'm increasingly confident I need to master what I can of my powers."

"I don't know if I can help with that, sir," Kaladin said. "Though we share a Surge, our abilities seem very different."

"Yes, but there is one who *can* help me. Unfortunately, he's insane. And so, Kaladin, I do not need you as a soldier right now. I need you as a surgeon. You are of the few who personally understand what it means to have your own mind betray you. Would you be willing to go on a mission to recover this individual and find a way to help him, so he can help me?"

"Of course, sir," Kaladin said. "Who is it?"

"The Herald Ishi," Dalinar said. "Creator of the Oathpact, Herald of Truth, and original binder of the Fused."

Syl whistled softly.

"Sir," Kaladin said, feeling unnerved. "Ten days isn't enough to help someone with *ordinary* battle shock. It will take years, if we can even find proper methods. To help a Herald . . . Well, sir, their problems seem far beyond mine."

"I know, soldier," Dalinar said. "But I think Ishar's malady is supernatural in nature, and he gave me clues to help him recover. All I need from you now is an agreement to help. And a willingness to travel to Shinovar in somewhat . . . odd company."

"Sir?" Kaladin asked.

"I'll explain later," Dalinar said. "I need time to think this over, decide what I really want to do."

Kaladin nodded, but glanced at Syl, who whistled again. "Ten days?" she said. "I guess it's happening. . . ."

Dalinar started back toward his meeting—then paused and reached for something on a nearby table. A flute?

Wit's flute.

"Lift had this," Dalinar said, handing it toward Kaladin. "She said that Dabbid recognized it as yours."

"It is," Kaladin said with awe. "How is Lift, by the way?"

"My lunch is gone," Dalinar said. "So I'd say she's doing fine. We found her spren once the tower was restored, and they have—for some reason—decided to begin carrying around a bright red chicken." He sighed. "Anyway, she said she found that flute in a merchant's bin down in the Breakaway. One who sells salvage from the Shattered Plains. There might be other things your men were forced to abandon there."

Huh. "Did she say which merchant?" Kaladin asked.

.•.

The Pursuer drew in a deep, angry breath as he woke.

Then he screamed in rage.

It felt good to have lungs again. It felt good to shout his frustration. He would continue to scream it. Killed. A second time. By that Windrunner. That insolent mortal, who thought his victory was due to his *skill* and not raw luck!

The Pursuer screamed again, glad for the sound to accompany his fury. His voice echoed; he was someplace dark, but enclosed. That made him pause. Shouldn't he . . . be out in the storm?

"Are you quite done, Defeated One?" a voice said in their language, but with no rhythm.

The Pursuer sat up, twisting to look around. "Who dares call me—" He cut off as he saw who stood on the other side of the room, lit only by a Voidlight sphere held casually in his hand: a sleek figure looking out a dark window, his back to the Pursuer. The figure had twisting horns on his head and carapace that reflected the light wrong. He always ripped off his natural carapace formations at each rebirth, then replaced them with metal inclusions. They were incorporated into his body by Voidlight healing and his own special talents.

El. The one with no title.

The Pursuer silenced himself. He didn't fear this Fused. He feared no one. But . . . to El, he did not complain.

"Where am I?" the Pursuer asked instead. "Why have I been reborn so quickly? I was on Braize for barely a day before I felt the pull."

"We didn't want to wait," El said softly, still facing away from the Pursuer. No rhythms. El was forbidden rhythms. "So we had it done the old way. The way before the storms."

"I thought Odium wasn't doing that any longer."

"Our new god made an exception, Defeated One."

The Pursuer grunted, picking himself up off the ground. "They gave your title to another, you know. A human."

"I've heard."

"Disrespectful," the Pursuer said to Derision. "It should have remained unused. Give me that Voidlight. I need to recharge myself, to earn back my legacy."

"Earn back?"

The Pursuer forced himself to keep his tone respectful, to not shout. The one with no title could be . . . difficult. "I will hunt the mortal who killed me," the Pursuer said. "I will kill him, and then anyone he ever loved. I will murder mortal after mortal until my vengeance is recognized, my atonement made. I assume you all know this, if you couldn't wait for me to be reborn. So give me that *damn* Voidlight."

El turned, smiling in the shadows. "It is for you, Lezian."

"Excellent," the Pursuer said, stalking forward.

"But you mistook me," El said. "When we said we did not want to have to wait for your rebirth, it was not your convenience that troubled us, but mine. I am very curious, you see, and you were the sole appropriate subject."

"Subject for what?" the Pursuer asked, reaching the window and looking out over Kholinar at night.

"Oh, to see if this really works." El raised the Voidlight sphere . . . and the Pursuer saw it was attached to a knife. Did the Light look wrong somehow? Warping the air around the gemstone?

"I think this might hurt," El said, then grabbed the Pursuer by the front of his beard. "Enjoy this final Passion, Defeated One."

He plunged the knife down as the Pursuer struggled.

And his soul ripped itself apart.

⁂

Kaladin walked the now-bright streets of the Breakaway, bathed in cool steady light from above. The transformation the tower had undergone already was amazing. The air had become as warm as it was in Azir, an envelope of temperate weather that extended out to the fields.

People breathed more easily now. The entire tower was not only properly ventilated, it had water running through hidden pipes into many rooms, like they had in rich cities such as Kharbranth. And that was just the beginning. While some rooms in the tower had once held normal wooden doors, many others had stone doors that opened to the touch. They hadn't realized how many rooms they'd missed while exploring because they'd been closed when the tower had last shut down. The place was truly a wonder.

He finally found the merchant shop Lift had told Dalinar about. Though the hour was growing late, the market was busy with people celebrating, so a lot of the shops were open, this one included. Kaladin was directed to a bin of salvage, and he began rifling through it, Syl on his shoulder. He found Rock's razor. And some of Sigzil's brushpens. And . . .

He held up a miniature wooden horse, carved in exacting detail.

Syl breathed out an awed sound.

"I lost this before coming to the Shattered Plains," Kaladin said. "I lost this in *Alethkar*. Tien gave it to me the day we were recruited into the army, and it was taken with my other things when I became a slave. How . . ."

He clutched the horse close to his chest. He was so amazed that he walked off, and had to come running back to pay for what he'd taken. After that, he trotted back toward the tavern. He'd promised earlier that he would meet Dabbid, Noril, and the others he'd rescued from the monastery sick rooms, to decompress from yesterday's events.

Kaladin would do as Dalinar asked, and go to save the Herald Ishi. That was for tomorrow, however. Today, Kaladin had another promise to keep. After all, he'd told Teft he would join these meetings and start taking care of himself.

⁂

Dalinar felt energized as he smelled the crisp cool air of the mountains. He stood at the very top of the tower, drinking it in while holding Navani, her warmth pressed against him. The sun had set, and he'd had enough of reports for the day. He wanted time with his wife and to look at the stars.

"I should have known you'd find a way out of it on your own," he whispered to Navani as Nomon bathed them in light. "I should have seen your potential."

She squeezed his arms. "I didn't see it either. I spent a long time refusing to do so."

Dalinar heard a rumbling in his mind. Not angry rumbling though. More . . . contemplative.

"The Stormfather doesn't know what to make of this," Dalinar said. "I think he finds it strange. Apparently, his Bondsmith and the Nightwatcher's Bondsmith sometimes had relationships, but the Sibling's Bondsmith was always apart."

"The Sibling is . . . curious that way," Navani said. "I'll introduce you, once they are ready. It might take them time."

"As long as it's within ten days," Dalinar said. "I can't guarantee what will happen after then."

"That deal you made . . ." she said.

"I'm sorry. I had to make an agreement while I had him. It isn't everything we wanted, but—"

"It's a good deal, Dalinar," Navani said. "Inspired, even. We will have peace, even if we have to give up Alethkar. I think we've all been coming to realize that was a probability. Instead, this gives us a chance. I just wish . . . That last bit you agreed to. That worries me."

He nodded. "Yes," he whispered. "I know."

This was his job though. To sacrifice himself, if need be, for everyone else. In that . . . In that Taravangian was right.

It still felt so wrong for Taravangian to be dead. Dalinar would never have a chance to prove to Taravangian that Dalinar's way was correct. Gone. Without a farewell. Burned away in another stupid plot to manipulate Szeth.

"At least we can stop the bloodshed," Navani said. "Tell our troops to hold position and wait for the contest."

"Yes," Dalinar said.

Unless . . . Should Dalinar have insisted the contest happen *sooner?* He didn't feel ready. But would he ever?

Something feels wrong, he thought. *Something has changed. We need to be ready for these next ten days.* He felt that truth like a twisting in his stomach.

"I feel your tension," Navani said.

"I'm second-guessing what I've done," Dalinar said.

"The best information we have indicates this contest is our most reasonable hope of success," Navani said. "And I doubt anyone the enemy presents can best Stormblessed."

"I'm . . . not going to pick Kaladin, gemheart."

"Why?" Navani asked. "He's our best warrior."

"No," Dalinar said. "He's our best soldier. But even if he were in peak fighting shape, I don't think he'd be our best warrior. Or our best killer.

"Wit says the enemy can't violate our agreement, and isn't likely to try to misinterpret it—not intentionally. In fact, Wit seems to think the victory is already ours, but he got what he wanted. Odium will remain trapped either way. I'm worried though. There's more I'm missing; I'm sure of it. At the very least, I think I left Odium too much room to continue fighting in the coming ten days."

"We'll find the answers, Dalinar," Navani said. "We have a goal now. If you can win this contest, that will be enough. We will find a way to live in this new world, with the singers in their lands, and humans in ours."

Navani squeezed his arm again, and he took a deep breath, intent on enjoying this moment. Storms, it felt good to be holding her. Beneath them, the tower's lights shone brightly in the night—and down in the corridors, it was positively *warm*. He'd had to come all the way up here to smell mountain air.

"I should have known," Dalinar repeated. "About you."

"I don't think so," Navani said. "It was a remarkable stroke of luck that I figured it all out."

"Not luck," Dalinar said. "Conviction. Brilliance. I was scared for you, but should have remembered when I was scared *of* you—and realized how much danger the Fused were in by trying to take your fabrials from you. You are incredible. You've *always* been incredible."

She breathed out a long, contented sigh.

"What?" he said.

"It's good to hear someone say that."

He held her for an extended moment of peace. But eventually, their crowns came calling. People came looking for Navani to settle something regarding the tower, and she was forced to leave.

Dalinar lingered on the top of the tower. He settled down on the edge, putting his legs over the side—the place where Kaladin had reportedly leapt into the darkness of the storm.

You were wise to give the Windrunner more time during his fall, the Stormfather said, approaching Dalinar. *You were wise to show . . . mercy.*

"It's an important concept to learn," Dalinar said to him. "The more you study it, the more human you will become."

I do not wish to become human, the Stormfather said. *But perhaps I can learn. Perhaps I can change.*

"That's all it takes," Dalinar said. "A willingness."

You are wrong though. I do understand mercy. I have expressed it, on occasion.

"Really?" Dalinar said, curious. "When?"

117

ONE FINAL GIFT

FOURTEEN MONTHS AGO

Eshonai hit the ground of the chasm in a furious splash. Above, the battle for Narak continued, and the rest of the listeners summoned the Everstorm.

She should be leading them! She was foremost among them! She leaped to her feet and shouted to a dozen horrible rhythms in a row, her voice echoing in the chasm. It did no good. She had been defeated by the human Shardbearer, sent tumbling into the chasms.

She needed to get out of here and find the fight again. She started trudging forward. Though the water came up to her waist, the flow was not swift. It was merely a constant, steady stream from the Weeping—and in Shardplate she was able to walk against the current. Her greaves flooded with chill water.

Which way was which? The lack of light confused her, but after a moment of thinking, she realized she was being silly. She didn't need to go either direction. She needed to go *up*. The fall must have dazed her more than she'd realized.

She picked a rough-feeling section of wall and began clawing her way up. She managed to get halfway to the top—using the awesome gripping strength of Shardplate, the Rhythm of Conceit pounding in her ears. But then the way the chasm wall bulged presented a problem.

In the darkness, she couldn't find a proper handhold, and the flashes of lightning above were too brief to help.

Lightning. Was that lightning too frequent, too bright, to be coming from other stormforms? Her own powers had been ruined by the water, naturally. She could barely feel any energy in her; it flooded out the moment it started to build.

What *was* happening? That was the Everstorm coming, wasn't it? Yes, she could feel its power, its energy, its *beauty*. But there was something else.

Listening to the howling wind, she realized what it was. A second storm. A highstorm was coming as well.

She attuned the Rhythm of Panic.

The two storms clashed, making the very ground tremble.

Clinging to the wall within the chasm, Eshonai felt the wind howling above. The lightning made her feel like she was blinking her eyes quickly, light and darkness alternating.

Then she heard a roar. The terrible sound of water surging through the chasm, becoming an incredible wave. She braced herself, but when the water hit, it ripped her off the wall.

It was here, within these highstorm rainwaters, that Eshonai's first battle began: the fight for survival.

She slammed into a rock, her helmet cracking. Escaping Stormlight lit the dark waters as they filled her helmet, suffocating her. She thrashed in the current and managed to grab something hard—an enormous boulder lodged into the center of the chasm.

With a heave, she pulled herself out of the water. A few precious moments later her helmet emptied, letting her gasp for air.

I'm going to die, she thought, the Rhythm of Destruction pounding in her ears. Water thundered around her, splashing her armor, and lightning spasmed in the sky above. *I'm going to die . . . as a slave.*

No.

An ember within Eshonai came alive. The part of herself she'd reserved, the part that would not be contained. The part that made her let Thude and the others escape. It was the core of who she was: a person who had insisted on leaving the camps to explore, a person who had always longed to see what was over the next hill.

A person who would *not be held captive.*

That was when her second battle began.

Eshonai screamed, trying to banish the Rhythm of Destruction. If she was to die here, she would die as herself! It was a highstorm. In highstorms, transformations came upon all people, listeners and humans alike. Within a highstorm, death walked hand in hand with salvation, singing a harmony.

Eshonai began summoning her Blade—but in a rumbling flash, her boulder shifted and she lost her grip. The Rhythm of Panic ruled her briefly as she was again submerged. Lightning flashing above made the water seem to glow as she was smashed into one chasm wall, then another.

Not Panic. Not your rhythms.

I reject you.

My life. My death.

I WILL BE FREE.

Sunken deep in the water, Eshonai summoned her Blade and rammed it into the chasm wall. For some reason, she thought she could hear its voice, far away. Screaming?

She clung to it anyway—holding steady before the current. She banished all rhythms, but she could not breathe. Darkness began to close in upon her. Her lungs stopped burning. As if . . . as if everything was going to be all right . . .

There. A tone. The strange, haunting one she'd heard when taking warform. It seemed . . . one of the pure tones of Roshar. It began a stately rhythm. Then a second tone, chaotic and angry, appeared beside it. The two drew closer, closer, then snapped together.

They melded into harmony, making a song of Honor and Odium both. A song for a singer who could fight, but also for a soldier who wanted to lay down her sword. She found this tone as, in the blackness, a small spren—shaped like a shooting star—appeared ahead of her.

Eshonai strained, reaching, clawing.

Her head came above water, and then her helm blessedly emptied. The rush of the river was slowing. She gasped sweet air, but then her hand slipped from her sword, and she slipped back under the water and was towed away—though with less force than before.

She attuned the rhythm. The Rhythm of War, the rhythm of victories and losses. The rhythm of a life at its end. To its beats, she resummoned her Blade and rammed it into the ground, holding it tightly as the waters slowed further.

She would not die. She would *live*. She *was* strong enough. Her journey was not at an end. *Not. Yet.*

She held on, belligerent, until the water slowed. Until the weight of her Plate was enough to resist the current without her effort, and she slumped against the bottom of the chasm, her back to the wall, water streaming over her.

She felt at her side, where the Plate had broken—as had her body. She bled from a deep gash here, her carapace ripped away. Each breath came as a ragged, sodden mess, and she tasted blood.

But in her mind, she cycled through the rhythms of her childhood. Awe. Confidence. Mourning. Determination. Then Peace.

She had lost the first battle.

But she had *won* the second.

And so, to the Rhythm of Victory, she closed her eyes. And found herself drifting in a place full of light.

What is this? Eshonai thought.

YOU WERE HIGHLY INVESTED WHEN YOU DIED, a voice said. It rumbled with the sound of a thousand storms, echoing through her. SO YOU PERSIST. FOR A SHORT TIME.

Invested? Eshonai thought.

YOU WERE RADIANT WHEN YOU DIED. YOU COULDN'T SAY THE WORDS, UNDER THE WATER, BUT I ACCEPTED THEM ANYWAY. HOW DO YOU THINK YOU SURVIVED THAT LONG WITHOUT BREATHING?

She floated. *So . . . this is my soul?*

SOME WOULD CALL IT THAT, said the Rider of Storms. SOME WOULD SAY IT IS A SPREN FORMED BY THE POWER YOU LEFT, IMPRINTED WITH YOUR MEMORIES. EITHER WAY, THIS IS THE END. YOU WILL PASS INTO ETERNITY SOON, AND EVEN I CANNOT SEE WHAT IS BEYOND.

How long? Eshonai asked.

MINUTES. NOT HOURS.

She had no eyes to close, but she relaxed in the light. Floating. She could hear the rhythms. All of them at once, with accompanying songs.

What did it mean, then? she asked as she waited. *Life.*

MEANING IS A THING OF MORTALS, the Rider said. IT IS NOT A THING OF STORMS.

That's sad.

Is it? he asked. I should think it encouraging. Mortals search for meaning, so it is proper they should create it. You get to decide what it meant, Eshonai. What you meant.

If I decide, then I failed, she thought. *I gave my people to the enemy. I died alone, defeated. I betrayed the gift of my ancestors. I am a shame to all previous listeners.*

I would think the opposite, the Rider said. In the end, you made the same choice as your ancestors. You gave away power for freedom. You know those ancient listeners as few ever have, or ever will.

That gave her peace as she felt her essence begin to stretch. As if it were moving toward something distant.

Thank you, she said to the Rider.

I did nothing. I watched you fall and did not stop it.

The rain cannot stop the bloodshed, she said, fading. *But it washes the world afterward anyway. Thank you.*

I could have done more, the Rider replied. Perhaps I should have.

It . . . is enough. . . .

No, he said. I can give you one final gift.

Eshonai stopped stretching, and instead found herself pulled toward something powerful. She had no eyes, but she suddenly had an awareness—the storm. She had become *the storm.* She felt every rumble of thunder as her heartbeat.

Watch, the Rider said. You wanted to know what was beyond the next hill. See them all.

She soared with him, enveloping the land, flying above it. Her rain bathed each and every hill, and the Rider let her see the world with the eyes of a god. Everywhere the wind blew, she was. Everything the rain touched, she felt. Everything the lightning revealed, she knew.

She flew for what felt like an eternity, sustained by the Rider's own essence. She saw humans in infinite variety. She saw the captive parshmen—but saw the hope for their freedom. She saw creatures, plants, chasms, mountains, snows . . . she passed it *all.* Everything.

The entire world. She *saw* it. Every little piece was a part of the rhythms. The world *was* the rhythms. And Eshonai, during that transcendent ride, understood how it fit together.

It was wonderful.

When the Rider finished his passage—exhausted and limping as he passed into the ocean beyond Shinovar—she felt him let go. She faded, but this time she felt her soul *vibrating*. She understood the rhythms as no one ever could without having seen the world as she had.

Farewell, Eshonai, the Rider of Storms said. Farewell, Radiant.

Bursting with songs, Eshonai let herself pass into the eternities, excited to discover what lay on the other side.

DIRTY TRICKS

W it strolled the hallways of Elhokar's old palace on the Shattered Plains, searching for an audience. He flipped a coin in the air, then caught it before snapping his hand forward and spreading his fingers to show that the coin had vanished. But of course it was secretly in his other hand, palmed, hidden from sight.

"Storytelling," he said to the hallway, "is essentially about cheating."

He tucked the coin into his belt with a quick gesture, keeping up the flourishes of his other hand as a distraction. In a moment he could present both hands empty before him. He added to the theatrics by pushing back his sleeves.

"The challenge," he said, "is to make everyone believe you've lived a thousand lives. Make them *feel* the pain you have not felt, make them *see* the sights you have not seen, and make them *know* the truths that you have made up."

The coin appeared in his hand, though he'd simply slipped it out of his belt again. He rolled it across his knuckles, then made it split into two— because it had always been two coins stuck together. He tossed those up, caught them, and then made them appear to be four after adding the two he'd been palming in his other hand.

"You use the same dirty tricks for storytelling," Wit said, "as you do for fighting in an alley. Get someone looking in the wrong direction so you can clock them across the face. Get them to anticipate a punch and brace themselves, so you can reposition. Always hit them where they aren't prepared."

With a flourish, he presented both hands forward, empty again. On his coat, Design made a peppy humming sound. "I found one!" she said. "In your belt!"

"Hush," Wit said. "Let the audience be amazed."

"The audience?"

Wit nodded to the side, where a few odd spren were following in the air. Almost invisible, and trailing red light. Windspren—but the wrong color. She was expanding her influence, that old one was. He was curious where it would lead. Also horrified. But the two emotions were not mutually exclusive.

"I don't think they care about your tricks," Design said.

"*Everyone* cares about my tricks."

"But you can make the coins vanish with Lightweaving," she said. "So it doesn't matter how many you hide in your belt. And if you do something amazing, everyone will assume it was done with Surgebinding!"

Wit sighed, tossing four coins in the air, then catching them and presenting one solitary coin.

"They don't even use those for money here," Design added. "So you'll only distract them. Use spheres."

"Spheres glow," Wit said. "And they're tough to palm."

"Excuses."

"My life is *only* excuses." He wound the coin across his knuckles. "The illusion without Lightweaving is superior, Design."

"Because it's fake?"

"Because the audience *knows* it's fake," Wit said. "When they watch and let themselves be amazed, they are *joining in* the illusion. They're giving you something vital. Something powerful. Something *essential*. Their belief.

"When you and the audience both start a performance knowing that a lie is going to be presented, their willing energy vibrates in tune with yours. It propels you. And when they walk away at the end, amazed but knowing they've been lied to—with their permission—the performance lingers in their minds. Because the lie was real somehow. Because they know that if they were to rip it apart, they could know how it was done. They realize there must have been flaws they could have caught. Signs. Secrets."

"So . . . it's better . . ." Design said, "because it's worse than an illusion using real magic?"

"Exactly."

"That's stupid."

Wit sighed. He bounced his coin off the ground with a metallic *pling,* then caught it. "Would you go bother someone else for a while?"

"Okay!" Design said excitedly. She moved off his coat and to the floor, then zipped away. His audience of corrupted windspren trailed after her. Traitors.

Wit started down a side hallway, but then felt something. A tingling that made his Breaths go wild.

Ah . . . he thought. He'd been expecting this; it was why he had left the tower, after all. Odium couldn't find him there.

He hiked to Elhokar's former sitting room and made himself available—visible, easy to reach. Then, when the *presence* entered the nondescript stone chamber, Wit bowed.

"Welcome, Rayse!" Wit said. "It's been not nearly long enough."

I noticed your touch on the contract, a dramatic voice said in his head.

"You've always been a clever one," Wit said. "Was it my diction that clued you in, my keen bargaining abilities, or the fact that I included my *name* in the text?"

What game do you play here?

"A game of sense."

. . . What?

"Sense, Odium. The only kind I have is nonsense. Well, and some cents, but cents are nonsense here too—so we can ignore them. Scents are mine aplenty, and you never cared for the ones I present. So instead, the sense that matters is the sense Dalinar sensibly sent you."

I hate you.

"Rayse, dear," Wit said, "you're supposed to be an idiot. Say intelligent things like that too much, and I'll need to reevaluate. I know you adjusted the contract, trying for an advantage. How does it feel to know that Dalinar bested you?"

I shall have my vengeance, Odium said. *Even if it takes an eternity, Cephandrius, I will destroy you.*

"Enjoy that!" Wit said, striding toward the door. "Let me know how the brooding treats you. I spent a century doing it once, and I think it improved my complexion."

So interesting, Odium said. *How did I never see you there, in all my planning . . . Tell me, whom would you pick as champion? If you were in my place?*

"Why does it matter?" Wit asked.

Humor me.

Wit cocked his head. There was something odd about this change in tone from Odium. Asking whom Wit would choose? Rayse wouldn't care to know.

Never mind, Odium said quickly. *It matters not. Whomever I pick, they will destroy Dalinar's champion! Then I will use him, and my minions on this planet, to finally do whatever I wish!*

"Yes, but where will you find that many willing horses . . ." Wit said, continuing on his way out the door. He started whistling as Odium's presence remained behind. That had gone *exactly* as he'd imagined. Except that last part. He slowed, turning the words over in his mind.

Was Rayse growing more thoughtful? Wit didn't need to worry, did he? After all this, Odium would be safely imprisoned, no matter what happened. There was no way out. . . .

Unless . . .

Wit's breath caught, but then he forced himself to keep whistling and walking.

A power *slammed* into him from behind. A golden energy, infinite and deadly. Wit's eyes went wide, and he gasped, sensing something horribly *wrong* about that power.

I have made an error, I see, the power said, soft and thoughtful. *I am new to this. I should not have pushed for information. It's all about giving you what you expect. Even a being thousands of years old can be tricked. I know this from personal experience now.*

"Who are you?" Wit whispered.

Odium, the power said. *Let me see . . . I cannot harm you. But here, you have used this other Investiture to store your memories, haven't you? Because you've lived longer than a mortal should, you need to put the excess memories somewhere. I can't see your mind, but I can see these, can't I?*

For the first time in a long, long while, Wit felt true terror. If Odium destroyed the Breaths that held his memories . . .

I don't believe this will cause you actual harm . . . Odium said. *Yes, it seems my predecessor's agreements will allow me to—*

Wit stopped in the hallways of Elhokar's old palace on the Shattered Plains. He searched around, then cocked his head. Had he heard something?

He shook his head and continued forward, looking for an audience. He flipped a coin in the air, then caught it before snapping his hand forward and spreading his fingers to show that the coin had vanished. But of course it was secretly in his other hand, palmed, hidden from sight.

"Storytelling," he said to the empty hallway, "is essentially about cheating."

He tucked the coin into his belt with a quick gesture, keeping up the flourishes of his other hand as a distraction. Then he heard a *pling* as something slipped free of his belt. He stopped and found one of his fake coins on the ground, the ones that could be stuck together to appear as one.

But just one half? That should have been safely tucked away in the little pocket hidden in his shirt. He picked it up, glanced around to see that no one had noticed the mistake.

"Pretend you didn't see that, Design," he said.

But she wasn't there on his coat. Storming spren. Had she slipped away when he hadn't been looking? He put a hand to his head, feeling an odd disorientation.

Something was wrong. But what?

"The challenge . . ." he said, tucking away the fake coin, "is to make everyone believe you've lived a thousand lives. . . . Make them *feel* the pain, the sights, the truths . . ."

Damn. It was wrong somehow. "You use the same dirty tricks for storytelling," Wit whispered, "as you do for fighting in an alley. Always be ready to hit them where they aren't prepared."

But no one was listening. Hadn't there been a couple of Sja-anat's minions following him earlier? He vaguely remembered . . . Design chasing them away?

Wit stared around himself, but then felt something. A tingling that made his Breaths go wild.

Ah . . . he thought. He'd been expecting this; it was why he had left the tower. Odium couldn't find him there.

He hiked the short distance to Elhokar's former sitting room and made himself available—visible, easy to reach. Then, when the *presence* entered the nondescript stone chamber, Wit bowed.

"Welcome, Rayse!" Wit said. "It's been not nearly long enough."

I noticed your touch on the contract, a dramatic voice said in his head.

"You've always been a clever one," Wit said. "Was it my brilliant prose that clued you in, my keen bargaining abilities, or the fact that I included my *name* right there for you to read?"

What game do you play here?

"A game of sense."

. . . What?

"Sense, Odium. The only kind I have is nonsense. Well, and some cents . . ." He glanced down at the coin he still held in his hand, then cocked his head.

I hate you.

"Rayse," Wit said, looking up, "you're supposed to be an idiot. Say intelligent things like that too much, and I'll need to reevaluate. . . . Anyway, I know you adjusted the contract, trying for an advantage. How does it feel to know that Dalinar Kholin, a simple mortal, has gotten the better of you?"

I shall have my vengeance, Odium said. *Even if it takes an eternity, Cephandrius, I will destroy you.*

"Enjoy that!" Wit said, striding toward the door. "Let me know how you enjoy the time with yourself. The Beyond knows, no one *else* can stand your company."

It doesn't matter! Odium roared. *My champion will destroy Dalinar's, and then I will use him and my other minions here to do whatever I wish!*

"Yes, well," Wit said from the door, "once you're done, at least try to remember to wash your hands." He slammed the door, then spun and continued on his way. He tried to find a tune to whistle, but each one sounded wrong. Something was fiddling with his perfect pitch.

Odium's presence had remained behind. Was . . . something wrong?

Don't trouble yourself, he thought. *This is working.*

After all, Wit's first face-to-face meeting with Odium in over a thousand years had gone *exactly* as he had imagined.

THE END OF

Book Four of

THE STORMLIGHT ARCHIVE

ENDNOTE

Burdens, Our Calling.
Songs of Home, a knowledge:
Knowing a Home of Songs, called our burden.

— Ketek written by El, Fused scholar of human art forms,
to commemorate the restoration of the Sibling

Poem is curious in its intentional weighting of the last line, where
Alethi poets traditionally weight the center word and build the
poem around it. Singers, it can be seen, have a different interpretation of the art form.

ARS ARCANUM

THE TEN ESSENCES AND THEIR HISTORICAL ASSOCIATIONS

NUMBER	GEMSTONE	ESSENCE	BODY FOCUS	SOULCASTING PROPERTIES	PRIMARY / SECONDARY DIVINE ATTRIBUTES
1 Jes	Sapphire	Zephyr	Inhalation	Translucent gas, air	Protecting / Leading
2 Nan	Smokestone	Vapor	Exhalation	Opaque gas, smoke, fog	Just / Confident
3 Chach	Ruby	Spark	The Soul	Fire	Brave / Obedient
4 Vev	Diamond	Lucentia	The Eyes	Quartz, glass, crystal	Loving / Healing
5 Palah	Emerald	Pulp	The Hair	Wood, plants, moss	Learned / Giving
6 Shash	Garnet	Blood	The Blood	Blood, all non-oil liquid	Creative / Honest
7 Betab	Zircon	Tallow	Oil	All kinds of oil	Wise / Careful
8 Kak	Amethyst	Foil	The Nails	Metal	Resolute / Builder
9 Tanat	Topaz	Talus	The Bone	Rock and stone	Dependable / Resourceful
10 Ishi	Heliodor	Sinew	Flesh	Meats, flesh	Pious / Guiding

The preceding list is an imperfect gathering of traditional Vorin symbolism associated with the Ten Essences. Bound together, these form the Double Eye of the Almighty, an eye with two pupils representing the creation of plants and creatures. This is also the basis for the hourglass shape that was often associated with the Knights Radiant.

Ancient scholars also placed the ten orders of Knights Radiant on this list, alongside the Heralds themselves, who each had a classical association with one of the numbers and Essences.

I'm not certain yet how the ten levels of Voidbinding or its cousin the Old Magic fit into this paradigm, if indeed they can. My research suggests that, indeed, there should be another series of abilities that is even more esoteric than the Voidbindings. Perhaps the Old Magic fits into those, though I am beginning to suspect that it is something entirely different.

Note that I currently believe the concept of the "Body Focus" to be more a matter of philosophical interpretation than an actual attribute of this Investiture and its manifestations.

THE TEN SURGES

As a complement to the Essences, the classical elements celebrated on Roshar, are found the Ten Surges. These, thought to be the fundamental forces by which the world operates, are more accurately a representation of the ten basic abilities offered to the Heralds, and then the Knights Radiant, by their bonds.

Adhesion: The Surge of Pressure and Vacuum
Gravitation: The Surge of Gravity
Division: The Surge of Destruction and Decay
Abrasion: The Surge of Friction
Progression: The Surge of Growth and Healing, or Regrowth
Illumination: The Surge of Light, Sound, and Various Waveforms
Transformation: The Surge of Soulcasting
Transportation: The Surge of Motion and Realmatic Transition
Cohesion: The Surge of Strong Axial Interconnection
Tension: The Surge of Soft Axial Interconnection

ON THE CREATION OF FABRIALS

Five groupings of fabrial have been discovered so far. The methods of their creation are carefully guarded by the artifabrian community, but they appear to be the work of dedicated scientists, as opposed to the more mystical Surgebindings once performed by the Knights Radiant. I am more and more convinced that the creation of these devices requires forced enslavement of transformative cognitive entities, known as "spren" to the local communities.

ALTERING FABRIALS

Augmenters: These fabrials are crafted to enhance something. They can create heat, pain, or even a calm wind, for instance. They are powered—like all fabrials—by Stormlight. They seem to work best with forces, emotions, or sensations.

The so-called half-shards of Jah Keved are created with this type of fabrial attached to a sheet of metal, enhancing its durability. I have seen fabrials of this type crafted using many different kinds of gemstone; I am guessing that any one of the ten Polestones will work.

Diminishers: These fabrials do the opposite of what augmenters do, and generally seem to fall under the same restrictions as their cousins. Those artifabrians who have taken me into confidence seem to believe that even greater fabrials are possible than what have been created so far, particularly in regard to augmenters and diminishers.

PAIRING FABRIALS

Conjoiners: By infusing a ruby and using methodology that has not been revealed to me (though I have my suspicions), you can create a conjoined pair of gemstones. The process requires splitting the original ruby. The two halves will then create parallel reactions across a distance. Spanreeds are one of the most common forms of this type of fabrial.

Conservation of force is maintained; for instance, if one is attached to a heavy stone, you will need the same strength to lift the conjoined fabrial that you would need to lift the stone itself. There appears to be some sort of process used during the creation of the fabrial that influences how far apart the two halves can go and still produce an effect.

Reversers: Using an amethyst instead of a ruby also creates conjoined halves of a gemstone, but these two work in creating *opposite* reactions. Raise one, and the other will be pressed downward, for instance.

These fabrials have only just been discovered, and already the possibilities for exploitation are being conjectured. There appear to be some unexpected limitations to this form of fabrial, though I have not been able to discover what they are.

WARNING FABRIALS

There is only one type of fabrial in this set, informally known as the Alerter. An Alerter can warn one of a nearby object, feeling, sensation, or phenomenon. These fabrials use a heliodor stone as their focus. I do not know whether this is the only type of gemstone that will work, or if there is another reason heliodor is used.

In the case of this kind of fabrial, the amount of Stormlight you can infuse into it affects its range. Hence the size of gemstone used is very important.

WINDRUNNING AND LASHINGS

Reports of the Assassin in White's odd abilities have led me to some sources of information that, I believe, are generally unknown. The Windrunners were an order of the Knights Radiant, and they made use of two primary types of Surgebinding. The effects of these Surgebindings were known—colloquially among the members of the order—as the Three Lashings.

BASIC LASHING: GRAVITATIONAL CHANGE

This type of Lashing was one of the most commonly used Lashings among the order, though it was not the easiest to use. (That distinction belongs to the Full Lashing below.) A Basic Lashing involved revoking a being's or object's spiritual gravitational bond to the planet below, instead temporarily linking that being or object to a different object or direction.

Effectively, this creates a change in gravitational pull, twisting the energies of the planet itself. A Basic Lashing allowed a Windrunner to run up walls, to send objects or people flying off into the air, or to create similar effects. Advanced uses of this type of Lashing would allow a Windrunner to make himself or herself lighter by binding part of his or her mass upward. (Mathematically, binding a quarter of one's mass upward would halve a person's effective weight. Binding half of one's mass upward would create weightlessness.)

Multiple Basic Lashings could also pull an object or a person's body downward at double, triple, or other multiples of its weight.

FULL LASHING: BINDING OBJECTS TOGETHER

A Full Lashing might seem very similar to a Basic Lashing, but they worked on very different principles. While one had to do with gravitation, the other had to do with the force (or Surge, as the Radiants called them) of Adhesion—binding objects together as if they were one. I believe this Surge may have had something to do with atmospheric pressure.

To create a Full Lashing, a Windrunner would infuse an object with Stormlight, then press another object to it. The two objects would become bound together with an extremely powerful bond, nearly impossible to break. In fact, most materials would themselves break before the bond holding them together would.

REVERSE LASHING: GIVING AN OBJECT
A GRAVITATIONAL PULL

I believe this may actually be a specialized version of the Basic Lashing. This type of Lashing required the least amount of Stormlight of any of the three Lashings. The Windrunner would infuse something, give a mental command, and create a *pull* to the object that yanked other objects toward it.

At its heart, this Lashing created a bubble around the object that imitated its spiritual link to the ground beneath it. As such, it was much harder for the Lashing to affect objects touching the ground, where their link to the planet was strongest. Objects falling or in flight were the easiest to influence. Other objects could be affected, but the Stormlight and skill required were much more substantial.

LIGHTWEAVING

A second form of Surgebinding involves the manipulation of light and sound in illusory tactics common throughout the cosmere. Unlike the variations present on Sel, however, this method has a powerful Spiritual element, requiring not just a full mental picture of the intended creation, but some level of Connection to it as well. The illusion is based not simply upon what the Lightweaver imagines, but upon what they *desire* to create.

In many ways, this is the most similar ability to the original Yolish variant, which excites me. I wish to delve more into this ability, with the hope to gain a full understanding of how it relates to cognitive and spiritual attributes.

SOULCASTING

Essential to the economy of Roshar is the art of Soulcasting, in which one form of matter is directly transformed into another by changing its spiritual nature. This is performed on Roshar via the use of devices known as Soulcasters, and these devices (the majority of which appear to be focused on turning stone into grain or flesh) are used to provide mobile supply for armies or to augment local urban food stores. This has allowed kingdoms on Roshar—where fresh water is rarely an issue, because of highstorm rains—to field armies in ways that would be unthinkable elsewhere.

What intrigues me most about Soulcasting, however, are the things we can infer about the world and Investiture from it. For example, certain gemstones are requisite in producing certain results—if you wish to produce grain, your Soulcaster must both be attuned to that transformation *and* have an emerald (not a different gemstone) attached. This creates an economy based on the relative values of what the gemstones can create, not upon their rarity. Indeed, as the chemical structures are identical for several of these gemstone varieties, aside from trace impurities, the *color* is the most important part—not their actual axial makeup. I'm certain you will find this relevance of hue quite intriguing, particularly in its relationship to other forms of Investiture.

This relationship must have been essential in the local creation of the table I've included above, which lacks some scientific merit, but is intrinsically tied to the folklore surrounding Soulcasting. An emerald can be used to create food—and thus is traditionally associated with a similar Essence. Indeed, on Roshar there are considered to be ten elements; not the traditional four or sixteen, depending upon local tradition.

Curiously, these gemstones seem tied to the original abilities of the Soulcasters who were an order of Knights Radiant—but they don't seem *essential* to the actual operation of the Investiture when performed by a living Radiant. I do not know the connection here, though it implies something valuable.

Soulcasters, the devices, were created to *imitate* the abilities of the Surge of Soulcasting (or Transformation). This is yet *another* mechanical imitation of something once available only to a select few within the bounds of an Invested Art. The Honorblades on Roshar, indeed, may be the very first example of this—from thousands of years ago. I believe this has relevance to the discoveries being made on Scadrial, and the commoditization of Allomancy and Feruchemy.

STONESHAPING

As I've had further occasion to study the use of Investiture on Roshar, and the curious manifestation of it known as Surgebinding, I've found occasion to ruminate further on the nature of Intent and Connection.

The power known as Stoneshaping, as practiced by the orders of Stonewards and Willshapers, is an excellent example of this. This ability manipulates the Surge of Cohesion, and is in many ways a cousin to the axial manipulation known as microkinesis—as both grant the ability to manipulate the forces that bind individual axi together. Fortunately, in my explorations, it appears that Stoneshaping is far less . . . explosive of a power, bounded by the rules that Honor placed upon it to protect from the mistakes that happened on Yolen.

Nevertheless, a practiced Stoneward or Willshaper can mold stone as if it were clay, weakening the bonds between axi. (Indeed, this can be done to other materials as well, I'm led to believe, but stone is the easiest and most common application.) This is not simply a chemical process. Normally, one might expect heat to be involved to excite the axi, but this is not the case. Indeed, it is the Intent of the user that is relevant here.

The stone senses the desire of the Stoneward, and the practitioner is able to shape it through desire as much as through physical force. I don't believe I properly understood the way Investiture responds to the conscious Intent of the user until I read of the interactions of spren and sapient beings on Roshar. There is so much to learn here and so much to explore.

I have sent my best agent to embed among the Stonewards. His research has been most illuminating. It suggests there are three ways we can look at the nature of Intent as it relates to Stoneshaping.

Willingness: Stone seems to be uniformly willing to obey the commands of a Surgebinder attuned to Cohesion. This is curious, as stone is often among the most difficult of materials to work with in Soulcasting—even more difficult than living beings, depending on those beings' emotional, mental, and spiritual states.

Why is stone so eager to change for a Stoneward or Willshaper? What about it makes it so likely to respond to their desires, to incorporate them, and to enjoy the result? Like a willing audience at a comedy, the stone lets the Surgebinder guide it.

Connection: The stone can sense the Intent of the Surgebinder, and even their past. I have reliable reports of stone reaching back through generations of Connection to display events, feelings, emotions, and ideas from long ago. It will shape the faces of Stonewards long dead. It will create pictures of events long forgotten. What I initially dismissed as an inferior form of microkinesis is, indeed, much more focused and—in some ways—more remarkable. There is a divining property to Stoneshaping I had not thought to find.

Command: The Stoneshaper must often make a Command, mental or verbal, to truly control the stone. This is much like many other arcana around the cosmere, and is in itself not that novel. However, I find electrifying the news out of the mountains of Ur, that their current queen seems to have been able to Command the creation of an anti-Investiture. Long theorized, this will be my first true evidence it is possible—and can only be created through Intent.

I think that perhaps Foil, deep within his ocean, would find this information supports my theories over his. And he'd do well to listen to me on this matter if he ever wishes to achieve control over the aethers, as he has insisted is his goal.